The
COMPETENT
AUTHORITY

The
COMPETENT
AUTHORITY

~ a novel ~

SHOVON CHOWDHURY

ALEPH

ALEPH

ALEPH BOOK COMPANY
An independent publishing firm
promoted by *Rupa Publications India*

First published in 2013 by
Aleph Book Company
7/16 Ansari Road, Daryaganj
New Delhi 110002

ISBN: 978-93-82277-60-6

1 3 5 7 9 10 8 6 4 2

For sale in the Indian subcontinent only.

Typeset in Adobe Garamond Pro by SÜRYA, New Delhi

Printed by Replika Press Pvt. Ltd., India

For Ruma, Pia, Shyon and Coco.
Thank you for the sunshine.

The head clerk in the big chair
The mildest man we knew
Who could ever dream or guess
His mind was such a zoo?

(*Abol Tabol*, Sukumar Ray)

CAST OF CHARACTERS

The Competent Authority—Anonymous and mighty, he rules the nation with an iron fist, which only a few can see.

Mehta—PA to the CA. Everything goes through him. Surrounded by pies, he wishes he had more fingers.

Hemonto Chatterjee—A lowly minion in the Central Bureau of Investigation. He is dogged, pessimistic, and deeply in love.

Banani Chatterjee—A schoolteacher, wife of Hemonto Chatterjee. Not as delicate as she looks. Lightning quick with a rubber truncheon.

Ram Manohar Pande—A policeman. Very similar to most other policemen, only more so. Many people, now dead, underestimated him.

Pintoo—A twelve-year-old mobile repair-boy. Works at Kader Khan's Mobile Shoppee. Undergoing changes.

Samrat—A genetically modified Alsatian. Bark worse than bite.

Sanjeev Verma—Beleaguered mine owner. His South Africans are beating the Maoists, but their vuvuzelas are driving him bats.

Mrs Verma—Wife of Sanjeev Verma, mother of Pappu. Deeply concerned about Sanjeev Verma's hard-earned money.

Pappu Verma—A sweet child. Kind, but slow.

Ramu—Pappu's servant. Or so Mrs Verma thinks.

Vinod—A six-year-old student of Pintoo.

Shanti-bai—Founder and matriarch of Shanti Nagar.

Tarun-da—Thirty-two-year-old JNU alumnus.

Ancient Headmaster—Elderly educationist. Well-versed in history. Tends to be crabby.

Ranvir Hooda—Loyal henchman of the Ancient Headmaster.

Dharti Pakar—Former management consultant, now spiritual force behind the ART OF BREATHING™.

The General—Head of the armed forces. He soldiers on, exhausted.

PM—Prime Minister, related to a long line of PMs. Attractive figurehead. Signs ordinances and chooses furniture.

Sam Kapoor—Manager, Bank of Bodies, Karol Bagh. Wishes he was back in the credit-card business.

The Chairman—Heads the Bank of Bodies. Suffers from a self-imposed speech impediment. Expects total obedience, which people would happily provide, if only they could understand what he's saying.

No. 2—Deputy to the Chairman. Rose through the ranks from No. 36. Compellingly smooth.

SECTION 1

1

'If I hear one more lecture from your mother,
I'm going to kill myself!'

Hiring a policeman was such a headache these days, thought Mr
Chatterjee, as he scooched under the steering wheel and checked how
much cash he had. It used to be so much easier in the old days. All you
had to do was pick up the phone, and within a couple of hours, you'd
have one at your doorstep. The rates were reasonable, the service was
good. Basically, the country was going to the dogs, with no work ethic
whatsoever. Of course, with his background in economics, Mr Chatterjee
knew what the problem was. A simple matter of supply and demand.
More and more people needed to hire one now, and the government
simply had not expanded the available pool of trained manpower.
Rampant inefficiency. What the hell was he paying his taxes for?

Mr Chatterjee was parked under a tree, in a narrow lane just next to
the police station. There was a shady character pissing against the wall in
the distance, his pee washing a crudely painted advertisement on the wall
which said: 'Dr U.R. Rehman, Sexologist. All sexual disturbances
available.' Just next to it was a huge bloodstain, about the same height as
a man's head. He felt a bit nervous, but he had his revolver on the seat
next to him, and anyway, the police station was only twenty feet away.
The police took a very dim view of people messing around with paying
customers.

He finished counting. He had about six thousand rupees, which
ought to do the job. No more fish for the next couple of weeks, he
realized sadly. He stepped out of the car, temporarily vegetarian.

The police station had a deserted look about it. There was no one at
the gate, and no jeeps parked outside. The only vehicle in the lot was the
abandoned hulk of a Tata Nano Especiale, rusting and covered in pigeon

shit. That's what happens when you buy a flashy car, thought Mr Chatterjee with satisfaction, as he walked up the steps and went in. He himself frequently took the metro—petrol prices being what they were—and got his bum pinched on a regular basis. The precipitous drop in the number of available women had led to a lot of men turning on their own kind.

No jeeps meant no officers, so Mr Chatterjee resigned himself to his fate and went off to meet the sub-inspector on duty. It turned out to be an old acquaintance, Pande—faded, fat, around forty, with a formidable moustache and lingering traces of good looks, somewhat marred by his habit of spitting paan in all directions. They had had dealings in the past. Pande had seven imaginary daughters, and for the last job, Mr Chatterjee had paid him with a very nice jewellery set instead of the usual envelope. Pande had been deeply moved. It was the little things that mattered.

At the sight of Mr Chatterjee, Pande shifted around in his chair, rearranging his belly by way of greeting, and shot out a quick paan salute against the wall to his right. It hit a Crime List blackboard, which was blank, testifying to the total absence of any law and order problems in the Safdarjung Enclave area. 'Chatterjee-sahab,' he said effusively, 'sit, sit. After a long time you've come. Chatterjee madam is OK?'

Since Chatterjee madam was the reason he was here, he didn't quite know how to respond to this. Instead, he got straight to the point. He had thought long and hard, and realized that there was no dignified way to broach the subject of assassinating a dog.

'Pandeji, there is a dog doing nuisance next door,' he said. 'My neighbour Aggarwal bought one six months ago. Alsatian. It was a security measure. Trying to save money. He thought he was being very smart. He told me, "Why waste money paying policemen? All the dog needs is rice and roti, sometimes a little sabzi. Very economical." Stupid fellow. Problem is, the animal barks at all times of night. And you know how hard Mrs Chatterjee works. She's a schoolteacher. Today's children, you know how they are. The stress is too much. Her health is getting affected. She cannot perform properly.'

It went down better than he thought. He had worried a little about how the stern son of many generations of Brahmins would take to the concept of dog elimination, however necessary it might be. Being Pseudo-Secular, he had very unclear ideas of the religious implications, although he knew that killing other animals like cows and pigs was the source of various complications. But dogs? It seemed vaguely unpleasant. A dead dog was obviously a matter for the local sweeper, and God help you if you couldn't find one in time. But that was after the actual demise. What about before? Difficult to tell. Which was why he had shrewdly (and completely untruthfully) worked in the dog-as-competition-to-police angle.

It seemed to have worked. Pande's face darkened, and a huge frown etched itself across his magisterial brow.

'How big is the dog?' asked Pande.

'Six months. So that means he's about four years old in human terms,' said Mr Chatterjee. 'Not too big yet.'

'Poor thing, only a child.' said Pande, completely unexpectedly, heaving a huge sigh. He slumped back in his chair, and gazed dolefully at the portrait of the Prime Minister on the wall. She looked stern but sexy. Mr Chatterjee waited apprehensively. He hadn't considered the extreme youth of the victim.

Pande finally dragged his attention back to his potential customer. 'Well,' he said, 'what has to be done has to be done.'

'By when, Pandeji?' asked Mr Chatterjee, leaning forward eagerly.

Pande opened a large register, which was, appropriately enough, dog-eared. 'Lots of cases, sir, lots of cases. Tuesday, one paper-wallah, his legs I have to break. Three confiscation cases on Wednesday. Next, traffic collection duty. Then there's a kidnapping, for which van is also required—saala Chaubey, don't know where he's taken the van for last three days. Slum clearance, two question-answer sessions, one rape case, one No. 3 treatment, riot duty . . . Not before next Monday, Chatterjee-sahab.'

God, one more week of domestic tension. 'Can't you possibly . . .'

'Sorry, sir, duty is duty. But your job will get done. Ram Manohar Pande has given his word.'

Mr Chatterjee passed the envelope to Pande, who rocked back in his chair and resumed his contemplation of the Prime Minister. Mr Chatterjee just hoped he had got the amount right. Discussing rates would have been in very bad taste, but if it was too little, young Samrat would keep barking and he'd never see his money again.

Why the hell can't they put together a decent rate card, like everyone else, he thought morosely as he headed for the door. But there was no arguing with the police. They were a law unto themselves. Warren Buffet had once tried to invest in the Delhi Police, given the multiplicity and the consistency of their revenue streams, but he had been unable to explain to them the mechanics of an IPO.

He glanced at his watch on the way out. Shit, he was late for work! Venky would get the first one.

He ran.

❑

Banani Chatterjee was an extremely tired woman. She was tall, slim and very pretty, with a pale, angular face and laugh lines that she insisted on calling wrinkles. People hardly ever noticed the sixth little finger on each hand. But there were dark circles under her lovely eyes right now, and her good nature was giving way to a certain snappishness.

It wasn't just the dog barking all the time. Conditions at work were not good either. Mrs Johnson, the principal, had recently ruled that all lessons would henceforth be conducted in rhyming couplets, as she was a great fan of Thiruvalluvar. She found his aphorisms pithy and enchanting, particularly the one about how even peacock feathers could be a burden, if the loading was done in bulk. She used it often when the management tried adding to her workload. If Thiruvalluvar could cover ethical behaviour, worldly affairs, and the love between man and woman with such insight and elegance, then surely her teachers could communicate a few facts in simple rhyme? In addition, slokas were a part of India's rich educational and literary tradition. Indeed, they were the form in which education had always been imparted by rishis and gurus. Mrs Johnson was a little vague about this latter part. She had a hazy impression of bearded men with topknots, sitting on mountains and spouting educational poetry with disciples clustered below them, sitting in the lotus position on conveniently located protrusions of mountain rock. Details she might not know, but that this was a part of their rich tradition she was clear. And tradition was increasingly becoming a good thing in modern India. The owners of the school were dead keen on tradition.

No amount of persuasion from the staff could change her mind. In fact, she had briefly introduced the lotus position for the students as well, until one of them had cracked up and beaned the biology teacher with a cricket bat. On the whole, it wasn't a good idea to push around the students these days, which was why Mrs Johnson reserved most of her petty tyrannies for the faculty.

Banani sat there in the staff room, clutching her head in her hands. Rhyming couplets, for God's sake. When was she supposed to get the time to compose them? Every evening, she sat down at home with her battered *Wren and Martin*, a collector's item since most bookshops had been vaporized. They were yet to be reconstructed. The Bureau of Reconstruction was working on a precisely defined reconstruction schedule, with retail outlets listed in order of importance, as per the recommendations of the Justice Kundu Committee and bookshops came very low on the list. Every evening she racked her brains, trying to convert the rules of parsing into poetry. With the stupid dog barking his head off. And her stupid husband with the TV blaring all the time. Recent success at work had also made her husband a lot hornier. So here she was, with her job on the line, thanks to sex, dogs and television.

Mrs Johnson ruled with an iron fist. She was the only member of staff with enough diamond jewellery to stand up to the parent body. Her loud authoritarian manner kept the owners on her side, despite the fact that she lacked any qualifications as an educationist. So far as her staff was concerned she was insecure, treacherous and unforgiving, quick to crush dissidents, and discipline those who didn't jump to satisfy her whims. She was not someone to trifle with. Banani needed to come up with something quick.

Wearily, she gathered her books and got up. It was time for English Grammar with Class VI. In the corridor, it was chaos as usual. Students of various sizes lolled about. Two boys having a wheelchair race zipped by, followed by a group of cheering classmates. A quiet little boy in spectacles was using a black felt-marker to add circular boobs to a picture of Mahatma Gandhi on the wall. He'd been busy for a while. The Rani of Jhansi next to Gandhi was now smoking what she could only hope was a large cigar.

Class VI, as always, had plenty to keep it occupied during the break between periods. Murali, a hulking brute who ought to be in Class IX, had one of his classmates pinned against the wall, and was busy trying to feel her up. The silly girl must have been too slow to draw her switchblade. Most girls now had one, and wounds inflicted in self-defence were generally ignored by the authorities. We're going to have to give them quick-draw lessons, thought Banani exasperatedly, like those gunfighters in the Wild West. This was Darwinian evolution in action. The predators were evolving, forcing their prey to do the same.

Murali had his back to her, and the class was whooping him on. Banani drew the rubber truncheon from her belt and whacked him over the head, using her other hand to page security. The girl managed to slip back to her seat, but Murali's skull was incredibly thick, so it took a couple more solid ones before he finally collapsed on the floor, the leering grin fixed on his face. With an efficiency born of practice, security was soon on the scene and they quickly removed the unconscious perpetrator. Murali's father was a cabinet minister, so they were likely to receive one of those 'Do-you-know-who-I-am . . .' statutory letters. Luckily, most students these days were VIP kids, so they tended to cancel each other out—cloutwise. And even the most doting parents realized that without the occasional bonk on the head, they'd have no school to send them to. They were quite sporting about it, actually.

The class had settled down now. A couple at the back were wearing Google Glass, which meant they were technically no longer on this planet. Banani let it pass, it meant two less to deal with. It was time for the immortal verse of *Wren and Martin*, academia's answer to Lennon and McCartney.

❑

Sanjeev Verma was extremely annoyed when his son Pappu blew his hand off. His own, that is, not Sanjeev's. You'd expect a ten-year-old to have more sense. Here he was, trying to deal with the bombing of his factory in the badlands, and now this. It was those damn commies. They'd been encroaching westwards for years now, bombing and murdering and taking over bit by bit. And those inbred buffoons of the Indian army did nothing. The kind of airs they put on. Like the rest of us are all Scheduled Castes or something, he thought darkly. Or Former Scheduled Castes, he should say. After the re-abolition of the caste system, the Scheduled Castes and Scheduled Tribes had been redesignated Former Scheduled Castes, and Former Scheduled Tribes, thus turning SC/ST quotas into FSC/FST quotas. By a strange coincidence, a combination of Scheduled Castes and explosives was the root cause of his domestic problem too.

Pappu and his slave, Ramu, had been conducting experiments on the terrace of their mansion on Prithviraj Road. Diwali was coming up, and Ramu had claimed, erroneously as it turned out, that he knew where to get firecrackers that were much better than the stupid Sivakasi ones. Pappu, who was partially deaf, needed firecrackers to be really loud for them to affect his life in any way. So he'd cheerfully handed over the bulk of his pocket money to Ramu. Ramu had rushed across to Shanti Nagar, as fast as his little legs could carry him. He'd negotiated with his cousin Bhure Lal through the barbed wire, and gotten what he needed.

The experiment had not been a success. Pappu had eagerly lit one of the firecrackers and held it to his ear. Ramu had yelled at him frantically. Realizing something was amiss, Pappu had held out the cracker at arm's length, smiling sweetly at his friend.

Now, in the aftermath, Mr Verma stood on his terrace, surveying the scene. Mrs Verma had her injured son clasped to her bosom. Their doctor, a high-priced purchase from Slaves R Us, was busy bandaging the stump. Ramu cowered in a corner.

Rage gripped Mr Verma. He felt like knocking the stupid kid's head off, but he took pride in never laying a finger on the domestic help. 'Take that chutia kid and put him in the incinerator,' he ordered his men, pointing to Ramu.

Mrs Verma looked up, completely appalled. 'Certainly not,' she said, in a voice that brooked no argument. She had had her nose remodelled to resemble Indira Gandhi's. IG noses had been all the rage about a decade back. Since then trends had come and gone, but she'd stuck with it. She felt it gave her authority. With a husband like Sanjeev, she needed all the authority she could get.

'You will most certainly not put Ramu in the incinerator. What would the neighbours say? Trade him in at the Bank of Bodies, instead. Our credit balance is very low. You know how expensive it is with poor little Pappu.'

Mr Verma gazed at his innocent, dipshit son, who was surveying his stump with a certain pride. His gaze softened. 'You're right, of course,' he said, 'I'll have to buzz them about a new hand anyway.' He turned to go.

'Order Express,' she called after him. 'If I hear one more lecture from your mother, I'm going to kill myself!'

2

'Hello, this is Bank of Bodies.'

Mr Chatterjee leaped out of his car and sprinted. The reconstructed CBI office was a thick, stubby finger of concrete, with poor lighting to make it harder for foreign spies to see anything. The guard was used to sprinting testers, so he waved him on with a smile. Mr Chatterjee straightened his tie and slowed his pace to a brisk walk as he entered the building.

He hurried down the narrow, dusty corridor. It was long, with a gloomy dark stairwell in the distance. On either side, intermittently, were narrow, tall doors of faded, cheap wood. Jutting out at right angles to each one, like a railway signal, was a thin band with the name of the room in thick white paint. Most of them were illegible. The ones with no names were the ones to watch out for. They contained Officers on Special Duty.

At the one which used to say *Testing Lab*, Mr Chatterjee went in. The lab was dazzling white, large, tiled, clean and cool. Professor Krishnan looked up from his desk. 'Hemonto,' he boomed, 'alas, you have missed the first customer. Come, sit, sit.' Professor Krishnan took great pride in pronouncing Mr Chatterjee's name right, with the fat, round Os in the middle. In the process, he invariably ended up emphasizing the word in any sentence he spoke. From this way of address, outsiders, particularly strangers, immediately got the impression that Mr Chatterjee was some kind of retard, and tailored their subsequent behaviour towards him accordingly. Mr Chatterjee truly hated him for it. Personally, he much preferred a quick firm handshake and a crisp 'Chat'jee' through clenched teeth, as a means of introduction. Instead, thanks to his boss, he came across as a dim bulb with a vowel problem. The horn-rimmed spectacles were self-inflicted, in honour of Dibakar Banerjee, his favourite director, who was luckily still alive. He had been conducting a symposium in Bulgaria when the bombs had dropped, wiping out the earlier version of Delhi.

But this was where the money came from, and God knows there was little enough going around these days, so he smiled brightly at his boss as he sat down at his workstation. 'Sorry I'm late, Professor,' he said, 'I know Venky's always getting the first one, but I'll start beating him now, just wait.'

An unusually sweet smile lit up Professor Krishnan's dark, lean, ascetic face. 'You fellows fight over your money. I am just interested in results.'

That was a fair enough description of the job market. Given that reconstruction was a top priority, all departments of the government were now under the Bureau of Reconstruction, until further notice, or the completion of reconstruction, whichever came sooner. The Bureau of Reconstruction had given market forces and capitalist principles a free hand, ruling that efficiency and speed took precedence over all else, except in areas of public or private enterprise deemed necessary for exemption by the Competent Authority. The result was that most jobs were now contract jobs. The only secure jobs, unless you were born into an army family, were in the Bureau of Reconstruction, which was expanding rapidly because the Chinese had left them with an awful lot to reconstruct. Most of the remaining population were, by and large, day labourers. Even the BoR itself contracted out at the lower levels. Generally, the government found hungry, desperate, co-operative, part-time employees quite addictive, and a pleasure to deal with. It left genuine government servants with much more free time, which they used to keep track of their money. Rumour had it that on the outskirts of Madurai, there was a temple dedicated to the man who had coined the phrase 'Public-Private Partnership'. Only government officers were allowed to worship there.

Mr Chatterjee stopped brooding and focused on the glass partition. The partition divided the lab into two, roughly equal, sections. On the other side, Venky sat across the table from the first catch of the day.

Mr Chatterjee opened up the file on his PC. He had to shake the mouse a few times. His requisition for a new one was still pending. The putative telepath who was being tested was a teller from one of the State Bank of India branches in Pune. No police record. A dumpy, cheerful-looking wife. And two children! Fertile. That put him automatically at the head of the class. Even slight traces of Skill 17 would get him in. No one really knew what the first sixteen skills were, because the files had been misplaced. But everyone knew about Skill 17. It was the ability to read minds.

He looked at the subject with renewed interest. He was a smallish man in his fifties. Bald, except for two tufts of greyish-white hair fringing his ears. Slightly round-shouldered. Completely innocuous. That's usually how it was. Maybe it was nature's way of compensating. Across the table, in marked contrast, was the slim, lithe figure of Venky. But for the huge headphones blocking off all sound, he could have been a tennis player, coiled up and ready to spring.

Venky spoke into his mike. 'Okay, Mr Kutty,' he said, wincing at the slight squealing of the ancient PA system, 'now we'll move on to Spatial Mapping.' He closed his eyes, concentrated. 'Where am I now, Mr Kutty?'

'You are on a beach, sir,' replied Kutty, timidly.

'Describe it, please.'

'Very bright and sunny, sir. The sand is very white. The sea is blue. Not like India, sir.'

In his mind, Venky was lolling somewhere in the Mediterranean. His parents had taken him there once when he was fourteen, before quarantine. Parts of his recollection were very vivid, other parts were sketchy. He was filling in the gaps in his mind.

'Anyone else around?'

'Not close by, sir.'

'How far can you see into the sea?'

'Till the end, sir. End is slightly blurred. Wait . . . where it meets the sky, I see writing, in big, black letters.'

'What does the message say?'

Kutty frowned. 'It says "The CA wears smelly socks",' he said finally.

Venky took off his headphones, pleased to have achieved his quota. One of his goals in life was to make sure that every day, he made at least one citizen of India say something rude about the CA. As a semi-government servant, he was supposed to keep the CA's existence a secret—in the interests of national security—but Venky rarely did what he was supposed to. With a confirmed telepath, the finder's fee was a sweet bonus.

Kutty was sent to the reception to wait while Venky gave them the low-down. 'Very high-level display of Skill 17, prof. It's amazing that he's lived with it all these years. It must be a zoo inside his head! We'll need to run basic sanity tests before roping him in. Or has that been waived now?'

Shovon Chowdhury

The BoR's requirement for telepaths was constantly growing while conversely, the supply had thinned to a trickle. The early sweeps had picked up most of them. And telepaths were fragile. Many went mad before anyone got to them, unhinged by all the honesty. Entry standards were constantly being lowered.

'Not yet,' said Professor Krishnan. 'Send him up for processing. Hemonto, take the next candidate.'

Mr Chatterjee went to the reception to pick up the next supposed telepath. Registered telepath for the BoR was a secure job, so a lot of optimistic fraud happened. Quite a few slipped through the first screening. Some were quite good. Last year, a down-on-his-luck godman had tried hypnosis on him. ('Sorry, maharaj, no elephant.' 'No, no, bete—that dark, long item in the corner of your mind—that is the trunk, see. Concentrate . . .') Messing with heads was an area where India remained light years ahead of the competition. Radioactivity had simply accelerated the process.

The candidate was sitting on a bench in the reception. He was huge. His shoulders hulked under a tent-like kurta. His eyes were slightly glazed. He was chewing gum, long and slow. He looked to be about thirty, but his expression was childlike. The little old lady in the bright silk sari, sitting next to him, sprang up. She came forward and clutched Mr Chatterjee's arm, fingers sinking into his sleeve. 'My son, Rahul,' she whispered. 'His talent works only when I am in his lap. May I attend also, please?'

Great, now we've got two-for-one offers going too. Kinky ones, thought Mr Chatterjee, hallucinating slightly. He led them into the lab.

❑

'Hello, this is Bank of Bodies,' cooed the operator. 'If you have the soul, we have the body. How may we help you, sir?'

The operator sounded nice, the rich warm contralto loaded with promise, but there was a time and place for everything. Sanjeev Verma was brisk and businesslike.

'I need one hand for Pappu Verma, Super Milky skin tone. You have the rest of the specs. The operation has to happen no later than tomorrow.'

'Just hold on, sir.' The gentle strains of a bhajan wafted over the phone, rendered contemporary and peppy by the judicious addition of a disco beat, rhythmic chants, and what appeared to be castanets adding that essential Latin touch. The whispered lyrics were in heavily sanskritized Hindi, and strove to establish a connection between the Bank of Bodies, Lord Krishna and the Competent Authority. Sanjeev gritted his teeth and waited. At least they weren't singing about the Twenty Point Programme, or the Six Ways Forward, or advising him to Work More and Talk Less. The remnants of the government had analysed the reasons for their massive defeat by the Chinese, and apparently an insufficiency of slogans had topped the list. In the decade since the war, a lot of work had been done in this area. The Bureau of Reconstruction now had a logo, and a small cartoon bulldozer as a mascot, and walking billboards with tall, spindly legs that stepped their way gingerly through traffic. Sometimes they stopped to sing.

'I'm afraid we have no Super Milky hands in stock, sir,' said the operator eventually. 'It will take us about three days. Would Thursday suit you?'

'No, it would not suit me,' said Sanjeev testily. 'Charge what you like, but I want a complete son by tomorrow morning.'

The woman at the other end of the line took this in her stride. 'Sir, as a Gold Card holder, we can offer you our Super Express Delivery Service, for those times when it just can't wait. There will be a 300 per cent premium, but your satisfaction is guaranteed.'

'Go ahead,' said Sanjeev, 'I'm depositing an eleven-year-old in prime condition today. See whether that covers it.'

'We'll have to go through the mandatory medical, but I'm sure it will, sir,' said the BoB representative reassuringly. 'In the meantime, can I interest you in one of our newest services, sir? At the Bank of Bodies, we don't just repair bodies, we enhance them. Our new Branolia Plus treatment consists of a series of 100 per cent triple-filtered brain tissue injections, which enhance intelligence without increasing the size of the head, unlike competitors. There are hardly any side effects. Subjects have gained admission to medical college, improved marital life, and memorized up to two hundred recipes. One of them is working on his first epic poem—a sequel to the *Mahabharata*. With our new Easy Buy instalment plan, you can start paying us only when you're smarter, and more easily able to earn extra money. So it, in effect, pays for itself. I can arrange for—'

Shovon Chowdhury

'Just get the hand. Tomorrow morning,' said Sanjeev, disconnecting. He had a bomb plot to deal with. For starters, he needed to get back to the badlands, and confiscate all the beer from the South Africans. They were taciturn but thirsty. He had actively considered buying a brewery, but even he was a little scared of the liquor mafia. They were heavily armed and twitchy.

❑

Pintoo was trying to explain to Vinod what cricket was when the siren went off. Shanti-bai had strictly forbidden the following of cricket in Shanti Nagar, on the grounds that it was detrimental to the character. There had been some mutterings of discontent, but she had quelled them with a cricket bat, which she had wielded personally. Consequently, when they came to 'C is for cricket bat', Pintoo found he had a lot of explaining to do. His young protégé, who paid him ten rupees a lesson, expected value for money. He taught him in the evenings, after they both came back from school and work. Later on, he would drop into Kader Khan's KK Mobile Shoppee, where he tinkered with mobile phones on a job-to-job basis. It was hard work, but it meant that he could pay Tarun-da for the little cot that he slept in; all in all, not bad going for a twelve-year-old. His mother had always told him he should stand on his own two feet, and he had started walking early.

The siren blared on and on. Vinod tugged at Pintoo's shirt, terrified. 'Boys or girls?' he whispered urgently. The fear in his eyes made Pintoo want to cry. He rushed to the door. The Medical Military Commandos from the Bank of Bodies were coming. What were they looking for? If they were looking for little kids, he had to get Vinod out of the way. Then he saw who was running, and he knew.

From the maze of alleys between the small buildings and shacks they ran, eyes straining, chests heaving, teeth bared in terror. Boys. Lots of boys. Some his own age, some younger. Mostly fair. It was clear the Medical Military Commandos were looking for Super Milky skin tone. Some rich bastard must want an urgent replacement. 'Don't go out,' he whispered to Vinod, and jogged off briskly, trying not to panic, quickly mixing in with a bunch of runners. They needed to get to the other end of Shanti Nagar, where all the proper buildings were. But how far away were the Medical Military Commandos? That would depend on where they had made the breach. The Self-Defence Force would fall back temporarily. They had a deal, which they hated, but the commandos were heavily armed. The boys would have to fend for themselves. There was some safety in numbers. The smell of fear was like glue. They jogged on, sweating steadily, hearts hammering, looking back from time to time. Bunch or scatter—that was the question every group faced eventually. And no one wasted breath talking. The group would come to an instant, instinctive decision.

This one was a scatter group. Suddenly, silently, the group started splitting up into twos and threes. Pintoo ducked into a side lane. No one followed. He was on his own. Good and bad. He sneaked a quick glimpse at the lane leading to the road. It was pretty dark. There was a clatter of boots, and he froze against the wall. They flashed past one by one, their dazzling white shapes in gleaming body armour broken only by the assault rifles and the red crosses on their helmets. The surgical staff carried surgical kits.

Pintoo stayed plastered to the wall, eyes closed, chest heaving. The boots faded away into the distance. Strangely, none of them had looked sideways into the lane. He crept out of the lane and peered around cautiously.

The rifle butt hit the back of his head with a sickening crunch. Strong hands caught him by his armpits and lowered him to the ground. The Medical Military Commandos were pleased with the success of their 7 plus 2 tactic, which they had rehearsed extensively. In this, seven men in the squad went ahead on their sweep while two men lagged around a hundred yards behind. Prematurely relieved victims who revealed themselves could thus be nabbed. It saved a lot of running. Collecting was hard work.

Pintoo was dimly conscious. They had set up a very bright light which shone in his eyes, then it moved away. Very faint, metallic sounds. Murmurs. Pain.

It took about half an hour. The surgeon surveyed the neatly bandaged stump. He was no butcher, and he hoped the kid would make it.

Pintoo lay flat on his back, drifting in and out of consciousness. The squad leader left a family pack of D-size Superreddy batteries next to him, and led his squad out. The Bank of Bodies preferred barter to cash transactions. Their market research had indicated that amongst the

Shovon Chowdhury

underprivileged, flashlight batteries were the optimum commodity. Superreddy supplied the BoB batteries; the BoB supplied Superreddy employees Full Body Cover. A tight little circle with no cash involved. There was no point in giving these people money, they were bound to squander it on drink.

Pintoo stared up at the sky. He could hear the boots of the Medical Military Commandos clattering away in the distance. It was dark now. The pain was so great he could scarcely breathe. It was like a living thing, growing inside him. And it was triggering something in his mind. What were all these things flashing in front of his eyes? How was he able to see so many things at once? He could see his mother, much younger, holding him in her lap and singing that sweet song that he always loved to hear. Then there she was cooking, a little older now, smiling down at him as he tugged on her pallu, and then, the last time he had ever seen her, waving him goodbye as he walked off to school. He could see his mother, older, younger, happy, sad, so many different mothers, even from times before he was born. He felt like he could reach out and touch her, touch her at any point in her life, but he couldn't move because of the pain. He could see places too, places he had never been to. All he had to do was focus his mind and look. He saw cities, cities that grew from little villages to concrete jungles, like a film in fast-forward, populations multiplying in front of his eyes. If he focused, he could stop and see a city for a brief moment in time, as if he had hit the pause button, and when he let go, it kept growing and changing as he watched. There was more, much more. It was all around him. There was no end to what he could see. Or even reach out and touch. If only the pain would stop.

A flame of agony shot through his neatly sliced stump, and his mind snapped back to the here and now. He could hear dogs barking in the distance. They seemed to be coming closer.

He knew they would be hungry.

3

*'For thousands of years, we Punjabis have been
the doormats of India.'*

The bananas were bright purple, and perfectly straight. Robbed of their curvature, glistening purply, they looked like tanned and fit brinjals. Each had a little sticker on it. Banani picked one up and examined the fine print. 'Hanuman Brand Super Banana', it read. 'These hand-picked, genetically-enhanced, superbananas have 221 per cent extra nutrients. Despite being purple, there is no radiation hazard. In fact, more properly, black and yellow are colours denoting radiation hazard, not purple. Had you paid more attention to the warnings issued by the Competent Authority, you would have known this. Hanuman Brand Super Banana is a fitting product for both human consumption, as well as a super offering for the supergod, Lord Hanuman. Don't forget to watch the exciting new adventures of Baby Hanuman, every night on the Cartoon Network.'

She peeled a bit of it. The inside was white. But was that the faint warmth of radiation that she felt? You could never be sure with fruits and vegetables. It all depended on where they had been grown. This could be a natural mutation, or it could be a feat of engineering. Or something in between. Anything deemed to be a change by the Competent Authority was subject to prior approval by the aforesaid authority. Approvals were infrequent. No, some company had probably quietly slipped these bananas into the market. And if a minister's wife took a liking to the superbananas, they were all in business.

The fruit-and-vegetable man stood impassively in front of his rickety wooden cart. He was obviously from Shanti Nagar. He came once a week to her house, just after she got back from school. He had never uttered a word to her which wasn't a price. Once, he had appeared to smile, but Banani wasn't sure. He always had a cloth wrapped around his head, covering half his face. Banani lived in fear that one day it would slip.

She had a bit of a thing for bananas. Hemonto hated them, but found her fondness for the fruit very funny. 'Ba-na-na for Ba-na-ni', he would prance around and chant, over and over, 'Ba-na-na for Ba-na-ni', rubbing

Shovon Chowdhury

a banana across the backs of his knees. Sometimes he would be in his underwear when doing this. This was completely out of character for her normally reserved husband, and she had no idea why bananas affected him this way. Consequently, she tended to eat her bananas in that oasis of calm between when she came back from school and he shambled home from office.

'I'll take six,' she told the man. 'I'll hide them this time,' she said aloud, wondering whether it would provoke a reaction. No flicker of expression crossed the half-face. He took out his dull, blunt knife and started hacking away at the bananas. They were tough, and clearly wished to stay together.

She was looking down the street when she saw the three young men on motorbikes, zooming towards them. Not good. She'd left her gun back in the house by mistake. Next door, Mr Aggarwal's Samrat started barking his head off. The bikers zipped by.

Banani felt a spray of dampness on her hand. She looked back at the cart. Unexpectedly, the fruit-and-vegetable man was foaming at the mouth, his single eye rolled back, one hand still clutching the knife with a superbanana impaled on it. Slowly, gracefully, he crumpled to the ground. He tried to pull himself up, chest heaving, but fell back again. The cloth slipped off his head. As Banani knelt down to help, she realized that his entire face was completely normal.

❑

As Mr Chatterjee had suspected, Kid Hulk, whose name was Rahul, turned out to be a dud. He had been pried loose from his mother, despite her loud protests. No, Mr Chatterjee had explained patiently, she couldn't sit on his lap, and yes, he could see she would fit, and of course he was a strong boy, but the presence of a third party tended to affect the emanation of mental radiation (a burst of inspiration on his part), and she didn't want to hamper his chances, did she?

Venky, who had earned his finder's fee for the day and was feeling pretty mellow, had been kind enough to lend a hand, more or less manhandling her into a chair in the observation area. As a concession, Rahul had been allowed to keep the red, plastic water bottle his mummy had thrust into his hands, along with an encouraging kissie. But once separated by the glass partition, he had switched off completely.

Mr Chatterjee had taken him through a whole battery of tests. Out of sympathy for his incandescent patheticness, he had thought of simple things, like a big red ball, and a piece of string. Somewhat desperately, he had tried projecting the image of the ball into his young friend's head, concentrating really hard, although he knew he himself had no telepathic skills. 'See anything round?' he had whispered cunningly, taking advantage of momentary inattention on Professor Krishnan's part. No reaction. Maybe I should make little cog sheets, he had thought gloomily, tiny cards with clearly visible illustrations, and flash them secretly. That's how he'd got through college himself. But who was he kidding? People had been shot for less. He had cleared his mind and visualized an extra-large ten-thousand-rupee note, hoping against hope that money would trigger off the kid's talent. The young man only continued to stare at the table, mouth slack, eyes blank, his only response a modest, well-mannered grunt. He was like a hippopotamus on sedatives.

It was time to raise the bar. Painstakingly, Mr Chatterjee had constructed a visual in his mind of the boy's tiny mother, dressed in a leopard-skin leotard, walking on a tightrope, with a luminous green umbrella in either hand. For good measure, he had decided to throw in an Auditory Receptivity Test, and made her sing 'Babul Mora' in a hauntingly deep voice, even more lugubriously than was traditionally the norm. He had a warm relationship with this song. On occasion, when his constipation was particularly bad, singing it helped open him up. He had assembled all the elements in his mind, and once he was sure that mummy was singing well and looking good, he had taken hold of the subject's hand. 'Come on, Rahul,' he had said pleadingly, 'tell me what I'm thinking.' I really need the money, he had added mentally.

He had got a reaction, but not the one he had hoped for. Rahul had remained slack-jawed; indeed, he seemed to be drooling a little. But there had been a furious banging on the glass. Mini Mom had leaped out of her chair and was hammering the partition with both fists, mouthing what appeared to be obscenities, thankfully damped by the soundproofing. Venky was trying to drag her away, but she was proving to be surprisingly resilient. What on earth was she so mad about?

It had hit him then. She had maintained from the beginning that they were a sort of double-act, but the question was, who was the ventriloquist, and who was the dummy? How far would a mother's love go? Had he been looking in the wrong place? Were they going to create history, and unearth two telepaths in succession? Would this mean interviews on television? Would they get to meet the PM and, oh, frabjous day, would she like him? As a favourite of the PM, would he not take a quantum leap, career-wise?

His reverie had been broken by Mini Mom, who had started behaving very oddly. She had clutched at her throat and started screaming. Her eyes had rolled back, the pallu of her sari had dropped (Mr Chatterjee averted his eyes), and she had collapsed to the floor, where she proceeded to twitch spasmodically. Faintly, very faintly, Mr Chatterjee had felt a sharp buzz in his own head, mildly unpleasant and insistent.

Abruptly, the buzzing had stopped. Mini Mom, perfectly in sync, had stopped twitching as well. Beyond the glass partition, her son sat slumped in his chair, gazing at her, sipping thoughtfully from his red water bottle.

Just across the corridor, Mr Kutty, in the process of being registered as a Registered Telepath, had created very little fuss. He had simply passed out quietly, falling to the floor in a neat little heap, his feet tucked under his body. He had always been thoughtful that way.

❑

Pintoo came to, opened his eyes, and found himself looking up at the sky. It was dark now, the stars obscured by the soot cloud that never went away, though it was thinner than it used to be. He could make out the faint outline of the grey, diseased moon.

That was when he felt the nose of the first dog, somewhere near his knee. Then another. And another. Snuffling, sneezing, probing. They were hungry, like every human and animal in Shanti Nagar. He could sense what they were thinking, in their crudely childlike way. They were thinking, where do we start. Which bit . . .

Pintoo knew he was going to die at that moment. He wished he could make them go away. He saw a place in his mind. He couldn't see it very clearly, everything was still hazy from the pain. But he knew it was connected to him in some way. And he sensed it was far away. He wanted the dogs to go far away.

He reached out with his mind.

He pushed.

❑

Mrs Verma was woken up by the sound of barking. She had just retired for a much-needed afternoon siesta. Pappu's operation had happened within an hour of collection, so Sanjeev had really delivered this time. You had to hand it to the man. Here he was, with Maoist guerrillas crawling all over his factory, yet he could still arrange for his son's vital surgery in double-quick time. A surge of affection rose through her fairly ample bosom.

Of course, he shouldn't have parked his factory so close to the border in the first place—something she had repeatedly warned him against. Who knew what could happen when it came to borders these days? Her father, for example, had ordered her strictly to stay away from them. Their family had gone through enough trouble getting across the old one, during the first partition, and struggled hard to get to where they had. They had come to Delhi with nothing but the clothes they wore. They had kicked and shoved and clawed, spoken in very loud voices, used their elbows liberally at wedding buffets, letting nothing and no one come in the way of their pursuit of the last kulfi, or the last paisa, until they had acquired enough farmhouses, and a mansion on Prithviraj Road.

'For thousands of years,' her father used to say, 'we Punjabis have been the doormats of India. Every time someone invaded, they would trample all over us, butchering our sons and raping our daughters. That is why, eventually, we became aggressive. It was a matter of survival. All because we were on the border.'

Bad enough that the borders kept creeping towards you, even if you kept still, without tempting fate any further. That chap Tughlak, he had the right idea, trying to shift his capital to where? Bhopal, was it? Or was that the gas place? She could never remember.

Sanjeev, of course, had completely ignored her painfully acquired family wisdom when he was setting up his factory. He had mumbled something about 'cheap' and 'refugees', and now here he was, infested with bombs and commies.

Still, he'd delivered when it came to Pappu's operation. He hadn't actually stayed around for it, of course. He'd left to see if he could hire the army again. It never worked, but he lived in hope. Leaving her to handle a hysterical mother-in-law, who kept manifesting on a variety of screens. She treated every one of Pappu's operations like it was the first

Shovon Chowdhury

one. Not to mention the sharks from the Bank of Bodies, who appeared to generate supplementary bills at the rate of at least one every fifteen minutes (they carried portable printers, and gave a five per cent discount against cash).

She'd gotten through it, finally. It had left her emotionally drained. She was a mother, after all, and however many times Pappu might go through this, she still lived through his pain. Once it was over, a nap was clearly called for.

And now, after barely five minutes—barking. Several dogs too, not one. She quite liked dogs actually (Sanjeev hated them). That wasn't the point. The point was—they didn't have any. Yet it sounded like they were . . . in Pappu's room?

She could move fast when she wanted to, and she was out of the room in a flash, pressing her beeper as she did. By the time she reached Pappu's room, she could hear the reassuring racket of boots coming up the stairs behind her.

There were three of them. Mangy little street dogs. They were clustered around Pappu, wagging their tails cheerfully. Pappu was using both his hands, old and new, to pat them. The new hand seemed to be working well. He looked up at his mother.

'Mama,' he said cheerfully, 'doggies.'

Half an hour ago, the house had been dogless. Where on earth had these mongrels descended from? For extremely good reasons, their security was supposed to be watertight. All the guards ought to be shot. But who was going to do that? She could hardly ask them to shoot each other. So then what?

As always, when dealing with a tricky domestic problem, she retired to the bedroom. She wasn't worried about the dogs. They seemed fundamentally harmless. Besides, cruelty to animals was something she simply could not abide. She was a lot like Maneka that way, and proud of it.

❑

The Competent Authority was busy going through a presentation on 'Survivable Tactical Nuclear Strikes in the Context of Proxy War'. Written by one of those overbred, overeducated and generally underworked idiots of the Indian Foreign Service, who thought they were God's gift because they'd done a little better in the Civil Services entrance exam. Fat lot of good it did them now. He ruled over them all. He was the only man in the country with the power to make notations in his own file.

He himself hadn't been born godlike, but had actually become so through a combination of quick thinking, utter ruthlessness, and a clear-sighted ability to grab hold of opportunities. By the time the war had turned half the country into a pile of shit, he had risen to the position of head of the Civil Services. The Prime Minister, who had stood tall for India in the face of Chinese aggression, had been obliterated, along with most of the cabinet. In hindsight, re-electing him had been a mistake, railway punctuality nothwithstanding. Like his idol, Hitler, the erstwhile PM had left no wife or children. His lack of blood relatives had caused utter confusion and delayed the process of selecting his successor. In the midst of this confusion, and under the cover of darkness, which had lasted throughout Asia for six months, the Competent Authority had re-arranged governance for greater efficiency. The war had wiped out most of Delhi and Bombay, along with large chunks of UP and Punjab. Punjab was hit by the Americans by mistake. They had been aiming for Islamabad, but some overspill had occurred. The top priority for the nation being reconstruction, the CA had set up the BoR and placed everyone under its supervision. Nothing else had been tampered with. Elections were held. Prime Ministers were appointed. Chief Ministers were elected. States were run. It was just that all decisions were taken by the Competent Authority. He remained anonymous, except to those he tyrannized. It was a temporary arrangement. Normal service would be resumed as soon as reconstruction was complete. But the contractors were very incompetent, and the process was taking longer than originally anticipated. He had expected far more progress in the last ten years. It was a sore point with him.

The paper the Competent Authority was reading actually made some interesting points in a detached, brahminical way, although the points were entirely theoretical. They lived in a world of theory, these Tam-Brahms. They ought to stick to papers on mathematics. Or astronomy. Hate was not an emotion that the Father of the Nation could afford. Had he been able to, he would have hated them. Supercilious bastards. And why did they have to put curd in everything?

The Competent Authority, on the other hand, lived in the world of practice, not theory. And as he went through the presentation, it was as if a bright ray of light burst upon him like a benediction. He saw it. He saw the solution that his nation sorely needed. The solution that would enable him to proceed with reconstruction at the pace, and with the degree of single-minded attention, that was truly called for. Some additional reconstruction might be required, but then, that was a skill that he and his mostly loyal staff had spent many years perfecting. All he needed was an excuse to set the wheels in motion. That, and a clean slate.

Ideally, he would have spent more time on this. However great the idea, though, the iron of discipline was in his soul, and if his agenda demanded that at 4 p.m., he would spend thirty minutes discussing the Haryanvi Horror issue with sundry law-enforcement officials, then he would certainly do so. His people needed him in various different ways. As he never failed to remind his boys, the concept of service was integral to the term 'public servant'. It was a heavy burden, but someone had to bear it. History had shown that no mere elected popinjay, however svelte, was in a position to do so. His Grand Plan (flowering, flowering at the back of his mighty mind) could wait for say, half an hour. Thirty years, thirty minutes—it was all a matter of perspective. Vision. Patience. Multitasking. Destiny. Humility. Ability. Responsibility. *The Seven Habits of Highly Effective Bureaucrats.* He owned one of only three copies that had ever been sold. They had run out of subjects towards the end.

Just then, to his considerable irritation, an e-mail marked URGENT floated towards him. Not that he was anti-e-mail, it was the timing that annoyed him (occupied as he was with thoughts of the future that the paper had sparked off). In fact, he much preferred dealing with the world at large through e-mail. As a humble servant of the people, he was anonymous. The fewer people who knew who he was, the better. Indeed, the fewer people who knew what he looked like, the better. It was a question of national security. Not for him the accolades and the medals and the kudos (he knew how to pronounce it correctly—how many Indians could say that?) that went with recognition and fame. He must stay in the background, doing what must be done, expecting no gratitude. Of course, some amount of human contact was unavoidable. Sometimes, people had to explain files in person. Accordingly, as per an addendum to the Indian Penal Code of 1860, revealing his existence had been made a non-bailable offence, on par with tweeting. Otherwise, he got most of his work done through e-mail. In an act of supreme boldness, he had tried to get internet connections for all government offices, but the Intelligence Bureau was still studying the implications. Of course, it helped that he didn't like meeting people very much. If he actually met too many of the people who were affected by his decisions, it would affect his decisions. Enchanted by this last turn of phrase, he quickly noted it down. It might look good on a marble slab somewhere. Having finished performing his duty towards posterity, he opened the mail. It was deeply disturbing.

'Between 3:25 p.m. and 3:35 p.m. IST, a surprise attack was conducted on the entire Registered Telepath Corps,' it read. 'Of our total strength of hundred and forty-seven, sixty-three were rendered instantly unconscious, and remain so. Their status remains uncertain until revival. Thirty-one others appear to now be clinically insane, although their exact status is yet to be determined. Three are deceased. The status of the remaining is unknown as of now. Kindly advise.'

The Competent Authority sat there, in his incredibly expensive, custom-built swivel chair, by far the finest chair in the land, staring at the wood-panelled wall. There were no pictures on it. He could hardly put up his own, unless someone suggested it, and his heroes had all cultivated a tradition of facelessness. He would have to postpone the meeting on the Haryanvi Horror by half an hour. Stern action was called for. Thought was required.

4

'No, sir, inspector-sahab, sir. Please, sir.
Not sub judice . . .'

When Pintoo could see again, he found himself on a mattress. He was still on the ground. He could smell the dust. As his eyes focused, he saw a patched-up pair of chappals, and severely cracked feet. Feet he had touched often.

The ancient headmaster sat next to him on a low stool, his dhoti hitched up. There was moisture in his rheumy old eyes. The headmaster

Shovon Chowdhury

was the oldest person in Shanti Nagar. Perhaps Shanti-bai, the eunuch who had helped found Shanti Nagar, was older, but these days she mostly stayed in bed, staring into space, her fighting days long over. She still knew the best swear words, though. There was a lot you could learn from her.

The headmaster was ancient but extremely active. He still rode his bicycle and even polished it himself—using spit to discourage thieves. At school, they were always discussing how old he might be. Ninety-seven was a popular figure. One of the students had once asked him his age, and had had a wooden chalkboard eraser thrown at him. It missed. 'I have eaten so many students,' he had yelled feebly, 'do you want me to add up all their ages?'

'At least you still have one good hand,' said the headmaster, gently. Pintoo looked down at his hand, and the horror washed over him again. He forced himself to look around. Where was he?

He was in one of the volunteer clinics. A basin, a few cupboards, a table. A tired, angry doctor, holding up an X-ray against a dim bulb. The health-worker was very cheerful. She came and knelt down next to him, a bowl of something in her hands. He could smell the starch in her sari.

Vinod came in like a small whirlwind, yelling. He sank to his knees beside him. 'Fucking haramis,' he raged. The headmaster rapped him on the back of the head. 'Fucking haramis,' he repeated, crying angrily. Pintoo smiled at him. His Hindi vocabulary was already very strong, it was the English that needed work. 'Why do we have defence-force-wallahs if they won't fight? They should catch those motherfuckers and cut off their dicks.'

'I'm all right,' whispered Pintoo. The Self-Defence Force was small, they worked for no pay. They spent most of their time scrounging bullets and guns wherever they could, but they still had very few. They could just about defend Shanti Nagar with what they had, and couldn't waste it fending off body thieves. It was all a question of balance. Balance was bad, though. Look what it had done to him. There were things he wanted to do. But right now, he was too weak.

Vinod sat there, clutching Pintoo's one good hand. A crowd had begun to gather. Some were angry and bitter, and he could hear their murmured cursing. Others looked on, silent and expressionless. They were all there, the sweepers and cooks and drivers, the people who worked on computers, and the people who worked on phones. White-collar workers, in T-shirts and grubby pyjamas, office-wear carefully wrapped away for the morning. A few of the bombed people, blackened, scarred and twisted, tattered rags covering the bits no one wanted to see. They were all represented. All the people who ruined the landscape, who spoiled the perfection of reconstructed streets and elegantly mannequined window displays, demoralizing the bold and the beautiful. Through this crowd, using his knobby elbows to good effect, came Tarun-da.

He stood at the foot of Pintoo's mattress, gazing down at him sadly. He was tall, thin, with an unruly mop of curly hair, and a big, bushy beard that radiated nobility. When he delivered speeches, his beard took on a life of its own, stiffening when resolve was required, swelling to meet rising challenges, pointing when pointing was called for. In repose, it rippled like a gentle sea. He had wrapped himself up tightly in a dirty grey shawl. He was the secretary-general of the People's Vanguard Party (R.T. Pal Group). It was rumoured that he kept himself wrapped tightly in a shawl to prevent the party splitting any further. He was also the elected Block Officer of Transit Camp 2, where the government had dumped low-income survivors just after the war. It seemed like a good spot because there were already some other low-income people squatting nearby. They had emerged out of the metro, led by Shanti-bai. Transit Camp 2 had become permanent many years ago, once people realized that they were not actually in transit. Shanti-bai had incorporated it into Shanti Nagar, since no one else seemed to want them, along with the memorials for dead people, just beyond the ruins of the Red Fort. 'Living people need the land more than dead ones,' she had said.

Tarun-da spoke. 'Do not think, Pintoo,' he said, firmly and penetratingly, 'that we will take this lying down. I can only imagine the pain you feel. Eradicating this ill from our area is one of my first priorities. I will be raising the matter with our military authorities. Never think you are alone. United, we will grow stronger . . .'

Someone threw a mutant tomato at him. This particular strain was far too squishy to eat easily, but was extremely useful at political meetings. Radiation-hardened skin made these tomatoes explode only on impact. Some of the more thoughtful residents always kept a few handy.

There was no actual malice intended. Tarun-da meant well. He worked hard for his voters, although they would have voted for him anyway. After the years of chaos, some of the older residents welcomed the return of the true-blue politician. The empty poses, the awful slogans, the heartfelt insincerity—it was a link to a lost past, and a sign of hope for the future. It took tremendous optimism to chalk out a career plan based on broken promises. And yet, here, amidst this squalor and desperation, this unique form of optimism had reared its head once again. He represented the memory of a simpler, better time.

However, Tarun-da felt he owed his public more effort, speech-wise. He and other pioneers would after all be laying the foundation for the political system of the future. History was watching them. He had obligations, to the Great Helmsman, as well as to His Little Helper, R.T. Pal, author of *The Smaller Red Book*. He had learnt to take mutant tomatoes in his stride, with a minimal loss of dignity. That took practice, particularly if they managed to get you in the face. Tarun-da always carried a small face-towel slung over his left shoulder, dirty white with splotches of red. The red stains were stubborn, and besides, who had the water? At least the stains were red, the colour of revolution.

Undeterred, Tarun-da continued. 'The time for struggle is soon coming,' his voice rose. 'Our brothers of the Maoist Council in the east are pushing steadily, supported by the enlightened petty bourgeoisie of the Protectorate. Soon our day will come. Our day to rise. To rise up and avenge this evil deed that has been committed here today . . .'

Tarun-da's voice kept getting louder and louder. Pintoo felt dizzy and weak again. He had to stop him. He was going mad. He closed his eyes and saw Tarun-da in his head. He thought of a place just outside the volunteer clinic, in the dusty narrow lane where his voice wouldn't be so loud. That was where Tarun-da had been standing, five minutes ago, asking a passer-by what the fuss was about. He wanted Tarun-da to be five minutes ago, in the lane outside, not yelling. He pushed.

Tarun-da vanished from the foot of the bed, quietly and instantly. The headmaster nodded his doddering old head shakily, vaguely uneasy. A hushed silence fell over the crowd.

Then, after a minute or so, there was Tarun-da, pushing his way back through the crowd, repeating his movements step for step, standing in front of him again. Like a rewind, thought Vinod, awestruck. Tarun-da found himself unable to speak and stood there, breathing shallowly, fear in his eyes. The crowd melted away, mumbling nervously. The headmaster stared out into space.

❑

The fruit-and-vegetable man had stopped frothing at the mouth. Banani stood there looking down at him, frowning. This man needs medical attention, however scruffy he may be, she thought. I need to get him into the house. She raised her chin and determinedly walked down to Mr Aggarwal's residence next door.

They had never actually met their neighbour, of course. They lived in a part of Delhi where such things were frowned upon. They had peeped at each other through half-drawn curtains. She had heard whispered reports about his drinking from her maali. The floor-cleaner had refused to comment, sticking out her tongue and shaking her head grimly. The cooking-person said he seemed the shopkeeper-type, low-class. The garbage-woman preferred not to talk to her, and she respected that.

So she was clueless about Mr Aggarwal, apart from the fact that his dog Samrat was driving her nuts. Still, an emergency was an emergency. She rang the bell and waited. After a while she tried the door. It was open and she pushed. She peeped into a dimly-lit sitting room. She called out a couple of times. No reply.

Somewhat relieved, she went back to where the fruit-and-vegetable man lay. It's just you and me, veggie man, she thought, sighing. She bent down and grabbed him by the armpits, trying not to think about her fingers. It'll wash off with soap, she told herself resolutely. She dragged him, huffing, resting on the way, till she got him into her house. She dumped him in the corridor, and once again stood there, looking down at him.

This was a completely new situation for her. The police automatically arrested anyone who reported an accident. The fees for release varied depending on the type of accident. She couldn't afford to get arrested, as they had sunk most of their funds into the Samrat case. Plus this was a person from Shanti Nagar, which made it a lot more complicated. They were semi-independent, weren't they? She had never quite understood how that worked. The place had sprung up on the outskirts of the city around ten years ago, soon after the Chinese nuked New Delhi, after the Dalai Lama was reincarnated on Indian soil and the Prime Minister had publicly fed the child a small piece of dhokla with peppermint chutney. It was just the excuse the Chinese had needed. The Politburo, which was by this time almost entirely military, had recently determined that China could no longer rise only through peaceful means. It was also perilously close to 2030, when Merrill Lynch had predicted that the Indian economy would overtake China's. It seemed very unlikely, but the Politburo had great faith in Merrill Lynch, an organization which managed most of their personal funds. Since their objective was to destroy the Indian economy, they had avoided the usual border skirmishes and moved straight to obliteration. It was a question of efficiency. From the ashes had emerged New New Delhi, richer and cleaner than before (except for the Dead Circle). In their only act of the war, the Americans had responded immediately, and obliterated Pakistan. This was deeply unfair, but the ISI had killed many American soldiers, and the American plan had been ready for a very long time. The American president had been re-elected by a huge margin.

Maybe she should just call the fruit-and-vegetable man's friends and ask them to take him away, Banani thought. But who were they? How could she get in touch? And didn't he need a doctor first?

The fruit-and-vegetable man partially solved these problems by regaining consciousness. 'He has come,' he said, abruptly, sitting up quite smartly. He wiped the spittle off his face with his cloth. 'Kalki avtar has come. After many years of sin, now everything will be all right.' He stood up. 'I must go and inform the others. What could be greater news than this?'

Banani made him sit down and gave him a glass of water. The glass was one of the good ones, but she figured she'd wash it longer than usual. 'What happened to you?' she asked.

'I felt him come,' he said, simply.

'But how do you know it's Kalki avtar?' persisted Banani, used to dealing with ten-year-olds.

'What else could be so bright?' the fruit-and-vegetable man asked. 'And besides, the sins have piled up. It is long due.'

Banani was quite miffed. Not a word of thanks. And here she was risking a police case for him.

'And what's this big drama with the face cover? Your face is perfectly fine,' she said, crossly.

The fruit-and-vegetable man hastily started rearranging the cloth over his head. 'My whole family was dissolved in fire. Their skin and their flesh melted off their bones. Or so I am told,' he whispered. 'I was in Janakpuri at the time. My burns started later. Only left side. Can't you see?' he pointed to his smooth, unblemished cheek.

This was getting scary. She wished he would go. It showed on her face. He scowled darkly.

'Now everything will change. I will get reward for being a good person. My past suffering will gain meaning. And that way, I am here . . .'

The bark made them both jump. It was an introductory sort of bark. Samrat stood in the doorway. I left the door open, thought Banani, terrified. Samrat was a big, zebra-striped Alsatian, cross-bred especially to adorn the homes of the rich, his face only slightly horsey. He loped across the room and placed himself between them, facing the fruit-and-vegetable man. He smiled up at him, tail wagging.

The fruit-and-vegetable man let himself out, thankless to the last, muttering ominously about the new era that was about to arrive.

Banani knelt next to Samrat, fondling his ears. So now we're friends, she thought, amused. Funny how things work out. Then it dawned on her. Hemonto would have to call off the cops. But that Pande fellow was probably outside right now, getting ready to lathi-charge. She clutched Samrat's neck, shivering.

❑

Ram Manohar Pande chewed his paan with small circular movements of his jaw. He was on his best behaviour. He had been assigned an official investigation, with clues and suspects and reports and everything. An actual court case, even. He hitched up his belt and took a look around.

He was standing in the foyer of Sanjeev Verma's Prithviraj Road mansion. The foyer had a redundant semi-circular, open staircase that you could choose to ascend or descend from the left or the right, depending on moods or camera angles. Down such stairs, both left and right, countless heroines had tripped gaily, singing melodiously, sometimes swinging their ecstatic mothers-in-law in circles as they did so. Or slid down banisters, their bums testing the woodwork.

Framed by this monumental staircase stood Pande and Sanjeev Verma. 'Some new technique is being used. Do you get me? How can three dogs get into my son's bedroom just like that? Some new technology is involved. The commies must have got it from the Chinese. Big-time haramis these Chinese are. Like the fathers of the British, but with no clubs-shubs.'

No comment seemed called for, so Pande maintained a respectful silence. Genuine investigations were unfortunately free jobs. But it took a lot of clout to get one started. This was obviously a big man. Perhaps he even had a photo with the PM. The big man wanted information.

'Have any other things like this been reported?' he asked. 'What's the trend?'

Pande cleared his throat, 'Some sort of ghapla is always on, Verma-sahab. Terrorist infiltration in Shanti Nagar. Jat protests in Mehrauli. Ladies and gentlemen at Jantar Mantar. Hurting of public sentiment. No special trend. Let me talk to your guards first. May not be such a big thing.'

Pande clumped off to the guardhouse. It was obviously one of the guards. Verma's only son must have had a child marriage with the daughter of some industrialist. He and Verma had possibly gone to college together. They might have sworn eternal friendship. Possibly they had ridden around on a motorcycle together, singing songs, as in the film *Sholay*. Now industrialist was trying to marry his daughter to a better prospect, for which the first child-husband had to die. So his people bribed the guards. An even bigger man than their own big man, they would not have been able to say no. But why the dogs? As a cost-saving measure? To show contempt? What could lead to such hatred?

On the other hand, one of the other members of the family might have smuggled the dogs in as a prank. Rich people were unpredictable that way.

The guards were little help. Fresh from the villages, still smelling of the mustard fields, they could barely speak. Except for one, the head guard, an oily little veteran called Ram Din, who called him 'inspector-sahab' about sixty times and saluted frequently.

'We are always supporting the police, inspector-sahab, you are like our elder brothers,' he said, hunching up and rubbing his hands. He smiled charmingly. His dental condition was shocking.

'So much indiscipline in society—what else is there but you? My son had applied for police also, but he got rejected. Because of double kneecap—many of our children have had this feature since the war, which blessed us all in different ways. Injustice was done to him. If your leg bends more, then that should be good, no? Better flexibility. Police should also be flexible, inspector-sahab—isn't that an advantage? Can you put in one letter for him? We will try again. Always it was my dream—my son will become policeman. I will be known as father of policeman. Perhaps father of inspector, also. It would fill my heart, fully.'

They were standing outside the guardhouse. Pande spat paan into a nearby flowerpot. 'Cut the shit,' he said briefly, thrusting out his belly threateningly. 'Which one of you motherfuckers let the dogs in?'

Ram Din seemed shocked by his crudity. He managed to look fearful and forgiving at the same time. 'We were all playing cards, inspector-sahab, I swear. We saw nothing. See, they are still there on the table.'

Pande clipped him one over the ear. Ram Din cowered. 'Saala, you think I'm an idiot? You just put those cards there. I can check. I am an investigator. I can check for fingerprints. Do you even know what a fingerprint is? I can read the sign of your fingers on the cards.'

This was not, strictly speaking, true. They hadn't had a fingerprint kit at the station since 1962. But these people were too primitive to understand such things.

The head guard was awestruck. 'You are an astrologer, sir? In addition to inspector?' He held out his hand. 'What is there in my fate, sir?'

This was too good a cue to be missed. Pande brought his lathi down on the outstretched hand with a horrible thwack, and grabbed him by his greasy hair. 'Do you want to be sub judice?' he hissed into his ear. 'I'll arrange it. Thirty-forty years we can pull the case. You'll be cleaning latrines and giving maalish in the thana for the rest of your life.'

Ram Din was petrified. 'No, sir, inspector-sahab, sir. Please, sir. Not sub judice . . .' He was on the verge of tears. 'I am a poor person, sir.'

Pande gestured to his constables, who came up and dragged the man off to the van. Back to the thana for interrogation. Pande hated interrogations. His arms ached afterwards. Sometimes his fingers slipped while he was placing the electrodes. He was getting old. Soon he would have to pass on the torch to the younger generation. As, indeed, had so many generations before his. Tradition. It was what made a nation great.

An imported butler drone was floating nearby. It was perfectly spherical, with a single eye mounted on a stalk, which helped it to look around corners. It was observing their every move.

'Tell Big Man Verma that we have a suspect,' said Pande to the drone, and climbed into the van.

5

'Bark like a dog.'

Like a battle-scarred veteran returning from war, the Rajdhani Express groaned and creaked into New New Delhi Railway Station, riddled with fresh bullet holes, and dented in various places by stones and the odd grenade. It only went as far as Patna, since Calcutta was now in a foreign country, but even though its route was much shorter than it had once been, it was fraught with danger. The Maoists loved moving targets. Personnel regularly sought transfer to Southern Railways, where the worst you could expect was having a stainless steel mug of coffee thrown at your head. The South had escaped largely unscathed in the war, except for the virus attack on Hyderabad, and the amphibious attack on Pondicherry, claimed by the Chinese in symbolic retaliation for historic French atrocities. This gave Southerners a healthy majority in parliament. It meant very little, since the CA decided everything, but it felt good, and it gave them control over the canteen menu.

The hospital car was packed to the brim, the arms and legs of the injured poking through the windows. Mr Chatterjee gaped at it, slack-jawed, conserving his energy for when he would need it. He was completely exhausted and slightly weepy. He shook himself and started focusing on the disembarking passengers.

He was sitting on a bench on Platform No. 7 on the Paharganj side. He'd been at the railway station since morning. At first, as he went from platform to platform, he had made feeble attempts to dust off the benches before sitting down. Then he had compromised, and merely avoided the damp parts. Now he could feel a faint stickiness in the seat of his pants, seeping through the fabric and laying cold fingers on his buttocks, and he didn't care.

New New Delhi Station was a monument to normalcy in this time of reconstruction. The old station had been right in the middle of the Dead Circle. The new one was constructed as an exact replica, near the airport. The old station used to have a Paharganj Gate and an Ajmeri Gate, both of which had been vaporized. To compensate, the Northern Railways had nostalgically installed two small gates on either side of the new station, and named them Ajmeri and Paharganj, thus continuing the tradition. Ajmeri Gate had two elephants with trunks intertwined. Paharganj was adorned with two stone lions, yawning. Most people called them the elephant gate and the lion gate.

The station had been bright and new eleven years ago. Clean, shiny, and somehow wrong. The public had known what to do. So had the railway authorities responsible for it. After eleven years of hideous misuse and neglect, now it really was an exact replica. Until you took a closer look at some of the passengers, of course.

Which was one of the reasons why Mr Chatterjee hated railway stations. It was the crowds. Crowds made up of all kinds of people. And these days, 'all kinds' covered a fairly broad spectrum.

A few yards away a coolie was having an incident. A few people still had seizures, from time to time, though not as often as before. He had dropped the luggage he was carrying and sunk to his knees. He was trying to pry open one of the suitcases, gibbering. The fat auntie who had hired him was protesting, pulling feebly at his red tunic. By this time, the coolie had the suitcase open. He had found a tin of tooth powder. He pulled out the stopper and started pouring it down his throat, head thrown back, Adam's apple bobbing furiously.

Probably on drugs, thought Mr Chatterjee gloomily. A lot of them were. Maybe I should have done drugs, he thought. Maybe that would have been fun. He had never known anyone who did. He had had no idea where to get them from. Nobody had ever offered him any. Venky was the slick type. He would know. Perhaps he should ask.

On cue, Venky slid down on to the bench next to him. He looked at Mr Chatterjee, worried. He held out a paper cup. 'It has vodka in it,' he said, 'it'll do you good. I'll take this train. You relax.'

Now this was a caring side of Venky that he had never seen. Mr Chatterjee felt a lump growing in his throat. They could fight over cases, they could argue over money, but at the bottom of it all, in this dog-eat-dog world, Venky cared for him. Should he cry now? It seemed like the right thing to do. Perhaps a sip of vodka first.

Kutty and Mini Mom both passing out simultaneously at the Telepath Lab had been no coincidence, they had soon discovered. Telepaths across the city had been affected in various strange ways. They had soon found themselves in a briefing session with the CBI director, Mr Jogi Prasad Sinha, of the Bihar cadre. He was a shifty-eyed specimen with formidable white eyebrows and a walrus moustache. He was malcontented. His promotion had been delayed because of his involvement in a fodder scam. This was extremely unfair. He was very fond of cows. He had been due for promotion two years ago, but at the time they had said that seniority was not a criterion. Subsequently, when the criterion was changed to merit-cum-seniority + suitability, he had been made director of the CBI. An officer on special duty from the Bureau of Reconstruction sat discreetly to one side. Director Sinha had first berated them for not anticipating the attack on the telepaths. It was a colossal failure of intelligence, and an inquiry commission of forty MPs would be set up, as soon as they were free from the other committees. One day's pay was to be deducted. A notation was being made in Professor Krishnan's file. As and when temporary staff like Venky and Mr Chatterjee came to deserve the recognition of a file, notations would be made in theirs also. Professor Krishnan himself seemed largely unaffected, although he was careful to look apologetic.

However, the Director had continued, fighting the enemy threat was currently higher priority. Punishment would occur subsequently. Preliminary analysis had indicated four possibilities:

a) The Chinese had developed a new weapon targeting telepaths. This weapon was based in China. This would require action against China. CBI to procure evidence.

b) The Chinese had developed a new weapon targeting telepaths. This weapon could only be used locally, not long distance. One or more Chinese infiltrators would have entered New New Delhi, carrying this weapon. CBI to identify infiltrators.

c) The Chinese had infiltrated and compromised the entire Indian telepath network. Chinese secret agents had been secretly meeting all telepaths, and implanting commands in their minds through hypnotic suggestion. All these commands had been programmed to go off at the same time, causing the incident of this afternoon. All telepaths and those associated with them to be subjected to thorough CBI investigation. Those who were contract workers, with no fixed loyalty to the BoR or the Republic of India, would be under particular suspicion. This meant them, the Director had pointed out with relish.

d) The Chinese had sent in a telepathic mutant with extraordinary powers. He was lurking somewhere in Delhi. CBI Telepath Team to launch an immediate city-wide sweep to locate the miscreant.

There was a brief hush as everyone digested the analysis. The Competent Authority had not yet indicated what the result of their investigation should be, said the Director, so they were to pursue all four possibilities until further notice. Venky had a question.

'Director sir, as per point c, are we not under CBI investigation? If so, how can we participate in point d?'

Director Sinha had gazed at him serenely. 'Both will proceed in a simultaneous manner. You will be both hunter and hunted.' His PA had guffawed, and then quickly subsided, his appreciation registered.

But Venky had more questions.

'There are only six of us. How are we supposed to sweep the city?'

Director Sinha had already thought of this and had a plan in place. 'Professionalism in the CBI is uncompromising! Even if six months is required, every inch of Delhi must be scanned. At the same time, urgency is also paramount, due to the emergency situation. Work smarter, not harder! Apply modern management principles.'

Professor Krishnan had led them back to the lab, pondering modern management principles. Logically, if this was a one-time attack, the evil-doer would be trying to escape. New New Delhi Railway Station was a good place to start looking. They would scan all major departing trains, particularly those headed east, and look for evil. In case they happened to find evil, they would take it back to headquarters, and beat it up until it confessed.

So here they were, flopping on a platform bench, exhausted. Both Venky and he agreed they didn't have a hope in hell of catching anyone. It was true that their brains were mildly sensitive to telepaths. Chatterjee could feel a slight tingling when he was near one. A strong telepath might project a bit further. But their main technique was sitting with a subject, visualizing things and testing them. You could hardly do that to a trainload of passengers. So they had settled on the technique of randomly testing anyone who looked suspicious. Or Chinese. Venky actually didn't give a shit, but Mr Chatterjee sincerely tried to feel that elusive tingle. Lives were at stake. Moreover, he wanted to make the world safe for Banani.

The passengers had started emerging from the Rajdhani. Venky's eyes lit up as he spotted a voluptuous young woman in a hipster sari, carrying a vanity case. 'See, Hemonto, that girl. Don't you think she looks suspicious? She looks highly suspicious to me. I think we should talk to her.'

'Give it a rest, Venky,' said Mr Chatterjee, covering his face with a wet handkerchief and leaning back. Hours of concentration had left him with a raging headache. Ignoring his advice, Venky leaped up with a single bound, and strode off purposefully. So this was Venky's idea of taking the Rajdhani for him? He closed his eyes, sighed and resumed searching, face still under the wet handkerchief.

His mind heard what his ears heard. No more and no less. Sometimes, on good days, he could pick up the odd stray thought. A person touching his mind once and then gone forever. He had followed a pretty secretary in the office around for weeks last year, after catching that one beautiful thought, convinced it came from her. She had stapled his tie to his shirt, and his pants to his underwear for good measure.

Today was not one of those good days. He would have to test someone who looked suspicious. He pulled the wet handkerchief off his face and sat up. He steeled his gaze and focused on the passengers. Venky came back abruptly and sat down, a fraction of his former cheery self. 'Fish scales,' he said briefly, lapsing into broodiness.

None of the passengers looked suspicious to Mr Chatterjee. Some looked tired. Some looked hungry. Some looked innocent. Some looked angry. Some murmured to their Gods. Some grappled with babies. Some touched the ground. Some looked lonely. Some looked scared. Some looked hopeful. Most looked like they needed a cup of tea.

None of them looked suspicious. Welcome to the remnants of the big city, boys and girls, thought Mr Chatterjee. I hope you make it.

He stood up. He was all clipped again, all of a sudden. One of his uncles had been a colonel, and sometimes he channelled him. He took the morose Venky by the arm, and pulled him up. 'Time to go,' he said, decisively. 'I have a wife to go home to. You need a bath.'

They picked up Professor Krishnan from Platform No. 6, forcing him to throw away his bhel puri, overruling his feeble protests.

Professor Krishnan took out his little notebook as they went down the steps to where their white Ambassador Classic Turbo was parked discreetly, next to all the other white Ambassador Classic Turbos. 'New New Delhi Railway Station—completed,' he said with satisfaction, and marked a flamboyant tick-mark in his notebook with his fat-barrelled pen.

❑

Director Sinha of the CBI was meeting with the Competent Authority and it was not going well. 'Bark like a dog,' said the Competent Authority, glaring at him.

'Excuse me, sir?' said Sinha nervously, wondering whether this was some sort of coded instruction which he was misunderstanding. He was expected to know all about code. Was he being tested on his ability as Head of Intelligence?

He wasn't. 'Get down on all fours and bark,' said the Competent Authority. 'And make it realistic.'

Sinha looked around the room. No one of equal or senior rank from the Bihar cadre was there to support him. Two of his subordinates were with him, as was the omnipresent Mehta, PA to the CA. Plus the PA to the PA. Plus the tea boy, who was serving tea with no expression whatsoever. He looked faintly Chinese. Probably a spy.

With some difficulty, he got down on his knees and barked. 'Arf,' he said, 'arf, arf.'

'Now wag your tail,' ordered the Competent Authority. Obediently, Sinha waved his fairly large backside from side to side. The only option I have, he thought as he wiggled, is to make those two subordinates of mine do the same thing once I get them in my durbar. Doubtless they would in turn do the same thing to their own underlings. Thus did the techniques of governance percolate down to the grassroots.

The Competent Authority had it all worked out. Like many of his lessons, this one too worked at many levels. Gautam Buddha had been very similar that way. He looked around at the others in the room. 'Can anyone tell me why the Director is barking?' he demanded.

This was a tricky area. The right answer could lead to immediate promotion. On the other hand, the wrong answer could, at the very least, lead to further animal impressions. After a brief pause, it emerged that none of them knew why the Director was barking.

The Competent Authority explained. 'This demonstration works at two levels. The people we are dealing with are dogs, and less than dogs.

They are scum. They are filth. In Spain there is a saying—to be a bullfighter, you must learn to think like a bull. And it is important for us here in India to apply global best practices. Mehta,' he turned to his PA, sitting across the room, 'can you name any other global best practices?'

Mehta thought deeply. 'Usage of condoms, sir?' he said eventually. The Competent Authority threw a paperweight at him. It missed. 'If we are fighting dogs, we must learn to think like dogs. And we are fighting dogs. Calling them human is an insult to humanity.' He made a gesture to Mehta, who noted down this last phrase. 'The Director has not been thinking like a dog. So I am helping him. But at another level, it is also a punishment. Can anyone tell me why this man is being punished?'

It turned out nobody could.

The Competent Authority smiled gently at the barking Director. 'You may stop barking now, Sinha,' he said kindly, 'for you have to listen.' Sinha stopped barking and got off his knees. The tea boy, evidently a thoughtful fellow despite being Mongoloid, discreetly handed him a glass of water.

The Competent Authority got up and went to the map. 'The CBI analysis of the attack which the Director has presented is completely flawed and lacking in . . . lacking in what, Mehta, tell me? Begins with V.'

'Vision, sir,' said Mehta, hip to the boss.

'That's right—Vision. That is precisely what it lacks,' said the Competent Authority. 'I have a Master Plan, which I have not shared with you, but which you should have guessed.' He pointed to the right side of the map of India. 'What do you see here?' he asked, stabbing the map viciously.

That was an easy one. 'The traitorous slime of the Bengal Protectorate, sir,' said Sinha, eager to redeem himself.

'Correct,' said the Competent Authority, benignly, 'except that you should emphasize the word "traitorous" more when you say that. Not to mention the word "sir". Mehta, please make a note.' Mehta made a note.

'What is the history of the Bengal Protectorate?' asked the Competent Authority. This was a tough question. Luckily, it was rhetorical.

'I will tell you the history of the Bengal Protectorate,' continued the CA, to the immense relief of all present. 'Because Bengal was so pathetic, so insignificant, so unable to contribute to the well-being of India, so arrogant just because Rabindranath Tagore and Amartya Sen won Nobel Prizes, so unwilling to consume the various products manufactured by a thriving economy, so attitudinally opposed to any form of advancement, so infected and infiltrated by the anti-national Maoists, so keen to push inferior players into the Indian cricket team, so supportive of all forms of perversion and subversion that . . . that . . . What was I talking about Mehta?'

'The history of the Bengal Protectorate,' supplied Mehta obligingly, dabbing some of the froth off the CA's mouth with the corner of his handkerchief.

'Correct,' said the CA, 'the state of West Bengal, due to its insignificance, was hardly affected by the war. They did not make the sacrifices that the rest of us did. The people of Bombay made sacrifices. The people of Delhi made sacrifices. Even the people of Jammu and Kashmir—they too made sacrifices. The Chinese missiles missed Bangalore, because they thought the airport was next to the city, otherwise they, too, would have made sacrifices. But not the mutinous dogs of Calcutta. And what was the result of this? Were they grateful? Were they relieved? Did they come forward to help the task of reconstruction? No, they did not. Instead they became traitorous pacifists. They demonstrated on the streets. They refused to be targets, not understanding the national interest. Their so-called leaders encouraged them in their cowardice. What was the end result?'

They all knew what the end result had been. However, they felt it was better not to mention it. It tended to put the CA in a bad mood.

The Competent Authority provided the answer. He was unveiling his grand strategy. Petty things like moods paled into insignificance. 'They indulged in sedition,' he said bitterly. 'They seceded from the Indian Union, like their treacherous Muslim brothers before them. Just because of a few bombs. Just because Delhi and Bombay were slightly damaged, and they feared for Calcutta. In any case, Delhi is now reconstructed, and in Bombay they are waiting for real estate prices to reach the right level. But did it help them?'

Everyone shook their heads regretfully.

'They were penniless, the stupid fools. They had no money to pay salaries even. They had no economy. What economy will a bunch of useless Bengalis run? They had not understood the whole basis of

Centre–State relations, after complaining about it for years. So what did they do? They sold Darjeeling to China. Darjeeling! My brother-in-law had gone on honeymoon to Darjeeling. It was a nice place. And they sold it! It became part of the New Territories of China. And what did they do with the money? Wasted it! Within five years, they were back to square one, with no money, and no future. In their time of dire need, did they turn to us, their countrymen? No, because they are *traitorous* scum. They invited in a Chinese Governor, and became a Protectorate. A satellite state of China. Bloody communists. They betrayed us in 1942, they betrayed us again ninety years later. But why is this connected to yesterday's incident with the telepaths? Can anyone tell me?'

Once more, nobody could.

'On the face of it, it is not. Forget about telepaths for a moment. Let us consider strategy. This Bengal virus is a cancer which is gradually spreading west, in the form of the Maoist vermin. It has infected Chhattisgarh. It has infected Bihar. It has infected Orissa. It must be stopped, once and for all. Here, we must borrow lessons from the past. What did the last war teach us?'

'It taught us the art of reconstruction, sir,' ventured Sinha, still eager to get out of the doghouse. Literally. His wife was mad at him too. She felt his support for her NGO was inadequate.

'Of course, of course,' said the CA, secretly pleased. 'But that is not the main thing that the war taught us. It taught us the glory and the power of this nation that we call India or Bharat. It taught us that we can fight such a war and survive, even against the Chinese. It taught us that there is nothing that can destroy us as a nation. It taught us that there is nothing they can destroy that we cannot rebuild. If we can survive war with China, what hope does this puny Protectorate have? Filled as it is with evil Bengalis with unhealthy eating habits. They will be too busy getting the bones out of their fish to resist us.' The PA to the CA's PA, who was a Bengali himself, edged towards the door nervously.

The CA was on a roll. 'What does this have to do with the incident with the telepaths this afternoon, you may ask. You do not realize, do you?'

They nodded their heads, not realizing.

'A civilized nation like ours cannot just attack its neighbours, even neighbours who are treasonous ex-citizens with vile personal habits.

Diplomacy demands a casus belli, which is a Latin term, meaning excuse. Go out and get me my excuse. Do not be afraid. Even if the Chinese interfere, we will survive. Do you not see?'

They saw. They had seen nuclear war before, which made it easier to visualize.

'Now do you realize why I was so annoyed?' the CA asked Sinha. 'You come to me with a detailed analysis by your so-called analysts, giving four separate scenarios involving the Chinese. Who wants Chinese culprits? China's too big. China's not the problem. Give me Bengalis. Give me the Protectorate. Give me my casus belli. The time is ripe.'

There was silence as everyone digested this.

Sinha went first. 'Clearly, sir, we have been misguided. On reflection, it would appear to me that the culprits are the Protectorate, not the Chinese.'

The CA looked for his paperweight. Mehta picked it off the floor and passed it back to him, but the moment had passed.

'I don't know who the culprits are, you moron,' he thundered, 'that is what you are paid to find out. But we can officially blame it on the Protectorate, and take the necessary action. Maybe you would like to go to Calcutta and deliver our strongly-worded protest personally?'

'No, sir,' begged Sinha, 'please not that. Anything but that. Don't send me to Calcutta, sir. Some of them are cannibals.'

Once more, the Competent Authority was secretly pleased. Due to contamination, the supply of non-vegetarian food in the subcontinent had become somewhat restricted. At his suggestion, the CBI had for several years been spreading rumours and news reports that the citizens of the Protectorate, unable to curb their base cravings for flesh, had begun to eat each other (*Daughter-in-law consumed in hideous dowry death scandal!*).

'Whether you are sent to Calcutta or not depends on your performance,' he told Sinha sternly. 'Find me the culprits of this attack. Find me the real culprits. And dig out a Protectorate connection. We will find out the truth. Then we will twist it. Then we will take action. Is that clear?'

Director Sinha had many questions, but some sixth sense warned him that now was not a good time to ask them.

As they trooped out, the CA turned to Mehta. 'What is next on my agenda?'

'One of the victims of the Haryanvi Horror case would like to meet you, sir,' said Mehta, 'both he and his BMW have suffered severe damage, sir, mainly at the backside. The investigating officer is also with him.'

'Send them in,' said the Competent Authority. BMW ownership guaranteed a five-minute audience. He could hardly spend all his time discussing strategy, tempting and appropriate though it might be. What kind of a leader was he if he lost touch with his people?

6

'I cannot conceive of a situation, sir, where they would knowingly serve you Haryanvi chicken.'

Banani was getting increasingly stressed. It was late, past nine in fact. Hemonto wasn't back yet. She had tried calling his office, but everyone was out. The software had been quite friendly, and wished her all the best with her mobile phone application, which had been pending for seven years. She didn't qualify economically, but she had requested one on compassionate grounds. Meanwhile, Samrat was sniffing around her sofa suspiciously. The zebra-striped Alsatian's owner appeared to have vanished. She'd checked next door on Mr Aggarwal several times. Had something swallowed all the men in the neighbourhood?

It was a bad time for that to happen. Somewhere out there, sub-inspector Ram Manohar Pande was skulking. Hemonto had told her all about him. She could visualize him, a brute in khaki, with claw-like hands and coal-red eyes, looking up from his skull-crushing to sniff the air. For all she knew he had already tiptoed in, and was hiding behind the curtains, ready to spring. Was that the outline of a large belly behind one of them?

Samrat would have noticed, surely. He continued to investigate the sofa, oblivious to lurking Pandes. Thankfully he hadn't peed on anything yet. She had no idea how you got a dog to do it. Perhaps there was some sort of secret signal? 'Samrat,' she called. He turned his head. She pointed to the bathroom and made some moderately obscene gestures. He stuck his tongue out encouragingly. She gave up.

The TV was on in the corner. Normally she hated it, but right now it warmed her. She felt like Hemonto was home, that he might shamble out of the bathroom any minute, tripping over his pyjamas as he came.

A flurry of activity on TV caught her eye. On-screen, curtains were rising, trumpets were blaring, and a diamond tiara was being hydraulically lifted onto a splendiferous pink column. Femina BoB Miss India Universe was being crowned. For a number of years now, the contestants had been genetically screened and enhanced, with the Bank of Bodies throwing in those essential spare parts to add that all-important finishing touch. Recently, the public had grown sick of all the perfection, so contestants were being marred with little imperfections. The winning contestant, for example, had three breasts, a bold leap into the unknown.

Hemonto wouldn't miss this ever, thought Banani. Something must have happened to him. She got up, decisively. She didn't want to hang around here, with her husband missing, and Pande looming somewhere in her future. She bitterly regretted getting mixed up with the police. Why had she forced poor Hemonto to go? Because of Samrat, of all things, who had turned out to be quite a sweetie-poo.

She jotted down a quick note and marched out of the house, whistling to Samrat on the way. They both got into the battered Maruti van. Driving out alone at this time of night was not a good idea. But she had to find Hemonto. And she had a large mutant dog with her. There were easier victims to pick on.

❑

Mr Chatterjee just missed his wife. He drove home like a zombie, exhausted beyond belief. He had rejected Venky's cheerful offer of one for the road with horror. Venky had taken this quite sportingly, and gambolled off in search of entertainment.

The house was empty. The TV was on. Normally, Banani would have been lying in bed, eating achar out of a jar and reading Agatha Christie. Despite all her complaints about her workload, she always found time for this. Mr Chatterjee found it strangely soothing, looking at her like that.

She wasn't there. 'I want to stretch the limits of convention,' said Femina BoB Miss India Universe. Mr Chatterjee gazed at the TV, slack-jawed, transfixed by her cleavages. For a moment he thought he was seeing double. Then he realized she had three breasts. Freaky!

He tried to drag his eyes away, mortified. What was he doing? His wife had disappeared, and here he was ogling breasts in triplicate. The cleavages shifted a little on the screen, enabling him to spot the yellow sticky note.

'GONE TO YOUR OFFICE' it said, in Banani's large fluid scrawl. From what he had heard, his office was full of the CBI. They were being thoroughly investigated. Banani didn't like being investigated, and could often be extremely sarcastic. The CBI never got sarcasm.

Mr Chatterjee sprinted out of the house.

❑

Pintoo had been practising all evening, sitting on the porch of the clinic, facing the street.

The pain was still fresh, but he gritted his teeth and carried on. The sooner he figured out what his powers were, the sooner he could destroy the Bank of Bodies. And that would be just the beginning. He started with little rocks first, ones that were just out of reach. He concentrated hard on each one, and pushed. They rose high in the air, trembling, hovered briefly, and fell back to earth. He sent them higher and higher. The higher they went, the harder they fell. He filed this fact away for future reference, like Galileo had done before him.

After a while, Pintoo started trying rocks that were further away, and heavier. That was harder. He felt slightly out of breath afterwards.

The crowd had melted away after he had pushed Tarun-da, and only the doctor and one of the nurses remained at the clinic with their new patient. They said nothing but kept glancing warily at him from time to time. Now the nurse approached him and handed him a glass of milk, which he drank without protest. She took the glass and walked back in, radiating disapproval.

A scrawny little street dog was trying to slink past on the other side of the road. Pintoo scowled. He remembered how the dogs had tried to eat him when he was lying helpless. He decided he didn't like dogs anymore. He was going to become a cat person, like the Cat Lady of Nizamuddin, who had shifted her cats to Goa to save them from the bombs. He focused on the dog, and the street he was in, and peered back at the street through time. The street changed as he looked further and further back, the shacks disappearing one by one, the street itself narrowing down to a dirt track, eventually vanishing so that all he could see was a shattered landscape, with twisted cars and bodies everywhere, and the ruins of a big, red wall in the distance. This must be a long time ago, before Shanti Nagar even existed. A fire engine rushed past, sirens blaring, and a black cloud rose in the distance. He shifted his focus back until he could see the street as it had been just a few minutes ago. He closed his eyes and pushed the little dog backwards, just a little bit.

The dog vanished. Pintoo waited patiently. The dog emerged round the corner again, retracing his footsteps. He slunk past Pintoo, nervously this time, taking care to avoid his eyes, his tail well between his legs. Pintoo now knew what he had done to Tarun-da. He had pushed him so hard, he had gone into the past. But this time, with the dog, he had been able to see where he was pushing. It was a question of concentrating hard enough.

Vinod arrived, looking sheepish, carrying his English alphabet book. 'Take a holiday today, Pintoo,' he said. 'You just lost a hand.'

'Give me the ten rupees,' said Pintoo. 'Sit down. It's time for your English lesson.' He might have lost a hand, but that was no excuse. He could still speak English. His mother had always hated excuses.

As Vinod settled down, Pintoo felt a sense of grim satisfaction. He would have to practise some more, of course. But once he was ready, he knew exactly what he would do first. The anticipation was so thick he could taste it. The expression on his normally amiable face was unpleasant. Vinod eyed him nervously. 'M for Madam Sonia,' he read, from his alphabet book, his voice barely a whisper.

❑

The Competent Authority experienced a moment of self-doubt as he bit into a chicken leg. He was not a person used to self-doubt. It irritated him.

'Mehta!' he yelled. The Competent Authority didn't like anyone watching him eat, so Mehta made himself scarce at dinner-time. Scarce, but within earshot.

He materialized. The CA looked him straight in the eye, poising in mid-chew. 'Mehta,' he barked, 'are you sure this chicken is not from Haryana? It tastes funny.'

This was a serious accusation. It was directly linked to the male-female ratio in Haryana. Through a judicious combination of many years of female infanticide and general meanness, Haryana had managed to reduce its male–female ratio to approximately 10:4. Many of these women were old and wrinkled, and spent most of their time pointing at the men and cackling, squatting on their haunches in the dust, slapping the ground in their merriment. The paucity of young women had made the male population increasingly desperate, leading to frequent assaults on various types of livestock. The common wisdom was that you should avoid eating Haryanvi chicken, because you never knew what had been in it.

Mehta looked suitably horrified. 'I cannot conceive of a situation, sir,' he said, 'where they would knowingly serve you Haryanvi chicken. However, I will check the challans to note point of origin.' A chicken leg whizzed past Mehta's head as he backed out of the room. He would turn vegetarian for a while, the CA decided, at least until the poultry and livestock situation improved. 'Send the General in,' he yelled behind Mehta.

The General had been waiting patiently in the visitor's room, leafing listlessly through a six-year-old issue of *High Society* magazine ('*They demanded extra dowry because of my radiation burns, and look at me now!' says PM's niece after plastic surgery*). An after-dinner meeting with the Competent Authority was not his favourite way to end the day. A lot depended on whether the man had liked his dinner or not. But sometimes such meetings were unavoidable. Late night briefings were when the Competent Authority shared his secret plans and dreams, replete with fevered visions and unspeakable consequences. It was when he was most inspired and most resistant to reason. The General had taken charge over a year ago. In all that time, he hadn't slept peacefully even once. He had already started grooming his successor.

Mehta popped his head in, noting the haggard expression on the General's face. It pleased him. He took great pleasure in keeping the General waiting at least half an hour every time he came, and never offered him any tea. His pleasures were small, but they gave him great joy.

He cleared his throat. The General looked up. Mehta gestured curtly (but not too curtly) with his head towards the CA's room across the corridor, and snapped his fingers.

The General gazed at him steadily. 'Are you trying to say something?' he asked, politely. Mehta decided not to push it. You never knew with these faujis. 'Sir is calling, sir,' he said, leading him in.

Throwing the chicken leg had made the Competent Authority feel much better. He was actually in a jovial mood. He offered the General a bidi, which he respectfully declined. The Competent Authority lit up, and said cheerfully, 'The time has come for action, my military friend. This morning, I read a paper on "Survivable Tactical Nuclear Strikes in the Context of Proxy War", and in the afternoon, depraved saboteurs from the Bengal Protectorate have provided me the perfect excuse—they have launched an attack against our brain fries. The evidence is not yet in my hands, but it soon will be. The time for action is coming.'

The General sat down carefully, and gazed at the Competent Authority's plump, slightly sweaty face. This was somewhat unexpected. Routine calls for army help to annihilate communities, localities, parties, families, college students, farmers, housewives, and other forms of opposition were quite normal, and dealt with strictly on a case-to-case basis. The annihilation part usually got toned down to heavily-armed parading. On occasion, they dragged people out of their houses and booted them around a bit. In the east, in the badlands, it was war, of course. The Protectorate armed the Maoists, and the Maoists tried to kill them. That was different.

But now this evil little man wanted to nuke Bengal. He had friends there, for God's sake! He disapproved of nuclear weapons. The last lot had turned the country into a toilet bowl. A toilet bowl which had re-armed promptly, taking great care this time to acquire missiles which could both fly and explode, and was now run by a madman whose arrogance and incompetence were exceeded only by his megalomania. He was going to have to be very careful.

The Competent Authority sat across the table gazing at him, radiating bonhomie. He was graceful enough to allow for a period of adjustment. It was a big concept, undoubtedly. People tended to let details obscure their vision. He picked up a pencil to note down this last bit.

'The Chinese,' said the General, alarmed at how he croaked it out. He gripped his swagger stick harder, seeking strength in its knobbiness.

The Competent Authority frowned. 'I don't follow,' he said.

'The Chinese will nuke us if we nuke Bengal,' said the General, going for the simple approach.

'Of course not,' said the CA, indignant at the very thought, 'this is purely an internal matter. What we do in our own backyard is our business. What about the Beijing Incident of '22? We didn't interfere then.'

Well, it didn't involve nukes, for starters, thought the General. Just a few military men demanding immediate punishment of Japan, which was promptly delivered, marking the point where China became, finally, a full-fledged military state.

'The issue of the Bengal Protectorate is disputed, sir,' he said aloud, firmly enough. 'The Bengalis would choose to believe they are independent. The Chinese believe they are in their sphere of influence. We believe they are part of India. The Americans believe they are rebel Chinese. It's a lot like the film *Rashomon*, sir, where there are multiple truths and multiple perspectives.'

It was a good try, but it failed. On a few memorable occasions, the General had managed to steer things so that he ended up having an intellectual conversation, smoking a bidi or two, and marching off into the night.

Not tonight. The CA was feeling masterful and historical.

'The Chinese have no say in this,' the Competent Authority said, not so cheery any more. 'Bengal has always been a part of India. A handful of communist rascals cannot change that.'

'Well, if they're part of India, then we're nuking our own people. No one's ever done that before.'

The General had decided to revert to simple. He was feeling slightly dizzy now.

The Competent Authority smiled again. 'But they can't hit back,' he said triumphantly. 'Once you accept the Chinese are out of the picture, where is the danger? And if there is no danger, then why should I live with this cancerous growth of degenerates, who are constantly gnawing away at the borders of India like ideologically-misguided chipmunks?'

'The Chinese are never out of the picture,' persisted the General, doggedly. 'They could use this opportunity to crush us once and for all.'

The CA leaned forward, holding the General immobile with his gaze. The General felt his resolve weakening. There was a reason why this man had risen to become the head of the administrative service, superseding grizzled and wily veterans who could make vast sums of money disappear with a flick of the wrist.

'That's exactly what I read in that paper by that Madrasi.' The CA hissed, 'Even if China does attack, they cannot crush us. We can survive. We have survived. We just have to be more Tactical. Our strategies have to be Survivable. What is stopping the completion of reconstruction? The cancer of the Bengal Protectorate. It swallows up our arms, our men, our willpower. We can be rid of them. Yes, we may be affected, too, if China responds. But *we can build again.*' He grabbed hold of both the General's hands, rubbing their palms with his thumbs ardently. 'That is what we *do.* We'll do it better this time, I promise you. We'll get everything right. We just have to start with a clean slate. Get the right contractors. Allocate sufficient funds. Follow proper procedures. Encourage public-private partnership. We have the experience now. You'll see. We will become like a combination of Singapore and Switzerland. The key to their success was a smaller population. How much the world will come to admire us!'

The General's head was reeling. Maybe this was the solution. Blow everything up and start over. A clean slate! How often had he dreamed of an India without so many of the bad things the army had to put up with. A fresh start in a clean world, with discipline, esprit de corps, bagpipes . . .

God, he was going mad too. How on earth had this lunatic come to be in charge? It had happened without warning. Most things the government did were insane anyway, and promotion in the civil service was automatic. At some point, a genuine madman had slipped in, and no one had noticed until it was much too late.

He had to assert himself. He stood between the nation and the deluge, like some other character he had once read about. He was fuzzy on the details, but it hadn't ended well.

'Sir, we are not yet sure whether an act of aggression has occurred. Let the CBI present its findings. If we act without evidence it looks bad, and foreign magazines will criticize you. The image of the country will suffer. Meanwhile, I'll have my staff do a full situation analysis. We can discuss this further once that is done.'

The Competent Authority sat back in his chair and looked at him thoughtfully. The man still had some spine left, evidently.

'Oh, go play with your toy soldiers,' he said, sulkily, 'don't take more than three days. Dismissed!'

Once the General had gone, the Competent Authority smiled. He would get there. He always did. It was just a matter of time.

7

'The leds nid more beer.'

A bullet smacked into the wall behind Sanjeev Verma's head, and he ducked under the table with the swiftness and fluidity that comes from long practice. Sounds of gunfire and explosions filled the air, overlaid with the continuous drone of vuvuzelas. It was driving him bats.

'Why do they keep playing those things?' he asked his assistant.

'It demoralizes the enemy,' replied his assistant from behind the photocopier. He was disgruntled. The Burmese had taken over from the Japanese as the world's leading manufacturers of photocopiers. They were making them smaller and smaller, which made them harder to hide behind.

'What about their friends?' Verma asked, plaintively.

It was six in the morning, and around a hundred Maoists had launched a full-scale assault on his factory. They could go without sleep, or food, or rest, those bastards, they were born not needing them. These days, they were well supplied by the Bengal Protectorate with drones and mortars and even a few light tanks, although there was a fat lot they could do with those in the jungle (except pose for pictures maybe, and impress the commie chicks). Of course, most of the commie chicks were fighters themselves and liked collecting balls as souvenirs. They compared them amongst themselves around their campfires, like little boys with their marble collections, while their menfolk looked on nervously, crotches twingeing. It had become that kind of war.

Verma raised his head gingerly and took a look out the window. His South Africans were giving a good account of themselves, less than fifty yards ahead, some maintaining a steady rate of fire, while others were picking and choosing their targets, blowing long blasts on their vuvuzelas every time they scored a hit. Luckily, there wasn't too much to defend.

Verma's factory was really just a big quarry with a shed to one side, and a ramshackle cluster of shacks where the slaves lived. Calling it a factory made Verma feel like more of an industrialist, but the only structure was the shed, and the only important thing in the shed was the cash box. If the historians ever gave this epic confrontation a name, it would be called the Battle of Verma's Cash Box.

The Maoists were backing away into the forest now, dragging their wounded along. They weren't here to flatten the factory, or take it over. They were just raising some hell. Piling on the pressure. Making him wonder once more whether it was really worth it.

A few of them paused to fling a few last bombs into the quarry. They always started their attacks by bombing the quarry, and always killed many of the slaves when they did so. This confused people on both sides, especially the younger Maoists. Weren't they supposed to be helping the poor and downtrodden, and if so, why were they blowing them up? There were economic forces at play, a senior comrade had explained, and they needed to take a long-term view of the matter. Depriving the capitalists of labour and means of production was their first priority, after which they would drive them from their lands and reclaim it in the name of the proletariat. But if we blow up all the proletariat, then who is going to reclaim the land, a young Maoist had asked. The young Maoist was transferred to another unit, soon after, so the rest of them never got to hear the answer.

The Maoists melted away. After waiting for a decent interval, the South Africans leaped up from behind their sandbags, and put their vuvuzelas to their lips. The jungle trembled to the sound of the victory cry of a full-grown South African platoon. A dog howled in the distance. Verma felt like joining him. But like the senior comrade, he too, was aware that economic forces were at play. He needed to check how much damage they'd done. It would all come out of his pocket. He had no insurance. He had tried to get some once. On learning the location of his factory, his agent had fainted instantly, hitting his head on the solid marble counter of the Country Club Bar.

❑

Verma came back to his office enveloped in gloom. Most of the slaves were dead. Almost all of them had been in the quarry. They were behind on their quotas, and the supervisor had been working a double-shift. It was easy to order double-shifts when you didn't have to pay double. It was frustrating. This was typical of the narrow penny-pinching thought process that Verma was trying so hard to rise above. Now he would have to buy a whole new set, and God only knew how much it would cost this time.

The local labour market was currently in a state of flux, because the population was unable to make its mind up. One minute they were rushing into India, fleeing Maoist oppression, the next minute they were rushing into the Liberated Zone, fleeing Indian oppression. It didn't take much time for them to gather their belongings because they had never had any. How on earth were you supposed to buy them or sell them if they refused to stand still? One solution would have been to round them all up and keep them in one place, but that would have meant feeding and clothing them even when they weren't needed for work, a concept so completely alien to everything Verma held dear that he threw up a little in the back of his throat.

Captain Kruger came in and sat down grumpily, setting his beer mug down on the table with a resounding bang. He didn't drink straight from the bottle like the others, he had a position to maintain.

'The leds nid more beer,' he said, sucking the juice out of each word and spitting out the core.

Verma groaned. He wasn't afraid for Kruger to see his pain. The 'leds' were already drinking their body weight in beer every day, and it all had to be imported because Indian beer gave them the trots. The South Africans were fantastic mercenaries, second only to the Israelis, who were even better because they were completely unfazed by the local situation. It was a picnic compared to home, and they'd always liked hanging out in India anyway. The Russians had been early favourites, until they knocked off a few owners and took over their operations (they were now significant players in the mineral business, known for their slick suits and killer parties). Factory owners were allowed to hire only foreign mercenaries, because the government disliked the use of Indian troops against its own people. It's true what they say, thought Verma, we really are integrated with the global economy.

But more beer? Verma did a quick mental calculation assuming a 20 per cent increase and tried hard not to whimper. Just because his profit margin was over 10,000 per cent, did it mean it wouldn't hurt?

'I'll see what I can do,' he said weakly.

'You do det,' said Kruger, 'and mek it fast.'

He swept up his beer mug and lumbered off, keen to avoid chitchat. He didn't like talking to the boss. He smelt funny.

It was almost dark now. Verma could hear the faint cries of injured slaves, somewhere in the distance. No doubt someone would remove them soon.

He looked sadly at his cash box. The lamp gleamed a feeble yellow, indicating that his funds were running low. He needed money to buy new slaves. He needed money to buy more beer. He needed money to buy more holoporn, which was the only thing that kept him going during lonely nights in the jungle.

He called his wife. Her face came up on his screen.

'Are you listening?' he cooed.

Mrs Verma gritted her teeth and chewed on her straw. She had been sitting on the patio sipping a mojito, watching the sun go down in her garden when her husband had called.

He was up to something, she knew, when he said 'Are you listening' in that gooey voice he used when he'd messed up big time. It was unnatural, and slightly unnerving, like hearing an Alsatian bleat like a sheep.

'What horrible thing do you want me to do now, Sanjeev?' she asked, hoping it didn't involve women.

'You need to send me a kalmadi,' he said, shame-faced.

Mrs Verma blanched. On the whole, she would have preferred it if it had involved women.

'A hundred crore? Are you feeding everyone money there? They can make do with rice, you know.'

Verma was cut to the quick. It had been a rough day. People had been trying to kill him. Virtually all his slaves were dead, which meant no production for at least a week. Large South Africans had been menacing him for beer. So what was with all the sarcasm?

'Why don't you come over here and do it instead?' he demanded. 'The South Africans can't guard the whole quarry—they can just about protect me and the money. The commies keep coming in and blowing everything to hell. The few workers I have left have run away. The local headman knows this, and he's going to charge us a bomb to get a new crew. I've got a shipment next week I'm going to miss, and no shipment means no money, but if I don't pay the minister his share by Monday, he'll get me for human rights violations, illegal electric connections, and serving beer without a permit. If you're so smart, why don't you solve everything?'

'Import,' said Mrs Verma, crisply.

'What do you mean import? The beer? It's Danish. It costs so much, it's probably peed directly into bottles by the royal family.'

Mrs Verma shuddered. Sanjeev could be so crude sometimes. Civilizing him was a full-time job.

'I'm talking about the workers,' she said frostily, 'why don't we import them from Haryana, from Slaves R Us? They're much cheaper there, and even after transportation costs, you'll save money. We'll hire an armoured combat vehicle—the new one from Chevrolet. It has a bomb-proofed undercarriage.'

Verma was awestruck by his wife's sagacity. The Haryana slaves would be stronger too. These junglee types were much too feeble. As far as he knew, for he left their feeding to the supervisors, they mostly ate leaves and berries, possibly some puffed rice.

'While I'm sorting out your labour, you'd better do something about security,' said his hawk-nosed helpmeet. 'Instead of all these drug addicts and Christians, get yourself some good Indian army boys. They'll do the job for rum. You'll save a packet.'

'It's still against the law,' said Verma, exasperated, 'you know how hard I've tried. But the buggers won't listen to reason. They keep saying they're busy in Jharkhand, where they have to reoccupy parliament, and they can't do more than four or five districts at a time. Over here, the Maoists don't touch government buildings, just us.'

'Then get the law changed. What kind of businessman are you? Here I am, handling your labour problems, and supervising the maalis at the farmhouse, and catering to your mother's whims and fancies, and trying to stop your sister from turning into a lesbian, and meeting Pappu's teacher on Open Day, and you can't get the government to change one little law? What is the point in having all these BMWs if you cannot achieve this much? What would your father or grandfather say if they saw you now? Isn't the Competent Authority's assistant your cousin-sister's brother-in-law? Even with a relative at the top, you're unable to do some management?'

She was right. At the rate security costs were going up, he might as well take South African citizenship, given how much he was contributing to their economy. He preferred not to, though, it was apparently a very violent country.

'I'll see what I can do,' he said sulkily, and switched her off.

He cracked open the reinforced steel door of his office and stood outside for a moment, breathing in the early morning air. The smell of cordite was still heavy. The sound of a single shot rang out from somewhere in the jungle, followed by the low-pitched drone of a solitary vuvuzela.

It was time to go to Delhi and do some managing.

8

'Who are you to teach me religion?
You think you're very clever?'

Ram Manohar Pande was in a foul mood. There were too many dogs in his life. It was undignified. This was not what he had signed up for. He had joined the police twenty years ago. It seemed like yesterday. Time truly flew when you were having fun. He remembered the first time he had gone back to his village, after getting selected. They had treated him like a God. Secure job. Guaranteed income. Prospective mothers-in-law by the dozen. Huge dowries. Respect from the local police. Gestures of respect, mainly in the form of laddoos, from every major criminal in the area. He was a big city cop, part of the Delhi sarkar, mai-baap to the nation. His fellow villagers were mightily impressed. His neighbours knew that it was just a matter of time before their land became his. Several of them had emigrated, bowing to the inevitable. Prior to him, their community had contributed to Delhi a pickpocket, an autorickshaw driver, and a ticket collector with the Indian Railways. The ticket collector had been the village's symbol of urban success. Each of his promotions was discussed and analysed in graphic detail. He was successfully supporting over one hundred family members. But once Pande hit the big time, the ticket collector's lustre had faded. After a few years, he and his family had shifted to another village, uninfested by

Delhi big shots. Pande had borne him no grudges, he was a Brahmin too. But he recognized that the village wasn't big enough for the two of them.

What would his brotherhood think if they knew what he was doing now? The dog motif in his life was beginning to bother him. The bulk of his private income this week would be generated by killing a dog in Safdarjung Enclave, as per instructions of that wimpy Bengali fellow with the spectacles. Bengalis and South Indians tended to overpay. Plus they were very polite. The best kind of customers to have. In order to maintain his reputation within this customer base, he would have to kill the dog. It was a simple job, but undignified. He planned to get the case out of the way first thing tomorrow morning, before breakfast, preferably.

Coincidentally, his one genuine investigation at this point, with the Verma boy, also involved dogs. He felt vaguely insulted, but given that a big shot from Bungalowpur was involved, he had to solve the case. Bungalowpur was the first part of Delhi they had rebuilt, with roads as smooth as Kareena's cheeks, and landscaped roundabouts with musical fountains. No buses ever ran in Bungalowpur, because if you needed a bus, you didn't need to be there. The trees there were extra leafy, and gigantic airborne blowers did their level best to keep the atmosphere pure. It was like Mount Kailash without the climbing. Not only would this Verma fellow have a photograph with the PM, he would also have slept with numerous heroines, and donated much gold to temples. Such people were not to be trifled with. So here he was, pursuing his last lead, at the ART OF BREATHING™.

Sanjeev Verma's head guard, the oily little man who admired the police, had revealed nothing, despite their best efforts. Usually, whether guilty or not, once a suspect ended up in their hands, he confessed to something. Not him. In fact his sunny good nature had rapidly evaporated, to the point where he started threatening them, and asking which villages they came from. This had made them nervous, maybe he had connections they were unaware of, so they let him go after a while. They even gave him a glass of water before he left. The head guard's unwillingness to confess had left Pande with a problem. If the guards, instigated by a business rival, had not smuggled dogs into the Verma premises, then how did they get there?

One of the maids, a free woman from Shanti Nagar, had provided a valuable lead. She was fond of Pappu, who was fundamentally benign, and didn't want to see him get hurt. Her lead confirmed Pande's theory of an arranged child marriage that had gone badly wrong. It was true that Pappu Verma was a mere stripling, who had spent the last few years in Class IV, but his goose was already cooked. His parents had mated his soul with the teenage daughter of a fellow industrialist, one Juneja, although the maid could not confirm whether he and Sanjeev Verma had ever sworn eternal friendship or not. The girl, a bit of a firebrand, was loathe to forsake her beloved, a surprisingly sensitive gym instructor called Rocky, and had strenuously objected to the match on the grounds that a) Pappu was eleven, and they wouldn't let him into nightclubs, and b) he was kind of special, wasn't he?

With the union of so much money in peril, her mother had swung into action. She had dragged her child to a counselling session with her guru, hoping to erase her hard drive with his magnetism. This session had occurred just two days prior to the appearance of the dogs in Pappu's bedroom. The miracle worker in question was renowned for his ability to levitate in the lotus position, under appropriate conditions. Perhaps he had used his tantric powers to help his devotees. Pet tricks were not known to be his forte, but he might have expanded his portfolio.

Which was why Pande found himself standing in front of the ART OF BREATHING™ building, a vision in steel and glass, all of twenty-seven stories tall, in the heart of New New Delhi, constructed thanks to permissions granted by a besotted bureaucrat. In a city of bungalows, the ART OF BREATHING™ building was like the Eiffel Tower, only holier.

Dharti Pakar, the creator of the ART OF BREATHING™, was the last real suspect he had after the head guard had fizzled out, and Pande was sure he could pin something on him. By all accounts he was not to be trusted.

Many of the rich English types had become his disciples over the years, but Pande was not fooled by this. This was simply their way of pretending that they too were true Hindus, alive to concepts like sanskar, parampara and the need to recover temples. But they were not true Indians. Their children thought in English and dreamed of America. Many of them were secretly Pseudo-Secular. Pande had a grudging respect for those who admitted it openly, in this day and age. He had broken many such skulls, though the contents had revealed nothing. Still, they lived by certain principles, misguided though they might be.

Even his sweeper knew that saffron was the true colour of faith. But these people all dressed in white. Just to show off. See, they were saying, I can afford detergent and water, while you can't.

The guards too were dressed in spotless white uniforms, and armed with the latest Kalashnikovs. Nothing but the best for Guruji. Everyone else had Black Cats, but for him, only white would do.

They made him feel inferior and smelly, him with his ancient pistol and mouldy old khakis. He was on duty twenty hours a day. When was he supposed to wash? It made him angry. He itched to break a head or two. Where was a rickshaw-wallah when you needed one?

It must have shown on his face, because the guards backed away hastily. Pande smiled wolfishly, filled with the vigour of his investigation, and the aching hope of a false move on their part.

The reception was huge, the high domed ceiling holding the promise of heaven beyond it, a towering artefact of pure white marble and glass. This travesty of Hinduism extended to the liberal use of incense, he noted. The air was thick with it. Expensive stuff, too, not the cheap agarbattis he used for his own puja. *Strength through Breathing*™ said the large translite behind the reception desk, in six-foot-high letters.

The girl at the reception was pretty, which helped curb his mounting rage. She was fair and chubby, with an impossibly large red bindi in the centre of her forehead. Her sari and blouse were pure white, except for a thin saffron border. It suited her complexion. She could easily have been one of the nubile nymphets in a Santoshi Maa film. There'd been a revival of Santoshi Maa films recently, and nubile nymphets had played a big role in this. For some reason they kept finding themselves immersed in water, usually the river Ganga in spate, and it took a long time before they could find dry clothes afterwards.

'I need to meet Guruji,' said Pande, less peremptorily than he had originally intended. 'It is an investigation authorized by the PMO.'

The reception girl had a certain amount of discretion when it came to visitors. She had actually been hired for her brains, not her beauty. A lot of nubile women had become Teachers of The Way™, accessible through Outlook Express, and, for a select few, in person too. That had seemed too much like hard work to her. Besides, there were many Teachers of The Way™ while there could only be one Guardian of the Portal of Bliss™. Plus the working hours were more reasonable. Who wanted to chat with confused Americans in the middle of the night?

'Please take a seat,' she said, gesturing to one of the plush sofas. 'Guruji could be anywhere in the building. Can I offer you some badaam milk?'

Pande found himself completely disarmed by this yummy morsel, and said, yes, badaam milk would be fine. He settled down on one of the sofas. Even if they made him wait for an hour or two, he found the prospect quite agreeable, what with the clean, cool atmosphere and this young woman at hand. Perhaps he could switch sofas periodically, and view her from different angles.

'Wake up the old man,' whispered the reception chick into her headphone, 'I have a real sample at the reception. If he's not out of here in five minutes, you're back on the footpath.'

Guruji's assistant was an MBA from one of the premier institutes, (with a variety of global alliances, and a fully air-conditioned equestrian enclosure) but he knew when not to argue. Five minutes later, Pande was in the Presence of the Lord™.

Guru Dharti Pakar was surprisingly good-natured and down to earth, with a disconcerting tendency to giggle at the slightest provocation. 'You are a policeman,' he said, with penetrating insight, once Pande had settled down in one of the chairs opposite his gaddi.

Guru Dharti Pakar sat on a dais about three feet above ground level, reclining against a fluffy white pillow. He had started his career as a management consultant, before realizing that his talent could be put to better use. His brief flirtation with film production had ended once he realized that the industry was being undermined by the underworld. Who do these people look up to, he had asked himself, once his own position in the food chain had been made abundantly clear to him. The burden of their sins gave them a hankering for religion, he had observed, and once this had become clear, so had his career path.

Pande felt vaguely frustrated. Ever since he had entered this building, he had found it hard to sustain his anger. These people were complete frauds, obviously, but they were so good-humoured and good-natured about everything he was finding it difficult to sustain his rage. Pande had spent most of his life hating something or somebody. His many enemies made him who he was. This giggling fraud had somehow, magically, left him bereft of the crutches that gave his life meaning. He was happy, and this annoyed him.

'Yes, baba, I am a policeman,' he found himself saying, talking more politely than he had in many years. 'And I have a question I must ask you.'

'The answer is clear to me,' said Guru Dharti Pakar promptly, 'whatever you may think, whatever your doubts may be, you are a good person. There are times when you wonder whether it is so, but it is so. Your only problem is, you are not breathing correctly. Breathing solves everything. As a first step, cross your legs like me. Even if you cannot achieve the padmasana in its most perfect form, it does not matter. So long as the padmasana you achieve is the padmasana in your own mind, it is the padmasana. Disregard the texts—they were not meant for the modern world.'

Mesmerized, Pande found himself trying to pull up one of his jackbooted feet over the opposite thigh, but he simply wasn't flexible enough. The aloo paranthas had done this to him, he thought, angrily. He would go home and kick his wife, who, not satisfied with being sonless, had now shamed him in front of this big person.

'Never mind, beta,' said Guruji, beaming, 'it is possible to do the padmasana even in your mind. If you tell yourself it is so, it is so. Now clasp your nose with your fingers and seal your nostrils.'

Pande was aware that the situation was rapidly going out of his control, but he sealed his nostrils nevertheless.

'Now take a deep, deep breath,' trilled his mentor. 'My air is very pure—all radioactivity has been cleared by the application of soul force. Fill yourself with my air. Fill yourself with my purity.'

Belly straining against his tunic, Pande filled himself. One of his buttons popped and landed at Guruji's feet, like an offering.

'Now imagine all your anger and hatred is a liquid,' said Guruji, 'unplug your nostrils. Keep your mouth closed. Let it flow out in a gentle, healing stream.'

Pande let go of his nose and let the anger flow out. It didn't work. There was too much of it. He felt moderately refreshed, but the hatred still burned, deep inside his brain. He sat there, silent, sad, disappointed, ashamed, looking down at his boots, which weren't even clean. What must Guruji think of him?

Guru Dharti Pakar gazed down at his pupil with sympathetic eyes. A hard case, he reckoned, wondering how to get rid of him. He had met many policemen. This one was just like the others, only more so. He could sense the coiled-up violence in him, just waiting to be unleashed. He would need careful handling.

'My son,' he said, beaming, his voice sweet and low, 'do not be distressed by your failure. It takes a certain amount of practice to achieve serenity. Often it cannot be achieved alone. Guidance is needed. Here, let me appoint for you one of my Teachers of The Way™.'

He opened a drawer in the small desk next to his levitating throne marked with five small stars (the one below had four) and took out a stack of photographs. He offered them to Pande. 'Indeed, why don't you yourself choose one that suits you? She will guide you in person. The telephone numbers are on the back. For the police, there is no official charge. Whatever you give out of the goodness of your heart will suffice.'

The bastard was actually asking him for money! Pande sprang up, enraged. He no longer cared whether this simpering fraud was a big person or not. He was the police. Nothing and nobody could touch him. Pyjamas turned yellow when he raised his voice. Who was this giggly little pansy in a silly white dhoti that he thought he could ask him for money? And lecture a Brahmin on religion? He had an unusual surname, for one thing. A sure sign he was hiding his caste.

He grabbed the pictures from Guruji's hand and flung them in his face. He climbed up on to the dais and caught him by the throat, pushing him backwards and pinning him down, grinding a heavy knee into his chest. Guruji reached feebly for the alarm button, but it was too far away.

'Who are you to teach me religion?' roared Pande, back in his element. 'You think you're very clever?'

Dharti Pakar, rapidly turning purple, shook his head, denying this. His eventful and extremely pleasant life flashed before his eyes. He didn't want it to end just yet.

'Now I ask the questions, and you answer. Is that clear?' demanded Pande, hoping with all his heart that Pakar would refuse. Sadly, he agreed. He let go of his throat. Guruji sat up, gasping.

Pande took hold of his beard. It was silky-smooth, freshly-shampooed, and almost slipped through his fingers.

'Do you have any dogs?' he asked, yanking once by way of punctuation. Guruji's mind whirled rapidly, trying to figure out the right answer. Pande yanked again, hard, snarling.

'Many, my son, many,' he babbled, 'so many families are under my care. Their dogs are my family also. All living beings are my family.'

'What kind?' hissed Pande, with another tug. 'Tell me what kind.'

Dharti Pakar had frequently lectured on out-of-body experiences. Now he was having one.

'All kinds, I have all kinds,' he said desperately, 'Alsatian, cocker spaniel, dachshund.'

Pande tugged again.

'What kind do you want?' he pleaded, desperate.

'Street dogs,' said Pande, 'how about street dogs?'

Even in the midst of his pain, Guruji was offended. 'What kind of people do you think I mix with?' he demanded feebly. 'The Shanti Nagar type or what?'

Pande let go of his beard and sat back. He looked at his face closely. This man had tried to lecture him about the Truth, but it was he, Pande, who knew all about Truth. He extracted it at the station every day. He knew it when he saw it. He saw it now.

Slowly, deliberately, he spat out a long stream of paan juice at the quivering fraud. It landed in a beautiful line, diagonally across the front of his kurta, bright red and glistening, making him look like he'd been gunned down by an AK-47. It was a pleasing image.

'Never ask a policeman for money,' he told the cowering godman, 'and never lecture a Brahmin on religion. If I find out you have, I'll come back and break your legs.'

Pande strode out of the Presence of the Lord™ and into the long, cool corridor, wondering where he should go next. It was turning out to be not such a bad day after all. He was sure he would find many more leads to pursue, and many more people, high and low, to interrogate. They might have given him a genuine investigation, interrupting his daily routine, and hampering the pursuit of his livelihood, but no mother's son would have the guts to give him a deadline. He could take sixteen days, or he could take sixteen years. It was all up to him.

Dharti Pakar crawled to the intercom and called reception. 'How many fashion models are there in the building?' he asked, hoarsely.

'Six, Guruji,' came the prompt reply. They had position locators attached to them, for emergencies.

'Send them all in,' he whispered, 'immediately.'

He needed to get back in touch with his inner self.

9

'Hey, kid. Looks like you had an accident
with that hand.'

Pintoo stood there, across the street, looking up at the sign. BANK OF BODIES, it said, in large chunky letters. *'If you have the soul, we have the body!'* it said just underneath. The colour scheme of the building was red and white, just like a hospital.

But then it was a hospital, wasn't it? A very special kind. They made a lot of money doing what they did. The customers came in big cars, and wore fancy clothes. They bathed a lot, and smelled heavenly.

Pintoo rarely left Shanti Nagar. He didn't need to and the city made him nervous. But he had no choice. He had gone to Tarun-da and asked him for the address. Wordlessly, Tarun-da had given him a small chit of paper, avoiding his eyes.

'If you're going to be late, don't take the metro,' he had murmured as he was leaving, 'it could be dangerous.'

Tarun-da hadn't spoken to him much since being rewound. He was nervous of the new Pintoo, but he'd get used to him. Pintoo didn't have the time to reassure him, he had things to do, things he was still figuring out. But he was clear about what he needed to do first, and it involved the Bank of Bodies.

He walked up to the big glass door. The two guards in their red-cross helmets looked at him suspiciously. He was low-class, and missing a hand. Clearly he was the donor-type, not a customer. One of them moved forward, threateningly. 'Oy,' he said.

Pintoo closed his eyes and pushed. The man was only six feet away. He was lifted off his feet and hit the wall with a loud smack. He collapsed. The other one raised his rifle by reflex, backing away. Pintoo could see the whites of his eyes. He pushed him too, upwards this time. He kept him in mid-air for a bit. The guard dropped his rifle and threw his arms and legs about, like a man trying to swim. Pintoo let him drop and went in.

It was cool inside. The air smelt fresh. The foyer opened into a large hall with many counters with little windows, like any bank. *Deposits*, said one set of counters. *Withdrawals*, said another. Pretty girls in saris sat behind each one. There were cheerful posters on the walls. *Gift your parents the best!* said one, *The gift of life!* It showed a nice-looking white-haired man, in a spotless kurta, bouncing a happy baby on his knee. Pintoo gazed at it. He had never seen a kurta so white, except on television. Another poster showed a beautiful woman dressed as a bride, smiling shyly. *Gift your husband the best!* it said, *The gift of beauty!*

It was all very quiet. The customers spoke in soft voices. The girls murmured back softly. None of them seemed to be missing anything.

A hand caught him roughly by the elbow. 'You want your money, go to the back,' said a voice. Pintoo turned. He found himself looking at a handsome young man. He looked like a movie star. His hair was phenomenal. He wore a badge that said *Customer Service*. His grip on Pintoo's elbow tightened.

'Come with me, you idiot,' he said, 'you'll frighten the customers.' As a policy, the Bank of Bodies forbade the mixing of donors and customers. It made some customers uncomfortable. He was probably a voluntary donor, desperate for cash.

'You can't sell it here, you fool,' he hissed.

'Fuck you,' said Pintoo.

He hit him like a hammer with his mind. The man flew off his feet, sailed backwards, and hit one of the glass-paned counters. The glass shattered all over the pretty young girl behind it. He made a huge painting by a promising young artist fly off the wall. It floated in the air briefly, flapping this way and that, as if unsure where to go next, before it finally fell face flat on the floral arrangement at the centre of the lobby, like a drunk coming home to his wife. That was when the screams began.

He focused on a bank of computers, and they rose up together. He smashed them. He walked down the counters, smashing them one by one. He smashed swivel chairs against tables. He took a large mahogany desk and hurled it across the room, strewing paper and free keychains with the Chairman's face on them. He ignored the screaming people. He didn't care about the people. For now, he wanted to smash up the place. And once he had destroyed it, he would go after the truly evil people, the people behind the BoB, the people at the top.

He went through the building, room after room. He went through rooms with stacks and stacks of files. He flung them all about, sent them sailing out the window and into the corridor. He started pushing the other way too. He could do it much better now. He took whole cupboards and sent them away. He sent them ten years away. He sent them fifty years away. He found an operating theatre full of medical things, and he smashed them. He found a room full of rifles and helmets and he sent them back a long, long way, back to when he hoped they wouldn't even know what a rifle was. He found jars and freezers and vacuum-sealed tanks and hurled those back too. He didn't smash them, he didn't want them to break, he didn't want to see the things inside, the arms and legs and livers and hearts and blood and (preferably pale) skin, just like his. He found rooms full of money and rooms full of paper. He made it all disappear. He found computers and tablets and sleek little machines with blinking lights. He smashed them all. Part of him was scared. What else would he find here? Would he find heads, preserved whole, like pickles in a jar? Would he find strings of arms and legs, hung out like clothes on a washing line? Would he find dustbins with bits and pieces that had been thrown away? Would he find whole bodies floating in huge glass vats, bodies of people he knew? Would he find them huddled over someone, actually taking something from someone, smoothly and cleanly with steely sharp scalpels? He didn't care. He couldn't be scared. He couldn't be weak. He would never let them do this to anyone again. He didn't feel tired. He didn't feel pain. He smashed and smashed and smashed.

Dimly, he could hear people screaming. He sensed people running past him. 'Security!' screamed a voice, high and quavering. Security had left the building long ago. They were only brave with the weak. He longed for them to come.

It was getting quieter now. Hotter. He could smell smoke. Some of the rooms were burning. It wasn't so cool and pretty now, was it? Where was their air conditioning now? He could hear sirens in the distance. It didn't matter. He was almost done.

The last room he found was bigger than the rest. It was very quiet and very empty. It had a lovely thick carpet and fat little sofas. There were no posters on the walls, just lots of wood. And bookshelves, with lots of books, bound in leather. It looked like a rich man's study, not an office. In the serials that his mother used to watch, evil fathers-in-law strutted in rooms like this, brandishing canes and twirling their moustaches.

Pintoo paused, standing in the middle of the room. He was panting slightly. The atmosphere here was so peaceful. There was a big wooden desk at one end of the room, and a huge black chair behind it. On the desk was a black computer, a few papers, and framed pictures of a smiling pale woman and two small, pale children, dainty little fairy creatures in beautiful clothes. A small, brass plaque said *Sam Kapoor, Manager.*

There was the faintest of scratching noises. Pintoo peered under the desk and found him there. One of Sam's Gucci shoes had scraped the chair. He had managed to stop his teeth from chattering, but his shaking legs had given him away. Pintoo gazed down at him.

Sam was having a very bad day. His first phone call of the morning had been from a retired union minister, complaining about defective livers. They were in the medical joy business, as a consultant had once famously told them, but they weren't magicians. The man had drunk himself silly, and reduced his liver to something more like Swiss cheese than anything human. He had been told that his transplanted liver, while of prime quality, would need gentle handling, one-year warranty or no one-year warranty. But did he listen? No, sir, he went straight back to half-a-bottle of Scotch a day. Indian livers weren't built to handle such quantities of Scotch, it just didn't work that way, they'd argued with him. Then the man had wanted a foreign one, for God's sake! Where on earth was Sam supposed to get one—kidnap a diplomat? Not that there were many diplomats left in Delhi. The climate didn't suit them, the bulky protective suits they wore made it hard to move around, plus the children kept throwing stones at them. As a result they tended to huddle in their sad little ghettos, just as they had in the long-ago past.

Now here he was, crouching under a desk, the whole building a shambles, about to be hideously abused by some lunatic slum kid. He had sent memo after memo about the need for improving security, and streamlining the collection system, but no one ever paid the slightest attention.

It wasn't supposed to work out this way. These should have been the golden years of his career. He had spent many years in the credit-card business, and done very well out of it. But there was no escaping the shabbiness of it. It was the defaulter side that he couldn't handle, with all the lame excuses and the whining. When he got the BoB offer, he took it instantly. The Bank of Bodies was a class apart, constantly appearing in the Ten Most Admired Companies in India. Plus he didn't have to deal with all that unpleasantness any more. He was able to make a genuine difference to his customer's lives. That was all he really wanted to do—provide genuine satisfaction and make lots of money.

And this is where it looked like it was ending, abused and battered by loony ex-politicians and murderous slum kids. What had he done to deserve this?

Pintoo gazed down at Sam, who was trying to adjust his tie. So this was the big boss. He looked so pathetic, crouching there trembling. This was who had caused so much pain to so many. This was who had been selling them off in bits and pieces. This foolish thing.

Sam was nothing if not resilient. His brain was always working, however bleak things might look, that was his strength. If he couldn't talk down one snotty little kid, how could he have come this far?

'Hey, listen, kid,' he said, emerging from under the desk, 'looks like you've had an accident with that hand. I don't know what your problem is, but how about I organize a free hand job for you, top quality, A-1, 100 per cent match. Maybe a big, strong heart too. You could be a sports champ. You could try skiing. The babes are awesome.'

Sam Kapoor was very close to death at that moment. Pintoo raised him, high up, till his head touched the ceiling. He held him there while Sam gibbered. Why should this man live, Pintoo asked himself. He would find some way to harm people as long as he lived. He would be scared for a day or two, but then he would go back to his old ways. And he had the power to stop this. He could drop him from up there. He could raise this big, heavy desk and finish him off with it.

But he couldn't do it. What would his mother have said? She used to be so gentle even though her life hadn't been easy. She had worked as a maid in the city, leaving every morning and coming back every night, ever since Pintoo's dad had died, and their pension got unavoidably delayed. She always spoke softly, and never complained. One day she had gone to the city and had never come back. 'Yes, yes, take all the good people,' Shanti-bai had said when she heard the news, shaking her fist at the sky. 'This is why I don't trust you.'

Pintoo carefully lowered Sam down into his plush leather chair. Sam started dusting himself, frowning slightly. He was tripping without scoring. This was new. Pintoo relaxed, his mind savouring the peace for a moment. 'At least I've finished your Bank of Bodies. You can't hurt people any more. If you try building it again, I'll come back,' he told Sam, cheered by the thought.

Flopped bonelessly in his leather chair, Sam gaped at him. Then he started laughing. He couldn't help it. He laughed and laughed. 'You've got a Head Office problem, man,' he wheezed, tears streaming down his face. His whole branch junked by a psychotic kid with the wrong address! He sat up. 'You realize this is the Karol Bagh branch, don't you, kid? Was your problem even connected to this branch? If not, tell me which branch, and relax. I'll take care of it. I'll make them pay. They can't get away with this sort of thing, you know, doing what they did. I'll take it to customer service and escalate. I'll escalate big time.'

Pintoo stood there, staring at Sam. His plan was going to need more work, he suddenly realized. A lot more work.

10

*'Have you ever come upon your husband whispering
secret instructions in Chinese[?]'*

Banani was relieved when she finally reached the CBI building. Driving through Bungalowpur made her feel like an intruder, with its water cannons lurking near every roundabout, poised to spray the unwelcome, and the battered barricade drones floating overhead, ready to block public access instantly. The CBI building was more like home ground, lowly though Hemonto might be. She effortlessly parallel-parked and got out of the vehicle, dragging the zebra-striped Alsatian with her, telling him not to be such a big baby.

The security guard recognized her and saluted—she often brought Hemonto lunch during the summer holidays. She came straight to the point.

'Where is he?' she asked. 'He hasn't come home yet. He's not meeting some lady, I hope?' she continued, more as an opening gambit than a real question.

The guard eyed Samrat nervously and stuck his tongue out, embarrassed. 'No, no, mem-sahab, what are you saying? You should not even think that.' He was very fond of Banani. She was one of the few English-types who treated him like an actual human being.

'Big ghapla with all the akaashvanis. Many fell sick, some of them also died. He and Venky-sahab and others had to do overtime duty. But how much overtime can they do? By now they should have reached home. You should not have come out so late.'

A man stepped out of the shadows. He was wearing a bush shirt and trousers, both of which were changing colour constantly. This was because he was undercover. He was holding a notebook and had a pencil tucked behind his improbably large ear, genetically engineered for acute hearing. As a CBI officer, he was a superior kind of investigator, with access to superior data, compared to the Jat peasants of the regular police. He knew that one of the suspects had a wife who was a babe. This was clearly a babe, although somewhat on the slim side.

'Are you Banani Chatterjee?' he asked, getting the balance just right, cultured but firm.

Banani looked him up and down. He was a stranger, but seemed well-educated enough.

'Yes, I am,' she said.

Samrat didn't seem to object to him, which gave her additional confidence.

'Please follow me,' said the man, whose bush shirt was currently light blue. 'I have a few questions to ask.' He was politely determined. His last job had been a disaster. He had mistakenly filed a chargesheet in a case that had been successfully kept pending for the last thirty years. In the process, he had almost ruined the CBI's unblemished track record of never having solved a defence case since India became independent. Only prompt action by an alert Director Sinha had saved them from disaster. He needed to redeem himself. CBI officers with access to telepaths were suspects in the telepath case, and the CBI was therefore investigating itself to see if it was guilty of any wrongdoing. It was up to him to reach the right conclusions. Director Sinha was depending on him.

Banani followed him into the building. The guard opened up one of the waiting rooms. 'I am just outside,' he said pointedly, as he left. Banani sat down in one of the uncomfortable plastic chairs with Samrat curled up on the floor next to her and waited for him to speak.

'Are you Banani Chatterjee, wife of Hemonto Chatterjee?' asked Bush-Shirt-Man. Banani nodded.

Bush-Shirt-Man consulted his notes. 'Do you know any Chinese people?' he asked.

'I don't think so,' said Banani, 'but we have a couple of friends from Nagaland. Does that help?' She could be mean when she wanted to be. Kids never got sarcasm; she didn't get to do this much in school.

'Of course not,' he replied.

He went on to the next question. 'Have you ever come upon your husband whispering secret instructions in Chinese over the phone in the middle of the night?'

'No,' said Banani, 'but sometimes he does whisper in Bengali. His mother lives in Calcutta.'

That was actually question number seven, so he chose to ignore it at this point in the proceedings. 'Has your husband revealed to you any plots he is involved in that are designed to undermine the unity and integrity of the Republic of India?' he asked.

'Not to the best of my knowledge, no,' said Banani. 'He's deeply concerned about the state of the Republic of India, but he hasn't tried to undermine it yet,' she added, somewhat injudiciously.

'May be undermining nation', Bush-Shirt-Man wrote in his notebook, glad to get a piece of evidence at last.

Mr Chatterjee burst into the room at this point, glasses askew, his normally neat hair in disarray. 'What are you doing with my wife?' he demanded, uncharacteristically loudly. She looked very tired, and that made him angrier still.

'You are a suspect in a plot against our nation, the Republic of India,' said Bush-Shirt-Man with enormous dignity.

'Suspect?' yelled Mr Chatterjee, 'suspect! I've spent the whole bloody day trying to find out who did it. That's why I'm late. I didn't have time to make a bloody phone call. That's why she's here. And I'm a bloody suspect?'

'Yes,' said the CBI officer, firmly, 'your name is on the list. You were informed at your briefing session. You either forgot, or chose to ignore it. I will be arresting you seven days from now, as per the personal instructions of the Director, CBI. His PA has given me this in writing.'

Mr Chatterjee glared at him. 'If you're going to arrest me in a week anyway, why are you asking my wife all these questions in the middle of the night?' he demanded.

Bush-Shirt-Man was appalled. 'Obviously I have to collect evidence first,' he said, trying not to take this personally. 'What kind of an operation do you think we run?'

Banani stood up and took his arm, gazing up at his face. 'Let it be, Hemu,' she said, feeling weak all of a sudden. 'Seven days is a lot of time. Who knows, in seven days, maybe the horse will learn to sing.'

She put her head on his shoulder and leaned against him. Mr Chatterjee put his arm around his wife and held her close.

'May we leave now?' he asked politely, not angry any more.

Bush-Shirt-Man stepped back and gestured expansively to the door. Ruthless in the pursuit of justice he might be, but he remained fundamentally courteous.

11

'What names should I put in the strongly worded protest,
which I may or may not send later?'

The CA felt the need to get in touch with his compassionate side, so he extended the meeting with one of the victims of the Haryanvi Horror case for another five minutes. Besides, he had already postponed this meeting once, which called for some extra solicitude.

The pain of his experience was etched on the face of the young man sitting across from him. The CA already had a reasonable idea of the nature of the injury inflicted upon the well-nourished victim. Many cases had been reported recently, and the lad was sitting very gingerly on the edge of his seat.

'CA uncle, he takes a bunch of bananas,' whispered the victim, hoarsely, 'those modified, straight ones. He bends down, behind the BMW, and he . . .' he paused for a moment, unmanned by the horror of it, 'he shoves them up the exhaust pipe, one after the other, one after the other!'

'That must hurt a lot,' said the CA, sympathetically, feeling slightly nauseous. He loved his own BMW more than his children. It made sense. The BMW was here. His children were in America.

'It does,' the young man replied, moaning softly at the memory. 'And that's not all he does . . .'

The CA glanced at his watch. All this sympathy was a strain, and his head was now beginning to hurt. He rang for his PA.

'Mehta,' he said, yawning, 'assure this young man of our best efforts in this case. Let him know that I am confident that thanks to his cooperation, we will apprehend this repulsive criminal, the so-called Haryanvi Horror, sooner rather than later. Let him know also that his sacrifice has not been in vain, and accordingly a note will be made in his file. And that in future he should refer to me as CA sir, or CA ji, rather than CA uncle.'

Mehta whisked the young man to another room to inform him of all these things. The CA leaned back, content. He spent some time reviewing his Grand Vision. The future unfolded before his eyes, rosy and full of construction. The Great Builder. That was what the history books would call him. Or perhaps, the Architect of New India. Simple and austere, yet with a certain majesty. There were arguments in favour of the Father of the New Nation too. He liked the Gandhi angle in that one. Yes, a time would come, a happier time, when he would tear off his mask of anonymity and reveal himself. The people had a right to know. He would leave out the bit about the flood relief scam, though, and the fact that he'd declared a thirty-day curfew in Thiruvananthapuram to prevent the spread of dengue, and that he had gone to Europe to investigate helicopter bribery but had mostly eaten pizza instead, and brought back a small memento for the PM. Some of his actions as a junior officer were easy to misconstrue, which was why he resolutely opposed excessive computerization. Computerization meant that files would have copies. With paper, all you had to do was make sure that improperly attested xeroxes were inadmissible as evidence. Of course, he was in no way against technology. Technology meant progress. He supported progress. He was keenly interested in the internet, for example, and had set up a commission to study it.

He decided to call up the CBI Director and yell at him. 'Where's my Hourly Status Report?' he shouted, causing Director Sinha to spill coffee on it. Sitting in his room, Director Sinha looked up at the CA's face on the screen, petrified, knowing the CA could see everything. He had been about to fax it. 'It's seven minutes late,' yelled the CA, 'if I wanted them in sixty-seven minutes, I would have called them Sixty-Seven Minute Reports, not Hourly Reports. Isn't that so?'

Sinha desperately tried to wipe the coffee off the report with shaking hands, smudging the ink and rendering it illegible as he did so. There had to be an easier way to do this.

'What are these reports called?' demanded the CA. Education was a constant process. A teacher could never rest.

'Hourly Status Reports,' recited Sinha, abjectly. He needed to take speed-typing lessons immediately. The crux of the problem was that each hourly report was taking over an hour to type.

'Have you found any evidence implicating the Bengal Protectorate yet? Have you proved that they are behind the telepathic attack? Please don't make me angry,' said the CA, dangerously calm now.

'No, sir,' said Sinha, who felt like crying. Should he? He had never tried that approach before. Would the CA show mercy, or would he write 'tends to cry at meetings' in his file? Director Sinha was unfamiliar with mercy. His children were scornful, and his wife never showed him any.

'Or perhaps the culprits were the Chinese themselves? I am not averse to this conclusion. Do you have any proof? Should I include it in the strongly worded protest, which I may or may not send later?' The CA knew he was being very ironic. He also knew it was wasted on these buffoons.

'Sir, we have not found any culprits, sir, neither false nor genuine,' said Sinha pathetically. 'However efforts are proceeding with full force, sir. Sir, we have already covered the railway station and the airport, only a few main points in the city are left. Plus the Dead Circle.'

'WHAT DID YOU CALL IT?' roared the CA, glaring into the screen. Sinha shrank visibly and cringed in his chair. A posting to the Andaman and Nicobar Islands shimmered faintly in the distance.

'Nothing, sir. Sir, nothing,' he quavered, 'I did not use the term Dead Circle, sir. Other people use it sir, less-educated types. Sir, I never use it. Never. Somebody else said it, sir, not me.'

'Grab your left ear with your left hand,' said the CA, in a voice like iron. Sinha grabbed his left ear with his left hand. He shut his eyes so he wouldn't have to look.

'Now twist—keep your grip hard—twist anti-clockwise. Good. Now clockwise. Please keep repeating. Anti-clockwise. Clockwise. Harder.'

The Director of the CBI twisted his own ear for a while. He spared

Shovon Chowdhury

himself no pain. The CA had an uncanny talent for spotting insincere self-punishment. The consequences of non-compliance were inconceivably hideous. He considered himself fortunate that it was his ears and not his nipples.

The CA observed his teaching methods in action. This would teach the man not to use rude language in future. He would be a model servant of the state from now on, language-wise. The CA finally gestured to him to stop. Sinha let his hand drop, but remained sitting upright, rigid with fear.

Yes, it was true that reconstruction in the Connaught Circle area had been unavoidably delayed. Perhaps another thirty or forty years would be required. Yes, the radiation had proved difficult to eradicate. Yes, a few deranged people insisted on hanging around there, making public spectacles of themselves. Yes, the debris and the garbage had combined in odd and unexpected ways, creating substances which the municipal corporation was still unable to categorize or analyse, much less eradicate. It was hardly paradise. But for an official of the government to call it the Dead Circle! Monstrous!

Well, at least they were being thorough. He expected the reports to come in any minute. Sinha's obedience as an officer was legendary, it was the fodder scam that had briefly besmirched him. The CA had all the evidence against him, of course. Whenever he felt bored, he could threaten him. But not just yet. Maybe it was time to call the General instead, and tighten the screws there a bit. Ask him to mobilize a few divisions. Draw up a few scenarios. Calculate collateral damage. Get him used to the whole thing. That was the good thing about war games. They made war seem like a game.

He disconnected. No longer transfixed by the CA's gaze, Sinha flopped back in his chair, weak with relief. What had he been thinking? He would have to ask his boys to speed up the investigation. He needed to show some actual results. It seemed like an odd thing to do, but there was always a first time for everything.

❏

Luckily he wasn't at the Dead Circle at that time, or his gloom might have deepened. Mr Chatterjee was, though, and he felt like he was having an out-of-body experience with no assistance from Dharti Pakar.

The Dead Circle was a huge circular patch of earth, rubble and deeply corroded metal, several miles across. The original inhabitants were all gone, vaporized on impact. It was now a garbage dump, located conveniently in the heart of the city, its surface covered with over a decade of decaying garbage. It formed a slimy, glistening coating over the debris, punctuated with the occasional colourful polybag, and little bits of skeleton. If there was ever a circle from which all manner of human disease and misfortune and horror could emerge—this was it.

Nevertheless, people lived here. The Competent Authority thought of them as deranged, and they probably were, even though the sanity bar was much lower these days. But this was their home.

Some were squatters who didn't want to leave the big city. They didn't want the walled-off village life of Shanti Nagar. Here, they could step out of their homes and walk the streets. It was their democratic right. Arson and riots were often used against them, in the hope that malls could follow, but they always came back. Then there were the sweepers who were expected to live with the garbage, fashioning little huts out of the more durable debris. There was also a good sprinkling of psychopaths and degenerates, whom Shanti-bai had kicked out of Shanti Nagar. 'They should go live with their own kind in Delhi,' she had said. 'It's better for them. Some of them could become ministers.'

The city had pushed all of them back—the good, the bad, and the ugly, bit by bit—remorselessly, as builders blessed by the Bureau of Reconstruction ruthlessly reclaimed every habitable patch of the city, until they found themselves with their backs to the Dead Circle. So that was where they had settled down, a human buffer zone between the rest of the city and its blasted, rotten core.

The leaders of the Dead Circle were the shopkeepers. Their forefathers had run the shops in Connaught Circle, basking in the glory of rents that never changed. They still did. Their mental and physical condition tended to deteriorate rapidly, but business was good, so their financial condition improved. Their costs being low, the Dead Circle shops were famous for stocking the cheapest goods in the city. Stocks moved off their shelves fast. Rumour had it that some of it moved while still on the shelves. Some members of the public reckoned that while living there was out of the question, how much harm could radiation or disease do to a few bars of soap in a couple of days? The key to transactions here was

Shovon Chowdhury

getting in quick, buying quick, and getting out quick. Hanging around to count change wasn't an option.

Mr Chatterjee had never ventured into the Dead Circle, so he was transfixed by what he saw. He gaped at a bejewelled housewife, one of the many hunters of bargains, standing in front of a monstrous mini van, briskly directing a coolie on the loading of large cartons full of soap, pulses and detergent. The coolie's face and arms were a mass of sores, although he was thoughtfully wearing rubber gloves to avoid smearing the merchandise. He was quite cheerful, and engaged in happy banter with his temporary employer. 'How much soap does your family need, madam?' he asked, grinning. 'Or are you giving baths to the whole neighbourhood?' His patroness smiled indulgently, pleased with the prices she had got. Was it Mr Chatterjee's imagination, or were the boxes emitting a faint glow? Well, most soaps promised a glowing complexion— it looked like this lot would really deliver. The coolie dumped his load and hobbled off happily, all set for the next consignment. The satisfied housewife carefully wiped the backseat of her car with a dainty handkerchief, tossed it away, and climbed in.

Mr Chatterjee felt slightly dizzy. Was nobody sane any more? What on earth was that woman thinking? Were there no limits to what people would do for a discount? Had she failed to notice the lethal condition of her cheerful helper? Why on earth did she need six cartons of soap? Soap won't wash your sins away, madam, he felt like calling after her, you have to work much harder than that. But he was far too polite to do any such thing, of course.

He was standing in front of a rickety, crooked signboard that said 'Chawla General Store'. The edges of the metal board were slightly corroded, as if eaten away by acid, or rats with super-strong teeth. Quite a spacious emporium, although dimly lit. Like the best restaurants, they weren't too keen on letting you see what you were getting. It was as good a place to start his investigations as any. The Director had called them all in that morning, and urged them to accelerate the investigation. Usually when he was briefing them, the Director would make inverted commas with his fingers whenever he mentioned the word 'investigation', but not this time. The Competent Authority wanted them to get to the bottom of the telepath attack mystery, and until they did they would be chasing down every lead, no matter how slim. Which was why Mr Chatterjee,

Venky and Professor Krishnan were all about to enter the Dead Circle to see what they could find, apart from bargains.

Venky had gone slightly pale, as they entered, but once he spotted Lifeboat, the health and beauty store, he perked up a bit. 'I'll cover the ladies, don't worry,' he whispered to Mr Chatterjee reassuringly, and trotted off, ever optimistic. The Dead Circle seemed like an odd place to be seeking health and beauty, thought Mr Chatterjee. Their prices were probably exceptional.

Professor Krishnan had pottered off too, eagerly seeking junk food. He was crazy about it. His wife kept him on a tight leash, feeding him a strictly vegetarian, home-cooked diet, so he spent his working hours pursuing his darkest culinary fantasies. He had scooted off down a dingy bylane, attracted by the sound of frying. Mr Chatterjee tried very hard not to imagine what he might be eating right now.

Which left him with the responsibility of conducting any actual investigations. Mr Chatterjee's inherent sincerity prevented him from emulating his gambolling colleagues. There was also Banani to consider. Given that he was going to be arrested for the crime in, what was it now, six days, his only hope lay in catching the culprit—assuming there was one. Otherwise, he would be a gone case, and then who would take care of her?

He marched resolutely into Chawla General Store. The name was reassuringly familiar. There used to be a Chawla General Store in his neighbourhood as well, when he was a kid. Perhaps Mr Chawla would be a sort of pillar of society of the Dead Circle, in a diseased but well-informed and well-mannered sort of way. A person with his finger on every pulse. Assuming, of course, he had fingers.

Mr Chawla turned out to be a pudgy, amiable chap in a laundered beige silk kurta, with several gold chains around his comfortably fat neck. He was reclining behind a low desk, on a well-upholstered gaddi, partly because of tradition, and partly because he had no legs.

'Come, come, sahab,' he said effusively, 'what can I provide for you? Ranjeet!' he yelled. The coolie promptly emerged from the shadows, complete with rubber gloves, with an empty carton in his hands.

Mr Chatterjee flipped open his ID, like they did on American TV serials. He didn't get to do it too often, although he practised at home a lot. Banani had caught him once doing it in front of the mirror, and had had hysterics for fifteen minutes.

'Chat'jee,' he said, very clipped, not parting his lips too much, 'CBI Investigator, TP Department.'

'Oy, govmint!' said Mr Chawla, erupting in mirth. 'Oy, Ranjeet, we have a babu from the govmint. Such a big day today is! Our fortunes have opened up, totally! Oy!' He almost fell off his gaddi, wiping his streaming eyes and steadying himself with his other hand.

'So, govmint babu,' he said, once he had recovered slightly, 'what have you come for? Have you come to give electricity connection? Or maybe sweeper service for front road? Or wait, wait, water, it must be water, no? Clean corporation water we'll get. Oy Ranjeet, don't sell all the soap, we'll need some soon.'

Ranjeet started giggling too. That Chawla-sahab, he was just too funny.

'Or, wait,' said Mr Chawla, making his eyes all round and googly. Clearly, the man had an aptitude for theatre. 'Perhaps we should be scared,' he said, in a deep, quivering voice. He clutched his pudgy hands to his chest. 'Have you come to check our licence, govmint babu? Am I not registered properly? All forms not submitted? Am I permit expiry case? Will you fine me heavily?' He sat there, shivering in mock fear.

Mr Chatterjee felt vaguely embarrassed. He didn't know why, he couldn't quite put his finger on it. His father had been a schoolteacher, with all of a Bengali schoolteacher's respect for Education and Culture. He had always railed against shopkeepers, the banias, those uncultured money-grabbers with their bottomless greed, who had brought the country to rack and ruin. Yet here he was, an educated man, with a job which involved reading and writing, standing in front of a bania, embarrassed. It was confusing.

'Look,' he murmured finally, 'I'm sorry about the electricity, and the water, and the sweeper. I'm not really a government officer, I'm temporary. But there is something threatening our country, and I have been asked to investigate. I need your help. I'm only trying to do my duty. Can you give me five minutes? I would appreciate it.'

Mr Chawla eyed him soberly. 'Please sit down,' he said quietly. 'Tell me what you have to say. Ranjeet! Get the babu a sharbat. Or wait,' he turned to Mr Chatterjee, 'I don't suppose you want to drink my sharbat, do you?'

Mr Chatterjee squirmed, shame-faced. 'No matter,' said Mr Chawla, cheerfully. 'It must be a big threat to the country, no, for a spectacled babu like you to risk the Circle?'

Mr Chatterjee adjusted his glasses and cleared his throat. He told Mr Chawla about the attack on the telepaths. He told him about the Chinese or Bengali aggressor they were seeking. He told him about the frustrating, pointless search he was conducting. He told him how his colleagues were more interested in junk food and babes than saving the country. He even told him how he was scheduled to be arrested next week, and how he was afraid of leaving his wife a helpless widow in a harsh, cruel world. The man had a sympathetic face. He told him everything.

The bania waited patiently for him to finish. He massaged his wobbly jowls thoughtfully. 'Achcha,' he said, 'so it's a terrorism case?'

Mr Chatterjee nodded, hoping the man would tell him what to do next.

'It may not be the Chinese or their chamchas from Bengal, you know,' said Chawla, thoughtfully, 'other candidates are also there.'

Mr Chatterjee had never stopped to consider this. Who else could it be but the Chinese?

'It could be Maoists,' mused Chawla, answering his unspoken thought, 'but Maoists today fight face to face, like real men. Army is having a tough time. They do bombing-shombing also. They sabotage very expertly. However, what do I know, I am just a poor shopkeeper.' He sighed gustily, enveloping Mr Chatterjee in a cloud of fragrant paan masala.

Mr Chatterjee looked up, his heart quickening with hope. This man probably knew exactly what to do. He was just dragging it out a bit, milking the drama.

He was right. Mr Chawla's eyes were twinkling. 'Since it is a sabotage case, I think I should make a phone call. There is a man I know who deals in such matters. Pucca professional. I'll use speakerphone. Then you can hear also.'

He dialled a number on the immaculate purple phone on his desk and punched the speaker button with the air of a conjurer about to pull off a major trick.

'Hello, this is Al Qaeda,' answered a cultured voice at the other end, 'how may we help you?'

Mr Chatterjee stared, open-mouthed. Chawla winked at him cheerfully.

'Oy, Ali,' he boomed, 'don't be so stylish, yaar. Chawla this side. One friend of mine needs some help. Shall I send him?'

'Certainly, Chawla-sahab,' said the voice at the other end, cordially, 'as you know, any friend of yours is a friend of mine.'

'Chalo, then,' said Chawla, 'I'll just send him. Don't blow him up or anything, he's a nice person.' He rang off.

Chawla scribbled out a little chit and handed it over, grinning hugely. Mr Chatterjee held it in his nerveless fingers. What mythical beast was this that had suddenly shambled out of antiquity? A name that mothers used to scare their children. A long-lost footnote in the history of terror. He would have been less surprised if he'd been asked to meet a unicorn. And a lot less likely to pee his pants.

'They're just around the corner,' said Chawla helpfully, deeply satisfied with the effect he had produced.

Mr Chatterjee got up to go. His actions were mechanical. His mind was blank.

'Oy, Chatterjee-sahab,' Chawla called after him as he was leaving. Mr Chatterjee turned back to look at him.

Chawla met his eyes. He was no longer smiling. 'Consider this, Mr Chatterjee,' he said softly, his expression glacial, 'if there was one place on earth where you would expect to find the last of Al Qaeda, one last corner of this world—which place do you think that would be?'

❏

'So how did you mess it all up?' asked Pintoo. His stump was hurting and he was feeling crabby. But he had work to do. He'd been given these powers for a reason. His mother would have been deeply disappointed if he just sat around, moaning about his hand. 'It's hard for people like us to help others,' she used to say, 'but do what you can.'

'Excuse me?' said Tarun-da, nervously.

They were sitting in the Party office, a small shack with a fading red flag on top, right next to the open drain that ran down the west wall. Tarun-da had chosen this spot to show they were a party with a difference. The stench was terrible. Membership was slow. But that suited Pintoo. His lessons with Tarun-da and the headmaster were rarely disturbed. He now realized that smashing the Bank of Bodies was going to take longer than he had thought, given their extensive retail network. He couldn't solve everything by just pushing things. He had to think. Besides, it was more than just the Bank of Bodies. Something must have gone badly wrong for everything to be so screwed up. He needed to learn more, so that he could try and unscrew things.

'See, I'm just a kid, right,' said Pintoo, 'you're the adult. Whatever the current scene, it's all thanks to you people. It must have required a lot of work to make things this bad. I've seen other countries on television. What was it you did that turned this country into such a mess?'

'It was the capitalists,' said Tarun-da, without hesitation.

'What did they do?' asked Pintoo.

'They sucked the blood of the people, till they became bloated, like leeches.'

'Could you give more detail?'

'There was one man in particular who ruined us, with his unholy vision. Before him, corruption was there, but it was small. He taught us many new things. I cannot mention his name because his children are very ferocious, and their lawyers might hear me,' said Tarun-da. 'They fly around in small helicopters, with powerful microphones, identifying those who have to be silenced. As a child, he started by selling onion pakoras, which he sold in good numbers, but onion pakoras were not enough. Through all manner of trickery, and some amount of hard work, he grew from strength to strength. Whether it was about twisting laws or twisting people, he was always in the forefront. He dared to dream big. He was a man with a simple vision. All he wanted was everyone else's money. If someone had strangled him when he was a little baby, it could have saved the nation. But then again, what harm has a little baby done? Maybe if someone had stolen him from the hospital, and donated him to the Ramakrishna Mission? Today the Ramakrishna Mission could have been running the country. All of us would be receiving very good education and eating terrible, but nutritious food. If only someone could go back in time and change his destiny, how different our lives would be.'

Pintoo got up and gave Tarun-da a hug. He couldn't help himself.

'Tarun-da,' he said, 'you're a genius!'

Suddenly, he knew what to do.

12

*'Dr Vijay, why don't you do medical examination
on this lady?'*

When it came to buying people, women did it best. It was just like vegetables. No self-respecting Delhi man with a wife, mother or sister would ever be caught dead buying vegetables. Rumour had it that your dick fell off instantly. As a result, over the years, the women had developed tremendous skill at assessing natural produce.

Like all domestic purchases, this too was something Mrs Verma took pride in doing well. So here she was, at the cavernous warehouse of Slaves R Us, a few miles off Panipat, a place where thousands had died on several occasions, to help make someone or the other the ruler of Delhi.

The elderly manager eyed her warily. He was one of the thirty-seven cousin-brothers who owned the store. Their village had cornered the trade in people. For the first few years they had sold at the local mandi, with little regard for shopping environment, or customer delight, and no one had ever complained. All that had changed when one of the younger cousin-brothers had returned from America, mightily impressed by the concept of large format retail verticals.

'You can't stop progress,' he'd argued, although most of his cousin-brothers couldn't see why not. They'd been doing it for years.

The young spark was a favourite of the patriarch, however, because he massaged his feet, and hadn't married an American. His views had prevailed in the end. Cash flows had improved significantly. Extracting the cash remained a challenge, because their clientele consisted almost exclusively of Delhi matriarchs, never the easiest people to deal with, what with their prows like battleships, and their noses like scimitars, and diamond rings that could easily double as knuckledusters.

This one was a regular customer. He knew her well. Getting money out of her was like squeezing water from a stone.

He hitched up his dhoti and adjusted his turban, ready for battle.

'Greetings, Owneress,' he said, coming forward with sincerely folded palms.

'Put up the AC,' said Mrs Verma crossly, 'as it is you'll take the price of this showroom from my pocket. At least let me enjoy it.'

The manager made an imperious hand movement, and a little boy who had been leaning against a nearby wall scampered off to find the remote control. He was the only one who understood all the buttons.

'I'm buying in bulk, so you're paying for delivery,' announced Mrs Verma.

The manager grunted non-committally.

'First, I need a doctor. Sanjeev has disposed of the last one.'

The manager shook his head sadly. He never ceased to be amazed by the wasteful habits of the aristocracy. He raised his voice.

'Kindly come here, Dr Vijay,' he said.

A bespectacled young man got up from a nearby desk where he had been working on his computer. He held a steaming cup of tea that he had been sipping from.

'Yes?' he said, politely.

Slave R Us displayed its merchandise in their natural habitat. It was a trick they had picked up from Big Bazaar. Graduates and above sat at desks; labourers squatted under plastic trees; airline staff stood ready with trays full of airline food; domestic staff sat around in simulated living rooms, getting up once in a while to do a spot of dusting.

'An excellent young man from one of the best medical colleges,' said the manager, patting Dr Vijay on the shoulder. 'His family recovered his medical fees and made a good profit on him. Eats very little. Highly capable. Dr Vijay, why don't you examine this lady?'

Dr Vijay was reaching for his rubber gloves when Mrs Verma stopped him. This whole demonstration thing was getting completely out of control.

'I'm not paying one paisa more than I paid for the last one,' she declared firmly, drawing her sari down to cover more of her bosom, suspecting the manager was getting an eyeful. She'd seen the women around here. Scrawny little things. No wonder the men got a little frisky. It was their own fault for not feeding them.

The manager was appalled by her suggestion that she acquire the doctor cheaply.

'Owneress, what are you saying? The cost of food has gone up so much. He's a doctor, we give him brain food. Also we keep buying him all these expensive books. Price of everything has gone up. I'm a poor man, please don't do this to me.'

'Don't talk nonsense,' said Mrs Verma, unmoved. 'Poor? You could buy me on this side of the river and sell me on the other, you fraud. Same price. No discussion. Load him in the helicopter.'

The manager sighed and gave Dr Vijay a nudge.

Dr Vijay gulped down his tea and went off to pack.

'Now let's get down to my main business,' said Mrs Verma, 'I need fifty labourers for our factory in Chhattisgarh.'

The manager looked puzzled. These kinds of requirements were usually handled locally. Chhattisgarh was a thousand miles away.

Mrs Verma was prepared for this.

'Those Bihari villagers are too weak,' she said quickly, 'mining is heavy work. I need some good, strong Jat boys.'

The manager seemed satisfied by her explanation. He walked down the aisle to a well-equipped gym, where a few husky young men in loincloths were admiring each other.

'Oy Rajinder,' he called out.

Three men came forward, smiling confidently, flexing their muscles. The manager turned to Mrs Verma.

'Best quality boys from our own village,' he said proudly, slapping a nearby bicep. 'Raised on the best wheat and desi ghee. They have been sold to raise money to buy wives for their brothers. It is very sad, but what to do, times have become like this.'

They certainly looked strong, although Mrs Verma didn't like the way they were checking her out. Not her problem. They'd be working with Sanjeev. They would eat a lot, though, and poor Sanjeev was already moaning about extra beer. But fifty boys like this would make a big difference to productivity. Some of them could even be trained to fight . . .

The manager knew he'd made a sale. He named a price. They argued. They sat down at the table recently vacated by Dr Vijay and had a cup of tea. They argued some more.

'Throw in three kitchen boys and you have a deal,' said Mrs Verma eventually.

'You know the terms,' said the manager, promptly, 'thirty-six month EMI, 50 per cent to them, 50 per cent to us. After three years, you can renew the contract, or go in for exchange offer. Naturally, we cannot give any guarantee or warranty. After all, these are human beings.'

Her phone rang urgently. It was Sanjeev. The reception was bad, his face was blinking on and off on her screen. He looked harassed.

'Where are you, darling?' asked Mrs Verma. 'I'm shopping at Slaves R Us. I thought you'd be in Delhi by now to try and get the army to help you out.'

'I'm still in the jungle, you stupid cunt! The Maoists shot down my helicopter again.'

The picture went fuzzy. She could hear the sounds of gunfire, accompanied by vuvuzelas. She was shocked by his language, but decided not to make an issue of it just then.

'Do you want me to come and pick you up?' she asked solicitously.

'Of course I want you to come and pick me up, you silly bitch!' roared Verma, 'I'm getting my arse shot off here. And get me another helicopter pilot. This one's dead.'

'Mek sure about the bier,' whispered Captain Kruger, who was standing next to Mr Verma.

'I'll see what I can do,' said Mrs Verma frostily. The line went dead. Sanjeev was completely exasperating. How the hell was she supposed to find a helicopter pilot in Panipat?

'Do you happen to have a helicopter pilot in stock?' she asked the manager, who had maintained a respectful and sympathetic silence.

'One of the village boys actually was a helicopter pilot,' said the manager ruefully, 'but we just hanged him yesterday for marrying a girl from the same sub-caste.'

Mrs Verma gave a cry of rage, horror and despair.

'What the hell is wrong with you people?' she demanded. 'Do you think helicopter pilots grow on trees?'

'No,' admitted the manager, slightly sheepishly, 'but in this case he is hanging from one.'

'It should have been you,' said a wizened old crone, who was squatting in a nearby corner. Mrs Verma hadn't noticed her before. Now that she looked, she could see several old crones all over the showroom. They were squatting on the ground, so they were hard to spot. Enjoying the air-conditioning, no doubt. Or perhaps they had always been sitting here, and the showroom had been built around them.

The manager ignored her.

'I am sorry we are unable to fulfil this requirement,' said the manager, with dignity, 'I will place an order immediately. For your current order, kindly give me delivery details. As you know, we deliver to any location in India which is not radioactive, within seventy-two hours.'

Mrs Verma filled the delivery form, swiped her card, and rushed off to rescue her husband, reminding herself to pick up some beer on the way.

13

'They kept talking about some place called Turkman Gate.
No one knows why.'

The Competent Authority sat in the Prime Minister's room, shaking his legs and nursing an erection. It was the first one he'd had in months, and it made him uncharacteristically cheerful. It was hidden behind the solid oak of the massive desk, his rigid little secret.

Everything about the PM's room was huge. It was the size of a smallish football field. Instead of spectators, the walls were lined with portraits of ex-PMs, lugubriously viewing the proceedings. Except three, each and every one of them had been massacred by terrorists, so their depression was understandable. The current PM was related to several of them.

The large room was actually an act of kindness on the Competent Authority's part. As the actual power of the Prime Minister had diminished, the bureaucrats had made the room bigger and bigger. It seemed only fair. To mark the culmination of the process, the Competent Authority had now expanded it to stadium-like proportions. He also had the hots for her, and was hoping this would make her happy.

He gazed at the object of his affections, mesmerized. Of course, she was getting on a bit, but her skin remained milky-white and impossibly smooth. Her party men always raved about how her body language helped them win elections, and, man, could he hear her talking! A tiny bit of drool dribbled down his chin.

There was a big box of tissues on the table, which the PM pushed towards him without looking up. She was busy reading the Republic Day proposals, but her peripheral vision was extremely acute.

How had she ended up in the clutches of this nasty little man? She had started out all those years ago, full of hope and optimism, confident that she could make things better. She had tramped up and down the country, broiling in the sun and choking on the dust, wooed every conceivable caste and creed, including some she had no idea existed, worn every possible form of costume and headgear, memorized slogans in a hundred dialects, squatted on the ground of a thousand villages, smiled her dazzling smile on a million TV screens. Because it was what she was supposed to do. Because it was her destiny. Because she believed she could make a difference. Only to discover that there was very little she could actually change, except for her furniture. Provided she wasn't in a hurry. Otherwise, as elected representatives, the only function of people like her, the ministers in her cabinet, and other MPs, was to take their share and keep the files moving. They were the public faces of the biggest mafia racket in human history, otherwise known as the Indian Administrative Service. The Indian economy was still big. Not all taxpayers had been vaporized. Data still flowed through submarine cables. Young men from Rampur were still speaking Texan. Mehrason's Mega Store was still selling gold. Middle-class remnants were still buying soap, and chappals, and anti-radiation swimsuits. Foreign Direct Investment continued to be significant, although the foreigners preferred to monitor their investments from home. Relations with Switzerland were at an all-time high. Many rupees were being generated. And not a rupee changed hands without passing through the IAS, with the police by their side for pest control. Foreign Mafiosi often dropped by on secret study tours, braving radiation in pursuit of knowledge.

She finished reading and looked up at the Competent Authority. The Competent Authority looked back, benevolently. His legs were shaking at an astonishing rate, and his eyes seemed slightly glazed.

'Is it entirely necessary for me to lead the parade riding a missile?' she asked, plaintively. 'Wouldn't a horse be more appropriate, if anything?'

The Competent Authority beamed at her. It would actually fulfil one of his kinkier dreams, but he was well bred enough not to voice this directly. Finesse was called for. 'Madam, this is what your public wants to see. They see you as a twenty-first-century Goddess Durga, riding the twenty-first-century version of a lion—the symbol of our power, progress, and manhood.' He croaked a bit on the last word.

'Don't you think it's the tiniest bit undignified?' she persisted. 'After all, the Bushes will be watching, not to mention that ancient Chinese fellow. If he gets too excited, he might injure himself.'

'And what could be better for India?' responded the CA smoothly.

'Your family has a long tradition of making sacrifices for the nation. Do you not think it is worth it? We researched the concept, and the focus groups went wild. It would probably mean at least fifty more seats in the next election. You owe it to the party, madam, if you will excuse my interfering in the political process. We have things working smoothly. Leave everything to us.'

The Prime Minister sighed. The only decision in her hands, evidently, was what to wear. Riding breeches seemed the logical choice. Perhaps a Stetson, to keep Bush happy. Along with leather boots and a riding crop, to goad the missile on. She decided not to share this with the Competent Authority at this point. He was worked up enough as it was.

She turned her attention to the rest of the parade. There were plenty of floats, as always. Many of them symbolized the culmination of nearly a hundred years of progress. One float was a mobile mountain of rice, sixty-feet high, to represent self-sufficiency in food. Not cooked, hopefully. Sachin Tendulkar, she noted with relief, had politely declined the opportunity to sit inside a gigantic replica of the World Cup, a celebration of the nation's cricketing prowess. There were plenty of missiles, over and above the one she was riding, including a rather sweet arrangement of smallish missiles in the shape of a lotus. A contingent of marching men with spades over their shoulders represented the Bureau of Reconstruction.

'Why are they marching with spades?' asked the PM looking up. 'Wouldn't bulldozers be more appropriate?'

The Competent Authority scowled. This was a sore point with him. It was the obvious thing to do. People kept asking him about it. He had made the last person who asked him hop on one leg for two hours. 'They could not move fast enough,' he said, sulkily, 'Besides, the idea was tested with the public. They kept talking about some place called Turkman Gate. No one seems to know why.'

The Prime Minister did, and she winced slightly, it was an incident from the past that was best left buried there. It was time to move on to the state of the nation. She always asked the CA a question or two about the state of the nation. It showed she was on the ball. Hopefully, someday, she might be able to influence something not involving clothes, make-up, television or votes.

'What are we doing about this Haryanvi Horror?' she asked. 'The media is having a field day. Some of my friends are complaining. A lot of them own BMWs. I noticed a lot of graffiti, too.'

The Competent Authority cursed, deflated in more senses than one. His legs stopped shaking. This unspeakable creature was becoming something of a nuisance. The media was indeed having a field day. They hadn't had so much fun since the Monkey Man. TV crews were cruising the city in the hopes of catching him live. Decoy reporters were, with understandable reluctance, driving around in hired BMWs in the hope of becoming the next victim. Artists' impressions of the maniac were being created and speculated over. Most showed an enormously tall peasant, lantern-jawed and steely-eyed, in a white dhoti and a yellow kurta, brandishing a huge lathi. SMS jokes about backdoor entry and molested tail-pipes were spreading like wildfire. Mysterious graffiti had been cropping up all over the city, with messages like 'Haryana Zindabad!' and 'Up the Aristocracy!' Each was accompanied by a crudely drawn banana. If the man appeared in public and stood for elections, he would probably win in a landslide.

He had tried hard to hide all this from the PM. He had appointed roaming squads to instantly erase the graffiti and replace it with more appropriate BoR slogans such as 'Together we will build a better future!' and 'Don't be bitter on Twitter!' and 'Have you reported a neighbour today?' But they hadn't been fast enough. He made a mental note to transfer the officer concerned to the Bengal border for life.

'The situation is under control, madam,' he lied smoothly. 'All the victims are being compensated with a new BMW and a bottle of Johnson's Baby Oil. Investigations are making rapid progress. An arrest is imminent.'

The PM could easily make out when the Competent Authority was trying to hide his incompetence. He tried to be cagey and reassuring at the same time.

She was deeply disturbed by this Haryanvi Horror phenomenon. Crime affected the poor, mostly, where they sorted it out locally, or the middle class, where the news channels raved and sneered for a week or two. Now here was this creature, this slavering maniac, who was making sure that nothing and no one was safe. Lurking behind bushes, skulking behind lamp-posts, jumping her friends without the slightest reason or provocation. A perverted pimpernel, buggering the rich and cheering up the poor. For all she knew, there was a whole band of nihilists at work, training in some secret hideaway, practicing on rubber dolls or straw dummies under some crackpot drill master. ('On the count of three—one, two, three, forward—dhotis UP! That's the way . . . don't let go of the banana . . .')

She had requested the General to intervene, but the General had declined, arguing with some passion that sex crimes and auto vandalism were not yet under the purview of the armed forces, and as long as he was around, he intended to keep it that way.

That reminded her of the other thing that was bothering her. 'Why is the army beginning to mobilize?' she asked the Competent Authority, looking him squarely in the eye.

'Purely routine, madam,' said the Competent Authority, 'if there is one lesson we have learnt from the past, it is that we must be Ever Vigilant. When our enemies think of us, the first word that comes to their minds should be Vigilant. "Those Indians, they are very Vigilant," they must say to themselves. We must take no liberties with such a Vigilant Nation.'

He liked saying the word Vigilant, he realized. It rolled so nicely off the tongue. Maybe he should add it to his description in the history books—The Vigilant Father of the Nation. It had a certain ring to it, just like Gandhi, but more specific.

The Prime Minister eyed him apprehensively. She didn't know which scared her more—the Competent Authority, in full flow, driving her in strange and unpredictable directions, or the Competent Authority in a state of temporary catatonia, playing fantasy numbers in his head. She had often considered getting herself a pet telepath and hiding him next door, just to read his mind. She had never done so, partly because the CA kept a vice-like grip over all telepathic resources, but also because she was genuinely scared of finding out what was inside his head. Some closets were best left unopened.

The Competent Authority noticed the fleeting strangeness that passed across the face of his beloved, and quickly assumed an expression of extreme competence. He pushed a file forward.

'One last thing,' he said casually, 'there is this ordinance you need to sign. Purely routine. The wheels of government must keep rolling. For us to do these boring things, we sometimes need your signature. And a very elegant signature it is too, if I may say so.'

Women liked flattery. It was a well-known fact. He held out a pen for her. The pen was smooth, just like him.

She glanced through the document. It was gobbledegook, as usual. Terms like 'situational analysis', 'mobilizatory imperatives', and 'anticipatory aggression' floated before her eyes. As always, after approximately twenty-two clauses and sixty-three sub-clauses, it ended with the phrase, '. . . as per the direction of the Prime Minister, or in absence of the Prime Minister due to unavoidable or other circumstances, the relevant competent authority.'

She never really knew what she was signing anyway, but she had a bad feeling about this one. There was nothing much she could do. If she didn't sign it now, it would re-materialize on her table in the middle of fifty other files, and she would sign it then.

She signed the file and handed it back to him. The Competent Authority tucked it under his armpit and got up. He shook her hand with warmth and vigour.

'I will take your leave, madam,' he said, 'I do not wish to impose any further on your busy schedule. I look forward to seeing you on Republic Day.'

I'll bet you do, thought the Prime Minister sourly, as he lumbered off. She waited till the door had closed behind him, and then she reached for one of her seven telephones. It was the only one she used. She had no idea what the others were for. It was time to make some calls.

14

'Plus Mr Chawla supplies us essential goods on credit,
so naturally we of Al Qaeda are grateful to him.'

Riot duty was the most tiring part of a policeman's job, and Ram Manohar Pande was tired. He was more of a solo artiste, essentially. Mobs were a different game. Some people thought it was just a simple matter of egging them on, or standing by quietly while they did their thing. Terms like 'gross' and 'negligence' were frequently bandied about. But actually, it involved a lot more skill, the nudge, the wink, the well-placed lathi blow, selecting exactly which of the victims to arrest. Keeping a sharp eye out for journalists. They could be quite sneaky sometimes. He'd almost been caught on camera once. He'd managed to break the man's skull just in time. Soft living and soft skulls seemed to go hand in hand. If Pande had been a man of words, rather than a man of action, he might have written a paper about this.

The man of action was currently taking a well-deserved break, reclining against a convenient doorstep, slightly out of breath. He'd taken his boots off, and Bhiru, one of the thana sub judices, was massaging his feet. He'd brought him along especially for this purpose. After thirteen years, he had grown quite fond of the fellow. He was a well-trained domestic, always eager to please. Of course he mumbled somewhat, since most of his teeth had been broken, but he was satisfactory in most other ways.

The usual post-riot clean-up was going on. A few of his constables were rooting through debris in the smouldering shops, hoping against hope to find something valuable. This was unlikely. The looters had been pretty thorough. A few ripped and torn banners were the only remnants. The bodies had been piled on one side of the street, and somebody had gone to get the kerosene. A well-fed gentleman in a safari suit had just finished loading goods into his van, and was driving off with a cheery wave. Pande smiled back, glad to have given satisfaction. He ran a tight operation. It was a matter of professional pride. So few people took pride in doing the job right these days. Personally, Pande blamed it on the decline in educational standards. His own imaginary daughters all went to very good schools, but in the real world, there weren't any. The whole country was just one big bucket of shit, and there was nothing a man could do about it.

He kicked Bhiru away from him, his momentary good mood spoilt. He was in his socks, so it wasn't much of a kick. He started putting on his boots so he could do it properly. Bhiru, a veteran with years of hard experience, scampered off to the jeep and started dusting Pande's seat, taking care not to bend over too much. With some foresight, he had filched one of the case files and shoved it down the back of his dhoti, but there was no point in taking chances.

Pande stood up and yawned. Tomorrow morning he would get up bright and early, and set off on his expedition into Shanti Nagar. That rich fake guru had been right. The only place you were likely to find tame street dogs was Shanti Nagar. The dogs that had mysteriously materialized in Pappu Verma's room could only have come from this source. That was the key to the Verma case. He was making progress. He had a lead. It was quite addictive, this investigation thing. Point A led to Point B, and then Point C, and so on and so forth. A man could get used to it. If he cracked this case, maybe they would transfer him to the CBI. The rations were much better, there was air-conditioning, tea was served by bearers in clean uniforms, and the biscuits were manufactured by reputed companies. He might even get a swivel chair, something he had secretly always lusted over. Perhaps a desk with a brass nameplate.

With the brass nameplate shining in his mind, Pande felt decisive and masterful. Now was the time to finish off that stupid dog assassination job too. If he left right now, he could be done in about an hour. He would march into that Aggarwal fellow's house, locate the dog, and shoot it. If the Aggarwal fellow objected, he would shoot him too. The Banerjee chap had not specifically asked him to shoot his neighbour, but Pande was feeling generous, and didn't mind throwing in a freebie.

Pande grabbed Bhiru by the neck and shoved him into the back seat. He got behind the wheel of his jeep, started it up with a single, masterful flick of his wrist, and drove off, skilfully avoiding the outflung arm of one of the corpses.

Behind him, the gutted shops smouldered on, sending little curly fingers of smoke up into the bitter, grey sky.

❑

'Save the country? Who'll save the country? You'll save the country?' said the ancient headmaster, galvanized. They had just finished Pintoo's math lesson. The headmaster's method of instruction was simple. He slapped him when he got the answer wrong. As a result Pintoo could never do more than an hour of math at a time. His cheeks hurt too much. The ancient headmaster was currently the only person in Shanti Nagar who didn't fear him. Pintoo had asked him why. 'Because I'm too old to care, you son of a donkey,' he had said, slapping him. Right now, Pintoo was trying to put in a spot of research before heading home to Tarun-da's, taking care to stay out of range.

'You'll save the country?' repeated the headmaster, drooling scorn.

'Yes,' said Pintoo, from a safe distance. If he could stay uninjured long enough, he might be able to learn something which would help him change things for the better. He had a few ideas. Whatever he did, they could hardly get worse.

The headmaster paused to digest this.

'Well, someone has to,' he said, eventually.

'So if there was one thing,' said Pintoo, 'if you could go back in time and change one thing. One thing that could save us from living like this. What would you do?'

'Find Indira true love,' the headmaster said, cackling unexpectedly. 'She was alone for too many years, that lady. Maybe if someone had been by her side, giving her hugs from time to time, her heart would have been softer. Then perhaps she would not have hated us so, and turned us all into her servants, and gifted us the culture of chamchagiri, and made us an aristocracy of idiots, and allowed every manner of corruption to thrive, so long as the corrupt bowed deeply as she walked by.'

Pintoo had never heard of this Indira person, but engineering romance sounded like a tricky business. Affairs of the heart were notoriously dodgy, and hard to put a schedule to. His consciousness was becoming cosmic, but he wasn't stupid.

'Our arses have been taken in so many ways,' he said, morosely, 'it would take a magician to solve anything.'

'In my life, I heard of only one magician,' said the headmaster. 'In those early years, when nothing was fixed, if he had lived a few more years, perhaps he could have done something. At least he would have rid us of the IAS. But an RSS man shot him. Otherwise he would have lived longer. His eating habits were very regular, like mine, and he cleared his bowels frequently.'

'Who was this?' asked Pintoo.

The headmaster closed his eyes for a moment and smiled.

'Mahatma Gandhi,' he said.

❑

The Al Qaeda office turned out to be quite cosy, with a small desk in one corner, and a compact little sofa and coffee table combo in the other. It could have been a local real estate agency, right down to the plastic flowers on the desk, except for the large portrait of Osama Bin Laden that dominated the wall. There was an expression of ineffable sadness in his hypnotic, loony eyes. Given the way things had worked out, this was hardly surprising.

Ali was at the desk, hunched over his computer when Mr Chatterjee came in. He was wearing headphones. Mr Chatterjee's legs were trembling violently, and he badly needed to sit down. Ali put a finger to his lips and waved him towards the sofa, grinning. He looked amiable enough, but also extremely lean and fit. He could probably snap his neck like a twig.

Mr Chatterjee flopped down bonelessly, feeling sick and dizzy. He felt like his brain was floating two or three feet above his skull, an independent entity cut loose from conventional moorings by an overdose of weirdness. He had more or less lost track of why he was here, what he had originally set out to do, what time of day it was. He vaguely remembered worrying about Banani, but he wasn't sure why. There also seemed to be an arrest floating ahead somewhere in his future, but he couldn't recall having committed any crime, barring fudging the occasional expense voucher. He needed guidance. Maybe Ali could provide it. He looked at him hopefully.

'No, I can't get you any uranium, love,' said Ali, into the headphones. 'I know there ought to be some lying around, but the fact is they used up most of it. Also, while I don't know your husband very well, that doesn't make for such a good birthday present, does it? How about some tribal art from Bastar instead? Or some nice candles from the Blind School? Radioactive? No, I'm afraid they're not radioactive. Well, all right then. Goodbye.'

The moment he had heard 'Al Qaeda', Mr Chatterjee had imagined a commanding hook-nose and kohl-darkened eyes, perhaps a goatee, like the sheikh he had once seen shopping for shoes at the Oberoi. But Ali was pleasantly nondescript. He could have been from anywhere. You could imagine sitting next to him at the dhaba, and never once noticing him. He wore frayed blue jeans and a Bob Marley T-shirt. *Ja Rules!* said the T-shirt. Mr Chatterjee had no idea who Ja was, and why he should be ruling. No doubt all would be revealed in due course.

'All part of the service,' explained Ali. 'I do get some odd inquiries, though. Like a spot of tea?'

Mr Chatterjee nodded, relieved. It seemed like he was not going to be blown up immediately.

'What service?' he asked.

'Well, I do information, don't I? Didn't Chawla-sahab tell you? Oh, I see. He's a sneaky little sod, isn't he? He just sent you off to meet Al Qaeda. He has no conscience, that man. He's like something out of Dostoevsky.'

An intellectual! Mr Chatterjee cheered up slightly.

'He's a decent bloke, on the whole,' said Ali. 'This place is a shithole, but he does the best he can. Plus Mr Chawla supplies us essential goods on credit, so naturally we of Al Qaeda are grateful to him.'

Mr Chatterjee was intrigued by the 'we of Al Qaeda' bit. How many people could possibly fit into an office this size?

'Are there more of you?' Mr Chatterjee ventured timidly.

'No, just me,' said Ali. 'So it's all on my head, innit? All that shit we pulled, over all those years. I spent the last few years in Karachi, but then it started getting hot, and I don't mean the weather. We thought we'd be fine, because who can ever tell what's going on in Karachi, and who's killing who and why. But those mini hunter-killer drones were wiping us out. There was nowhere to hide. You couldn't even take a dump in a loo with a window. So I slipped into Delhi, just in time for the bomb to drop on us. Talk about timing. The rest of the lads were in Pakistan, which is where they all ended up after they wrapped up in Mali. All that French food was too much for them. Then the Yanks planted mushrooms all over Pakistan. They're partying with the virgins now. That pretty much makes me the last one, doesn't it?'

Ali looked reflectively at Mr Chatterjee. 'You're around the same age as me, you know what it was like. Babies with their skin on fire. Rows of corpses laid out on Yusuf Sarai. Little kids lifting sheets, looking for their mummies. It was just too much suffering, is what it was. You keep hanging onto hatred because it's the only thing you know, and the anger's been inside you since school, and it doesn't go away easy, the things they called you. But it got pretty ugly in Somalia, executing teenage girls with firing squads. That's when it started for me. The doubt. I was never much of a fan of blowing up schools, anyway. It's just that I was angry for so many many years. Those nazi dicks, the ones that put shit on my sister's head, they were defending England, they said. I though I'd give them something to defend against. I bought into the whole story, about how it was a war, and there were bound to be casualties. But not any more. I've seen Yusuf Sarai. I'm done with caliphs. God is big enough to take care of himself. I've got some skills. I try to help people. It can't change what I did, but it's the best I can do.'

Mr Chatterjee took a moment to take all this in. This new version of Al Qaeda was a lot different from what he had expected, a sort of Middle Eastern version of the Little Sisters of the Poor. What was clear, though, was that he wasn't going to get blown up immediately, and consequently, his brain started functioning again.

'How do you help people?' he asked.

'Information,' said Ali. 'We're in a state of Emergency, so you need a special permit for a mobile. Just in case you spread rumours or hurt sentiments. It was a temporary measure introduced ten years ago. The government doesn't issue many permits. People need information. I know how to get it. It's what I used to do, mostly. Where's the best place to sell bananas today? Is my husband really shacking up with that floozie? Is it safe to plant crops in Faridabad? Where can I find a wife? What does the BBC say? Is Tendulkar still batting? How can I emigrate to Bangladesh? Why does he keep puking like that? What is this constitution thing people keep going on about? Does the Competent Authority have a rate card? How do I get adopted by the Gandhi family? Where can I find an honest judge? Is that just a pimple on my dick, or should I see a doctor? People have a lot of questions. What's yours?'

'I want to understand what's going on,' said Mr Chatterjee.

'So did Marvin Gaye,' said Ali, 'but you're going to have to give me a bit more to work with.'

Mr Chatterjee told him everything, starting with the attack on the telepaths. Ali listened carefully. He was very still when he listened. Eventually, he went to the computer on his desk, and tapped away, humming cheerfully under his breath. 'It wasn't the Chinese,' he said. 'They have only one agent in New New Delhi, and he's obsessing over the PM, currently. Probably a pervert.' He tapped on. 'The city's full of Maoists, as usual, but it wasn't them either. No increase in activity before or after the event. I'm not surprised. They don't do much. They're mainly into vague menace.'

As an intelligence agent himself, Mr Chatterjee was shocked and awed. This man was a thorough professional. His motivations may have changed, but his core competence remained formidable.

'How do you know all these things?' he couldn't help asking.

'Well, Al Qaeda was virtual, wasn't it?' said Ali. 'It's how we kept it running. I was one of the backroom boys. Spent a lot of my time planting fake Osama sightings. Osama spotted at Honolulu Airport. Wife of Tora Bora farmer patches up Osama's underwear. Is Osama in Peru? Stuff like that. Kept them confused for years. Planting information, finding information, it's much the same thing. You have to know your way around.'

'So what really happened?' asked Mr Chatterjee. He had always been sceptical of the Chinese agent theory. People in authority always assumed there was a Chinese saboteur lurking behind every bush, but Mr Chatterjee reckoned the Chinese had better things to do. He felt a twinge of sympathy for colleagues who had just been directed to keep Chinese restaurants under twenty-four-hour surveillance. On the other hand, at least they were eating well.

'Well, a Bank of Bodies branch got trashed yesterday,' said Ali, 'something wiped it out. No one knows what, exactly. The company says they're closed for routine maintenance.'

'But you know what happened, right?' said Mr Chatterjee admiringly.

Ali smiled a quick smile.

'The manager's an up-and-comer called Sam Kapoor. He's in a mental hospital right now, babbling like an idiot, although I don't know how they can tell the difference. I'm reading his transcripts. He's been going on about some kid from Shanti Nagar. Destroyed the place with his mind, apparently. That's a new one.'

'But how is this connected to my investigation?' asked Mr Chatterjee

'Two acts of sabotage close together?' said Ali. 'There's usually a connection. Trust me, I know. In the old days, *we* were usually the connection. Looks like the kid, if you ask me. He did something to your telepaths, too. It's not just Sam's mind he blew.'

Ali was the first true professional in any field that Mr Chatterjee had ever met. He could see that he was in very competent hands, although he remained apprehensive.

'So what do you suggest, Mr Ali?' he asked respectfully.

Mr Ali looked at him thoughtfully.

'Why are you so keen on this?' he asked. 'You can't be the only officer on the job. Most of them must be drinking beer and eating tangri kebabs. Even if you do get to the bottom of it, you won't get any credit. So why waste your time?'

'I'm going to be arrested for this in a few days,' said Mr Chatterjee. 'The CBI informed me of this officially. My wife isn't very practical. If I go to jail, what will happen to her?'

Ali was delighted. 'So romance rears its ugly head!' he said.

He jackknifed to his feet. He was, as Mr Chatterjee was to discover, a very decisive person. He caught him by the arm and pulled him up. 'Let's get moving, chum. Sitting here isn't going to solve your problem, is it? Kid's in Shanti Nagar. That's where we need to go.'

He folded up his computer and put it in his pocket. He picked up another one and wrapped it round his waist, under his shirt. He slid open the door and stepped out into the hot air, raising his face to feel the heat.

'It's a long time since I did any fieldwork,' said Ali. 'Takes me way back, it does, to the old days in Camp Abu Jihad.'

'Are you some kind of commando, sir?' asked Mr Chatterjee, shyly.

'Well, I'm better than those Saudis,' said Ali. 'Bunch of nancy boys. But what can you expect from a country that abolished slavery in 1962?'

15

'Please do cooperate with the authorities in the creation of this atmosphere, with immediate effect.'

Completely unaware that her husband was now in the clutches of a semi-mythical terrorist organization, Banani was having a quiet afternoon, quite worn out by the events of the previous day. She lay on her stomach on the bed, chewing the tip of her pencil and thinking about the book she was trying to write. She could feel Samrat at the other end of the bed, snuffling at the soles of her feet. The Alsatian seemed to have taken up temporary residence in the Chatterjee household, especially as it appeared its owner hadn't reappeared yet. It was miraculous how much Samrat had calmed down. It was probably because he had company. Mr Aggarwal used to keep him chained to the gate, where he had spent most of his time barking his head off. Samrat took one last sniff at her feet, decided she wasn't edible, and went and lay down on a nearby rug.

Banani had taken half a day off from school. Besides all the excitement with Hemonto, Mrs Johnson, the principal, had been particularly rampant this morning. As part of reintroducing the school to the ethos of traditional India, she had decided that all lessons would be conducted with light instrumental music in the background. She seemed to be under the impression that the gurukul system of education, apart from involving rhyming couplets, had also involved sitars and veenas as mood-setting devices. In her mind's eye, she visualized nubile yet demure young women in purple Kanjeevaram sarees strumming delicately with expressions of deep devotion. Her Christian upbringing left her a little handicapped in such areas, but she was working on it.

It would also, she felt, soothe the savage breasts of the student community. On this last point, Banani tended to agree. Her students needed all the soothing they could get, although personally, she would have preferred a cattle prod. Her rubber truncheon was proving to be grossly inadequate.

The scheme, while conceptually sound, had been implemented less than perfectly. Within a week of it being introduced, each classroom had been installed with a top-of-the-line sound system. *The Best of Anoushka Shankar* was downloaded instantly. The trouble started once the music started playing. The students, while supporting the idea in principle, expressed a desire to play music of their choice. Mrs Johnson, who believed that the bedrock of modern education was student-teacher collaboration, agreed at once.

The new music policy was implemented by the time the second period started. Consequently, Anoushka Shankar made way for Bhojpuri rap, several of the latest filmi hits, and various Sufi disco remixes, competing against each other from adjacent classrooms. So far, Banani had refused requests for the Honey Bunny Orchestra, and Fuck Your Mother, although she was willing to consider the Brooklyn Raga Massive. She and Hemonto had made out to their music once.

By the middle of the third period, students began expressing their views on the volume. Mrs Johnson, who was pretty much going with the flow by now, agreed. In effect, this converted the background music into foreground music, much to the delight of the majority of students. One or two may have objected, but once the volume was raised, no one could hear them.

By the end of the period, Banani had more or less given up any attempts at teaching, with or without the aid of rhyming couplets, which was fine since she hadn't written any. Instead, she sat on top of her desk, facing the class, gently waving her legs to the beat.

Where are you, O Moon Face?
How do you do, O Moon Face?
Let's get to it, Moon Face,
Why not do it, Moon Face?

The ode to lunar beauty seemed to go on and on. Some of the back-bench brutes were doing subtle pelvic thrusts, although they remained seated while doing so. But with this kind of rousing stimulus, it was only a matter of time before their bums detached themselves from their seats and they jumped one of their female classmates. Banani tightened her grip on her rubber truncheon and tried to look fearsome. Maybe I should transfer to kindergarten, she thought. The kids are smaller, and the boys still think girls have cooties.

The note from Mrs Johnson came just before the lunch break, just as a couple of prime specimens had begun to look decidedly twitchy. 'From the desk of Mrs Johnson', it said, as always, in a typeface that was bold and supple yet feminine. Mrs Johnson was a connoisseur of typefaces. She was constantly changing the typeface in circulars and test papers, usually at the last minute. Exams frequently started late as a result. This didn't matter too much, as students were routinely passed in all exams in order to discourage nasty things like competition. Since this got them out of the school faster, the faculty supported the system wholeheartedly.

'It has come to my notice,' the notice began, 'that the New Musical Policy is being imperfectly implemented by certain members of the staff. Mr Gupta, our self-defence instructor, has come up with what I believe to be a constructive suggestion. Henceforth, the first five minutes of every period are to be designated as the Meditation Moment. During this time the students and the teacher should, with their eyes shut, commune in harmony with the music. Lesson should start only after an appropriate atmosphere has been created, as was the case with our noble forebears. Please do cooperate with the authorities in the creation of this atmosphere, with immediate effect. Dissidents and non-cooperators will be dealt with severely. Jai Hind!'

Banani pondered over this. It was all very well for Mr Gupta. He was trained in self-defence. She tried to visualize herself meditating with her eyes closed at the beginning of every class. She didn't want to imagine what would happen in the classroom for five whole minutes while she wasn't looking.

Give it to me, Moon Face,

Don't you shoo me, Moon Face,

Gimme gimme gimme Moon Face! belted out the lunar devotee, right on cue.

Banani decided this was a good time to fall sick. Sick enough to miss two or three days. In two to three days, there would be a riot, and the musical meditation programme would be 'temporarily suspended'. It might even happen in two to three hours, but why take chances?

The moment the bell rang, she took herself to the school doctor. She pantomimed puking. He raised an eyebrow. Banani raised three fingers. Dr Davidar was a staunch ally of the teaching staff, a strong advocate of euthanasia for students, and in Mrs Johnson's view, distressingly unpatriotic. But he was a good doctor, and good doctors were hard to find these days. Most were in the UK, the rest had been enslaved by the glitterati. Dr Davidar wrote out a prescription for her, and recommended she take three days' sick leave, effective immediately.

So here she was, lying in bed, working on her book. Barring the occasional police siren (or were they ambulances?), it was blissfully peaceful. Samrat was snuffling and coughing, trying to make conversation, but Banani ignored him.

Banani had been working on her book for several years now. It was going to be a series of biographical sketches of great Indian teachers. Banani had wanted to be a teacher since she was eleven. She had started with dolls and teddy bears, and moved up to little children. She had never felt a moment's doubt.

Her immediate inspiration for the book was her grandmother, who had also been a teacher albeit of a different sort. She had lived on the outskirts of Calcutta. Post retirement, after a moderately hilarious and debauched life, she had started a school in a nearby village. It had been hard work, and she had been viewed with considerable suspicion. Grabbing land in the name of building a school was a time-honoured tradition. Plus, an educational trust was a good way to mop up dollars. Many village elders were not yet convinced that education was a good thing, particularly if it meant children of different castes sitting together.

The teachers at the nearest government school (conveniently located only six miles away by foot) saw it as lethal competition, although their competitiveness didn't extend to actually teaching. Party work took precedence.

Given all this, any plans to start a school had to be thoroughly scrutinized by various bureaucrats.

The old lady did not give up. She taught in the open air, under the trees. She relentlessly pushed files where they needed to be pushed, and smiled away at the village elders till her cheeks ached. She invited them to her house for cups of tea, and let them spit paan on her walls without shuddering once.

She got her way in the end, after seven long years. Once a few of the children started learning how to read and write, and helped their parents fill in bank slips and check ration cards, the villagers started taking a more practical view of the caste situation. One of the elders had suggested that the lower caste kids sit on the floor, to maintain some distinction. The old lady had called her policeman friend, who had called in the local barber and shaved the elder's head.

The school had grown over the years. Some of the kids had made it to college, a couple even got into IIT. Not all of them came back, but some did. On the whole, the school prospered.

Banani's book had started with her grandmother's story, because she wanted people to remember her. Then she had started investigating. She realized that in the years before the war, many people had quietly done solid work in the field of education. Since the war, of course, information was harder to come by. She knew nothing much was happening around New New Delhi. Times were hard, and people had grown harder. Maybe it was better elsewhere. There was little news of Calcutta, for example, but she hoped the teachers of the Ramakrishna Mission were keeping up the good work. Banani had devoted a whole chapter to them. They had changed a lot of lives, and they deserved to be remembered.

Samrat broke her chain of thought. The sound coming from deep inside him was something she had never heard before, a rattling, ugly growl, low but rising in volume. He was on his feet, facing the door, his fangs bared. The expression in his eyes was deeply unpleasant.

Someone was at the door.

Banani's heart lurched sickeningly as she realized who it might be.

16

'War is not for the faint-hearted.
Are you faint-hearted, General?'

His radio crackled to life again. 'Warning, warning,' it warned, 'missile aimed at Beijing is being rebounded by Satellite Defence Systems. Destruction of missile imminent. Starting countdown. Sixty . . . fifty-nine . . . fifty-eight . . .'

The Agni Attack on Beijing! If it failed, the war could still be lost! Captain Navalkar quickly switched to Space Mode. He had options here. He could launch a Space Shuttle attack from Vayu Space Base. Or he could use the Anti-Satellite Satellites to take out the Chinese Anti-Missile Satellites. Quick as a flash, he decided on the A.S.S. option. The Space Shuttle would never get there in time.

'A.S.S. Command, this is Navalkar speaking. I am transmitting co-ordinates for your target. Commence firing immediately. Remember, the nation is depending on you . . .'

There was a tap on his shoulder.

'Busy, Navalkar?'

Captain Navalkar lunged for the pause button (and missed) and leaped to his feet. Beijing was being atomized on the computer screen behind him, but he was too busy trying to salute. He stood awkwardly to attention, his arm entangled in the wires of his headset.

'You're a bloodthirsty little bugger, aren't you?' said the General, mesmerized by the mushroom cloud on-screen. 'How many Chinese did you kill today? Twenty million? Thirty?'

Captain Navalkar glanced down reflexively to check the Collateral Damage Score, but he stopped himself just in time. He snapped back to attention.

'Testing a War Game, sir,' he said, briskly, 'designed to help develop tactical skills in real-time environments.'

Tanya chose this moment to appear on-screen in a negligee, a glass of wine in her hand. 'Come home and come to bed, tiger,' she lisped seductively, 'you did a great job for the country today.' She froze, and the new high score message flashed on the screen.

'Get into my office, Navalkar,' said the General, wearily, 'and switch that thing off before someone sees it.'

He tried to sound annoyed, but he was pretending. He liked the boy. He was bright and optimistic. These days, he needed all the optimism he could get.

Navalkar scurried after the General.

'What's up, boss?' he asked, as he sat down in the General's office.

The General gazed at him steadily.

'Sir,' said Navalkar hastily. He assumed an expression of efficient humility, and sat up straight.

'I'm scheduled to call the Competent Authority,' he said.

Navalkar rolled his eyes and made gagging noises.

'I want you to sit outside range and observe the meeting. Let me know what you think afterwards. The army needs your gigantic brain.'

Navalkar looked hurt, but pulled his chair to the side discreetly.

The General dialled the CA's number. The CA appeared on-screen, munching a very large leaf of lettuce.

'Ah, General,' he said, between chews, 'to what do I owe the honour?'

'You asked me to call you at four,' said the General, politely.

The CA considered this as he devoured his lettuce.

'Always have lots of green items,' he said eventually. 'I have recently given up consuming non-vegetarian food and my health and disposition towards the world in general have improved immeasurably. I'm thinking of giving up bidis also, I now smoke only two a day, one in the morning, and one before I go to bed. You army-wallahs have far too much rum and red meat. Green things are good for you. In the old days, that might have seemed unpatriotic, but now the colour green is perfectly safe. Lettuce is quite good, particularly in winter, but there are other good green things too.'

Was this why the CA had asked him to call? To advise him about salad? It seemed unlikely, but with the Competent Authority, you could never be sure.

'Will that be all, sir?' he asked, semi-hopefully.

'You have such a sense of humour,' said the CA, oozing charm and goodwill. 'It's one of your more attractive features. No, I have a simple question. The best questions in life are simple, as a great man once said. I think it was me. My question is this. How come you haven't crushed the Maoists yet?'

From the corner of his eye the General could see Navalkar gaping at

Shovon Chowdhury

the screen, slack-jawed in astonishment. It was the first time he was seeing the management.

'It's not that we're not trying,' he said, carefully. 'I have a sum total of seven divisions on the ground, across Chhattisgarh, Bihar, Jharkhand, and Andhra Pradesh. I lost eighteen men today.'

'Come, come, General,' said the CA, contradicting his own advice about all things green and picking up a tomato. He took a large bite. Juice dribbled down his chin. 'Don't call a minor police action against a few pathetic Maoists a war. You have such a nice, big army with such a nice, big budget. Paid for by the Indian taxpayer. The Indian taxpayer expects more value for money. This is like using a cannon to shoot a mosquito.' He paused with his mouth full and picked up a pen to write the last bit down.

No comment seemed called for. The General sat looking at the screen, stony-faced. The CA was pushing on all fronts. The General was trying to delay mobilization against the Protectorate, and sticking to computer simulations, white papers and opinion pieces in the *Indian Express*, using the CBI investigation as an excuse. The CBI could be relied on to make an unholy mess of everything. But the Maoist operation had been going on for the last twenty years. It was an existing war. The General could hardly refuse to pursue it.

'I do not wish to interfere in military strategy,' said the Competent Authority, 'but you have thousands of tanks. Many of them are fully functional. Why don't you simply roll in and squash them like the loathsome bugs they are? End it now. Why drag this out? Would Rommel have acted this way? Would Napoleon? Would Netaji Subhash Chandra Bose?'

The General sighed. This wasn't the first time he had received tips on strategy from the CA, and it wouldn't be the last. Like all senior bureaucrats, the CA was an expert on practically every subject under the sun. It was the chair. It constantly radiated waves of expertise into his brain, via his backside.

'It's not quite so simple, sir,' said the General. 'For one thing, the Maoists look remarkably like the local population, so it is not always easy to know who to crush. They're also swimming in Chinese weapons. This is not a bunch of tribals with bows and arrows. This is a bunch of tribals with tanks and artillery. They control over 25 per cent of our remaining land mass. They're well supported by elements in the Bengal Protectorate, the way the Taliban was supported by the ISI. This war has been going on for a very long time. Officers from the south are getting restive. It's quiet down there, and they don't see why they should be fighting north Indian wars forever. Splittists did very well in the last elections. There are only so many Udipi cooks I can find, and the Maharashtrians and the Biharis get upset if we serve too much sambhar. It's the only thing they agree on.'

The CA swallowed the last bit of his tomato and decided to change tack. He twinkled roguishly.

'Now, now, General,' he said, 'don't be so downhearted. As a leader, it's your job to inspire the troops. That's what leaders do. That's why I'm so cheerful all the time. I happen to know that things are not as grim as you're making them out to be. I have my sources too, you know. Isn't it true that we just recaptured Darbhanga district in Bihar? Yesterday, around four? I believe you are keeping information from me, General, which is very, very naughty.' He waggled a finger at the General humorously. His finger grazed the screen, leaving a watery, red trail of tomato juice. It reminded the General of footage from the Third Gulf War.

'If by "recapturing", you mean taking possession of the District Magistrate's bungalow, then yes, sir, we have. However, there are eighteen blocks and over two thousand villages in Darbhanga, and it's been a number of years since the District Magistrate had much to do with any of them. We'll take six months to recapture those villages, one by one, and need at least forty thousand men to hold them. The local Maoists will vanish as we do this. When we're halfway through, they will reappear, wipe out a few platoons, and take some of the villages back. We will then have to re-recapture them. If the British had controlled India this way, every man, woman and child in their country would have been in uniform, and over here. I would also like to point out that, more than re-capturing Darbhanga, what we've actually done is prevent Patna from being encircled by elements of the Fifth Tribal Division.'

'Bold strokes!' said the CA, picking up another tomato. 'What we need is bold strokes! This is precisely why we must take the battle beyond. We must get to the heart of the matter. Who is supporting these evildoers? Who is helping them divert our attention, so that we cannot focus properly on reconstruction? The vile, fish-eating, traitorous Bengalis of the Bengal Protectorate, aided and abetted by the Chinese!'

He sprayed the screen with tomato juice as he spoke, 'We must open a second front. How was World War II won? By opening a second front. Learn from military history. Don't let the cost of the last war scare you. War is not for the faint-hearted. Are you faint-hearted, General?' He made a note on his pad: cardiac tests for all senior military personnel. War and medicine went hand in hand, he realized.

'No, sir, I am not,' said the General, with dignity. 'But I would like to repeat that there is the danger of a response from China. They have far more nuclear weapons than we do. This course of action is not advisable.'

'General, I have heard your advice,' hissed the CA, all traces of bonhomie now gone. 'I also gave you an order. We are attacking the Bengal Protectorate, not China. Try not to confuse one with the other. Just because the Governor is Chinese, do not get the wrong impression. In any case, he is too depressed to do anything, because of the lack of economic progress and the scarcity of concubines. There are no nuclear weapons in the Protectorate. Therefore, there is no danger of nuclear war. Evidence of the Bengal Protectorate's treachery will be in our hands in less than a week. I will apply special pressure on the CBI to ensure this. You had better be ready by then. Do I make myself perfectly clear?'

'Yes, sir,' said the General, woodenly.

The CA leaned back and resumed munching. The screen went black.

The General looked across at Navalkar.

'Holy Mother!' said Navalkar, ashen-faced.

'I doubt that your mother will be able to do much about this,' said the General, 'get me the Prime Minister instead.'

17

'Why was he trying to remove my clothes?'

It was a busy day in the potter's neighbourhood inside Shanti Nagar. Women were running to and fro with earthen pitchers on their heads. Men with buckets huffed and puffed to keep pace with them. Children carried mugs, pots, pans and anything else they could find. All the people who lived in the sturdy little shacks were out on the dusty street. It was Bathing Day.

Ali and Mr Chatterjee had entered Shanti Nagar through the South Gate. Ali was on good terms with the guards there. Just next to it was the potter's locality. They were standing there now, in the middle of the forty-foot road, sweating in the hot sun, watching the mass of humanity swarming all around them.

Once a week, according to a pre-arranged schedule, different localities were allotted extra water for bathing. The catch was, you had to collect it in person, to each as much as they could carry. Which meant the whole family had to pitch in. One such family, around thirty strong, was shoving its way past them in an enormous scramble, carrying buckets, pitchers, mugs, bladders, cooking pots, even plastic bags and lemonade sets, anything that could hold fluids; arms and legs and clay and plastic were all jumbled up into an enormous water-collecting organism which spoke in many voices. The head of the family, a large man with a heroically twirly moustache, was right in the heart of the throng, herding them on like sheep and roaring at the top of his voice. He was supporting a water tank the size of a baby elephant, strapped to his back. Mr Chatterjee wondered how on earth he'd carry it back once it was full.

As he stood there, ruminating about this, an elderly granny straggler caught hold of his arm to rest for a bit.

'Welcome to Shanti Nagar!' said Ali, clapping him on the back. 'Some people think it's a dump, but that's only because they've never been to Bradford.'

The granny let go of Mr Chatterjee's arm and tottered off feebly after the rest of her family. She was carrying two buckets. Mr Chatterjee was wondering whether to go after her and offer to help when the stench hit him like a physical blow. It was a horrible, gut-wrenching miasma, a thick, slithering presence, pouring over him from somewhere behind his right shoulder. Mr Chatterjee turned around, filled with dread, to face the source of this pungent decay.

It emanated from the grubbiest, dirtiest man that Mr Chatterjee had ever seen. He had grubby, bushy hair, and a grubby, bushy beard. A cloud of flies floated just above him. He clutched a grubby shawl over a patched, brown vest, his fingernails black to the roots. He reached out with one of his filthy hands and plucked at Mr Chatterjee's shirt.

'Ten rupees for five, sir,' he hissed, 'ten rupees for five.' He gave the shirt another tug, pulling it half out of Mr Chatterjee's pants. Mr Chatterjee clutched his shirt to his stomach possessively and shrank back, traumatized. He looked at Ali.

'Back off, brother,' said Ali, giving the man a little push. 'My friend doesn't mind a little dirt,' he said, smiling. He pushed back a hand that was reaching automatically for his Bob Marley T-shirt. 'I'm fine too. I'll give you a shout if we're dating or anything.'

The grubby man promptly pulled out a business card from the unspeakable recesses of his shawl and handed it over.

'It has my landline number, sir,' he told Ali, 'please call me when you have a requirement.' He shambled off, the cloud of flies keeping leisurely pace with him.

'Why was he trying to remove my clothes?' asked Mr Chatterjee in a querulous whisper, as he rearranged his shirt with trembling fingers.

'He's a black-market dhobi,' said Ali. 'The dhobi caste does all the washing in this part of town. They get a special quota of water. Sometimes others use their bathing quota to get in on the action. They do it cheap. If the dhobis catch the blacker, he's had it.'

The hectic activity around them continued. Some people were coming back now, their quota collected, occasionally resting (their water containers at their feet) before moving on. There was a lot less talking now.

'This is Shahrukh Colony,' said Ali. 'Shanti-bai couldn't stop them from naming the whole place after her, but she did give the names for all the colonies. They're a little eccentric.'

'Why Shahrukh Colony?' asked Mr Chatterjee.

'She used to fancy him when she was young,' said Ali. 'Let's hit the colony office. I know the secretary. He usually knows what's going on.'

The colony office was a small, neat, white building in a part of the neighbourhood where there were fewer shacks and more houses, adorned by a giant hand-painted cutout of a soulful Shahrukh Khan. The building had a wide, open verandah on one side, facing a dusty square meant for meetings. They had plans to build a shopping mall there eventually, but no one had told Shanti-bai yet. Mr Madan Mohan Tyagi, Secretary of Shahrukh Colony, was sitting on the verandah, feet up on the railing, reading a newspaper. He got up when he saw Ali. He was of medium height, a wiry, knotted stick of a man with a weather-beaten face and leathery hands. His expression was forbidding. It was designed to minimize requests from the community. He believed in conserving energy.

Ali explained why they had come. He was surprisingly open about the nature of their investigation. Mr Chatterjee had thought the whole process would have a lot more cloak-and-dagger to it, but apparently everybody involved was going to go about it quite openly. Mr Chatterjee derived a certain comfort from this thought.

Mr Tyagi heard Ali out patiently. He scowled.

'I don't know what Chinese spy he is looking for. There are no Chinese in my locality, nor anywhere else in Shanti Nagar. They poisoned our earth and fouled our water. There is no support for any Chinese here.'

'You think I don't know that?' said Ali. 'But you usually know what's up. Can you give us a clue? Any kids been acting funny lately? Making everyone a little nervous, maybe?'

The secretary stared at Ali. He said nothing. Time passed. Mr Chatterjee fidgeted restlessly, but Ali remained perfectly still.

'There is a boy,' he said eventually. 'If you promise not to harm him, I can get you a darshan.'

'It's nothing like that,' said Ali. 'Man's from the CBI. Just needs to solve a case.'

They both laughed uproariously. Mr Chatterjee felt slightly hurt.

'How is the Jeep Scam of 1948 going, by the way?' asked Mr Tyagi, revealing an unexpected humorous streak. 'Have you found any new leads?'

'Leave him alone,' said Ali, 'just show us the way to the boy. Man needs to see him, shake hands with him, take a picture maybe. Then he goes home to his wife, gives her a big hug. Files a report. Everyone forgets about it. Nothing to worry about.'

'How about the Irrigation Scam?' asked Mr Tyagi. 'Is it true they were irrigating Switzerland? Is that why they have all the lakes?'

'Stop it, will you,' said Ali. 'Besides, he's not like the others. He doesn't have any money.'

'He should be living here then,' said Mr Tyagi. 'Go talk to the headmaster of School No. 1. He lives in Ping Pong Colony. Possibly he can help you.'

Shovon Chowdhury

They got up to leave. 'One more thing,' said Mr Tyagi. They turned. 'For the first time in years, things are looking hopeful,' he said, 'please don't cause any trouble.'

Ali gave him a grin. 'Trouble's already here, boss,' he said. 'We just want to find it.'

❑

Ram Manohar Pande arrived in front of the Chatterjee house and parked his jeep. Something occurred to him as he got out of the vehicle and he drew his revolver. He yanked his sub judice out by the collar, and shoved him towards the Aggarwal residence. 'Go in there and get me the dog,' he told him. 'Bring him out here on the footpath. I want to sit in the jeep and shoot him.' He was constantly using his sub judice for menial tasks, but he realized now there were so many ways in which this creature could make his life easier. It was all a question of proper training.

'Sir, I'm scared of dogs, sir,' said Bhiru, cowering fearfully, 'he'll bite me. I'll need injections.'

Pande kicked him all the way from the jeep to the gate. 'You're refusing, you rascal?' he said. 'Would you prefer a bullet in the backside or what?'

Bhiru scampered off, whimpering to himself.

He was back a while later. He delivered his report from the safety of a conveniently located bush.

'Not there, sir,' he said, apologetically.

'What do you mean not there?' demanded Pande, 'He has to be there. I was told he is there.'

'House is empty, sir,' insisted Bhiru.

Pande stormed off to check for himself. The sub judice was right. The door was open, but the house was empty. It looked like it had been empty for several days. He stalked from room to room, snarling, a bit like a dog himself.

He came out in a towering rage. Perhaps there had never been any dog in the first place. How dare that spectacled prick make a monkey out of him? What kind of game was he playing? Pande was fed up of all these dogs. How was a man supposed to keep track? Dogs appear in Pappu Verma's room out of thin air. Dogs vanish from this Aggarwal's house into thin air. What kind of tamasha was this?

Ram Manohar Pande decided that enough was enough. This Chatterjee had been making a monkey out of him, and it was time for him to pay. Of course, strictly speaking, he had already paid, since Pande had collected in advance. But money wasn't everything. There was such a thing called respect. He had heard an elderly retired commissioner give a lecture on respect once. Respect was a vital bond, he had said, between the police force and the local community. The local community needed to respect the police. This weedy, clerical babu had been yanking his chain, which was not respectful, and he needed to be taught a lesson. It was a matter of principle.

Pande marched up to Chatterjee's door, revolver at the ready. He decided to follow proper police procedure and ring the bell. Let Chatterjee open the door, then he would shoot him. It would all be done by the book. Besides, his foot was hurting too much to kick the door in. He would have to inspect Bhiru's backside—it was suspiciously hard.

He rang the bell for a while but no one opened the door. Then it struck him that that clerk was probably one of those conscientious types who actually went to work on time. He certainly looked it. But Mrs Chatterjee ought to be there. She was the one who had originally made the fictitious complaint. She was the one who deserved to be punished. Although he had never actually met her, he had heard she was very attractive. Pande hammered on the door impatiently, excited by all the possibilities.

Suddenly a dog started barking from inside, and he heard frantic female whispering. He stood there frozen, as the full significance of this sank in. The dog was in the Chatterjee house! With Mrs Chatterjee! They were talking to each other!

They had not asked him to shoot a non-existent, hypothetical or magically vanishing dog, he now realized. They had actually kidnapped the dog themselves, and then covered their tracks by filing a false police complaint. Pande could see it all now. He could see Mr Chatterjee telling his wife: 'Don't worry about that Pande fellow. He's one of those illiterate village types. He's too stupid to figure all this out. He can't speak English like us.' He could hear their laughter. It went on and on.

He needed to hear cries for mercy. That would make the laughter stop. That would teach these English types not to mess around with Ram Manohar Pande.

Shovon Chowdhury

He stepped back, aimed at the lock and fired, once, twice, thrice. He pushed the door and it swung open. He walked in, the laughter still ringing in his ears.

❑

'What would *you* do to make everything better?' asked Pintoo.

They had just finished the letter N, and he was feeling mellow. So what if his pupil was six years old? He was still human. It was mostly his future they were all concerned about.

'Give everyone lots of money,' said Vinod.

Pintoo smiled weakly. His stump still hurt, especially in the evening.

'That would take a lot of time. Use your brain, no? Think of yourself. If you could go back and change one thing in your life, what would you change?'

'I'd go back to last year and stop Preeti from kicking me in the balls,' said Vinod. 'It really hurt. She said it's OK for girls to fight dirty. Shanti-bai said so. Also, she said that if girls keep doing this, then the gandu-type people won't be able to have children, and life will be better for everyone.'

Shanti-bai's views on justice were simple and direct.

'So what you're saying is, if we go back and give some people vasectomies, our lives could get better?'

'Maybe,' said Vinod, who wasn't sure what a vasectomy was.

'It makes sense,' said Pintoo. 'The question is, who? The headmaster or Tarun-da could help me with that.'

'Ask Kader bhai,' said Vinod, 'Kader bhai knows everything!'

Kader Khan of KK Mobile Shoppee often gave Vinod and some of the other children free games, and he was always very up-to-date on cool stuff.

'I think I'll do that,' said Pintoo. Kader hadn't built a business by the time he was sixteen by being an idiot. He would check first thing tomorrow, when he dropped in for work after school.

'When will you destroy the body bank?' asked Vinod. 'Shouldn't you do that first? Supposing they come for me?'

'I'll do that,' said Pintoo, 'soon. But there's more to it than the Bank of Bodies. Our lives are shit because bad things happened. I want to stop some of the bad things. I have to do it quickly. I don't know how long I'll stay this way. First, I need people to help me decide. Then I need people to help me do it. I may have to force them, but it has to be done.'

'Once you finish, will you stop?' asked Vinod.

'I hope so,' said Pintoo.

18

'Gwum which wum woo.'

'We need to dwiversify,' said the Chairman of the Bank of Bodies, transfixing his subordinates with his piercing gaze. His subordinates nodded reverentially. Several of them wrote down the word 'dwiversify' on their little pads. The two youngest directors, seated at the far end of the table, as befitted their station, looked at each other gravely and nodded. Everyone waited with bated breath for further details.

When it came to design, the boardroom of the Bank of Bodies owed more to the 'Bank' part than the 'Bodies' part. Although it was not a bank in the financial sense, and despite being truly state-of-the-art when it came to medical technology, the boardroom was a throwback to a kinder, gentler era, when a man was known by the depth of his carpet. Between the walls, the mammoth table, and the fully equipped bar in the corner, it contained enough wood to destroy a small forest. The walls were covered with pictures of the Chairman. The Chairman with the Prime Minister (he was asleep). The Chairman with famous cine-star Mallika. The Chairman with champion wrestler Dharam Pal. The Chairman with author Arundhati Roy. The Chairman with danseuse Rukmini Devi. The Chairman with a painting of the Chairman. Being in the boardroom gave the Chairman a deep sense of comfort. Wherever he looked, he could see himself, and this was good.

What exciting new direction would the Chairman take them in today, wondered the board members. Their eyes were fixed on the Chairman. So were their ears. In one or two cases, quite literally, since some of the ears were detachable. They were huddled against the back of his chair, trying to make out what he was saying. The Chairman said very little, and when he did, he mumbled. He usually kept a hand cupped in front of his mouth when he spoke. The mumbling was not, as rumour had it, because of a lifelong devotion to the motion picture *Godfather*. Its roots were much deeper. As a child, the Chairman had frequently been spanked by his mother for having bad breath. 'I can see the germs,' she would say, keeping his mouth open with an iron grip, 'they're crawling around inside.' How much ever he brushed his teeth, she could still see the germs, and smell the horror of his breath from across the room. So now, whenever he had to open his mouth in public, he kept it carefully covered (usually, as at present, with a handkerchief). He didn't want his subordinates to spot the germs or find out about his breath.

'Gwum which wum woo,' said the Chairman.

The littlest director, who was supposed to record the minutes of the meeting, wiped his brow and licked his pencil. He looked imploringly at No. 2.

No. 2 cleared his throat. 'The Chairman makes a very good point here,' he said smoothly. 'If our business is to expand, we need to go beyond the rich and focus on the poor as well. We need to expand our market. What do the rest of you think?'

The rest of them thought this was simply brilliant, and demonstrated this by breaking into spontaneous applause. The Chairman, who had begun to nod off, woke up with a start.

'Poo too poo,' he said.

No. 2 picked up the ball and ran with it. 'Our problem, of course, lies in the revenue model. The poorer sections of society have so far been a source of raw material. Our current basket of services is too expensive for them to be considered customers. So the question is, what kind of service can we provide them?'

'Ligion goo noo model,' said the Chairman.

'The answer lies in religion,' said No. 2, without missing a beat. 'While we go off searching for new markets, we cannot ignore our old ones. We have to look at a business that not only brings in new customers, but expands our portfolio of services for existing customers. Religion is the one thing that binds this nation together. From the highest to the lowest, everyone sets aside a portion of his or her disposable income on religion. Amongst the poorer sections, they may do without education, or water, or food, or homes, or any semblance of a future— but they cannot do without religion. The most ignorant and pathetic of priests can easily convince them to sacrifice their sons and sell their daughters, give away the clothes off their backs and the roof over their heads, give away their last rupee, even make them borrow rupees, and not give a single thing in return.'

'Not us, not us!' said the Chairman, galvanized into lucidity by all the rupees.

'Not, as the Chairman says, us,' continued No. 2, promptly. 'We are not in the business of taking money and giving nothing in return. If we enter this field, and provide even a moderate return, or even the appearance of a moderate return, we change the entire dynamics of the religion industry. If we get our product mix right, I believe we can gain significant market share in the very first year of our operations. The question is, what return do we offer?'

'Goo whwee goo,' said the Chairman.

'Exactly,' said No. 2, with just the right amount of admiration in his voice. He faced the rest of the board. 'What do the rest of you gentlemen think?' No. 2 enjoyed torturing the directors occasionally. It kept them on their toes, and reminded them that the Chairman wasn't the only person they had to worry about.

The directors goggled helplessly. One or two were veterans, though. They knew how this script played out.

'I think it's a wonderful idea,' said one of them, 'it's amazing that none of our previous chairmen ever thought of it.'

'I couldn't agree more,' said No. 2. 'The trick lies in what he just told us—that we should keep doing what we do. *Our* religious service will come with a concrete return—the promise of long life, health, and happiness. We will no longer provide Medical Joy to just the rich, we will provide Medical Joy to the entire nation. Every man, woman and child in the country will be our marketplace. The problem is, our services are very expensive, so how can we possibly get a proper return on investment? After all, there is a limit to how much money the average citizen will be able to spend on religion. Traditional religion provides some empty words and a few cheap ceremonies in return, so profit margins are very high. Our medical services could be integrated into the reward system of our religion. But our medical services are very expensive. So how can we make the numbers add up?'

'Wottery,' said the Chairman promptly. 'Woo weepteke,' he added, in order to clarify.

Shovon Chowdhury

'Precisely,' said No. 2. 'The answer, as the Chairman rightly says, is to offer, not a guaranteed return to everyone, but instead, the *chance* of a big reward. Most religions are built on the same principle—they increase your chances of salvation, but only the truly faithful are redeemed. Only a handful actually gain. Namely, the Lottery Principle.'

'Wottry wet twum ligion,' interposed the Chairman.

'Absolutely,' said No. 2, beaming, 'lotteries are a better, more honest business than religion. In a lottery, at least a few people gain something concrete, and are seen by the rest to do so. In a religion, all that the customer gains is hope, and the possibility of return at some point in the undefined future. Our religion will combine the best elements of both. We will go for the low-value, high-volume segment, that is, the poor. We will reinvest a fraction of our revenue to provide Medical Joy to a few lucky customers. These visible symbols of success will draw in more customers. We will apply professional management techniques to the marketing and operations aspects of this new faith. The beauty is, this new product can be offered to our existing customer base as well. After all, the rich deserve religious salvation every bit as much as the poor. They're human too.'

'Go on, go on,' said the Chairman, dropping his handkerchief in his excitement.

No. 2 nodded deferentially. He owed his position in the company to the fact that he was the only one who could understand what the Chairman was saying. But it did no harm to occasionally demonstrate that he also had a brain the size of a planet.

'How should we start this process?' he asked. The directors shifted uneasily, hoping the question was rhetorical.

It was.

'Every successful religious business has been started by a messiah. We need one. We could, of course, pick someone off the streets and put him through a rigorous training course. But ideally, I think that messiah should be someone genuinely special. Personally, I think a child would be good. Children are easier to control.'

No. 2 was a bachelor.

'The question is, how do we locate the right person?'

He thought for a minute.

'I think the answer lies in our original subject of discussion,' he said eventually. 'We met here to discuss the unfortunate incident at our Karol Bagh branch.'

'Wuddy Wam,' grumbled the Chairman.

'Yes, certainly it was mainly caused by the incompetence of the manager, Sam Kapoor. Despite our very comprehensive selection and training programmes, the occasional incompetent does slip into the system.'

Several of the directors shifted uneasily. No. 2 smiled at them. 'But the point is, the destruction of that branch was apparently caused by a child. A child with extraordinary powers. A child with a grudge against the Bank of Bodies. A child who is currently our enemy. I propose that we locate this child, take care of his grievances, and groom him to be the messiah of our new Religious Services Division. As Sun Tzu once said, the best way to tackle an enemy is to turn him into an ally.'

No. 2 was truly audacious. He didn't mind quoting Chinese philosophers in a public forum.

He looked at the Chairman, who nodded benignly.

His gaze swept the rest of them. 'Do I take that as confirmed, then?'

The directors nodded vigorously.

'Then let it be so noted,' said No. 2.

The littlest director so noted it, and gave No. 2 a look of heartfelt gratitude.

Snacks were served. They were prawn cutlets—the Chairman's favourite.

The sounds of munching filled the air.

19

'Joking with the police, haa?'

The PM was doing her weekly scam review when the General was announced by her PA. She asked for him to be ushered in immediately. When he walked in, she gestured for him to sit, and said, 'I'm doing the laundry.'

The CA's office gave her a detailed note every week, listing the scams of the week, their approximate value, and what she ought to say about them.

Shovon Chowdhury

'Here's a good one,' she said, 'it's the Schoolbook Scam.'

The Schoolbook Scam was relatively small. It involved vendors who supplied textbooks to government schools. Most textbooks supplied by the government had been supplied right on schedule, but due to deadline pressure, the vendors had skipped the printing stage and gone straight to binding. So they were all blank. Most of these blank textbooks had mysteriously materialized at local grocery stores across the country, where they were being sold as notebooks.

'What could you possibly say to defend that?' asked the General.

'Well, for one thing,' said the PM, 'the livelihoods of many hardworking shopkeepers are involved.'

The General's eyes bulged, but he managed to maintain a dignified silence.

'Plus the teachers have everything in their heads. So the students just need to take notes.'

'What teachers?' asked the General.

'You're not supposed to ask that question,' she said. 'But the good news is that when it comes to the Money Printing Scam, we're taking prompt and effective action.'

The Money Printing Scam involved the illegal printing of large amounts of money, which only the government and its favoured industrial conglomerates were allowed to do. None of it was counterfeit, because actual Government of India printing presses were involved. In effect, a few people with the right connections had been getting money hot off the press, which saved them the trouble of going to the bank, or actually earning it.

'That's a relief,' said the General. 'What are we doing?'

'Anyone found in possession of such money goes to jail,' said the PM.

'But if they're printed legally, how can anyone tell the difference?'

'You're not supposed to ask that question either,' said the PM. 'In fact, spreading unnecessary rumours about this gets you arrested for sedition. The owner of the newspaper that broke this story is having his home demolished. They're building public latrines on the site.'

The Competent Authority had a thing about latrines. While he was willing to put up with the public, he didn't like them doing it publicly, particularly against trees. He also liked taking away land from people who had been disobedient, and then getting the public to piss on it.

'Let me get this clear,' said the General. 'This means that anyone found in possession of money can be picked up at any time, and charged with undermining the national economy?'

'Looks like it,' said the PM. 'Try not to have any money. Although I suppose if anyone tried to arrest you, a platoon of jawans would materialize instantly and machine gun everyone in sight.'

The General chose not to respond to this. He waited patiently while the PM went through the rest of her scam notes. It never failed to depress her.

'How much money do they need!' she exclaimed.

'Well, those fancy cars cost a lot of money,' said the General. 'The CA has a whole collection.'

The PM felt a twinge of guilt before she remembered that wasn't what she wanted to discuss. She wanted to know what the CA was up to. He was being especially charming. She had her suspicions, and they were horrifying. She looked across the room at the portrait of one of her relatives for inspiration. He'd had his share of troubles too.

The General cleared his throat.

'What do you want to know?' he asked.

'Tell me what's happening.'

The General sipped his water and eyed the PM. He was fond of her. He remembered the vivacious young woman who had filled them all with such hope. Hope was such a precious commodity—they all owed her a debt of gratitude for having provided it, however briefly. But he knew very well that she had little or no actual power. What was the point in involving her?

'That vicious little reptile is up to something,' insisted the PM. 'Let me help you.'

The General considered the PM thoughtfully. The blood of generations of great leaders flowed through this woman's veins. At the very least, they had done an awful lot of leading. How could it make things worse?

'There's a file you passed the day before yesterday,' began the General. 'Let me explain to you what you signed.'

❑

'Joking with police, haa?' said Pande, as he squeezed. 'It was very funny, no? Laugh, saali, why don't you laugh? I want to hear you laugh.' The veins stood out in his forehead. His hands were around her neck. He was glaring down at her madly.

Banani was pinned to the bed by his bulk, fighting to breathe, his monstrous belt buckle cutting into her flesh. Things had happened fast. Pande had shot open the door and Samrat had leaped out at him. Pande had fired at the dog and missed, then slipped into the house with surprising dexterity. Samrat had swerved into the next room, startled by the gunshot and Pande had shut the door on him, blocking it with a heavy chair. He had then stalked from room to room, smashing doors, until he had found Banani cowering in the bedroom. Now he was administering justice, which he liked to be swift.

'What's wrong?' he asked, squeezing harder. 'Am I not funny?'

The blood was rushing to his head, making it hard for him to hear, which was why he never heard Samrat. At the very last moment, he saw Banani's eyes flicker, but by then it was too late. He felt a sharp pain in his buttocks. He tried to twist around, but now he was pinned down himself, by fifty kilos of angry dog, savaging his fleshy bits. Banani slipped out from under him, pausing only briefly to catch a breath before she picked up a copy of *A Suitable Boy* from the bookshelf and hit him over the head with it. Hard. Unable to handle so much literature, Pande collapsed, face down on the bed, unconscious.

Less than five minutes later, Banani was outside. She had assaulted an officer. Her house was now a crime scene. She was a fugitive from the New New Delhi police. What was she supposed to do? And where was Hemonto? She had almost been massacred by the cop he had hired. She felt the urge to have a conversation with him, which she would do whenever her throat stopped hurting.

Bhiru popped up bashfully from behind the bush. He held out the keys to Pande's jeep. 'Madam, you keep this,' he said, 'I'll tell him you overpowered me.'

'Thanks for letting the dog back in,' said Banani. 'That was you, wasn't it?'

'Pande-sahab, his behavior with women is not so good,' said Bhiru, shamefacedly, 'and besides, you're a teacher.'

'Well, thank you,' said Banani. 'You're a good man. Will you be all right?'

'My requirements are very little, so most of the time I'm OK,' said

Bhiru. 'You should go to Shanti Nagar. The police aren't allowed there. He can't catch you. He wouldn't dare create gadr in Shanti Nagar.'

On the basis of her brief acquaintance with Pande, Banani wasn't so sure. Nevertheless, it was bound to be safer than New New Delhi. She took the keys from Bhiru. Samrat trotted up to Bhiru and sniffed him, licking his leg briefly. He approved.

'Can you take care of him?' asked Banani.

Bhiru scratched his head, 'Maybe he can threaten people so that they give me food,' he said. 'Or I could hide him in your bathroom till Pande-sahab goes away.'

'The second plan sounds much better,' said Banani, as she climbed into the jeep and gunned the motor. She had always wanted to drive a police vehicle. She switched on the siren, crashed into gear, and took off.

❏

'This Windows Phone is completely useless,' said Pintoo, chucking it on the table.

Kader Khan swung off his feet. At sixteen, he was just a few years older than Pintoo, but he was Shanti Nagar's leading mobile entrepreneur. He was sitting at a table amongst a bunch of other tables, keeping an eye on the staff and watching holoporn. The holograms were gorgeously realistic. Working conditions at Kader Khan's KK Mobile Shoppee were a mixture of good and bad. The lighting was dim, but the porn was state-of-the-art.

Kader Khan swiped the air and the writhing bodies vanished.

'I guess this means you can't stop it from crashing?'

'It's Windows. It's crashing. It's what it does,' said Pintoo.

'I suppose you're still expecting to be paid?'

'I was hoping for a raise.'

'Sure,' said Kader Khan, promptly. 'How much?'

He had a strict policy of not messing with superpowered employees.

'One hundred an hour more?'

'Fifty.'

'Done.'

The two boys smiled at each other, relieved that it was over.

'I have no idea why you even do this anymore,' said Kader.

'I have to earn a living.'

'Did you get the answer to your question yet?'

'What question?'

'The one you've been asking everyone in Shanti Nagar. What do you think went wrong with the country? Very deep. You should sit under a tree and think about it for fifty years. Then you might find the answer. Meanwhile, everyone knows you've been asking everyone you can find. You even asked Asha behn at the Lucky Lucy Travel Agency. She thinks you were trying to get fresh. She doesn't mind. She says your balls just dropped, so naturally you're a little frisky.'

'What do you think the answer is?'

'I'm just a simple guy, running my stomach. What do I know? But mostly it's all crap because of the bombs, isn't it? First you start making them, then you start thinking about using them. Then, you think, I'd better use them before they do. We should have stopped the government from making bombs. That just seems like common sense to me. My dad used to say that if we hadn't done that second test at Pokhran, Pakistan would never have gone openly nuclear. They were never scared of us after that, and the Chinese saw that, and that gave them ideas.'

Pintoo thought about this for a bit.

'Is there any particular type of porn I can get for you, boss?' he said. 'I can hack some down if you want.'

'I'll shout if I need you,' said Kader.

20

'How can he be refusing puris?
They're his favourite.'

Mrs Verma was beginning to think that her doctor wasn't taking her seriously. He was nodding his head and looking sympathetic, but it all seemed a tad mechanical.

'He only had four puris,' she said, trying to inject a sense of urgency into the conversation, 'he never takes less than six.'

'Dear me,' said the doctor and assumed an expression of concern.

'We even made him that dry potato thing with jeera and pepper that he likes.'

The doctor knew all about the dry potato thing. They frequently gave him the leftovers. Completely bland. An insult to the tastebuds. He came from a land where the fish was inflammable. His family were poor fisherfolk. Most doctors came from poor villages. Rich city kids had better things to do, although he had never clearly understood what. His family had traded him in to pay off generations of debt. It was ironic to think that if he hadn't studied so hard, he would still be with his family, swimming in the sea every day, and wearing clothes appropriate to the climate. He hoped at least his brothers and sisters were having fun and buying lots of fish with his EMIs.

'Have you been feeding him anything new?' he asked, with the air of a man keen to get to the bottom of things. There was no medical crisis here. Mrs Verma fed her son enough for a family of five. Entire villages in the badlands survived on less. It was a wonder Pappu didn't burst.

'Nothing that I can think of,' said Mrs Verma, eyeing the doctor suspiciously.

'Have there been any changes in the cooking staff?' he inquired delicately. Mrs Verma had an imperious manner that went with her IG nose, and the cooks often bore the brunt of it. They were always running away to Bangladesh, despite the hazards involved in the journey. Good cooks were in high demand there. Plus the standard of living was much higher.

'It's the same cook,' said Mrs Verma impatiently, 'I'm telling you it's that hand. I told Sanjeev not to be in such a hurry. God knows where they get these things from, they must be full of all kinds of diseases. There's no concept of quality control in this country.'

'You're right,' said the doctor promptly. 'The hand is the culprit. He must be suffering from some infectious disease of unknown origin. Should I conduct tests?'

'All of them,' said Mrs Verma. 'You have the list. But is that enough? How can he be refusing puris? They're his favourite. He has to keep up his strength until the test results come in.'

'I'll make sure they do them immediately,' said the doctor. 'Meanwhile, perhaps we should discuss some of the details of your upcoming tummy tuck . . .'

A maid burst in, face flushed, panting.

'Madam, madam, Pappu bhaiyya is throwing all his toys away,' she cried.

'Oh my God, it's affecting his brain!' moaned Mrs Verma, and rushed off to find Pappu. The doctor followed reluctantly in her wake. They didn't need medical help here, he thought, they needed tranquilizers. He made a mental note to add some to their vitamin supplements.

❑

Pappu was on the balcony. The railing was super-high, because he sometimes got confused about which floor he was on. However, he could reach the top if he really stretched and that was what he was doing. He had just tipped a brand-new Batman action figure over the edge when his mother arrived on the scene.

'Oh my God, Pappu, we got that for you from New York!' she wailed, making a despairing lunge and just missing. Batman dropped like a stone, showing no inclination to swoop, soar, glide, or apprehend passing criminals.

'Whee!' said Pappu. He picked up a Game Boy, a model that had been on the market for less than a year.

'No!' cried Mrs Verma, snatching it away from him, and clasping it to her bosom. 'What is wrong with you?'

Pappu was quite used to his mother throwing hissy fits. He remained unperturbed.

'They need them,' he said simply, pointing downwards to the street. 'They don't have any.'

Mrs Verma looked down. Two grimy little boys looked up at her, grinning. The mother of such a kind boy was undoubtedly very kind herself. Maybe she would throw even bigger things down.

Taking advantage of his mother's momentary inattention, Pappu picked up a teddy bear and flipped it over the railing. It was a genuine Winnie the Pooh. Mrs Verma uttered a heart-rending cry.

The doctor noticed something odd at this point, and felt a spark of professional interest for the first time since he'd come to this house. The boy was using only one hand, which was natural. He had just undergone surgery. It always took time to adjust to new parts. But he was using only his new hand, not the old one. This was something worth investigating. He made a mental note.

Mrs Verma had other things to worry about.

'Pappu Verma, why are you giving away all your toys to those dirty little boys?' she demanded, hands on her hips. 'They're purchased with your father's hard-earned money.'

'They remind me of Ramu,' said Pappu.

❑

Late that night, Mrs Verma sat on Pappu's bed, stroking his forehead while he slept. He tossed and turned fitfully.

'I miss Ramu,' he whispered in his sleep. He sounded very sad.

Mrs Verma blamed herself. She should have taught him not to get attached to slaves, but he was her only son and she didn't like being mean to him. This was the result. He'd begun to think of them as pets, actual human beings, even. He was too young and too trusting to understand that these people would always take him for a ride. It was in their nature. It was hard to explain these things to Pappu. Even she had to admit that he was a few chairs short of a dining set.

But what could she do about Ramu? After the firework incident which had blown off Pappu's hand, Sanjeev had deposited Ramu at the Bank of Bodies. Most probably, they had already disassembled him and stored him in several jars. She could only hope against hope that they hadn't processed him yet.

Pappu whimpered in his sleep, and continued calling out Ramu's name. Such an affectionate boy, she thought, ruffling his hair. He would suffer in life because of it. As long as she was around, though, she would do everything she could to protect him.

She had to go to the Bank of Bodies. Assuming he was still alive, she had to bring back this child that her son had grown so attached to. Failing which, she would get someone very similar. It was the least that a mother could do.

21

'You're going to talk about class struggle, aren't you?'

'So, this whole Hindu-Muslim thing,' said Pintoo. 'When did it start?'

He was sitting with the ancient headmaster and Tarun-da under a pipal tree like the Buddha, as per Kader Khan's suggestion.

'They started it!' said the headmaster, before realizing that there was no one to point to. Tarun-da smiled and shook his head.

'You're going to talk about class struggle, aren't you?' said Pintoo apprehensively.

'My youth was spent on your question,' said Tarun-da, who was thirty-two. 'I did my PhD thesis on communalism. At JNU we were against it.'

'Yes, but how did it start? Who lit the first match?'

'There were complex socio-economic forces at play,' said Tarun-da. Pintoo was disappointed. He couldn't do much about those.

'It was Jinnah,' said the ancient headmaster, 'it was Jinnah who started it. Shaitan! Badmaash! Betrayer of salt! He spat out the nipple that suckled him!'

'There were faults on both sides,' said Tarun-da sagaciously. 'You cannot blame Partition solely on Mr Jinnah, although my grandfather used to do it regularly. Our side also tried many monkey tricks.'

'Who's talking about Partition? That was a circus! I'm talking about Direct Action Day. After that, the very meaning of the word "action" changed.'

'It was just another riot,' said Tarun-da.

'Just another riot? You're a Bengali and you can say this? Go ask your grandfather, why don't you?'

The ancient headmaster was drooling with rage and his dentures threatened to pop out, always a bad sign. Pintoo stepped in. 'You can beat him up later, sir,' he said, 'first tell me the story.'

'The first Muslim to visit India was Mahmud of Ghazni,' said the headmaster. 'He had married too many women and had run out of money, due to which they were criticizing him day and night. This is a common problem in the Muslim community. What year did he come in? Why are you looking at my face? Tell me! I have already taught you this. What year? Tell me!'

He glared at Pintoo.

'1001?' said Pintoo, getting ready to duck.

'That is correct,' said the ancient headmaster. 'He destroyed many temples and killed many people for the glory of Allah, although the plunder he kept for himself. His family lived in great splendour, until they were plundered by Muhammad Ghori. Seeing their example, many others followed, raping and looting and causing all manner of disturbance. In fact, due to lack of seating arrangements in his own house, one Persian fellow even stole the Peacock Throne. But that was later. After the first few waves, one of the invaders thought, why should I eat only once, when I can eat continuously, especially if I can get my mother-in-law to stay in Samarkand? Accordingly, he set up shop in Delhi, after disposing of Prithviraj Chauhan, who was generous and brave, but annoyed many people, so that when it was his time to die, no one came to support him.

'Over time, many Indians became Muslims, after which things became very mixed up. Lot of adjustment was required. Over a thousand years, across thousands of villages, disputes were happening constantly, like Mohun Bagan vs East Bengal in Calcutta. Ten-twenty people were getting killed all the time. Someone wanted someone's land. Someone wanted someone's wife. Someone wanted someone dead. Someone wanted to be head. The Hindu-Muslim part was just an excuse. But what are ten-twenty dead people in India? Ten-twenty people are dying all the time. No one notices such things, because a lot of extra people are always available. Then the British came. Initially they pretended to be humble traders, but they were worse than any lala, soon they wanted everything. They started dividing people, Hindu against Muslim, Gurkha against plainsman, Maratha against Maratha, because throughout the world, this is what they do. Whenever you see a country in two pieces, like Western and Eastern, or Northern and Southern, or Islamic and Democratic, you will know that the British have been there. Also, very few people know French in such places, which is a further clue. But after a while they had to start educating Indians, because someone had to write minutes of the meetings and keep track of all the money, and so some people became educated, and they started looking around, and they said, "Who are we? Are we monkeys?" And so they began to fight against the British. One of them was Mr Jinnah.'

'Mr Jinnah was Indian?' said Pintoo. 'I thought he was Pakistani, and evil.'

'He was very much Indian,' said the ancient headmaster. 'You judge for yourself whether he was evil or not.'

'I must object to this kind of demonization,' said Tarun-da, firmly. 'You are distorting Pintoo's value system. At this rate, you'll turn him into a cat's-paw of the reactionary Hindu right wing.'

'I object to your beard,' said the ancient headmaster, 'but do you hear me complaining about it? Let me finish my story. Mr Jinnah was the proper English type. He ate ham sandwiches and hated religion. He was very similar to Mr Nehru in this regard. On the other hand, Gandhiji kept singing bhajans, which Mr Jinnah objected to. Finally they parted company on this issue and Mr Jinnah founded the Muslim League and demanded a country called Pakistan on the basis of religion, which initially he had objected to, but now he was strongly in favour of. Many Muslim landlords and preachers supported him, because he could speak proper English, and they needed someone like that. But Gandhiji and Nehru were very clever, and Lady Mountbatten was favouring them, and he was unable to get his Pakistan. Then he decided only Direct Action could achieve Pakistan, and he declared Direct Action Day, a day on which all Muslims would rise and demand Pakistan. In case people misunderstood, he explained very clearly what Direct Action meant. Nehru was silent. Gandhiji was silent. Nobody tried to stop him. They thought he was bluffing, which is strange, because Mr Jinnah was not known to be a bluffer. "Do you think I will sit with folded hands? I also am going to make trouble," he said. The danger was greatest in Calcutta where the Muslim League was in charge and a holiday was declared and newspapers published detailed instructions for the rioters, including exact points at which processions would start, and the number of Muslim League workers deputed to each mosque. I think they were giving away a chopper with every annual subscription. Still nobody did anything. The local British chief was a fool and believed everything Suhrawardy the Chief Minister said, because by that time all the intelligent Britishers had gone back to Britain, leaving behind only the fools and the criminally violent. CM Suhrawardy asked the police to be sympathetic, so subsequently when the riots began, they were very sympathetic towards everyone except the victims and when the case became tricky, they ran away. Thousands of people died on that day, and in the week that followed. They kept hacking and chopping, hacking and chopping, Hindus and Muslims both, and the bodies piled up in the street, and the gutters flowed with blood. Then, for revenge, all Hindus were wiped out in Noakhali, and thousands of Muslims were butchered in Bihar, and so the circus began. Hindus and Muslims in Bengal never trusted each other again. People talk about Partition, as if it were all one thing, but they do not see the differences. Partition in Punjab was forced. Partition in Bengal was voluntary. They did not want to live together, ever again, the Bengalis. Because of Direct Action Day. Because of the Great Calcutta Killings. Because it was not ten-twenty people, it was thousands. Because it was no longer a small thing, it was politics, it was tactics, it was a game. Jinnah and Suhrawardy made it a game. They showed the way to everyone who followed.'

Pintoo made a small tick in his little notepad.

'That's one,' he said, quietly. 'I'll need a good man for that one.'

'I disagree with him totally,' said Tarun-da, while the ancient headmaster was recovering his breath. 'In my view, it was the *Ramayana*.'

'You're against Hindu scriptures?' asked Pintoo, who had never really discussed religion with Tarun-da before.

'No, the television programme. I myself do not want to disengage the proletariat from religion, as this could affect the popular support for the Party. But my study on communalism at JNU showed that the root cause behind the proliferation of communalism was the telecast of the *Ramayana* in 1987. Before that, television was only used for speeches, sitar recitals, and documentaries on fertilizer. By producing the *Ramayana* at that exact moment, with fertilizer as the only other viewing option, the history of India was transformed. Before that, Lord Rama was a figure seen only in temples, or a face we imagined while listening to devotional music. Suddenly, he was a handsome man with nice shoulders on television. He was a God we could see. He was a God we could love. He was a God whose temples achieved added significance. Whole families were mesmerized. Earlier, Hindus were not that militant. But afterwards, when the man of the house leaped up and said, "I'm going out to beat up some nuns," or, "I'll be right back after I massacre some Muslims," his wife would just smile and say, "Carry your umbrella, dear, and don't forget your tiffin." It was no coincidence that the Babri Masjid was destroyed soon after. Since then, militant lunatics have become stronger and stronger. Some Muslims were always difficult. But with both sides like that, what country can you have? You have to stop them from making the *Ramayana*, Pintoo, at that exact point in time. Give them alternative suggestions. We know all the hit movies since 1987. All producers like superhit ideas. Please let's give them some, like *Bunty and Babli*, or *Man With Warm Heart Will Whisk Away Bride*. Let them make the *Ramayana* later, when brains will not be washed so thoroughly.'

Pintoo looked down at his notebook, frowning.

'Stop Direct Action Day,' he said. 'Convert India's top five billionaires into missionaries from Ramakrishna Mission. Find Indira Gandhi true love. Stop nuclearization. Give vasectomies to select VIPs. Stop production of the *Ramayana*. Save Mahatma Gandhi. That's a very long list. I may not have the time. We can't do all of this. We have to choose.'

Repairing a mobile phone was easy, Pintoo realized.

Repairing a country, not so much.

22

'87 per cent of those surveyed would prefer a religion with genuine miracle content.'

No. 2 was addressing his fellow directors in the plush Bank of Bodies boardroom. He was slightly irritated because he was having to make his presentation in a brightly-lit room. No. 2 liked having his audience staring hypnotically at a bright screen, while his voice made telling points in the dark. However, the Chairman had strictly forbidden any dimming of lights in the boardroom. In his view, this prevented people from being able to see the various pictures and paintings of the Chairman, which was a privilege he did not wish his loyal colleagues to be deprived of under any circumstances. In addition, he was afraid of the dark. In his childhood, his father had often leaped into his bedroom in the middle of the night, pretending to be a ghost. His theory being that this would help strengthen his son's nerves, and prepare him well for the challenges of adult life.

No. 2 did not let this frustration show, of course, and remained on the surface the compelling smoothie he had always been. 'You're bound to get involved in some kind of number two business,' one of his teachers had predicted after observing him closely. The name had stuck.

'At our last meeting, our Chairman had enlightened us with a vision,' he said, smoothly and compellingly. 'As the next step in the evolution of BoB, he had suggested a lateral and entirely logical extension from the Medical Joy business to the business of Organized Religion. Today, we take the first step in transforming this vision into a reality. Over the past two days, we have conducted extensive research amongst our potential target audience to determine the desired features of our religion product.'

The littlest director, sitting at the extreme end of the table, was busy taking the minutes. He wrote down 'religion product' with a flourish and gazed at it admiringly. What a dynamically innovative company he worked for! He couldn't wait to go home and tell his wife all about it.

'The results of this research have been analysed by some of the finest minds in our company, including my own,' continued No. 2, 'I will take you through them one by one.'

The Chairman hid a yawn behind his handkerchief. He hated research meetings. Like Steve Jobs, a sage from long ago, he always knew exactly what to do, and saw no reason why the flow of his omnipotence should be interrupted by asking customers for their opinion. Some of his minions were rather fond of such things, however, and he tended to humour them in this regard. Sometimes, he even stayed awake.

'87 per cent of those surveyed,' said No. 2, 'would prefer a religion with genuine miracle content. For example, turning ten-rupee notes into hundred-rupee notes.'

The Chairman was much excited by this. 'Can we actually do that?' he exclaimed, dropping his germ-preventive handkerchief in his agitation.

'Not yet, sir. But we're working on it,' said No. 2, reassuringly, while secretly congratulating himself on getting the Chairman's attention.

'A better-looking spouse was the second most popular expectation from the new religion. Interestingly, more women mentioned this than men. The curing of incurable diseases was another item on the wishlist. As you can see, there is an inherent strategic fit between the new religion product and our core business of Medical Joy, which involves cosmetic enhancement and the replacement of defective organs through donor contributions. Frankly, it's quite astonishing that none of our previous chairmen drew this obvious conclusion.'

The Chairman smiled fondly at No. 2. He always knew the right thing to say.

'Several other desires were expressed by our customers,' continued No. 2. 'The ability to convert female offspring into male offspring. The ability to terrorize government officers at will. Better mileage from automobiles. A freeze on the price of vegetables. A permanent solution to premature ejaculation for males, and the ability to have an actual orgasm with existing spouse for females. Better housing, more money, and a general desire to avoid the consequences of past actions. So clearly, our customers expect a strong miracle content in their religion.

'The next area we probed was the expected profile of the figurehead or guru of the product. Any thoughts on this, gentlemen? I know we discussed using the Shanti Nagar child last time, but let us keep our minds open to other possibilities,' said No. 2, arching his eyebrows coyly. 'There is an obvious answer, you know.'

The other directors fidgeted nervously. They hated being put on the spot. Bitter experience had taught them that, in such cases, there was no such thing as the right answer.

No. 2 sighed gustily. 'The answer is staring you in the face, quite literally, and from multiple directions. We need a personality to lead our religion, someone who can inspire mindless devotion in the masses, someone appropriately godlike. Who else but our esteemed Chairman could possibly fit the bill?'

It was the Chairman's turn to be alarmed, and he fluttered his handkerchief at No. 2, signalling frantically. He had no wish to be constantly surrounded by thousands of members of the germ-infested public, however adoring they might be.

No. 2 shook his head sadly, 'But of course, that is not an option,' he said, to the immense relief of the Chairman. 'The Bank of Bodies, and indeed, the nation's business community, could not possibly spare him. But we do have a candidate in mind. Moving on to the next point. When we asked our customers about preferences in gurus, 67 per cent expressed a preference for an attractive female guru. Pursuing this line, and bearing in mind the examples of other gurus who have in the past generated significant revenue streams, we asked about the attractiveness of a religion which advocated free sex. 82 per cent confirmed that they would give such a religion a try, and were willing to pay substantial enrollment fees.'

No. 2 paused and surveyed his audience. Altogether too many statistics were being discussed, he realized. Several of the older directors were beginning to look distinctly glassy-eyed. It was time to cut to the chase.

'So it boils down to two options,' he said, 'we can launch a religion with a significant sex content, or we can launch a religion with a significant miracle content. These are the two products with the maximum revenue potential. It is for this august assembly to debate, discuss, and arrive at a direction for me and my team.'

'Ngff Sex,' mumbled the Chairman. He hadn't had sex in years, and saw no reason why anyone else should. It was a matter of principle.

'Miracles it is then,' said No. 2 amiably, thereby marking an end to the discussion and debate. 'Of course, in the case of a religious product driven by miracles, our guru or mascot would have to be a genuine miracle worker. Anyone remember anything about the Shanti Nagar kid we mentioned in passing at the last meeting?'

'He sent Sam to the loony bin!' said the littlest director, glad to be able to make a contribution.

No. 2 smiled benignly at his junior colleague. 'I would have put it more elegantly,' he said, 'but in essence you are right. We have knowledge of a genuine juvenile miracle worker thanks to the garbled testimony of our ex-employee Sam Kapoor, until recently manager of our Karol Bagh branch, who is currently incapacitated by virtue of being clinically insane. Sam interacted most closely with the young fellow, but the testimony of other witnesses also confirms his existence. The problem is, while we know he exists, we don't know exactly where he is in Shanti Nagar. Any ideas on how to locate him?'

'Send in the Medical Military Commandos!' said the littlest director, who now had the bit firmly between his teeth.

'Under normal circumstances, I would agree with you,' said No. 2 kindly, 'after all, that is how we collect our donors, thanks to whose contributions we spread Medical Joy. However, given that we wish to recruit the child, as opposed to harvest him for body parts, I think more finesse is called for. Locating a single child in an area as huge and heavily populated as Shanti Nagar is a task in itself. No, this appears to be a job for Jasubhai the Collector.'

Jasubhai the Collector was a very old associate of the Bank of Bodies, going back to the days when it had merely dealt in money. Jasubhai had originally helped the Bank collect overdue loans. From this, he had graduated to collecting the people who owed the money. Showing commendable business acumen, he had expanded the scope of his organization to cover both collection and disposal, and had been of immense service to BoB on innumerable occasions. As the business had grown, so had the need for his services. He was well-informed, well-connected and admirably discreet. Moreover, his rates were reasonable.

'Make a note, will you,' said No. 2, gesturing to the littlest director, judging it time to give the man something menial to do and thereby put him back in his place. Let them fly briefly and then bring them back to earth with a dull, sickening thud. That was his understanding of human resources management.

'Make sure he's in my office by tomorrow morning.'

The littlest director made a note and subsided, chastened. He hated it when No. 2 was mean to him.

'This brings us to one final point—the question of licences,' continued No. 2, who was eager to wrap up now. He could hear a gin and tonic calling him.

'After the last round of liberalization, we no longer need licences. However, we do need sixty-seven different approvals from nine government departments, none of which are referred to as licences. Any alternative suggestions?'

No. 2 now looked at the littlest director invitingly. The littlest director gazed back blankly. He judged, correctly, that he had made enough contributions for one day.

No. 2 gave him an approving smile. The lad would go far, provided he managed to stay on the right side of the Chairman.

'Bljee,' mumbled the Chairman, who was also quite keen to wrap up the meeting. It was time for his nap.

'I should have thought of that myself,' noted No. 2. 'It's time to call Balaji the Fixer. Between Jasubhai and Balaji, they'll have the whole thing sorted.'

Balaji the Fixer, another old associate, fixed everything. You just had to name it, and Balaji would fix it for you. Duplicates of film stars so that businessmen could claim they had slept with film stars. Liquor licences. Up to thirty seconds with the PM. Expert witnesses. Amateur witnesses. Amateur witnesses, who, over time, became expert witnesses. Amnesiac witnesses. Minority witnesses. Hostile witnesses. Unreliable witnesses. Incompetent witnesses. Penitent witnesses. Foreign witnesses. Indeed, Balaji had considered specializing in witnesses, and even designed a logo. But he knew he would miss the variety. He fixed things. It was what he did. Each job was a new challenge.

Balaji and Jasubhai, the dynamic duo, mused No. 2, as he watched his fellow directors shuffle out of the boardroom. It usually boiled down to the two of them. Getting the basics right. That was the key to success. The rest was all powerpoint.

23

'Who are these guys, Grandpa?
Should I fuck them?'

The ancient headmaster crossed himself, and cowered behind his desk, trembling. He could be surprisingly spry and had made the transition from drooling on the charpoy to cowering behind his desk in more or less a single bound.

'Begone, Satanic One!' he quavered, making feeble gestures of defiance with one hand and covering his genitals with the other. Ranvir Hooda, his trusty doorman, was nowhere to be seen. Probably behind the cowshed, doped to the gills. The odour of cow-dung improved his high.

Mr Chatterjee questioned the wisdom of Ali's approach. Ali maintained that handing out business cards gave a more professional touch, as befitted an organization that had been very particular about medical benefits and leave travel allowance, and was intimately familiar with Outlook Express. It hadn't worked with the ancient headmaster, who had been semi-comatose until he saw the card, which simply said, 'Mojtaba Ali, Al Qaeda', at which point he had sprung up, and was now making various gestures intended to ward off evil.

'Sir, I am Bengali, sir,' ventured Mr Chatterjee tentatively, hoping to salvage the situation.

'What type?' demanded the ancient headmaster. 'Actual, or Bangladeshi?'

'Actual, sir, genuine,' said Mr Chatterjee, realizing he may have just made things worse. For some reason, Ali was trying hard not to laugh.

'Netaji Subhash Chandra Bose was a Bengali,' said the ancient headmaster, thoughtfully. He eyed the Satanic One, who winked at him.

His cheerful demeanour softened the venerable educationist. He seemed like a pleasant enough young man, although evil. The old man tried to unbend himself, and found he was stuck. His spinal cord was not what it used to be. Mr Chatterjee and Ali came forward, carefully pulled him upright and guided him back to his charpoy. The old man reached out and grabbed Ali's forearm, pressing the flesh to reassure himself that he was real, and not some djinn or shaitan.

'Are you carrying any bombs?' he demanded querulously. Ali smiled and let him check, submitting himself to a fumbling but thorough inspection. The headmaster was surprised to find the computer film clinging to his chest, and peered near-sightedly at it for a while. Computers came in many forms, and Ali used most of them, depending on circumstances. The headmaster eyed Ali shrewdly.

'You're the modern type, is it?' he said.

'Doing the best I can,' said Ali modestly.

'So what does Al Qaeda seek in Shanti Nagar?' asked the headmaster once he had reinserted his hookah into his mouth.

Ali explained Mr Chatterjee's assignment, the danger to his innocent wife, and dwelt on the overall meritorious nature of Mr Chatterjee's quest. Listening to him speak, Mr Chatterjee was mildly uplifted, although generally pessimistic. Even though he was bound to be massacred by Al Qaeda, or executed by a Bureau of Reconstruction firing squad, or have his brain mangled into mush by a renegade telepath, he would meet his end with his head held high, as a Man Who Had Done His Duty. His father would have been proud. When he met him soon, in the afterlife, he would tell him all about it, maybe have a drink or two.

'We just want to find out the truth,' said Ali.

The ancient headmaster eyed Ali unblinkingly, poker-faced. His hookah bubbled away cheerfully.

'What will you do with the truth?' he asked.

'He just has to file some sort of report,' said Ali. 'If they like it they might not arrest him, and then he can keep looking after his missus. She's a bit slow, apparently.'

The ancient headmaster hesitated.

'Pintoo has been very busy studying these last few days,' he said, eventually. 'He is trying to find out what went wrong. Whatever little history I know, I have taught him. Now that communist Tarun is teaching him. He is a fool, that one, but he has knowledge. Communists are very studious. Perhaps that is what destroys their brains. Pintoo is trying to decide what to do. He should not be disturbed.'

'I was part of history,' said Ali. 'In fact, I'm a specimen. That might be helpful.'

The ancient headmaster looked at Ali, and at Mr Chatterjee.

'A Mohammedan terrorist and a Bengali gentleman,' he said thoughtfully. 'Yes, you could be useful. I think you may meet him.'

Mr Chatterjee was not entirely reassured by this, although Ali seemed pleased enough.

'So, where do we have to go, masterji?' asked Ali.

'You do not have to go anywhere,' said the ancient headmaster, 'Ranvir will take you.'

Ranvir appeared right on cue, moderately high but generally mobile. On spotting the two strangers he hitched up his dhoti and took a firmer grip on his lathi.

'Who are these guys, Grandpa?' he asked. 'Should I fuck them?'

Ranvir was his manservant, and very loyal, despite the low pay. He covered his living expenses through supplementary menacing. The headmaster threw a duster at him, hitting him on the side of the head with an accuracy born of seventy years of practice.

'Mind your tongue, badmaash,' he said. 'These are guests. If anybody has to be fucked, I'll let you know. Take them to Pintoo at Tarun's office.'

Ali got up and touched the headmaster's feet. 'Thank you, sir, for your guidance.'

'Whether guidance or misguidance I do not know,' said the ancient headmaster. 'Soon we will all find out. God go with you.'

❏

Ram Manohar Pande had Bhiru by the throat, pinned against the wall. Given that Bhiru was approximately four feet tall, his feet were dangling in the air, kicking feebly. He was bare bodied, because Pande had ripped off his shirt and shoved it down the back of his pants, to staunch the bleeding from his buttocks.

'That's all I know, huzoor,' he croaked. As a sub judice for nearly thirteen years, he had often longed for death, but now that it was looking him in the face, he wasn't so sure.

Pande squeezed harder.

'Are you sure she said Shanti Nagar?' demanded Pande, spraying Bhiru with spittle. Bhiru gagged helplessly. If Pande's hands didn't kill him, his breath certainly would. Why hadn't he stayed back in the village like his mother had asked him to?

'God promise, sir,' he said, 'she said she was going to Shanti Nagar, and drove off in your jeep. I was behind that bush over there, doing small job.'

'Why didn't you stop her, you harami? You're my fucking servant, and you let her steal my jeep?'

'What could I do, sir?' sobbed Bhiru pitifully, 'I am so small. The mem-sahab was much bigger than me. I thought better to give you information by hiding and listening. If I had tried to stop her, all you would find is my dead body, then what clue would you get, sir? How will you arrest without clue, sir?'

Bhiru was well-versed in police procedure. Clues were vital to police investigations. You caught a person, beat him to a pulp, and made him say things. The things he said were known as clues. These clues helped solve cases and, thereby, close files. The whole process was known as investigation.

Pande had a throbbing headache, but he could see some logic to the actions of his pathetic sidekick. He was fundamentally a man of justice, so long as justice was presented to him in terms he could understand. He let go of Bhiru's throat. Bhiru collapsed at his feet, where, out of sheer force of habit, he started weakly cleaning Pande's shoes with his dhoti. Pande kicked him in his Adam's apple.

'So don't give me false clue, bastard. She went to warn her husband, didn't she? The weedy little babu with spectacles. She paid you to lie to me.'

Bhiru was too busy having a coughing fit to answer the question. Pande waited impatiently. He briefly considered another kick, but even he could see that this would only delay matters further, and he was in a hurry. In this respect, he was better than his father who had never known when to stop.

Bhiru recovered eventually.

'Sir, if she paid me, where is the money?' he asked reproachfully. 'Search me. Do I have any? Have I ever had any? Did my father ever have any? Have you ever given me any? Did anybody ever give me any?'

'Achcha achcha, OK,' said Pande, feeling his eyes moisten unexpectedly. Perhaps he should have treated his sub judice better. It was not unheard of to do so. Some other officers had even arranged to have their sub judices married, with proper dowry and everything, and filled their thanas with little sub judice children.

'OK, OK, you get up,' said Pande, kicking him in a sympathetic sort of way. He was telling the truth, evidently.

Pande stood there thinking, as Bhiru crawled off to a safe distance, nursing his abused throat. His head and his buttocks were throbbing with pain and he was finding it hard to think. He was deeply confused, which made his head hurt even harder. The last he remembered, he was about to give that snooty little bitch what she richly deserved when that monstrous dog attacked his posterior. The next thing he knew, he had gained consciousness on the bedroom floor, with a lump the size of Chhattisgarh on his forehead. He had assumed that it was that cowardly little shit of a husband, the bespectacled babu, the bastard who had introduced this whole dog motif in his life. All these dogs that were now refusing to stay put, and routinely appearing and disappearing all over the place. It was a wonder he was still sane.

One thing was clear. He was a police officer. He had been assaulted in the course of his duty. For that, someone had to die.

He beckoned to Bhiru.

'I have to go to Shanti Nagar to kill people,' he said. 'You go straight back to the thana. Don't try to be clever.'

'I am not clever, sir,' said Bhiru, simply. 'You know I am stupid, as you tell me regularly. Do one thing. Why don't you give me your handcuffs? I'll go back to the thana and handcuff myself to your chair, so I can't escape.'

This seemed reasonable. His years of training had not been wasted, Pande thought with some satisfaction. He gave the handcuffs to Bhiru, along with the key.

A young stud on a 1000cc Rajdoot bike was just passing by. Pande stepped into the middle of the street and stopped him. He cuffed him on the side of the head and knocked him off the bike, following up with a quick boot to the groin. He removed the boy's helmet and put it on his own head. Riding without a helmet was against the law, and Pande was nothing if not law abiding. He revved up, adjusted his still-throbbing buttocks on the seat so the pain was manageable, and drove off towards Shanti Nagar, where they would soon learn all about justice. No mother's son was going to stand in his way. Spectacular retribution loomed large in the near future, beckoning him on seductively.

Bhiru watched him go from the footpath. He would have to hop over to the house and fetch Samrat, who was locked away in one of the toilets. As per Banani's advice, he had given up his plan of using Samrat to menace people for money, although it seemed reasonable enough to him. Perhaps Samrat would prefer the cleaner environment of his village, where the sunlight peeped through once in a while. He knew his little nephew would be pleased. He looked at the handcuffs in his hands. He fondled them lovingly. High-quality stainless steel. He should be able to sell them for a hundred rupees at least. Enough to buy him a train ticket back to his village. Once he got there, he would stay there.

The big city was no place for a poor man.

24

'Servant resented this pressure to end affair,
which he was enjoying regularly.'

The Self-Defence Force boys were no match for the Medical Military Commandos. The latter were financed by the Bank of Bodies, which provided its troops the absolute best in training, equipment, facilities and intoxicants. Their motivation levels were extremely high. Some of them were American AfPak veterans who were fed up of winning hearts and minds and happy to be doing a job that involved shooting people.

The Medical Military Commandos could not rampage at will, however. Farming bodies was like any other form of agriculture. Over-harvesting was inadvisable. If they pushed it too far, they would have a full-scale uprising on their hands. What with one thing and another, they would probably end up obliterating Shanti Nagar, especially if the government got into it and was feeling particularly masterful. Which would leave them with no raw material. The BoB had tried growing people in situ, under laboratory conditions, but the whole process cost far too much money and took far too long. Collection was the only cost-effective option. So the BoB and Shanti-bai had struck a deal, and the Medical Military Commandos came in not more than twice or thrice a week, collecting only against immediate orders.

Thus they existed, Shanti Nagar and the BoB, in a state of horrid equilibrium. The Self-Defence Force boys watched, cursing, gripping their rifles till their knuckles hurt, and waited. Every month, they trained a few more boys and gained a few more weapons, but it wasn't enough to repulse the Commandos. Their time would come; meanwhile they stayed sharp, and trained hard.

The police were different. They were on the payroll. It was one of the first things Shanti-bai had done, and she'd paid well above the market rate to make sure they stayed away. Out of gratitude and respect for her, they had never asked for a hike. It suited them fine. It was extra income, and they already had their hands full with all the shenanigans in the city.

Which was why, when Ram Manohar Pande rode his bike right through the gate, doing well over a hundred, and mowing down a rookie guard in the process, it was a bit of shock for the SDF. Two of the other guards picked up their wounded colleague while a third levelled his light machine gun at Pande. He was a tough young man who had left a dead family behind in the strip mines of Chhattisgarh, and the gun in his hand was rock steady.

Pande struggled to his feet and drew his pistol. He smiled his terrible smile. Low-caste scum didn't scare him.

The young guard smiled back. 'Payday is next Monday, uncle,' he said, 'what happened? Didn't get your share?'

Pande swallowed his bile. The two-paise person had a machine gun. But his rage would see him through.

'I need to go in, motherfucker,' he hissed, 'don't try to stop me.'

'You know the rules, uncle,' said the young guard. 'Whoever it is you are chasing, you can't follow him here. Otherwise stop taking the money. Then we'll see.'

His gun didn't waver. Nor did his smile.

Pande hesitated. In his mind, he was grabbing this piece of shit and hacking off his arms, as depicted in the movie *Sholay*, thereby rendering him tragically unable to play Holi, or point guns at officers of the law, or hug widowed daughters-in-law. Unfortunately, this did not seem to be an option at this point in time. Pande knew his reflexes were not lightning-quick. Usually, this hardly mattered, as the recipients of his justice were poor and weak. But somebody had been feeding this scheduled caste, and they had even given him a machine gun. So now, instead of cleaning bathrooms, he was threatening policemen. That was the problem with big cities. They had drifted too far.

It was time to apply strategy. Pande knew what strategy was. The OC of his thana had explained it to him a couple of times. There would be rare occasions, he had said, when a police officer would find himself in a position where he was unable to solve a problem by applying electric shocks to the testicles. In such cases, the concerned officer would have to apply his brain, and fabricate some kind of story which would enable him to reach his ultimate goal—Closing The File. Incest, adultery, and lecherous servants usually played important roles in such stories. Strategy was a rare and wonderful thing; shrewdly, Pande had memorized a few good ones used by other officers, and now seemed like a good time to roll one out.

'Look, fucker,' said Pande, cordially enough by his standards, 'let me tell you the full story. Then you judge. This is a special case, involving the OC of my thana. His neighbour was a medical doctor, but he was a loose character. Doctor's unmarried sister was living with doctor and spouse. She also was a loose character, naturally. Sister was having an affair with servant—one more loose character. Doctor was having affair with wife of colleague, yet another characterless person. Doctor demanded that sister stop having affair, but sister would not listen, giving example of his own affair. Servant resented this pressure to end affair, which he was enjoying regularly. Servant contacted doctor's colleague and informed him of doctor's activities with his wife, which he was unaware of. Both then entered house of doctor and shot him repeatedly, late at night, while all concerned were under the influence of alcohol. Unfortunately, one bullet went through the window and penetrated skull of my OC in the next flat, who was reading *Times of India*, leaving him spot dead. According to coroner, it bounced off, his skull was very strong, but the concussion was too much.'

The guard was fascinated by this complex web of deceit and lechery. It was better than TV. But he didn't lower his gun.

'There's lots of excitement in the big city, uncle,' he said, 'but what's that got to do with me?'

'The killers have run away to Shanti Nagar,' said Pande, 'and I was on guard at the OC's house. I have to find them, or my story will finish. Try to understand, it's not a normal person who died—it was the OC. Don't take my backside like this. I have to go in.'

The guard hesitated, but he could see the man's point. He wore a uniform himself.

'I'll give you two hours,' he said, 'but if you try anything clever, I'll come after you and shoot you. Is that clear?'

'It's clear,' said Pande, giving him a smile that chilled the young man to the bone and caused him to have serious second thoughts about his generosity.

But before he could say anything Pande was already striding off into Shanti Nagar, lathi in hand, itching for action.

25

'Would you recognize Gandhiji if you saw him?'

A band of women were sorting mushrooms by the side of the road. Little boys were putting them in polythene packets. Little girls were putting labels on the packets. They were doing their respective jobs intently and seriously, little fingers moving like quicksilver.

One of the little girls gave Banani a shy smile, and she smiled back.

She walked up to her. 'Where's the local school?' she asked the little girl.

The little girl paused, a label held delicately between finger and thumb.

'My school, or the big one?' she asked.

'Which is better?' asked Banani.

'Oh, my school,' said the girl. 'It's the best. We have no chairs or tables, but Auntie is very kind. The big school has that really old headmaster. He's mean. He throws things at you. And he spits a lot when he's shouting. And he smokes a hookah and makes the room smokey.'

The big school sounded remarkably like Banani's own, although with a rustic touch. It was the last thing she needed right now. Mrs Johnson's face floated in front of her eyes and she suppressed a shudder.

'I'll go to your school, sweetie, since you like it so much,' she said. 'How do I get there?'

The little girl gave her detailed directions.

❑

Ali and Mr Chatterjee were sitting on a bench outside Tarun-da's house. Ranvir had asked them to wait, while he went inside to announce their arrival.

A giant black crow descended from a nearby wall and hopped up to their feet, looking for food.

Mr Chatterjee shook his head and the crow flew off, cawing hungrily. It perched itself on a nearby wall and looked at him, head cocked to one side, calculating the odds of getting away with a bite out of him. Mr Chatterjee eyed it nervously.

'Isn't he a beauty?' said Ali. 'Better keep an eye out.'

Ranvir re-emerged. 'Pintoo will see you now,' he said. 'That sisterfucker Tarun is also there, but you can ignore him—nothing he ever says makes any sense. He's a communist. Take your shoes off before you go in. And remember, if you try any stunts, headmaster has told me to smash your heads. I like smashing heads.'

They went in. It was a single room, dimly lit, but cosy, with many bookshelves. A bust of Lenin was placed on the floor. A man and a boy sat together on a narrow cot. The man had a beard, and was wrapped in a shawl. The boy was around twelve. He had a freshly-bandaged stump. He looked pale and delicate and feverish. His eyes were very bright. He was studying them closely.

'Please sit,' he said, beckoning them to the bed.

'He looks like the government type,' said Tarun-da, dubiously. Government types were not popular in Shanti Nagar. Regarding Al Qaeda, they were neutral.

Mr Chatterjee sat down next to the boy. Ali settled down on the floor, and awaited further developments.

'Why are you here?' asked Pintoo.

Mr Chatterjee was feeling more relaxed now, unaware that his situation was about to become supremely weird. He had feared that Shanti Nagar would be full of diseased, mutant horrors, but these two looked quite normal, except that the man's beard appeared to be moving slightly, and the boy was injured, and should have been in bed. Otherwise, he looked like a nice kid, just unusually intense for a twelve-year-old.

'There was an attack on the telepaths three days ago, something fried their brains. The official line is that it's the Chinese, but they decided that without finding out anything,' said Mr Chatterjee.

Tarun-da and Pintoo exchanged glances.

'I'm investigating. I'm also a suspect. They're going to arrest me in a few days if I don't get to the bottom of this. If that happens, my wife will be alone. I worry about her. She's very innocent.'

'Would you recognize Gandhiji if you saw him?' asked Pintoo.

'Well, he's on all the currency,' said Mr Chatterjee, puzzled. Ali shifted uneasily.

Pintoo picked up three slips of paper from the table. He put one of them in Mr Chatterjee's pocket. 'This is the right one for you,' he whispered in his ear. 'Read it later. I'm sorry, there's not much time. I don't know how long my power will last. Do the best you can. Stand up straight.'

Mr Chatterjee stood up straight. Once again, he was letting events take their own course. He felt himself slipping and sliding, bewildered flotsam on the raging tide of his peculiar destiny.

'Banani might come here looking for me,' he whispered. 'If I don't come back, please keep her safe from a man called Ram Manohar Pande.'

Pintoo nodded. He stepped back, and closed his eyes. He pushed.

Mr Chatterjee vanished.

Ali was on his feet instantly. 'You'd better get him back or I'll gut the whole lot of you,' he said, quietly.

Ranvir grabbed him from behind and held him tight. His arms were like tree trunks. 'Speak properly, motherfucker,' he barked.

Tarun-da sat on the bed, terrified. They had been living in fear that Pintoo would crack up at some point. He was hardly the only strange person in Shanti Nagar, but he was by far the most powerful. Tarun-da was his local guardian. He shuddered to think what Shanti-bai would do to him if she found out he'd lost control of the boy.

'What are you doing, Pintoo?' he whispered, urgently.

'Do you know what's happened to me?' asked Pintoo. 'Because I don't. I have to be quick. There's no time to waste. We don't know how much time we have.'

He looked at Ali, who was struggling to break free of Ranvir. Ali was mortified. He was losing it. He was horrified that a buffalo like Ranvir had gotten the drop on him.

Pintoo put a slip of paper in Ali's pocket. 'His middle name is Shaheed,' he told him, 'because he martyred so many people. You're a terrorist, right? You're the best man for the job. You want to do good? Do this. I like your T-shirt, by the way.'

He stepped back and closed his eyes.

'Bollocks,' said Ali.

Pintoo pushed.

26

'You think you're tough, fattie?
I'll show you who's tough!'

The Competent Authority was busy reading a report on the Shakahari Sena. Apparently, a well-armed team of activists had liberated a Chinese restaurant in Defence Colony. As per their standard operating procedure, they had liberated the whole building, as well as the two houses on either side. First, they had roundly abused all customers and ejected them from the premises, regardless of whether they had finished their chop suey or not. Then they had thrashed the cooks and lit a holy fire in the middle of the kitchen, forcing them to swear the Oath of Vegetarianism. All offensive foodstuffs, including garlic, had been burnt in the street outside, along with the furniture. The premises had been thoroughly cleansed, using a combination of holy water and Dettol. A few live chickens had been released from captivity, and they were currently on their way to a rural retreat, where they would live out the remainder of their natural lives in peace and quiet, unmolested and undigested. The owner was absconding, his game plan no doubt similar to that of the chickens. The flag of the SS now fluttered proudly above the building and armed volunteers stood guard outside, keen to meet any unsuspecting customers who might come around looking for wontons.

The organization was able to do all this because it was a religio-political organization, and hence the normal principles of law and order did not apply. The police never interfered with it, and on the rare occasions when a leader was briefly arrested, senior police officers would salute repeatedly and hold open doors for them. Sympathetic police constables occasionally joined in the mayhem. The Home Minister often had tea with the Chief Shakahari, and they exchanged Diwali gifts made from pure, 100 per cent vegetarian silver, wherein special patented Swiss technology was used instead of goat membranes to purify the metal.

The Shakahari Sena was, in fact, an organization of global significance. It had strong support from the USA. The Secretary of State, himself a vegetarian, made donations to it, as did most of Hollywood. Since the resolution of the Tibet issue, it was the next big thing. Liberated buildings in India were occasionally visited by Hollywood starlets, which did wonders for recruitment. The American Embassy tended to turn a blind eye to its activities, so long as it left McDonald's alone. They also saw its members as shock troops against Islamic Terror, which was aggressively carnivorous. None of the Americans could pronounce Shakahari, though, so they called it the Vegetarian Defence League instead.

So the VD League had attacked a Chinese restaurant, mused the CA. Was there any geopolitical significance to this? Could it in some way help him bring his master plan to fruition? The problem was, Chinese restaurants in Delhi were about as genuine as Indian restaurants in London. The chow mein tended to contain healthy doses of succulent paneer, the chilli chicken was reassuringly tandoori-flavoured, and requests for chopsticks were usually met with a mixture of horror, sadness and disappointment. People from the Northeast had earned good money over the years, pretending to be Chinese, figuring that was what people in Delhi thought they were anyway. Since the war, they had come out into the open. Most Chinese restaurants were thus largely devoid of Chinese characteristics.

But then again, did the Chinese know that? They were notoriously hyper-sensitive. Perhaps they would react violently to the denigration of anything with the word 'Chinese' in it, the taint of tandoori notwithstanding.

The CA was mulling over the possibilities when Mehta slithered in and announced that a BoB delegation had been waiting to see him for an hour, and that the Chairman had begun to make threatening gestures with his handkerchief, so would it be OK if they disturbed him now?

The CA indicated that it was OK. Making the high and mighty wait interminably in his poky little waiting room had always been one of the undiluted pleasures of his job. Over the years, his room had expanded massively, but he had ensured that his waiting room remained supernaturally oppressive. Ventilation was rudimentary, and his bearers were under strict instructions to delay glasses of water for as long as humanly possible. He liked having his room to himself, and he hated it when people came in to disturb him.

But mercy was also an essential part of the character of any great man, and the CA felt it was time for him to show some. Hence he allowed Mehta to bring in the high-powered delegation. He loved watching them from his table, as they emerged from the little hellhole into the awe-inspiring hugeness of his office. Just being able to breathe again usually filled them with gratitude, and made them less demanding, and more amenable to any whims and fancies that might strike him.

The Chairman of BoB lumbered in, followed by No. 2, with a recently de-institutionalized Sam Kapoor bringing up the rear. The Chairman and Sam were sweating through their expensive suits, the CA noted with pleasure, although No. 2 still looked like a freshly-minted fashion model. It was a superpower that he possessed, and it had played a big role in his reaching the position of No. 2. One of his rivals had scrimped on shampoo, and he was now No. 27.

The CA gestured magnanimously for them to sit. Mehta, having undergone a long and strenuous apprenticeship under the CA, knew what was expected of him. He always carefully counted the number of visitors the CA was about to have, and ensured that there was one less chair. The CA liked to watch at least one person stand and fidget at all times. He found it soothing.

In this case, Sam was the standee. Life had been rough on him lately, and he could feel a crying jag coming on. Plus his feet hurt. During his time in the Dr P.P. Chandrashekhar Homeo Psychopathic Institute For The Criminally Insane, he had not worn shoes, as this was considered inappropriate for inmates with homicidal tendencies. His clothes had soon followed.

Now that he was back amongst the relatively sane, nudity was no longer acceptable so he was wearing shoes which hurt his feet. The shirt chafed his skin. He fingered his collar uncomfortably. He was miserable. He bit his lip to stifle a sob and shuffled from foot to foot.

'I believe BoB has a proposal for GoI,' said the CA. 'GoI is ready to hear it. You have half an hour.'

The CA sometimes liked to refer to himself as the Government of India, which was, after all, what he was. The third person was his natural state of being.

'Indeed we do,' said No. 2. 'It is a proposal that will change the face of the nation, even more than you have already done.'

The Chairman grunted from behind his handkerchief, wishing he hadn't scoffed that last prawn cutlet at lunch. He was also deeply uneasy at not being the most powerful man in the room. He missed his chair.

Unbeknownst to him, Mehta had given him a particularly fragile and uncomfortable one. He was hoping that it would eventually collapse under the Chairman's weight. He liked to watch fat people fall on their backsides. He saw every overweight visitor to these chambers as a quivering mass of potential. Pratfalls were an almost daily occurrence. Mehta had a very basic sense of humour.

The CA inclined his head regally, indicating that they should commence proposing to GoI.

'My colleague Sam Kapoor will take you through it,' said No. 2. 'He is one of our brightest young stars, until recently the manager of our Karol Bagh branch, which he helped make one of the most profitable in India. He had a slight mishap involving the underprivileged, but I am glad to say he is now fully recovered. Do go ahead, Sam.'

Sam switched on his wristwatch projector and focused his first slide on the wall. He was a bit miffed that No. 2 had referred to the trashing of his entire branch as a 'slight mishap'. He had almost given his life for the BoB, and sacrificed his sanity, yet no one seemed to appreciate it. He felt very sorry for himself. He wiped a tear from the corner of his eye and pointed to the first slide. Luckily he'd been having irrational mood swings lately, so he knew he would soon be fine. More than fine, quite possibly.

'VISION 2100,' said the first slide. 'A FOOLPROOF PLAN FOR RELIGIOUS WORLD DOMINATION.'

He stood quietly for a moment, letting the full power of his awesome title sink in. He was very proud of the word foolproof, which he had slipped in when No. 2 wasn't looking.

'We at BoB are patriots,' he began. 'While we are interested in profits for the company, we are also constantly asking ourselves a simple question—what could be profitable for the nation?'

The CA smiled benevolently. He liked this question. He was also intrigued. He had never really thought of the BoB as selfless national benefactors, but he was open to new ideas. Flexibility was one of his strong points. He kept a yoga teacher in the basement.

'It is true that we are committed to the business of Medical Joy,' said Sam, quietly slipping off a shoe, 'but every business needs to grow. When it came to diversification, we asked ourselves another key question . . .' He flipped a button.

'WHAT IS OUR CORE COMPETENCE?' asked the next slide.

'The moment we thought of you, Mr Competent Authority, sir, we decided to name our strategy the Core Competence Strategy, in your honour. Because your Competence goes to your very Core, along with many other excellent things like . . . like . . .'

'Simplicity,' said No. 2, smoothly stepping into the breach.

'Mggmf,' added the Chairman, not to be left behind.

'And sagacity,' translated No. 2, 'as our Chairman so perceptively points out.'

'Right,' said Sam, back in his stride, 'lots of good stuff. Anyhow, we sat and thought, what is the Core Competence of this nation? What matters to the common people the most? Let me show some of them to you, to provide inspiration. Let their innocent faces tell their own stories . . .'

He flipped through several slides, with pictures of common people on them. They were all his old buddies from the asylum, smiling cheerfully into the camera, except for Electric-Bill-Man, who was nibbling on an electric bill, and the Snake, who was looking down at it. Apart from Electric-Bill-Man, who wore a loincloth, the others were all naked.

'As we gaze into the warm, gooey eyes of these common people, what do we see?' asked Sam. He paused expectantly, awaiting comments. He liked his presentations to be interactive.

The Chairman mumbled disapprovingly from behind his handkerchief. No. 2, rendered temporarily speechless by the successive images of nude lunatics was unable to translate.

'No one? Anyone? Someone?' asked Sam, who was feeling quite perky now. 'I'll tell you what you see. You see a yearning for religion. Seeing this, we had an Awesome Vision. This was the Awesome Vision.'

He flipped a slide. No. 2 closed his eyes, dreading what was to follow. Not rehearsing with Sam had been an error on his part, he realized belatedly.

'TOTAL WORLD RELIGIOUS DOMINATION' said the next slide.

'Right now BoB heals only bodies,' said Sam, slipping off his other shoe. 'Thanks to the wide availability of spare parts. But spirituality is also widely available in this country, and with this, we can heal their souls! Their souls, man!' He did a little jig.

The CA was perplexed. He had not seen such enthusiasm in quite some time. It seemed wrong, somehow.

No. 2 started to get up from his chair, but Sam was unstoppable. He was in the zone. He could feel the force.

'And it's not just in India that souls need healing,' he declared, 'it's everywhere across the world!'

He picked up a coaster from the table and tossed it across the room, narrowly missing a small statue of the CA that had been standing quietly on a nearby shelf, harming no one. He turned back to his audience, who were so obviously loving it. He was really getting through to them.

'What we lost through the bomb, we can regain through religion!'

The CA frowned. He disapproved of any discussion regarding loss through bombs. In his view, through his efforts, the Bureau of Reconstruction had successfully repaired most of the damage. Thanks to them, the nation was cleaner and stronger, barring the odd pile of rubble here and there.

Mehta was watching Sam admiringly. He hadn't seen anyone get away with so much hanky-panky since the President of Burkina Faso and his six wives had come visiting in '32.

Sam flipped to the next slide, which had only a large, red question mark on it. It winked on and off, and pulsed eerily.

'But in order to set up this fresh, new, world-dominating religion, there's one thing we need. Guess what that one thing is? Someone? Anyone?'

No. 2 groaned and covered his face with his hands. The Chairman was agitatedly chewing his handkerchief.

Sam turned to the CA. 'How about you, fattie?' he asked him cordially. 'Any thoughts?'

The veins stood out on the CA's forehead. He tried to speak, but he was choked with rage. Mehta thought the CA would reach for his metal ruler now, the one he kept in his desk to use on visitors who irritated him, but it seemed inadequate under the circumstances. Perhaps he should go and get the riding crop, kept behind the filing cabinet especially for such occasions.

Sam could see the CA was unhappy, and he felt his own mood shifting from euphoria to anger. What, this fattie was mad at him now? Was he going to beat him up too? What was this, let's-all-laugh-at-Sam-then-beat-him-up-week?

'You think you're tough, fattie?' he roared, ripping off his shirt and twirling it round his head. 'I'll show you who's tough!'

He struck a dynamic Bruce Lee-like pose and flung out a hand. 'Fly away, fattie,' he commanded, 'I'm pushing you . . .'

The CA sat in his chair, transfixed. He was genuinely scared now, his rage evaporating in the face of this unbridled lunacy.

'Fly, damn it,' roared Sam, 'fly up against that wall and smash your head . . .'

Luckily, Mehta had already pressed the magic button, and a squad of gigantic commandos burst in. They grabbed hold of Sam, who had paused to unbutton his trousers, and dragged him off, cursing. 'If a grubby little slum kid can do it, why can't I?' demanded Sam as they grappled with him. 'I'm an MBA, for Chrissakes!'

No. 2 and the Chairman got up hastily and retreated towards the door. No. 2 paused briefly.

'Some people cannot handle the presence of greatness,' he said, tactfully. 'Our young colleague obviously cracked up under the strain. We'll submit our proposal in writing, and perhaps catch up over a cup of tea?'

There was a cup of tea on the table. The CA picked it up and hurled it. It narrowly missed the back of No. 2's head as he slipped out.

27

'Have. You. Seen. A. Weedy. Little. Shit.
Wearing. Glasses?'

Ram Manohar Pande was standing in the middle of No. 3 Market in Shanti Nagar, lathi in hand, watching unfettered capitalism at play, aghast. It was essentially a narrow lane, with street vendors sitting on the ground on either side, hawking their wares. Up ahead in the distance, at the end of the road was a dilapidated cinema hall with shimmering lights.

The vendors were selling fruits and vegetables, cheap nylon saris and slightly better cotton ones, plastic mugs and buckets, earthenware crockery, sweets in glass cases, little wooden toys, torches and padlocks, hawai chappals and dainty slippers, brassieres and steel knives. There was even a milkman pouring out milk from an aluminium cup while his cows stood nearby. Several cows had more than the regulation number of udders, which Pande found interesting. Did that mean they gave extra milk? These people must have bred them specially. They were wily, all these milking communities.

But that wasn't what bothered Pande. What bothered Pande was that all the vendors looked so cheerful. Why were they not cowed down, beaten, furtive? Why were they not looking around fearfully for policemen? How could they look so well-fed and happy? Obviously, this was because they were not performing their duty of supporting the police. Pande tried to mentally calculate the loss of revenue that this vast sea of vendors represented. It was significant.

As he walked past them, no one cowered, no one shrank and no one saluted. He felt like a chicken magnate who suddenly comes upon a hidden valley, a short walk away from the poultry farm, and finds hordes of chickens roaming wild and free.

Pande had seen many severe cases of mutation over the years, but this was by far the worst. This was an entirely new species. It was like his whole world had suddenly turned upside down.

'Twenty, twenty, twenty, twenty,' said a voice from behind him. 'Twenty, twenty, twenty,' it added for good measure.

Pande swung round, and found himself face to face with a slim young man with a neatly brushed moustache, wearing dark glasses, and a red handkerchief round his neck. His white shoes gleamed.

'Twenty, twenty, twenty,' said the man persuasively, 'latest Digital Rajnikanth movie, boss. Full power. Superhit. Rajnikanth, sir, lighting six cigarettes with one match, doing sunglass triple flip, adjusting dhoti, punching gorilla—all with one hand. Not to miss. Twenty, twenty, twenty.' He held out a bunch of tickets invitingly.

The power of lifelike animation had kept Rajnikanth alive long after his passing. His descendants, who owned the copyright, were among the richest people in India. It helped that none of the bombs had reached Madras. It also helped that they had, in fact, reached Bombay, thereby wiping out his biggest rival, Digital Amitabh, along with most of the rest of the city.

If the hawkers had made Pande angry, he could now feel his rage growing to monumental proportions. A ticket blacker was actually asking him to buy a ticket! The audacity! He glared at the blacker, raising his lathi, and the blacker, a recent immigrant from New New Delhi, wisely decided to take his business elsewhere.

It was clear to Pande what this place needed. It needed justice. It needed order. It needed the iron hand of the law. Plus, he himself needed information on that weedy little Chatterjee and his whore of a wife, who thought they were so clever.

When in need of information in a market, Pande always used a simple method, and there was no reason why today should be an exception. He grabbed hold of the nearest vegetable vendor and started thrashing him.

'Have. You. Seen. A. Weedy. Little. Shit. Wearing. Glasses?' he asked, in between blows. He paused for a moment to see whether the question had registered. Blood was pouring out from the man's forehead, but he had taken care not to smash his mouth. The man stared at him, unable to believe what was happening to him. Why the hell isn't he scared, thought Pande. Why do I see no fear in his eyes?

He started thrashing him again. 'How. About. A. Tall. Young. Whore. With. A. Wheatish. Complexion?' he inquired.

Strong arms grabbed him from behind. Pulled him away from his victim. How dare they? Who were they? Even terrorists never dared come this close, they shot from a distance.

He felt a fist hit his stomach. Again. And again. It really hurt! He felt tears come into his eyes. How could they treat him like this? Was he not an officer of the law? First, his buttocks and privates had been assaulted, then his head, and now his stomach. All in less than twenty-four hours. The condition of the country was deteriorating unimaginably.

He was on his back now, and there was a foot on his chest. He could dimly make out a sea of faces all around him. He tried hard to focus, blinking away his tears, so he could remember their faces for the future. But it was getting dark, and there were no streetlights.

'You're in the wrong place, you fat fool,' said a hard voice. 'We don't do things that way here.'

'In Shanti Nagar, even vegetable sellers are human beings,' said another.

'Let's drown him in the nala,' suggested a third. 'That way he can eat shit and die.'

'That's enough,' snapped a voice that sounded faintly familiar. The other faces moved back, and now, gazing down at him, was the young guard from the gate.

'I knew it was a mistake letting you in, you old harami,' said the guard. 'That's why I followed you from the gate. This is not your father's garden, that you can beat up anyone you feel like. You're a Brahmin, you have God's mobile number, you'd better pray that Dinesh will be OK, otherwise no God can save you.'

He straightened up, his machine gun riding his hip, and gestured to the crowd. 'Tie him up,' he said. 'We've never had filth like him in here before. We'll take him to Pintoo. He can decide what to do with him.'

He looked down at Pande thoughtfully.

'Use lots of rope,' he added, 'and make sure you tie him tight.'

28

*'Calcutta. And don't fly too low.
I've been shot down once this week already.'*

'Motherfucker, how are you?' said Verma.

'Sisterfucker, how are *you?*' said Mehta.

They slapped each other on the back. They were more than just cousins, they were old friends. They had grown up together in an old kothi in West Patel Nagar, which the patriarch had obstinately refused to leave long after they could afford Prithviraj Road. Someone knocked him off, eventually. Everyone suspected the eldest daughter-in-law, but no one said anything. They didn't want to get into her bad books. The police were paid off, and the servant who had the least amount of service in the household was arrested. He got twenty years, but his family lived happily ever after, so it was a win-win.

'Bastard, it's all good.'

'Sonofabitch, take a seat.'

Pleasantries thus dispensed with, they got down to business.

'Yaar, you need to crack the army for me, yaar,' said Verma, making it sound like a minor request.

'Perhaps you would like to sleep with the PM also?' enquired Mehta politely.

He was reclining in a plush sofa, a very different man from the one who skulked in the shadows in the CA's room. In his own lair, he was at ease—the most powerful man in the country. The CA took the decisions, but the files came to him. He was the Lord of the Files.

'Boss, I'm getting fucked,' said Verma. 'Those Maoist fuckers are attacking all the time, and those South African goons I have are too busy blowing their trumpets to shoot straight. Mostly they're drunk, and they drink only imported stuff.'

Mehta hissed in horror.

'The bells of my business are ringing, boss, my backside is being taken full power. At this rate, I'll have to cutlo from Chhattisgarh.'

He mourned for the days of his father, who had died long ago of AIDS, although everyone was told pneumonia. It was a time when mining barons had owned entire states. Chief Ministers used to polish their chappals, their wives would dry their feet with their hair. Their relatives would romp amongst the ministries, swapping with each other once in a while, just because they could. Those were the good old days. It was different now. The CA and his people owned everything. The rest of them had to manage on scraps. It was totally unfair.

'The Maoists are getting bolder,' said Mehta. 'Some of the power companies have also been complaining. Work is getting hampered.'

'So do something, bhai. You are the mother-father. Everyone is looking towards you.'

Mehta did not deny this. He sighed, oppressed by the weight of expectations.

'Everyone wants the army, Sanjeev bhai. Nowadays ministers accept only army protection. Some of them require tanks. Their helicopters are escorted by fighters. Commandos are protecting school canteens and beauty parlours owned by their girlfriends. When they go swimming, they expect submarines nearby. It's a prestige issue. Other than that, most active units are in the war zone, where the Maoists are in force. Your area is one of the pacified areas. "Situation Normal," says the magistrate. If I reduce any minister's security for that, they will chew my brains.'

'And if my business goes to the dogs, what will your officers eat?'

Mehta made a dismissive gesture. He was happy enough to do Verma occasional favours, but he didn't want him getting too uppity.

'There's enough to eat, don't worry. Parties like you are falling out of the trees all the time. One will go, others will come.'

'Can't you arrange at least eight-ten?' whined Verma. 'They're taking my arse, man.'

Mehta looked at him thoughtfully. Recent developments could have a strong bearing on this man's life, he realized, given that he was geographically slap bang in the middle of it. As his childhood playmate, he ought to at least warn him of his impending doom, even if it meant revealing secrets for free that he ought to, strictly speaking, be charging cash for.

'There will be a requirement for extra soldiers soon,' he said finally. 'We might get into a war with the Bengal Protectorate. A small one. The CA is in a bad mood.'

'You're fucking kidding me! I'll be flattened like a roomali roti. I'm right in the middle. And are they out of their fucking minds? What do they mean, war with the Bengal Protectorate? The Chinese will get into it. This time they'll finish us off. The only Indians left will be living abroad.'

'This has nothing to do with the Chinese,' said Mehta, sticking to the party line. 'Forget about big things. Handle your own affairs. Whatever mining you have to do, do it in the next five-six days. At least I'm warning you.'

Verma said nothing but 'fuck' for a while. Mehta asked for some tea.

'This is bullshit, man!' said Verma. 'We've got to stop this, I'll get totally fucked. I'm going to Calcutta. My partner Agarwal is there. He's a cool customer. He knows the government. It takes two hands to clap. We'll make them apologize or something.'

'You're talking like a fool,' said Mehta. 'Big forces are moving, there's nothing you can do. Just pack it up quickly and put the money somewhere else. Not so close to the border this time.'

'I'm going to Calcutta,' said Verma obstinately, and left.

What did Mehta know? He was just a chamcha, although a solid gold one, with diamonds on the handle. All his power came from kissing someone's arse. He did things differently. You had to go out and grab things. No one was hanging around waiting to put food in your mouth. You had to make it happen.

There was one other thing that he had. He had money. Agarwal knew all the right people in Calcutta. Together they would be unstoppable. Everything boiled down to buying and selling, and that they were both pretty good at.

'Calcutta,' Verma told his pilot. 'And don't fly too low. I've been shot down once this week already.'

❑

Meanwhile, back in the city, his partner in joy and sorrow was lowering the hammer on a quivering minion.

'What do you mean you can't give me a refund? I demand that you return my goods immediately!'

The customer service executive stood there petrified, his mind wiped clean by all the sound and fury. They had given him only eleven days of training, and none of it had prepared him for anything like this. He would not achieve an erection for the next three weeks.

'Glub,' he said.

Mrs Verma had decided that offence was the best method of defence, and had charged into the BoB like a stampeding rhino. All work in the branch ceased as everyone crowded around, eager to watch her dismantle their colleague.

'Madam,' he croaked, 'this is not a cold storage. You can't just change your mind and take things back.'

'Do you want me to have you all arrested?' she demanded. 'You're nothing but a bunch of 420s!'

She waved a statement in his face. 'You're showing a credit balance of one ten-year-old boy. The boy I deposited was twelve. This is fraud. You're cheating me of at least 20 per cent.'

'Do you have a birth certificate to prove that?' asked the executive, faintly, clutching at straws.

'As if any of them have birth certificates! I have three cousins from his village who can vouch for how old he is. They remember the blockbuster movies from the year he was born. What more proof do you need? Now stop messing about and give me the boy back. Or do I have to call the Chief Justice of the Delhi High Court? I have him on speed dial.'

She did, as a matter of fact. The CJ's nephew had got her a great deal on a farmhouse. Everyone had everyone else on speed dial in Delhi, or so everyone said. They got a lot of it every day, the staff at the BoB, they could tell who was bluffing. Not this one. The service executive gestured with his head, and one of the others scurried off to storage. God help them all if the boy had already been processed.

He hadn't been. He came up in the elevator and stumbled out into the lobby, blinking in the bright light. He wore threadbare white pyjamas and a grey vest with a little red cross. He looked much thinner, but he was Ramu. At the sight of Mrs Verma he smiled faintly. He seemed weak.

'What kind of tamasha is this? You've not even been feeding him properly. What kind of third-rate people are you? You pretend to be a medical organization? I can expose you on television. They will strip you naked in front of everybody. My friend Sameer is the MD of NCTV. You think you can keep fooling the public like this? You should be ashamed of yourselves.'

She grabbed Ramu by the wrist and dragged him towards the door.

'Please, madam,' begged the executive, little beads of sweat on his forehead, 'not NCTV. Anything but that. Is there anything else we can do for you? A free baby credit? A signed photograph of the Chairman?'

He assumed she had deposited a family member by mistake. It was not unheard of. It was the pace of modern living. To err was human.

'I'm letting you go this time,' she said, 'but you better be more careful from now on. I'm not one of those two-paise customers that you can do what you like with.'

Now that she had what she needed, she decided to go a bit easy, she had the future to think of. She needed quality service from the BoB. It was best not to make enemies of the staff. It was just like a restaurant, if you weren't careful, they could mess with things behind your back. While you were unconscious, they could make one boob slightly bigger than the other, or transplant skin which peeled in winter, or give you a bladder that was just a smidgen too small.

'Just help me get the boy to the car,' she said. She even smiled at the executive. He stumbled back, tottering.

She had brought only one car, so Ramu got in the back seat with her. She was too tired to protest. She leaned back and closed her eyes. Ramu snuggled closer. He put his head in her lap and put his arms round her waist and promptly fell asleep.

She sat there, stunned, not sure what to do. She was being hugged by a servant. She had always known that having a son like Pappu would mean she would end up in strange and unexpected places, boldly going where no mother had gone before. This seemed to be one of those places.

'Let's go home,' she told the driver, softly. 'And turn the music down.'

29

'How do I get to a man called Suhrawardy?'

Mr Chatterjee lay on the ground, eyes closed, fighting waves of nausea. He had always been prone to motion sickness. He remembered vomiting three times during one six-hour trip to Darjeeling, when he was a little boy. His father had suggested leaving him somewhere on the bank of the river Teesta and going on, but his mother had managed to dissuade him, arguing that it was to some extent their fault too, for giving him way too much kurkure and mango juice.

He wasn't sure exactly what Pintoo had done to him, but he had a hunch that this had been a much longer trip than the one to Darjeeling.

Cautiously, he opened his eyes, first the left one, then the right, and he was dazzled. The sky! It was so bright and blue. The clouds were so pure and white. Not at all like the murky, grey skies and bitter, black clouds that he was used to. How come the sun was so much brighter?

He sat up, astonished and smelt the air, which was fresh and clean. Much like the oxygen bar he had been to in Tokyo in the days when Indians were still allowed to travel. He took a deep breath, filling his lungs with it, not really caring for that brief moment where he was. He felt the blood rush to his head. He was high on breathing! Banani had often suggested that he get high on life, instead of whisky, especially after the fourth or fifth, but he had never thought that this was actually possible.

He was sitting on the footpath, he realized. He must have been lying here for quite some time. What a strange place, he thought. Does no one here care if they see someone lying on the street? He might have been dead for all they knew, or grievously injured.

He looked around him. It was a broad footpath, and it looked as if it had been recently swept. On his left was a huge sign that said REGAL

CINEMA; under the lettering was a giant poster of Raj Kapoor and Nargis, gazing soulfully into each other's eyes.

As he looked at the people walking by, he began to wonder. Their clothes were so strange. Many wore Gandhi caps, and many more were in dhotis. What amazed him even more was the number of Englishmen. The few foreigners he knew of in Delhi lived cowering behind embassy walls, sorely missing the days when Delhi belly was all you had to worry about as an expatriate in Delhi. Here, the foreigners were roaming around openly, some of them in shorts, even. Many were in uniform. The predominant fashion motifs on this street seemed to be khadi and khaki.

None of them were mutants. All of them had their eyes and ears and noses exactly where they ought to be, no one had any extra limbs or even fingers, none of them were covered in sores, none of them had strips of dead blackened skin hanging from them. No wheelchairs or mechanical limbs. No blind cows bumping into lampposts. No armless, legless people rolling on the ground, biting ankles and begging for money.

He heard the clip-clop of hooves. A tonga was passing by, bells ringing merrily. A young couple, newly married from the looks of it, sat in the back. The young man was shyly holding his wife's hand, and pointing to the beautiful circular park just beyond the road. It was covered in lush green grass and scattered with quaint, wrought iron benches.

With a mounting sense of panic, Mr Chatterjee realized what he was looking at. It was the Dead Circle. Except it wasn't dead. Instead of the blackened, slime-encrusted pit he had visited recently, it was a pretty green park. Instead of unspeakable giant rats, skittering in the debris, there were cheerful young couples and retired senior citizens, relaxing on the grass. The buildings all around were intact, as far as the eye could see. Elements of the skyline seemed faintly familiar.

He was still in Delhi, but he was a long, long way from home.

Suddenly Mr Chatterjee remembered the little piece of paper Pintoo had slipped into his pocket. Read it later, he had said.

With trembling fingers, Mr Chatterjee took it out of his pocket and read it. Then he sat down on the footpath, knees trembling. Once again he was having an out-of-body experience, a really bad one this time

The note had three words written on it in block capitals, a childish scrawl. Pintoo had taught himself how to write with his left hand, but he could still only do capitals.

SAVE MAHATMA GANDHI, said the note.

As Mr Chatterjee bent over to vomit into the gutter, he couldn't help but notice how clean it was.

❑

When he regained consciousness, the first thing that hit Ali was the smell of fish. Rich, pungent and briny—with a hint of decay. This was not the mild, innocent fish that was tandooried every evening by his neighbourhood kebab vendor. This was formidable fish, fish that boldly declared its presence, fish that, once consumed, would stamp itself on you at the cellular level and define your character in strange, unpredictable ways. This was fish whose odour could transform, cleanse and purify you. Ali would never forget this odour for the rest of his life.

The second thing that hit him was cool, fresh water, which was being liberally sprinkled on his face. The water, too, was completely different—not the foul, brackish stuff he had drunk all his life. It was sweet and clean and tasty. He licked his lips greedily, content to just lie there for the moment and enjoy this wonderful gift. Had he died and gone to heaven? Could it be that all the propaganda about martyrdom was really true? Had his old teachers in Al Qaeda been right all along? Were the thirty-six virgins even now fighting over who would serve him first? Or was it seventy-two? Possibly succulent melons from Tashkent were also being sliced up as he lay there, soon to be served up on silver platters by off-duty virgins or apprentice bum boys. The fish didn't quite seem to fit, though. None of the briefing sessions had ever mentioned the presence of rotting fish in paradise . . .

'Poor man,' said a woman's voice, 'his stomach is growling. He must have worked too hard all day and fainted from hunger. Ramzan fasting is hard on these poor labourers.'

'It may not just be Ramzan,' said another woman. 'The price of food has gone up so much, perhaps he has not eaten for a long time. The war is long over, but those banias are still making money.'

Bengali! They were speaking Bengali! Ali knew the language well, mainly because it was his mother tongue. His father had driven a taxi in Preston, and called it Ali Baba Taxi Service, after his son. As a result, Ali had been mockingly called Ali Baba throughout his school years. The mockery had been vicious. His father had pretended to love Bengali, even though he couldn't speak a word of it. He often lied to passengers about going to Dhaka every year, and the beauty of village life, before popping into the pub for a pint or two. Ali had made it a point to learn the language well, and his stint with the HUJIB boys had helped him brush up. He'd been appalled by all the poverty there, and realized that maybe life hadn't been so hard in the UK after all. Old Owl Face had sent him to evaluate Bangladesh as a future base, once the Frogs started infesting Mali. It was easy to underestimate the French, and not always the right thing to do. He had also been asked to bring HUJIB upto scratch on the internet, an area in which they were lagging, but they were too busy killing bloggers. He remembered the HUJIB boys well. They were particularly bloodthirsty, and fond of poetry. These girls were speaking a different dialect, though, from a coastal area called Chittagong. It was the language of Professor Surya Sen, a man who had briefly liberated his district from the British, with the help of a handful of schoolboys.

What on earth was he doing in Chittagong?

Ali sat up abruptly and found himself face to face with two dark young women in slightly grimy cotton sarees—slim, wiry and vibrantly alive. At this point, they had less than a week before they would die horribly.

'Am I in Chittagong?' asked Ali, getting straight to the point.

The two young women burst out laughing, covering their faces with the ends of their sarees and peeping out shyly at him in the midst of their merriment.

'Merciful God, he's been hit on the head,' exclaimed one of them, 'let's take him to a doctor!'

'It's the smell of your fish, Angoor,' said the other woman. 'It's driven him crazy. I knew this would happen one day. You use too much salt, and you don't know how to buy fish. Just like you didn't know how to choose a husband.'

'You're in Calcutta, you silly man,' said the older girl. 'It's true I am making loitta fish, Chittagong style, but that's because we used to live there. My father brought us all to Calcutta after the Japanese bombed our house. We used to be zamindars there,' she added, proudly.

Her friend hooted in derision. 'Zamindars. Hah! Jamadars, more like. All you refugee-types claim you were zamindars. And look at you now. Fourteen people living in one room in Bagbazar. They would all be starving if you weren't such a good cook and running this hotel.'

Ali looked around. The 'hotel' consisted of three rickety tables and a few benches, with a crude thatched roof. Nearby, on the ground, were some large aluminium drums with food in them. One of them contained the fish. He assumed the others were for people to puke in.

Angoor and her friend hauled him off the ground and helped him sit on one of the benches.

'Anyway, you rest for a while,' said the young woman. 'You're obviously mad, but you look harmless. Would you like a little bit of fish?'

Ali said no.

Angoor looked at him thoughtfully. 'You know, I thought you were a labourer, but you don't talk like one. Your clothes are very funny. Why do you have a picture of the demon Mahishashur on your chest?'

Ali was still wearing his Bob Marley T-shirt.

'He's a baul singer from Murshidabad,' said Ali.

The young woman eyed him suspiciously, but she held her peace.

'You said something about Japanese bombs,' said Ali, 'but it was the Chinese wasn't it? I don't remember the Chinese bombing Calcutta.'

'Either you're very clever, or you're very stupid,' said Angoor.

'But he is very handsome,' added her friend, giggling, 'and smart enough to avoid your fish!'

'That's true,' said Angoor grinning. 'See here, mister. I don't know what Chinese you're talking about. The Japanese attacked us, but the British drove them away. Netaji helped the Japanese, but now he is hiding in the Himalayas. He will come back when the time is right. Then things will improve for all of us. But these are all big things, and we are small people. All I know is that the war has been over one year, and the price of rice and fish and everything else has gone up three times. It is those bastard banias who are doing this. My father says we should slit their throats. But that's nothing. That's just big talk. Especially after he's had his bangloo. We may not get to eat, but they all get to drink. Luckily, it's Ramzan so things are better right now. But all the men are very irritated. They are hungry, and tired, and they have no money, and either they miss their drink or they drink on an empty stomach. And Jinnah-sahab is sitting in his big mansion, in the dark, with no wife to comfort him, and God alone knows what his intentions are.'

Her mood had changed as she spoke, and now she looked tired and frightened. More than anything else, this unnerved Ali. She looked like a girl with spirit to spare. It was time to find out where he was.

Ali took out the little slip of paper the boy had shoved in his pocket. 'STOP DIRECT ACTION DAY,' it said.

So that's where he was. Calcutta, just before Independence. 1946, wasn't it? The boy was right, thought Ali.

He looked at Angoor, who had been observing him quietly.

'I need help,' he said. 'Will you help me?'

'Depends,' she replied.

'Then tell me this,' he said, 'how do I get to a man called Suhrawardy?'

30

'I am only interested in kalchar.'

As the obligatory Robindro Shongeet came to an end, the PM discreetly switched off her iPod. Her family had always supported art and culture in principle, but she preferred to do it from a distance. Pretending to run the country was a full-time job. She used to wear her hair in a short bob, and she looked pretty cute in it, even if she said so herself. Many people had remarked on her resemblance to her most formidable ancestor. She was honestly flattered at first, but as she grew into her role, which for the most part seemed to consist of feigning interest in speeches that went on forever, she had grown her hair longer to hide her earphones. It was rumoured that one of her predecessors had kept a powerful audio receiver under his turban, although this was more for instructions than entertainment.

She was at a Satyajit Ray Appreciation Evening at the High Commission of the Bengal Protectorate in Chittaranjan Park, just next to No. 1 Market, where all the fish lived. The lights in the auditorium were dimming. The film was about to start. She would get through the film somehow, but it was the appreciation session that she was dreading. She prayed it would be short.

The film was about a man who found a stone that turned everything into gold. The man wore terrible black shoes and had a face like a frog. But he was funny. The Calcutta they showed was a lot cleaner than the Calcutta she remembered. There were Englishmen in high places, and the clothes were hilarious. It was cheerful, simple, and mercifully short.

In due course, the appreciation session began and it was time she contributed something. She looked down at her notes, created for her by the PMO.

'I think Kali Banerjee was a genuine titan of Indian cinema who was given far too few opportunities to shine,' she said.

She actually thought nothing of the sort. The actor in question bore an uncanny resemblance to a permanent secretary who had caused her much grief when she was younger, constantly calling her 'Your Highness' and bowing and scraping like a comic opera major-domo. Sometimes it felt like her life was filled with an endless procession of arseholes, lining up before her single file, one after the other, one after the other, as far as the eye could see.

Out of deference to her contribution, the rest of the panel said nice things about Kali Banerjee for a while. This was followed by a long discussion on the true meaning of satire and the role of the satirist in modern society. Mark Twain and Molière were dragged in, kicking and screaming. The PM couldn't see much sense in satire, personally. All you had to do was read the newspaper in the morning. Who could make up stories like that?

The appreciation session meandered to an end. It was time for fish fry with mustard.

She put on her party face and made a beeline for the Bengal High Commissioner. He was a short, round man who was fond of his food. He was wearing an ankle-length orange, batik print gown, similar in shape to those preferred by the poet Rabindranath. His views on playing the host were simple and direct. He provided a congenial atmosphere and he provided excellent food. After that, he led by example.

'Have some fish fry,' he said through a mouthful.

The PM broke off a small piece and nibbled on it.

'Have fum muftard too,' he said.

The PM added a spoonful of mustard. She had donated her digestive system to the nation long ago. Her staff would have an antacid ready on her bedside table. They had been with her family for years.

'So how's the mood back home?' she asked. 'I hear your army boys are getting a little itchy.'

The High Commissioner wrinkled his nose as if offended by the smell of gunpowder at a celebration of celluloid.

'I am only interested in kalchar,' he said. 'My primary mission here as

High Commissioner is to disseminate the kalchar of the Bengali nation.'

He emphasized the word nation, in addition to the word kalchar, and he did it with pride. The Bengal Protectorate was just like the old American Confederacy, except with fish and film criticism instead of cotton and slaves. The PM usually made it a point to say 'state' whenever she said 'nation', but this time she let it pass.

'So should I be talking to your culture minister back home then?' she inquired sweetly. 'He must be the most powerful man there.'

The High Commissioner tittered.

'He is more interested in pisci kalchar than kalchar. He owns 20 per cent of the fish farms in the country. I hear he's so fat now, he can barely move. He cannot recite the words of a single Robindro Shongeet.'

The PM waited patiently. The man was a gossipy old queen. He was bound to give her something. She watched him chew on his fish fry, liberally lathered with mustard, his brain temporarily disconnected by his taste buds.

'The local central committee decides everything,' he said, swallowing the last bit and reflexively reaching for another one. 'I don't know what they're thinking because I don't know Chinese. You should talk to Comrade Bijli Bose. He always knows what is going on.'

'Bijli Bose is still alive?' she asked disconcerted. In the old days the CBI or RAW or one of the agencies which were her eyes and ears would have provided her with this sort of information but now she was only told whatever the CA deemed fit.

'He is very much alive, and his brain is very sharp. He has been eating only the choicest fish for over one hundred years. I believe the Chinese have used some special techniques to resurrect and preserve him, out of gratitude for the services he provided them. Traces of his DNA were found on a whisky glass.'

Bijli Bose was an old friend of the family, sometime ally, sometime enemy, always loyal to the nation. They hadn't realized that the nation in question was China until it was far too late. He was much more than just a traitorous stooge, however. He was the architect and the poster boy of the CPI(M), their Rasputin and Elvis rolled into one. He was the bartender who had mixed the lethal cocktail of totalitarianism and sympathy for the underdog that had dragged an entire society down the tubes in less than a single generation. If she wanted to know what

Shovon Chowdhury

was going on in the Bengal Protectorate, she could do much worse than ask Bijli Bose. But she would have to be careful, he was a sly old buzzard.

'What else is going on?' she asked the High Commissioner. 'Do you get any news of Calcutta at all, or do you have to watch television to find out?'

'The Chow Mein Riots have been unexpectedly ferocious,' he admitted. 'Section 144 was declared. Tear gas was used. Mounted police had to be called in. It is very ironic, because for once the Chinese were trying to do a good thing. They were trying to introduce their subjects to a better class of noodle, using much less oil, and cooked in the proper way by registered practitioners. However, the Chow Mein Sellers Union of Gariahat proved to be a powerful force, particularly after the martyrdom of local strongman Potla. The property damage caused was substantial. But through their efforts, we have gained culinary freedom. We wanted greasy mutton noodles with deep fried onions, and by God, we are getting them. It is one small step forward in the struggle.'

As the High Commissioner of the Bengal Protectorate, a tributary state of the People's Republic of China, he ought not to be speaking this way, she thought. But most people in Bengal were pretty confused right now.

The good news was that the natives were restless. She needed to talk to Bijli Bose. It was going to be tricky. No one ever knew whose side he was on. Usually it was whoever had the best scotch. She would call the aviation minister tomorrow. Air India always had some good stuff stashed away. She also had to meet the Japanese Ambassador. Then there was Prime Minister Lee in Taiwan. He'd been asking a lot of questions lately, sensing something was in the air, but she hadn't been able to have a proper discussion with him as the CA had all her phones tapped.

Things were getting really complicated. What would her formidable ancestor have done? She should have spent more time with her. One thing was for sure: she would have found a way to beat them.

31

'Don't just stand there gaping. Go get a doctor!'

Banani arrived at Tarun-da's house just a few minutes after Pintoo had made her husband disappear. The tired lady at School No. 6 had been having trouble managing her class, so Banani had stopped to help her. After she revealed that she was running from the police, the woman had suggested that she meet Pintoo.

Ranvir was asleep on the doorstep, cradling his lathi. His mouth was open and he was snoring. Banani tapped him on the shoulder. Ranvir leaped up, brandishing his lathi, the picture of instant vigilance.

'You think I didn't see you?' he asked. 'I saw you coming a long distance away. I was waiting for you to come closer to see if you were going to try any tricks.'

Ranvir peered at the woman. He was short-sighted, but he tried to hide the fact. He didn't want to encourage evil-doers. Judging by the chalk dust all over her, this woman was a teacher. Ranvir saluted. After years of serving the ancient headmaster, he had a profound respect for educationists.

'May I see Pintoo?' she asked politely. 'I need his protection. I'm being chased by a lunatic policeman who wants to kill me.'

Ranvir bristled indignantly. He was loyal to the teaching fraternity. He hated policemen. The situation seemed tailor-made for him.

'I'll solve your problem,' he said confidently, 'just tell me where the sisterfucker is. After that, you leave the rest to me.'

'That's very kind of you,' Banani replied, 'but let's see Pintoo first.'

Banani was horrified by the boy's stump. It had been crudely bandaged, and the bandage was flecked with spots of blood.

She took the damaged hand in hers, and looked at it. She looked up at Tarun-da.

'Are you the guardian of this child?' she demanded.

Tarun-da nodded shamefacedly.

'Well, you're doing a terrible job,' said Banani crisply. 'He needs fresh bandages. Where can we find a doctor?'

She looked at the boy.

'Who did this to you?' she asked.

'Medical soldiers,' said Pintoo. 'It doesn't hurt so much, but it itches sometimes.'

Banani swore lavishly. Many of the words she used were unfamiliar. They waited respectfully for her to finish. She had only been here a few minutes, and already she was teaching them.

'Everyone around here keeps saying you'll protect them,' she said, 'but who's protecting you?'

'Tarun-da's here, and Ranvir's an ex-commando, and the headmaster's really good with his duster. Besides, I can do things. I destroyed the Bank of Bodies,' he said, with justifiable pride.

'Really?' said Banani, impressed.

'Well, I did one, but then I realized it's only a branch,' admitted Pintoo. 'We're working out the next step. There's not much time. This could be temporary.'

'While you're being a hero, you know what else could be temporary? Your life. If that gets infected, you're in trouble.'

Tarun-da was gazing at Banani admiringly. Both her beauty and her spirit were attractive to him. His beard rippled gently.

'Don't just stand there gaping,' said Banani. 'Go get a doctor!'

SECTION 2

32

*'The grub's gone to hell since all the cooks
went to Pakistan.'*

Mr Chatterjee had been walking for nearly an hour when he saw a woman on sale, right in front of the refugee camp. It was the first thing that reminded him of home. It was just like Bid 'n' Win Day at Slaves R Us.

He had stumbled away from the Dead Circle, now gloriously and disconcertingly undead, and walked through the city in a daze. It was like seeing your hometown in a funhouse mirror, distorted in strange and unexpected ways. There were no Bureau of Reconstruction slogans on the walls. There was no rubble, and no abandoned vehicles. The streets were full of children. No suspected Maoists were being shot while trying to escape. The air was so fresh it made him dizzy. There were no armoured vehicles into which he could leap at the first sign of trouble. Hardly anyone carried any weapons, leaving most of the populace defenceless. No one was digging up anything. No one was building anything. No one was pretending to dig or build anything, hiding behind *Work in Progress* signs and drinking cups of tea. No horns blared. No one was dragging anyone out of their cars and beating them up. No injured pedestrians cried out weakly for aid. No women were being molested. No crows were pecking at corpses. There were even Muslims on the streets, out there in the open, and none of them were handcuffed. Where was the familiar cacophony of sirens? Where were all the police cars, the ambulances, the VIPs? Where were all the billboards for Burn Free, guaranteeing pre-war skin at post-war prices? And yet, it was still all recognizably Delhi. This was version 7.0, the one the British had left behind before transferring their attention to soccer. It was indifferent and cold, quiet and exhausted, drained by the upheavals of independence

179

and partition, waiting to see what happened next, apprehensive of fresh horrors.

As he watched the auction, he felt his jangled nerves begin to settle. The whole process was comfortingly familiar. The young woman stood on a raised platform, her sari wrapped demurely around herself. She wasn't enthusiastic, but she wasn't cracking up either. It was six months since Partition, she'd seen much worse.

A few plump men in dhotis were raising their fingers and bidding discreetly. Some were customers, while others were wholesalers, buying at source. The auctioneer was equally polite, raising his voice only once to inform the crowd that she was a good Punjabi girl, she was not converted or anything, and could cook both veg and non-veg. In case they still felt she needed to be purified, he added, there was a priest at hand who would do it for free, except for a nominal fee for the Ganga water.

He was extremely professional, just like the floor managers at Slaves R Us. Mr Chatterjee felt a bit homesick. He and Banani had always wanted a domestic slave of their own, but all they could afford was five part-timers. This was why they never got invited to any of the bungalow parties. Mr Chatterjee was confident that if he got to know just one of the bungalow families properly, they could escape the tyranny of their birthright and transcend their lower middle-class origins. But it was all a pipe dream. He knew they would never be able to afford the EMIs on a slave. Still, there was no harm window-shopping.

He sidled up to one of the traders in the front row. 'How much is the EMI on this one?' he whispered.

'Bhai, tell me in Hindi,' said the trader, 'we're independent now.'

Mr Chatterjee explained the concept of EMIs to him. The trader laughed uproariously. 'Bhai, you have understood the opposite. I deal in cash only. I count notes with my toes. I am not a giver of EMIs, I am a taker of EMIs. Do you require EMIs? I can give you loan, 5 per cent per month, very cheap.'

Mr Chatterjee politely declined the offer and looked on longingly. The girl was soon picked up and another one took her place, shivering but determined, with glittering eyes. She was going to live. The bids were hesitant. Mr Chatterjee shook his head. No one was going to pick up a slave with eyes like that.

'See anything you like, babu?'

The voice dripped with scorn, and a faint Scottish accent. Mr Chatterjee turned and found himself face to face with a young British officer. His face was red, his eyes were dead, and his tunic was half unbuttoned. There were unexpected streaks of grey in his hair, and fatigue had etched deep lines into his face. Mr Chatterjee felt unaccountably embarrassed that a foreigner should be watching this display. What they did amongst themselves was a different matter. But then again, this was 1948. Maybe this young man wasn't so foreign after all.

'Well, if it offends you so much, and it's against the law, shouldn't you be doing something about it?' he murmured.

The officer sighed. 'Haven't done anything in the last six months . . . why on earth would I start now? Don't want to break the winning streak, do we?'

He lit a cigarette, and squatted down on the kerb, Indian style. He'd learnt how to do it from the Sikhs. They had squatted all over Asia together, these past four years. The jungles of Kohima. The hills of Burma. The streets of Singapore. The pretty boulevards of Saigon, which they had machine-gunned with maximum prejudice. He was a long way from Lower Islington.

'What the hell were we doing in Saigon, can you tell me—putting the Frogs back in charge? My Sikhs used to ask me that all the time. "What are we doing here, sahab?" they'd ask. "We have no quarrel with the Annamites." Neither did I, so I told 'em to drink up their rum and try missing when they shot someone. The whole thing was completely pointless. I've seen the local lads, they're a tough bunch. Uncle Ho and his merry men. They'll kick the Frogs back into the sea before you can say crepe suzette. The Frogs'll be too busy cooking lunch to stop them.'

'Are you eating better these days?' asked Mr Chatterjee, who was not a fan of French cuisine.

'The grub's gone to hell since all the cooks went to Pakistan,' said the young warrior moodily. 'Besides, who feels like eating after watching what you people have been doing to each other? If we'd known you were like this we would have left years ago. And it's not like it's over. We'll probably go to Kashmir next, where we'll shoot lads we used to mess with. I can tell you one thing. When I get off the boat, the first thing I'm going to do is go meet Winston bloody Churchill. I know exactly what to do with that cigar of his.'

Listening to the officer relate his woes, Mr Chatterjee felt normal service resuming in his brain. It was true he had seen some ups and downs lately, but compared to the travails of this young man, his own problems seemed trivial. He hoped he really did get to meet Churchill and turn that roly-poly racist inside out. And if he, a junior officer, squatting on the footpath, could dream of meeting Churchill, why couldn't Mr Chatterjee meet Mr Gandhi? It wasn't that preposterous. Here, in 1948, he wasn't a face on a banknote, he was a living, breathing human being, who bore a close resemblance to Ben Kingsley.

When he met Gandhi, he would shake him by the hand, and warn him of the danger to his life. He would be careful while removing his shoes, so that they didn't mistake him for a shoe-chucker and shoot him. Where he came from, leaders preferred crowds to be barefoot.

Once he had finished his cordial chat with Gandhi, and perhaps shared a cup of tea with the great soul, he would make doubly sure he was safe by going to the police station and registering an official complaint. Everyone always said things were much better under the British, so he was sure the police would be sympathetic, professional and quick. There, too, he might have a cup of tea. With that, mission accomplished, he would go home and find Banani.

How was he supposed to go home, though? He had no idea. But that was a question for another day. First, he had a job to do.

The young captain reached out and pulled himself up with his hand on Mr Chatterjee's arm.

'I'm sorry if I was rude,' he said, mustering a smile, 'it's been a bit rough, the last few years. But it's not your fault, is it?'

'It's all right,' said Mr Chatterjee, feeling unaccountably sorry for him, 'I understand.'

'Can I walk you down somewhere? You look like you've got money. Things could get tricky for you around here. Life's a little cheap right now.'

'Don't worry,' said Mr Chatterjee. He didn't feel like adding to the young man's sea of troubles. 'But I'd be obliged if you could give me some directions. How do I get to Birla House?'

'Want to see Gandhi, do you?' said the officer. 'I've half a mind to do it myself, one of these days. The fellows back home will find it awfully strange if I tell them I spent two years in India and never once saw him. Bit like going to Paris and not seeing the Eiffel Tower.'

He glanced at his watch. 'If you make it quick you might just get there in time. What you need to do is take a tonga from over there,' he said, pointing a half-mile down the road. 'Tell them to take you to Albuquerque Road. Ask for the prayer meeting. Everyone knows where it happens. And watch out for pickpockets. Not everyone goes there to listen to Gandhi, you know.'

It was 1948. At least one of them was going to come with a gun.

Mr Chatterjee hurried off down the street, looking for a tonga.

33

*'May I offer you a cappuccino,
Signor Authority?'*

The Competent Authority was swinging in his hammock, humming a little tune. He liked the idea of running the nation from his hammock. No one had ever done it before. He liked the idea of staying in mid-air while he repaired everything, his feet only touching the ground once the ground had been sufficiently purified. The touch of his feet would be the final act of purification.

The CA was in his magnificent underground bunker, built to ensure the maintenance of essential services in the event of war and to protect him from its consequences. It had lead-lined filing cabinets, built-in electromagnetic pulse protectors, and bulletproof TV screens, to ensure uninterrupted viewing in the face of enemy firing. There was nothing else on the walls except a big red map of China. There was a plentiful supply of potassium iodide tablets, in an aluminium trunk marked 'Private'. After the last war, the Ministry of Health had made a packet hoarding potassium iodide tablets. The personal wealth of all concerned had increased significantly, along with the death toll. The health minister had made enough money to build an underground tunnel to Yangon, through which he had escaped, but not before leaving behind a secret stash of tablets for future governments.

Hanging in a hammock protected the CA from extreme ground shocks, which were inevitable during a heavy nuclear attack. Buildings above would shatter and crumble, and collapse into piles of sod, but he would suffer nothing more than aggravated swaying. The hammock was of very good quality. It held him in its grip gently, but firmly, just like he held the nation.

A solicitous metal tentacle tapped him on the shoulder.

'May I offer you a cappucinno, Signor Authority?' said the bunker. (It was a luxury model made in Italy.)

'Maybe later,' said the CA.

As a result of the lack of shelters, as well as the lack of potassium, casualties during the last war had been severe. With typical dynamism, the Competent Authority had set about rectifying this. Three varieties of bunker had been constructed, with lead shielding for VVVIPs (this was him), concrete shielding for VVIPs, and packed-dirt shielding for VIPs. All three types were equally effective, but lead was much more prestigious. Low-income radiation shelters were also under active consideration, but even after downsizing, the size of the population made things difficult.

The massive steel doors parted briefly, and Mehta shimmied in, naked, holding a file in one hand and a battered black bag in the other. The bag contained the nuclear button, which he guarded with his life at all times, except once or twice when he had forgotten it in the men's room at the Delhi Gymkhana. He was naked because everyone had to take their clothes off before entering the bunker in order to prevent Hot Particle Damage, from particles carried in on clothing. It used to make him uncomfortable, but he had gritted his teeth and thought about the money. Nowadays, he quite enjoyed the sense of freedom it gave him. Sometimes he struck statuesque poses when he thought the CA wasn't looking.

'Put down the file and push my hammock,' said the CA. 'Don't let go of the bag.'

'Sir, the CBI is not making any progress in the telepath case, sir,' said Mehta.

The telepath case had catalysed his thinking, and helped his Master Plan come to fruition, so to speak, but did he really need an excuse to complete his vision? A small part of him said that he did, but many other parts of him questioned this. Now that the majority of women were sterile, it was true that it was only a matter of time before the Switzerland or Singapore type population scenario, which he dreamed of constantly, would soon come to pass. But the years of service had made him weary.

He wanted to start the task of proper reconstruction now, and see it blossom in front of his eyes. He wanted to reveal himself, once and for all, as the Saviour of the Nation. Due to his anonymity, the people did not worship him. They deserved to pay for their ingratitude. Was it wrong to expect a little bit of worship after all that he had gone through?

'Sir, the CBI is not taking matter seriously, sir,' said Mehta. He was a tattler. 'Their telepath team is being very casual, sir. Mostly they are relaxing in bars.'

'Why have they only got brain-fries working on the case?' asked the CA crossly.

'It was as per your instructions, sir,' said Mehta. 'You only were saying about that bullfighter case, that we should learn to think like a bull, so they thought, case involves telepaths, let us send telepaths to investigate. No one knew they would be so thirsty, sir. Previous track record did not indicate.'

'Ask them to put some normal people on the case as well,' said the CA. He was beginning to worry about the CBI. They hadn't solved a case in years. It was important to keep them on their toes, in case he ever needed them to actually find out something.

'Bring me my breathing tube and my swimming trunks,' said the CA. It was time to do a practice run in the immersion tub, which would protect him from the firestorms that would soon rage through New New Delhi. Mehta brought him his gear, and helped him emerge from the hammock. The CA pulled on his swimming trunks and stepped into the tub. As he floated in the tub, fully immersed, he felt a deep sense of tranquillity wash over him. When he was a child, his mother had ensured that he had no friends, to keep him free of bad influences. Here, underwater, breathing through a tube, he had reached his mother's ideal. He was utterly alone and at peace.

Things had become clear once he had read that paper on Survivable Nuclear War. For one, it had quoted liberally from conservative scientists in America who believed in global warming, now that the oil was almost gone. Saudi Arabia was out of stock, for example. There was nothing much to do there now, except hang around with camels, and maximize souvenir sales in holy places. Their preachers no longer had the money to rear poor boys on hatred. Their princes no longer lived lives which made Caligula look like a nun. Their religious police no longer beat up people, they collected fines for their salaries instead. The Americans claimed that the accelerated pace of global warming would cancel out nuclear winter. It made perfect sense. It meant that he was free to act. The telepaths were just an excuse. The Maoists were just an excuse. The Protectorate was just an excuse. What he really wanted was China. He would provoke them in various ways, and soon, very soon, the cleansing process would begin. They were very easy to provoke, now that the army was fully in charge.

The Competent Authority dozed off in the immersion tank, smiling a smile of the purest bliss.

34

'Keep threatening me, you little turd.'

'I've often wanted to destroy the Bank of Bodies,' said Banani, 'but they've got too many guns. How did you manage to do it?'

Pintoo picked up a banana from a pile of fruit on a tray, which looked suspiciously like an offering. His hand felt much better. The auntie was right, a fresh dressing really did make a difference. Tarun-da peeled the banana for him. The sight of Pintoo sitting there, happily munching a banana made him seem less threatening, somehow. He was a child, after all. Banani had faith in her own ability when it came to children. But what was it that he could do, exactly? A liberal medical research environment and high doses of radiation had borne some strange fruit over the years. One of the boys in her class started floating whenever he was nervous. They had to tie him to his chair during examinations. Another suffered from lethal flatulence which often left classmates unconscious, but no one had figured out a remedy for that yet. Whatever the child was producing was defying chemical analysis.

'I can push things,' said Pintoo. He didn't want to reveal too much, because people might be terrified. Terrified people did stupid things. He wasn't Superman. All someone had to do was creep up from behind and hit him on the head.

'Some things I smash. Some things I vanish.'

'How big are these things?'

'As big as a person. I haven't tried anything bigger till now.'

'How many people have you vanished?' asked Banani, taking care to keep her voice steady. She could panic later, once she had all the facts. 'And shouldn't you have asked their permission?'

'Two, so far,' said Pintoo. He had no idea why he trusted Banani, but he did. 'It has to be this way. Who's going to listen to me?'

'Where did they go?'

'One's trying to save Gandhiji. The other has to stop a big riot in Calcutta in 1946, because it taught Hindus and Muslims a new technique which they didn't know about before.'

'Why?'

'At first I could only think about destroying the body bank, because they took my hand. It may take time, but I'm still going to do it. The thing is, at least for a while, I seem to have this power. There's much more that I can do. I'm an old guy, but there are little kids like Vinod to worry about. He deserves a better life. I'm trying to make things better by changing what happened. The headmaster and Tarun-da have been helping me.'

Banani glared at Tarun-da. She should have guessed that this bearded leftie type was chewing the child's brains. She had several friends from JNU, of whom she was very fond, but she would never in a million years leave any of them in a position where they could influence impressionable young minds. Especially a mind that could make people vanish.

Tarun-da avoided her gaze and swallowed guiltily. He was saved from further interrogation by a tremendous commotion outside. It sounded like half of Shanti Nagar had turned up.

'Wait outside,' said a take-charge voice. 'Hold the motherfucker tight. Let me go in first.'

A dark young man with a light machine gun riding his hip, strode in, came to attention and saluted. He couldn't click his heels because he was wearing sneakers. The lack of proper military boots rankled.

'Master Pintoo, sir!' he barked. 'I have brought you a prisoner.'

The young guard from the main gate liked acting all military. One day, the Shanti Nagar Self-Defence Force would be a proper army, and then they would kick serious butt. He was constantly preparing for that day.

The ancient headmaster, who had been dozing in an armchair, was woken up by all the barking. 'Why are there soldiers yelling in the room?' he demanded feebly. 'RANVIR! Fuck this man!'

Unfortunately for him, Ranvir was nowhere to be found.

'I've never had a prisoner before,' said Pintoo. 'What kind of prisoner is he?'

'Very dangerous prisoner, sir,' replied the guard. 'He beat up Dinesh the vegetable seller very badly, for absolutely no reason. It took six people to thrash him and tie him up. He's like an angry buffalo. Now you decide what to do.'

Four or five people dragged Pande in. He was still struggling violently. They had thrashed him mercilessly, and bound him up super-tight, but he was still full of mustard, describing in graphic detail what he would do to them once he got them to the nearest thana.

As soon as he was dragged in, two things happened. Banani leaped up like a frightened salmon, searching wildly for a way to escape. Pande started spitting and cursing.

'So there you are, saali,' he said, baring his paan-stained teeth. 'You thought you could escape from me, hah? See all these nice little low-caste people have brought me to your hiding place. Where did you think you could hide, you whore?'

He heaved, and actually managed to haul himself forward a few steps, along with his whole entourage. The guard moved quickly, reversing his machine gun and clubbing him over the head with it in one smooth motion. Pande sank to his knees, growling like a rabid dog. Banani cowered in a corner, completely and utterly terrified. She could handle many things in life, but Ram Manohar Pande was not one of them.

'Watch your tongue,' said Pintoo.

Pande spat at him. The guard swung his machine gun back again like a club and stood poised, loosening his hips for the swing. Pande spat at him too. 'Keep threatening me, you little turd. My day will come. Then you see what I do to you. Showing me a machine gun . . .'

Tarun-da stared at Pande, appalled. He had rarely stepped out of his home, let alone Shanti Nagar, and he had never actually seen a policeman in the flesh. His knowledge of oppression was mostly theoretical. But he had seen pictures in books. A slice of history had entered his room. From Jallianwalla Bagh to the Trilokpuri Incident to the Nagpur Massacre, for over a hundred years, regardless of changes in management, it was creatures like this, dressed in khaki like this, with paunches like this, who had suppressed the forces of revolution and oppressed the toiling masses. They had jeered and sneered and leered at the poor, and destroyed their lives as per their whims and fancies, breaking their bones and violating their women, killing their children and burning their homes. And here was one of them, a ranting, slavering blast from the past, breathing fire and oozing menace, standing right here in his very own living room.

Tarun-da took off his chappal and started beating Pande over the head with it. 'Capitalist swine!' he said. 'Running dog of imperialism! Oppressor of the proletariat! Reactionary cat's paw! Petit bourgeoisie!'

Pande sank to the floor, temporarily deflated. All this English was way too much for him. In addition, his head was beginning to throb. The repeated blows were beginning to have their effect. His skull might be thick, but there were limits.

Pintoo sat on the bed, swinging his legs, looking down at Pande.

'Where. Did. You. Hide. Chatterjee?' Pande gasped out to Pintoo.

Banani popped up from behind the bed.

'You've met my husband?' she asked. 'Why didn't you tell me?'

Tarun-da and Pintoo glanced guiltily at each other.

'Yes, we did,' said Pintoo. 'He was worried about you. We promised him we would protect you, and we will. Even from this.' He touched Pande with his foot. Pande snarled.

'Where is he?' asked Banani, with mounting dread. 'What have you done with him?'

'We'll tell you everything,' said Pintoo, 'first, let me take care of this man, like I promised. Then you'll be safe, and we can talk.'

Banani sat down, wishing she had a God to pray to. All she could do was wait.

'Nothing can save you from me, you whore!' roared Pande from the floor. 'I'll teach you a lesson and nobody's father will stop me!'

The guard raised his gun but Pintoo gestured for him to stop.

'Set him loose,' he said.

The guard looked at Pintoo as if he were insane.

'Now we'll have some fun,' said the ancient headmaster, cackling.

'Please,' said Pintoo to the guard, 'don't be scared.'

The guard untied Pande. Two of the others pulled him to his feet. Pande leaped forward, hands outstretched, growling. He didn't care if there were a hundred people in the room, he would get his hands around the bitch's throat. Then he would squeeze.

Pintoo pushed him, hard. It took less effort this time. His gift was getting stronger and better with practice. Pande flew through the air and hit the opposite wall, his head hitting brick with a crunch. He slid down and lay there with his back to the wall, stunned.

There was a hushed silence in the room.

Pintoo got off the bed and walked up to Pande. He stood there, looking down at him.

'You've got a thick head,' he said. 'And you never stop.'

Pande moaned. But he was recovering quickly. If he pretended to be hurt, the child might bend down. Then he would snap him like a twig. Then, while the others were distracted by the disaster and moaning over the little shit, he would get hold of Chatterjee's wife . . .

'You're pretty strong, too,' continued Pintoo thoughtfully.

Tarun-da protested. He could see where this was going.

'No, no, Pintoo,' he said, 'not him.'

Pintoo stood there, thinking.

'He's an animal!' yelled Tarun-da. 'You can't trust him.'

Pintoo ignored him and looked down at Pande.

'You always get what you want, don't you?' he said, almost affectionately. 'Nothing can stand in your way. You keep on going till you get it.'

'I'll get you, you little shit,' hissed Pande, malevolently.

'No, you won't,' said Pintoo, smiling.

'You see,' he said, turning to Tarun-da, 'he's the right person.'

'How can you say that?' said Tarun-da, horrified.

'You said this was an impossible job.'

'They're all impossible jobs,' said Tarun-da, momentarily depressed.

'But we still have to try,' said Pintoo, 'and he is the right person. We need someone stupid enough to fight the whole Indian army.'

'And I don't want him anywhere near her,' he added.

Tarun-da nodded. Who knows, he thought. He might even make it. He'd seen a little of Pande. He would never bet against him.

Pintoo reached down and shoved a little slip into Pande's pocket. Pande tried to grab his hand, but the kid was too quick for him. He was feeling a little exhausted, in truth, though he would die before he admitted it.

'Do this job and I'll bring you back,' said Pintoo. 'I'll try to find a way to make you less angry.'

Pande spat at him. 'Go make your mother angry,' he said.

Pintoo pushed.

35

'It wasn't me. It was the hand.'

It was a red-letter day at the Jawaharlal Nehru Indira Gandhi Rajiv Gandhi Sonia Gandhi Rahul Gandhi Priyanka Gandhi Museum (formerly known as the National Museum). They had started naming everything after all of them, because now there were too many of them to name individual things after. When it came to building nomenclature, safety first was the guiding principle.

The PM was at the JNIGRGSGRGPG Museum to inaugurate a new wing, dedicated to twentieth-century India. It had been an eventful century, and the exhibits showed it. There were animatronic models of Bollywood stars, mouthing dialogues and swivelling their hips, although not both at once. There was a Kashmiri stone-thrower inside a glass case. He looked disturbingly life-like. There was a cutaway view of a call centre, with rows and rows of cubicles. Some perverted japester had rearranged the little dolls, and a colossal orgy was now in progress. There were stones from the mosque, and stones from the temple, side by side. They looked remarkably similar. There was a statue of Mr Toilet, hero of sanitation just across the aisle from Zia-ul-Haq, the Pakistani dictator, oozing menace and brilliantine, but a little hard to recognize because they hadn't put on his moustache yet. A life-sized replica of the satellite Aryabhatta floated above their heads. People were trying not to stand directly underneath it. There was a rickety and elaborate steam-powered money-vanishing machine, which promised to make money disappear if you put some inside. There was an exact replica of Mahatma Gandhi's spinning wheel. It was broken.

Once the inauguration was over, the PM remained seated on the dais, waiting for the photographers to finish. She always made time for them. They were the only friends she had. The PM had delivered a stirring anti-war speech, in the hope of creating an atmosphere where missile launches would be frowned upon, but the CA had ensured that no TV channels were present. This was a bad sign. It meant he was deadly serious. Banning TV channels was a masterstroke. There wasn't much she could do with photographs, except look sad and disapproving.

It was strange to see so many children in one place. The teachers were making half-hearted attempts to control them, but as far as she could see, they were pretty much going berserk. One little boy was running down the aisle, whooping, holding the detached limb of a statue over his head, followed by three of the wheelchair kids. One of the kids had an even smaller child tied to the back of his wheelchair, who was watching the world zip by with a slightly bemused air. How had they managed that?

Forming a small bunch in front of the dais was the usual crowd of chamchas and fixers, all hoping to catch her for a minute or two. Her audiences seemed to be composed exclusively of people with files to push. She hadn't met any genuine members of the public in years. Of course, the party still showed TV clips of her visiting poor people in their humble homes, but this was achieved by shooting her against a blue screen on the lawn, and later inserting the relevant scene. They might be putting her in porn movies for all she knew, with an eye on the youth vote.

The favour seekers shifted restlessly, waiting for the photography to finish. She would spend the obligatory five minutes mingling with them, and a lucky few would drop a few words in her ear. Her private secretary whose hearing was acute would note down the words and the person. He in turn would drop a word into the ear of whoever was handling the file. 'They spoke to the PM,' he would say, without further elaboration. No one ever asked.

Balaji the Fixer had come to fix the PM. He stood near the dais, biding his time. The PM's private secretary was on retainer with him, so he always knew exactly where she was. He was wearing sophisticated clothes. He had shaved several times, and splashed himself liberally with aftershave. He had practised shaking hands with his wife. He was glad the PM was the modern type. He hated prostrating himself. It was difficult to speak with your lips kissing the floor and this often caused complications. He had once ended up with a contract from Bata instead of Tata. The client had been most understanding, and had quite happily set up a footwear factory instead of an automobile factory and paid him his full fee. It was things like this that made him proud to be Indian. He dried his palms with a handkerchief. 'Good evening, madam. The weather is particularly fine, is it not?' he muttered under his breath.

The photographers were winding up. She would be stepping down from the dais soon. From the left or the right? Judging that was crucial. He rocked on his heels, and swayed from side to side.

Just then, he felt a stabbing pain between his legs and looked down. A little boy, around eight or nine, dressed in a grey school uniform, was holding his scrotum in one hand and squeezing them. He was looking up at Balaji's face with an expression of mild interest. He squeezed harder. 'Eeeee,' said Balaji, trying to keep his voice down. What were you supposed to do if you were assaulted by a schoolboy in the presence of the PM? None of his investigations into etiquette had provided him with any clues.

'MotherFUCKER!' he cried, as the child gave a hearty yank.

A hushed silence fell across the room. The children paused in their acts of vandalism and stared at him, open-mouthed, delighted. The PM was quickly hustled out by her guards. She withdrew reluctantly. This was the best thing that had happened at one of these bashes in years. She peered over her shoulder to check out the little boy. He was still going at it with gusto. The future of the nation was in safe hands, she could see. The future of Balaji, not so much.

Mrs Johnson materialized, mortified. 'Little boy!' she said. 'Let go of that man immediately. The Prime Minister is watching you!'

'No,' said Pappu obstinately, 'he's a bad man. He's from the Bank of Bodies.'

Balaji tried to focus on the boy through a haze of agony. He looked more closely at the hand, which was refusing to let go. It was surgically attached to the wrist. A customer! Why was he being attacked by a customer? Donors he could understand, which was why he never got out of his car in the poorer parts of town. But customers? The irony was inescapable. He was being attacked by the hand that fed him.

'Help,' he whimpered.

Mrs Johnson plunged into the fray. She could be accused of many things, but lack of boldness was not one of them. She grabbed hold of Pappu's hand and pulled. A huge struggle ensued, during which Balaji the Fixer lost consciousness. Pappu tried to hold him up, but he was too heavy, he had to let go. Mrs Johnson dragged him away and spun him around.

'What's your name?' asked Mrs Johnson, tremulously. She only remembered the famous kids. The rest were just a blur.

'Pappu Verma,' said Pappu, proudly. Several of the older boys came over and slapped him on the back. A couple of the girls waved at him shyly. The school had a new hero.

'Why did you do this?' demanded Mrs Johnson.

'It wasn't me,' said Pappu, giving birth to an immortal school catchphrase. 'It was the hand.'

Mrs Johnson frogmarched him back to the schoolbus. She was going to call in the boy's parents and give them hell, customer service be damned. Then she was going to call the boy's class-teacher and give her hell too. Then she was going to have a drink—several drinks, actually.

❑

Balaji was standing in front of No. 2, holding an ice pack to his loins.

'I was attacked by a child at the museum,' he said.

'I assume you were trying to molest him,' said No. 2, who could conceive of no other reason for Balaji to visit a museum.

'I never laid a hand on the kid,' protested Balaji hotly, 'I was trying to catch the secretary's eye and he grabbed me.'

Privately, he had to admit that there had been a sexual element to the encounter. Balaji was always ruthlessly honest with himself in his mind. His life was such an elaborate tissue of lies and deceit that it was easy to get confused, so he periodically took the truth out and had a look at it, just to make sure it was still there.

'Did he mention any reason, or was it more of a public service?'

No. 2 didn't like Balaji very much. He considered him to be a necessary evil, and spent as little time with him as possible.

'He's a customer,' said Balaji. 'He's angry with the BoB.'

'That's the second attack on us in a week,' mused No. 2. 'Of course, the first one involved substantial property damage, whereas in this case it was just you, but it was an attack nevertheless. You're sure this wasn't a donor child?'

'It was a fat little kid,' said Balaji sullenly. 'Name of Verma.'

'Verma? Are you sure?'

'I'm sure,' said Balaji. He'd checked with security afterwards. He always kept track of people who'd done the dirty on him.

'Don't try any stunts,' said No. 2 who knew exactly how Balaji's mind worked. 'Let me take care of this.'

If this kid was linked to the Shanti Nagar kid, then they had a pretty big problem on their hands, No. 2 figured. He had presented his plan on diversification into Religious Joy as general time-pass for the Chairman. He had only half-believed the story of the superhuman child, based as it was on the testimony of that gibbering idiot Sam Kapoor. Having majored in behavioural science in business school, he was more inclined to believe that it was some form of mass hallucination triggered by group hysteria, rooted in subliminal guilt. However, it was now clear that this was no longer the case. All the evidence pointed to the existence of an actual, genuine, or bona fide child. He would have to find out as much as he could about him immediately. Unless he was won over, he could cause significant damage. That was the fundamental flaw in their business model, lucrative though it maybe. The raw material could fight back.

36

'A piece of string is cheaper than the life of
a trained soldier.'

'That's not how you do it, boy,' said Ali softly.

The young man leaped like a startled faun. It was one of those sticky Calcutta afternoons and he was sweating profusely, the grenade clearly visible through his muslin shirt. He was standing next to a big car, trying to look casual. One of his hands was inside his shirt. Ali could see it through the sodden fabric, clasping and unclasping spasmodically. Typical rookie. For starters, he was wearing a white shirt—not the best way to hide explosives.

'What are you talking about?' asked the boy, stuttering. He was thin and gangly, with all the fluid assurance of a baby giraffe. Whoever had sent him to do this job was completely insane. Or desperately short of volunteers.

'Why don't you take your hand off the pin for a minute?' said Ali, 'Come on. Take your hand out. I'm asking you nicely.'

As he tried to get the kid to relax and not blow them both up, he was reminded of his salad days, training apprentice martyrs in Bora Bora. They had come from all over the world to Camp Abu Jihad, all those warriors for Allah, from Switzerland and Sudan, from Chechnya and Chittagong, from Putney and Pittsburgh. It had been like Harvard with suicide vests. They even had a company song and a mission statement. He could see the recruitment poster they should have made. Join Al Qaeda. See the world. Meet interesting people. Blow them up.

This one was just like those eager, young half-wits, except not so excited about virgins. Back then, the whole problem had always been that none of them got enough sex. If they had, the appeal of martyrdom would have been significantly lower. Once you took out virgins as incentive, all you had left was melons. Who would massacre innocents for melons? Fat Mike back in Preston would have killed anyone for food, of course, but he was more of a French fries man.

'Come on, lad. Take your hand out,' said Ali, 'just for a minute. You can put it back in after.'

The boy took his hand out, unable to take his eyes off Ali.

'See?' said Ali. 'The pin's still there, isn't it? It's not going jump out on its own. So you don't need to keep clutching it, do you?'

The boy looked at his hand, felt for the grenade nestling in his bosom, and nodded at Ali, awestruck. Ali felt the muzzle of a revolver jabbing him in the back.

'I don't know who you are, but you better leave the boy alone,' said a hard voice. Ali turned, slowly and carefully. This one was in a different league, dark and compact, with a face like a stone. His revolver was hidden in the folds of a newspaper.

'Good afternoon,' Ali said. 'Do you mind if I just finish instructing the kid? It'll come in handy later in life, assuming you let him have one.'

Not a muscle moved in the man's face. 'Do you think this is a joke?' he asked.

'I think you should do it properly,' said Ali.

There was a flicker of interest in the man's eyes.

'Perhaps we should sit in that tea shop over there, and talk like gentlemen,' suggested Ali.

'My target will go away,' said the boy. He was simple, and single-minded, like all of them had always been. Ali felt a pang. He put a hand on his shoulder.

'Boy, this is a British officer's car, but he's not here. It's just his wife. It's parked in front of Firpo's. She's having weak tea and dry, crumbly cake with her friends. She's just a poor woman who'll be back in England next year, where she'll bitch about the food and miss the sun, while her husband listens to cricket on the radio. What's the point?'

'They beat my brother to death,' said the boy.

'Would he want you to die?' asked Ali gently, putting an arm round his shoulders. 'Come and have tea.'

The tea shop was just like the ones he remembered from Dhaka, long ago, and far in the future. A little boy scurrying from table to table. Incredibly hard biscuits in a filthy jar. Rickety benches. The newspaper man who would let you read his newspaper, provided you listened to his views on the news. Industrial-strength tea in little clay cups which left a little bit of mud in your mouth with every sip. Why would anyone want to go anywhere else?

'Who is that man on your chest?' asked the boy, pointing.

'He's a revolutionary poet,' said Ali. These guys would get it. They were just the right audience. 'I'll sing something for you.'

He stood up and sang 'Get Up Stand Up', drumming on the table with spoons. The patrons applauded politely when he finished. He sat down again. The tea shop helper brought him tea.

'I like the chorus,' said the hard man, thawing slightly.

'The words are easy to remember,' said the boy.

'And here's another thing that's easy to remember,' said Ali. 'A piece of string is cheaper than the life of a trained soldier.'

'What do you mean?' asked the hard man.

'What was your plan?' asked Ali. 'The boy would stand near the car, see the target and pull the pin, provided he didn't pee in his pants, right?'

The hard man said nothing.

'Well, suppose he fixed the grenade to the bottom of the car, and tied a string to the pin? Suppose he ran the string along the gutter to a lamppost twenty feet away? Suppose he saw the target, bent down, and pulled the string? Boom!'

'Boom!' said the boy, pleased.

'That could work,' mused the hard man.

'That *has* worked. A thousand times. Even better, fix the grenade to the bottom of the car. Tie a string on the pin. Fix the other end to the door. Target opens door. Boom! Of course, you could also ask yourself what's the point, since they'll be gone by next year anyway.'

'Why are you telling us all this?' asked the hard man.

'Why do you care? Once I give you the knowledge, can I take it back?'

'In that case, you should come with us to our mess. There are others who should hear you.'

Ali was pleased to receive the invitation. If he had to stop Direct Action Day, he needed to infiltrate the lawless elements. They would be in the thick of the action. What better way to do it than by becoming guru-cum-scientific advisor to a group of hardcore lunatics, teaching Jihad 101, Elementary Subterfuge, and Advanced Explosives?

He followed his new comrades down the road, 'I Shot the Sheriff' playing in his head. Ali felt alive for the first time in years. He had no doubt his career was going to end here in Calcutta. There was no other way this could play out. But he was going to do some damage before he was through.

37

'I'm letting him go because I'm on temple duty.'

Pande woke up with sand in his underwear. He was still groggy and disoriented from the numerous beatings (and one biting) he had received, although he was recovering rapidly. Despite his enormous paunch he was physically tough, it was his mental recovery that was taking longer.

He was more accustomed to being the abuser than the abusee, but in a little over twenty-four hours, he had been bitten by a dog, thrashed by vegetable sellers, threatened by a scheduled caste, and battered by a street child, all of whom were his prey in the natural order of things. In order to regain his self-esteem, he would have to exact thorough and prolonged retribution from the nearest innocent bystander. Not that anyone was ever actually innocent. Who would know this better than him?

Unfortunately, there didn't seem to be any bystanders in the immediate

Shovon Chowdhury

vicinity. He had woken up face-down in the middle of the desert. As he staggered to his feet, the searing heat hit him hard. All he could see for miles around was sand, punctuated by a few scraggly little bushes here and there. Finally, he spotted a truck far away in the distance and started walking in that direction. His spirits lifted. Truck drivers were his friends, a source of small but regular income. If he reached the highway and caught the next truck, he could be reasonably sure of money, liquor, and somebody to thrash.

As he walked, he took out the piece of paper the child had given him. 'STOP THE POKHRAN BLAST' it said.

Pintoo was a boy of few words.

Pande mulled over this. Despite being a man of action, Pande was not completely illiterate. He knew that the Pokhran blast being referred to was a nuclear test. But they had done two—one in 1974, and one in 1998. Which one was Pintoo referring to?

Either way, he was in the past and he was in Rajasthan, which he had visited before. It was the armpit of the universe with too much sand, too many camels, not enough to drink and limited earning potential for enterprising officers of the law.

As a devotee of mythological TV serials, where the miracles flew thick and fast, Pande was hip to the supernatural. Even in some of his favourite family soaps, where the in-laws wore phenomenal amounts of jewellery and behaved badly, the narratives tended to switch between the past, the present and the future, depending on which actors were asking the producer for more money. So he was familiar with the concept of time travel. However, he had never expected to actually do it himself, nor had he expected to come across an incarnation of Vishnu in Shanti Nagar. He was a little puzzled that Vishnu had chosen to incarnate himself as a slum child, but who was he to question the Gods? They were prone to eccentricity.

Pande drew the line at very little, but messing around with the Gods didn't seem like such a good idea. He was under divine instructions to do something about this bomb blast, so that was what he was going to do. It was a bit like being on temple duty. He remained slightly confused, but this much was clear—an avatar of Vishnu outranked both his SHO and the commissioner, so for the time being, he was under new management.

He needed to evolve a plan of action. There were several points to consider.

a) A nuclear bomb was a military weapon, so it would be controlled by the army.
b) The army were a bunch of bastards who paid no attention to the police. If he tried to beat them up, they would shoot him.
c) He could not, therefore, catch hold of the nearest soldier and thrash him till he told him where the bomb was, and how to switch it off.
d) He wasn't sure whether the bomb would have a switch. A fuse, more likely, or something electronic. If it had a fuse, he would simply remove it. Or he could pour some water on it, thereby causing it to short circuit. If it was small enough, he could dunk it in a bucket of water, but for this he would need a bucket. Alternatively, he could carry the water in a bucket, and pour it on the bomb, but this would leave him with only one hand free for beating up people.

However, this was all in the future. First, he had to find out where the bomb was, and get close to it, with or without a bucket. This would mean ploughing through numerous army jawans, who would be disrespectful, uncooperative, and well-armed.

By now Pande had reached the edge of the highway and he stood there, waiting for a vehicle to hijack. Soon enough, a taxi emerged in a cloud of sand, but Pande—on the verge of stepping out—stopped. The taxi driver was a sardar. These bloody sardars were everywhere, even in this shithole! Sardars were typically very large and carried knives, so as a matter of policy, Pande avoided confronting them unless he was with other policemen and outnumbered them. Moreover, he seemed to recall that some of them had been terrorists in this era, and he had no desire to mess with terrorists. They always had better weapons than the police.

He let the taxi pass. He pondered over his problem. What could he do to get into an army camp? It seemed like an impossible task for a sub-inspector from Safdarjung Enclave. He didn't even have a water cannon. Not that he often got one back home. Ministers' children often borrowed them for rain dances, or they were lent to film producers who wanted to re-create riots.

Terrorists! That was the key. Back home, there were no terrorists, except for the Maoists, and they were an army. But this place was full of them. They came in a wide variety of flavours. This was one area where the army and the police had always cooperated. In fact, some senior police officers, motivated by a misguided sense of duty, had died fighting terrorists. Perhaps he could pose as a Dedicated Policeman, in Hot Pursuit of a Terrorist. That would get him close to the army.

All he needed was a sub judice. Once he got hold of one, he would beat him up until he agreed to be a terrorist, drag him down to the army camp where the bomb was, and tell them he had foiled a plot to sabotage the bomb. He would then be invited in, lionized by all and sundry, plied with expensive army canteen alcohol, perhaps even be given a woman or two. He knew all about what went on in those army camps, his uncle had served in the Northeast. Once his hosts had subsided into a drunken stupor, he would procure a bucket from one of the bathrooms and sabotage the bomb, thereby fulfilling his religious duty.

Pande was very impressed with himself. He would be the first one to admit that brainwork was not his forte, but he had successfully hatched a cunning plot. If he kept on at this rate, even if he didn't get the CBI job he dreamed of, perhaps he might get a teaching post at the Police Academy, where tea was served in cups and saucers, along with fresh pakoras. The atmosphere here was suiting him. Rajasthan might not be such a dead loss after all. Maybe he should ask for a posting here once he got back.

Another taxi was approaching, and having ascertained that the driver was reasonably small, Pande stepped into the middle of the road. He waved his lathi imperiously and gestured to the passengers to get out. An impossibly large number of them, two or three entire families by the looks of it, emerged from the taxi grumbling. They didn't grumble very loudly, though. Pande was proud and pleased to see that his uniform commanded the same respect here that it did back home.

He grabbed the nearest passenger by the front of his kurta and pulled him close.

'What year is it?' he asked, kicking him hard in the testicles, thereby rendering him incapable of speech.

'Arrey, this policeman is drunk,' said a pimply youth, grinning toothily, 'he's forgotten everything!'

Pande cracked open his skull with a casual flick of his lathi and turned to the remaining passengers. 'It's 1998,' said the boy's mother, weeping into her pallu, 'it's May of 1998. Please don't kill him.'

'You could have said that in the beginning,' said Pande, wiping his lathi on the boy's dhoti. 'Go away, all of you. You can take the boy. Make him control his mouth. Next time he won't be so lucky. I'm letting him go because I'm on temple duty.'

Pande hopped into the now empty taxi and slapped the agitated driver on the back of his head.

'Where are we?' he asked him.

The driver pointed to a milestone, too scared to speak.

'POKHRAN, 10 KM' it said.

'Take me to the nearest police station,' said Pande, slapping his head once more for good measure.

38

'We will combine the best points of Pearl Harbor with the best points of D-Day.'

'Why don't we attack China?' the CA asked the General. 'It's big. It's close. It's hard to miss.'

The General was looking at him thoughtfully. He chose his words carefully. 'We don't have to attack China just because it's big, or close,' he said. 'We can hit small targets too. Technology has improved a lot.'

The CA pushed out his lower lip. It made him look like a disgruntled baby. He had woken up bright and happy this morning, and in his mood of sunny optimism, he had felt that if he took a vivacious approach to the whole thing, he would be able to sweep the General along with him and set events in motion with a twinkle and a smile. But the General was still being grumpy and uncooperative. Honestly, he didn't know why he bothered. He grew noticeably less twinkly.

'We could take back the Bengal Protectorate in a day,' the CA said sourly, 'I just have to give the word. The only reason we haven't done it so far is to avoid giving offence, because the Chinese claim that Bengal was originally part of China, just before the Ice Age, and they're very sensitive about such things. The Bay of Bengal, too, is part of the South China Sea, apparently. This is based on recently discovered historical evidence that shows the Ming Emperor Long Wu once peed out of a porthole while sailing through.'

'The Maoists are in between,' the General said.

'See, this is where you need to be bold,' said the CA, 'like Alexander the Great, or me. Boldly go where no general has gone before. When people look at you, they must point their fingers and say, there goes the boldest man in the history of the Indian army. What would the boldest man in the history of the Indian army do, General?'

Throttle you like a chicken, thought the General.

'I have no idea,' he said, 'you're so much bolder than me. What would you do?'

'Forget Bengal! We'll attack China! We'll sail there. It will be a turning point in Indian history. We'll wade ashore, singing patriotic songs, holding our weapons over our heads, and capture their beaches. History will be our guide. We will combine the best points of Pearl Harbor with the best points of D-Day.'

The General blanched in horror.

'We don't have enough boats,' he said feebly.

'My dear General,' said the CA, 'this is why you should study geography more. War is all about maps. What do you see there on the map, nestling near the foot of India, shaped like a paramecium?'

'Sri Lanka,' said the General dully.

'Exactly! They are an island nation. They are bound to have lots of boats. Just like the British. We will borrow them. Are you learning anything from this? This is what I do as a matter of habit. Combine a sense of history with a sense of geography. You must learn from this. Of course, it's too late for you, but you should pass this knowledge on to younger family members. Tell them I said so.'

'Perhaps we should re-look at the plan to invade Bengal,' said the General, unable to believe that he was saying this aloud.

'Bengal is too insignificant,' said the CA, 'and the message is too indirect. We have to send them a clear message. The Chinese only understand simple messages. They're not subtle like us. I big. You small. I want. I take. That's how they think.'

This was true, the General realized. When they had destroyed Bombay and Delhi in the last war, the message they had sent was quite simple: we want you dead.

'I need some time to digest this,' said the General, with a hint of desperation. 'Not all of us have your vision. I need to run scenarios.

Evaluate options. Get Navalkar to play some more war games. Arrange for swimming lessons. Wake up the navy. These things take time.'

The CA smiled fondly at him. The General was hooked, but still thrashing. He just had to reel him in.

'Let's not be too late,' said the CA, 'we don't want to lose the initiative. Who knows what might happen next?'.'

❑

After the General left, the CA smiled to himself. He was pleased, but not ecstatic. The General was on the same page now, but he was still a marginal notation. He would take his time. He would drag his feet. He would nitpick and quibble. The process would be slow, and this bothered him because bold people were never slow.

It was time for some diplomacy. He needed to talk to the Foreign Ministry. They were notably incompetent, the exact opposite of him. He would let them loose on the Chinese, with emotional and ambiguous instructions. If he played his cards right, they could be at war with China by Monday. He would also need to involve the PM, just to make sure. He had to see her anyway for the Commonwealth Games, which were starting next week. The games were entirely online now, and there were some glitches in the software. The international media was having a field day. He refused to let this ruin his mood. He had started the day sunny, and by God, he was going to end it sunny, even if he had to terrorize people to stay that way.

Besides, how could he not be sunny? He was going to meet the PM. At the thought of meeting his beloved he felt a warm glow in the pit of his stomach. Together, they had work to do. He was confident in the inability of the Foreign Ministry. But when it came to triggering diplomatic incidents, he preferred the hands-on approach.

39

'Apart from money, we will also offer to tranquilize Sam and present him as an offering.'

The Chairman of the Bank of Bodies was disgruntled. His attractive young secretary had just read him the latest quarterly report, and the results were not good. His prawn cutlet lay half-eaten on his plate. Disconsolately, he brushed a few crumbs from his bib and sighed.

Rumours of war had been circulating amongst the rich and famous, who formed the bulk of the BoB's customers. Most of them felt they might need replacement organs soon, so they were holding on to their deposits and withdrawals were down. Expenses were shooting up. Acquiring organs was cheap for the BoB, but holding them was expensive and involved the use of the latest cryogenic techniques. Every extra month that they had to store an organ, they lost money. Their business depended on a smoothly flowing pipeline, where an organ was neatly and quickly removed from a donor, and then neatly and quickly inserted into a customer.

Of course, a war would also mean a boom in business for the BoB, with bits and pieces missing all over the place, but the Chairman was not consoled by this thought. Wars were uncertain things. During the last war, they had certainly seen an upswing in revenues, but the previous Chairman and three other directors had been reduced to radioactive sludge, so the outcome had not been wholly positive.

They were facing problems on the supply side too. In the past, the BoB had solved inventory problems by simply throwing away old organs and getting fresh ones, but the rumours coming out of Shanti Nagar were disturbing. They might face greater resistance than they had in the past, according to information provided by Jasubhai the Collector. That would mean strengthening the Medical Military Commando squads, which would drive up costs. The Chairman felt very sorry for himself. All he wanted to do was run an honest, clean business and make a decent profit for his shareholders. Why did everything have to be so difficult?

'Wgn wnmf wummp?' he asked No. 2 from behind his handkerchief, hoping he would come up with something.

No. 2, as usual, was able to oblige.

'We need to take swift action to improve results in the next two quarters,' he said. 'Which means we need to speed up our plans for dwiversification, and quickly roll out our Religious Joy business by Quarter 2, so that the revenues start kicking in by Quarter 3.'

'Wqt wudy faam!' exclaimed the Chairman, exasperated.

'Yes, it's true, Sam has created a bit of a problem,' admitted No. 2 ruefully. Sam's attempt at using his non-existent superpowers on the

CA, and his repeated use of the term 'fattie' had led to a situation where relations between the BoB and the government could only be described as frosty.

'I think we should avoid meeting the CA,' said No. 2, 'who, between you and me, Mr Chairman, displays disturbingly megalomaniacal tendencies.'

The Chairman grunted. He hated megalomaniacs.

'Instead, I think we should submit our proposal in writing, which is what we should have done in the first place. Files are the lifeblood of the government. They made us what we are today. Files can be managed. Balaji the Fixer will help. Once we tell him who and what to fix, he will fix it. Some expenditure will be involved, I'm afraid.'

The Chairman groaned piteously. No. 2 was sympathetic, but unbending. He allowed his eyes to moisten a bit, to show that he was hurting too.

'However, if we are submitting a proposal in writing, our business plan has to be robust. For one thing, we need to recruit our religious figurehead, who will form the basis of our Religious Joy business,' he said.

'Fwk?' asked the Chairman.

'Yes, the freak,' said No. 2. 'In fact, his recruitment will also help our Medical Joy business. As you know, our relations with Shanti Nagar are somewhat rocky at this point.'

'Wuddy wam!' grumped the Chairman. He could see the rascal's fingerprints everywhere. After the episode with the CA, the Chairman had demanded that Sam be disassembled immediately, and stored in jars, but No. 2 had stopped him, mumbling something about using him later. The Chairman considered this to be a high-risk strategy. The man was a menace to society in his opinion, and ought to be dismantled immediately.

'Well, yes, on the Shanti Nagar front, too, Sam seems to have made himself unpopular, but this is only natural, given that he was removing their organs. Which brings me to my point. We need to get Shanti Nagar back on our side. To do this, we need to recruit this boy Pintoo, by offering him a career path and large sums of money.'

The Chairman groaned again.

'No, sir, I fear I must be firm in this case,' said No. 2. 'A few D-size batteries will not do the trick. Apart from money, we will also offer to tranquilize Sam and present him as an offering. The child can do with him as he wishes.'

The Chairman beamed. He liked this part of the plan.

'In this way,' said No. 2, 'we will buy out key elements of Shanti Nagar society, including Pintoo, as well as some of the people around him. This will help streamline supplies for our Medical Joy business, whilst providing us with a figurehead for our Religious Joy business.'

Even the Chairman had to admit he was impressed. No. 2 might be a loathsome, smarmy creep, who put far too much Brylcreem in his hair, but there was no one to beat him when it came to elaborate plans for world domination. When the day came for the Chairman to pull the lever, thereby opening the trapdoor under No. 2's feet and plunging him directly into the Processing Department, he would do so with regret. Perhaps he should remove his brain first, and keep it for personal use.

Astonishingly, there was even more.

'The other aspect of the business we have to consider is distribution. In other words, where will we sell Religious Joy from?'

'Wgt wig wnchs, gpd git!!' said the Chairman, pretty sure No. 2 was going to suggest opening new shops and spending a whole lot more money. It was sickening. Three requests for money during the course of one meeting was a crime that deserved death, in his book. His hand crept towards the lever.

'Please bear with me,' said No. 2, presciently, 'I am not suggesting we spend any more money. But the branches we have really won't do, you know. Luckily, I have an idea for a strategic alliance which would mean no additional investment.'

The Chairman removed his hand from the lever.

'Our customers at the BoB branches are of a particular type, Mr Chairman,' said No. 2. 'However, our Religious Joy business will be a high-volume, low-margin business, involving middle-class and even poor customers. We don't want the two to get mixed up, do we? Heaven forbid, but if they all come to the same branch, some of our BoB customers might come face to face with donors!'

The Chairman choked on his handkerchief. His attractive young secretary patted him on the back. The possibility of donors and customers coming face to face was their single biggest nightmare as the incident at Sam's branch had showed.

'Yes, I know,' said No. 2, once the Chairman had recovered. 'It's a terrible thought, isn't it? My proposed strategic alliance can prevent this. The question we have to ask ourselves is—who else is a key player in the business of Religious Joy? Who already has a distribution network that stretches across the length and breadth of the country? Who is using a vague sense of religiosity and excellent dental work to lighten the wallets of millions of our countrymen as we speak?'

The Chairman tried to think, but he couldn't. He was still limp from the thought of donors entering the sanitized, ethereal environs of his beloved branches.

'Our logical ally is Dharti Pakar of the ART OF BREATHING™,' said No. 2. 'A man who has offices in every nook and cranny of India that has not been obliterated by the Chinese. A man whose limpid eyes are like fathomless pools of eternity. A man who has an assortment of supermodels at his beck and call. A man who expertly fills countless people across the nation with an amorphous sense of well-being. A man whose offer to eradicate Maoism with the power of positive thinking has been foolishly spurned by the government. With such a man as our distribution partner, our Religious Joy business cannot fail. All we need to do is recruit the slum child; take some good photographs; announce the first lottery, three lucky winners of which will receive personal miracles; and run a huge advertising campaign. By Quarter 2, revenues should be up by 23 per cent.'

The Chairman burst into applause, dropping his handkerchief in his elation.

'And that's not all,' continued No. 2, visibly chuffed with the effect he was having on the Chairman, 'as you know, the wives of the rich and famous find Dharti Pakar unreasonably attractive. Once we have him on our side, guess which powerful and influential person will stupidly agree to everything we say?'

'Me, me!' said the Chairman.

'No, not you, sir,' said No. 2 indulgently, 'I am referring to Mehta, the PA to the CA. He is a devotee. If the holy man makes a request, he cannot say no to him. He will smoothen our way to the CA. We have suffered some minor setbacks, but there is no reason for concern. BoB will continue to flourish under your capable stewardship. All I need is your permission to strike the necessary alliances.'

The Chairman reverentially held out a prawn cutlet to his brilliant henchman. They munched together in companiable silence, totting up revenue figures in their heads.

40

*'Original model outlet on the left, duplicate model
outlet on the right.'*

Banani was squatting on her haunches, buying bangles from a little girl with unnaturally large feet. The bangles were pretty. The child was dishing out some expert sales patter.

'Your arms are really strong, didi, see, you can wear bangles right up to your elbows.'

This was true. Years of wielding a rubber truncheon had toned her forearms, biceps and triceps.

'Mobile, mobile, mobile,' said a voice in her ear, 'mobile, mobile, mobile.'

Banani found herself squatting next to a disreputable man of indeterminate age. He drew some leaflets from his vest and spread them out like a fan. They were slightly sweaty. Banani was fundamentally law-abiding, but she couldn't help taking a look. She kept her voice down when she spoke, just in case.

'I need to make a phone call,' she whispered.

'Come,' said the man, springing to his feet, 'I will take you to Chatpat Singh.'

He disappeared into one of the lanes just next to the market with Banani hurrying after him. The lane grew progressively narrower, till Banani was almost walking sideways. The gutter was as wide as the lane, putting her sandals in jeopardy. At one point, the mobile man leaped nimbly over a young pig coming the other way, leaving Banani standing in front of it. The pig eyed her reproachfully before stepping into the gutter. Banani resumed pursuit. The pig rolled over on its back and sighed.

The lane opened up again, and she could see a little bit of sunlight. Suddenly there were tiny shops on either side, each one a little box in the wall, gaily painted and festooned with bunting, overflowing with mobile phones of every description. Banani felt like she was in the middle of a crime wave. She had never seen so many mobiles together in one place.

At the sight of her, the snoozing shopkeepers were galvanized into action. They rubbed their faces and hitched up their pants. They reached out their hands from both sides of the lane. Cries of 'Didi!', 'Genuine!' and '50 per cent discount for beautiful ladies!' rent the air. One of the men held out a phone. 'Auto-colour-changing panel, madam. Just see the beauty!' The phone shimmered eerily, changing from green to blue and back again. 'Didi! Change colour to match clothing! Matching handbag free!'

Banani paused. The handbag was nice too, and her old one was getting shabby . . .

The mobile man doubled back, took her by the elbow and dragged her away. 'You are Pintoo's local guardian,' he said seriously. Banani hadn't thought about it, but it was probably true. It couldn't be Tarun-da or the headmaster, they needed local guardians themselves. 'You will buy from Chatpat Singh directly. Best price! Full guarantee!'

Chatpat Singh turned out to be a bespectacled youth of around fourteen, wearing baggy shorts and a Nokia T-shirt. The T-shirt was a genuine antique. He sat on a wooden chair in the middle of a huge shed, playing a game on his mobile with intense concentration. All around him sat boys of various ages, hunched over little tables, fiddling with mobile phones. Light instrumental music played in the background. Fans whirred overhead. He ran a clean operation, unlike his deadly rival, Kader Khan. 'WE REPAIR ALL KINDZ OF MOBILE' said a sign on the wall.

'I got you a customer,' said the mobile man. 'She has a requirement.'

Chatpat Singh gave her a bright smile. 'Good afternoon,' he said, putting on a cap that said 'CP Mobile'. 'Welcome to CP Mobile. We cater to all your mobile requirements. Whatever your problem, one of our boys will find a solution. We can handle any model. Obsolete is not a word in our dictionary. Company service is on your left, CP service is on your right.'

'What's the difference between company service and CP service?' asked Banani.

'Company service is provided by the original manufacturer of your handset, while CP service is provided by CP,' said the young tycoon.

'So what's the difference?' asked Banani.

'Company people sit on the left, CP people sit on the right,' said Chatpat. 'Also the company people are wearing badges.'

Banani took a closer look. They were.

'Well, if you're so clever, you would have known that I don't have a mobile. I need to use one.'

'Then please proceed to the retail outlets in the back,' said Chatpat Singh. 'Original model outlet on the left, duplicate model outlet on the right. Both are equally good. It's a question of peace of mind.'

'I just want to make a phone call,' said Banani. 'Isn't there a public phone booth or something?'

'Ownership is much better in the long run,' said Chatpat Singh, 'otherwise you end up paying a lot of hidden costs.'

'Well, I can't get a SIM card anyway,' said Banani, 'my income level doesn't qualify.'

'The system is different here. We will get you an international SIM. That's what all of us use. The government cannot ban those. At CP Mobile you get bulk rates which are very reasonable.'

'How can I pay for an international SIM?'

'We have drop boxes all over Shanti Nagar. Customer service is our only passion.'

'Well, all right, I'll buy one,' said Banani. 'I think I'll buy the one you're using. But I'd like to try it once first.' All she needed to do was make one phone call.

Chatpat Singh knew when he was beaten. He took off his cap. 'What's the number?' he asked, not so corporate any more. Banani gave him Mrs Johnson's mobile number.

Mrs Johnson appeared on the screen. There was a dazed look in her slightly protruding eyes. She had a few hairs out of place. She peered near-sightedly at the screen.

Banani was clutching at straws. She suspected that Hemonto was out of mobile range, but she was hoping against hope. Pintoo had described the uncle he had sent to rescue Gandhi, but it wasn't as if Hemu was the only geek in Delhi. He was her geek, though, so while stopping Pintoo from blowing everyone up was her first priority, she had to spare some time to find her husband. Perhaps Pintoo was mixing him up with someone else. If he was still in Delhi, he was bound to go looking for her in school.

'Banani?' said Mrs Johnson. 'Where have you been?'

'I'm busy,' said Banani briefly. 'I had to leave in a hurry. Did Hemonto come looking for me?'

Mrs Johnson brought her phone very close to her face, which made her nose look unnaturally large.

'How do you discipline a parent?' asked Mrs Johnson.

When it came to problems, she tended to focus on her own.

'First, tell me about Hemonto,' said Banani.

'Haven't seen him,' said Mrs Johnson.

So that was that. Pintoo was probably telling the truth. Banani couldn't help feeling upset. First, he had set a homicidal policeman on her tail and then he had gone off to 1948, without even letting her know. Once she found him, she would have a few things to say.

'How do you discipline a parent?' repeated Mrs Johnson. Her urgency was genuine. She had never done it before, the school treated parents like paying customers, deserving of every solicitude that money could buy.

'Why do you need to discipline parents?' asked Banani. Such a need had never cropped up before. When children threw shoes at teachers, the school bought them new shoes. Even the parents who'd thrown a beer party for Class VI had been fully reimbursed.

'Do you remember a boy called Pappu Verma, from your class?'

'Maybe,' said Banani, carefully, sensing some blame coming her way.

'Well, do you know what your student has done?'

Banani braced herself.

'He grabbed a senior corporate executive by the balls, right in front of the Prime Minister!' said Mrs Johnson, and burst into tears.

'Someone must have told him to do it,'

'He hasn't done this to anyone before?'

'I would have noticed,' said Banani dryly.

'Why would anyone do such a thing?' wailed Mrs Johnson.

'Has he suffered from some kind of trauma recently?' she asked.

'No, nothing,' said Mrs Johnson, who didn't have the faintest clue.

'I'm fairly sure he has,' said Banani, 'I think you should try to find out.'

'What do I do with the parents?' asked Mrs Johnson, remaining focused on her primary problem. 'Can't you come and talk to them? You're so good at it. You know all the details, like their names, and their marks, and things like that.'

'I'm busy,' said Banani, thinking of Hemonto. Where was the poor man? What was he eating? How would he survive for more than twenty-four hours without his pyjamas?

'Look,' she said, 'you can't let this pass, or they'll be mooning the Republic Day parade next. You have to be tough with these parents. Accuse them of bad parenting. Tell them you know there's something going on with Pappu and then find out what it is.'

'But that's so rude! How can I talk to parents like that?'

'That's easy,' said Banani, 'just pretend they're teachers.'

❏

It was evening. Banani was sitting next to Pintoo on the porch.

'Can you see him?'

'Yes.'

'Is he all right?'

Pintoo closed his eyes.

'He's going into a police station. He doesn't look happy, but he doesn't look scared.'

Mr Chatterjee was about to officially warn the police about the threat to Gandhi's life, after which he was hoping they would leap into action in one fluid motion, like the gazelles on the National Geographic channel.

'Can you bring him back?'

'I don't know.'

'Will you please try?'

'From tomorrow.'

He knew he could do something about it, but right now he was busy looking back over the years and listening. Tarun-da and the headmaster had taught him a lot about history, but the best way to learn history was to watch it happening.

41

'Was it recently you got hit on the head,
or was it a long time ago?'

The first man Mr Chatterjee asked for directions to a police station tried to sell him a house. He was completely nondescript in his crumpled white dhoti and kurta and certainly didn't look like a plutocrat. He was a middleman, a son of the soil, the eternal backbone of Delhi.

'Very good house, sir,' said the agent, whispering. 'Going cheap. Five-bedroom, British-style bungalow, price includes maali, cook and driver, although security guard has unfortunately disappeared. Cook can cook continental also, which looking at you I'm thinking you will like. House belonged to Mohamedan gorment officer, now lying vacant. Only one-two such properties are left, Hindu gorment babus have mostly picked up, but this one we kept for good buyers. Why should gorment babus get everything? You also deserve a home, no?'

Possession was immediate, apparently. All he had to do was walk in. Mr Chatterjee had no doubt that as they spoke the exact same thing was happening across the border.

'But how do you know I can afford a brand-new house near India Gate, even if it's going cheap?' asked Mr Chatterjee.

The agent smiled, amused by his humility. 'Arrey, sir, you are wearing English-type clothes, that too of very good quality. Anyone can see you are a big man. Not only that, you are asking me how to go to police station. Whoever goes to police station, unless policemen take them there? All us small people, we stay as far away from police station as possible, no good can come from visiting. But you, sir, you are smiling sweetly and asking, "Which way to the police station?" as if it's a horticultural garden. Obviously you are a big man, that's why I'm offering you a house that's suitable for your status. In case you're hesitating because it's a Mohammedan house, I can put you in touch with my cousin. He knows a priest who can speak very fast. The ceremony will be quick.'

Mr Chatterjee was both repulsed and reassured by this. On the one hand, it was reassuring to know that he looked like a person of status. Perhaps people would be more likely to pay attention to what he had to say. Given what he had to do, credibility was key. On the other hand, it seemed he looked like someone who would happily participate in a gruesome and reprehensible housing scam. He noticed that his friendly companion had carefully avoided mentioning whether the previous owner was recently deceased, or had merely emigrated to Pakistan. On the whole, he was better off not knowing.

'Look,' he said, 'I am very grateful for this hot tip you are giving me.

But first, let me finish my business with the police, then maybe I will come and see your property.'

The agent shook his head. There was no reasoning with a madman. He gave him directions to the nearest police station and they parted as friends.

Five minutes later, sitting in front of a bemused sub-inspector, Mr Chatterjee was overwhelmed by a feeling of déjà vu. Everything was eerily reminiscent of his first meeting with Pande at the Safdarjung Enclave police station which was where all of this had started. The same grimy table, covered in files. The same crime chart with illegible chalk scribbles on it. The same wanted posters—carefully designed to ensure that absconding criminals were completely unrecognizable. The same rickety fan, rotating asymmetrically on a long, creaky pole. The same paan-stained walls. He half expected to find Pande sitting in front of him, and in truth, the officer on duty was strikingly similar, with a spectacular paunch and a general air of lazy menace.

Maybe they'll have a rate card, thought Mr Chatterjee hopefully. He'd always heard that the British were efficient. Maybe they had a proper system with fixed prices. That would make his life so much simpler. What was the going rate for preventing the assassination of the Father of the Nation, though? It was a hard thing to put a price to. And how on earth was he going to broach the subject? Mr Chatterjee knew what would happen if he told them the truth, that he had been sent from the future by a twelve-year-old, and was armed with information about future murder cases. He would be dragged off to the nearest asylum, no questions asked.

The sub-inspector was eying him warily, equally puzzled. He had never had a rich person sit in front of his desk before. Rich people followed simple rules in Delhi. Rich people called up the commissioner, who called up the deputy commissioner, who called up the SP, who called up the SHO, who came into his room and kicked him on the backside and told him to do whatever the rich people wanted him to do. That was the natural order of things. Why on earth was this man sitting in front of him like this? Did he not have a telephone? Was he perhaps recently arrived from some far-off place like Burma, and unaware of the system?

The only explanation was that he was insane. The sub-inspector had an elderly uncle back in his village who was insane, so he knew how to deal with such people. The trick was to humour them and in case they got violent, to knock them senseless with a quick blow to the head. Sometimes they had to be tied up. He kept one hand under the table, surreptitiously clutching his lathi.

'What service can I do for you, Your Lordship?' he asked, smiling his most charming smile.

'I have news about Gandhi,' said Mr Chatterjee cautiously.

'Ahh,' said the sub-inspector appreciatively, putting on an improbably attentive expression.

'He is going to die soon,' said Mr Chatterjee hoarsely.

'Well, Bapu is an old man,' said the sub-inspector, indulgently, 'he has lived a long and fruitful life. All of us must die eventually.'

'No, no,' said Mr Chatterjee. 'They're going to kill him.'

'Achcha,' said the sub-inspector, approximating concern. 'Who are these badmashes who would do such a thing?'

'It's the RSS,' said Mr Chatterjee, wishing he had paid more attention in history class. 'There's a man called Godse, plus there were two others. I can't remember their names.'

The sub-inspector was sympathetic. 'That's only natural,' he said. 'Was it recently you got hit on the head, or was it a long time ago? Would you like me to hit you on the head again?' he added hopefully. 'Sometimes a second blow is beneficial in cases of memory loss.'

'Nathuram!' said Mr Chatterjee, remembering. 'His name is Nathuram Godse. He's going to kill Gandhi.'

The sub-inspector pretended to think about this.

'Well, there's a Nathuram who lives just down the road,' he said eventually, 'but he's not a murderer. He makes sweets. His laddoos are very good. Of course, if his laddoos were stale, and he gifted a box to Gandhiji, then perhaps . . . but even then, Bapu would get food poisoning, I think. It wouldn't kill him. Don't worry, I'll have a word with Nathuram. If he gives any laddoos to Bapu, I'll make sure they're fresh.'

Mr Chatterjee could see he wasn't getting through. This was not how he had envisaged the situation playing out. On the bright side, he wasn't being instantly institutionalized, or chucked into a jail cell. But somehow, this was worse.

'There is a conspiracy to kill Gandhi,' he said urgently. 'Nathuram

Godse is involved, plus one other Godse, plus a third person who's name I can't remember. Also Sardar Patel!' he added, with a burst of inspiration, remembering dark suspicions his grandfather had expressed about the Home Minister when he was a child.

The sub-inspector frowned. He was beginning to revise his opinion. Was the man drunk? He didn't smell like it. But he had heard that rich people drank special kinds of rare, expensive alcohol, which had no smell.

'Your Lordship,' he said sternly, 'are you suggesting that the Home Minister of India is involved in a conspiracy to assassinate the Father of the Nation?'

'No, no,' said Mr Chatterjee, 'perhaps I got that part wrong. It was Savarkar who was the leader, plus somebody from the RSS. They are all from Maharashtra.'

'I see,' said the sub-inspector, gravely, pretending to make a note. 'Then the matter is simple. There are not many Maharashtrians in Delhi. As soon as I come across some, I will arrest them. Then Bapu will be safe. If they are still in Bombay, then the matter is not under my jurisdiction. It's for the Bombay police to take action. I can send them a note, of course, but they will ignore it. They always do. But if these Maharashtrians are in Delhi, don't worry. You take it that the matter is taken care of.'

'They'll shoot him with a pistol,' said Mr Chatterjee desperately. 'His last words will be "He Ram".'

The sub-inspector made a note of this. 'Understood,' he said, crisply. 'Maharashtrian. Carrying pistol. Devotee of Rama. Nothing could be simpler. We'll arrest him in the next hour or two. Would you like me to arrest Sardar Patel also, or should we let him be for now?'

It was time to give up.

'No, that's OK,' he said numbly.

'Any other service I can provide you, Your Lordship?' the sub-inspector asked, quite pleased with the way he had handled the whole thing. He relaxed his grip on the lathi.

'No, thank you,' said Mr Chatterjee. They shook hands. Mr Chatterjee left the police station.

From the point at which his life had taken a sharp left turn into the richly bizarre, all he had done was stumble from Point A to Point B, and thence to Point C, and so on and so forth. He was lost without Banani.

She usually told him what to do. But if he wanted to see her again, he had to take charge now. He was going to find a park. He was going to sit on a bench. He was going to think. The police were going to be no help. It wasn't so different from home, after all.

42

'I will get the Dalai Lama's statue polished and inform the Ministry of Information and Broadcasting.'

The Competent Authority was gazing adoringly at the PM while she went through the file he had just placed on her table. He had placed it slightly out of reach, which had forced her to bend forward and allowed him to take a deep breath of her perfume. He was holding his breath for as long as he possibly could, savouring her heavenly aroma and going slightly pink in the process.

The PM suppressed a shudder and thought wistfully of her formidable ancestress, who was famous for being able to reduce men to mush with a single glare. A British interviewer who had dared to question one of her decisions had received such a tongue-lashing that he had never had an erection for the rest of his life. People across the nation still spoke in whispers in front of her photograph. Several of her ministers had worn adult diapers throughout their ministerial careers, and in some cases, beyond. She had been frequently mocked at the beginning of her career, and she had carefully noted each and every mocker. When the time came, she had systematically and ruthlessly crushed each and every one of them, doing it so thoroughly that not even their memories had remained to mock her; till one day, when she looked around her, all she saw was a sea of quivering sycophants, and that was pleasing to her.

Well, there was good and bad in everyone, and over the years, people had come to have rather mixed feelings about her. Personally, the PM remembered her as affectionate, but busy. The one thing she was sure of was that she wouldn't have been sitting here being sniffed by a civil servant.

The PM flipped through the file, trying to lean back in her chair as far as she possibly could. It was the Alternate Chair proposal, which her PA had already heard about from Mehta and passed along to her, but she pretended she was seeing it for the first time.

He hadn't really come about the Alternate Chair proposal, of course. He needed her help to create a diplomatic incident with China. But he was good with women, and he knew that, being a woman, she would be entertained by a discussion about furniture, which would enable him to enjoy her invigorating presence just that little while longer.

The PM looked up at him, relieved to see that he was no longer having one of his usual fits or seizures.

'So what do *you* think of the Alternate Chair proposal?' she asked.

'A shining example of innovation in governance,' replied the CA.

The Alternate Chair proposal was a brilliant new scheme to help the government grow smoothly. While the need for more civil servants was growing by the day, space was a constraint. One of the bright young sparks in the CA's office had come up with the excellent idea of hiring two bureaucrats for every chair, and having them come to office on alternate days. This way, each government office could have twice the number of officers.

The CA had been enchanted by both the simplicity and cost-effectiveness of the proposal. His only misgiving pertained to the chair-sharing aspect. After all, the power of every government officer came from his chair. If each officer was given 50 per cent less access to his chair, would this weaken him in some mysterious and unforeseen way? Would enough power, knowledge and authority still rub off onto his bum to enable him to perform adequately?

It was a question that had caused the CA several sleepless nights, but in the end, the prospect of doubling his empire at a single stroke had been too delicious to ignore.

'Do we really have the money to hire so many extra officers?' asked the PM dubiously. 'Why not reduce them? Couldn't people work a little harder instead?'

'No, no, madam,' said the CA, aghast at this unholy twist to the conversation. 'Our people work long hours under inhuman conditions and face frequent assaults from the public. How much more can they do? The Bureau of Reconstruction in particular needs to expand, as I foresee a lot of reconstruction in the near future. A few other ministries need people too, such as tourism.'

'But we don't have any tourism!' protested the PM.

'All the more reason for us to prepare thoroughly for when we will,' said the CA. 'However, we *could* make a few cuts in the Foreign Ministry.'

The CA was extremely annoyed with the foreign secretary who had been unable to mould the world according to his wishes, despite repeated instructions and frequent guidelines. The foreign secretary's excuse was that the foreign minister had never travelled more than two hundred miles from his hometown of Nagpur, and thought Tokyo was a type of attaché case. The CA had pointed out that several US presidents had been very similar and you never heard any of their staff whining about it.

The PM signed the file and waited for the CA to get to the point. The General had already called her and warned her that the CA was up to no good, and practically begged her to buy him some time. She had promised to try, but once the CA was riding a hobbyhorse, unhorsing him was no easy task.

'I want you to insult the Chinese,' said the CA.

The PM raised an eyebrow.

'Am I allowed to do that?' she asked.

The CA simpered coyly. 'The PM is allowed to do whatever she wishes,' he said.

'And why do you want me to insult the Chinese?' she asked.

'Who am I to want you to do anything?' said the CA, humbly. 'It is the nation that requires this of you.'

'Okay, then,' said the PM, 'why does the nation require me to insult the Chinese?'

'The Chinese have committed acts of telepathic aggression,' said the CA, 'as a prelude to military action. The evidence will soon be in my hands. We must show them that we are not afraid of them by insulting them. We must cause them to lose face. Once they see we are fearless, they will be too scared to attack. We will then be free to finish off our little local action against the Protectorate. The Chinese must be kept on the back foot. On behalf of the nation, you must be obnoxious.'

'Did you have any specific insults in mind?' asked the PM, fascinated.

'Of course, of course,' said the CA, glad to see she was coming around, 'I have made a list, so you can choose your favourite.' He took a small piece of paper out of his pocket, and fished out his reading glasses.

'The first option, and possibly the best, is to unveil a statue of His Holiness the Dalai Lama in front of India Gate,' he said. 'I have had a statue made especially and kept ready, for just such an occasion. Your love for art and culture is well known, so you would come across as a truly cultured person, while insulting the Chinese at the same time. It's a very nice statue. He looks very holy.'

'But the last real Dalai Lama died years ago. The new one only lasted a few days. Dharamsala was one of the first places they blew up in the last war. And only about 20 per cent of the people in Tibet are Tibetan these days. Do the Chinese really care any more?'

'Oh, they very much care,' said the CA. 'For one thing, the pacification of South Tibet is running behind schedule. Joy has not been unconfined.'

'What other insults do you have on your list?' asked the PM.

'Well, we could sabotage their bid for the Olympic Games. They desperately need another one. People are getting restless.'

'What else?' asked the PM.

'We could send a strongly worded accusation, alleging that the Maoist rebels in our country are inspired by Chairman Mao.'

'Aren't they?' asked the PM, now genuinely puzzled.

'Yes, of course they are,' said the CA, 'but we're not supposed to say that. We've pretended there's no connection for sixty years.'

The sheer variety of schemes was impressive.

'Did you think up all of these yourself?' she asked.

The CA smiled modestly. 'I may have helped with one or two. Which one do you like best?'

'None of them,' said the PM, crushingly. 'Why don't we just support independence for Taiwan?'

The CA was shocked. Such haste was unseemly.

'They would launch a nuclear strike immediately. It is the one subject on which they will brook no argument.'

'Well, I don't like any of the others,' said the PM. He could ask his hellish minions to cook up some more.

'Madam,' said the CA, 'I must insist that you choose an insult. The nation requires you to do this. I will wait here quietly while you give the matter more thought.'

The PM sighed. The General had asked her to hold him off, but when did the CA ever listen to anything she said?

'Let's do the Dalai Lama thing then,' she said, judging that this would be the least offensive.

The CA beamed.

'So now that I've agreed, let me get this straight,' asked the PM, 'you think, if we put up a statue of the Dalai Lama, the Chinese are going to be too scared to declare war?'

'With the Chinese, anything is possible,' said the CA. 'Besides, we don't want to fight a war. We just want to show them we are not afraid, so they don't attack us.'

'Shouldn't we be afraid? They're about fifty years ahead of us!'

'Evolution is not everything,' said the CA, cut to the quick. 'Plus, we are on the verge of full reconstruction!'

'So basically, we want to prevent them from attacking us by doing things that will provoke them into attacking us?' asked the PM. She could feel her head spin, which was how she always felt at some point during any meeting with the CA.

Despite the allure of her fragrance, the CA was beginning to find the PM annoying.

'Madam, trained professionals have considered these matters long and hard before reaching these conclusions. I will get the Dalai Lama's statue polished and inform the Ministry of Information and Broadcasting. They will let you know when and where you will be required.'

He waddled off grumpily, clutching his list. The nation deserved to see better leaders. There was no question. When the time was ripe, he would reveal himself to the public, in all his glory. The process had already been initiated. The phrase 'Competent Authority' was now featuring far more regularly in notices, billboards and press releases. He would have to avoid anything overtly dictatorial, of course, like an oddly shaped moustache, or a throne. But the wheels were in motion. He had momentary pangs at the thought of betraying his beloved, but if she was going to be annoying, then she deserved it. He closed the door behind him with a bang.

So now the CA had his diplomatic incident, thought the PM, and they were all one step closer to the edge. Fat lot of good she had been. The General would be ashamed of her. But at least she had managed to talk to Bijli Bose, using an untapped line at the Bengal High Commission. As usual, he had been full of suggestions. There were others she could talk to who might help her come up with ideas to thwart the CA's plans.

He could smell her all he liked, but the Competent Authority was going to discover that this rose had thorns.

43

'We make bombs for Hindus also.
Our products are equally effective on both.'

A line of Muslim League volunteers was marching down the narrow lane, waving their fists and brandishing freshly printed green flags.

'Pakistan! Pakistan! We'll fight and we'll get Pakistan!' they roared.

A small group of Hindu boys glowered resentfully as they marched past. One of them was rolling up his sleeves, but the others were holding him back. All that was needed for the situation to explode was a tiny little spark. People were peering down from the rickety balconies above, and how long before someone got the bright idea of dropping something on the marchers' heads?

However, Ali's new friends didn't seem too concerned and continued towards the Matongini Mess. Just then they saw the old man waving his crutch and cursing, a solitary figure in a tattered British uniform, walking towards the mob.

'IF NETAJI WAS HERE, HE WOULD KICK ALL YOUR BACKSIDES!' he roared.

'Hang on a minute,' said Ali to his new buddies. He hurried over to where the old man had planted himself in the middle of the road, directly in the way of the procession. Ali grabbed hold of his elbow but the old man shrugged him away.

'Islam is in danger!' said a voice from the approaching mob.

'As if Islam is a child's toy,' said the veteran, 'that any bloody fool can endanger it!' He was wheezing a little from all the yelling.

The mob was very close now. Ali braced himself and considered his options. He was unarmed so he didn't have too many. He could whip out his Pocket PC and play a video of Osama Bin Laden, but he wasn't sure how much good that would do. He could have scrambled their brains with his ultrasonic brain scrambler, but he had exchanged it years ago for a washing machine, making himself cleaner, but less lethal. He stepped in front of the old man and balanced on his toes, getting ready to drop kick the leader in the Adam's apple, cursing himself for becoming a slave to technology, and wishing his jeans weren't quite so tight.

The mob simply went around them, paying them little heed. A few boys threw the old man ironic salutes, and performed a goose-step or two. None of them touched him. Not all the salutes were ironic. The old man spat at them. He gave them the old battle cry of the Indian National Army. 'Jai Hind!' he roared, waving his crutch defiantly, looking small and lonely. Ali dropped a coin in his begging bowl.

'British not paying your pension, sir?' he asked, sympathetically.

'They called me a traitor and stopped my pension,' said the man hotly. 'I am no traitor! It is they who betrayed us, letting our families starve while we fought for them. Anyway, let Netaji come back. Then we will be free, and I will get my pension, and a medal from the government.'

Even though Subhash Chandra Bose had been officially declared dead over six months ago, Ali was yet to come across a single person in Calcutta who referred to him in the past tense.

'I have to get back to my friends,' said Ali, 'but try not to be so reckless, uncle. The times are not good.'

Ali followed the hard man and the trainee up the narrow, dingy stairs of Matongini Mess. Since time immemorial, young men from all over Bengal had yanked themselves away from their mothers, come to Calcutta, and stayed in messes. They were labyrinthine buildings with an inexhaustible supply of poky little rooms, common bathrooms tastefully appointed with a hole, bucket and mug, besides endless balconies to hang dhotis from. The inhabitants of these buildings were either students, or office babus, or unemployed, along with the odd gentleman of leisure with no particular goal in life. Most of them were poets. They were painfully thin, with concave chests, thin, scrawny necks, and disproportionately large heads. It was like living in the middle of a lollipop convention. Ennui was rampant. Eyesight was poor. Tuberculosis was widespread.

The dining room was dank, the walls sticky with cooking oil and grime. Mashima, the chubby and forbidding auntie who presided over this wheezy flock, spent so much time cooking that it left her with very little time for cleaning. As soon as she finished preparing and serving a meal, she'd begin the next one. Her husband was fond of the races and she needed the income. He also spent a fortune on canvas running shoes, although he never actually did any running.

Three young men were at one of the tables, having breakfast, which consisted of rice as hard as Japanese bullets, a bowl of watery dal and a single piece of fish. 'Juice, mashima,' murmured one of them, and she grudgingly poured him a libation of pungent, oily gravy.

The hard man, who was called Robi, introduced them. 'Bhanu, Johor and Chinmoy,' he said, 'and you've already met Topen,' indicating the young man Ali had saved from blowing himself up. 'We are the Very New Young Men's Bodybuilding Society, dedicated to facilitating violence against oppressors.'

They didn't look like they did much bodybuilding. Johor was cuddly. Bhanu and Chinmoy were skeletal. Topen was tall, cheerful and radiantly good-natured. Robi told them why Ali was here. They sat down together at the table.

'I have a poem,' announced Bhanu. He'd just finished it and didn't like to keep his public waiting. His ambition was to drink himself to death, like his idol Devdas, but he couldn't afford it yet. While he was waiting for his economic circumstances to improve, he was composing long and passionate odes to a purely hypothetical loved one who was probably Madhubala. He unfolded a large sheet of paper. 'Shhh! Not in class!' said Johor. Bhanu put the paper away.

Ali felt the old familiar rush that he always did when he was moulding young minds. He smilingly waved away the little bowl of fish being offered by mashima, who had a high regard for professors, and was conscious of their need for brain food. The faces of his old students, now mostly vaporized, floated in front of his eyes. Simple village lads, they'd been sold by their parents. Suicide bombing was a vertically integrated industry in Waziristan. Villagers in that part of the world provided both the hardware—in the form of belts, bearings and detonators, and the software—in the form of their sons. This was the local equivalent.

He held up the grenade that he had taken from Topen on their way to the mess.

'What is this?'

The trainee terrorists looked at each other, puzzled. Was this a trick question? They were already suspicious about this new instructor whom Robi da had suddenly foisted on them. He looked just like a local person, what could he know about terrorism? Had he been a retired Russian anarchist, the kind of instructor they secretly longed for, it would have been different. Someone cultured and historical, who would tell them inspiring stories, supply them philosophical ammunition, and shower them with anecdotes and esoterica. Robi-da was too strict and frankly, not very cultured.

'Most people think of this as a grenade,' said Ali, 'but you can also use it as the main component in an IED, which is what we're going to talk about today.'

His student body perked up. This was the challenging part. He had to give them some information, but he had no intention of making them any more lethal than they already were.

'An IED is an improvized explosive device, typically used against vehicles. The first rule to remember about using an IED is, don't blow yourself up.'

This was new. There had never been much emphasis on self-preservation at the Very New Young Men's Bodybuilding Society.

'It's pretty simple. If you don't blow yourself up along with the bomb, you can blow someone up again tomorrow. What you need is a trigger, so that the bomb and you are not in the same place when it detonates. There are five ways to trigger an IED. You can use remote control, infra-red, magnetic, pressure-sensitive, or tripwires. We'll be working mainly with tripwires.'

Technological options were a little limited here. He'd asked about hot spots, but no one had been able to help, except one slightly exhausted man who had directed him to Sonagachhi where all the working girls lived.

'So remember the first rule, lads. When it comes to IEDs—we want you in one piece. What if I don't have any tripwire, you may ask, does it mean I have to stop blowing people up altogether? This is where the Molotov cocktail comes in.'

The Molotov cocktail wasn't any more lethal than any bomb these young revolutionaries would know about so it was okay to talk about it; importantly, it had only recently been invented so it would hold their interest.

'You pour petrol in a bottle, put in a fuse and throw it, I think,' said Robi.

'It works best with a mixture of kerosene and petrol,' said Ali quickly, 'plus a small amount of egg whites, animal blood, tyre tubing, motor oil, or sugar. It makes it sticky, and concentrates impact.'

'Russians are always the best at bomb-making,' supplied Topen happily.

'It's Finnish, actually,' said Ali, unable to resist. 'The Finns used it *against* the Russians, who were practicing on the Finns before they attacked other people, since they were small and lived next door. When someone asked the Russian called Molotov, what about all these bombs you're dropping on Finland, he said, they're not bombs, they're food packets. So the Finns called them Molotov Breadbaskets. Then a Finnish professor invented this bomb made from liquid, and they said it was a drink to go with Mr Molotov's food, and they called it the Molotov Cocktail. So it wasn't really discovered by Molotov, or named in his honour. It was aimed at him.'

'Russians drink petrol?' asked Johor, perplexed.

I need to drop the clever stories, thought Ali, and stick to blowing up things.

'Let's move on to a field exercise,' he said. 'I'm going to teach you the basic principles of infiltration. We're going to infiltrate a terrorist cell. I hear the Muslim League is planning something on Direct Action Day. Our job is to get in. Anyone who can lay his hands on any plans or blueprint gets extra marks.'

'You could go with Topen next time he makes a delivery,' said Robida.

'Excuse me?' said Ali.

'The Muslim League only pours the kerosene. They don't light the fire. It's Suhrawardy's goondas who will do everything. He used them to steal the election. He'll use them on Direct Action Day. We know all of them. We make bombs for them. This is fundamentally an economic activity for all concerned. That's why we're called the Very New Young Men's Bodybuilding Society. Everyone knows bodybuilders are good at making bombs. It gives us credibility. That's why we're so keen you instruct us. It keeps us at the forefront of knowledge. What Bengal thinks today, India thinks tomorrow!'

'But you boys are Hindus! How can you make bombs for the Muslim League?'

'Don't worry,' said Robi, seeing that Ali had misunderstood the situation. 'We make bombs for the Hindus also. Our products are equally effective on both.'

'So you're doing this for the money,' said Ali.

'It's going to be a long war,' said Robi, 'we will need the money to fight it.'

'But the British are going soon,' said Ali.

'Yes, they are and we will hurry them on their way. But their servants will still be here. It will be their Raj now. They are duplicates of the British, except that whatever are the few redeeming virtues of the British, those they do not have. True freedom will come when we eliminate them all. Right now they are fighting over who will get what. What do you think Direct Action Day is all about? The forces of feudalism will savage each other like wolves fighting over a piece of meat. We are helping reduce their ranks so that our job is easier later.'

'But you'll kill a lot of innocent people,' said Ali.

They'll never stop fighting, he thought. They'll all have their reasons. They're all going to die cursing each other till the very moment the bombs drop and the hot wind snatches away their breath.

'People die in revolutions,' said Robi pleasantly.

'Sure they do,' Ali said, not wanting to get into a pointless debate, 'but I'd still like to meet the Muslim League. If you really want me to help you, I need to understand your customers better.'

44

'This boy has emerged as a Rajnikanth!'

I should have stayed with the Manipur Rifles, thought the Medical Military Commando as he flew backwards through the air. He hit the barrier and stuck to the barbed wire, about six feet up from the ground. He found himself right next to one of his comrades, who hung limply, eyes staring, little pools of sweat collecting in his plexiglass visor. His fear shone brightly in the headlights of the RMV parked just behind the barrier. It was a six-wheeled behemoth, shiny white with a huge red cross and machine guns at the front and rear. It bore no logos or insignia. The

Bank of Bodies preferred not to use it as an advertising medium. Across the barrier, beyond the open ground of the transit zone, the SDF boys were setting up a bazooka on a nearby roof. They raised a cheer as another of the Medical Military Commandos went flying through the air. This one did a little backflip before he hit the barrier. Pintoo was improving with practice and he was adding little flourishes to please the crowd.

'Perhaps we could sell tickets,' said Tarun-da, 'and raise some much needed revenue. My available budget is rather low.'

His available budget was zero. No one ever gave Tarun-da any money. The people of his locality didn't mind voting for him since it seemed to make him happy, but there was no way they were paying him anything. The way they saw it, public servants were just like public toilets—free for all and slightly stinky.

The rest of the MMC squad were huddled together, backs to the checkpoint, cowering behind their shields. They were too scared to raise their rifles. They were hardened veterans with nursing degrees, handpicked from government hospitals across the nation for their ferocity, but this was like trampoline practice without a trampoline. If this could happen to them for merely entering Shanti Nagar, what would they incur if they shot someone? They had no desire to find out. They were going to hang around just long enough to make it look like they had tried.

'Sixer! Sixer! Sixer!' chanted the crowds from the roofs all around.

Pintoo stepped out. He focused on a commando. He closed his eyes. He held out his hand in a dramatic gesture. He didn't really need to do this, but it looked much cooler. It was only a matter of time before he started wearing his underwear over his pants. Pintoo made a magic move, and the commando flew up in the air. He soared over the transit zone, arms and legs flapping in a grotesque parody of flight, cleared the barbed wire barrier, and landed on the roof of the RMV, right in front of the rear machine gun. The machine gunner leaped up, jumped out, hit the ground, and ran. The crowd roared again. Someone started bursting firecrackers. From the distance came the faint sound of dhols.

Pintoo took hold of another commando and raised him vertically in the air before making him pirouette like a ballet dancer. Then he let go of him abruptly and the man crashed back amongst his huddled buddies.

'This boy has emerged as a Rajnikanth!' said one of the spectators admiringly.

The survivors of the collection squad were inching back step by step, still on their haunches, but the gate was far away. They had charged in confidently as usual and were already halfway through the transit zone before the involuntary flying lessons had started. Some of them, who had heard vaguely of the havoc some kid had created in a BoB branch began to put two and two together but by then it was far too late. One of them now stood up and raised his hands. He was unarmed, and wore a surgeon's smock and rubber gloves. He realized that he was holding a scalpel in one of his raised hands. He looked at it, as if in astonishment, and quickly handed it over to an equally astonished commando.

'Little boy, please let me go,' he said, 'I'm a doctor. I abhor violence. I'm very sympathetic towards slum people. If you want, I can provide almost free treatment before I leave. I do this regularly, to help the public.'

Everyone fell silent, including the dhol players. Pintoo looked at him closely. His stump was throbbing, as if his missing hand was trying to tell him something. The doctor wore the same green cap and the same green mask. The scalpel he had just disposed of looked just the same. His smock was just as blood-stained and his boots were just as shiny and black.

Banani put a hand on Pintoo's shoulder. 'Let me take care of all of them,' she said.

She stepped forward. She closed her eyes. She held out her hand, palm upwards. The doctor and the rest of the MMC squad froze. What powers did this woman have? Had everyone in Shanti Nagar been blessed by the divine? Would flames shoot out of her fingertips? Would she massacre them with her mind? Would she magically transform them into eunuchs, in honour of Shanti-bai?

'Please, Owneress, have mercy on us,' begged one of them, 'take the doctor instead. He's the real badmaash. He knows how to read and write. We're just poor village boys with no brains. We do whatever they tell us to, because our families need to eat.'

Banani lowered her superpowered hand. 'Will you do whatever *I* tell you to?'

They nodded fearfully.

'Stand up,' ordered Banani, 'and drop your weapons.'

They dropped their weapons.

'Now drop your pants. All the way. Down to your ankles. Good. Now run away from this place, and never come back!'

The commandos hobbled off with their pants around their ankles, the crowd jeering them on their way. The doctor had a BoB logo on his underwear, a cartoon bulldozer with a big, happy smile. Little children started throwing stones. Some SDF boys darted in and scooped up the discarded weapons. The dhol players drummed up a crescendo. The MMC squad struggled back into the RMV. Once they were in, it reversed up the narrow lane, back into New New Delhi, where everyone knew their place and a rifle butt was enough to keep them there. The machine guns on top of the RMV were gone. The SDF boys had removed them, along with the ammunition. Someone had artistically modified the red cross, so that it now had blood dripping from it.

Shanti Nagar erupted with joy. People came out on the streets, cheering, hugging each other and screaming themselves hoarse. Cries of 'Pintoo Baba Zindabad!' rent the air. Even the workers from the mini foundries gathered, blinking in the unfamiliar sunlight. They worked double shifts and hardly anyone had ever seen them outdoors in the daytime.

'Auntie, that was brilliant!' said one of the SDF officers. 'You snatched away their izzat. They can never come back.'

Banani scowled. She didn't like people calling her auntie.

Another soldier ruffled Pintoo's hair. 'Thanks to this champion, we can drive away the body-snatchers anytime they come.'

'Why just drive them out, we can follow them,' said the officer.

'We can take over their head office and drag the big bosses out of their rooms.'

'We can make them give back what they stole.'

'An eye for an eye!'

'A hand for a hand!'

'Let's also go to the Dead Circle and pick up some TV sets!'

'Mutton stew from Karim's.'

'Silk saris from Nalli!'

'Handicrafts from GK II!'

'Smart cars from Defence Colony!'

'To Delhi!'

'To Delhi!'

It was a familiar cry, uttered by many over the years.

Banani was appalled. They were progressing from underdogs to overlords with dizzying speed.

'Shut up!' she said, using her best juvenile-management voice. The SDF boys subsided, and came sharply to attention. They recognized top brass when they saw it. The invasion of Delhi was going to have to wait. Banani grabbed Pintoo by the shoulders and pulled him forward.

'Does he look like a security guard to you?' she demanded. 'He's a child. Do you think we're going to waste him so you can play Age of Empires?'

'His power belongs to all. He should do what is best for all,' said the officer. He remained at attention, eyes straight ahead. They could hear the roars of the crowd in the background. No one had ever roared for them before.

'Let Shanti-bai decide that,' said Banani, in a burst of inspiration, 'we'll take him to her first thing in the morning. Do you have any objection to that? Or would you rather march to Rashtrapati Bhavan right now?'

The soldiers shook their heads. No one messed with Shanti-bai. She didn't need superpowers. Her tongue was enough. Banani looked at Pintoo, who was grinning at a girl on a nearby balcony and flexing his bicep.

'As for you, young man, isn't there something you promised to do for me?'

Pintoo nodded.

'You vanished my husband without his permission. You didn't even give him time to pack his pyjamas. Now you have to find a way of getting him back. Follow me!'

Banani marched off. Pintoo followed her meekly. The soldiers broke up and joined the party in the streets. It would go on till dawn.

❑

Balaji the Fixer was the first one to find out. His tentacles ran deep. Even his moles had moles, and none of them trusted each other. He called No. 2 immediately.

'Sir, that child I was telling you about, he made an entire MMC squad fly out of Shanti Nagar!'

No. 2 was at the Annual PETA Fashion Show. As part of its corporate social responsibility programme, the Bank of Bodies sponsored it every year. PETA had widespread support amongst the glitterati.

Shovon Chowdhury

'Did we provide them with any form of aerial transport?' asked No. 2, just to make sure.

'No, sir, he made them fly like birds with his mind! He removed their trousers in mid-air!'

A girl in an asparagus bikini was walking down the ramp. No. 2 hated coming to these things. He was always haunted by the fact that someone might have peed in the champagne. But he knew he wouldn't have to stay for more than half an hour. Soon, the lust-crazed sons of politicians and policemen would leap on stage, maddened by all the model flesh, after which all hell would break loose and he would be able to make a quiet exit. Some of them were already getting restless, and fingering their revolvers.

A man strode out wearing an anti-radiation codpiece fashioned out of half a coconut shell. The rich boys subsided a bit, intimidated by how buff he was, and sucked in their stomachs self-consciously. He was quickly followed by a girl in a negligée made out of lettuce.

No. 2 pushed his way to the exit, through the panting crowds, his mind working quickly as he tried to figure out what to do next. They would have to get to the kid right away, he thought, plus they would have to get in touch with the godman. 'This means we need to speed up things with Guru Dharti Pakar,' he told Balaji. 'Have you fixed him up yet?'

'Sir, that type of fixing you will need to do personally,' said Balaji, sheepishly. 'I have lined up everything. A small darshan from the Chairman is also required.'

'Set it up,' snapped No. 2.

As he stepped into his limousine a single shot rang out followed by screams. It sounded like the party had started.

45

'If you have no electricity, you can always use a car battery.'

The terrified taxi driver drove Pande right up to the doorstep of the police station and held open the door as he stepped out.

'You can get lost now,' said Pande by way of thanks.

Home again! For Pande, joy was an unfamiliar emotion, except when he was beating someone up. Yet here, in a totally non-violent context, he could feel it. He had been wrenched from his roots, and dragged through slums, and flung through time and space by capricious divinities. He had been spat on by scum and preyed on by those who should have been his natural prey. Terrorizing the passengers of the taxi had mitigated the pain to some extent, but now, at last, he could feel the true healing begin. The same old frayed underwear hanging from drooping washing lines. That old familiar atmosphere, an unforgettable cocktail of fear and loathing, fatigue and despair, urine and sweat, apathy and menace. He was home. He could feel his batteries recharging. He smiled.

The constable on guard flipped him a salute as he bounded up the stairs, and Pande saluted right back. 'Is the Small Babu in?' he asked. The Big Babu was the officer-in-charge, the monarch of all he surveyed. The Small Babu was the senior sub-inspector, Pande's counterpart, and the man who was really in charge. The guard gestured with his thumb and Pande walked in. A tea boy scuttled past, carrying a wire basket full of glasses, and Pande smoothly lifted one with a skill born of long practice.

Five minutes later, he was sipping tea and batting the breeze, surrounded by his peers. He'd adopted the role of an investigator from Delhi, which was semi-true.

'So do you break the hands first, or the feet?' asked one of the junior sub-inspectors, a mere stripling whose paunch barely cleared his belt. They were comparing techniques, as professionals often do when they get together.

'That's a good question you've asked,' said Pande, approvingly. With this kind of attitude, the young man would go far. 'In Delhi, we generally prefer to do the hands first, because it takes less effort. When you're conducting an investigation, it's important to conserve your energy. But also you have to assess the suspect, and understand which politician he is supporting. Is he gorment party, or opposition, or rebel politician supporter? If he is gorment, your Big Babu must call and ask permission first. Gorment party leaders usually don't give permission, and we have to release the suspect, unless you call when they're drunk. That's why my Big Babu always calls in such cases after 9 p.m. They can never remember what they said afterwards, so it's OK. If it's an opposition supporter, it's no problem, so long as the suspect is not a relative of the leader. You can go ahead and break his hands. But if it's a rebel leader supporter who is currently with ruling party, but also rebelling, then the matter can become complicated. I remember once I had a new Big Babu, he fell into this trap. He wanted to fight crime. He was very sincere. You know the type.'

They all snickered except for one of them who sat in a corner looking depressed. Not a team player, Pande could see. There were still a few such fools left in this day and age. In his era, such elements had been more or less successfully weeded out.

'So this new young Big Babu, he comes to me, and he says, "Pande, first I want to stop all the drug-dealers, and then, all the triple-X film-sellers." Why, I asked him, because they are corrupting the youth? "No," he says, "because I used to enjoy both in college, and I need to remove the temptation." He was basically an honest man.'

His audience made sounds of wonder.

'"So, Pande," he says to me, "do you know who the drug-dealers and pornographers in this area are?" And naturally I knew all of them, so I said yes. Then he asks what we should do to stop them, and I say, break their hands the first time and next time, break their heads. But first, you must check which party the criminals are supporting, otherwise there could be trouble. So he finds out that they are supporting the ruling party and I said forget about it, let's go after petty thieves or hooch-sellers instead; but he says, "No, let me talk to the leader myself." So he talks to the local MLA, who says, no, no, crime is bad, you must stop crime, do not worry and do your job. And then the Big Babu says to me, "See, Pande, an honest leader."'

His audience burst into uproarious laughter. One or two had choking fits, and Pande waited politely for them to recover.

'So anyway,' he continued, 'one Sunday I rounded up all of them, about twenty in all, and they were all lined up in the thana courtyard. One by one this young Big Babu asks them if they are drug-dealer, or selling porno and they're all simple, honest people so they say yes, looking very shy. So he makes them hold out each hand and he breaks them with his lathi, one by one, just like I taught him. He came from a good family, and he was not used to such things, and he got tired very quickly. "This is not something they taught me in college," he says to me. But he did not stop until he finished all of them. He was very determined, that boy. At the end, he told them to go away and not repeat this any more, or he would break their heads next time. So they saluted him and we took them to hospital for plaster-shaster. Then we burnt all the drugs, and made a mountain out of the DVDs in the main market and crushed them with a roadroller which I had arranged especially. My Big Babu told me, "Pande, you take care of all that, I can't bear to watch." Later, the people of the town took out a procession, and he was garlanded by the District Magistrate's wife.'

'So that means he actually did stop some crime, didn't he?' asked the quiet one in the corner, hopefully.

'Listen to this fool,' said Pande. 'I'm telling you this story for a different reason, you let me finish first. You see that leader, he had made a fool of us. It's true that he was a ruling party leader, but those badmaashes supported a rebel leader, his rival. So he got my Big Babu to break the hands of those who supported his rival, to show how strong he was. He was hoping the local goondas would all leave the rebel leader and join him. But the rebel leader had his own connections and with the blessings of the party, he put twenty court cases against my Big Babu, charging him with criminal assault, torture and a list of other things. "What is all this," my Big Babu asks me, not able to understand, "why are they prosecuting me?" "I told you to check carefully," I said, "but you did not check carefully enough. Now you'll have to rush to Calcutta twice a month and stand in front of the judge like a criminal." And that is what he did. The cases dragged on for years, and he spent most of his salary on lawyers, because if he depended on the gorment lawyer he would get the death sentence within one week, maximum fourteen days. For years, those criminals would come and bear witness against him. Always with their hands in plaster. It looked very bad in court, all those weeping men lined up, all of them with plastered hands. They got a lot of sympathy. And the Big Babu, he became poorer and poorer, thanks to all the legal fees and because he refused to earn extra from bribes. The rest of us in the thana offered him a share from the collections many times, because he was a young boy who had just made a mistake, but he never accepted. Luckily, after four years, the rebel leader joined the opposition party, as a result all the cases were dropped. So, brother, there are two things you can learn from this.'

'What are those two things, uncle?' asked the young man who had originally asked him for expert advice.

Shovon Chowdhury

'First, before thinking of breaking hands or legs, find out which party the suspect is supporting. Get the proper picture. That is very, very important. And second, try to avoid any plaster-shaster, or any such thing which can be shown in court. That is why in Delhi we often prefer electric treatment. If you have no electricity, you can always use a car battery.'

'There is another thing we learn from this, brother,' said the local Small Babu, who had been listening approvingly as his team was being educated. 'All politicians are motherfuckers!'

There was much cheering and applause and clinking of tea glasses.

'Nothing could be more true,' said Pande. 'We are what we are thanks to them.'

They observed a brief silence as they dwelt on this fact.

'So tell us about your investigation, brother,' said the Small Babu, sensing that the morale in the room was dipping slightly. 'You are our guest. It's our duty to help you.'

Pande leaned back and loosened his belt. He had worked it all out on the way in the taxi. He continued to be impressed by his rapidly burgeoning intellect. Once he got back, a promotion would be his for the asking. Air-conditioning was just a heartbeat away.

'Is there some army camp nearby, in a place called Pokhran?' he asked casually.

'Army, air force, both,' replied the Small Babu, 'but what is that to you, brother? We police have no dealings with army people. They treat us like cockroaches. Their officers strut about like film stars.'

Pande smiled sympathetically. 'You're talking about army-wallahs here? You should see the ones in Delhi, what they think of themselves!'

'What do you want in the army camp?' asked the Small Babu suspiciously. 'The Pokhran one is where the bomb blast happened in 1974, which made every Pakistani go back inside his mother. It's a very secret place. You're not doing something anti-national, I hope? Stomach is stomach, but nation is nation.'

'If that's what you think then I'll leave,' said Pande, half-rising. It was a bit of an effort, because theatrics was not his strong suit, but he managed to make his chin quiver.

'No, no,' protested the Small Babu, realizing his mistake, 'please don't be like that. We did not mean to insult you. Tell us what help you require and we'll give it.'

Pande sat down again. They were absurdly easy to manipulate. At the end of the day, they were a bunch of village bumpkins, not a metropolitan sophisticate like him.

'It's OK,' he said, 'it's good that you're careful. It's a question of the nation. It's a matter concerning army purchase department.'

The Small Babu smiled knowingly. Of course it would have to be the purchase department. However arrogant they might be, the army was mostly honest. But the purchase department!

'One don back in Delhi has become too big,' said Pande. 'He's made crores doing number two business in liquor. Now he is no longer supplying to the commissioner for free, he is actually charging money, saying who are you, I know the home minister.'

'What a rascal!' exclaimed the Small Babu, scandalized.

'Yes,' agreed Pande, 'that's what happens when small people become too big. That's why we have to teach this don a lesson. It seems he gets his supply from the army canteen store. We'll need to identify who all are involved and get them to sign confessions. We'll connect them to the don. Then we'll put him inside and teach him some manners. It's a prestige issue!'

'You tell your commissioner-sahab his prestige is in our hands,' said the Small Babu, slapping the table in his agitation. 'We are all together in this matter!'

Pande had worried a little about this part. Why would a booze baron in Delhi smuggle stock all the way to the capital from this flea-bitten pisspot in Rajasthan? But his comrades hadn't noticed this loophole, they were too infuriated by the insult to the commissioner, and they were busy roaring about the world going to the dogs; it was time to take a stand, it was, the commissioner was like a father to them all, and if need be they would travel to Delhi themselves and beat up this chutiya don, by God they would!

Pande waited for them to calm down before proceeding.

'So tell me, then, how do I get into this army camp to find the suspects?' he asked.

'It's the purchase department, no?' said the Small Babu. 'They buy from all over town, both in Pokhran and in Jaisalmer. Guns and bullets and uniforms come from Delhi, but butter and biscuits and rice and vegetables they buy from here. It's easy. Just say you have found some wholesale trader who is doing ghapla with their food supply. Make it sound like a big scandal, they'll get very nervous. Say it's something to do with officers' food. Their officers are very stylish. I have heard the generals like to have puris with small Nainital potatoes for breakfast. Take some person along with you as the culprit, and say you want to do joint interrogation. Once you give this excuse and get inside, you can find out all about this liquor tamasha and get the evidence against that bastard don.'

'Thank you for your excellent suggestion,' said Pande. 'I'll need a sub judice to take with me. Do you have any sub judices handy?'

The Small Babu laughed, amused by his question.

'Of course, we have sub judices, how many do you want? We can even pick up a fresh one. But, I have the ideal candidate. He actually used to be a vegetable seller. He'll be very suitable.'

He turned to one of his boys. 'Is Hukum there? Bring him.'

'Right now may be a little difficult,' said the officer, looking very sheepish. 'We did not know there would be immediate requirement.'

'OK,' said the Small Babu, 'no problem, we'll send him to the doctor, by tomorrow he'll be OK. Then you can take him to the army camp. If you teach him, he'll understand what to do.'

Pande was pleased. He knew coming to the thana had been the right idea.

The quiet man in the corner spoke up.

'Shouldn't you find out more about the army camp and the officers first? That's what investigating officers do. Otherwise what are you going to do, march up to the guards and say "Take me to the canteen"?'

This was pretty much what Pande had been planning to do. He usually always got his way so long as he shouted loudly enough. But the man had a point, although he didn't like his tone.

'What are you suggesting?' Pande asked him, swallowing his bile.

'There's a journalist called Joshi, sits in Jaisalmer,' said the quiet one. 'He's a smart fellow, and he's very interested in the army. If you go meet him, he can give you some information. I always do that. Sometimes people in Rajasthan also do investigation.'

I'll give you something to investigate once I'm through, you little shit, thought Pande, but he forced himself to smile. The fact was, he also needed to learn a bit more about this nuclear bomb thing. It was hardly likely to be displayed on the parade ground with instructions for sabotage pasted on it, although with the army you could never be sure.

'Thank you for your suggestion,' he said. 'Of course it is a good idea. Give me his address. While your sub judice is getting treatment, I'll go and see him.'

'Would you like us to give you a jeep?' asked the Small Babu, eager to make up for the rudeness of his colleague.

'No need,' said Pande, 'I'll take a taxi. That's how I came.'

That was one more thing, across the ages, which Delhi and Rajasthan had in common: transportation was never a problem for the police.

46

'It's not over till the bomb drops.'

The PM's time was precious. The General kept his update crisp. They were meeting in one of her guest bathrooms, hoping to avoid bugging by the Competent Authority. The General had a fly swatter in his hand, in case one of the mini spy drones got in. They were perfect yellow spheres with smiley faces. They were supposed to give citizens friendly advice and helpful information, but over time they had also started collecting fines and looking for seditious elements. All of them reported to the CA.

'He wants me to invade China by boat,' said the General.

'By boat?' said the PM in some disbelief.

'By boat,' said the General gravely.

'Will he join us?'

'I doubt it.'

'Can he swim?' asked the PM.

'I'll ask him next time we meet. Have you managed to do anything?'

'Well, I've been helping him create a diplomatic incident.'

'Good God! What did you do?'

'I agreed to unveil a statue of the old Dalai Lama.'

'Bloody hell!'

'Was that wrong? The man's dead. It's just a statue. It's not like it was an android simulacrum from Honda or anything, like the one we used to replace Uncle Mannie towards the end. No one could tell the difference, except the sniffer dogs. They barked at it all the time.'

The General sighed. There was no doubt about it. The quality of management had declined over the years. With every generation, the blood was getting diluted.

'I didn't want to,' said the PM, sensing the General's displeasure, 'he just kept bombarding me with more and more options until I cracked and said yes to this one. Plus he was smelling me.'

'Why don't you announce an emergency cabinet meeting?' asked the General. He was secretly very impressed by emergency cabinet meetings, where a myriad security retinues merged and mingled, like a kumbh mela with Kalashnikovs, and ministers entered and left the PMO with uniformly grim impressions, and smiled mysteriously at the press as they got in and out of their cars. It lent an air of gravity to whatever the proceedings were, the feeling that unspecified momentous events were imminent. As the host of these meetings, the PM was not as impressed. They mostly involved snacks and snoozing, and the ritual kissing of feet.

'I suppose I could set one up,' she said dubiously. What else could she do? Media coverage was never a problem, but what would she get them to cover?

'Perhaps I could launch a local chapter of the Campaign for Nuclear Disarmament,' she said.

'It's a little late for that,' said the General.

'But we never actually hit them with anything. They were the ones who bombed us. Don't we still have the upper hand, morally speaking?'

'That's only because most of our planes stayed on the ground and none of the missiles were ready to launch. It wasn't for lack of trying.'

It was a bitter time, and both of them remembered it vividly. It was in the days before the Competent Authority had taken over. The previous PM had been in charge. He was a Man of Steel. Re-election had made him steelier. By the tenth year of his rule, he was unmanageable. He was not someone to back down in the face of Chinese aggression. All those years of ruling he had done, holding meetings, winning elections, signing files, issuing orders, standing tall, and what had it all amounted to? Nothing. As an insider, she had always known that some money was being lifted here and there, and a few things were bound to run a little behind schedule, and some of the things the government bought were not exactly top notch, or might not even exist. But that was just the way things worked. Until the day the missiles failed to launch and the planes never flew, and the trucks broke down on the way to the front, and the Man of Steel had died, thinking that's funny, I could have sworn I signed for all of those, as the flames seared the cities, and the ground turned to glass, and the poison blew in the wind.

'What about all your foreign friends?' asked the General.

'President Lee in Taiwan could help,' she said. 'Our kids went to college together. But how do I talk to him? The CA has me bugged all over. I'm not sure even this bathroom is safe.'

This was true. The Competent Authority was in love. Reviewing all her messages made him feel closer. He had spent many a happy evening reading and re-reading her e-mail, and stalking her on JabMe, the revolutionary new social network where every user received a personal floating robot with a boxing glove that administered jabs to the kidney whenever a new message came in.

'I might have friends in high places, but there's not much I can do,' said the PM, momentarily depressed. 'It's up to you. You have to get us a truce with the Maoists. It's the only way to stop him. Once we have peace, he can reconstruct to his heart's content. That's his main problem, isn't it? The Maoists are bleeding us, and hampering reconstruction.'

The General wasn't so sure. He'd seen glimpses of the CA's vision. Either way, a truce with the Maoists seemed unlikely.

'The Maoists don't trust us. They won't meet us. We keep shooting them when they try.'

The PM sat up suddenly, setting off the flush by mistake. 'Why don't I come with you?' she said. 'Wouldn't that be a game-changer, or something? "PM personally reaches out to Maoists." It might actually buy us some time.'

'You can't step out of this building without the CA finding out,' said the General.

The PM pursed her lips and frowned. She kicked her heels on the bathroom tiles. She had often thought of lurking undetected amidst the populace like Haroon Al Rashid, but lurking was much harder these days. It was the Haroon Al Rashid bit that gave her the idea. Unlike Haroon bhai, she was a woman. It would have been easier for a woman to lurk in Baghdad.

'You leave that to me,' she said, briskly, 'just set up the meeting.'

'How do I do that? We don't talk to the Maoists.'

'Just catch any journalist in Delhi,' said the PM, 'most of them are Maoists. They'll fix it all up for you.'

'What about you?' asked the General.

'I think it's time to meet the Saudi Ambassador,' she said, 'it's a long time since I had tea with him. I'll invite his wives too. He won't say no, because it's me.'

'Is this the time to have a tea party?'

'Who's the Prime Minister?' asked the PM tersely. 'You or me?'

She put a hand on the General's shoulder and pulled herself up. Her knees really hurt these days. But she managed to give him a smile.

'Trust me,' she said, 'it's not over till the bomb drops.'

47

'I kept telling her, why don't you keep going in the bushes like we have always done, but she said no.'

He was small, frail and stooped, and leaned heavily on the two young women on either side of him as he slowly made his way to the dais.

Mr Chatterjee couldn't get over how tiny he was, and how old he looked. In the newsclips of his youth, Gandhi had been a robust figure, radiating vitality, striding ahead of people half his age as they marched their way to Dandi. This was not that Gandhi. This was a pale, sad shadow of the man he remembered.

'They're not feeding him properly,' said an old lady disapprovingly. Her husband grunted.

'I'm telling you,' said the old lady, 'the food they are cooking is not tasty enough, that is why he is not eating. Everybody requires tasty food, even saints. We should give him some of our food.'

'Perhaps he will survive your cooking, being a great man,' said her husband doubtfully.

'Who is greater than you?' demanded his wife. 'You've survived well enough all these years!'

'Anyway, he only takes goat's milk and lemon juice,' said her loyal spouse, keen to avoid controversy.

'Goat's milk!' said the old lady, shocked. 'Why can't he drink the milk of a normal-sized animal? No wonder he's so small. Who can maintain their size on goat's milk? Thank God we are carrying milk from our buffalo. Come, come, we must make him drink some.'

She bustled ahead, followed by her reluctant husband.

She wasn't the only one, Mr Chatterjee noticed. Many others were carrying offerings of some kind or the other, morsels eked out from their hardscrabble lives. There were masses of people all around. Some were standing, some were on their knees, and some were bowing low before him, as he made his way slowly across the well-manicured lawn, flanked by immaculate flower beds. The grounds of Birla House were filling up as he watched. They came in their cars, and their tongas, and on foot, and they were streaming in through the little gate. There was little or no security. Mr Chatterjee tried scoping the joint, like a proper detective, but there wasn't much scoping to do. The whole place was wide open. Anyone could shoot him from anywhere. Gandhi reached the dais and slowly sat down. He gazed out at the crowd with a lost expression in his eyes.

'Why isn't he saying anything?' whispered a nearby devotee. 'Is he angry with us for some reason?'

'No, no,' said another, 'there's some defect in the microphone. See, someone is trying to fix it.'

'It must be the goras,' said the first man, darkly, 'still making mischief.'

'That's not the case,' said someone else, who was well-versed in current affairs, 'Nehru has married the lat-sahab's wife. They are like our in-laws now. It must be those bastard Pakistanis.'

The microphone crackled to life. Gandhi began to speak. His voice was high, clear and strong. For some reason, he was talking about travel permits in South Africa.

'Why is he talking about South Africa?' asked someone.

'It's his ancestral place,' said someone else. 'If something happens there, it's only natural that he will be concerned.'

Mr Chatterjee looked around, desperately trying to spot Godse. Godse was Maharashtrian, he knew. What did Maharashtrians look like? The only Maharashtrian person he could recall was Tendulkar, and Tendulkar looked just like anyone else.

As Mr Chatterjee watched Gandhi on the dais, he remembered that he had been shot while walking, so perhaps he was safe for the time being.

Maybe all he had to do was come at four in the evening every day and keep an eye on Gandhi as he walked. Ideally, he should become a devotee and join his inner circle, but he had a morbid fear of enemas. He could mingle with the crowd, though, and stalk him down the pathway. That's what Godse had done. Was he brave enough to take a bullet when the time came? He didn't think so. He wanted to see Banani again. And how long could he keep this up? If Gandhi went to Pakistan, was he going to stow away on the plane? No, this had to end here. He tried to remember what else detectives did. They conducted interviews, he recalled, and asked penetrating questions. He looked around for someone to interview. Everyone was gazing at Gandhi with rapt attention, except one man who was gazing at Birla House. A rich farmer in a clean turban. He was wondering whether he could build one just like it in his village and how he would stop people from peeing on its walls.

'It's a lovely house, isn't it?' said Mr Chatterjee.

'This pure-white finish is OK for the city,' said the farmer, 'in the village, maintenance is a problem. People may use it to dry cow dung patties. But, it is the correct place for Gandhiji. He is fasting so much, he should be comfortable.'

'Why is Gandhiji fasting?' asked Mr Chatterjee.

'Oh, you know Bapu,' said the rich farmer, ceasing his contemplation of Birla House. 'He's always fasting. Frankly, I don't think he requires much food. But he must be eating sometimes, otherwise he would not need to go to the toilet. And he must be going to the toilet. After all, if he does not go to the toilet, then why does he keep telling people to build them? All the time he is telling people, "Go and build toilets." My wife also started nagging me, saying, "Bapu says build a toilet, you should do that, you are a rich man." I kept telling her, "Why don't you go in the bushes like we have always done." But she said, "No, Bapu says build a toilet." Not only that, we have to keep cleaning the toilet also. My back hurts from all the bending and sweeping, and all the sweepers are laughing at me, but my wife says you should learn from Bapu, he also cleans the toilet daily . . .'

There was no doubt the farmer could have spent the rest of the evening fulminating about toilets, but Mr Chatterjee needed information.

'Why is he fasting right now?' asked Mr Chatterjee, patiently.

'The case is very complicated,' said the farmer. 'Like the case of

Vishwanath's cow back in the village. Vishwanath had two sons, and only one cow. They tried to share the chuchis of the cow, saying the front ones are yours, and the back ones are mine, but the adjustment did not work out very well, and there were many disputes during milking. Other people in the village also got involved, and there were many suggestions and much confusion. The national case is also similar. The British had to divide India fast, because Mountbatten wanted to get his wife out of the country as quickly as possible. She was exchanging intimacies with Pandit Nehru and the English King was writing letters to Mountbatten, saying this is wrong, and you are shaming the family, and after this no one will want to marry my children. Because of the rush, they could not find anybody else to do the partition, so they sent a very old man, with very little brain. His eyesight was poor, and he could not see maps properly. Also they made some mistakes while counting people, so that there were many Hindus left in Pakistan, and many Muslims left in India. The Sikhs were everywhere, because everyone forgot about them. After that there was a lot of killing. Everyone killed and killed and killed, but still they could not finish the job, so the work is still going on. We have four-five Muslims in our village, but they are good fellows, so we did not touch them. Now some people are realizing that perhaps this is not the best way.

'All this time Bapu was in Calcutta, because Bengalis are very ferocious, and the goat's milk there is very good. Then the Bengali goondas threw away their weapons. Some of them even cried. Others retrieved their weapons later, because after all, this was their livelihood. A little while ago Hindus in Pakistan started being killed, and people came to Bapu and said Bapu, please go to Pakistan and tell them to stop, and Bapu said, but in Delhi in front of my eyes you are killing each other and so I will stop eating. I must say this is a very powerful technique. My wife has started using it, and the situation at home is very different. It was effective in Delhi also. Everybody has stopped fighting, and they signed a peace pledge, and fed each other sweets. So now Gandhi will go to Pakistan. Jinnah-sahab is already regretting bitterly. When he sees Bapu, he will burst into tears. They will embrace in full view of the public, and everything will be fine.'

Mr Chatterjee wasn't so sure. From what he'd heard, Jinnah was a tough nut, unlikely to be bothered by a few smouldering corpses. But you never knew. Gandhi had performed many miracles. Mr Chatterjee continued his investigation.

'Have you seen any suspicious characters around here?' he asked.

'Yes, Shyama Prasad Mukherji,' said the farmer promptly. 'He is the leader of the Hindu parties. He refused to sign the peace pledge. He was the only one. People say his heart has become hard since the Great Calcutta Killings of '46. He made Bapu very sad.'

There were a few people milling around in front of the wall, behind where Gandhi sat, and Mr Chatterjee watched them anxiously. Were the police insane? Why were there arbitrary people standing behind Gandhi and why was no one clearing them away?

A tall, dark man was fiddling with something on the wall. It looked like a box wrapped in cotton. He knew everyone could see him so he kept his eyes half-closed in order to avoid detection. Then, he took out a box of matches, lit one, and applied it to a fuse. When the fuse started burning, he walked away quickly, looking back nervously.

'Stop that man!' screamed Mr Chatterjee. Was he the only one who'd seen him? Was everyone blind? Or was it just that all eyes were on Gandhi? He started to run towards the wall, shoving people out of the way as he ran. The murderer was supposed to use a pistol, he knew, and this was a bomb, but there was no time to think about that.

The bomb exploded, throwing up huge chunks of the wall. Madan Lal Pahwa, a man of limited intellect but unlimited rage, was scurrying around, trying to find the way out. He had remembered to bring the bomb, but he had forgotten to check out an escape route. Birla House was in an uproar, with people screaming and running in all directions. Near the podium a young woman scooped up her toddler in her arms and pointed at the would-be assassin, who still hadn't figured out where the gate was.

'He's the one,' screamed the young woman, 'he's the one who tried to kill Bapu!'

To Mr Chatterjee's utter astonishment, Gandhi was still talking.

'Why should it be that one with a white skin cannot have a dialogue with one who has brown skin?' asked Gandhi, completely unperturbed. 'Why should Indians have to fight for their legitimate rights?'

He was still talking about Indians in South Africa. Meanwhile, Indians in India were trying to kill him.

'For God's sake, someone cover him,' screamed Mr Chatterjee, but no one did, and Gandhi carried on.

A soldier and a policeman had grabbed hold of the bomber and pinned him to the wall. While all eyes were on this drama, there was no reason why one of his accomplices couldn't have simply sauntered up to Gandhi and shot him, but no one did. That was, in fact, the plan, but the others had run away and jumped into the taxi waiting outside, leaving their Punjabi comrade to the tender mercies of the authorities. They had never liked him much anyway.

Gandhi finished his speech, and appeared to notice the pandemonium for the first time.

'There is no need to panic,' he said, conversationally, 'perhaps the army has conducted some kind of bomb test.'

The bomber was dragged off, shouting and struggling. Mr Chatterjee stood there, his heart hammering in his throat. Was it over? Was Gandhi safe now? In some strange way, had his presence changed the course of history?

Realization dawned on him gradually. He remembered what this road was called back home. Tees January Marg. Thirtieth January Road. Named for the day Gandhi had been killed. Today was the twentieth.

Ten days before he was killed, an attempt had been made on Gandhi's life. In broad daylight. In front of thousands of people. In the capital of India. Ten days later, in the same place, at practically the same time, Nathuram Godse had walked up to Gandhi and shot him. No one had done a thing to prevent it. There was no point in trying to dig up evidence and presenting it to the authorities. The authorities had all the evidence they needed. They were letting the murderers play little practice matches, so that they could get it right on the big day.

If everyone wants him dead, how do I help him, thought Mr Chatterjee, almost losing hope. But then he remembered the vast and unconditional affection he had felt around him. Six more months. Even if he could buy him six more months, surely he could make things better? Perhaps it was a forlorn hope. Perhaps there was nothing he could do. But who had ever realized the power in a lump of salt?

As he turned to go, he saw the rich farmer. He stood rooted to the spot, ashen-faced, not so jolly any more. Something had been bothering Mr Chatterjee, and he couldn't help asking.

'You never told me what finally happened in the case of Vishwanath's cow,' he asked.

'They solved it very simply,' said the farmer, 'one brother killed the other, and he kept the cow.'

48

'If Jinnah-sahab won't pay for legs,
let him break them himself!'

'Why do I have to stay in the truck?' said the littlest goonda, who didn't see why he had to miss all the action just because he was fourteen.

'Because someone has to hand out the weapons,' said Nazimuddin, 'now eat up your biryani before it gets cold.'

Topen looked at the little goonda sympathetically. He had the same problem back at the Very New Young Men's Bodybuilding Society. No one ever let him do anything. He had come on behalf of the Society to understand the explosive requirements of the Muslim League's unit in Metiabruz. The VNYMBS was completely impartial. They sold bombs to everyone. Ali had used his terrorist training skills to infiltrate them. Now he was using them to infiltrate the Muslim League. He was here to stop Direct Action Day, the first and nastiest football match in a long series of football matches between Hindus and Muslims. The Muslim side was looking good. They were stoking up on protein and carbs. As Topen and Ali sipped their elaichi tea, having politely declined dinner, their leader Nazimuddin was explaining why.

'Mohammedans eat meat,' said Nazimuddin, chewing on a fatty piece of mutton, 'and meat generates heat. That is why we are good fighters. Non-violence is for those who eat grass, like Gandhi. The Muslim League has taken no foolish oath of non-violence, so we will fight, and we will win. We'll fight and get our Pakistan!'

There were around ten men at the rickety table and they raised a cheer, somewhat muffled because their mouths were full of biryani. They were listening to their leader with rapt attention, but taking care to methodically shovel in the rice and meat as they did so.

Most of these men were in it for the meat. It was more about physiology than ideology. History might have been different if they had more to eat, Ali thought. It could still be different if he played his cards right. He was just one man, but that didn't matter. He was Al Qaeda. He was the virus. He could infect any system. He was going to find out exactly how this riot had happened. He was going to figure out how stop it. When his time came, he was still going to go to hell, of course, but they might turn the temperature down just a bit.

'Brother Suhrawardy is handling the police,' said Nazimuddin, reaching for a seekh kebab. 'As Chief Minister, he is their father and mother.'

Ali hadn't checked out the local police yet. He was allergic to police stations. But he had no doubt they would be a testament to Suhrawardy's parenting skills.

'Boats will ferry our people across the river to Howrah, early in the morning,' said Nazimuddin, gulping down meat. 'Trucks with petrol drums will be waiting for our fighters on the other side. We have plenty of petrol. Every Muslim League minister was issued a special petrol ration just for this purpose.'

A happy sigh went around the room. It was good to be on the side of the law. Thanks to Brother Suhrawardy, they weren't pimps and thieves and extortionists anymore, they were government servants.

'How do we carry the loot?' asked one of them, a future minister with an eye for detail.

'Everything has been organized, son,' said Nazimuddin. 'The trucks will be full of petrol. You use the petrol to burn Hindu houses and shops. You use the choppers and pistols to kill anyone who tries to come out. You use the truck to carry back the loot. You bring in a full truck, you go back with a full truck.'

His followers made appreciative noises. There was a reason why Nazimuddin was their leader. Professional planning made such a difference.

'But remember one thing, boys, this is not a shopping expedition,' he said, twinkling roguishly at them, 'we need to keep track of the score also.'

'Do we get paid before or after?' asked the future minister. Nazimuddin nodded approvingly. The boy would go far. He was destined for greatness. He tore a long strip of meat off a haunch of mutton and stuffed it in his mouth. Juice trickled down the corner of his mouth, staining his beard.

'Don't worry about money. All the good Muslim shopkeepers have contributed. We told them it was important, or we might mix up their shops with Hindu shops, and mistakes could occur. They understood instantly. The rate is fixed, same price across Calcutta. Ten rupees for a murder, five rupees for a half-murder.'

'If I break a leg, will I get two rupees at least?' asked one of the boys. Everyone laughed, although one or two looked worried, wondering what a half-murder was, exactly, and foreseeing ugly financial disputes in the near future.

Ali suppressed the urge to kill them all, then and there. He could do it easily enough. They were grossly out of shape. They had discussed murder often enough, back in the day, but at least there had never been any witty repartee, or side-orders of shammi kebabs.

'Since we're talking about making money,' he said, 'have you considered the opium trade?'

'Who is that man on your shirt?' asked Nazimuddin, transfixed by Bob Marley.

'He's Al Maruli,' said Ali, 'a great Muslim leader. You probably haven't heard of him. Works mostly in the Caribbean.'

'Arrey, what are you saying? Who amongst us has not heard of the great Al Maruli?' protested Nazimuddin. 'He is a legendary figure in Calcutta!'

'I read about him just the other day in *The Statesman*!' said one of his thugs.

'My cousin met him in Rangoon!' said another.

'He is a Sufi mystic who sings songs about revolution,' said a third, with uncanny prescience. 'Sometimes he falls down when he has had too much hashish.'

Ali couldn't help smiling. They were Bengalis all right. If they were to have a family crest, it'd probably bear the legend *Death Before Admitting Ignorance* in bold gothic type, supported by rampant koi fish and embossed with a tiger taking a nap. The question was, could he make them an offer they couldn't refuse and save a few lives in the bargain?

'There's a lot of money in the opium trade,' he said, 'much more than this five-rupee ten-rupee game. Flowers are worth more than people. They grow it in Afghanistan. There's not much else to do there.'

'Afghanistan is a long way from Howrah,' said Nazimuddin, munching on an egg smothered in gravy, and belching. Ali had never seen anyone belching and eating at the same time before.

'It's just a question of building supply chains,' he said, 'I can put you in touch with some of the talibs.'

'What would students in spectacles know about opium?' hooted Nazimuddin. 'It seems to me you have been smoking some yourself.'

Ali clicked his tongue irritably. He had forgotten that it was 1946 and the Taliban were just a distant gleam in the eye of some unborn Saudi cleric.

'The Pathans of the frontier would be glad to lend a hand,' he said hopefully.

Nazimuddin almost choked on his egg. They laughed uproariously. They really were in a very cheerful mood.

'The Pathans have all become vegetarians!' said Nazimuddin, wiping a tear from his eye. 'They are followers of Gandhi. They wear red shirts and get bullied by their wives. If you slap Khan Abdul Ghaffar Khan on the cheek, he will turn the other cheek and say, sir, please slap this one also, it's feeling lonely!'

This sounded most unlike any Pathans Ali had ever met, but if so, it was not an atmosphere conducive to drug dealing.

'How about outsourcing?' he said.

Nazimuddin looked at him suspiciously. Was the boy trying to maaro some English? He hated it when people did that.

'I don't know what that word is,' he said, ripping the top layer off a lachha paratha with an air of veiled menace.

'It's the way of the future, boss,' said Ali. 'Look at it this way. You've got ten men here and you're the leader. If each of them does ten murders and ten half-murders, that's a total of one hundred and fifty rupees, which all of you share.'

'Ten rupees per murder is too little,' said one of the boys, 'we should not get less than twelve rupees.'

'Or at least eleven rupees and fifty paise,' said someone else.

'And what about legs?' demanded a third. 'Why should we be breaking legs for free? If Jinnah-sahab won't pay for legs, let him break them himself!'

Nazimuddin was now eying Ali with acute disfavour. Why was he messing with the minds of his boys? Was the man a communist? He didn't like communists. They were tricksy.

Ali hastened to reassure Nazimuddin.

'I'm just trying to help, chacha. Your production capacity is limited. You're fighting each other for revenue. Your revenue would grow exponentially if you outsource basic functions, leaving yourselves free to do what you do best, which is getting contracts to murder people.'

The crowd was silent now, and listening with rapt attention. They found him incomprehensible, but strangely fascinating.

'First, you have to get some poor farm boys from East Bengal. Will that be a problem?'

They shook their heads. There was never any shortage of poor farm boys from East Bengal.

'They'll be your field agents. You pay them four rupees per murder, and two rupees per half-murder. The rest is your profit.'

Nazimuddin looked at him with dawning appreciation. One of the boys leaped up and protested hotly.

'Saala, you've come to cut us out! You want villagers to take our livelihood!'

'You're not getting it,' said Ali, 'each of you becomes a project leader. You'll have ten field agents, who'll do ten full murders and ten half-murders each. You pay six hundred rupees, and you earn fifteen hundred. It's like printing money.'

'Wah!' exclaimed Nazimuddin. 'Bahut khub!'

'Plus think of the productivity. Instead of a hundred murders, you'll be doing a thousand!' said Ali. It was an incredibly complex scheme, and Ali was confident that with him around to misguide them, he would be able to drag the process out till at least Christmas, by which time Jinnah would give up, and perhaps retire to a little cottage somewhere near Savile Row.

'If you keep using the word murder it doesn't sound nice,' said Nazimuddin, revealing an unexpected streak of delicacy. 'Why don't you call them goals instead?'

'There's no limit to the number of goals you can score,' said Ali. 'All you need is enough players.'

'There you have put your finger on the problem,' said Nazimuddin. 'Village boys don't like coming to the city. The city water doesn't suit them.'

'But think of the opportunity!' said Ali. 'With enough players, you could run every match in the country. We should go to Mr Jinnah with a proposal!'

Ali was feeling a little optimistic now. With some luck, in the fullness of time, he might have the whole of the Muslim League punching clocks and filling time sheets. They would indulge in meaningless, casual sex and fantasize about killing their supervisors.

'All these things will take time,' said Nazimuddin.

'But think of the revenue!'

'I always think of the revenue,' said Nazimuddin, with simple, sad dignity, 'but you have not understood the nature of Direct Action Day, or the nature of Mr Jinnah. These days he is sleeping on the floor. Do you know why? To practise for sleeping in prison. This is a gap in his bio data. Mr Nehru is far ahead of him in this regard. He has spent many more years in jail and also written many books. This is Mr Jinnah's big chance. He will lead the masses, like Gandhi. He will make the supreme sacrifice for Pakistan, and wear prison pyjamas. He will stand in court and make memorable speeches. He is also not someone you can say no to easily. Suhrawardy has tried several times, and it has affected his health. He keeps a wet handkerchief on his forehead while sleeping. There can be no compromise on Direct Action Day. We must satisfy him in this matter, then the rest we can see.'

They were clearly committed to their plan, which in essence was to keep killing innocent people until someone begged them to stop and gave them whatever they wanted. It was a simple plan, suitable for simple minds. But it had led to the birth of a nation. Some elements within it had learnt the lesson well, and used it lavishly.

'I'll draw you up a business plan,' persisted Ali, 'that'll make things clearer.'

Nazimuddin stood up too.

'Of course, of course,' he said. 'You are trying to benefit the rural youth of Bengal, we are very much with you. But in the meantime, don't forget our order.'

Topen tapped his notebook reassuringly. He had noted down their explosive requirements.

'You can get another 20 per cent out of him if you try,' whispered Ali to one of the goondas on his way out. Things looked tough here, but there was no harm in sowing a little discord.

It was time to meet the other side.

49

'I can see the strings,
you camel-fucker!'

Ram Manohar Pande was in a foul mood as a result of being taken in by false advertising. It was all the fault of the taxi driver who now stood at a discreet distance, cowering. Pande had hijacked him on the highway near the Pokhran police station and slapped him around a bit until he had agreed to take him to Jaisalmer, where he was going to meet Joshi the journalist, who would tell him about the key people in the local army camp, and give him more information about this nuclear bomb blast that he was supposed to prevent, as per the instructions of the avatar of Vishnu who had used his divine powers to transport him here, post which he would no doubt receive two to three boons from the grateful deity. He hadn't yet decided what he would do with the boons, but one of them would certainly involve the Bengali bitch who had led him a merry dance all over Delhi, and embroiled him in some kind of utterly incomprehensible dog-related confidence trick.

In an attempt to avoid further corporal punishment, the taxi driver had prattled merrily throughout the drive to Jaisalmer, sharing with him tidbits about local culture, cuisine and places of historical interest. He had talked a lot about how Jaisalmer was the city of gold, and even had a legendary golden fortress, which people came from far and wide to see.

Pande had found this information hugely exciting. A city of gold! In the Delhi of his era, thanks to the war, what you got to see was mostly rubble. But he had heard that India had once been a rich country, so a city of gold was not inconceivable. The Golden Temple in Amritsar still had a lot of gold, of course, but it was also guarded by armed and militant sardars, and hunter-killer drones in tiny turbans, and presented very little opportunity for enterprising policemen. From what he'd seen of the Rajasthanis, they were lily-livered wimps, and hardly likely to object if he collected a chunk or two. He regretted not bringing a bag.

His first sight of Jaisalmer had been acutely disappointing. 'See, sahab,' the taxi driver had said, 'the city of gold!'

Everything all around, from the bus stops to the shopfronts to the statues, was carved out of pale, golden stone. Up above, on a nearby hill shimmered a Rajasthani fort, made from the same material. People with nothing better to do flocked around it, gawking, taking pictures, buying bangles, and sipping Coca Cola. Guides and touts hopped about like crows at a garbage dump.

Pande had almost murdered the taxi driver on the spot, but he couldn't see too many other taxis around and didn't fancy walking back to Pokhran. So he had just slapped him around some more and ordered him to take him to the Hotel Moti Mahal where Joshi was supposed to meet him. Getting a transfer to Rajasthan didn't seem like such a bright idea any more. Pickings would be slim.

He had arrived slightly early, so he was standing in front of the hotel watching a puppet show. He had reached the conclusion that the people of this region mostly spent their time selling puppets to each other. There was a puppet shop every two to three feet in this town, and the ones who weren't selling puppets were performing puppet shows—like the sprightly little man in the lurid turban whose puppets he was observing in grim silence with arms folded.

The puppets were grotesque, with impossibly long arms and legs. Were these people idiots or what? Did they never look in the mirror? Did they see anyone walking around with ridiculous arms and legs like that? It offended his sense of anatomical correctness. The hero appeared to be some sort of king, who was killing Muslims by the truckload with a large tinsel-wrapped sword and periodically leaping in the air for no good reason. He had brought along his wife or concubine, who was dancing a filmi dance to encourage him, complete with hip jerks and reverse buttock flips. Both of them were dressed in pink, and both had little bells on their ankles. For once in his life, Pande was rooting for the Muslims. The whole thing was a travesty. The man was making a fool of him. Pande watched with mounting rage, until he couldn't bear it any more.

'I CAN SEE THE STRINGS, YOU CAMEL-FUCKER!' he roared, 'WHAT KIND OF AN IDIOT DO YOU THINK I AM?'

He snatched a puppet from the puppeteer's hands, ripped off an arm, and started beating him over the head with it. The taxi driver rushed towards his taxi to get Pande's lathi, hoping against hope that his negligence would be forgiven.

A pudgy man in a safari suit tapped Pande on the shoulder. 'Are you Inspector Vijay?' he asked politely.

Pande had always dreamed of being an inspector. Now had seemed as good a time as any. He had named himself Inspector Vijay because that was what Digital Amitabh was always called in the movies, and he was a big fan. In honour of his idol, he too had misplaced his mother soon after birth, and looked forward to being reunited with her at some climactic moment, once it was revealed that the blind beggar woman who lived down the street and sang devotional songs outside his bedroom window was none other than she.

'How did you recognize me?' asked Pande, pausing to catch his breath.

The man smiled, revealing yellow teeth. 'I took a guess,' he said, gently disengaging him from his victim and tossing the man a coin. 'My name is Joshi. Come, let us go into the hotel and have a cup of coffee. All that hard work must have made you thirsty.'

Pande felt his mood improving. He liked having coffee in posh hotels. It made a nice change from snatching food from street vendors.

They walked into the restaurant. It was indeed very stylish, with a glittering gold chandelier, plush purple carpets and shiny red sofas. The napkins were green. Pande surrendered himself to the lap of luxury.

'I hear you are conducting a sensitive investigation,' said Joshi, after they had finished ordering, 'how may I help you?'

'Tell me about this nuclear bomb-shomb,' said Pande, who didn't like beating about the bush.

'It was a long time ago,' said Joshi, 'in 1974. Indira Gandhi was going to be defeated in an election by a man who kept a pet monkey, even though she beat the Pakistanis in the war, and this would have been very humiliating. Her father never lost an election in his life. She was a very proud woman.'

Pande could feel himself getting annoyed again. He was fed up of the way various forms of wildlife kept popping up in this case. He might as well be in a zoo.

'So there were rumours that she had rigged the election, so she wouldn't lose to the monkey-man. No one could ever say no to her, not even election officers, because she was the only one with balls in the country. But as the rumours grew, she needed to distract the people, so she burst a nuclear bomb in Pokhran. So then there was great joy and celebration, and everyone said, see, now we are a truly great nation. We may not be able to feed everyone, or clothe everyone, or give everyone jobs, but we can certainly blow everyone up, thanks to the miracle of technology. But the Supreme Court was not impressed, and the next year they declared her guilty of rigging, whereupon she declared the Emergency, and became the Maharani of India. Then she got careless and called an election, and all the poor people threw her out. So the bomb didn't really help her much. But why do you want to know about all this? It was all so long ago.'

Pande hadn't come here for a history lesson, but he could see that Joshi was very well-informed, and he could get a lot of information from him without even beating him up, which was quite relaxing. However, he knew he would have to handle the matter of the second Pokhran Blast with great care, without revealing that he was from the future, or what his true purpose was.

'What about any new nuclear bomb-shomb?' he asked.

Joshi gazed at him thoughtfully. This man wasn't as much of a country bumpkin as he looked. He seemed to be privy to some top-secret information. Some alcohol might be in order. But he decided to take the unlubricated approach first. The prices at this hotel were sinful.

'Perhaps if you could share something with me?' he said carefully. 'I might be better able to guide you.'

An extraordinarily elderly waiter tottered up to their table, deposited a plate of pakoras and tottered off again.

'I don't know anything,' said Pande simply, through a mouthful of hot pakora. 'That's why I'm asking you.'

Joshi decided not to take any more chances. After all, the first time he had seen this man, he had been savagely beating up a puppeteer with his own puppet. He might as well give him whatever he wanted, and then hang around in the hopes of picking up a story.

'Government has tried to do more bomb blasts,' he said, 'because the scientists needed to practise. The more you practise, more the performance improves. Like cricket. Or sex. But the Americans are always causing problems.'

Pande frowned.

'What is it of their fathers'?' he asked.

'They want to be the only experts in nuclear bombs. That way, everyone has to listen to them. But we need it too, so we can bomb the bastard Pakistanis! We can teach them a lesson they will never forget!'

Pande eyed him sourly. He had seen what the bomb could actually do. It was obviously fools like this who had caused it all, waving and cheering and saying stupid things, right until the moment the bomb dropped on their heads, and the sand popped like popcorn, and the skin peeled off their flesh in long black strips. He should show this moron some of the people in the Dead Circle—that would cure him of his enthusiasm. Pande was beginning to see why he had to do what he was trying to do. But he wished the man would stop talking about international politics. It was giving him a headache.

'How do the Americans cause problems?' he asked.

'They keep stopping us,' said Joshi, 'we have tried to do testing in 1985, 1995 and last year, and each time they find out in advance and they stop us. The American ambassador comes to the PM's house and he has tea and sandwiches, and he shouts at him, so then the PM stops the testing and the scientists all go home and cry in their pillows or beat up their wives, depending on their mentality.'

'How do they always get to know?' asked Pande. 'Do the faujis tell them everything or what?'

'The faujis are not like that,' said Joshi, whose brother was in the army, 'although one or two will tell you anything for a bottle of Blue Label. It's their only weak point. No, the Americans can stop us because they can see us.'

'How can they see us?' demanded Pande. 'America is thousands of miles away.'

'They have satellites, high up in the sky,' said Joshi, 'from there they can see everything.'

'You mean, like aeroplanes?' asked Pande, puzzled.

'No, no,' said Joshi, 'much higher than that. They have special cameras. Cameras so powerful, they can read a piece of paper in a soldier's hand on the ground.'

Pande eyed the journalist suspiciously. Was he trying to make a fool of him? Why did everyone always try to do that? This sounded like a complete cock-and-bull story. He rolled up his sleeves, trying to make it look casual.

'Believe me,' pleaded Joshi, 'it's true. The Americans have lots of money. They can do anything. Their women even have artificial breasts.'

Pande had not known that the Bank of Bodies had branches in America too. As an Indian, he felt quite proud. But he could see a weak point in Joshi's story.

'So what if they have these special cameras?' he said. 'Why can't we do blasting underground? Or are these X-ray type?'

'No, they are not X-ray type,' said Joshi, 'and actually, blasting does happen underground, in the desert. But to place the bomb, they have to dig a big hole in the sand, with bulldozers and lots of soldiers. Even if they do not spot the activity, they can see when the sand is disturbed. Then they know some bomb-related activity is occurring. That's when the ambassador comes to the PM, and has tea, and yells at him. Last time the ambassador gave the PM a proper slide-show presentation, to show the pictures they had taken. The quality of photography was very good. He was astonishingly rude. Some of the Indian diplomats took notes, so that they could say similar things to the Bhutanese and Bangladeshis in future.'

Pande was perplexed. The Americans were like Gods, with their special planes and their artificial breasts and their magic cameras. Yet a second Pokhran blast had certainly happened, despite their superpowers. He felt a little depressed. What could he do, on his own?

Joshi watched him closely. He had a hunch he was on to a big story, although why the government had entrusted a top-secret mission to a semi-literate psychopath was a mystery. He could see that the man was getting discouraged. If he kept him on track, he would get his story.

'Perhaps you should visit Khetolai,' he suggested.

'What is this Khetolai?' asked Pande. 'Is it in Mizoram or what?'

'It's a village near Pokhran,' said Joshi, smiling. 'It's the closest village to the bomb site of 1974. They may know more than anyone else about such matters.'

'That's a good idea,' conceded Pande.

'Can I come with you?' asked Joshi, trying to hide his eagerness.

'No,' said Pande, 'you ask too many questions. That's the problem with you paper-wallahs. When you're talking to police, always remember—we ask the questions, not you. If I need anything further, I'll contact you.'

He got up to leave. Joshi wasn't too disturbed. He had his own sources in Khetolai. They'd keep him informed.

'When you go there, don't kick the goats, or the deer,' he called out as Pande left. 'The people there love animals. They're Bishnois. They look peaceful, but they can be ferocious.'

Great, thought Pande, that's all I need. More animals.

50

'Did I call you today and say, "Subramaniam, kindly come and give me a lecture on Psychology"?'

On Monday, the CA received his first Threatening Note from China. It was a pleasant surprise. The CBI had been overly intrusive in its investigation of Chinese restaurants. For some time China had been pushing for the recognition of all Chinese restaurants worldwide as Chinese territory. The proprietors of such concerns received stapled visas when visiting China, since they were going home. Any mistreatment of them was considered a slap in the face of the Motherland. While he was secretly pleased with the result, he had used the opportunity to chastise CBI Director Sinha, who had been standing on one leg outside his office for the last three hours. Sinha had also been babbling something about Shanti Nagar. The CA had ordered Mehta to gag him. He hated it when anyone mentioned Shanti Nagar.

The threatening note showed that like all his plans, this, too, was working out perfectly. He liked it when entire nations responded to his actions. It helped place the earth-shattering greatness of his being on an appropriate geographic canvas: Him the CA, vs China. The CA vs the USA. The CA vs the United Arab Emirates. The CA vs the European Community. It made him a key player in the Game of Nations.

Guiding destiny was not an individual sport, however, and even the CA needed support, which was why he had called in Subramaniam, his Foreign Affairs Advisor. Subramaniam was Tamil. The CA was deeply prejudiced against his race.

Subramaniam cleared his throat gently. 'The Threatening Note, sir,' he said, adroitly combining the servile and the urbane. 'Do you not wish to share it with me?'

The CA picked up the sheet of paper from his desk. It really was quite remarkably rude. The Chinese were rather good at this sort of thing. They had thousands of years of practice at pouring scorn and contempt on inferior races.

'The Pseudo-Democratic, Neo-Colonialist so-called Republic of India is hereby warned that it should desist from conducting further acts of imperialist aggression against Mother China with immediate effect. Prosecution and harassment of Chinese citizens, or anyone resembling Chinese citizens, must cease immediately. No further encouragement of splittist tendencies on the Chinese mainland (currently defined cartographically as three kilometres west of Patna) will be tolerated. Pathetic attempts at mobilization by Indian forces have been noted and will draw an appropriate response from the People's Army if continued. Any further hostile acts, devious acts of subterfuge, acts demeaning or disrespectful in nature, or any other objectionable acts committed against the Republic of China, its citizens, or its allies, will be considered acts of war and dealt with accordingly.'

The CA looked up at Subramaniam. They were on the verge of making history, he knew, and it filled him with pride. Subramaniam chewed his pipe thoughtfully. He sighed and shook his head.

'Typical, really,' he said. 'Quite, quite typical. I have frequently written on the subject of the Chinese psyche, and how their unique quality of aggrieved superiority is a filter through which all their actions and utterances must be viewed. Throughout the past few centuries, they have never felt that the normal rules of diplomacy governing the transactions between nations apply to them. On the one hand, they have been the victims of colonialism and imperialist aggression, and they believe the rest of the world owes them restitution. Married to this is a tendency to rewrite history—witness how the Cultural Revolution has been erased from their group mind. Once you factor in their invincible sense of moral, cultural, racial and now, military and economic superiority, you have a paradigm—a truly unique paradigm. In my opening speech to the Re-Non-Aligned Nations at Geneva, I had—'

The CA snatched the pipe out of Subramaniam's mouth and dropped it into his spittoon.

'When I want a lecture on psychology, I will let you know,' he said menacingly. 'Did I call you today and say, "Subramaniam, kindly come and give me a lecture on psychology." Did I?'

Subramaniam shrank visibly in his chair. 'No, sir, you did not,' he mumbled, wishing he was in Geneva.

'So just tell me one simple thing,' hissed the CA, 'how soon will they declare war?'

Subramaniam recovered his poise somewhat, disarmed by the childishness of the question. Honestly, these laymen were such simpletons!

'War? There will be no war. Most of China's neighbours have by now learnt the art of decoding the semantics in Chinese pronouncements. In fact, in a paper I presented at Brussels—'

The CA grabbed hold of Subramaniam's tie and yanked him forward. He pulled him inch by inch across his desk till he was half out of his chair and semi-prostrated, giving the CA a bird's-eye-view of his bald patch. The CA maintained his grip on the tie with one hand and picked up his stainless steel ruler with the other. He rapped Subramaniam on the head thrice, not hard enough to break his skull, but with sufficient force to ensure he would feel it when he combed his hair the following morning.

Mentioning Brussels had been a mistake, Subramaniam now realized, trying hard not to inhale an inconveniently placed safety pin.

'Soon. War. Very. Soon,' he mumbled, his lips mashed against the fine teak wood of the CA's desk.

'How soon?' persisted the CA.

The impulse to say tomorrow morning was practically overpowering, but Subramaniam was, in his own peculiar way, a man of integrity.

'Have. We. Really. Mobilized?' he asked.

The CA let go of his tie. Subramaniam flopped back in his chair, took off his spectacles, and started cleaning them. The CA waited patiently, letting him finish.

'We have not actually mobilized, have we, sir?' asked Subramaniam eventually. 'I saw no mention of it on television.'

This was a sore point with the CA. He snapped a pencil in two moodily.

'That damn fool General is dragging his feet,' he said. 'He is a coward and a traitor who doubts our ability to win this war.'

Privately, Subramaniam doubted it too, but it wasn't his area. His colleague Mullapudi could deal with that one.

Aloud he said, 'Then, sir, I would offer two pieces of advice. One, please tighten our security, as the Chinese seem to be privy to our internal discussions. And two, unless we actually do mobilize, I do not see any immediate threat of war.'

The CA sat and brooded about this for a while, glowering at nothing in particular. 'You can go now,' he said, finally, with a dismissive wave of his hand. The man was an idiot. If the Chinese were this angry over restaurants, imagine what they would do once the PM unveiled a statue of the Dalai Lama live on national television. His minions had despatched the statue to Tirunelveli by mistake, but as soon as it was back, he would make it happen.

51

'His Highness is demonstrating classic symptoms of
Alien Organ Syndrome.'

Mrs Verma was meeting her psychiatrist. She had bought him on eBay and kept him in the basement of her house. The basement was extremely well-appointed, with a home theatre, surround sound, and a cappuccino machine. Nutritious meals were sent in regularly through a slot in the door. But he craved pizza, which Domino's refused to deliver because it took fifteen minutes to reach the basement from the gates of the Verma mansion. He had often contemplated mentioning this to Mrs Verma when she came to discuss her mental disturbances with him.

Pappu Verma was fascinated by the little balls hanging from a titanium alloy frame on the psychiatrist's desk. He pulled one ball and let it go. Click clack went the balls. He clapped his hands. Mrs Verma watched him sadly. It was balls that had necessitated a consultation with the psychiatrist. Specifically, those of Balaji the Fixer, whose scrotum Pappu had squashed in full view of the public at the JNIGRGSGRGPG Museum, causing immense distress to the Prime Minister, Mrs Johnson, and most notably, Balaji, whose second round of surgery was scheduled for Monday. During a mildly disciplinary meeting with Mrs Johnson, Pappu had remained unrepentant and said that it wasn't him, it was the hand. As a defence, Mrs Verma had to admit this was brilliant, but she found his overall pattern of behaviour highly disturbing. He appeared to be suffering from some form of reverse kleptomania with kinky elements. Mrs Verma had decided it was time to seek a professional opinion.

Shovon Chowdhury

The doctor listened patiently to the whole story. He thought long and hard. He looked up at the ceiling. He looked down at the floor. He looked at Mrs Verma. He looked up at the ceiling again. Mrs Verma reached for the can of mace she always kept in her handbag.

'It appears the hand has developed an aversion to BoB executives,' said the psychiatrist, sensing peril.

'What do you MEAN!' said Mrs Verma. 'Are you on drugs? It's a hand, for God's sake. It doesn't have a brain.'

The truth was the psychiatrist didn't have a clue. Ever since he had been bought by Mrs Verma he had discovered that the family was dysfunctional in a variety of ways, but the kid was something else altogether. In his opinion Pappu was loony as a bandicoot. There was no good way of conveying this to his mother. As their resident mental-healthcare provider, he would inevitably be held responsible. A soothing and plausible diagnosis, on the other hand, could bring him one step closer to pizza. His mind filled with visions of cheese.

'Well,' demanded Mrs Verma, 'don't you have anything else to say?'

'Pepperoni,' said the psychiatrist by mistake.

The man was just like her mother. All she could think about was food. She spent whole days in cyberspace planning their meals, manifesting unexpectedly on kitchen monitors, driving the cooks to distraction.

'Perhaps you'd like to spend some time in a government hospital, taking care of radiation victims,' said Mrs Verma, 'it might take your mind off food.'

'His Highness is demonstrating classic symptoms of Alien Organ Syndrome,' said the psychiatrist, promptly. 'Along with what may be the early stages of Involuntary Psychic Confluence.'

'You just made all that up, didn't you?' said Mrs Verma.

'Am I an alien now?' asked Pappu.

'No, sweetie,' said Mrs Verma, giving him a hug.

'It is wrong to say that I have fabricated everything,' said the psychiatrist. 'The logic is such that even non-medical people can understand. The existence of phantom pains is a well-documented fact, whereby recent amputees feel the pain of an absent limb. But what about the limb? No one ever considers that. In India, such limbs are frequently reattached to people other than the original owner. We have a vast amount of data generated from such procedures. It is an area in which we lead the world.

This data shows that in certain exceptional cases, the new limb can cause unforeseen complications, unpleasant side effects, and unexpected consequences, unless and until prompt action is taken.'

'What kind of prompt action?' enquired Mrs Verma.

'A reversal of the surgical procedure is required. This will cause the young master some inconvenience, but I am sure a substitute will soon be found, one with no wireless connections to the donor. The current hand seems to have inherited certain prejudices and predilections from its original host.'

Given that she had just forced the BoB to refund Ramu, she dreaded the thought of asking them to take the hand back. It made her look whimsical, but if it had to be done, it had to be done. Unless this idiot could suggest an alternative.

'Isn't there anything else we can do?' she asked.

'We could wrap his head in aluminium foil,' said the psychiatrist, 'which could interfere with the transmissions from the donor.'

'He's a boy, not a sandwich!' said Mrs Verma. 'Get a grip.'

'How about gold foil?' suggested the doctor. 'That would give him the sort of premium appearance befitting his status. Perhaps it could be shaped like a crown.'

'We're not putting anything on his head,' said Mrs Verma, firmly, 'think of something else.'

The psychiatrist hesitated. Another solution had occurred to him. But how far was he willing to go for pizza?

'We could kill the source of the transmission,' he said reluctantly.

This would mean hiring a hit squad and going to Shanti Nagar. She could have brought some of the South Africans down from the mine, but they were striking to protest the lack of imported beer. Productivity had declined steeply. That was another thing she really had to do something about while Sanjeev faffed around in Calcutta.

'Let me see how it goes at the Bank of Bodies first,' she said. 'They're the ones who created this mess. Come, Pappu!'

The lift arrived, radiating happiness. Moments later, they were gone, leaving the psychiatrist sitting in his chair, dreaming of pepperoni pizza.

52

'When I was younger, perhaps, you could have made my dreams come true. At least two-three times a day.'

'When I was a little girl,' said Shanti-bai, 'I looked like a little boy.'

She was a eunuch! Banani was astonished. She had been rather relieved to find that Shanti-bai was just a little old lady in a white sari, much like her widowed aunties back in Calcutta. Her natural expression was one of grim disapproval. That was familiar too. She had thought her face looked mannish, but she had assumed that to be a natural consequence of the ageing process. Most of her grandparents resembled each other.

A chicken squawked impatiently, demanding Shanti-bai's attention. Shanti-bai swished at it with her broom irritably and the chicken fluttered back still squawking. Shanti-bai looked at the recently divorced husband and wife, who were contesting possession of the bird.

'Do one thing,' said Shanti-bai, 'cook the bird. You have one leg-piece, she can have one leg-piece, everyone will be happy.'

'This is a wrong ruling!' protested the man. 'You are making us eat our future!'

Shanti-bai cackled and clapped her hands. 'Oh, see everyone! One son of a vakil has come here! If you have any court cases give them to him, everything will get solved!'

'It's all right,' said the man sulkily, 'you decide. But give us a proper decision.'

'I'll tell you what,' said Shanti-bai, 'you give me the chicken, I'll eat it. You keep the feathers: you can make two cushions, and keep one each. That way, whenever you are resting, you'll remember her. I've also not had chicken stew for a long time. Ranjeeta, boil the water, a chicken is coming . . .'

'This not correct, Shanti-bai,' said the woman, 'think properly, no? You're not trying hard enough.'

Shanti-bai turned to Banani. They were sitting on her doorstep, with Pintoo crouching at their feet, surrounded by a wide variety of supplicants. A group of SDF boys stood amongst them, eager to press their case of launching a career of conquests à la Age of Empires, using Pintoo as their secret weapon. Even though Banani had demanded they let Shanti-bai decide, she was feeling nervous now. There was a certain whimsicality to Shanti-bai's decisions. They could end up in Moscow by Friday.

'See these people!' said Shanti-bai, turning to Banani. 'I have retired who knows when, still they won't let me go. I keep telling them I'm too old to dance now, and if I cannot dance, then what use am I? They have to solve their own problems. But no, every day they come and say, Shanti-bai, I have to wipe my nose, should I use a handkerchief, or is the end of my dhoti sufficient; or Shanti-bai, my mother won't let me marry the meat seller, will you help me, or should I run away, and other such useless things. I try to give them very bad advice, hoping they will stop coming, but they'll follow even that rather than think for themselves.'

'Now that we are here, you must help us,' said husband and wife together, showing a remarkable degree of unity for people who couldn't stand each other. Shanti-bai looked at their faces for a while, mumbling obscenities under her breath.

'You're not cursing us are you, Shanti-bai?' asked the woman, nervously. Everyone knew a eunuch's curse was lethal, second only to that of the Income Tax Department.

Shanti-bai pointed to the woman. Her voice was clipped and business-like. 'You will keep the chicken. You will take better care of it, being a woman. He will probably give it too much to drink, or drown it in the commode by mistake.'

The man opened his mouth to protest. Shanti-bai raised her broom threateningly. 'You will keep the eggs. Whatever money you make from selling eggs, you will share fifty-fifty. Of course, this means you will have to stay together to manage the whole affair, even though you hate each other. Perhaps she will cut off your manhood in the middle of the night, while you are sleeping. Then you can come here and become one of us. I need someone to press my feet.'

The man seemed unperturbed by this. They left together, followed by the chicken, who was relieved at her narrow escape.

'Bas, jao,' said Shanti-bai, waving her broom at the crowd, 'today's show is finished.'

'What about our case?' asked the SDF captain.

'What case could durwans possibly have?' asked Shanti-bai. 'Did someone trim your moustaches while you were sleeping? Perhaps your palms are too calloused from gripping your lathis? I can give you some moisturizer for that.'

The captain was a tough cookie. He held his ground, unbowed by all the sarcasm.

'The boy Pintoo defended us from the Medical Military Commandos yesterday,' he said. 'He made them fly out of Shanti Nagar like birds, except for one, who flew like a helicopter.'

'You were getting a helicopter, you should have left also,' suggested Shanti-bai, 'then you would not be here bothering me.'

The men murmured unhappily. The captain protested.

'Shanti-bai, this is our golden opportunity! We can make all your dreams come true. Just give us the boy and see what we do! We have been practising.'

Shanti-bai looked him up and down. He was nicely constructed.

'When I was younger, perhaps, you could have made my dreams come true. At least two-three times a day. But nowadays I prefer reading. I am unable to understand your meaning. Could you explain more clearly?'

'If Pintoo is with us, we can crush the city people, who are our enemies. The whole of Delhi can be ours. We will get you a nice flat, where you can bathe in a bathtub, and keep potted plants on the balcony. No one can stand before Pintoo! God has blessed him!'

Shanti-bai pressed her hands on her thighs and stood up slowly. 'Ranjeeta!' she called. 'Get me a sari, and some bangles!'

Ranjeeta appeared almost instantly. She always kept a set handy. She was a tall young hijra with crimson lips and rolling hips. Her sari was electric blue, and edged with silver. She had come in from the city and settled down with Shanti-bai. She liked it here. There was less money to be made, but more fun to be had.

'Here you go,' she said cheerfully, holding out a neatly folded sari for the captain. The bangles were on top. They twinkled insultingly.

'Why are you doing this?' he asked tearfully. 'We are working so hard to protect you. Why are you shaming us?'

Shanti-bai looked puzzled.

'How can I shame you?' she asked. 'You want to make a little boy fight for you, all you big strong men, what shame could you possibly have? See, this sari is a very nice colour, it will suit your complexion.'

Ranjeeta pouted and held out the sari invitingly. The captain backed away from it, ashen-faced. His men backed with him, in perfect unison, terrified into synchronicity. They backed away down the street, keeping their eyes warily on the sari, feeling reflexive twinges in their rapidly shrinking loins. Ranjeeta followed them for a short distance, making delicate, suggestive hip movements.

Soldiers were doing an awful lot of retreating in Shanti Nagar these days, thought Banani. It was probably a good thing.

'Why don't you come inside for a cup of tea, dear?' asked Shanti-bai.

Banani looked at her in surprise.

'What,' said Shanti-bai, 'you think a eunuch cannot learn English? Have you addressed the United Nations? I have. A Saudi prince wanted to marry me once. I don't blame him. I used to be super hot.'

'I'm sorry,' stammered Banani.

Shanti-bai put a hand on her cheek. Her hands were huge.

'I've heard about you,' she said, 'someone like you is very necessary here. Now that you've come to Shanti Nagar, we will not let you go. Come inside. You too, little superman,' she said, turning to Pintoo.

'Are you going to dance now?' asked Pintoo.

'Only on Fridays, dear,' said Shanti-bai. They went inside.

The room was spare and simple, with a cot, a bookcase, and a digital poster of Gandhi on the wall. He was marching to Dandi. The clip was a seamless loop. In Shanti-bai's room, he never stopped marching.

Shanti-bai lay down on her cot. Ranjeeta put on the kettle and came back to press her feet. Banani and Pintoo sat on the ground. They sat quietly for a while. It was very peaceful.

'Can I ask you a question?' said Banani.

'The story of Shanti Nagar?' said Shanti-bai intuitively.

Banani nodded.

'I was on the metro when the first bomb dropped,' said Shanti-bai, 'the train stopped at Rajeev Chowk, and never started again. Many rich people died that day, because they were in their big cars on the streets, while we were underground. The station soon filled up with survivors from above, although many did not survive long. I saw a little baby. It had no skin. Its eyes had melted. But still it was fighting to live. It died in my arms. For a long time I sat there, with the baby, until someone took it from my lap and said Shanti-bai, stand up, you must help us. He was known to me. He was from my ward, where I was the councillor. I stood for council elections as a result of a joke played by some young men. They came to me and said Shanti-bai, you must stand for elections. Be shameless and clap your hands, and show the world what we think of these corrupt politicians. I remembered what my old nayak said, when I was a young woman. There are only two ways for hijras to earn a living, he said—prostitution and politics. At least in politics you can serve more than one person at a time. So I agreed and I campaigned, and as I did, the logic of my actions became increasingly clear to me. I am a hijra. I have no family. I have no sons, for whose sake I will steal your money. I have no religion. The Muslims think I am Hindu, the Hindus think I am Muslim. I am a member of a community where everyone is alone and everyone is together. Who can lead the country better? Who can get the work done better? If work has to be done, who will say no to me, knowing the alternative is a hijra's curse? I said these things and people listened and they voted for me in very large numbers. I won by 50,000 votes. After I was elected, I never let them down. Until the day the bombs fell. Some of the people from my ward were in that train, and in that station. I was confused and grief-stricken. I may not have family, but I had people I loved, and I knew I would never see them again. We could hear the hot wind roaring above, and the cries of the dying below. It was a dead man who told me what to do. He was dead, but he was still speaking. He pulled on the hem of my sari as he lay on the platform. "Are you not the famous Shanti-bai?" he said. Each word was an effort for him. "Why are you not helping these people? Are you a eunuch or what?" He laughed and laughed, lying there on the platform, and then he died, and I saw his courage and although I am shameless, it shamed me, and I stood up. The first thing I had to get was food. I sent them to the fancy coffee shops, up and down the line, where a sandwich costs as much as a good man's wage, and collected whatever we could find. We were there for a month, and I rationed the food. There was none for the dying, but I walked amongst them every day and talked to them, and they understood. It was harder with the living. Each one was alone, and some were mad. Later, we took the mad ones with us and many are still here today. They do what work they can. Sometimes they throw tomatoes. If Tarun has given any speeches recently, you will have seen them. To the others, the lonely ones, I gave new families. The doctors, plumbers, computer people, cooks—each one was a group and I put them all together. Get to know each other well, I said, these are your families now. The office babus were a difficulty. We did not know what to do with them. We assigned some to each family as apprentices, hoping they would learn something useful over time. In this way we spent the next few weeks, down in Rajeev Chowk station, surviving and planning and getting to know each other. We could see what was happening above on the station's TV monitors. Not all the rich people had died. Some were on holiday. A few were in bunkers. Soon rich people from all around also started coming, from Chandigarh and Jaipur and Lucknow, attracted by all the vacant plots, many of which were still radioactive. This is not the first time Delhi has been depopulated, and it will not be the last. Land falls vacant. New people appear. I realized that this was our chance too. Our chance to build something new. Emergency had been declared by then, and the Bureau of Reconstruction had already been formed. But they had a lot of reconstructing to do. It was clear they would start with the ministers' bungalows, and then the places where the wealthy people lived. It would be years before they reached the poorer parts. Years that we could use. So I marched them all to Chandni Chowk station, where we emerged into the light. Do you see that red wall over there?' she said, pointing. 'That's where the Red Fort used to be. They used to say he who rules the Red Fort rules Delhi, but now there is no Red Fort. Just us.'

Pintoo gave her a hug. Banani wanted to, but she felt shy.

'What do I do about him?' she asked.

'I won't tell you what to do,' said Shanti-bai, 'but there are a couple of things you should think about.'

This was a familiar technique. Banani used it in class all the time.

'Tell me,' she said.

'My friend Giridhar had a mutant rabbit. Giridhar was very musical, he used to listen to the radio a lot. One day, just after breakfast his rabbit began to sing. He sang ghazals in the style of Ghulam Ali. If you closed your eyes, you would think it *was* Ghulam Ali. Giridhar was immensely proud of his rabbit and people would come from far and wide to see him. Giridhar would make him sing at all times of day, sometimes without letting him finish his carrot. One day, in the middle of a performance, the rabbit flew away and never returned. What do you learn from this?'

'Don't make your rabbit sing too much?' suggested Banani.

Shanti-bai rapped her on the head with a knuckle. 'Pay attention!' she said. 'Your mind is drifting. How long ago did Pintoo start pushing people? A week? Ten days? You think I would not have known if it was earlier? How do you know this is all he can do? How do you know his powers are not evolving? Or should we wait till one morning he turns us all into monkeys, so that people can point at us and say, see, see, look what Banani's student did! And see over there, see, that's Banani herself, eating a banana!'

Shanti-bai could be mean when she wanted to be. Banani didn't feel like hugging her any more. But she did have a point.

'OK, I should investigate the extent of Pintoo's powers,' Banani said. 'What's the second thing you want me to think about?'

'Think about what Chameli did. Years ago, in Madhya Pradesh, many from the hijra community were elected to many positions by the public, just like me. But the losing candidates would regularly purchase the Chief Justice, and he would always disqualify them, saying, are you a man or a woman, and which box did you cross in your form, and are you aware that fraudulent ticking of boxes is one of the biggest problems facing the country? The hijras fought each case, and they lost each case, until Chameli took initiative on behalf of the community. The Chief Justice had a son, who was unable to find a bride, because he was extraordinarily ugly and had failed in the real estate business. It was unheard of in those days for the son of a judge to fail in the real estate business, and it was seen as a sign of extreme incompetence. Chameli was very beautiful, and hardly needed to shave, and smelt like heaven. Her fragrance alone was stronger than Viagra. Posing as the owner of a luxury flat she seduced the judge's son while refusing to indulge in full congress. He was like putty in her hands, except once or twice, when he hardened. He begged and pleaded, but Chameli stood firm. Only if he married her could he gain full access to the flat, and her, she said. Seeing that his son was losing weight, his father agreed. Many hijras came to the wedding, but then, many hijras come to every wedding so no one suspected anything until it was far too late. The boy's mother had some prior misgivings, but the Chief Justice ordered her to stick to cooking, which she did. It all worked out for the best in the end. The son was deliriously happy and his business flourished. The Chief Justice had to stop persecuting hijras and allow them to win elections, since his son was having sex with one on a regular basis. It was a small price to pay for domestic bliss. After all, the politicians who had been defeated by hijras were just one of his many sources of income, and by marginally increasing his rates elsewhere, he was able to support his family in the style to which they were accustomed. So, as you can see, all my stories do not have sad endings. In this case, joy was widespread, except for the defeated politicians, who immigrated to Switzerland so they could be closer to their money. It comforted them, although the cuisine was not to their liking.'

'I'm already married,' said Banani, 'and I don't like perfume.'

'That is not the point of my story,' said Shanti-bai crossly.

'It's hard to tell what the point of your stories is,' said Banani, 'I tell my kids stories too, but they're simple ones, like Jack and Jill, which teaches you not to run with a bucket.'

'It should be perfectly obvious,' said Shanti-bai, 'your little boy smashed up a branch, and made a few medical militaries fly away. Do you think that is the end of the Bank of Bodies? Do you think they will not come again? Pushing them out of your house is not going to solve the problem. You need to get inside their house, and destroy them from within. And is the Bank of Bodies the end of the story? Don't think I don't know what these people have been doing. They're playing gilli-danda with history-geography. The only plus point is that rascal police fellow is now far away. But what about today? Is there nothing else you can do about today? You're a clever girl, do some investigation, give the matter some thought.'

It sounded like a tall order, but Shanti-bai was not the sort of person you said no to. She was right about Pintoo too. Why were they assuming this was all he could do? There had to be a way he could get Hemonto back. There was a trick with mirrors she was keen to try.

They got up to leave. Pintoo ducked down and touched Shanti-bai's feet. Shanti-bai rapped him on the head with her knuckle.

'She's looking after you, who's looking after her? Find her husband, you little rascal! You think you're a magician? Proper magicians don't just vanish things, they bring them back also. First you learn properly, then you do such tamasha. Until then, stick to card tricks, and do whatever Auntie says. And press her feet for at least half an hour every day.'

'Will you do a tiny little dance for me?' asked Pintoo meekly.

'Come back in a week,' said Shanti-bai. 'If Auntie is happy with you, I'll consider it. Now go away. Why are you standing here gossiping? I'm retired. What's your excuse?'

Shovon Chowdhury

53

*'The honey is produced by spiritually uplifted bees,
who relinquish it voluntarily.'*

Guru Dharti Pakar was practicing his smile in front of the mirror, taking great care not to mesmerize himself when the voice of his yummy receptionist broke his reverie.

'The delegation from Bank of Bodies is here, DP,' she said through the intercom. She was the only one who addressed him as DP, a legacy of the days when he had been a management consultant and she had been his secretary. At the time, DP had stood for Dinesh Pawar. She had joined him as a young girl with stars in her eyes, impressed by his monumental bestseller, *Convert the Competition into Cockroaches*, or 3C as it was more popularly known. The stars were long gone, but the income was fabulous.

Dharti Pakar née Dinesh Pawar was mildly annoyed at being disturbed in the middle of his favourite pastime, but he was always unfailingly polite to the cream of society. It didn't get any creamier than the Bank of Bodies.

'Send them up,' he cooed into the intercom, getting up on to his pure-white, elevated mattress and assuming the lotus position. He took a fistful of rose petals from a bowl and sprinkled them artfully around himself.

The delegation from BoB was sitting in the reception area, where they were alternating between admiring the reception and the receptionist.

As always, the marble floors and ceramic walls of the reception area were clean, bright and shining white. A newly installed fountain, tastefully adorned with white marble cherubs, dominated the centre. A hologram of Guru Dharti Pakar floated above the water, gazing benevolently down upon the assembled masses.

A heavenly aroma permeated the atmosphere, delightful, delicate and intoxicating. No. 2, lolling about on a dazzling white sofa, found something about the aroma oddly familiar. He inhaled deeply and smiled. It was the smell of money.

'Guruji will see you now,' trilled the receptionist, ushering them towards the elevator at the end of the corridor. As he walked down the corridor, No. 2 started, shocked to see a figure he had seen innumerable times on television, holograms, and promodrones, standing next to the elevator. Had Guruji come down himself to greet them? Such an honour was unprecedented. No. 2 felt his heart swell with pride. BoB was, of course, a name to reckon with, but nevertheless, to be personally greeted by the holiest man in the land! He even seemed to be holding a placard of some sort.

On closer examination, the figure turned out to be a life-sized cut-out of Guruji, with the slogan 'LEAN ON ME' written invitingly above his head. The receptionist noticed No. 2's interest, and proceeded to explain.

'This is the newest initiative of Guruji,' she said, magically conjuring a leaflet and handing it over, 'it is the Personalized Guruji Support System. In times of trouble, people look to Guruji for support, but he cannot attend to all personally, although he is with them in spirit. Once you install the PGSS, whenever you are troubled, you can lean on him, in the comfort of your own home and he will support you.'

No. 2 was checking out the price tag for a PGSS—it was discreetly embedded in the shoulder of the cut-out. He was taken aback by what it would cost to have one; self-reliance seemed more viable, economically.

The receptionist had not risen to the exalted position of gatekeeper to the Doors of Heaven by mere coincidence. 'There is a cheaper alternative,' she said, quickly, 'we take a life-size replica of Guruji, made from the finest handcrafted vinyl and paste it on your wall. But this is only partially effective since, after all, part of the support in that case comes from the wall, rather than Guruji. But this . . .'

She slapped her hand rather familiarly on the cut-out, which emitted a reassuringly solid thud, like a BMW door closing.

'This image of Guruji is mounted on reinforced stainless steel, with a solid, cast-iron base. You can lean on him as much as you like, however obese you may be, and you will receive full support. It comes with a three-year warranty.'

She draped herself around the effigy alluringly. No. 2 had no doubt that if need be, she could instantly materialize a credit card machine.

'Maybe later,' mumbled No. 2, walking towards the elevator and beckoning to his entourage to follow. He was deeply impressed. He had been right about the enormous potential in the religion business, and the huge benefits of allying with this genius.

The lift doors opened with a happy sigh as they entered. As the doors closed, joyful song filled the air, performed by Shri Shri Yo Yo, who now sang about religion instead of rape, since he'd been to jail, and experienced it. The lyrics were indecipherable but soothing, the tablas numerous. All three sides of the lift were adorned with life-sized pictures of Guruji, presumably for visitors to lean on and take a quick, free sampling of his latest product. These people were thorough professionals. As No. 2 stepped out of the lift and into the chambers of His Holiness there was a spring in his step.

Guru Dharti Pakar's eyes were closed and he seemed to be meditating. 'Please be seated while I absorb your auras,' he said in his richly mellifluous voice, his eyes still closed, 'it will only take a minute.'

They sat at his feet on thick white dhurries, leaning back against richly embroidered bolsters, waiting while their auras were absorbed. No. 2 had brought four hangers-on with him, to give himself the stature that was appropriate to this meeting. They sat behind him, furtively checking the room, hoping to catch a glimpse of a supermodel or two.

Dharti Pakar opened his eyes and smiled through his beard. The one with too much gel in his hair was the money. The others were barely sentient. The leader was a smoothie. Dharti Pakar knew the type. A lot like himself, except he did it in boardrooms.

Dharti Pakar clapped his hands, and a trainee receptionist materialized. She wore a white sari and carried a tray.

'Please refresh yourselves with some honeyed water,' said the Guru. 'The honey is produced by spiritually uplifted bees, who relinquish it voluntarily.'

They reached up from the floor and took glasses of the divine liquid and drank obediently. One of the young hangers-on tugged bashfully at the girl's saree. She glared down at him, and he subsided. She collected the empty glasses and flounced out.

'I have read your proposal with great interest,' said Dharti Pakar, who had done nothing of the sort. All his transactions were situational. He figured it out on the fly, and made things up as he went along. All he knew was that they were money-grubbing butchers, lacking in finesse, and they were here for some sort of tie-up.

'I gather you wish to assist me in spiritually uplifting the masses,' he said, smiling benignly. 'This is a task that I am already undertaking, throughout the universe and beyond. What can you possibly do to assist me?'

The guy was a tough cookie, realized No. 2. The key to negotiating was taking the upper hand, and this bearded bandicoot had managed to do that in thirty seconds flat.

'It's not so much assist as expand, Your Holiness,' he said, with the utmost humility. 'We have identified someone whom we can position as a messiah-type person, and we want to build a Religious Joy business around him. We would welcome your support.'

Dharti Pakar was aghast. He had always lived in fear of competition from multinational corporations. That day had finally come.

'I would never refer to myself as a messiah,' he said modestly, 'although the phrase has been used by the *New York Times*. But as I perform my duty of spiritual awakening and spread the fragrance of love across the world, it is only natural that people tend to look up to me. Why would you need someone else? I, too, provide Religious Joy.'

'This child can perform genuine miracles,' said No. 2.

Dharti Pakar raised an eyebrow.

'In a different way,' added No. 2 hastily, 'I mean, you perform genuine miracles too, not fake ones or anything like that. What could be more miraculous than genuine love? Something which you spread on a daily basis. No, this child is more like a freak of nature, and can do extraordinary things, although not in the same league as you when it comes to spirituality.'

No. 2 was beginning to sweat a little. Religious chitchat was a tricky thing. Body parts were much simpler. The man was running circles round him, simply by wiggling an eyebrow. He needed to focus.

Dharti Pakar allowed him to sweat while he thought rapidly. A genuine miracle-worker. That too a child. A potential gold mine. All he had to do was get his hands on the kid. Unfortunately, children and dogs were inherently suspicious of him. He had been bitten by both on numerous occasions. He would need intermediaries.

'It is good that you have come to me,' he said, 'a child of such power needs spiritual upliftment. Otherwise he will exhibit destructive tendencies, like the children of Bungalowpur. Luckily, I am an expert in this area. I have solved the problem of terrorism in many parts of the world, including Papua New Guinea and some pockets of Somalia. My patented breathing technique soothes fevered minds and converts violent aggression into reasonable calm. It also improves cholesterol levels and leads to greater potency, although for a child the latter may not be so relevant. I have frequently offered my services to the government, in order to solve the Maoist problem. Had they heeded my advice, all these problems would have been solved long ago.'

No. 2 was annoyed. The robed rascal was planning to corner their asset, by offering some sort of consultancy. He had to be put in his place, and quickly.

'Your child-counselling skills are legendary, Your Holiness,' said No. 2, 'no doubt at some point we will take you up on your kind offer. But what we are currently interested in is your distribution network. I believe you have over 3,000 outlets across the country. This would be an excellent pipeline through which to channel our new product, the Religious Joy Lottery.'

'My dear child,' said Dharti Pakar, with an air of mild rebuke, 'we do not have "outlets"; we have centres for the dissemination of spiritual upliftment through peace, love, joy and breathing. How can anything to do with the divine soul be a "product"? It is almost as if you have come here with some sort of business proposal.'

No. 2 gritted his teeth. 'Perish the thought,' he said, 'but the fact remains that your centres would be a great help in our endeavour to provide Religious Joy to the masses. If the venture received your blessing, and perhaps even your divine presence in the odd TV commercial, joy would spread much faster. In return for your support, we would naturally make sizable donations to parties you believe to be genuinely deserving.'

Dharti Pakar inclined his head gracefully, but continued to look regretful, signifying that he was not yet entirely pleased.

'Is there any other small way in which we can be of service?' asked No. 2.

'Much as I would like to help you, my child, our current centres are very small. For the kind of activities you are describing, we will need a series of new centres, with access to the main road, built on much larger plots. They can thus be insulated from the noise and disturbance of everyday life, and yet command the advantage of central location. We should not overdo it, so in the beginning we should not have more than fifty. Or perhaps a hundred.'

Religion and real estate had always gone hand in hand in India. Bliss required space, preferably freehold.

No. 2 was stunned by the man's audacity. He could see project costs spiralling out of control. The whole point was to utilize his facilities, not create new ones.

'I was not aware that you had such a space constraint,' he said, sadly. 'Then please do bless us, Guruji, and we will perhaps talk to Sach Guru of Internal Engineering™. He is far less popular, so hopefully he will have the space to accommodate us.'

The upstart guru of Internal Engineering™ was Dharti Pakar's bitter rival, who had not only stolen many of his basic ideas, but also pretended to be different by wearing a turban, and having a beard that was dyed grey—as opposed to jet black.

'I cannot possibly allow you to become a victim of that charlatan,' said Dharti Pakar, trying hard to control his agitation, 'my conscience would not allow it.'

'But I have heard that his programme helps balance the pressures of a demanding career with the longing for inner peace,' said No. 2, innocently, 'while also giving good results for arthritis and epilepsy.'

'Then you have heard wrong,' said the holy man, firmly. 'It pains me to say this, but certain individuals are using marketing gimmicks and air-brushed images to fool the public. He also happens to use eye shadow.'

'But are they not particularly active in the field of music?' asked No. 2, twisting the knife. 'The Internal Engineering™ Choir is famous throughout the world and has several hit albums to its credit. This would be very helpful for pulling in younger devotees.'

Dharti Pakar smiled at No. 2 warmly, his eyes filled with compassion, suppressing the urge to bash him over the head with one of the vases levitating next to his mattress.

'When it comes to music, the ART OF BREATHING™ has the 10,000-Man Tabla Orchestra, which is listed in the Guinness Book of World Records. Never in human history have so many tabla players been assembled in the same place at the same time. I can assure you that as a sight to attract potential devotees, nothing can surpass its power.'

No. 2 bowed his head, but said nothing.

'I suppose on a trial basis we can start this new plan for spiritual upliftment from our existing network,' said Dharti Pakar, knowing when he was beaten. 'Some of my disciples will sit with yours and work out the details.'

'Is there any other way in which the Bank of Bodies can assist you?' asked No. 2, who knew the value of being gracious in victory.

'I gather you have a panel of the finest legal minds in the country,' said Dharti Pakar, resigned to squeezing out whatever he could. 'I would want the BoB to provide this joint venture with strong legal support, in case of any mishaps or misunderstandings with devotees.'

Mostly female ones, I'll bet, thought No. 2, privately.

'It will be done, Your Holiness,' he said.

And let that be a lesson to you, No. 2 thought. Never mess with the man in the Armani suit. Now all he had to do was wrap up the kid, and he was golden.

54

'We do gymnastics also.'

It was a bright sunny day and Mr Chatterjee was sitting in the park, reading the newspaper. The city had an air of exhausted frustration. Resentment filled the air like a fog. But at least he could see the sky again. A group of RSS volunteers drilled in the distance, marching up and down with their lathis on their shoulders. Their baggy khaki shorts fluttered in the breeze.

Mr Chatterjee was reading about Morarji Desai. He was surprised to find him in the thick of the action here in 1948. All he remembered of Desai from his schooldays was that he was once prime minister of India, drank his own pee, and had lived to the age of approximately a hundred-and-three. Desai had stoutly maintained that the two were connected, but despite this shining example, urine therapy had never really caught on in India. In fact, he had led a cabinet of what could only be described as mixed nuts. They had come to power after the 1977 elections, in which Mrs Gandhi had been catastrophically defeated, despite the fact that all her advisors had assured her she would win. Her advisors could hardly be blamed. One of her sons was mad keen on sterilization. Electorally, this had handicapped her. The people of India were fairly tolerant, and accepted that young princes needed their hobbies, but they drew the line at widespread non-consensual genital snipping.

Morarji Desai's Janata Party government was a group of worthies that counted amongst their number (besides their pee-drinking leader) a tall leader who never used soap (he preferred mustard oil), and another who was mortally afraid of dentists. After observing them for a year or two, the people had welcomed back Mrs Gandhi with open arms. Her government shifted focus from gonads, and concentrated instead on not uplifting people from poverty. Apparently though, Morarji Desai had done more than just drink pee and briefly run the country late in his career, because here he was, staring out at Mr Chatterjee from the newspaper, wearing a Gandhi cap and looking like a stern and disgruntled pixie with improbably large ears. He was the home minister of Bombay, and a noted Gandhian, but he didn't seem very concerned about Gandhi.

Somewhat reluctantly, Morarji Desai had asked J.D. Nagarvala, the deputy commissioner of the Bombay Police, to look into the attempt on Gandhi. Two officers from the Delhi Police had met him, and Nagarvala, with characteristic acuteness, had penetrated to the heart of matter.

'You are too junior,' he had told the officers, 'also you have no jurisdiction in Bombay. You should not be wearing those uniforms here. Please take them off and leave this place. You may put them back on once you cross the border of Delhi.'

Mr Chatterjee was momentarily diverted by a mental image of the two Delhi cops in their underwear, their uniforms tucked under their armpits, glumly boarding the train for Delhi. But the overall situation was not good. It was almost as if they wanted Gandhi to die.

The RSS squad had marched themselves very close to his bench now, and he had a ringside view of their drill, which did nothing to improve his mood. They had formed a square and were standing slightly apart, to give themselves room to brandish their lathis. They wore black caps, white shirts, and ridiculously long khaki shorts, a design that would be copied decades later by seven-time Wimbledon champion Pete Sampras. They took two steps back in perfect unison, raising their lathis over their shoulders, and then two steps forward, swirling the lathis over their heads and bringing them down at precisely the same moment. They repeated this move, over and over, crushing countless imaginary enemies of the nation, the concentration fierce on their faces. It all looked eerily familiar to Mr Chatterjee. Nothing had changed much in nearly a hundred years, except that, in his time, some of them wore Nikes.

Their leader was now close to Mr Chatterjee's bench, his eyes flashing with zeal behind the thick, bottle-glass lenses of his spectacles. He was a nondescript little man in his early forties, with a shiny bald patch and shoulders that were hunched from constantly skulking in corridors. He was the butt of all the jokes in the office canteen. But here he was a leader of men. He sensed a kindred spirit in Mr Chatterjee, who looked vaguely clerical, and in obvious need of salvation.

'Victory to Mother India!' he said by way of greeting, 'Myself Dadlani.' He gestured to his squad to continue drilling on their own.

Not sure what to do and not wishing to give offence, Mr Chatterjee essayed a sketchy salute.

'Don't salute me, salute the flag,' said Mr Dadlani, pointing to the saffron double triangle hanging limply from a freshly-painted flagpole. 'That is the true flag of Mother India.'

Mr Chatterjee had never saluted any other flag, and he saw no reason to start now. He smiled politely at the man and went back to reading his newspaper.

'This drill should not scare you,' said the officer, 'it is not meant for fighting. It is meant to instil discipline. We do gymnastics also. It's all about fitness.'

For Mr Chatterjee, this was a new perspective. Apparently, there was nothing to fear from these people, they were mildly eccentric gym enthusiasts with a master plan.

'See, not just the flag, the whole system of government is wrong. This whole thing of two houses of parliament, one upper house and one lower house—totally wrong. There should be three.'

Mr Chatterjee found himself getting interested. His work as a telepath tester brought him in touch with a wide variety of dementia. His nostrils filled with the familiar aroma of freshly blooming insanity.

'Three houses of parliament, you say? How interesting. Who will occupy them?'

Mr Dadlani sat down next to him. He was behind on recruitment, and this fellow with spectacles reading the papers looked like a prime specimen.

'It's not just the houses, it's how they're selected. See, at the top of the government will be the president.'

'I see. Like the American system?'

'Not at all like the American system. Americans are decadent and immoral.'

They were a lot more global in outlook than he had realized, thought Mr Chatterjee.

'Not at all like the Americans,' emphasized Mr Dadlani. 'The president will be elected by the Lok Sabha, which is the parliament of the people.'

'We get to vote?'

'No, no,' said Mr Dadlani, his eyes gleaming with enthusiasm, 'this Lok Sabha is not elected, it is *selected*. And it will not consist of people, it will consist exclusively of *teachers*.'

'Who does the selecting?' asked Mr Chatterjee, puzzled.

'See, that's the beautiful part. There will be no election-felection or nonsense like that. All these lower class people, in our history they have never ruled. They should not. Their brains are too weak, due to poor eating habits and lack of exercise. Only proper people should rule.'

'So who are the proper people?'

'The HRD Ministry!' said Mr Dadlani triumphantly.

Mr Chatterjee hadn't seen that one coming.

'The Human Resources Development Ministry will appoint the president?' he asked, awestruck.

'Naturally. What does the HRD Ministry do? It selects all teachers in the country. All the good, respectable, decent people. The HRD Ministry will select the best teachers whose records are on their files, and make them part of the Lok Sabha. Only primary and secondary-school teachers, mind you. College professors are corrupt people. Many of them are Communists. Others eat beef.'

'Who selects the HRD Minister?'

'Naturally, we do. That is why we focus so much on education, and run so many schools. Our top teacher will be the HRD Minister. After him, whoever becomes the top teacher, he becomes the HRD Minister. The minister will then select mostly our own teachers for the Lok Sabha, because our people are mostly good people. That will be the Lok Sabha. The Lok Sabha will then select a good person as President.'

'Not the HRD Minister?' ventured Mr Chatterjee tentatively.

Mr Dadlani was annoyed.

'You are mixing things up! His function is totally different. President is president, and HRD Minister is HRD Minister.'

'So the president runs the country then?'

'No, no, not at all. That's the beauty of it. The president nominates the Guru Sabha, which is the second house of parliament. He will select the best holy men of the country, the sadhus and the sanyasis, and they will become the Guru Sabha.'

'So the Guru Sabha runs the country?'

'At last you are beginning to understand. It is the holy men, selected by the learned men, who form the number-one house of parliament, although they are formed second, because the Lok Sabha, which is the number-two house, is selected first, by the HRD Minister, because they are required in order to select the president, who will then select the Guru Sabha. All legislation and all financial bills will be developed by the Guru Sabha, and once they are OK with it, only then can the Lok Sabha consider it. They cannot change anything, but they can humbly suggest.'

'What about judges?' asked Mr Chatterjee. 'Won't we have any judges?'

'Don't be foolish. How can a country survive without judges? The Guru Sabha will also function as the judicial commission. They will select Supreme Court judges. If any judge turns out to have bad habits, like listening to foreign music, or celebrating Valentine's Day, or wearing skirts, they will impeach him.'

'How about an army? Will we have an army?'

'Of course, we must defend ourselves from the enemies. See you are not paying attention. I told you there are three houses of parliament. You forgot about the third.'

'I'm sorry,' said Mr Chatterjee humbly.

'The third house of parliament will be the Raksha Sabha, or Defence Parliament. It will consist of heads of army, navy and air force, plus many retired soldiers with good brains and the right type of thinking. Whenever they feel the country is in danger, they can declare Emergency, and take over the country. Then they are in charge.'

'So the army can take over any time?' asked Mr Chatterjee.

'Any time,' said Mr Dadlani firmly.

'Isn't the whole thing rather complicated?' ventured Mr Chatterjee.

'Nothing complicated! The selection of a good HRD Minister is the key. Our success has been predicted by astrologers.'

The man had been trying to mould his mind. He had listened

patiently. It was only fair that he should listen now, while he had a go at moulding his. History might thank him.

'Sir, I have one suggestion from my side,' he said. 'Why can't you be more of a cultural institution? Our culture is under threat. Someone has to defend it. Traditional dance forms are being neglected. Modern music has become corrupted. Theatre is declining. Literature is languishing. Sanskrit is almost dead. Even vegetarianism is being questioned.'

'It's those Muslims,' muttered Mr Dadlani.

'It could be anybody,' said Mr Chatterjee, 'but my point is, first make Hindu culture strong. Take your time. Do it properly. Spend a lot of time and effort on the film industry. Meanwhile, your political people can work in Delhi to reform the political system. Your youth wing could do cultural shows. Different people could play different roles.'

'You are a genius, sir!' said Mr Dadlani. 'We had never thought of diversifying that way. We are just one organization, with many enemies. British and Muslim influences run deep. But this way we could divide up the work. There could be many such parties of slightly excited people, which will do good work across the country, wherever it is required. They can be like training grounds. Promising officers from junior parties can join head office. It will be like one big, happy family. I will immediately share your thoughts with my supervisor. We could call it the Sangh Parivar.'

He rolled the phrase around his tongue and savoured it. Mr Chatterjee watched him, horrified. 'Perhaps you need to think this through,' he said, weakly. 'I foresee trouble if you follow this plan.'

Mr Dadlani wagged a finger playfully. 'Now, now. Don't be cheeky. How can you foresee? Are you an astrologer? The best ones sit in Chandni Chowk. If you want to talk about the future, you must have proper qualifications.'

'Actually your earlier plan was also good,' said Mr Chatterjee, wishing he had kept his mouth shut. 'In fact, in that presidential system, wouldn't Gandhi make a good president? He's a teacher, and a sort of holy man, isn't he?'

Mr Dadlani's face transformed into a mask of hatred.

'Gandhi is a traitor,' he hissed, 'because of him, the body of Mother India has been torn apart. He is a lover of our enemies. He deserves only death. It will happen soon. There is no lack of right-thinking people in the country.'

Throughout their conversation, the volunteers had been drilling away with single-minded determination.

Two steps backward, lathi back. Two steps forward, lathi down.

Over and over again.

Mr Chatterjee picked up his newspaper, got up and walked out of the park. He didn't say goodbye to Mr Dadlani. But Mr Dadlani had given him an idea.

It was time to pay a visit to Chandni Chowk.

55

'The so-called democracy of India stinks with the smell of rotten fish.'

The door of the limousine opened and the Saudi Ambassador stepped out, followed by three women draped in black from head to toe. Was it his imagination, or did he hear a muffled giggle? The General wasn't sure. He bowed deeply to the Ambassador, who responded with a brief nod.

'You honour us with your presence, Your Excellency,' said the General.

The Ambassador smiled. He looked slightly less bored than usual.

'The honour is entirely mine, General. The Prime Minister tells me you fought very bravely in the Battle of Srinagar.'

'Many people fought bravely in the Battle of Srinagar,' said the General, trying not to remember. It had been up close and personal, house to house and hand to hand, in the rubble of a ruined city, against grim-faced Talibs and feral children, who continued to fight on long after armistice, because that was all they had ever done and that was all they knew.

'It was a long time ago,' said the General, 'what can I do for you now, Your Excellency?'

'Ask him to give you the limousine,' whispered Navalkar. The General quelled him with a glance.

'We have just come from a meeting with the Prime Minister,' said the Saudi Ambassador. 'Three of my wives wanted to meet her, since she is a woman. They asked very politely, so I permitted them to accompany me.'

One of his wives kicked him in the shin. The Ambassador pulled out a piece of paper from his capacious gown and began to read from it.

'My latest wife,' he read, 'the presence of whom has not led to the diminution of my affection for my other wives in any way, has requested that the famous hero of the Indian army personally show her the command bunker from which the war was conducted. In order to do so, he will have to be her relative. To achieve this status, he must drink milk from one of her sister-wives, who is waiting in the back seat of the limousine, whereby he will become a son of the family, and thereafter be permitted to escort her around the bunker.'

The General's head reeled. The things he had to do for his country!

A Saudi guard held open the door of the limousine. The General braced himself and prepared to step in.

'Score!' said Navalkar, clenching his fist. He really did love life in the army. The General licked his lips and took a step forward. The guard stopped him with a hand on his chest. A slender, bejewelled hand emerged from the depths of the limousine, holding a feeding bottle. The guard took it and held it out to the General. Predictably, Navalkar was gesticulating wildly at the official cameraman, who was raring to go. All three Saudi wives were shooting him too. He would end up on YouTube in thirty to forty seconds, tops, Comedy Central by lunchtime, the General thought. This could be a grievous blow to the morale of the troops. Or it could uplift them unreasonably. No doubt Navalkar would add a humorous soundtrack.

The General took the feeding bottle and placed the nipple to his lips. He took a tentative swig, then a bigger one. Someone had thoughtfully added gin. He mentally doffed his toupee to the Saudi princess, who had shown both class and solicitude in what must have been a tricky situation. Or maybe there was a row of bottles in the car fridge, so that she could instantly convert men into her relatives as and when required.

'Welcome to the family!' said the Saudi Ambassador, beaming. He held out his arms and hugged the General. The Saudis were less uptight these days, because they had no oil. Their fortunes had been declining for some time. The US market had taken a huge hit after Oprah started riding a bicycle. Consequently, they were a kinder, gentler people.

The junior wife stamped on his foot. The Ambassador hopped to the side. 'I think she would like you to take her on a tour of the bunker without further ado,' he said, through clenched teeth. 'If you'll excuse me, I will leave while I am still able to walk.'

He hobbled into his limousine, followed by his remaining wives.

The General led his guest back into the building. As soon as they entered the elevator, she pulled off her headgear.

'Damn, it's hot inside these things!' said the PM. 'How do they wear them all the time? They should get them air-conditioned, like space suits.'

'What on earth do you think you're doing?' asked the General.

'What does it look like I'm doing?' asked the PM. 'I'm making a break for it. The CA has bugs and drones all over the place. What else was I supposed to do?'

'What exactly did you do?'

'It was easy. I invited the Saudi Ambassador and three of his wives for lunch. Three wives went in, three wives came out. Zahira is still in my room. She's happy as a clam. She's having some friends over for a party. Sweet little thing.'

'And was it entirely necessary to make me drink from a feeding bottle?'

The PM grinned impishly.

'It was soya milk,' she said, 'besides, your troops need cheering up. Now take me to the helicopter.'

'Where are you going?'

'It's more a question of where *we're* going,' said the PM. 'Those Saudi beauties seem to have addled your wits. We've got to do a deal with the Maoists. Once we have peace, the CA can re-construct to his heart's content. Then maybe he'll stop messing about with China.'

'We can get to Ranchi in just under an hour,' said the General.

'Then drink up your milk and wake up the pilot!' said the PM. 'It's time to meet some Maoists!'

❑

At that very moment, unaware that the PM was trying to make a break for it, the CA was looking at a document on his table and feeling very pleased with himself.

He had just received a second Threatening Note from China, and it was much worse than the first one.

The PM had unveiled the statue of the Dalai Lama three days ago, in full glare of the national media. Ever since the CA had the home of a prominent media mogul demolished and replaced by public urinals, the media had been anxious to stay on his good side. A single phone call to every major TV channel had been sufficient to ensure full attendance.

The PM had been uncharacteristically inarticulate, mumbling defensively about how the Dalai Lama was a great religious leader revered by many Indians, and how he had always believed in a unified China, but her heart wasn't really in it. She knew the damage had been done.

The results had been spectacular and the evidence was on his table. The CA was reading the note aloud, enjoying its natural rhythm.

'The People's Republic of China,' he read, 'thoroughly and completely repudiates all attempts by the pathetic and desperate Indian leadership to encourage splittist tendencies amongst the vile remnants of the Tibetan splittists. The erecting of a statue of the traitorous, cowardly dog, the Dalai Lama is a slap on the shining round face of the Chinese people. The so-called democracy of India stinks with the smell of rotten fish, and is led by an unprincipled elderly woman whose so-called good looks are a figment of the imagination of the biased Western media. The noble and powerful people of China have only contempt for these foolish attempts at destabilization by the second-rate Indian people.'

The CA paused, overwhelmed by the eloquence. 'This is poetry!' he exclaimed rapturously. 'They must go through extensive training to be able to write like this! The last part is the best. This is where they come to their demands.'

He read out the last part.

'The People's Republic of China demands that the statue of cowardly dog Dalai Lama be destroyed by the inferior Indian army using sledgehammers and manual labour, since they are incapable of handling any form of modern weaponry. This should be done on live television, with three times the exposure given to the original unveiling. Once this process has been completed, which will undoubtedly be done with maximum inefficiency and incompetence, the she-witch Prime Minister of India is expected to personally put all the fragments of the so-called statue in a handcrafted leather bag, and then personally come to Beijing to place it at the feet of her overlord, suzerain, and intellectual superior, the Chairman of the Chinese Communist Party. In case of failure to comply with this simple instruction, the wrath of the Chinese people will be terrible to behold, and will never be forgotten by the ignorant, smelly savages of India, who smell of fish!'

The CA put down the paper, amazed that it hadn't burst into flames. He turned to Subramaniam, who had been cowering quietly in a nearby chair.

'So, Subramaniam,' he said cheerfully, 'you're the expert. Give me your expert opinion.'

Subramaniam was fully conscious of his expertise and normally he was never shy about expressing it. However, given the way the CA had behaved towards him the last time he had been here, he had decided that he would say as little as possible, in an attempt to avoid corporal punishment.

'They don't like fish?' he ventured tentatively.

'Anything else?' asked the CA, surprised.

'They're very angry?' said Subramaniam, fiddling nervously with his tie, a work of art in handcrafted silk which he had bought in Geneva. When, oh when, would he see his beloved Swiss lakes again?

'Is there anything else you would like to add?' asked the CA, dangerously calm.

'They hate Tibetans?' offered Subramaniam feebly.

'Mehta!' barked the CA. 'Bring me the cattle prod!'

Mehta leaped up, eager to serve. He loved watching the cattle prod being used on these Foreign Service types. He could think of no other type of people who deserved it more.

'The tone and style of this Threatening Note is significantly more insulting than the first one, with greater use of traditional Chinese epithets like smelly, stinky, and vile,' said Subramaniam, speaking very rapidly. 'It indicates a far higher sense of grievance than earlier, as exemplified by the greater contempt expressed throughout. Repeated specific insults aimed at the Indian leadership indicate a greater desire to cause loss of face. The reference to placing the leather bag at the feet of the CCP Chairman indicates a demand that the Indian leader kowtow, thereby ensuring that the Indian leader will not only humiliate herself, but also do so in a traditionally Chinese manner, thus comprehensively demonstrating once and for all the indisputable superiority of Chinese heritage, tradition, and culture.'

Subramaniam paused for breath and mopped his brow with his designer handkerchief, hoping against hope that he had averted electrification.

The CA considered his input for a while, feeling somewhat disappointed. 'What about military action? Do you anticipate any military action as a result of this?'

'I'm afraid not,' said Subramaniam, apologetically. 'The insult we have caused involves the erecting of a statue, which is not a military act per se. They have insulted us back tenfold, even if the PM does not kowtow. In general, the Chinese give military responses only to military stimuli. They're quite simple that way.'

The CA eyed Subramaniam balefully. He could see the man had given a professional opinion. He decided to desist from corporal punishment. In his capacity as Stern But Loving Father of the Nation, he took care not to abuse his parental privileges.

'You may go,' he said, dismissing him with a wave of his hand.

The CA could see that the time for diplomacy was over, and mere insults would no longer do the trick. He would need to think carefully about how to take it to the next level. He had many resources at his disposal—it was just a question of picking the right ones. He was going to create conditions appropriate for proper reconstruction, come what may. It would be the culmination of his glittering career in the Indian Administrative Service, whose greatness he embodied in full measure. He would drain the cesspools and clear away the deadwood. He would baptize them all in cleansing fire. He would undo all the mistakes of the past. A brighter, shinier, leaner India would emerge. Some sacrifices would have to be made, but how else could greatness be achieved?

He picked up the Haryanvi Horror file, which was becoming thicker by the day. This despicable sociopath, too, had taken things to the next level. His latest victim was the son of the Chief Minister of Delhi, a person even richer and more influential than the others, driving a BMW that was even bigger and more expensive, and which had a hit-and-run victim count running into double figures. In his case, the degenerate criminal had not only shoved a banana up the exhaust pipe and buggered him, he had used a knife to carve the word 'JUSTICE' on his butt. As always, he had committed his unspeakable atrocities and vanished into the blue, and if anyone had seen him, they were keeping quiet about it.

The situation was going completely out of hand. The Chief Minister himself had called the Competent Authority, demanding justice, as well as compensation for the disfigurement of his son. He needed the money. He had cornered much of the land next to the Yamuna, but real estate prices had plummeted after strange creatures had started climbing out of the river.

'Sanction free skin graft to victim from the Bank of Bodies,' wrote the CA in the margin of the file, and put it in his out tray.

The BoB owed him a favour or two, he reckoned. Besides, he had a hunch they would be coming back soon to seek his support, everyone did, no matter how rich or powerful. If they wanted to repair their relationship with him, they could start by repairing some VIP buttocks.

56

*'By the time this is over,
everyone in Calcutta will know my name.'*

As Mr P.K. Roy, the Congress leader in Bengal, gazed out across the assembled crowd, sitting on the dais like a podgy little potentate, he felt his heart swell with pride. This was a golden opportunity to revive the fortunes of his party in the state, and he was all set to grab it with his fat little fingers. Since Netaji Subhash Chandra Bose had been hounded out of the party nearly ten years ago, the Congress had fallen on bad days. Many had never forgiven Gandhi, who had shown undue partiality to Nehru, just because he was more photogenic and better at sucking up to the Mahatma, thereby demonstrating that when it came to the crunch, non-Bengalis always supported each other. Gandhi, thus discredited, could win no votes for the Congress in Bengal, which was why he rarely showed his face in Calcutta. But he, P.K. Roy, was now ideally placed to bring his party back with a bang.

He was standing on a street corner in Ballygunge where his boys had done a good job of gathering the crowd. There were several hundred of them, standing in the street, blocking the traffic. Blocking traffic was a time-honoured Calcutta tradition. The smooth flow of vehicles always had, and always would, take a back seat to the smooth flow of ideas.

He carefully arranged his dhoti, from which the rough borders had been removed to avoid chafing his delicate thighs, and cleared his throat. He smiled his oily smile, briefly raised his hands in benediction and delicately tapped the mike before he spoke.

'Brothers and sisters!' he said. 'Suhrawardy, the rice thief, thinks that we, the good Hindu gentry of Calcutta, are stupid. That's because he thinks only he is clever, and everyone else is stupid. But you yourselves tell me—are we stupid?'

The crowd hesitated, not entirely sure. The situation in Calcutta could in many ways be described as stupid. They had all been good friends just a few months ago, shouting in the streets for Netaji, during the trial of the INA soldiers. They raised a feeble cheer.

Ali was standing near the back of the crowd, trying to blend in. He was feeling the pulse of the city, and so far it seemed the Hindu pulse was weak. Perhaps there was still hope. Maybe it was true what some people said—it really was the Muslims who had caused all the trouble. In that case, he just had to figure out how to tackle the Muslims, which made his job only half as impossible as before.

P.K. Roy also noted the lack of enthusiasm, but he remained unperturbed. Thanks to Mr Suhrawardy, he had some powerful material. He was just getting started.

'The Muslim League of Bengal has declared a holiday for Direct Action Day. Do you think Suhrawardy the rice thief has done this so that they can sit at home and perform pujas?'

P.K. Roy hated Suhrawardy, the Chief Minister of Bengal and leader of the Muslim League. He'd been enjoying the loaves and fish of office for years now. Bengal was the only state in India where the Congress had no ministries. Other Congressmen tended to look down on their Bengali brethren, who had no money. All the money in Bengal was being shared between the Muslim League and the Hindu parties, who occasionally joined the government, when their funds were running low. If this meant that the Congress had to be more Hindu than the Hindu parties, then by God he would do it. In his own way, he was a historic figure. He was the first Congress leader to realize why his partymen always dressed in white. It was so they could take on any colour.

'Suhrawardy the rice thief will fill the streets with idle Muslims, who in any case have no work. What do you think they will do? Good Hindus will try to open their shops and do business and these people will try to stop them, because they are jealous! Muslims cannot make money. They can only loot! From the time of Mahmud of Ghazni, this has been the case!'

The crowd remained largely unmoved. None of them had met Mahmud of Ghazni. None of them were shopkeepers. They had limited sympathy for their local trader. His behaviour during the recent famine had been less than exemplary.

P.K. Roy could sense he was flopping. He put one hand to his chest and struck a leader-like pose. The crowd murmured expectantly. There was precious little entertainment in Calcutta, and they liked a bit of theatre.

'Mr Suhrawardy and the Muslim League have thrown down a challenge to us. I ask myself, what would my dear leader Netaji have done in such a situation. Would he have backed away from such a challenge?'

'NOOO!!' roared the crowd, galvanized by the magic name.

'What about you, all you right-thinking Hindus of Calcutta? Will you back away from such a challenge?'

'NOOO!!' roared the crowd.

Standing in the middle of them, Ali watched helplessly as their brains switched off one by one. Chests expanded. Fists were raised. Slippers were removed, and waved in the air. If they weren't presented with an enemy soon, they would probably beat each other up. P.K. Roy reminded him of his old maulvi in Preston, and not just because he was small, plump, had hot breath, a silver tongue, and was constantly urging them to blow up things. Where his maulvi was concerned, this had usually boiled down to a choice between blowing up synagogues and blowing up slags.

P.K. Roy surveyed his handiwork and smiled. He had them in the palm of his hands now. The power he felt was like a drug—better than the opium he drank with his milk every evening just before the quick trip to the local whorehouse.

'They want us to submit to compulsory hartal. I ask you, who are they to tell us when to observe hartal? Just because the Chief Minister is a Muslim, does this mean we have all become servants of the Muslims?'

The crowd roared, denying this hotly.

'We will hartal every day of the week if we want to,' he continued, prophetically, 'but only if we choose to do so. Therefore I urge all of you, keep your shops open, and assist others to keep their shops open. Show the Muslims we don't fear them. If we have drunk our mothers' milks, we must show Suhrawardy the rice thief that Calcutta is not his father's property!'

P.K. Roy beamed as the crowd went crazy. Father's property and mother's milk were two concepts which never failed to inspire frenzy.

A burly sardar, who had been sitting quietly on the dais, stood up and drew his sword. A silence fell over the crowd as they eyed him uneasily. He looked ferocious. Sardars had a reputation for violence. Was he going to leap off the stage and attack them? Did he realize that their support for bloodshed, although completely wholehearted, was largely metaphorical?

It was a tense moment. Ali, who knew his weapons, could see that the sword was blunt and rusty. It was meant for purely ceremonial purposes, such as urging people to butcher each other.

'Sat Sri Akaal!' roared the distinguished sardar. He was the leader of the local Sikhs—big, tough men, whose ancestors had defied Aurangzeb. Their hatred for Jinnah was atavistic. Their love for Calcutta was sincere. They would defend their adopted home to the last drop of everyone's blood.

'P.K. Roy-sahab is a leader, and he speaks like a leader. But I am a plain man, and I will speak to you plain. These Muslims want a fight? We will give them a fight!'

He thrust his sword through the air, skewering an imaginary Muslim.

The crowd roared its approval. In any fight with the Muslims, they resolved to be right behind him. He was better-armed than they were, and substantially larger to boot. What better place to defend their faith than from the back seat of his taxi?

'Don't forget what happened in the riots of 1926,' he said, making it sound like a recent football match. 'Then, too, the Muslims attacked us, and they were soundly beaten. If they try to start any hanky-panky, this time also we Sikhs will back the Congress and together, we will give them a solid thrashing!'

He seemed extremely eager to get cracking. The more professional elements were standing just behind Ali. They had no time for rhetorical flourishes. They were getting down to business.

'Have the Marwaris given the money?' whispered one of them.

'More than enough.'

'What have we bought with it?'

'We got US army revolvers, each with a hundred rounds of ammunition. The markin soldiers are going home, and they're thirsty. All they want is two hundred and fifty rupees and a bottle of whisky.'

'Have we had any practice with them?'

'What's to practice? Just point it at a Muslim, and fire.'

There was much merriment. An older man gave them tips on where exactly they should point.

Ali glanced back at them cautiously. They were pretending to be bystanders, but they were muscle in mufti. It was never hard to tell. From Beirut to Bangkok, from London to Lahore, from Peshawar to Patna, wherever he had met them, they always looked the same. It was the eyes. You could always tell from the eyes.

'What else do we have?'

'Acid bombs, lots of them.'

'Are the blacksmiths on the job?'

'Every Hindu blacksmith in Calcutta is with us. They are making spearheads and sharpening rods. The Very New Young Men's Bodybuilding Society is supplying the bombs. You get us the boys, we'll give them the weapons.'

'Boys won't be a problem. Only the Bihari rickshaw-pullers are refusing, saying they don't want any trouble.'

'The bhaiyyas never want any trouble.'

'That's why they'll die first. Them, and the milkmen. But we will avenge them.'

Ali felt a heavy hand on his shoulder, and turned around. He found himself facing a short, bandy-legged man of indeterminate age. His manner was Napoleonic, his hygiene questionable. He grinned, revealing rotting, paan-stained teeth.

'Going by the picture of the ganja baba on your chest, you are a devotee of Maa Kaali, isn't it?'

'BOM KAALI!' exclaimed Ali promptly.

The man touched his forehead and his chest deferentially.

'As a Kaali worshipper, you're not afraid of a little blood, are you?'

Ali adopted a ferocious expression and shook his head.

'We could do with a tall, healthy lad like you. Choose your weapon, and we'll sign you up.'

'What weapons do you have?' asked Ali.

'What weapon do you want? We have small knives, big choppers, sticks, rods, guns, and pistols. Do you play cricket? We can give you petrol bombs and acid bombs. Also something new called a Molotov Cocktail, invented by the professors at the Bengal Technical Institute. There's more than one way to kill a Muslim. See Langda over there? He was a wrestler, until a Muslim driver drove over his foot. Now we catch them for him, and he strangles them with his bare hands, like chickens. They hardly get time to squawk. Each man has his own preference. So what will it be?'

'Chopper,' said Ali.

In true Al Qaeda style, he was now a foot soldier for both sides. Did that make him a double agent or a triple agent? It was important to keep track. People in the field had often got confused, and blown up the wrong people by mistake, or settled down permanently in suburbia, where they experimented with different kinds of cereal, and menaced middle-aged white women at PTA meetings.

'Ah, the chopper. Good choice,' said the little man approvingly, 'I use one too, being a butcher by profession. I can teach you to use the halaal method—Muslims like it that way. Come tomorrow evening to Chittaranjan Sweets across the road, over there. Ask for Gopal Patha. They all know me.'

He slapped Ali on the shoulder and swelled up like a little bantam cock.

'Gopal Patha,' he repeated, as he strutted off, followed by his henchmen. 'By the time all this is over, everyone in Calcutta will know my name.'

Ali had no doubt that they would. Unless he did something to stop him. An idea occurred to him just then, a natural consequence of his now being thick with one giant dick on either side. It might not stop Direct Action Day, but it could still save thousands of lives. It all hinged on one vital question: did Gopal Patha like Kabiraji cutlets?

57

'Without your liver, how will you work?'

Pande poked the taxi driver in the back of the neck with a horny finger.

'How much longer to Khetolai?' he asked.

'Bas, five more minutes,' the driver replied, a little sulkily.

He was sulky because he was in debt. He was in debt because he had been forced to borrow money to buy diesel. All this gallivanting up and down Rajasthan had emptied out his tank. He had thought about taking a few paying passengers along with Pande so that he could at least earn something, but the thought of what Pande might do to them had made him desist. Long after Pande was gone, he would have to keep living in the area. He had briefly considered asking Pande for money, but some sixth sense had told him this was not such a bright idea. So he had gone to his usual moneylender the night before, and borrowed another five hundred rupees.

'Why don't you drink less?' the moneylender had asked, shaking his head sorrowfully. He was a deeply compassionate man whose sole desire was that all his clients should have long and productive lives, earning just enough money to pay him, but not so much that they could escape his clutches. People always blamed him when some poor, debt-ridden farmer committed suicide, which was monumentally unjust. What did he gain by the death of a paying customer? By the time such things happened, the wife usually had nothing left to pay him with, so if anything, his loss was the greatest of all. Besides, was it his fault if the banks never lent these people money? He even maintained accounts for them, because they couldn't read or write. What he was running was essentially a charitable enterprise. It was a shame that no one saw this.

'Drinking will destroy your liver, son,' he had told the taxi driver. 'Without your liver, how will you work?'

'It's not for drinking, uncle,' the driver had replied testily, 'it's for diesel. I have a policeman on my back and he's sucking diesel from me like it's Coca Cola.'

The moneylender had looked at him sadly and handed over the money. There was no possible advice he could give to a man in the grip of the police. He was beyond redemption.

Pande was aware that his protégé had borrowed money, and he was secretly quite touched. He would readily have terrorized any nearby petrol-pump owner into relinquishing some diesel, but the boy had spared him the trouble.

On the whole, he was feeling quite relaxed, after a nice lunch at a roadside dhaba. They had used too much chilli, which Rajasthanis were wont to do, but the food had been quite tasty. He had summoned the cook and made him eat a few red chillies raw, to drive home the point that he should use fewer in future, and while the man had been too busy choking to speak, what with all the tears and the snot and his throat swelling up, he had used sign language to indicate that he had understood. He had gotten off lightly. Chillies played a big role in police interrogation. They were cheap, and plentiful, and lent themselves to a variety of highly creative uses.

Khetolai was just off the National Highway, and the taxi was now bouncing down a narrow dirt track. It was just like the road he took back home when he was going to his village. The scenery was very different, though. It was completely flat, and extraordinarily yellow, without the faintest trace of green. The soil was yellow, the road was yellow, the pathetic little shrubs were yellow, even the houses up ahead were made of yellow brick and stone. Not like the mud-and-thatch huts of his own village. These were sturdy little single-storied houses with proper roofs. Some of them even had TV antennas. A prosperous little village. He liked prosperous little villages. They were rich, and he was the law.

As the taxi approached the village, he could see little bunches of goats and cows munching away and eyeing him, the cows placidly, the goats suspiciously. He could see what looked like deer in the distance. A village of herders. Probably lazy, never having put shoulder to the plough. Knocking them about would be easy. His father would have called this a holiday. His father had escaped a life of bondage in the family paan shop and become muscle for the local MLA. Even now, in his sixties, he could hammer a peasant to the ground with his fists. His boss had got Pande the police job, as a favour. Together, as father and son, they could have achieved much in the village, but his father was seldom sober, and often too angry to think.

The taxi stopped on the outskirts of Khetolai, and Pande hopped out. A wizened old man sat on a charpoy, drivelling into a hookah. His eyes were shut, and his feet were shaking gently to some ancient, distant music that only he could hear. He had smelt Pande coming from a mile away and remained unperturbed. He had seen many policemen come and go. He had nothing to fear because he had nothing to lose. The opium made him a little drowsy too.

There was no one else in sight. Pande strode up to the ancient relic.

'Where are all the atomic bomb blasts going on?' he demanded, with his customary directness. If Joshi was to be believed, and he saw no reason not to, this village was no stranger to radiation, having being lavishly irradiated by Indira Gandhi in 1974.

The old man opened one eye cautiously. At his age, he conserved as much effort as possible. He judiciously considered the question.

'There have been bomb blasts,' he admitted carefully.

Pande waited, slapping his lathi against his boot rhythmically.

'They made the milk taste funny,' the fossil ventured.

Pande waited.

'My wife vomited for three days,' he said, after a long pause, 'and she wasn't pregnant. She's given me fourteen children,' he added proudly, grinning a gap-toothed grin.

Pande's patience, an ephemeral commodity at the best of times, was being sorely tested. But he drew the line at beating up respected elders. Villagers tended to take a dim view of such things, and while he was happy to crack individual skulls, he didn't want to be jumped by the whole lot of them. Besides, it was a rich village. Some of them might have guns. His own was unreliable. Everyone else always had better weapons than him.

'I hope grandma got better quickly,' he said politely, 'but I don't want to know about old bomb-shomb. I want to know about new bomb-shomb.'

'You want to know about new bomb-shomb?' repeated the ancient one, keen to get things absolutely clear.

'Yes,' said Pande, taking deep breaths.

The old man thought.

Pande waited.

The old man thought some more.

He burbled into his hookah thoughtfully.

'I don't know anything about that,' he said eventually.

Pande was gripping his lathi so tight his knuckles hurt.

'Is there anyone else in this village who could tell me?' he asked. A vein throbbed faintly in his forehead.

The ancient villager observed the vein with great interest. One of his cousins had exhibited similar symptoms. He had keeled over one afternoon while milking a goat and died on the spot. He wondered whether to mention this to the policeman. Perhaps not. So long as he stayed away from goats, he ought to be okay.

'You could ask Irfan,' he said, not wishing to disoblige a dying man, 'or maybe Mangat Ram, if you prefer Hindus. I'd say Irfan. Although Muslim, he is very aware. Advocate Prakash in Jodhpur uses him for all our court cases against the hunters. He does not eat meat, so we allow him to stay. In any case, our guruji's original intention was that Muslims should also be part of us, which is why we bury our dead, but after Partition, things became complex.'

He closed his eyes, exhausted by all the effort. His repose was disturbed by an odd clicking sound. It was Pande grinding his teeth.

'Where can I find them?' he asked hoarsely.

The old man thought about this. He chewed and mumbled around his hookah like a baby searching for a teat.

'At the election meeting,' he said, finally, 'although why they are having an election meeting I have no idea. We always vote Congress. Always have. Always will. What's there to meet about? Billu's sister humping Budh Ram's cousin—that too in the afternoon in an open field—that's something to meet about. But why elections? Everybody knows we support Gandhiji's party, although it's true he hasn't come here in a long time. They must keep him very busy up in Delhi. I keep thinking of going to see him, but I don't like going to railway stations, even though Odaniya Chacha Station is nearby. The trains make too much noise. Mind you, Odaniya Chacha Station is not named after anyone's chacha, as it appears. When I was a boy, I used to think it was an uncle, not a railway station, but now I know it's named after the two villages it serves—Odaniya and Chacha. Here in Khetolai we have no station of our own, so we use theirs.'

He was very close to death at that moment.

Before Pande could say or do anything, he raised his hand and smiled.

'Wait, wait, I know what you will ask,' he said, as he began to discern a pattern to the whole conversation. 'You will ask, "Grandpa, where is this election meeting happening"—isn't it?'

Pande nodded mutely, not trusting himself to speak.

'It's over there, in the village square,' the old man said, pointing with the stem of his hookah. 'If you listen carefully, instead of standing here and doing bukbuk, you'd be able to hear.'

A flock of little boys, most of them naked, a few in ragged shorts, ran past, yelling 'Elec-sun, elec-sun, elec-sun!'

That was another clue.

Pande left his friend, philosopher and guide and followed them, pausing only to kick out savagely at a little dog who was passing by. The little boys froze, paralyzed by horror, and his erstwhile companion got to his feet, forgetting to drool in his agitation.

'Ey,' he said, staggering towards Pande, making threatening gestures with his hookah, 'Ey. We're all Bishnois here. We worship all animals. God is in every animal. You don't do such things to animals here, else it doesn't matter who you are, we'll break your legs, you watch us, we will.'

Pande raised his hands in a gesture of surrender. Fair enough. India was full of peculiar people. You had to respect their religion, unless you were part of a mob. It was ironic. For once he was being considerate and taking his frustrations out on a dog instead of wringing the old man's scrawny neck.

The village square was crowded. Men of all ages squatted on their haunches. Two men were standing, one old and the other younger. They were engaged in a lively political debate.

'Why can't we vote for the BJP this time?' demanded the younger man.

'We always vote Congress,' said the older.

'But the big sarkar now is BJP. Shouldn't we at least try them once?'

'No.'

'But it would help us to get money for the village. Money to repair the water tanks. Money to treat the sick people. Maybe build a road, even.'

'No.'

'But the Congress has never done anything for us. Shouldn't we try some other party?'

'No.'

'Why should we keep voting for the Congress? There should be some reason, isn't it?'

The Competent Authority 303

'We always vote for the Congress.'

Many of the villagers agreed with the young man. Much of what he said was quite true, even though his clothes were odd and he didn't wear a turban. But they were bound to vote for the Congress. It was their destiny to do so. The reasons for doing so were buried in the distant past, but there was no doubt they would do what they always did.

Pande had little patience with political meetings. So far as he was concerned, elections just meant enormous amounts of extra work, although you could pick up a few bottles and bits of loose cash if you kept your eyes and ears open. But the headaches far outweighed the benefits. What he needed right now was information.

He poked one of the squatting villagers in the bum with his lathi.

'Where's this Irfan?' he asked. 'I need to talk to him.'

The villager was not in the least bit put out. It was the normal way for a policeman to say hello.

'His house is over there,' he said amiably, pointing north.

Pande walked across the square followed by a flock of boys of various shapes and sizes, accompanied by goats, chickens, a small fawn, and an unexpectedly frisky calf. The boys had sensed that Pande was a Man of Action, and they were tagging along, eagerly awaiting further developments. They whispered to each other excitedly.

Irfan turned out to be a slim, dark, young man in a cream-coloured kurta and bright orange turban, with a quicksilver smile and kohl-rimmed eyes. He was sitting on his porch talking fondly to a goat, gently stroking its ears as he did so.

'They give better milk if you talk to them,' he told Pande, as if they'd known each other for years. 'They're very much like children that way. Love and affection give better results.'

He patted the goat on the rump and it trotted off.

Why don't you try a boot in the backside, thought Pande, see what kind of results you get then. But he kept this thought to himself. The people of this village were clearly insane, no doubt as a result of all the radiation.

'Please sit,' said Irfan, gesturing with modest pride to, of all things, a deck chair. Pande sank in. It would be difficult to leap out of this and thrash people he realized, but even hard-working officers of the law needed to rest once in a while.

Irfan brought him a glass of water and offered it to him a little tentatively.

'Some people avoid drinking our water,' he murmured. 'Because of the radiation.'

Pande took the glass from him and chugged it happily. It was the purest, finest water he had ever tasted. Water was a precious commodity in Rajasthan, so he asked for another glass.

'It's very difficult getting boys and girls from our village married,' said Irfan, as he poured him some more water. 'People worry about the food and the water.'

'Tell me about the bomb blast,' said Pande.

Small talk was not his forte.

'Well, I was a little boy in 1974,' said Irfan, 'but I remember what happened after. People started to get cancer and skin diseases. Some people, they would itch all the time. Strange sores and red marks and boils would appear on their skin. Even our animals were affected, as if Mother Earth herself had been poisoned. There was something wrong with the grass. It was evident that the government had poisoned all of us. But nobody protested. We are all very obedient here in Rajasthan. Government is like mother and father. Sometimes mother and father may do wrong things, but we still owe them obedience and respect. Or so the elders say.'

Pande thought they were a bunch of pathetic whiners. Compared to what he was used to, these things were like mosquito bites. He had seen rain that stripped the skin off a healthy human being in minutes. He had seen a newborn child cough out its lungs in front of his eyes. He had seen raw, red flesh bubbling like soup. He had seen every kind of deformity imaginable, and some that were beyond imagination. His wife had borne him only one child. It had lived for three minutes. What did these people have to complain about?

'I'm not interested in old bombs,' he said curtly. 'Tell me about new bombs. Where are the new bombs going to be burst, and when?'

'Achcha, you're interested in the new bomb, is it?' asked Irfan, highly intrigued. 'You must tell me one thing but—how did you get to know?'

'An avatar of Vishnu came to me in the form of a little boy and told me,' said Pande. 'Being Vishnu, he knew everything. It's his nature.'

Irfan's heart swelled with pride. 'You see, boys,' he said, turning to his juvenile spectators, 'even the Gods are interested in our bomb!'

'BOMB BOMB BOMB!' yelled the little boys, leaping up and down. The young calf tried to join them, but gave up.

Pande resisted the urge to fell them all.

'More important question is, how do you know?' he demanded.

'Oh, everybody in the village knows,' said Irfan cheerfully. 'We've known for at least a year. When the work first started, and they were digging in the sand, and many soft people from the city came pretending to be soldiers, then my chachu said to me, see, beta, they're building another bomb, just like they did last time, better get married now, later you won't find a wife, and sell off all the goats to your relatives in Haryana while the price is still good. That's what I did. I quickly had a baby also, because later on he might come out funny. So everybody here knows. Other people don't know because no one ever asks us anything, except for you.'

'Where are they going to burst the bomb?' asked Pande, slightly dazed. This wasn't quite as secret as the usual top-secret programme.

'Oh, any of the boys can take you, can't you, boys?' said Irfan. 'They all know where it is.'

The boys nodded eagerly and jumped up and down a bit more. One of them fell over and pretended to be dead as a result of being hit by the bomb.

Pande got out of the chair and walked away slowly, thinking. The whole thing had been much simpler than he had thought. Apparently everybody knew all about the bomb, at least in this neighbourhood. He now had sources who, while younger than his usual sources, seemed to be well informed regarding the venue of the explosion. Pande was keenly aware that excessive proximity to the actual explosion would lead to vaporization, liquefaction, or slow, lingering death. It was better to catch the bomb unawares. It was obviously at the nearby army camp so he would have to go there. He would pick up a sub judice, thrash him until he agreed to pose as a supplier of counterfeit Nainital potatoes and, by pretending to investigate this fraud, gain access to the camp, via the understandably nervous purchase department, who would themselves be thrashed if the brigadier found out that his potatoes were bogus.

As Pande clambered back into the taxi, he thought of the Americans, looked up at the sky, and smiled. There they were, sitting in their

Shovon Chowdhury

satellite, with their magic cameras that could count the hairs on a man's head, completely oblivious to the fact that hundreds of men, women and children down here had all the answers that they required.

58

'My husband wants a six-pack.
Do you have any in stock?'

Mrs Verma took her pen drive out of her handbag and plugged her mother into her compad. Different people used different devices these days, depending on budget, and inclination, and whether they had fingers. She preferred this one, with its tactile 3D keyboard. She liked pressing buttons. She was sitting in the back seat of her car and she needed some advice.

'So finally you decided to plug me in?' said her mother's voice. 'Is it Diwali already?'

'You can't spend five minutes in a week talking to me?' demanded her mother. 'Sixteen hours I was in labour with you. You were an extremely fat baby. And after that there were gulab jamuns.'

Limbo had not improved her mother's disposition. Mrs Verma was the unexpected success story amongst her siblings. She used to be dull, podgy, and prone to hissy fits. No one expected much from her. Her landing a dynamic mineral magnate like Sanjeev had come as a complete surprise, despite his disturbing predilection for bell-bottoms, which had made a brief comeback, along with meaningless songs in very high voices. Her two much brighter brothers, on the other hand, had belied early promise (or perhaps fulfilled it) and received lengthy prison sentences for stock-market fraud. They had been lamentably cavalier with large sums of money belonging to powerful and influential people. Her mother had railed at the injustice of it all. 'As it is nobody goes to jail for anything! Why this partiality? Only once in a while, they punish somebody, just to create show-sha.'

Every posthumous conversation with her mother was stamped vividly on Mrs Verma's brain. Freedom from the flesh appeared to have freed her mother from all restraint. And how had the software captured that shimmering edge of hysteria so perfectly? She shivered. Her mother was speaking.

'Too busy, haan? Busy, my foot! What are you busy with? Sanjeev does all the work. Poor fellow! Who knows what he is eating in the jungle? At least Pappu is eating well, thanks to my training. Pappu must be doing very well at school by now. He was always a bright boy. He reminded me of my uncle who supplied barbed wire to the army in the Northeast. He was the sole contractor. It was also his sole achievement. He lived a relaxed life otherwise. He was very clever. He was reading books all the time. Sometimes he paid cash money for them. Does Pappu purchase books?'

Mrs Verma was fairly sure that Pappu couldn't read. Besides, his reading habits were not the reason why she had double-tapped her mother. She had done so because she was confused and nervous, and needed her mother's advice about which of her psychiatrist's options she should choose. Both suggestions made her feel uneasy. She didn't fancy putting Pappu through yet another operation to reverse the original procedure. Neither did she particularly want to assassinate the original donor, thereby killing the transmissions at source, along with the source. The donor would be about the same age as Pappu. Just like Ramu, Pappu's slave. Would she be able to kill a little boy? Was she being a wimp here, with the sanity of her son at stake? Should she have grabbed an AK-47 from the armoury and rushed off to Shanti Nagar, instead of coming to the Bank of Bodies, where she would receive a feedback form and a complimentary mint? Was it natural to have these doubts? Her mother would know. She would be unambiguous.

Technology had made her mother stronger. The software didn't have to pause for breath. It was hard to get a word in edgeways. Mrs Verma eventually managed to convey the gist of her problem, once she had reassured her mother regarding Pappu's health, his diet, and the improbability of his running away with a girl from a third-class family. No, she said, with perfect truth, he's not making eyes at the little girl across the street. This was mainly because there was no little girl across the street. Pappu was the only child on Prithviraj Road.

The software pretended to consider the problem. The processor was fast and powerful, and for all she knew, her mother was simultaneously analysing weather patterns in Papua New Guinea. But it remained silent for a while, to convey the impression of thought. It was clever that way.

'First, make sure you pack lots of sandwiches,' said the matriarch, 'and take some coffee in a thermos. What's all this talk of running out with guns? Are you forgetting our position? Take the durwans with you. If once in a while they cannot shoot someone for the young master, then what purpose are they serving? Why are we feeding them? Each one of them has at least six rotis every night. I have seen this personally.'

'What about the bank?' murmured Mrs Verma. 'Don't you think I should try at the bank?'

'What's there to try? Did I raise you to be afraid of bank clerks? You march right in, and whatever refund-shefund you require, just take from them. One or two slaps can do no harm. It improves the circulation of the face. Just remember to remove their spectacles first. Nowadays spectacles have become very expensive, what with X-ray facility, surfing the internet and other peculiarities. Whatever paper you require from the bank, you demand it. Grab their necks and make them sign. What did I teach you when you were a little girl? No one will ever give you anything. You have to grab it from them.'

This was indeed what she had learnt at her mother's knee, in those rare moments of mother-daughter bonding. Mrs Verma could feel the strength coursing back into her veins. She rolled her neck and loosened her shoulders, the way her Scottish yoga therapist had taught her.

'Sit up straight!' snapped her mother. 'How many times have I told you to stop slouching?'

Mrs Verma yanked the pen drive out of her compad and threw it away, not caring whether the file was corrupted or not. She had plenty more at home.

Her driver had drawn up in front of the Bank of Bodies, stopping in the middle of the road, blocking traffic as much as possible, just the way she liked it, while facilitating her egress with a tip of his hat.

A pair of giant, disembodied eyes followed her from the electronic billboard across the street, which was being used by the Bureau of Reconstruction to provide guidelines from the Twenty-Three Point Programme. 'Respect Everyone. Suspect Everyone' it said. The eyes looked left. The eyes looked right. The eyes looked right at Mrs Verma, suspicion evident in their gaze. Mrs Verma turned away and stepped daintily between the broken slabs of footpath, avoiding a cracked sewage pipe with a quick shimmy to the left, till she was at the entrance of the Bank of Bodies.

The guards in their red-cross helmets stepped away, not wishing to mess with her. Mrs Verma entered the BoB foyer and stood there with her hands on her hips, looking down her Indira Gandhi nose, awaiting service.

The receptionist had no intention of provoking her. She remembered Mrs Verma from her last visit. She stayed behind the counter and checked out the emergency exit.

'How may I help you, ma'am?' she asked, her voice quavering.

'Get the manager,' said Mrs Verma, with a frozen, icy stare.

'It's for you, Mike,' whispered the receptionist, ducking down behind the counter where she kept a secret stash of coconut cookies and her country-made revolver. The clientele was volatile at the Bank of Bodies. They had extreme biological needs, lots of money, and were used to shouting at people to get their way. Sometimes they acted as if they were going to rip the required organs out of the nearest member of the banking staff. It was a good thing they had to check in their weapons at the entrance.

Mike Khanna came down the lift in a pensive mood. He was the new manager, and he was already in the doghouse with No. 2 for refunding a child to a customer. It was easy to tell that No. 2 was mad because he was being so nice to him. Whenever No. 2 was exceptionally polite and gracious to anyone, it was a sure sign that he was planning something unspeakably hideous. This morning No. 2 had remarked on his tie, and asked after his children, even though he was childless. The signs were unmistakeable. Not knowing when and where retribution would strike only made it worse.

Mike emerged on the customer floor, and instantly recognized the statuesque suzerain with the large handbag and a nose that looked disturbingly familiar. Was this retribution? It certainly looked like it. He ought to know. His ex-wife had dished it out liberally. He slipped on his gloves and stepped forward, hand outstretched, smiling.

Mrs Verma ignored his hand. 'What kind of monkey house do you run here?' she demanded.

She was the Refund Case. She had deposited a twelve-year-old, and

Shovon Chowdhury

then she had withdrawn him. Luckily, he'd still been in one piece, the Bank of Bodies had not yet perfected the art of reassembling a human being from individual components.

Mrs Verma had begun shouting.

'First, you tried to cheat me by taking a twelve-year-old and showing a deposit for a ten-year-old,' she said. 'Two years of food and drink and maintenance you just digested! Then you gave my son a defective hand. What kind of goods are you stocking? Do you even check the expiry dates any more, or are you like Modern Store Redux? I want the procedure to be reversed immediately, and a full refund! Plus free gifts for mental distress. My husband wants a six-pack. Do you have any in stock?'

Again with the refunds. The woman was incorrigible. You can't just give it back, Mike wanted to say. It's not like a salwar set. Or maybe it was.

'Well,' demanded Mrs Verma, 'are you going to reverse the procedure or not?'

'Of course,' said Mike. He rapped on the counter. The receptionist emerged, munching. 'Go get one of the surgeons from the canteen,' he said. 'And please bring the beneficiary, madam.'

'I think you misunderstood me,' said Mrs Verma. 'When I said reversal, I meant you have to return the hand to the original donor, not just remove it from my son.'

'Are you kidding?' asked Mike, shocked out of servility. He was beginning to see how his predecessor had lost his marbles, and was now romping unclothed at the Institute for the Criminally Insane. He had never heard of such a thing. There were no procedures or guidelines. Their interaction with donors was brief. Nothing had ever been returned before. Their customers were not the kind of people who returned things. Databases had not been maintained. Did a donor become a beneficiary in a case like this? What kind of precedent would it set? What would No. 2 do to him if he suggested it? Was that No. 2's hair floating in the air, just behind Mrs Verma's head, like a dark cloud of doom?

Mrs Verma flexed her forearms and prepared to whack him with her handbag. This usually happened later on in the proceedings, and was not a card she played lightly. She needed to get his attention. He was high as a kite, and it was only two o'clock. What kind of people was the Bank of Bodies hiring these days? She would have to have a word with the Chairman, next time they met at the Gymkhana.

The receptionist came back with one of the surgeons.

'Pinky said you needed a hand job, so I ditched lunch and came,' he said, eager to please the management. He looked Mrs Verma up and down, frowning.

'I'll go get a bigger scalpel,' he said.

'It's nice that you want to give the kid his hand back, Auntie,' said Mike, a trifle sadly, 'but no one here can help you. We don't have much of a relationship with donors. We're not geared up for it. You can fill in this form in triplicate, and keep two copies for your personal records. We'll send you several automatically generated messages, which may or may not be connected with your case. Eventually, we'll put you in touch with the call centre, and if you call them too much, they'll start calling you. You really don't want that to happen. You can't win against a bank. It's against the law. If you have any Plan B to help your little boy, you might as well go for it. I can tell you this much. The donor's name is Pintoo. He lives in Shanti Nagar. He drops in here once in a while and flattens the place, but he doesn't have a schedule as such. He did promise to come again, so I guess you could wait. There's a coffee machine in the corner.'

Although freshly invigorated by her own mother, Mrs Verma could feel her resolution begin to falter. Erratic flunkies made her nervous, and Mike was freaking her out. The information he had given her hardly made her any happier. If a refund at the bank was out of the question, the only option was a daring guerrilla attack on Shanti Nagar, at the head of her domestic security staff, most of whom had so far shown a deep aversion to violence. Or she could sit and wait for Pappu to get better. His condition might not be permanent. So many people had temporary crack-ups these days. Perhaps it was just a phase, and all she had to do was grit her teeth, ride it out and make sure Sanjeev remained blissfully ignorant. The poor dear was particularly downcast right now, having failed so far to find a gift suitable for the Governor of the Bengal Protectorate, whose blessings he required for some purpose or the other. Their attempts to procure a Kolkata Knight Riders cheerleader had come to naught, and they were now chasing after some sort of animal contraband, although Mrs Verma wasn't sure about the details. Sanjeev had been uncharacteristically cagey, almost as if he was embarrassed.

Everything depended on what Pappu did next. Or, for that matter, what he was doing right now, at home, with just Ramu and the psychiatrist for company. She also worried about their doctor. The lack of sunlight was beginning to affect him, just like the plants in the movie room.

59

'Instead, the police will play ping-pong with your testicles.
They're very good, because of all the practice.'

Mr Chatterjee had just been pecked by a parrot. His spirits, already low, had sunk even lower. How was he supposed to protect the Father of the Nation when he couldn't even protect himself from a small bird?

He'd been walking down Chandni Chowk, looking for astrologers when he spotted a flash of green out of the corner of his eye. It was a parrot in a cage hanging outside a tiny shop. *Pandit Jatindas Chaturvedi*, the board said. *Fortunes told. Futures predicted. Enemies mesmerized. Good success in cases of love.*

Mr Chatterjee had never seen a parrot before. Still vaguely nauseous from his encounter with the RSS man, he had felt the urge to communicate with an innocent creature. He had stuck his finger in the cage and said, 'Koochie koo.' The parrot had bitten him. It expected more respect.

Jatindas Chaturvedi, proprietor of the parrot, was a vision in saffron robes, with a large red tilak on his forehead, and a superbly sculpted white moustache. He had ushered him into his room, eager to explore his wallet. He was bandaging Mr Chatterjee's finger, muttering soothingly and looking at him keenly, trying to figure out what the market could bear. His eyes were bright and beady, just like his parrot's.

'Please allow me to tell your future,' he insisted. 'After the injury that Balram has caused you, naturally I will give you a heavy discount.'

Mr Chatterjee was an atheist, like his father and grandfather before him. He was a little hazy on procedure.

'Do I have to take my clothes off now?' he asked.

The astrologer laughed uproariously, much enthused by his ignorance. 'Just hold out your hand.'

Mr Chatterjee held out his hand obediently. Pandit Chaturvedi held it palm up and whipped out a magnifying glass.

'Made in Germany,' he said proudly, 'we use only foreign technology here.'

He peered closely at Mr Chatterjee's palm and mumbled to himself, his mumbles rising in excitement as secrets revealed themselves.

'Amazing!' said the Pandit. 'What a hand!'

'Dickhead!' said the parrot, not willing to be left out.

Unbeknownst to its owner, a group of American GIs, taking advantage of the fact that the parrot was housed in a cage facing the street, had been expanding its vocabulary every day while the Pandit took his afternoon nap.

'He speaks only English,' explained the Pandit, looking up briefly. 'He, too, is imported. In India today, trend is rapidly towards imported. Even Nehru is preferring Lady Mountbatten.'

He resumed his study of Mr Chatterjee's hand. There seemed to quite a lot of reading matter.

'Rarely have I seen a hand like this,' he said, eventually, returning it to its owner.

'Nothing bad I hope?'

'Well, to some extent you are suffering because Brihaspati is debilitated. This is causing egotism, sloth, and legal problems.'

Back home, the CBI would be arresting him for sedition in exactly three, or was it four days; all this time travel, made it hard to keep track. This could probably be termed a legal problem. He wasn't sure where the egotism and the sloth were coming from, though. Nevertheless, these things were subjective, and one out of three wasn't bad.

'What would you suggest I do?'

'You will require a talisman, and some astral remedies. Wear a yellow topaz ring on your right hand, repeat "Aum Brihaspataye namah" nineteen times every day, one hour before sunset and offer yellow sweets to birds every morning. The ring can be provided at a very nominal rate by my maternal cousin.'

'What else do you see?' asked Mr Chatterjee, a trifle nervously.

'You have come from very far away,' said the Pandit.

'Blow job!' said the parrot. They ignored him.

'Soon you will meet great people and you will do great things.'

'Will I succeed?' asked Mr Chatterjee.

'You have a great fear of failure. But if you look inside your heart, you will find the way. Plus there are certain remedies I can suggest.'

As a telepath tester, Mr Chatterjee had met many candidates who had pretended to read his mind, eager to get a government job. He was no stranger to carefully crafted generalities. But he couldn't help hoping against hope. Maybe the man truly had talent. It was an easy enough thing to test. Who better to test an astrologer than a man from the future?

'What do you think lies in the future for India?'

'Future is very bright,' said the Pandit, 'we have just achieved independence. Men like Patel and Nehru will take us to new heights.'

'What about Jinnah and Pakistan?' asked Mr Chatterjee.

'Jinnah will live for ten more years. On his deathbed, he will repent his sins, and Pakistan will re-join Mother India.'

'Bullshit!' said the parrot.

'How about China?' asked Mr Chatterjee.

'China and India will be friends forever. We will grow together in peace and prosperity.'

'Will we fight any wars?'

'How can the country of Gandhiji fight any wars? Inspired by our example, other people also will stop fighting. The world will change as per Gandhiji's requirement. His followers will be worshipped like Gods, particularly in India.'

So the man was a fraud after all, thought Mr Chatterjee. Superstition was like a cheap torch, his father had always said. All it did was keep you mostly in the dark. I really wish you weren't right, Dad, he thought, I could do with a little bit of magic right now.

'Cock teaser!' said the parrot, which was just about right.

He had to remember why he was here. He was here because an RSS man had mocked him for not being an astrologer. Astrologers were credible sources here, like the BBC. He needed to become one.

'I have come here from the future on a mission,' said Mr Chatterjee.

'Prove it,' said Jatindas, and waited, hands folded in his lap.

When it came to other people, his standards were rigorous.

Mr Chatterjee took his iPhone 27 out of his pocket and switched it on. The screen came to life. A bullet shot out of a gun, straight towards them. Rajnikanth flew past it, his cape flapping in the wind. He stopped in mid-air, hands on his hips, grinning a heavenly grin and the bullet bounced off his chest. It shot out of the screen, menacing them briefly, and vanished abruptly.

Jatindas got back off the floor, trembling. He eyed the device in Mr Chatterjee's hand apprehensively, but nothing else emerged from it. Once he had recovered from the shock, he began to see possibilities. This was genuine knowledge of the future. Imagine what he could do with an endless supply of the real thing. He could see a golden yellow hue suffusing his destiny, as befitted those successful in trade or commerce. But for all this to come to pass, he would have to first satisfy this person, who was bound to have come for some specific purpose.

'How may I help you?' he asked.

'I know when Mahatma Gandhi will die,' said Mr Chatterjee. 'Someone will shoot him. I have to stop it.'

'How can anybody shoot Bapu?' said Jatindas, genuinely appalled. 'Even the British could not do that! The hand will shake! The bullet will not fly!'

'The hand did not shake, and the bullet did fly. On January thirtieth. The day after tomorrow.'

'His body is so weak and thin, how can somebody shoot a bullet at him? What is this you have made me listen to?'

Mr Chatterjee waited silently. It might not be so difficult after all.

When Jatindas recovered, he was a different person. Even his moustache looked more business-like.

'What do you need to do?'

'I need to warn the right people.'

Jatindas stood up and started pacing about the room.

'I can take you to the most powerful person in the land!' he said.

'Nehru?'

'No, no, Mountbatten!'

Mr Chatterjee was surprised. This seemed very different from what he had been taught in school. He had always assumed that Independence in 1947 had involved some form of detachment from the British. Jatindas had no doubts, however.

'Arrey, everything is the maya of Mountbatten. All this ripping and tearing, blood and murder, it's all because of him, because of his hurry and his stupidity. Yet he is still sitting here in Delhi having tea and biscuits. If he is not the king in Delhi, then who is? After this, do you think any ruler sitting in Delhi will ever admit their fault in anything?'

Mr Chatterjee suspected prejudice, but he was on shaky ground, historically. About Mountbatten specifically, he remembered little, except that a learned uncle had once called him a popinjay. Not knowing what a popinjay was, he had imagined him as a little multi-coloured bird, hopping from twig to twig, blood on its beak. It was hard to think of him as the king of anything.

'Once we give Mountbatten-sahab the news, he will send all the paltans to protect Bapu. This much I will say, he is very fond of Bapu. Once the paltans are there, no one will be able to touch him.'

When it came to protecting human life, Mountbatten seemed like an odd choice, under the circumstances. But Jatindas was confident, and his concern for Gandhi was completely sincere.

'Only thing is, how do we establish your credibility? Why should he believe you? You must confidently tell him many interesting things about the future.'

'In the twenty-first century,' said Mr Chatterjee, 'it was widely reported that the Prime Minister of India was secretly replaced by a humanoid robot manufactured by Honda. Unfortunately, the robot was defective, and would automatically go on "mute" all the time. Ultimately it had to be withdrawn, after the battery malfunctioned publicly. Honda claimed it was excessive remote control usage.'

'See, this is the kind of story customers want to hear! You have genuine talent. There is a future for you in this business!'

'Can't I just show him my phone?'

'Don't take it with you. They'll find it when they check you at the gate. Then the police will step in. You will never get to Mountbatten. Instead, the police will play ping-pong with your testicles. They're very good, because of all the practice.'

So I enter the premises with no proof that I'm from the future, thought Mr Chatterjee, and then I impress a legendary historical figure with my natural chutzpah. So far as plans went, this one lacked substance. Ping-pong loomed in his future. His companion remained optimistic, though. The effect of Rajnikanth still lingered.

'Tell him a story about Nehru-sahab's future. They are good friends. He will love it. Add some masala. The trick is to tell a good story. If you tell a good story, then they will want to believe you. After that, tell him about Bapu, and we can save him.'

He looked to his Gods and raised and lowered his folded hands. He was brisk, business-like and sincere. Mr Chatterjee gained strength from his energy. He missed Ali. He missed his calm, and his strength, and his easy smile. He tried not to think about Banani, alone and helpless in a nightmare city, wife to an absconding seditionist. He had to finish this job and get back home to save her. He had to think of something really good to say to Mountbatten. Something that would stop him in his tracks.

'Go fuck a duck!' said the parrot.

That might do the trick, thought Mr Chatterjee. It even made sense. After all, someone had to say it to him, eventually.

60

'Onward to Beijing!'

The room was an almost exact replica of the CA's room, except it was in Ranchi.

'It feels just like home!' whispered the PM to the General.

'It ought to,' the General whispered, 'technically, you're still in charge here.'

This was true, although no Indian Prime Minister had wielded any real authority here for over twenty years, ever since the Maoists had liberated the Compact Revolutionary Zone, which straddled the Indian subcontinent like a blood-red Miss India sash.

The Cabinet Secretary of the Compact Revolutionary Zone was an almost exact replica of the CA. He had the same round body, topped off by an improbably large head, the same two little tufts of hair above each ear, connected by a few, thin, parallel strands that traversed the vast expanse of his bald pate, making him look like a small alien was trying to consume him from the top down; the same fat hands which he rubbed together constantly, reassuring himself with the feel of himself; and the same air of monumental self-satisfaction unblemished by any trace of doubt. The only difference was that he was much darker. He was like the CA dipped in chocolate.

The General sat next to the PM, his back ramrod straight, his hostility palpable. He respected most Maoists. He respected their commitment, and their discipline, and their skills in jungle warfare, although he could knock them back in a stand-up fight any day of the week. But it was a long time since this oily little panjandrum had done any fighting, and his wearing jungle fatigues was an insult to the uniform. At least the babus back in Delhi didn't pretend to be soldiers. His revolver was Chinese, and brand new.

'I love what you've done with the place!' said the PM brightly, jabbing the General sharply with her elbow.

'My revolutionary name is Inquilab, but you can call me Mamaji,' said the Cabinet Secretary. 'You are currently wooing your Muslim voters, I see.'

The PM sighed. She was still wearing the burkha, minus the veil. It seemed to have done the trick because she and the General had managed to get to Ranchi to try and work out a truce with the Maoists without attracting the attention of the CA.

'I welcome you in the name of the General Secretary, who shall remain anonymous,' said Mamaji, 'and the Communist Party of India (Maoist), and all right-thinking proletariat of the Compact Revolutionary Zone.'

And what do you do with the wrong-thinking proletariat, the PM wanted to ask, but she stopped herself just in time.

'I am quite familiar with the state of Jharkhand,' she said, 'I used to draw it for my children all the time. They could never get the shape right. Since then, I've been to Ranchi a few times, usually to meet the Chief Minister.'

'You just missed him,' said Mamaji, 'he was here only fifteen minutes ago.'

The PM was surprised. 'We still have a Chief Minister in Jharkhand?' she asked the General.

'We still have everything in Jharkhand,' said the General, 'you send them money every year. It's in the budget.'

'That's exactly what we were discussing when he was here,' said Mamaji. 'How to disburse this year's funds, after the necessary party contributions.'

'I can't believe we're still sending money here?'

'You always have,' said Mamaji, 'after all, it is for the benefit of the people. I'm sure you want your people to benefit, don't you?'

There was no arguing with that. Although most of the people benefitting were probably in this building. There always seemed to be enough money, although she had no idea where it came from. She had no idea where most of it went, either.

'Of course this is just a temporary arrangement,' said Mamaji, 'until the revolution is complete. While the struggle continues, we will rely on the existing administrative infrastructure. All district magistrates, block development officers, tehsil development officers, and gram sevaks have been issued revolutionary clothing, and copies of *Hold High The Bright Red Banner of Marxism-Leninism-Maoism*. Once the whole of India is liberated, we will replace this administrative infrastructure with something more suited to the needs of the masses.'

Good luck with that, thought the PM.

'I hear you're having some trouble with the People's War people,' she said.

'The People's War Group were imperfectly integrated and remain ideologically misguided,' said Mamaji, frostily. 'They persist in taking a parochial and non-proletarian approach. We are using forceful criticism to help them resolve their inner contradictions. In this, we are being supported by the People's Vanguard, the South Central Maoist Committee, the CPI (Kanai), the CPI (Kanu) and the Irritated Tribal Collective, although the Democratic Front is becoming alarmingly fascist, while the Anti-Landlord Alliance is regressing into feudalism, and the CPI (Kananbala) is neglecting its duties and increasingly focusing on theatrical productions which grow ever more elaborate. As to where Jangalmahal stands in this matter—who can tell what Bengalis are really thinking?'

'So you're fighting each other, and we just licked you in Meerut,' said the General with grim satisfaction. 'The Compact Revolutionary Zone isn't so compact after all. Maybe it's time to take a breather.'

'The assault on Meerut was merely a diversion while the First Tribal Division deployed towards Lucknow. We were waiting for the armoured units to finish training. The First War of Independence was won and lost in Uttar Pradesh. So will this one be. The struggle proceeds exactly as per our plans.'

'Don't you get tired of struggling sometimes?' said the PM. 'Don't you feel like taking a break, seeing what you've got, maybe kissing your children goodnight and actually sleeping next to them? Don't you ever feel like that?'

'I think peace and prosperity go hand in hand, dear lady. Where there is no prosperity, there can be no peace.'

'Would it help if we gave you a telecom company?' asked the PM. 'We've got quite a few of those lying around.'

'Well, my son is very interested in mobile phones,' said Mamaji thoughtfully, 'but I think we're not quite ready for that. Besides, we already have three mobile service providers. I doubt that another player will be viable.'

A pert, young guerrilla girl came in with a silver tray, and served them tea in exquisite porcelain cups. Mamaji held out a little bowl.

'Some salt?'

The PM raised an eyebrow.

'We do this to show solidarity with our tribal brothers,' said Mamaji. 'They cannot afford sugar.'

The General discreetly pushed his cup away, unwilling to participate in the ceremonial consumption of enemy salt. The girl was still standing there, staring at the PM. 'She's so old!' she said giggling.

'That she is,' said Mamaji, smiling, 'you can go now.'

'I'm sorry,' he said to the PM, 'the life expectancy here is around fifty, so she's never seen someone as old as you.'

The PM felt a sense of desolation so deep she could scarcely breathe.

'This is why I came,' she said, 'we have to stop fighting, for their sake. In exactly what way have their lives improved in the last thirty years, can you tell me?'

'Well, eventually . . .' ventured Mamaji.

'Fuck eventually,' said the PM, 'generations have died just as poor as they were born. What about them? Who's going to be left to celebrate the arrival of your revolution? Give it up and join the gang. Stand for elections. With your discipline, you're ten times the RSS. You'll win scary majorities. Then you can do some real good, maybe even make a buck or two. Get some good clothes instead of these jungle prints, which are quite frankly awful. Do it for this little girl, standing here looking at me like I'm a zoo animal. Go, chit!'

She waved her hand imperiously. The girl zipped off, grinning.

'So what do you say?' she asked. She was superb in that moment.

'You're scared of the Chinese,' said Mamaji.

'They could declare war any minute. The Competent Authority keeps prodding them, like a kid on the beach with a jellyfish. Except China is not a jellyfish, it's a huge country run by a huge army, which has lots of weapons and loves using them. Ever since they beat the Japanese, they've been practically unmanageable. And they're confident because we have our hands full with you, and they keep you well supplied. It's like the jihadis all over again. No one ever fights us directly. If we could sign a truce with you, it might make them stop and think. You could save the lives of millions of your fellow Indians. They may not live in the jungle, but they're human too, right? Just for a while. Then you can start fighting us again, whenever the Politburo thinks social forces are correctly aligned, or the Competent Authority chokes to death on a carrot, whichever happens sooner.'

'The General Secretary has been pondering this issue,' said Mamaji, 'anonymity gives him a lot of peace and quiet, and he utilizes this time to think. He has reviewed our situation, and asked himself, what would Chairman Mao do in a case like this?'

'Oh, great!' said the PM. There was nothing she dreaded more than lectures on communism.

Mamaji smiled to himself, enjoying her consternation.

'When the Japanese invaded China during the Second World War, the Chairman took the view that the survival of the nation took priority. He therefore entered into an alliance with the Kuomintang, and together they defeated the Japanese, after which he massacred the Kuomintang. The situation here is very similar. In this, as in all else, we believe the Chairman is showing the way.'

Not literally, the PM hoped. Chairman Mao's body had been filched from his mausoleum in a daring midnight raid by the ultra-Maoists a few years ago. Even as they spoke, he was probably showing the way to someone somewhere, albeit somewhat inflexibly. The PM tried not to think about what they could possibly be doing with him. Besides she could sense that Mamaji was on the verge of becoming unhinged. She knew all the signs.

'The Chinese are power-mad and decadent,' said Mamaji, 'just like the Japanese in World War II. We could join forces with you, execute a swift U-turn, and sweep the Chinese from the sacred soil of India.

Hardened by years of battle with each other, our troops will crush the cowardly PLA, who are only good for shooting unarmed civilians, and sometimes running them over with tanks. Genuine Maoists in China will rise in their millions to support us, and in one mighty swoop, we will create a Vastly Expanded Revolutionary Zone which will include more than half of all humanity. After that, what price the survival of the USA? Onward to Beijing!'

He was certifiably insane, of course. Too many years of living in the jungle could do that to a man. Plus the uncanny resemblance to the CA was a giveaway. Personally she blamed the chair, which looked suspiciously similar.

Given that he had been receiving a wide variety of military advice from the CA for quite some time now, the General felt himself slipping into a familiar groove.

'You can't just wake up one morning and decide to whack the Chinese,' he said, 'these things take planning. All these computer simulations make it look very easy, but there's actual people and equipment involved, and you've successfully destroyed the few roads that we had. I'll have my staff get to work on it.'

The PM gave him a look of dumb gratitude. He was getting really good at not fighting wars. But it was a strategy that could only take them so far. Their performance as peacemakers left much to be desired.

'This is more than I could ever have imagined,' she said, perfectly truthfully, 'I think we'll just go and digest this a little bit, consult the cabinet, maybe talk to a few television personalities . . .'

'Report to the CA,' said Mamaji.

'Well, I wouldn't call it reporting exactly, but certainly we will keep him in the loop.'

'You must see the new statue of the supreme leader,' said Mamaji, as he led them back to their car, which was waiting to take them to the airport. He would have to call ahead and ask them not to check their passports. It would seem rude, in the light of their freshly minted alliance.

The statue was just in front of the secretariat. The supreme leader was a small man, so the statue was gigantic. He was dressed in combat gear, with one arm pointing towards Delhi. Presumably they would now turn the statue around so that it would point towards Beijing instead. The face of the statue was covered with a very large red handkerchief, which fluttered bravely in the breeze.

They sat together in silence in the helicopter, shoulder to shoulder.

What we really need is a drug to counteract testosterone, thought the PM. Put that in the chapatis and everything will be hunky-dory.

'Onward to Beijing,' said the General in a dull monotone.

SECTION 3

61

*'They grew genuine beards, not the theatrical ones
with spirit gum.'*

'When is the big man coming?' asked Nazimuddin, a little indistinctly
because his mouth was full of mughlai paratha. At six annas a plate, it
was one of the star attractions of Sangu Valley Restaurant, home to a
mixed clientele of Bengali barristers, middle-class Englishmen, and men
who were closer to nature, like them. His men ploughed through their
food methodically.

'He's just outside. I'll go get him,' said Ali. 'I've convinced him that
Direct Action Day will be more effective if you celebrate it in other cities
as well. Please keep your weapons on display and ready to use. This is a
big contract. We need to look professional.'

This was Calcutta in 1946. He was reasonably sure the Sangu Valley
management wouldn't do much if they saw weapons, beyond removing
excess cutlery.

'What a business brain that boy has!' said Nazimuddin, as he left. 'He
is like a professor for making money!'

Gopal Patha and six of his musclemen were waiting just outside, in
front of Purno Cinema where King Kong was once more trying to climb
the Empire State Building with a fistful of blonde. They were nuts about
King Kong in Calcutta, and he was unleashed on the city on a regular
basis. Also currently popular was *The Boat Sinks*, based on a story by
Tagore, which was a lot like the Titanic, except that the vessel was
smaller, and wife-swapping was involved.

'Where were you?' demanded Gopal Patha, who commanded eight
hundred men. There was no remorse or apology in this one. Ali didn't
feel any either. He reminded him of his old boss Zawahiri, the owl-faced
Egyptian, a nasty little man with the personality of a codfish.

'Forgive me, Gopal sir,' he said. 'It took a little bit of time. They're very suspicious, which is only natural. They're good Hindu boys who spent years infiltrating the Muslim League. They grew genuine beards, not the theatrical ones attached with spirit gum. It's hard for them to trust anyone. But when they heard the great Gopal Patha himself wanted to meet them, they were willing to take a chance. Inspire them, like you inspired me, and you could add a private army to your forces, in the heart of the Muslim League.'

'What should I speak of?' asked Gopal Patha.

'Abuse Jinnah a lot,' said Ali, 'they like that. They're sitting over there. I'll just follow you.'

Gopal and his goons trooped into Sangu Valley. Ali skipped across the road and hopped onto a tram.

❑

He stood by the door, feeling the breeze on his face. He felt a quiet satisfaction. Between them, the two sheikhs would be in charge of at least a thousand local lads. On Direct Action Day, they would be leading all the action and reaction. One would act, and the other would react. Or vice versa. Sometimes both would act simultaneously. Sometimes no one would act, there would only be reaction. In times of extreme necessity, the reaction might have to occur just before the action which would have caused it. All of it would be very direct, up close and personal. What they lacked in finesse, they would make up for in enthusiasm.

By taking them off the board, Ali had probably saved a few thousand lives, which was a nice way to spend the afternoon. Business-wise, Sangu Valley Restaurant would suffer a minor setback. But he was confident that they would soon float back into contention on a sea of oil, some of which they had been re-using since the nineteenth century. It gave their food a distinctive flavour, and reinforced in Bengali minds the conviction that Bengali stomachs were fundamentally weak.

He peered over the shoulder of a man sitting by the window. He was thin, and his shoulders were bony. He was reading detailed instructions for a riot in his morning newspaper. The newspaper explained everything step by step, in simple, easy-to-understand language. It laid out the details of routes, locations and timings. It listed different places in Calcutta, Howrah, Hooghly and Metiabruz from where processions would start; all the processions would converge at the Ochterlony Monument by 11 a.m., where Chief Minister Suhrawardy would declare the games open with a rousing speech. 'It is the duty of all Muslims in India,' it said, rounding things off on a high note, 'to make this day a complete success, by securing a complete moral and physical purge of the nation.'

Ali felt his euphoria evaporating. These were fighting words, and he'd read a few in his day. He used to read *Saamna* and *Organiser*, in the pages of which Hindu firebrands breathed Hindu fire, looking for clues, responses, and material for his blog, *Modern Jihadi*. While they did scatter kerosene and matches with gay abandon, they had never printed an actual instruction manual.

Ali needed to get off the tram. He had to clear his head. He hopped off gracefully. Calcutta trams were the slowest mode of transportation in the history of mankind. It was faster to walk, but taking a tram was the gentlemanly thing to do. Getting on and off was also part of the fun. People waited till the tram was in motion, and then mounted or dismounted with grace and athleticism, displaying a variety of individual styles. Occasionally, someone fresh from the villages would use the wrong technique, and fall off backwards, or flat on their faces. Ali's own dismount was instinctively balletic. He received a polite smattering of applause from the passengers.

He was on Rashbehari Avenue. The Great Kali Temple was on the other side of the road. As he watched, a small procession marched past it, waving green flags and shouting 'Allah hu Akbar' and 'We'll fight and get our Pakistan!' They raised their voices as they passed the temple. Bystanders glared back at them resentfully.

All of Calcutta was one huge, sprawling market as far as Ali could see, like Portobello Road without Hugh Grant. There were shops everywhere. Most of them sold food or clothes, along with a few harmoniums and four-poster beds. One shop had a board which said, 'Punjabis, Rs 2.' This was not, as it turned out, a local branch of Slaves R Us where citizens of the state of Punjab were being sold individually, or in lots, but merely a retail outlet for kurtas. Since such kurtas were believed to be popular in Punjab, they were called 'Punjabis', a fact that actual Punjabis found highly amusing.

Ali found himself standing in front of a small, dilapidated theatre. The dimly lit front was adorned with a gigantic hand-painted poster, a bold and vibrant work of art that used every colour in the rainbow, plus a few that defied description. 'THE EMPEROR OF THEATRE, GHANASHYAM DAS, WINNER OF 34 GOLD MEDALS, IN AND AS, **LIFE OF NETAJI!!!**' it said. It featured Ghanashyam Das, who was alarmingly full-figured, in what the artist fondly imagined to be a field-marshal's uniform, pointing dramatically towards what might or might not be the Qutab Minar. An endless procession of khaki-clad figures marched off into the horizon, growing progressively smaller. Hitler, Tojo and Mountbatten stood together in a corner, gazing on in awe. There were large dollops of blood everywhere.

Right next to it was another, smaller poster, which was remarkably similar, with almost identical scenes and many of the same characters. 'COMING SOON BY PUBLIC DEMAND', it said, 'GHANASHYAM DAS IN AND AS, **LIFE OF HITLER!!!**'

It was too good a chance to miss. It could even be classified as research, and, besides, how often would he get a chance to see an emperor of the theatre? He knew what he had to do next. He just didn't want to think about it for a while.

Ali walked down the dark, narrow corridor, carefully avoiding the malodorous gutter that ran beside it, till he reached the booking counter and asked for a ticket. The man at the counter eyed him suspiciously.

'Are you the theatre critic from *The Statesman*?' he demanded.

The ticket man was under strict instructions to prevent the critic from *The Statesman* from entering at all costs, by physical force if necessary. Of course, the critic was short and balding, while this man was tall and elegant, with excellent hair, but there was no point in taking chances. Critics were cunning. Besides, the man had a picture of some African playwright on his T-shirt, which made him suspicious.

'No, brother,' said Ali, smiling reassuringly, 'I'm not from *The Statesman*. I'm from Palestine.'

A foreign visitor! The ticket man had heard that Ghanashyam Das was rapidly becoming world famous, but this was the first time he had met an actual member of his international audience.

'Please, enter,' he said, graciously handing him a ticket.

Ali strolled into the theatre, and was almost driven right out again by a solid wall of sound.

It was Ghanashyam Das, beating his chest and laughing, rocking the theatre to its rafters. 'ENGLISHMEN?' he roared, 'WHAT FEAR HAVE I OF ENGLISHMEN? I SPIT ON ALL ENGLISHMEN! DOES AN ENGLISHMAN NOT BLEED? GIVE ME YOUR HEARTS' BLOOD,' he declared, thumping his chest, and rattling the audience right down to the soles of their chappals, 'AND I WILL GIVE YOU FREEDOM!!'

A woman in the audience fainted. Several babies started crying. There was no need for a Palestinian to leave Palestine to enjoy this show, realized Ali. He could just stay at home and keep his ears cocked.

Ghanashyam Das stamped up and down the stage, hands on his hips, his jackboots threatening to break through the rotting planks. He was extremely fond of jackboots, and had insisted on wearing them throughout the play, even in scenes where Netaji had not, according to reliable sources, been jack-booted. But his affinity for them was inexplicably deep. Sometimes he wore them in bed. The great thespian rolled his eyes and flung out an arm, narrowly missing one of his fellow actors. 'BROTHERS AND SISTERS OF INDIA. IT IS BETTER TO DIE FREE THAN TO LIVE A SLAVE. ARISE, MY COUNTRYMEN, AND RUN TOWARDS THEM, WITH YOUR BAYONETS HELD AT THE PROPER ANGLE!'

A horde of khaki-clad soldiers rushed in from stage left and rushed out again, leaving the stage free once more for the Emperor.

'TO BE FREE, OR NOT TO BE FREE, THAT IS THE ONLY QUESTION,' he declared, and froze, awaiting applause.

The Emperor had taken the liberty of improving some of Netaji's speeches. One of his fellow players, now no longer part of the troupe, had timidly asked whether they should fiddle with historical speeches. The great man had blackened his face with boot polish, while delivering a brief lecture on the meaning of art.

Ali watched the show, enchanted. It reminded him of all the things he loved about India. It was loud, and spectacular, and heartfelt, and frequently bizarre. Any resemblance to actual events was largely coincidental. Who knew what had really happened anyway? Perhaps Hitler really had cowered before Netaji and apologized abjectly for not giving him enough troops, offered him apple strudel to make amends. Maybe Mountbatten really had been reduced to the depths of despair, with Nehru stealing his wife and Netaji stealing his troops, and had decided, in a moment rendered all the more poignant by violins, that it was time for the British to quit India. Was it so utterly improbable that Tojo had planted a bomb on Netaji's plane, jealous of the fact that he was so much taller and more charismatic than him? Did it really matter whether the INA had reached the outskirts of Delhi or the outskirts of India, so long as the music was rousing and they marched well? The Emperor of Theatre strutted and preened and struck dramatic poses. He really did look a lot like Netaji, with his chubby cheeks and his piercing eyes. The whole thing reminded Ali of the pantos he'd enjoyed as a kid.

The crowd was enjoying itself thoroughly, barring the infants, who were petrified. The crowd stomped and cheered and laughed and cried. 'Again, again,' they roared, whenever Ghanashyam Das laughed his booming laugh. 'Guru, guru,' they said, as he stood with his boot on the back of Tojo's neck, daring him to get up and insult Mother India again. (He didn't.)

Everyone got their money's worth, and left the theatre completely satisfied. So did Ali. He stepped out of the smelly, cramped theatre into the cold night air, face to face once more with the cold reality of his predicament. But for a precious hour or two, he had forgotten. For this he owed Ghanashyam Das, winner of thirty-four gold medals, a debt of gratitude.

As he walked away from the theatre, he thought about what lay ahead. Sure, he had saved some lives. Two groups of goons were going to blow each other away. But that wouldn't stop the catastrophe. There was only one thing that would. He had made some bad choices. He had regretted them. He had tried to make amends. Now it looked like his life had come full circle.

He had to become history's first suicide bomber.

62

'I'd rather pluck out my eyes with a blunt spoon.'

The Bank of Bodies delegation stood in Tarun-da's room, feeling decidedly out of place, like poultry farmers at a chicken convention.

Shovon Chowdhury

No. 2 looked around nervously; he could understand why the residents of Shanti Nagar would resent BoB employees. Nevertheless, none of the people present seemed to be missing anything, although with internal organs, you could never tell. As a general rule, No. 2 avoided meeting donors. It helped him stay objective. Unlike his ex-boss. His ex-boss used to be the head of the Medical Military Commandos and took great pride in being a field man. He could gauge the market value of a human being by just looking at him.

'See that man?' he would whisper in No. 2's ear at meetings (he himself had been No. 3 at the time), 'you could get 500,000 rupees for his liver. Kidney, around 700,000. Heart's no use, you can see the tobacco stains on his fingers.'

Luckily for No. 2, he had passed away after complications arising from a botched penis transplant, leaving the field clear for his own meteoric rise.

A boy came in, with an extremely pretty young woman. No. 2 was instantly smitten. She glared at him with naked hostility. He found that irresistible in a woman. The boy and the young woman sat down together on the cot. The woman placed a protective arm around him, as if she was afraid they might leap up any minute and try to snag an organ or two. Foolish woman. Did she not realize that there was a process involved? It's not like plucking mangoes, he felt like telling her. The ignorance of the common public never ceased to amaze him.

His face betrayed none of this. He looked sophisticated, calm and benevolent, like a foreign-returned uncle. He held out his hand to Pintoo, remembering in the nick of time to make sure it was the left one. Pintoo shook his hand gravely, and then held it palm up and looked at it closely. There were no marks of surgery, so it wasn't stolen, it was his own. He let it go.

'You really have some nerve, coming here,' said Banani to No. 2. 'The last one of you guys Pintoo met was a real specimen, that Sam Kapoor. He nearly had a sofa dropped on his head.'

'At the very outset I would like to apologize for the abominable behaviour of my ex-colleague,' said No. 2. 'The Bank of Bodies is more than happy to hand him over to you as a peace offering. It is for you to decide what to do with him.'

Banani could hardly believe her ears. These people were like cannibals, serving each other up like meat. What kind of sick, twisted mind would think up a plan like that? No. 2 beamed at her avuncularly. She felt like slapping him.

'You've obviously come here for something, you horrible man,' said Banani. 'Spit it out, and then explain to us why we shouldn't lock you up and never let you go.'

No. 2 shook his head sadly, clucking his tongue. Banani repressed the urge to look for something to hit him with.

'Should I fuck him now?' asked Ranvir, brandishing his lathi. He was rapidly transferring his loyalty from the ancient headmaster to Banani.

'Not yet,' said Banani.

'Well?' she said, turning back to No. 2.

'You are, of course, entirely correct. On behalf of the Bank of Bodies, I have brought with me a proposal which I believe will be of great benefit to the local community. I would urge you to put aside our past misunderstandings and hear me out.'

'Keep talking,' said Banani. These people were full of shit, but it was worth it for the information.

'Thanks to his exploits at our Karol Bagh branch,' said No. 2, 'we are now well aware of the talents of this remarkable young man. We want to help him use his talents to benefit the maximum number of people.'

'I had no idea that the BoB was a charity,' said Banani.

'There is, of course, a commercial angle involved,' admitted No. 2. 'We are proposing to run a Miracle Lottery, where the lucky winners will receive one free miracle from Pintoo. We would love to make it free, but there are administrative expenses involved. This way, the child can bring joy to people across the country. It would be lovely to help everyone, but we have to have some method of selection. Hence the lottery.'

He smiled apologetically.

The ancient headmaster, who had been conserving his energy, hawked noisily and spat on the floor, generating a surprisingly large amount of phlegm for someone in such an advanced state of desiccation. His point well made, he lapsed back into a comatose state. Tarun-da leaped up, fetched a damp cloth, and started swabbing the floor. Having spent several days with Banani, he knew what was expected of him. Banani nodded approvingly, making a mental note to have a chat with the headmaster next time he demonstrated sentience.

Since arriving in Shanti Nagar, Banani had rapidly taken stock of the situation. A doddering old crock and a son of Stalin had been messing with the mind of an impressionable young child, who quite possibly might be the most powerful human on the face of the planet, and considerable mayhem had already been unleashed, in the hope of rectifying past mistakes and making the country less of a toilet bowl. Someone had to make sure things didn't spin out of control. Given that Shanti-bai had expressed a preference for naps, and was working only occasionally, this meant that it was up to her. She also had to get Pintoo to do something about Hemonto. What was happening to the poor dear? How was he managing without his pyjamas and his toothbrush?

She turned to No. 2.

'So, we're getting into new businesses, are we?'

'We felt it was time to give back to society.'

'What about the arms and legs and organs and skin that you're taking from society?'

No. 2 had known this question would crop up. It was only natural that the people of Shanti Nagar would fail to see the bigger picture. As a thriving transnational, the BoB made vital contributions to the growth of India's economy, helping to maintain a GDP growth rate that was the envy of the world. The per capita figures now looked even more impressive thanks to the post-war drop in capita. But did the people of Shanti Nagar understand that? No. They persisted in complaining about a statistically insignificant number of surgical procedures that kept this mighty growth engine running. That was the problem with poor people. They lacked perspective.

On the other hand, this child was a truly stupendous asset. Once they had him in their grasp, there were no limits to what the BoB could achieve. Or he himself, for that matter. The Chairman was practically gaga, and it was he, No. 2, who was running the show. All he had to do was convince the Chairman to go in for some particularly complex surgery, slip the surgeon a rupee or two, and in a matter of days, the man would be spare parts, and he would be the new chairman. Competition was fierce in the BoB, and most chairmen ended up being disassembled by their successors. He would ascend the throne, and under his dynamic, yet wise leadership, the BoB would soar to new heights. He could see himself on the cover of *Fortune* magazine, the toast of Wall Street. 'No. 2

is No. 1' the cover would say. 'Indian Genius Shows The Way,' it would add in smaller type, beneath a picture of him smiling, perhaps with one hand resting casually on a globe.

It wouldn't be difficult. The editor was a customer.

If he had to temporarily suspend their harvesting operations in order to reach this goal, it was a small price to pay. Short-term earnings might take a hit, but it was the long-term that mattered. He was a visionary. The BoB needed his vision. He owed it to the BoB to become No. 1. The BoB needed Pintoo. He would do it for the BoB. With the child firmly under his control, say, in a month or two, they could resume operations in Shanti Nagar. Meanwhile, they could briefly divert procurement to Bihar, or even the Bengal Protectorate. The raw material was not so good, and it would mean a rise in procurement costs, but they would manage.

Banani was the key. It helped that he was falling in love with her. He looked deeply into her eyes, and sincerity shone from his gaze. Deep loathing shone from hers.

'My dear, dear lady,' he said, 'how could you possibly think that we would continue harvesting under these circumstances? If the little boy agrees to join our new venture, we would naturally stop immediately. Otherwise who knows what could happen? Our teams might pick up one of you by mistake. Although I must say, anyone who receives an organ from a spectacular specimen of womanhood such as yourself would be truly fortunate.'

Banani gaped at him, dumbstruck. Was this guy for real?

Tarun-da stepped into the breach. He hated dealing with filthy capitalist swine, but the history of revolution was filled with calculated compromise. Coincidentally, he too followed a Chairman. He didn't talk about it much. Since the Chinese had blown up half the country, the popularity of Maoism had diminished significantly in those parts of the country that were not under their control.

'So you promise to stop your raids into Shanti Nagar?' he demanded.

'Absolutely,' said No. 2.

'It's not that you'll stop on weekdays, and do little runs on Saturday and Sunday?'

'No, no, of course not.'

'Not even on National Holidays?'

'We're closed on National Holidays. Also, all banking holidays.'

'I think we should do this,' said Tarun-da, turning to Banani, 'at least the Medical Military raids will stop.'

'Pintoo stays here,' said Banani, who had reached the same conclusion. 'Your scientists don't study him, your managers don't manage him, your doctors don't dissect him, you won't even be in the same room with him. Is that clear?'

'You won't regret this,' said No. 2, as he got up to leave. There was no sense in pushing his luck any further. He had what he needed, except for one small thing.

'We still have to get government approval for our scheme. For this, I would be very grateful if Pintoo would join us for just a couple of meetings, one with Guru Dharti Pakar, who is eager to meet the team, and one with the Competent Authority, whose clearance is needed for everything. A small demonstration from the boy will be enough to establish our credibility, thus enabling us to bring joy to the lives of millions. After that, we will not disturb him.'

'You mean there really is a Competent Authority?' said Banani.

'I thought he was some sort of committee,' said Tarun-da.

'I've been seeing that name on lots of things these days,' said Banani, thoughtfully.

No. 2 was feeling thoughtful too. As senior executive of a company whose turnover exceeded ten billion yuan, he was one of the few people who had actually met the Competent Authority. Revealing his identity was an act which jeopardized national security, and rendered him prosecutable, under the sedition law of 1898, a gift from the British Government to the Indian Government, which the Indian Government had preserved, intact, in honour of the love they had once shared. In essence, the law made it illegal to dislike the government, but its specific applications were wide and varied. The rule was strictly enforced. Punishments for seditiously revealing the CA's identity were lavish and gruesome. On the other hand, his attraction for this girl was a deep and powerful thing. She was like a flower in the wild, untamed and free. He felt the urge to draw her into his circle of trust, despite the inherent peril.

'There is indeed a Competent Authority, my dear lady,' said No. 2. 'He controls everything. The PM's primary purpose is to appear on TV. She may soon be replaced. A digital model is under development. If, just once, we can demonstrate to the CA this young man's skill, and convince him of the robustness of our business plan, files will be signed, and all manner of good fortune will follow.'

'Well, if Pintoo's meeting this guy, then I'm coming with him,' said Banani.

'If she's going, then so am I,' said Ranvir, 'anyone touches her, I break their heads.'

Pintoo gave him a quick grin, and a high five with his good hand. 'If I'm meeting any big people,' he said, 'I want you with me.'

'How can I say no to the pleasure of your company?' said No. 2 to Banani. 'Perhaps you could join us for dinner at the club afterwards?'

'I'd rather pluck out my eyes with a blunt spoon,' said Banani.

'I look forward to it,' said No. 2, warmly. 'As soon as I have fixed up a meeting with Guru Dharti Pakar, I will let you know.'

63

'Go fetch my cheap chappals.
I'm going to Shanti Nagar!'

'Pappu has come back from school nanga poonga again,' said the maid. Despite the constant threat of being put in the incinerator, the female staff remained refreshingly honest when it came to the delivery of bad news. This was because the Vermas never followed the guards down to the incinerator to witness people being burnt to a crisp, so female victims usually slipped the guards a quick one against the wall and slipped out through the back door, free to trade their services to the next person who could provide them three squarish meals. It was trickier for men, particularly if they had no money saved up to bribe themselves out of trouble. As a result they tended to be a bit more obsequious.

'Again!' said Mrs Verma, appalled. 'Not even his underwear?'

'The boys in the bus refused to take his chaddis,' said the maid, who had been debriefed by Pappu, 'but he managed to take them off and give them away to a beggar boy as soon as he got off the bus. He was too quick for me. It's not my fault. The problem is I don't get enough nutritious food.'

Mrs Verma's late mother had spent many long hours in the kitchen lecturing the staff on the importance of cooking proper nutritious food, without which the physical well-being of her family would be severely compromised. This had had the unfortunate side effect of thoroughly sensitizing the entire staff to the value of nutrition.

'Is this a time to be discussing food habits?' demanded Mrs Verma. 'Where is he? Take me to him immediately.'

They took the elevator down to the arrival lounge, the one with the golden Ganesha, bifurcated staircase and the gigantic chandelier, where Pappu was waiting for them, fully clothed, while Ramu stood next to him, naked. Mrs Verma swung round and glared at the maid.

'I thought you said it was Pappu!'

'It was,' said the maid, 'subsequently, Ramu donated all his clothes to Pappu, who is now wearing them.'

'He didn't have any clothes,' said Ramu, by way of explanation.

It was like an epidemic. She could only hope that adults were immune. She made the maid stand slightly behind her, just in case.

She bent down and held Pappu by the shoulders. 'Why?' she asked Pappu. 'Why?'

'It wasn't me, it was the hand,' said Pappu cheerfully, holding up the hand for her to see. Mrs Verma looked at the hand. The hand waved back. The hand was never going to let her go, she could see. She had been trying to avoid making this decision, but things had gone too far. She simply couldn't afford to buy any more clothes, not while war clouds loomed over their mining operation, and poor Sanjeev was risking his life in a metropolis noted for its savagery, in a desperate attempt to save the family business. The doctor had been very precise. Pappu's terrible condition was linked to the hand, and she could either reverse the procedure and donate the hand back to the donor, or eliminate the donor, a twelve-year-old named Pintoo, who lived in Shanti Nagar. It was clear what she had to do. She pressed the red button on her domestic touchpad, the strap of which was tucked into her sari at the waist. She waited. She pressed it again. She waited some more.

'I'll go get a bag,' said Pappu, who could tell when mummy was going on an expedition by the set of her shoulders. 'Can I bring Ramu too?'

'No, you can't,' said Mrs Verma, who was vastly irritated by this sudden influx of little boys in her life. She pressed the red button crossly again. She stomped her foot, causing the chandelier to light up. She stomped quickly twice to switch it off (there was no point in wasting electricity), and stormed off to the guardroom, which was across the lawn, just next to the generator room. It was a seamless oval of cold, grey concrete, radiating menace. Several surveillance drones followed her as she walked, ever vigilant, flying around her head on humming-bird wings, chirping softly to each other. She stepped inside the bunker to find the guards playing cards.

'Rascals!' said Mrs Verma. 'God knows how long I have been ringing the bell! I could have beaten all your brains out with a cricket bat before you even noticed. You call this doing guard duty?'

They were momentarily stunned, but Ram Din, the head guard recovered swiftly. He said in what he hoped was a winning tone:

'Owneress, we are supposed to prevent people from outside getting in. No one told us anything about inside people getting out. Perhaps Sanjeev-sahab forgot to mention it when he was instructing us. It's only natural. He's so busy. In future, we will protect both the front-side and the back-side. We may need some extra staff, however. I have several cousins who are very willing and able, Owneress. Your security is vital to our prosperity. You just give me the order, bas, everything else I'll do.'

He was old and wily, this Ram Din. After being arrested by Pande as a suspect in the dog case, he had shown enough brass for them to let him go. He had a face like a walnut and terrible teeth. Sanjeev swore by him, because he had often rescued him from bars in his youth, but Sanjeev wasn't the one dealing with him now.

'We're leaving for Shanti Nagar in fifteen minutes,' said Mrs Verma, leaving the bunker, which smelled like unwashed socks. 'There's some work we have to do there for Pappu. I need six men with rifles.'

'Rifles,' repeated the head guard, following her out. He scratched his chest dubiously. He was wearing a grubby singlet over his dhoti. He preserved his uniform for ministers and in-laws. 'Nandu, bring a rifle!'

A young man emerged from the bunker, blinking. Mrs Verma noted with approval that he was wearing his jacket, although he had buttoned it up wrong in his hurry. He was clutching a gleaming Mauser Laser Rifle. The men might be dishevelled, but their equipment was immaculate.

'Does that thing actually fire?' demanded Mrs Verma.

The head guard took the rifle and brought it to bear on a flower pot with a surprising economy of movement. He was a veteran of Guwahati, and they had died hard and retreated slow. He cocked an eyebrow at his suzerain.

'Each shot costs fifty dollars, Owneress,' he said.

'Never mind,' said Mrs Verma, hastily. 'I'm sure Sanjeev buys nothing but the best.'

The head guard smiled. He'd known Sanjeev for much longer than her. He was a number one 420, that man. He would never buy an original if a duplicate was available.

'The boss is very particular about quality,' he said, 'whenever I bring him anything, the first thing he will always ask is Ram Din, tell me, is this quality? Quality is like some sort of disease with him. He cannot sleep without quality. You can rest assured.'

Mrs Verma looked at him thoughtfully. An extended sojourn in the company of this man was going to be extremely taxing. She should probably pop across to the pharmacy for some tranquilizers.

'Order an armoured van and a laser-proof Rolls Royce from Mega Cab,' she said. 'Ask them to be here in fifteen minutes. Get Hoskins to drive my vehicle. If anyone attacks us, he's the only one who'll run over them. I'll just pack and get Pappu and we should be ready to leave shortly after that. I'm getting in touch with the BoB for a surgeon on loan. Get the Rolls to pick him up on the way.'

When she was packed, she headed for the vehicles, Pappu in tow. Her son was skipping along, wearing his Iron Man backpack and clutching a stuffed puppy. Spot was horribly moth-eaten, and he smelled, but Pappu loved him more than anything else he owned.

When he had asked her whether he could bring him along, Mrs Verma had been quick to allow it. Now, she turned to the maid who was wondering whether she could slip her boyfriend in through the kitchen window while the management was out.

'Don't just stand there!' said Mrs Verma. 'Go fetch my cheap chappals. I'm going to Shanti Nagar.'

64

'Despair gripped the heart of His Excellency,
and Her Highness was his only solace.'

Admiral of the Fleet Louis Francis Albert Victor Nicholas George Mountbatten, KG, GCB, OM, GCSI, GCIE, GCVO, DSO, PC, FRS, First Earl Mountbatten of Burma, was annoyed by what he saw in the mirror. This was unusual, and his orderly quaked in fear. Mountbatten was frowning because two of his medals were missing. It was bad enough the staff didn't polish them properly, but now they were misplacing them entirely. As if he wouldn't notice. His medals were like children to him. He knew the shape of the Grand Cross of the Order of the White Elephant of Thailand like the back of his own hand. To the extent that anything could disturb his equanimity, the thought of venturing out in public improperly dressed certainly did. As it is he was still frazzled over the fiasco at Elizabeth and Philip's wedding, where his gifting the future monarch Gandhi's loincloth had caused a bit of a rumpus, even after he had explained that it was freshly spun. Moreover, Jinnah was mad at him for not attending his Christmas party in Karachi. Mountbatten had also just shot Edwina's substitute lover Malcolm in the buttocks during a hunting trip in Bhopal, although the matter had been hushed up. It was not the first time he had shot another human being. He had once shot the American Chief of Naval Operations in the foot while demonstrating his revolutionary idea for an aircraft carrier made out of an iceberg. Luckily, relations had been mended since, as had the unfortunate seafarer, although he still limped slightly, and had developed a marked aversion to ice. Churchill wasn't talking to him, Edwina was menopausal and in Madras, and even the faithful Yola was sulking. People thought they were doing it, but the very notion of giving away his precious bodily fluids to someone else was unbearably painful to him. He was under terrible pressure all round, and the desire to punish someone was marring his naturally sunny disposition, with fateful consequences for history. If someone had told Mountbatten this, it would not have bothered him. He was making history all the time.

He stepped out, resplendent, onto the lawns of Government House, where they were letting in all sorts of people these days. Film stars, fakirs

Shovon Chowdhury

and fat politicos mingled with mem-sahabs, missionaries and managing agents, along with a sprinkling of princes who looked deeply depressed, which was perfectly understandable, given that their thrones were very shaky.

Mr Chatterjee was eyeing Mountbatten nervously from behind a sickly bush. The garden was suffering from neglect. The flowerbeds looked slightly dishevelled. The trees were just a little bit unkempt. This was because most of the gardeners had other things to do, such as surviving Partition. Bearers in dull khaki circulated amongst the guests, the perfect foil to Mountbatten's incandescent whiteness. They managed to radiate disapproval while remaining expressionless, thanks to years of training in phlegmatism.

Mr Chatterjee was feeling anything but phlegmatic. He was paralysed by performance anxiety. His memories of Mountbatten were of a ghostly white figure in grainy pictures. Nothing had prepared him for the dazzling reality of the matinee idol who now stood just a few feet away, wondering whether Edwina was serving spam for dinner again. Mr Chatterjee felt weak in the face of his magnetism. He was here to convince Mountbatten that someone was going to kill Gandhi. But who was going to convince whom?

Jatindas joined him behind the bush.

'Now the rest is up to you. I got you in. Go tell him about Bapu.'

'What do you mean? I thought you were his private astrologer!'

'What astrologer will a Christian have? One local fellow on his staff, he is my patient. I asked him to get me in, along with you.'

'How did you explain me?'

'I said you are my cousin from Moradabad who wants to join the navy. Mountbatten loves ships. He keeps sinking them.'

Given that Moradabad was landlocked, his cover story lacked plausibility. But this was no time to quibble over geography. He had to rescue Gandhi quickly so that he could go back and rescue Banani.

He stepped up to Mountbatten, who was thinking about getting a massage. Despite being undercover, he wasn't much good at lying, so he decided to stick to the truth. It was much less confusing that way, and he was already confused enough.

'Your Lordship, my name is Chatterjee. I'm here from the future. There are many things I can tell you about your future glory, but before anything else there is something very urgent you must attend to.'

'Tell me just a little bit about that future glory thing first,' said Mountbatten. The man was clearly mad, but this would make a great story for his autobiography, which he had been working on since childhood.

Mr Chatterjee had given careful thought to this. The key to success in futurology was to make the story exciting. Jatindas had been crystal clear on this point. Accuracy was secondary. Emotional engagement was the key. It was time for the Ballad of the Highnesses. It was a delicate job, requiring tact and diplomacy.

'Once upon a time,' said Mr Chatterjee, 'in a land far, far away, His Highness, and his wife, Her Highness, lived in great pomp and splendour. Their stables were full of horses, and their elephant garage was full of elephants, and the natives waited on them hand and foot, sometimes both at the same time. But they wanted their people to be free, so they fought many battles with the Great Ogre of the West, who smoked cigars and was often naked. With the help of their great friend, His Excellency, a native prince, they achieved their goal, but in the process love bloomed in the hearts of His Excellency and Her Highness, as it often will when two attractive people are thrown together in tumultuous times. They were united by their love for the Holy Man, who encouraged them to see more of each other. The land was baptized in blood and fire, and His Excellency and Her Highness fought each fire bravely, and staunched as much of the blood as they could. Despair gripped the heart of His Excellency, and Her Highness was his only solace.'

'Excuse me,' said Mountbatten, 'but who are these people?'

Mr Chatterjee had been trying to maintain a veneer of anonymity in order to avoid future legal complications. But when he looked back at what he had been doing for the past few days, it seemed trivial. Why stop now, just when he was having fun?

'This may come as a bit of a surprise to you,' he said, 'but everyone thinks the Prime Minister is bonking your wife.'

Mr Chatterjee had read about sangfroid, but he had never seen any. Mountbatten now displayed it in full measure. It was like doing 'English with Urmila'.

'Really?' he said.

'Well, I don't know about the bonking,' said Mr Chatterjee, nervously, 'but flowers were exchanged at Wildflower Hall, and their passion was

Shovon Chowdhury

deep and true. It will be one of the legendary romances of human history. Books will be written. Films will be made. Given that Gandhi plays a supporting role, Oscars could well be awarded.'

Mountbatten said nothing. But his mind was whirling. There was scope here to be part of a legendary love triangle. Their names would echo through the ages. They would dominate popular culture. He had always wanted to dominate popular culture.

'But the subject of Gandhi brings me to why I am really here,' said Mr Chatterjee, who was beginning to have some misgivings about his strategy.

'Have you told anyone else anything about all this?' asked Mountbatten, drawing closer.

Mountbatten had not risen to the pinnacle of every profession he had entered by being the blithering nincompoop that people often assumed him to be. His mind moved lightning fast, and he jumped to some quick conclusions. This was a legend in the making, but he would control how it unflowered.

'Your Highness, there has already been one attempt on Gandhi's life just a few days ago,' said Mr Chatterjee. 'No one seems even mildly concerned. The plotters are still at large. They will kill Gandhi on 30 January 1948. Towards the evening, I think.'

'How dare you, sir!' said Mountbatten. 'Coming here and talking about killing Gandhi? Is this how you show your gratitude, after everything that he's done for you? I am quite frankly appalled. Had Jawahar been here, he would have thrashed you soundly.'

He collared a pair of passing policemen. 'Take this man away,' he said. 'He's involved in the plot to kill Gandhi. Inform Sardar Patel. Interrogate him until he reveals who his accomplices are.'

The policemen hesitated, but the Big Lord was wagging a finger. Who could argue with the finger that had split nations? Mountbatten frowned. No one important was here today, and, after he'd had a massage, he was eager to get back to his manuscript. He had a whole set of suggestions for improving things in newly independent India, including finding oil, being nicer to the Indian Civil Service, and, at Edwina's special request, more holidays for the Prime Minister. No improvements had been suggested for the police. He liked them just the way they were.

'Take him away,' he said, 'jaldi!'

The policemen proceeded with the formalities. One of them slapped Mr Chatterjee on the back of the head. 'Not in front of the Viceroy, sir,' whispered the other.

'Saala, threatening Gandhiji?' said the sergeant.

'Why are we stopping him?' muttered the constable.

The sergeant turned on him in a fury. 'You keep quiet, you,' he said. He grabbed Mr Chatterjee by the collar while his companion slipped a rope around his waist. 'Chal, move,' said the sergeant, yanking him. 'We are all sitting here. You think you can kill Gandhiji just like that?'

65

'Will we be, once more, mute spectators, to the betrayal of our brave sailors by a callous and insensitive government?'

Nearly one hundred years later, in a different office in the same part of town, the Competent Authority was gently swivelling in his chair, humming happily to himself and thinking about religion. The revised proposal from the Bank of Bodies to start their Religious Joy business was in front of him. It had occurred to the CA that this was a moment of monumental significance in the history of the nation. Religion was the one area that the bureaucracy had failed to penetrate, barring odd bits of paperwork pertaining to land. Even these files were often cleared with lamentable speed by officers who put devotion before duty. For millennia the entire Brahmin caste had supported itself on religion, but the Indian Administrative Service had dropped the ball on this one.

Now, through the miracle of public-private partnership, the government would enter the religion business. Soon it would be a public-sector enterprise, like steel, or hand pumps, or flood relief, and the brotherhood would benefit. He might become a bit of a religious figure himself, he could see. Years from now, officers across the nation would recall his historic expansion of government in hushed tones. In times of trouble, they would light agarbattis and pray in front of his picture with folded hands. 'What would the Competent Authority do in such a situation?' they would ask themselves.

In fact, there was no reason why this should happen posthumously.

Shovon Chowdhury

Why should his countless minions in the Bureau of Reconstruction be deprived of such solace, just because he was alive? It would be quite simple to designate 9 to 9.15 in the morning as the time for such contemplation, and no doubt productivity would improve enormously as a result.

The CA took out a memo pad, in order to issue the necessary guidelines. But first, he had to clear the BoB file. Or did he? He was still extraordinarily peeved by the behaviour of Sam Kapoor, who had struck kung fu poses in this room, and called him fattie. Insanity was no excuse. He would clear the proposal eventually, but there was no harm in making them sweat. In any case, if he cleared a file the moment it arrived on his desk, what sort of ghastly example would he setting for those who looked up to him? No, the file needed to go round the block a few times, perhaps even be misplaced once or twice, to make sure the BoB knew who was boss.

His thoughts were broken by the sound of sizzling. His emergency hotline was ringing. Who had dared call him on this line? He was the one who declared emergencies. He punched in, and CBI Director Sinha appeared on the screen. He looked pale and worn, his eyes looked haunted. He was awash in a sea of troubles. To begin with, his wife was furious, after a News Laundry exposé which had revealed that many of the beneficiaries of her NGO for the disabled were, in fact, abled. Demands for a CBI inquiry were rising, and Director Sinha had been forced to promise that he would be investigating himself shortly, as soon as he was finished with other priority cases. But which priority case should he deal with first? Should he deal with the telepath case, or the LOL case? He had been assigned the LOL case by the CA shortly before the telepath case. It, too, was of critical national importance. It had something to do with the internets. Apparently, the acronym 'LOL' had been appearing with mysterious regularity on web sites across the country. Who was this LOL? What was his agenda? Was a foreign hand involved? The CA was keen to know. He had told Sinha that the LOL case was his top priority. But he had later told him that the telepath case was his top priority too. Which one did the CA want first? And by priority, did the CA mean he should solve the cases, or dissolve them? During his last conversation, he had gathered that the CA actually wanted solutions, which was unheard of. Nevertheless, he had given his own telepath team a free hand to roam the city, and brought back his best investigator from the Motor Vehicle Centre on Panchkuian Road. Information was trickling in. Much of it was coming from Shanti Nagar. This was a further complication. The CA hated any mention of Shanti Nagar. The last time Sinha had named the place, the CA had gagged him and made him stand on one leg for three hours. This made reporting a tricky affair.

'Sir, I cannot give you any details, sir,' said Sinha, 'but everything is going fine.'

'Could you be more specific?'

'Certainly, sir,' said Sinha, who had decided to take the conservative approach to specificity, just to be on the safe side. 'Specifically I wanted to tell you that all those things you asked us to do are being done, sir. The second thing, as well as the other thing. Genuine investigation is happening, sir. I brought Utpal back from Motor Vehicles, sir. He had once almost solved a case, but I managed to stop him just in time. He is ideal for this purpose, sir. He is ably supported by several junior officers who almost filed proper chargesheets. Here also, I managed to intervene in time. These people are highly indisciplined, sir, but they may cater to your current requirement, which is very specific. Very good job is being done, sir.'

'This is your status report?' asked the CA.

'Sir, yes, sir,' said Sinha.

'Get on the treadmill,' said the CA icily. 'The one I installed in your office for this purpose, along with the tank of piranhas. Start walking. Increase the speed once every five minutes. While you do so, think about what you did wrong.'

'Sir, could you give some kind of guideline, sir?' asked Sinha, desperately.

The CA flipped off the screen. Sinha was not the brightest of sparks, but he was obedient. He would continue increasing the speed till he collapsed. The CA spent a moment thinking about him, running harder and harder and going nowhere. It pleased him. It was all being recorded, so he could watch it later, at leisure.

He resumed his study of the BoB file. He picked up a pen to make a notation in the margin. It would have to be either illegible, or cryptic—ideally both. After a moment's thought, the CA put a very large question mark on it, and signed his name with a flourish. Much time would be spent exploring the full significance of this question mark, he knew. Did it mean that the CA was questioning this proposal, they would wonder. Or had he simply failed to understand it? Or was he questioning the officer who had put it on his table? Or was this question mark, in a larger sense, questioning the filing process itself? The CA liked being enigmatic, it made his people think harder. He was like a drill master for the brain.

The CA added another question mark, underlined both for greater emphasis, and rang for Mehta. Mehta oozed in, removed the file from his desk and headed straight for the scanner. Balaji the Fixer paid good money for copies of all BoB files, and Mehta loved money in a deep and personal way.

The CA switched on the television and watched the news with a sense of satisfaction. He had reason to be satisfied. His plans were bearing fruit. A screaming graphic jumped out of the screen. 'DOES THIS MEAN WAR?' it said, while a cute little mushroom cloud billowed merrily in a corner. Exciting military music played in the background. An elderly angry man in spectacles appeared on the screen, dressed in a combat jacket and gripping a microphone. Little wisps of smoke were coming out of his ears.

'I'm reporting live from a helicopter flying over the Indian Ocean,' he said, 'where, just a short while ago, I was witness, ladies and gentlemen, to what can only be described, as an outrage. A vessel of the Indian Navy has rammed a Chinese submarine. In what any civilized modern nation would regard an Act of War, one of the Indian seamen, who was merely waving and cheering after the event, and fell overboard, was shot by the Chinese. Chinese sources claim they thought he was trying to board them. We salute this gallant hero of the Indian Navy, Able Seaman Maninder Singh Lovely, yet another innocent victim of naked Chinese aggression. The question is, will the powers that be do anything in response, or will we be, once more, mute spectators to the total betrayal of our brave boys by a callous and insensitive government?'

Massed violins swelled up. The CA turned down the volume.

The General burst into his office without warning. For once he was neither composed nor immaculate.

'What the hell have you done?' he demanded. He was practically stuttering with rage.

The CA smiled at him. He knew all about the General's little trip to

Ranchi. He was showing gross disrespect for civilian authority, of course, but in this, his moment of triumph, the CA could afford to let it pass. Magnanimity was one of his many virtues.

'It's more a question of what the hell you've done, is it not?' he said. 'After all, you're the one in charge of the armed forces.'

'You know bloody well I had nothing to do with this,' spat the General, 'how did you pull this off?'

'Do you think each one of those soldiers and sailors and airmen is really under your control?' hissed the CA. 'Especially the sailors, who spend long weeks at sea? There are patriots who understand what needs to be done, even if you do not. If there's a weak link in the chain, I know what to do.'

'You won't get away with this,' said the General.

'You are no one to tell me what I can or cannot get away with, my dear General,' said the CA, 'but I'm willing to overlook your outburst since you've been under a lot of stress lately. Here, have a carrot,' he said amiably, picking one up from a jar on his desk, 'they're good for the eyesight, as well as blood pressure.'

The General could think of several things to do with the carrot, but he restrained himself. 'The Chinese are mad, but they're not idiots,' he said, half to himself, 'they're not going to go to war just because we bumped into their submarine.'

'I suggest you study history more,' said the CA, cheerfully. He looked at him and his eyes twinkled.

'Besides,' he said, 'every little bit helps.'

66

'Tell your Brigadier to avoid the potatoes.'

The Guard Captain eyed Pande with acute disfavour. There had been an unprecedented flurry of VIP visits lately, and his nerves were already frazzled. Besides, he was a Gurkha in the Rajasthan desert. It was unnatural. He always seemed to have sand in his clothing and he missed his wife, who was back home enjoying the fresh mountain air, and most probably, his cousin.

'No slip, no entry,' he repeated patiently.

Pande was being patient too, and feeling very proud about it. There was no doubt that he was rapidly becoming officer material. The night before, while beating up the sub judice whom he had brought along today as part of his cunning plan, he hadn't lost his temper even once. He had just kept on thrashing him without abusing him or misbehaving in any other way, until the man had understood that he was expected to play the role of an agent of potato dons, who were hand in glove with the purchase department and guilty of supplying counterfeit Nainital potatoes to the Indian army. He was standing right behind him now, dressed in a grimy vest and a crumpled dhoti, his mouth shut and his eyes carefully downcast. Pande had put a rope around his waist, in time-honoured police tradition, and the man was obediently following him around.

'Police and army are like brothers,' said Pande, ingratiatingly, 'what is a small thing like permission between brothers?'

It was astonishing. He was actually being polite to a Nepali, and not gagging or choking or anything. Maybe it was time to expand the range of his future career options, he might even do well in the PR department when he got back. PROs had cushy lives, sitting mostly in AC rooms and flirting with female journalists. Plus the booze was on the house, and of much better quality. Sometimes they got cream biscuits.

'I'm sorry,' said the Guard Captain, 'but if you don't have a slip, I can't let you in. This is a top-secret facility. It's not like the cantonment in Delhi, where you can stroll in and play a football match.'

'My job also is top secret,' said Pande, 'but I'll do you a favour and tell you the story. That way, you won't face firing squad later. See, people are taking advantage of Brigadier's good nature, and doing here and there with his breakfast. I can't tell you anything further, except that mafia dons, country liquor and senior politicians are involved. It's a smuggling case. You don't want to help smugglers I hope? Or are you also involved?'

The Guard Captain reeled back in horror. This was the first time he was hearing of the Brigadier's good nature. Someone had been tampering with his breakfast? What kind of lunatic would be foolhardy enough to do such a thing? The only thing worse would be to tamper with the Brigadier's scotch, a crime so hideous that the Guard Captain felt dizzy just thinking about it.

'This is not some drama you've cooked up?' he asked weakly.

Pande felt a twinge of sympathy for the man. If the same thing had happened to the police commissioner, his own reaction would have been similar. Failure to cooperate in such an investigation would have meant immediate crematorium duty.

'It's no drama,' he said, 'Purchase Department may be involved. That is why I have come. I want to have a quiet word, or the whole thing will become a big sho-sha. We should try to make some adjustment, and solve the matter, before Brigadier-sahab gets involved.'

The Guard Captain gestured to one of his guards.

'Take these men to the Purchase Department. Once they finish, bring them straight back here.'

'Arrey, why trouble the poor man in the heat?' said Pande, who was beginning to enjoy pretending to be a kind person. 'You just give us directions and we'll find the place.'

This, too, was part of his cunning plan. Once inside, and free to roam, he would hide the sub judice behind a convenient tank or artillery piece, and then search the camp for the bomb. Given the amount of damage that it could do, it was bound to be fairly large, and hence easy to locate. If he found a smallish soldier hanging around on his own, he could beat the information out of him, thus making things go much faster. Once he found the bomb, all he had to do was render it unfit for active duty. If it had a fuse, he would remove it. Otherwise, he would pee on it, thereby causing it to short circuit. He had realized that carrying a bucket would lead to a lot of unnecessary questions, and besides, why carry water when he could make some himself? He had drunk several large glasses of water before leaving. Yes, there was no doubt about it. The more time he spent in Rajasthan, the smarter he was becoming.

'I'm sorry,' said the Guard Captain, 'my man goes with you. This is the best I can do. Otherwise, go back to your thana and sort things out over the telephone.'

Pande could feel his new-found bonhomie evaporating rapidly. This stupid-son-of-a-dishwasher was ruining everything. How dare he suspect him like this? It was an insult to his uniform. He ought to teach him a lesson. But the sisterfucker was armed with a sub-machine gun, while all he had was an ancient service revolver and a metal-tipped lathi. Even vegetable sellers and sneak thieves had more firepower than he did. It was as if the police force in India was designed solely to oppress unarmed poor people.

He swallowed his pride and smiled at the Guard Captain.

'It's your village. You make the rules. I'll go with your jawan.'

The soldier led them into the camp. Pande strode after him, the sub judice trotting just behind him at the end of the rope. The camp was very basic, a collection of simple, single-storied sheds surrounding a central parade ground. It seemed practically deserted. Most everyone was indoors, because of the heat.

At the entrance to the parade ground stood a rusty green tank, mounted on a rickety platform, adorned with a shiny brass plaque.

'Pakistani tank,' said the soldier, proudly. 'We captured it in '71.'

Pande paused for a moment and looked at it closely, intrigued. He had never seen an actual Pakistani flag before. It seemed like they were still causing trouble here.

As he pretended to study the tank, another cunning plan sprang full-blown into his head. He wasted no time basking in its brilliance. He yanked on the rope and pulled the sub judice closer.

'Remember what you did when I kicked you in the balls yesterday?' he whispered. 'Do it again, right now. Don't stop till I tell you.'

The sub judice collapsed to the ground, clutching his stomach, and began to moan piteously.

'Oh God, it's happening again,' said Pande, 'same thing happened yesterday evening. He's having fit-shit. Go get the doctor, quick!'

The soldier looked at the sub judice uncertainly.

'Go!' roared Pande.

The soldier had been a pickpocket before he joined the army, and policemen still made him nervous. He ran.

'Stay there. Keep doing that,' hissed Pande to the sub judice, and set off towards the nearest shed. Once he'd reached it, he cautiously opened the door a crack. Several soldiers were sitting inside in their underwear, playing ludo.

'Oy, uncle!' called out one of them cheerily. 'See boys, a maternal uncle has come!'

Pande beat a hasty retreat. One thing was clear. Security was mostly restricted to the gate. Once someone was in, it was a picnic.

He ran a quick check on the trucks parked at the other end of the parade ground, their contents hidden by heavy tarpaulin. There was nothing inside but some stainless steel containers marked with strange yellow and black symbols. Special rations, most probably. Trust the army to get fancy food, while people like him had to make do with dal and roti. Nothing that looked remotely like a bomb. Just beyond the trucks was a shed marked *Prayer Room*. Pande felt no desire to pray, so he ignored it.

The next shed was some kind of canteen. Pande stepped in, exhausted by all the searching, hoping to sneak a cup of tea. At one of the tables sat a group of officers, and they were like no officers Pande had ever seen before. Some of them wore glasses so thick, they would obviously be blind without them. None of them looked fit enough to be in the army, despite the uniforms.

Their leader was an energetic little man with a wrinkled brown face and wild white hair, like the Odissi instructor of his OC's wife. When he took out a cigarette, three men leaped forward to light it for him. This was a smoker friendly period in the nation's history. Things had been very strict when Pande was a little boy, and his father had always raised a little extra cash before Diwali by terrorizing smokers. 'My son is with Delhi Police,' he would say. 'Pay up immediately or he'll come with his water cannon.' After the war, people had bigger things than lung cancer to worry about.

Pande leaned closer, hoping they would inadvertently reveal the location of the bomb. Nothing they said made any sense.

'Has Charlie gone to the zoo?'

'Not yet. Probably tomorrow.'

'And is Bravo saying prayers?'

'They've had a rehearsal.'

'How about Taj Mahal, Kumbhakaran and White House?'

'Progress on Kumbhakaran is slow.'

'Is Sierra serving whiskey in the canteen yet?'

'Actually, sir, we're Sierra. We're serving the whiskey.'

'God save me from code names. Only my wife doesn't have one.'

'She does, sir. It's Mumtaz Mahal.'

'Who suggested it? Give him a promotion!'

They laughed uproariously.

There was nothing to be learnt from these mad people. Serving in the army had obviously affected them mentally. Pande gulped down his tea moodily and left the canteen. This investigation thing was hard work, and not always fruitful.

The sub judice was still writhing on the ground where he had left him, while a doctor examined him anxiously. Their escort stood next to them, chewing his lip. He glared at Pande accusingly.

'I also went to look for a doctor,' said Pande by way of explanation, not caring much whether he was believed or not. The doctor was perplexed. He had never seen a case like this before. Nothing seemed to give the patient relief, and he obstinately refused to answer any of his questions.

Pande stared down at doctor and patient.

'All that studying you have done, all that money your rich father paid, but still you can't understand what medicine is required, can you?' he said. 'Even though you're a reading-writing person.'

The doctor looked up at him helplessly.

'I'll show you the medicine.'

He kicked the sub judice in the backside, hard.

'You can stop now. Get up,' he said curtly.

The sub judice leaped to his feet and handed Pande the end of his rope. He followed obediently as Pande headed for the gate.

'I have nothing more to do here,' he told the soldier, 'so I am leaving. Tell your Brigadier to avoid the potatoes. They are not actually from Nainital. And he should shoot one or two of the clerks in the Purchase Department. Time to time he should keep doing that. Then everything will be OK.'

In the backseat of his taxi, on the way back to the thana, he pondered his next course of action. The bomb must be somewhere else. The people in that village seemed to know all about it. Some of them had even been around for the first one in 1974, which had galvanized goats and petrified poultry. During his first visit to Khetolai, he had been much too mild. What he needed to do was go back there, thrash as many people as possible, and get them to tell him everything they knew about the bomb. If necessary, he would beat up the livestock too, just to try something new. Pande leaned back in his seat, and felt a weight lift from his mind. He slapped the taxi driver on the head affectionately.

'Put on the radio,' he said amiably, 'play some music-shusic.'

67

'Fighting, fighting, fighting, fighting,
never stop, never not!'

Banani felt a tug on her pallu and turned round. It was a little monkey with the face of a curious child.

'Shoo,' said Banani, gently removing her sari from its clutches, 'come back later, I'll try to find you a banana.'

The monkey scampered off. Banani turned back and scanned the crowd. She urgently needed to have a word with Pintoo, but Pintoo was busy. A dispute was in progress, and Pintoo had been brought out to deliver a judgement, in case the parties failed to adjust. Shanti-bai had been trying to broad-base the dispensation of justice in the hope that they would take her retirement seriously. 'Do I still have to wipe the shit from your bums?' she had asked, demonstrating graphically. 'Why don't you try to do some things yourselves?'

The dusty street had been turned into an al fresco court, with ramshackle chairs for Pintoo and the accused, and sheets on the ground for the accusers. The public was left to fend for itself. The accusers were the bartanwalis of Shanti Nagar, who made their living trading stainless steel utensils for old clothes. They bought the utensils from a wholesaler, plied their trade through the day, and sold the clothes in the market in the evening. There were over a hundred of them, squatting on their haunches in the street, their sarees protecting their heads from the hot afternoon sun, looking like a congregation of exotic, multi-coloured birds. Their faces were hidden, but their voices were loud.

'See how fat this Muthu Chopra has become, stealing money from poor people,' said one of them, gesturing at him with the palm of her hand. 'He's so fat, his wife doesn't let him do it any more, because she can't breathe when he's on top of her.'

'Maybe he'll give us a discount if you do it with him, Gulabo,' said one of her companions.

'Maybe he'll give us a discount if you promise not to,' said another.

Muthu Chopra and his partner Venu Chopra sat in their rickety chairs, glowering at them. Their faces would have darkened, except they couldn't get any darker. Their shirts were unbuttoned, revealing thick gold chains nestling on hairy breasts. They were two of the most successful businessmen in Shanti Nagar, soap makers from Tamil Nadu who had changed their names from Thevar to Chopra, hoping this would help them pass off as Punjabis, thus paving the way for them to do business with the locals, of whom they were deeply suspicious. They had invented a soap which needed very little water. Water was in short supply everywhere, and Shanti Soap (along with footwear, clothes, chiki and papad) was one of Shanti Nagar's most successful exports. They had named it Shanti Soap in honour of Shanti-bai. They supported several hundred people, and they were hard but fair. With Shanti-bai around, there was no other way. Over the years, they had come to see the merit of it. Being accused of profiteering rankled, but women were women. Who could control them?

The bartanwalis of Shanti Nagar needed soap, to keep their steel shining, and to wash the clothes they traded. They saved money by doing it themselves. Some of them were fertile, and they had made a pact with the dhobis, who viewed all encroachments on their livelihood as acts of war. They gave them a few children, both male and female, in return for the right to wash. Now the Chopras had raised soap prices, putting their livelihoods in jeopardy.

'How many more houses do you need, Muthu?' demanded their leader. 'Children you don't have. Or have the working girls raised their prices too? Have their pussies become more expensive? Should we go talk to them?'

The assembled women jeered good-naturedly at him, and offered to cut it off, thereby saving everyone the trouble. It was unlike any court that Banani had ever seen and she had to admit it made a refreshing change, the proceedings were vastly more entertaining. The crowd was abuzz, the atmosphere electric. Personally she was rooting for the girls, although they needed to have their mouths washed out with soap. Perhaps it was because they couldn't afford any.

'Soap doesn't come out of my backside,' said Muthu, chewing out every word. He hadn't become rich by giving in easily. 'We need material to make it. If material costs go up, what am I supposed to do? If my father had a chemical plant, would I be wasting my time with beggars like you?'

'Let go of such nonsense!' said the head bartanwali. 'And we're not beggars, we put money in your pocket. Foreign people you charge extra if you like, but we are your neighbours. What kind of badmaash steals money from neighbours?'

There were murmurs from the crowd. Public opinion was shifting in favour of the ladies. Tarun-da, whose sense of timing was not good, decided that it was time to lend a hand to the masses. He stood up, swept his shawl over his shoulder, marshalled his wriggling beard, and was instantly stentorian.

'Muthu Chopra go far away! Shanti Soap management down down! Fighting stopping never not! Accept injustice never not! Imperialist chemicals out out! Brothers and Sisters, will we allow these capitalist swine to oppress working women like this? Foil the nefarious plans of US oil companies. Black hands of Muthu Chopra, break the hands, grind the hands! Management decision not accepting, not accepting, never not! Enemy of people Muthu Chopra go far away, far away! Fighting, fighting, fighting, fighting, never stopping, never not!'

There were catcalls from the audience. Someone threw a tomato. Someone else asked Tarun-da to go home and hang himself with his shawl. A third person pointed out, quite reasonably, that Muthu was already black all over. A few of them linked hands and started singing about how they might be black, but so what, they had big hearts. A Mexican wave was building up. A well-aimed slipper caught Tarun-da on the bridge of his nose.

The head bartanwali frowned. Thanks to Tarun-da, just when it seemed like she had the upper hand, the whole thing was degenerating into a first day first show for Virtual Salman. She gestured to her girls. A few of them pulled Tarun-da down, giggling, pinching his cheeks and playing tag with his beard. 'Why so much anger?' whispered one in his ear. 'Meet me behind the cowshed and I'll make you happy.'

The head bartanwali took advantage of Tarun-da's temporary retirement from the field of play. 'Stop getting rich on your neighbours, Muthu,' she said, raising her voice, 'what money you make from other places, we have no share in that. But don't suck the blood of your sisters.'

The crowd stopped singing. They didn't like all this talk of mistreating sisters. If Shanti-bai found out, she would be very annoyed with them. 'What were *you* doing while it was happening?' she would ask. Each one felt her eyes boring into them.

Muthu Chopra knew when he was beaten. While the others were singing, he had been thinking, and doing some quick maths in his head.

'You can stop giving these filmi dialogues,' he said coldly, 'we'll do something for you. Our factory closes at ten. If you come after that, I'll give you the material, you use my machines for two hours, make your own soap, keep what you make. We'll charge you for material only. But make only for your own use. If you try to sell in the market, I'll cut off your hands. And don't lecture me on sisters. I don't know any brothers and sisters. I do business, I only know money. That's my offer. Take it, or go to hell.'

It was a good offer. The bartanwalis took it. A few of them offered to dance for him, but he wasn't in the mood. He stalked off, followed by his grumbling partner. They danced anyway, and there was much merriment in the street.

Banani looked up at Pintoo, who was sitting on a chair perched precariously on some bricks, to make it higher than the others. She was relieved that his judicial powers had not been invoked. So was he.

'Did you like being a judge?' she asked, smiling.

'Didn't have to judge much,' said Pintoo.

She caught him by the elbow, gently but firmly, and took him inside Tarun-da's house. Tarun-da hadn't yet managed to escape the attentions of the bartanwalis so they had the place to themselves.

'You and I need to talk, Pintoo,' she said.

'I'll just do potty and come,' said Pintoo hastily.

'No, you won't,' said Banani, who was well acquainted with hysterical bowel movements. 'Sit here on the bed.'

He sat on the bed. She stood by the doorway, looking down at him thoughtfully. He might be able to move mountains with his mind, but he was twelve.

'How is he doing, Pintoo?' she asked.

Pintoo frowned, and concentrated. Mr Chatterjee was sitting in a prison cell, a look of horror on his face. He had just tried to use the toilet.

'He's in a very secure place,' said Pintoo cautiously, 'but I don't see Gandhi uncle anywhere. He must be at a meeting. Or maybe he went for food. Though he doesn't eat much. My mother always said the women around him should have fed him more.'

Banani was unable to concentrate on Gandhian food habits. Delhi in

1948 was not a nice place to be. Not that Delhi ever had been. From Nadir Shah to the China Incident, from the Mongol Invasion to the Bike Bandit Raids, Delhi had always been a perilous spot for its residents, fair game for warmongers, ravishers, bombers, ethnic cleansing agents, property dealers, VIPs, OBCs, bulldozers, Britons, BMWs, ballistic missiles, and Officers on Special Duty. The plagues of Delhi had been lavish and biblical. If you were a Delhiite, you never knew who was going to get you. The problem was they had too much money. People had been trying for years to solve this problem by taking all of it. Delhi always survived, but they had chewed it thoroughly, and the marks of their sharp little teeth were all over its body. But this was 1948, one of the darkest periods in the city's history. The wounds would be fresh and bleeding. Carcasses would be rotting in the streets. Once Gandhi fell, the earth would shake, like it always did when a big tree fell. It was a natural part of the mourning process. She had to get Hemonto out of there.

'Have you tried getting anyone back?' she asked.

'I have an idea,' said Pintoo, 'I'll need a mirror. Just give me two days to work it out. I have to practise with Ranvir bhaiyya. I need a strong guy.'

His mistake had been in sending people he didn't know, he now realized. He could see anything he wanted, but he could touch only those he knew. But could he send them and bring them back?

A group of bartanwalis burst in, carrying a tray full of sweets.

'Pintoo-beta, sweeten your mouth,' said one of them, 'it's a happy day. We didn't need your help, but we knew you were there for us. Come, come, have.' She held out the tray.

Banani peered at the tray suspiciously, She knew the standards of hygiene in Shanti Nagar were unbelievably appalling. She also knew resistance was futile, but it was hard to give up the habits of a lifetime.

'Where are they from?' she demanded. 'Is it safe for a child to eat them?'

'Arrey, a new-born baby can eat them!' exclaimed the head bartanwali. 'These are from Hari Om Gupta's sweet shop, the pride of Shanti Nagar. Whole of Delhi eats them. He uses 3,000 litres of milk every day. Some of the cows give green milk,' she added, proudly.

Banani took a closer look at the sweets. Some of them were white, and some of them were green. Was it her imagination, or were the green ones throbbing slightly?

'Try those,' said the head bartanwali, pointing, 'those are the best. Very tasty.'

Banani, who was already having quite enough adventure, picked up a white one, and passed another to Pintoo.

The bartanwali waited, hesitant. Banani took a small nibble out of her sweet, and gave her an encouraging smile.

'Didi, there was one more thing,' she said shyly.

'What?' asked Banani.

'We heard that you're a teacher.'

'That's true,' said Banani, 'although I haven't done much teaching the last few days.'

The head bartanwali, who was actually quite a young woman, looked nervous and vulnerable, a far cry from the spitfire who had just defied Muthu Chopra.

'What can I do for you?' asked Banani, putting a hand on her arm.

'None of us can read or write,' said the young woman, 'we had to work too hard, and there was no one to learn from. We can do all our calculations in our head, but for keeping records and suchlike we have to pay a clerk. We have to depend on him. Even at the bank we need his help. Could you teach some of us a little bit? Maybe people would respect us more.'

'Come to me first thing tomorrow morning, around six,' said Banani, promptly. 'Not more than ten of you together. It'll take time, but that's not a problem.'

She glanced at Pintoo, who was munching on his sweet. It was a green one.

'I think I need to be here for a while.'

68

'If Pakistan is ever created, will it be my picture on the bank notes?'

Writer's Building was an imposing red brick edifice, the symbol of British power in Bengal. The guards at the gate were pretty imposing too, although not British. The place was still under British rule, but not many of the British were in evidence. They were busy packing, mostly.

The guards blocked his way, and demanded to see his pass, although they did so politely. His clothes were strange, so it was hard to tell whether he was a VIP or not but they were taking no chances. Khaki was out and khadi was in, but there were no instructions regarding cotton or denim. In matters of clothing, Gandhiji had made things very confusing.

'I'm here to see Mr Suhrawardy,' said Ali, 'with secret orders from Mr Jinnah.'

The guards backed off instantly, and Ali walked through. They courteously pointed out which way he should go. As a result, they failed to detect the small pack of explosives strapped to his chest. He had just enough for two.

His footsteps echoed as he walked the gloomy corridor. He could hear the creak of ancient, weary ceiling fans, and the rustle of fugitive sheets of paper, freshly escaped from their files, fluttering languidly in dusty rooms. A dog sneezed softly somewhere in the distance, getting ready to settle down for the night amongst the filing cabinets. Long dead British administrators gazed down at him sadly from the walls as he passed by, collars rigid and upper lips stiff, barely able to suppress their disappointment at the kind of riffraff they were letting in these days. The building was almost empty. All the babus had left in perfectly synchronized unison at 4:30 p.m., exhausted by a long hard day of ceaseless labour.

In its own way, this was a pilgrimage for Ali. Writer's Building was a historic landmark on the World Terrorism Map, an interactive tool which he had developed during his teaching days, where a mouse touch on the correct locations led to the popping up of a small burkha-clad hottie, who gave a brief description of the paradise that awaited successful graduates, with particular emphasis on the succulence of the melons. Ali had done a lot of research to select the right cities for the map. Calcutta was one of them. Long before Palestine, or Munich, or New York, dedicated young men armed with crude pistols and raw courage had stalked these halls, while Englishmen hid under tables, gibbering. Some would call them terrorists. But the targets of their terror had spent long, languorous hours sipping Darjeeling tea, and listening to Beethoven on the BBC, while millions of men, women and children had died in an endless succession of famines. It was all a matter of perspective.

India had evolved a lot since then. Things were much more civilized. The perpetrators of such negligence were no longer terrorized with bombs and handguns. All they had to fear was a few gentle questions in parliament, and some light grilling from sympathetic TV anchors.

Suhrawardy's PA, a dapper young man in neatly pressed trousers and a freshly laundered shirt, greeted him courteously, and asked him to take a seat while he went in to inform his boss. He wasn't surprised to see Ali. He gave the impression of being quite used to strange visitors dropping in late in the evening. It was known that Suhrawardy was the patron saint of half the lowlifes in the city. He knew many of them personally, and often attended their weddings. In fact, Writer's Building wasn't the only landmark Ali was going to see today. The man he was about to meet was a bit of a landmark himself. If you took an anthropological view of terror, Husain Shaheed Suhrawardy was the missing link. He was the point at which slaughter had become organized.

The PA came back.

'Please follow me, sir,' he said, and led Ali into an enormous room, wood-panelled, dimly-lit and richly-furnished. Suhrawardy was reclining in a plushly-upholstered armchair, and gestured for Ali to take a seat. He gave the briefest of nods to his PA, who instantly dematerialized.

Suhrawardy had neither horns nor fangs. No forked tail undulated behind his chair, and no flames emerged when he opened his mouth. He was a plump, jowly man with the air of a prosperous butcher. A matrimonial advertisement would have described his complexion as wheatish.

'I believe you bear tidings from our maximum leader,' he said, with a hint of sarcasm, 'please enlighten me. How may I be of service to him?'

They hated each other, Ali realized. Then why was Suhrawardy working so hard to make Direct Action Day a smashing success? Just to show that he could?

Suhrawardy's face revealed nothing. Ali licked his lips and cleared his throat. 'Mr Jinnah would have given this in writing, but times are uncertain, and he preferred that I tell you in person.'

'I promise to give you just as much respect as I would give Jinnah-sahab himself,' said Suhrawardy. 'Do proceed.'

'He wants you to disregard what you read in the newspapers about Direct Action Day. That's just a negotiating tactic. He trusts you to enforce law and order in the city. Above all, the Muslim League must maintain its reputation for an honest and just administration, he said.

"Tell my good friend Husain," he said, "that I trust he understands the need for rhetoric, but we must not allow rhetoric to compromise our principles, or our basic humanity.'"

Suhrawardy smiled broadly. He eyed Ali indulgently, like a cow watching a calf at play.

'See, now I know you're lying,' he said, without the faintest trace of resentment, 'would you like to know why? Because of three things. First, I am not his good friend, because I am not good enough. Second, he never calls me Husain, he calls me Suhrawardy, as if he is the principal and I am a schoolboy. And third, Mr Mohammed Ali Jinnah always means what he says. He is not two-faced like Gandhi. He is a straight person, unlike the rest of us, and that is why so many of our brothers trust only him, despite the fact that he wears English clothes and eats ham sandwiches. Wherever he leads, they will follow, even if he walks them straight into the sea. The rest of us are all such rascals, you see. We do not possess his integrity. They prefer an honest lunatic to a sensible rogue.'

There was little that Ali could say to this.

'So why not tell me why you really came?' asked Suhrawardy. 'Why are you so concerned about Direct Action Day?'

'It's not going to go well,' said Ali.

'How do you know?' asked Suhrawardy quickly. 'Do you have any information?'

'You'll tear Bengal apart. They'll never put it together again. Some of us will end up driving taxis in Preston.'

'Nothing like that will happen,' said Suhrawardy, without conviction. 'The British won't allow it.'

'The British will be paralyzed by the things you do to each other. They'll hurry back home and drink a lot, hoping to forget,' continued Ali, 'they'll never mess about in someone else's country again. And here, here in Bengal, Hindus and Muslims will never trust each other. When the time comes to choose, the Hindus will spit in your faces and tell you to take a hike. You'll be remembered as the man who destroyed his motherland.'

Suhrawardy sank back in his armchair, his face ashen. He still looked like a butcher, but he wasn't so jolly any more.

'You can stop this,' said Ali. 'You can ask your men to step down. Otherwise thousands are going to die.'

'Otherwise thousands are going die,' mimicked Suhrawardy savagely, 'you make it sound as if I will kill them personally. You make it sound as if everything is in my hands. Do you know where Mr Mohammed Ali Jinnah sleeps these days? He sleeps on the floor. Members of the Delhi Gymkhana are aghast, and he may be blackballed. His pyjamas are no longer pristine and spotless. His childhood ayah cannot stop weeping. Do you know why he is doing this? He's practising to sleep in jail. He expects disturbances on Direct Action Day, and he expects to be arrested. If I don't give him the disturbance he wants, how long will I be in the Muslim League? He is the great leader. I'm just a simple politician. I do what I have to do to survive. If Pakistan is ever created, will it be my picture on the bank notes? Will it be me that they call Qaid-e-Azam? Will it be my effigy the Hindus will burn during Ramlila? Stop chewing my head and go talk to him, if you're so concerned.'

'He's sitting in Delhi. You're sitting here.'

'Brother, the game is being played in Delhi. Everyone wants to be captain. I am not even the reserve goalkeeper.'

'Why don't you talk to Gandhi?'

'In matters of power, Gandhi is very much like my brother-in-law's nephew, Anwar. Whenever there is brain curry, Anwar refuses to share it, in the hope that it will increase his intelligence and make him smarter than us. We keep telling him that the most he can expect is to achieve the intelligence level of a goat, but he refuses to listen, and he refuses to share. Gandhi is just like that. In 1938, I was in the KPP, and he refused to join hands with us. He believes in democracy, but only as long as he has a majority. Then just the other day in UP, first he made an alliance with the League, then he kicked us out when he found he had enough votes. Gandhi just wants to eat us all up. We cannot be separate. We have to be inside him. In this current situation, he is Anwar, and we are the curry. But this curry will not be so easily digested.'

'Direct Action Day will last a week,' said Ali, quietly. 'You think you can light a little fire, and put it out quickly, just to make a show? But the poison won't go away. That's how you poison a country, bit by bit, lighting little fires all over its body. This is the first spot. You're the first poisoner. The one who showed the way.'

He put his finger on the button.

'Even last year I tried to join the Congress,' said Suhrawardy, sadly.

'My last chance to escape Jinnah. But Azad refused me. He must be jealous of my good looks. Or perhaps he was just being Gandhi's parrot, as usual.'

Ali hesitated. He gave it one more shot.

'What would Chittaranjan Das say if he saw you now?'

Suhrawardy leaped up, his face contorted in fury.

'Don't take his name!' he said. 'Don't you dare take his name. You are not worthy to discuss him. He was taken away at fifty-five, while Gandhi lives on forever. This is the mercy of the Almighty. Leave me in peace. I have nothing more to discuss with you. Do what you have to do, or go.' He sank back into his chair.

So this was it. This was how his life would end. In an act of violence. As an explosive device. Just like the poor, dumb boys from Kandahar and Waziristan. This is what Pintoo expected of him. However hard he might have worked, however much he might try to atone, it all boiled down to his expertise in putting together a suicide jacket. He had started down this road to teach the chavs back in Preston a lesson or two, after they put a lump of shit on his sister's head. She had walked back from school not knowing, she couldn't feel it through the scarf. He had never forgotten her face that day, and the rage had lasted a long time, and made him do things he knew he should never have done. But hadn't he made up for at least some of it? Hadn't he tried to help others the best he could? What was the point, if it was going to end this way?

He couldn't do it. He took his hand off the trigger.

He left then, stepping away softly, leaving Suhrawardy alone with his thoughts in the gathering darkness.

69

'They may expect you to practise the Thirty-Seven Acceptable Behaviours for Pathetic Inferiors.'

The Japanese envoy flickered in and out of focus, offering quick glimpses of the fat lady sitting behind them during moments of transparency. The restaurant had been emptied, out of deference to the PM's visit, but a few token diners had been strategically placed to preserve the illusion that she was amongst the common people. The diners had been carefully screened in advance, to ensure that they would raise nothing controversial and maintain an air of understated sycophancy. This was the only way she was allowed to meet commoners, a long-standing family tradition.

The Japanese envoy was pixilating alarmingly. There was no doubt the quality of Japanese workmanship had declined over the years. They couldn't even project their diplomats properly any more. There was a crackling noise, and the digital simulacrum did a little shimmy, before disintegrating into a fog of dancing white particles in the shape of a seated man. The interpreter stood behind him, beaming encouragingly at the PM while he waited for normal service to resume.

Due to a variety of health hazards, the Japanese had stopped visiting India in person. Instead, they maintained all diplomatic courtesies through simulacra. Personally, the PM found them highly entertaining. She had often suppressed the urge to poke one in the belly with a fork, just for fun. The envoy snapped into focus, but the audio was still out. A stream of gibberish emerged from his mouth.

'. . . Manchester United,' said the envoy, smiling.

The Japanese were under the impression that she was a football fan. The truth was she hated football. She had better things to do than watch hairy men trying to knee each other in the groin. But she never said anything, to avoid hurting their feelings. Extreme courtesy brought out the competitive streak in her.

'Yes, me too,' she said, smiling back.

'Manchester United,' said the interpreter. He smiled also.

The PM had no idea why this meeting was taking place. There was no way for her to contact the Japanese without written permission from the CA, so this private tete-a-tete was entirely at their initiative.

The envoy spoke. 'My wife sends her love to your adorable children,' said the interpreter. Her children were in their thirties. Neither of them wanted to be Prime Minister. They had seen their mum doing it, and it looked like a bum job to them. The PM was determined not to insist that they carry on the family tradition as had happened in the past. As she waited for the envoy to come to the point, she thought grimly that it seemed wrong to end her career as a ventriloquist's dummy for a deranged bureaucrat.

'My son used to watch a Japanese cartoon,' she said, 'where agents of a

Japanese superpower roam the world, protecting the innocent and defending the weak. Sometimes they baked bread. It was all very realistic, except for the pink hair. Do you allow pink hair in your armed forces?'

The interpreter interpreted. The envoy spoke.

'As a matter of fact, we do,' said the interpreter. 'The hair gets covered by a helmet. It does not impair the ability to point a gun.'

'Did you ever watch this cartoon? What did you think of it?'

The envoy spoke. 'The message was very inspiring,' said the interpreter, 'and the battle armour was very cool. The theme song by Android Attack spent three weeks at No. 1. Many of us dream of a Japan like that. A proud Japan. A heroic Japan. A Japan with awesome hair. But with a dragon in the neighbourhood, caution is called for. We catch fire very easily. We have fought one war, and we were lucky to get off lightly. How about your own little monster? Rumour has it that he too is quite frisky these days.'

She had a momentary vision of the CA gambolling in his underwear for some reason. It was terrible. She glared at the interpreter.

'He can't have said frisky,' she said, crossly. 'Are you sure he said frisky? Can you even say frisky in Japanese?'

The interpreter and the simulacrum briefly conferred.

'Prone to sudden movement,' said the interpreter, who had just looked it up. 'Most often applied to describe lambs. Yes, this was what he intended to convey. He believes the CA is in the mood for some sudden and extreme action. He has a reputation for whimsicality.'

Whimsical didn't even begin to describe it. The CA was extremely gung-ho. So was his dusky doppelganger in the Compact Revolutionary Zone. Even though news travelled slowly in the jungle, it was only a matter of time before they hooked up, and marched off arm-in-arm towards Beijing, with the General bringing up the rear, or flew in on the backs of missiles, not knowing that they had no actual warheads, since vast sums of money had been spent, not to purchase weapons, but to purchase the concept of weapons, whose hypothetical existence would scare evildoers into instant, quivering submission. Perhaps they would have white papers inside instead, or scornful articles from the China Study Group, which would rain down on an unsuspecting enemy population, bludgeoning them into surrender with syntax, and petrifying them with their polysyllabity. The General had more or less given up

Shovon Chowdhury

since the submarine incident and was busy trying to delay mobilization by making an unholy hash of the logistics, issuing orders that contradicted themselves on a variety of levels, and putting idiots in key positions. He was batting like a champion. He couldn't do it forever. It was up to her now.

'The CA wants to blow us all up,' said the PM. 'Things are untidy, and he has a passion for neatness. He hasn't said so specifically, but he's been smiling a lot lately, and I know it's not all me. Or maybe he really does have a grand strategy, which involves threatening the Chinese into giving him what he wants. This is not a good idea, given that China is a very large army with a country attached, just like Pakistan used to be, and we're extremely weak. Unless our billionaires lend us their armies, which were created through public-private partnership in order to protect our natural resources from internal and external aggression. It's unlikely. They spend most of their time on United Nations duty. The pay's much better, and they have shareholders to think about. Some of them are heavily armed. Once the Chinese massacre us, it'll be down to just you and them.'

The envoy listened to the interpreter gravely. He did not seem overjoyed at the prospect.

'You'll have to change your eating habits,' said the PM. 'Give up an island or two, maybe a few of the floating cities. They may expect you to practise the Thirty-Seven Acceptable Behaviours for Pathetic Inferiors. Sony and Honda will shift to Hong Kong. The Emperor will have to become a member of the Communist Party, and may have to do some gardening. You'll have to let Serve The People open branches in Japan, and drink lots of coffee that's been peed in by disgruntled female party members. All of them have to do two years compulsory service at Serve The People, which is bigger than McDonald's. Not to worry. I'm sure it'll work out eventually. If I were you, I would start taking Mandarin lessons.'

'His Excellency is already well versed in Mandarin,' volunteered the interpreter. The envoy smiled and nodded, but a frown creased his brow. He said something to which the interpreter listened carefully. He took a moment to compose himself. He took a deep breath. He leaned forward and gazed deeply into the PM's eyes. 'Does the fire still burn within you?' he asked.

She wasn't really sure. Sometimes she suffered mild heartburn. But a whole lot of people had looked up to her once, and sometimes even cheered, even though she had never much enjoyed being a performing monkey. She owed it to them to make an effort.

'If you have any suggestions, I'll hear them,' she said.

The envoy spoke. 'I would like to give you a personal message,' said the interpreter.

'Thank you,' said the PM.

'You're welcome,' said the interpreter. Sometimes he anticipated.

The envoy spoke softly now. Both she and the interpreter leaned closer. She took a quick glance around to see whether anyone else was listening. Her eyes locked momentarily with a nearby diner, who smiled and waved a small India flag. The envoy finished speaking.

'My interpreter will hand you a small white box,' said the interpreter. 'Inside the box is a mobile phone. You can use it like a conventional device, and call whomsoever you choose. Your privacy is guaranteed. All calls to the Japanese Prime Minister will be free of STD or ISD charges. Please keep it out of the reach of children, as usage by any unauthorized person will trigger the detonation of a microscopic thermonuclear device, which will vaporize anyone within a radius of six feet, thereby preserving confidentiality.'

The interpreter put his hand into his trouser pocket and presented the phone to the PM. He was beaming.

'So sorry,' he said, 'but maybe Japanese technology is not so bad?'

'You still have a few tricks up your sleeve,' she admitted.

The first person to call was President Lee in Taiwan, obviously. She had to sit down and figure out exactly what to say. Maybe she should call up Subramaniam and do the exact opposite of whatever he suggested. She would also have a chat with the General in private. His morale was plummeting. He needed some good news.

70

'Mummy, my hand is getting louder!'

The Rolls Royce hit a pothole, and Pappu flew up and hit his head on the ceiling. 'Wheee!' he said. He was freakishly immune to head injury.

Even a Rolls Royce was no match for the municipal corporation of Delhi. Roads in Delhi had been deteriorating steadily ever since the annual Commonwealth Games had gone online, sponsored by betyourshirt.com. Hovercraft had briefly come into vogue, but poor people had kept hitching rides underneath them, and their pneumatic underbellies were often punctured by the horns of reclining cows, leading to a resurgence in the popularity of flightless vehicles. Hovercraft were now only allowed in Bungalowpur, where they were least required, since the roads there were as smooth as a baby's bottom. In this leafy paradise, they were the standard form of transportation, demonstrating vividly that the people who lived there were a cut above the rest. It was not uncommon to see rich young lovers making passionate love in their two-seater hover cars, nestling in the welcoming branches of the gulmohar trees, labouring under the misapprehension that height rendered them invisible. Lacking the ability to fly, the police could only look on indulgently, and shoo away people whose cameras looked professional.

Right now, though, Mrs Verma and her posse were reaching the parts of Delhi Lutyens had never reached. The roads here were more theoretical. She had replaced the view of the neighbourhoods they were traversing with beaches in Goa, the music system was playing Remo Fernandes, and the air was heavy with Calvin Klein's Obsession for Interiors. But nothing could insulate them from the ferocity of the ride. Bouncing up and down in her seat, Mrs Verma rapped on the glass separating them from the driver, who had come free with the car.

'Mr Hoskins,' she said.

'Yes, mum,' said Mr Hoskins, originally of West Riding, Yorkshire.

'Please try to drive more carefully.'

'Certainly, mum,' said Mr Hoskins, 'as soon as we get to a road.'

He was quite looking forward to Shanti Nagar. They had good beer there, though they kept it quiet, and they were always happy to share with a working lad. Might be nice to put up his feet up for a while. There was a lot less shooting and looting in Shanti Nagar, a lot less of the old drama and hungama. He might even settle down there when it was time to pack it in. He had sounded a few of them out, and they seemed quite fine with a Brit staying over, although Shanti-bai had warned him not to start anything funny like last time.

The intercom crackled. 'Little Lord, live long long! Little Lord, zindabad! Down with foes of Little Lord! Little Lord, remain undead!'

It was her massed henchmen in the armoured car behind them. 'Say it once more, brothers!' said the Ram Din, the head guard.

'We're not standing for election,' said Mrs Verma, through the intercom. 'Shut up and keep your eyes on the road. Watch out for enemy riflemen.'

'There are no riflemen, Owneress,' said the head guard, 'just one peanut seller. Give the order, and I'll leap out of this vehicle and procure some. If you want, we can kidnap him, to ensure regular supply.'

It was good that their morale was high, but their overall approach was far too festive. No one seemed to see that this was a life and death matter for Pappu. She opened her mouth to speak, and felt hot breath on her earlobe.

'Martini?' asked the surgeon, she had hired from the Bank of Bodies for this expedition. He was sitting behind them, and making full use of the mini bar. Usually he had to make do with a hip flask on field trips, so this was heaven. The car hit a big one and his olive flew in the air, coming to rest inside one of Pappu's shoes. Pappu had taken his shoes off in the hope of quickly lowering the window and chucking them to a beggar the moment he saw one. His little kit bag would swiftly follow. It was several hours since he had helped anyone, and he was feeling restless. He held up his hand and twiddled its fingers. He let it go limp, and it came up, trembling, like a hound scenting its prey. It wanted to go to Shanti Nagar. He could feel it.

'Mummy, my hand is getting louder!' said Pappu.

'Could you drive a bit faster, Mr Hoskins?' said Mrs Verma, trying not to panic.

'Certainly, mum. Be a bit bumpy, though.'

Bumps didn't bother him. After twenty-five years in India, he had an arse made of iron. This was his chance to teach some capitalist bloodsuckers the true meaning of fear. Ultimately they would all be lined up against a wall and shot, but until then, this would have to do. His grandpa would have been proud of him. He'd never cut a picket line in his life. He flipped off the seatbelt sign and joyfully revved the engine.

❑

'Tarun-da, a group of Dilli-wallahs have come here asking for Pintoo,' said the Self-Defence Force guard, 'one of them just threw up on my shoes. Should I let them in?'

Tarun-da looked up at the screen and chewed his lip. Banani had gone to meet Shanti-bai, which meant that he was in charge. What would Banani have done?

'I can feel him,' whispered Pintoo, looking up from his homework, 'he has a piece of me.'

Tarun-da shivered. 'Let them in,' he said.

71

'Our eminent panel of experts gives its views on which Chinese cities should be bombed first . . .'

'The Parliamentary Committee Investigating Poverty has presented its annual findings, sir,' said Mehta.

'Speak faster so I can forget quickly,' said the Competent Authority. His time was precious. The Parliamentary Committee was a selection of babalog who occasionally discussed poverty to show that their hearts were in the right place. It was only fair that they should focus on this issue since their fathers had caused most of it, by sucking out pretty much all the money in the country. They seemed unaware of this, and they had been investigating the root causes of poverty by taking their SUVs to places where the roads were very bad. Sometimes they rolled down their windows and interviewed poor people, but none of them could explain why they were poor. The CA regarded their amateurish efforts with undisguised contempt. Such things were best left to the professionals. He took a brief nap while Mehta quickly read out the executive summary. Having finished, Mehta waited respectfully until the CA opened his eyes.

'What about our genuine poverty alleviation measures?' asked the Competent Authority.

Mehta flicked a switch on his pinky ring and projected a graphic.

'Sir, forty million people have fallen below poverty line in the last one year, due to excessive food inflation. However, if we use the Monty Constant to redefine poverty, poverty line reduces by 10 per cent every year and in the fifth year, we should achieve the Ahluwahlia Equilibrium. At this point, once the poverty line is close to zero, a further five-year projection shows a sudden and drastic reduction in the number of poor people, to practically zero. If implemented properly, this can make poverty history in less than a decade.'

The contribution from the fabled bureaucrat of the early years of the twenty-first century had been invaluable. Without him, India might never have been able to solve the problem of poverty. Now at least there was hope.

'Subramaniam and the General are waiting outside, sir.'

'Send them in,' said the Competent Authority.

The two men trooped in. The General was truculent; Subramaniam was breezy. They sat down in front of the CA, hunched up deferentially, their knees touching the table. Subramaniam adjusted his tie, cleared his throat, and looked at the General. The CA smiled at him encouragingly. Last week's meeting with the CA had dented both his skull and his confidence, but since then, he had managed to get through another meeting without physical violence, and he was feeling much more relaxed. His reservoir of pomposity was practically bottomless, so recovery had been swift. All the CA expected him to do today was explain the fundamentals of geopolitics to this soldier, and bring him in line with government policy. The man was clearly a yokel. He would be like putty in his hands.

'The Competent Authority has asked me to debrief you on the current geopolitical situation, which is exceedingly complex,' said Subramaniam, smiling reassuringly at the General, and hoping he wouldn't be too dazzled by his brilliance. 'But don't worry. I will avoid technicalities and explain it to you in layman's terms.'

The General glowered at him resentfully. He got enough nonsense from the fat frogs in the defence ministry, who were forever looking for new ways to insult and demean the armed forces, which made them feel like real men and doubtless helped them with their erectile dysfunctions. Now he was going to be lectured by this oily little pimp from the foreign office.

'I must say your navy boys have created a bit of a situation here, General,' said Subramaniam, wagging a finger humorously, 'all in high spirits, no doubt, but the consequences could be quite far-reaching.'

The Competent Authority grunted menacingly. All this banter was testing his patience. He disliked having his patience tested.

'What is required here is an application of the Doctrine of Offensive Defence, whereby we must defend ourselves from the consequences of our aggression by striking a more aggressive posture,' said Subramaniam, rapidly, getting the hint.

'You mean now that they're angry, the best thing to do is make them even more angry?'

Ah, the charming simplicity of the military mind! It was wonderfully refreshing.

'Well, the solution is counter-intuitive, and not immediately apparent, I must admit,' said Subramaniam, 'but consider the situation. We rammed a Chinese vessel, an act of unprovoked aggression.'

'But they shot our sailor,' said the General angrily, 'we're the ones who took casualties. All they need is a bloody paint job!'

'You need to put the symbolic importance of resources in perspective here,' explained Subramaniam patiently. 'In the Chinese system, individuals do not matter. A naval vessel, on the other hand, is an extension of the nation. By ramming it, you are ramming China itself, which is completely unacceptable. I can assure you that they are planning military action as we speak. It is imperative that we make them reconsider such a course of action, by making it clear that we will respond with equal force. That's why we need to strike an aggressive posture.'

'Perhaps you would like me to bomb Beijing?' suggested the General.

'No, no,' said Subramaniam, 'that would be excessive. All we want is a bit of forward movement. Some hints of mobilization. Perhaps a border incident or two. Just enough to keep them on the backfoot.'

'I've got a better idea,' said the General, 'you're a diplomat. Why not try some diplomacy? It's a lot cheaper than mobilizing thousands of troops.'

Subramaniam smiled sadly. This was the problem with dealing with inferior intellects. It was like trying to teach a foreign language to a resentful chimpanzee.

'Thank you for your suggestion, my dear General,' he said, 'I can assure you that diplomatic channels are very much open. What we require is some military activity to supplement our efforts.'

'I'll hold a few flag meetings on the frontline near Patna,' said the General sullenly, 'that's the best I can do right now. Full mobilization will take at least ten more days. You should be happy. It used to take three months. Of course, it helps that we now have so much less of everything.'

He'd been getting quite good at not fighting war lately. But he knew events were no longer entirely under his control.

❑

Events were under even less control than the General thought, because even as they spoke, Professor Krishnan was being interviewed on national television. He had just bought himself a chicken tangri kebab, when an angry old man in spectacles had thrust a microphone in his face. In his old age, the legendary TV anchor who had once demanded the nation's attention from his studio had been forced to supplement his income with fieldwork, which made him angrier still.

He was standing next to the rubble of a dilapidated flyover, destroyed years ago and never rebuilt. A small food bazaar had sprung up amidst the debris, much patronized by commuters on the way to the nearby metro station, inside which eating, drinking, peeing and all other bodily functions were strictly prohibited, and attracted long jail sentences. Consequently, people often stopped in the bazaar for a quick bite, followed by a quick pee behind one of the ruined pillars. Twisted girders and scattered blocks of shattered concrete formed convenient chairs and tables, for those in the mood to dine al fresco. Professor Krishnan had booked a table by placing his clipboard on a misshapen chunk of rusting iron, and was on his way back to it with his booty when the Angry Old Man had accosted him. He and the others had been investigating reports of a possible rogue telepath in the area, but it had turned out to be an escaped household slave high on smack. The police had arrested the man and were returning him to his rightful owner, along with the smack, but Professor Krishnan—mesmerized by the array of greasy delicacies at the flyover food bazaar—had decided to take a quick snack break. He had spent long moments agonizing over the many choices on display, like a child on a first visit to Disneyland. Should he try the gol gappas, being made with great dexterity by the one-armed man with the supernaturally large thumb? Or should he take a journey into mystery with the bhel puri, packed with a variety of ingredients of indeterminate origin? Or perhaps the frothy white lassi, sprinkled with pista, glowing seductively in the evening gloom? The lighting here was sparse, presumably so that people couldn't examine what they were eating too closely. Eventually he had settled on the tangri kebabs, unable to resist the lethal combination of deep-frying, recycled oil and militant spices.

And now here he was, caught red-handed on national TV. If his wife was watching this, he was dead meat, just like the drumstick. If any of her many friends were watching it, he was even deader. He desperately shoved the evidence into his pocket, and tried to assume the expression of a man not at all interested in roadside snacks.

'I'm here with a top agent of the CBI, bringing you, our viewers, once more, an exclusive scoop,' said the Angry Old Man. 'Secret invaders may be attacking, but the CBI, as always, is too busy snacking. Enjoying your chicken leg, Professor?' he asked.

Professor Krishnan was now in a state of complete panic. His mission was compromised. He had caused a famous TV personality to recite a rhyming couplet about the CBI. His predilection for unsanitary non-vegetarian food stood starkly revealed in all its greasy grandeur. His immediate future was bound to consist of a series of lavish and spectacular punishments, meted out by Director Sinha, the Competent Authority, and his wife. They would probably take turns, one of them whaling away while the others rested.

The Angry Old Man moved in for the kill.

'So tell us all about it, Professor. The nation wants to know. You don't mind the nation interrupting your meal, do you?'

'No,' said the Professor uncertainly, wishing Venky was around. He was so much better at handling these things. Even Chatterjee would have been helpful, but he had disappeared mysteriously.

'What the nation wants to know is very simple,' said the Angry Old Man, 'has there, or has there not, been a massive attack on our telepathic forces, a band of brave young men and women who have dedicated their brains to the country?'

'Maybe,' said the Professor. Non-committal. Vague. That's what he needed to be. He should be able to manage. That's what people thought he was most of the time anyway.

'Maybe yes, or maybe no?' asked the Angry Old Man cunningly.

'Maybe yes?' ventured Professor Krishnan.

'Am I to take it, Professor Krishnan, that you are confirming, to the nation, live on *Why Now?* that there may have been an attack on our telepathic forces?'

'Maybe,' said Professor Krishnan, cautiously.

'Is that a yes or a no?' asked his tormentor.

'Yes,' said Professor Krishnan feebly, weakened by his aura.

'And there is absolutely no chance, Professor Krishnan, that this was some kind of accident?'

'No,' said Professor Krishnan, thinking it was high time he denied something.

'Come on, Professor. Tell us the truth. It's the Chinese, isn't it?' he said, going straight for the jugular.

'Maybe,' said Professor Krishnan.

'Have you unearthed, as yet, any actual evidence of Chinese involvement?'

'Not yet, but we will by next Tuesday,' said Professor, eager to send a message to his boss, who might be watching, that he was still on the case and hard at work.

'You can state this with certainty?'

'Absolutely,' said Professor Krishnan firmly.

The Angry Old Man turned to the camera. His manner was grave. 'Ladies and Gentlemen,' he said, 'you have just heard a senior official of the CBI confirm to us that we have been, once more, the victims of Chinese aggression. It is clear that our own attack on the Chinese submarine was just the first step, in what surely has to be, a massive retaliation. I must thank Professor Krishnan for helping us break this news to the Indian public, despite the considerable jeopardy to his distinguished career . . .'

He gestured for the camera to pan across to the Professor, who, thinking the interview was over, had fished the chicken leg out of his pocket. He waved it at the camera forlornly.

'Ladies and gentlemen, you have been witness to a momentous moment in Indian history!' continued the Angry Old Man. 'The moment when we, as a nation, may have finally decided to stand tall. Join us after the commercial break for our special feature, "India At War", where our eminent panel of experts gives its views on which Chinese cities should be bombed first . . .'

Three hours later, the General called the PM.

'The Chinese just started mobilizing,' he said, 'they should be ready to attack in three days, maybe less. If you have any bright ideas, now would be a good time to share them.'

72

'I'm not here to do tourism. I'm here to know everything.'

Pande strode through Khetolai, itching for action. He carefully avoided the ancient relic whom he had almost assassinated during his last visit. He was sitting in exactly the same position as before, on the same charpoy, hookah stuck firmly in his mouth. Perhaps he had died and no one had noticed. Or he might have achieved some form of nirvana, and risen above eating, sleeping and moving, instead drawing all necessary sustenance from his hookah. Such a thing was not unheard of. A holy man Pande had known back in his village used to claim that he had achieved a similar state through the assiduous practice of yoga, and no longer needed to pee.

A little yellow dog remembered him from his last visit, and barked a greeting, wagging its stubby tail. It was an extraordinarily poor judge of character.

Pande had entered the village five minutes ago, pausing only to thrash the taxi driver for driving too slowly, but he had already acquired a posse of little boys who skipped after him, occasionally calling him uncle and begging to borrow his revolver.

Pande had a good memory for places and a great sense of direction, thanks to his years spent as a neighbourhood cop, when being in the right place at the right time used to make all the difference to his income. He was looking for Irfan, and he knew exactly where to go. Irfan had seemed rather knowledgeable about bomb-related matters, and Pande looked forward to extracting from him the sum total of all his knowledge with the maximum amount of prejudice. His last visit had been exploratory, and it had made sense to tread carefully. But the time for caution had passed. The bomb was going to explode any moment. The holy child expected him to prevent this. He was confident that this village had all the information he required. All he needed was stern resolve and a strong right arm.

The village was relatively deserted, apart from the little boys, and a motley selection of livestock, who were roaming about with remarkable confidence. It was a searing hot afternoon and most of the villagers were indoors, unaware that a police raid was in progress.

He had assumed that Irfan would either be asleep, or cavorting with his four-legged friends, given the strange habits of the people in this village, but to his surprise, he was not, although there were several goats close by, in case he wanted a quick cuddle. He was reclining in his deck chair, reading a newspaper. Pande was shocked. The man could read! No wonder the people in this village were so uppity. Some misguided individual had been teaching them how to read and write. For centuries, the Mughals, the British, and sundry other rulers of India had avoided making this mistake, sensing, correctly, that nothing good could come of it. And here was this yokel reading a newspaper, just like the gentry. He wasn't even standing up to greet Pande. Pande felt the rage building in him. But he also felt a little nervous. This village was unnatural.

'Police uncle! Police uncle!' piped the little boys, leaping up and down like tadpoles with the gift of speech. Irfan lowered his newspaper.

'Inspector-sahab,' he said, smiling, and now he did get up; he folded his hands in greeting. The goats shied away nervously, thereby demonstrating the little-known fact that goats are smarter than dogs.

'Welcome back to our village,' said Irfan, 'have your investigations been successful?'

'My investigations have gone to hell,' said Pande bitterly. 'Those faujis were no help at all. But you can't fool me. I know all you people in this village have full information about bomb-shomb. The time for fun is over. Now you have to tell me everything.'

He brandished his lathi, and swished it in the air a few times to test its balance.

'Certainly I will tell you,' said Irfan cordially, 'everyone here knows, so it's hardly a secret. Exactly what information do you need?'

Pande was taken aback. He was unused to information being proffered freely. He hesitated, not sure how to proceed.

'Would you like to see the test site?' asked Irfan. 'It's only five minutes' walk from here.'

'I'm not here to do tourism. I'm here to know *everything*,' said Pande, hoping the man would object and bring things back on track.

Irfan grinned, 'Sometimes the answer is already with you, but you cannot see it.'

'Speak straight!' barked Pande, infuriated by his grin. 'This is not some type of children's game that I am playing here.'

Shovon Chowdhury

Irfan remained unfazed. He had met enough policemen, and he always made it a point to be consistently cordial. It kept them off balance.

'It's funny you should mention children,' he said, 'no one knows more about the bomb than the little ones, and they have been following you all this time. Isn't that true, Ashok?'

One of the older boys, who had been tugging meditatively at his penis for want of anything better to do, drew himself up proudly.

'The soldiers beat me up regularly,' he said.

'Me too,' said one of others.

'And me!' said a third.

'I get beat up much more than the rest of them,' said the smallest boy, revealing a hitherto unsuspected competitive streak.

They started beating each other up, yelling foul military curses.

Pande scowled. So these were his sources. There was no way he could treat them like normal sources. If he plied them with country liquor, for example, their mothers would object. And even Pande drew the line at brutally thrashing children. He cuffed one of the boys on the back of the head half-heartedly.

'Where's the bomb?' he demanded.

'Over there,' said the boy promptly, pointing towards the horizon.

'Take me,' said Pande.

His little helpers disentangled themselves from each other and led the way. Pande followed. Irfan put down his newspaper and joined them. He snapped his fingers, and his goats trotted after him, along with a small baby fawn. Pande sighed.

They walked towards the outskirts of the village, their progress periodically hampered by the boys, who occasionally felt the urge to perform military drills. Pande let them be. The place was having a strange effect on him. He was finding it harder and harder to sustain his habitual state of rage. One of the goats, partial to ambulatory snacking, was nibbling at the edge of his uniform, and Pande shoved him away listlessly instead of bashing his brains out. He tucked his lathi under his armpit. It would see no use today. He could see a desk job looming in his future.

They were climbing a large hillock now, and there was grass under their feet. 'This is where we graze our goats usually,' said Irfan, 'but for the last two months the army has forbidden it. They don't want us to come near this place. Naturally, the little boys don't listen. They get beaten up regularly by soldiers.'

'They broke my leg,' said one of the boys cheerfully, pointing to an entirely unblemished limb.

They reached the top of the knoll. 'Get down now, or they'll see us,' hissed one of the boys, and they lay flat on their stomachs. Pande did so with difficulty. He wasn't built for subterfuge.

He found himself looking down on a rolling plain. There were a few sparse bushes scattered across the landscape, otherwise it was all sand as far as the eye could see. In the distance he could see the barracks he had visited only recently. In the centre of the scene before him was a dome of golden granite.

'That's where the scientists sit when they do their tests,' said Irfan. 'Their leader has long white hair like a dance teacher. He comes to our village to buy cigarettes.'

'They wear soldiers' clothes and pretend to be soldiers but they're not. They talk funny and they keep dropping their rifles,' said one of the little boys. 'We all know they're fakeloos but we pretend that we don't. We salute them and call them captain. Sometimes they give us toffees. Ashok took a cigarette once.'

'I did not,' said Ashok, indignantly.

Pande remembered the strange group of officers he had seen in the army canteen. So they were professors pretending to be soldiers. He was impressed by their cunning. Pande had never come across such a case before. Criminals in Delhi never bothered with disguises, depending more on mass amnesia and collective blindness.

'There are a lot more soldiers today,' whispered Irfan, 'I think the bomb is going to blast very soon. That officer is looking nervous. We must leave. I have to warn the others. We must cover the water, and take all the animals to a cool, dark place.'

Pande looked at him scornfully. Ignorant peasant. As if covering the water or hiding the goats would make any difference. He ought to come spend a week in the Dead Circle, hang out with some of the locals, pay a quick visit to the skinless colony, walk down the street of the rolling beseechers, feel the scaly touch of the double-fried children. That would give him something to think about.

Shovon Chowdhury

In the sand dunes below, bulldozers were pushing around huge mounds of sand in random patterns. As they watched, the soldiers laid out thick black cables, and placed canisters on a mound they had just created.

'Every day, for the past few weeks, this is what they do,' said Irfan, 'every day at exactly this time. Now watch the bulldozers.'

The soldiers moved back and the bulldozers moved forward, pushing sand over the cables and the canisters, burying them. They moved round and round on the small hill they created, shifting the sand, and changing the pattern of the dunes.

'It's a very strange thing they do,' said Irfan. 'There's no head or paw to this thing.'

Pande remembered what Joshi the journalist had told him, about the Americans sitting in the sky, watching to see if India was trying to blast a bomb so that they could stop it by yelling at the Prime Minister, although they would also serve him cucumber sandwiches while doing so. He could see no reason why they should bother. After all, they were paying for the bomb with their own money. What business was it of the Americans? But listening to the journalist, he had gathered that Americans were prone to conspiracy theories, although the exact purpose of such conspiracies was not always easy to fathom.

Watching the bulldozers at work, Pande thought that if he could see them, wasn't it likely that the Americans could too? Why weren't the faujis concerned about this? Perhaps because the Americans were on a snack break. He had heard that Americans ate a lot. Or perhaps they too had some TV programme similar to *Indian Idol*, or *How Many Fingers*, which the whole nation stopped to watch.

Pande lay there, thinking, oblivious to the chattering boys. They can see everything, Joshi had said. They can read the time on an officer's wristwatch, sitting up there in the sky. He could feel his mind analyzing facts with lightning speed. The climate in this particular Rajasthan continued to suit him. The air was purer, more oxygen was reaching his brain. He knew how to complete his mission now. After all the trouble he had gone through, it was actually going to be quite simple.

He struggled to his feet, adjusted his belly, and hauled up one of the boys by the scruff of his neck.

'Is there a carpenter in your village?' he demanded.

The boy wriggled free quite easily. He was used to escaping from soldiers, who were a lot fitter than police uncles.

'Yes, there is,' he said, keeping a safe distance, 'but you should pay him only after he finishes the work, otherwise he gets drunk and starts singing songs. Sometimes you have to wait for the wood. He can only take what the trees give him.'

'His wife is fucking the headman!' said one of the others, who believed in sharing complete information with the forces of law and order.

Pande ignored this. 'Can anyone paint?'

'Yes, yes, I can,' said one of the smaller boys excitedly; 'I'll go get my brush right now!'

Pande looked at him dubiously. He would have to do. Luckily, what he had in mind was fairly rudimentary.

'Chalo, let's go,' he said, 'we have work to do.'

He brushed the sand from his khakis and walked briskly down the hill. He was going to stop the Pokhran blast. He was also going to teach those arrogant army-wallahs a much-needed lesson. In future, they would behave better with policemen.

And if he succeeded, he mused, with a sudden flash of understanding, maybe the Dead Circle wouldn't be so dead after all.

73

'We must remain united in the face of opposition from non-Bengalis.'

The corporal punishment ceased once they were outside Mountbatten's line of sight. The policemen had been on duty, non-stop for as long as they could remember, and while they had put on a show for the Big Lord, they reverted to their practice of doing as little as possible as soon as they could. They bundled Mr Chatterjee unceremoniously into the back of the police jeep.

'Who's this beauty?' asked the driver, impressed by his clothes.

'He was arrested by the Big Lord personally!' said one of the constables. 'He was planning to kill Gandhiji.'

'Why just him?' muttered the driver, and crashed the jeep into gear. The jeep lurched forward and Mr Chatterjee almost fell out. The head constable caught him by the collar. 'Easy, brother,' he said. 'We don't want you patkoing before you reach the thana.'

The other constable eyed him critically. 'He doesn't look very fit,' he said. 'I would have thought they would get someone fitter to kill a big man like Gandhiji. Why did they choose a spectacle-wallah like this?'

'You need to know English to get close to Gandhiji. Look at Nehru and Jinnah. Of course, Jinnah was too English, that was the problem. He was maro-ing too much English all the time. Gandhiji didn't like it. When he told him, Jinnah got offended. That's *his* problem, he gets offended too easily. Big people get offended, and as a result, small people get fucked in the arse. That's our tradition.'

'How's your cousin in Kishanganj?' asked the driver.

'Arrey, don't ask. He wants to stop killing Muslims, but the leaders keep saying do more. Apparently the revenge for Calcutta is not complete yet.'

'But is anyone doing any calculation?'

'They are not revealing any targets or numbers. It's all in their heads. My cousin is worried. Crops are suffering, and harvest time is coming soon. When the same leader comes as the zamindar and asks for his share, what is he going to do? At that time he won't let him go.'

'This is very bad trend that has started,' said the younger constable, who was a bit of a thinker. 'The public is handling law and order personally. Ideally, we should be doing all these types of things. That's how it was under the British. Now the British have gone, no one is following any rules.'

'Nobody has gone, baba,' said the head constable soothingly. 'Everything is just the same. Ultimately all these things will be our responsibility. Right now, some confusion is going on because of Partition. The police alone cannot get rid of all Muslims. That's why the public is also contributing.'

As a student of history, Mr Chatterjee found this fascinating. As an individual, he was petrified. The police here were even more brutal than the ones back home, if such a thing could be imagined. He could expect no mercy.

They drew up in front of the thana in a cloud of dust. It was uncannily similar to the one back in Safdarjung Enclave where he had met Pande to discuss the elimination of his neighbour's dog. His adventures had begun in one police station, and it was only fitting that they should end in another. They tugged on the rope around his waist and led him inside. The room was dank and stinky, the atmosphere redolent of fear and sweat. Here too, the crime board was blank, testifying to the total absence of any law and order problems in the locality. It was like coming home. Giving up was such a relief. What had he been thinking? Who was he to change history? He was just a lowly telepath tester, with a minor talent for mind games. His biggest achievement had been marrying Banani. Each day with her had been a miracle, and he had spent most of his time expecting a notice from the government, explaining that it had all been a clerical error and his marriage was now dissolved. I hope she finds someone nice, he thought, she deserves someone who loves her.

They pushed him down in a chair, roughly. 'You wait,' said the head constable, 'the Big Babu is coming. He'll decide everything.'

Mr Chatterjee tried to imagine what the Big Babu would look like. He would be imposingly paunchy, with cold, cruel eyes and a thick right wrist like a tennis player, thanks to decades of vigorous lathi wielding. His revolver would be a relic of World War II, which was perfectly understandable here, given that it had only ended three years ago, but not so explicable in his own era, where most criminals had GPS-enabled laser rifles. He would use it to shoot him while he was ostensibly trying to escape, along with any witnesses who needed eliminating, and receive a medal and a cash prize for solving the Gandhi Murder Mystery, while the real culprits went on to become pillars of society. His nose would be bulbous, his breathing heavy. Chairs would creak ominously when he sat in them. His minions would cower, and hand him implements as and when he needed them.

A diminutive, flabby priest in a saffron silk dhoti breezed into the room. His face, his hands, even his little feet—everything about him was plump. Everyone stood up and saluted, except Mr Chatterjee. He was generally deferential to the priesthood, but he drew the line at saluting.

'Saraswati Puja happens only once a year,' said the priest. 'You people are all buffaloes, but I respect learning. I gave you strict instructions not to call me during my rehearsal. What did I tell you? Call me only in the case of more than fifteen fatalities. What sky has fallen on whose head that you had to disturb me like this?'

'The Big Lord captured an assassin!' said the junior constable.

'The Big Lord couldn't capture your grandmother!' said the priest. 'What is all this bloody nonsense?'

The head constable shifted feet uneasily. 'We were at the Governor's House looking for biscuits,' he said, 'when the Big Lord gave this man to us, saying he was trying to kill Gandhiji. We didn't actually see him make the attempt or anything, as Gandhiji was not present at this time. One of the bearers told me he was getting a foot massage from the Big Mem, which sounds unlikely. Perhaps he was resting after the recent bomb attack which none of us are investigating.'

The priest eyed Mr Chatterjee dubiously. He did not look like an assassin, and he had seen many recently. On the contrary, he looked like a man of culture, with whom he might be able to discuss poetry. He missed culture. Culturally speaking, conditions in Delhi were arid. 'What's your name?' he asked, not barking too much.

'Chat'jee,' said Mr Chatterjee in his favoured, clipped and professional manner like his uncle who used to be a director in Berger Paints.

'Chatterjee?' boomed the priest, delighted. 'I also am Chatterjee!'

He turned to his assembled minions. 'You people go. I'll take care of this personally. And bring us some tea!'

He crossed over to the big desk and sat behind it.

'You must forgive my attire,' he said. 'Normally I am very particular about dress code.'

Mr Chatterjee was trying not to say too much, but he attempted to convey through body language that he too was very particular about dress code.

'You are from Calcutta? What is your full name?'

'Hemonto Chatterjee,' said Mr Chatterjee.

'Hemonto? Like the singer? Ahahaha. So melodious! "At your door, there is stan-ding a yogi-i-i!"'

He sang it well. His costume lent him authenticity.

'This Mountbatten is a bloody phool, I tell you!' said the priest. 'First day he came for duty, I told Mrs Chatterjee, are you listening, this one has only pure cowdung inside his head. But even for him this is too much. He cannot tell a gentleman from a littleman? That too at his own tea party?'

Mr Chatterjee allowed himself the luxury of a small smile.

The priest leaned forward. 'We Bengalis must stick together. See what

Bengal has become? No more than a pimple on the map of India. And to think that at one time the country was ruled from Calcutta! What is India but a union of Calcutta and Bombay and Madras, plus Hyderabad once the Nizam has been terrorized by Mr Patel? Yet today we are just a negligible fragment. It's all very pathetic.'

Little did he know. There was much worse in store, but this did not seem like the right time to inform him that Bengal was going to be communist for most of the next century.

'Ever since the betrayal of Netaji,' said the priest, 'the situation has been deteriorating rapidly. Many in Bengal still support the Bose family, and the Congress bosses are violently against the Bose family. Consequently, the Congress is displaying anti-Bengali bias. Their attitude became obvious after Partition. Where is the compensation for Bengalis? Punjabis are getting all the benefits, Bengalis are getting nothing. It's all prejudice. Meanwhile, all the Muslims went mad crying for Pakistan, without any clear idea about geography. Now see their condition. Of course, we also could have been more generous in the matter of Dhaka University. In matters of education, such pettiness is avoidable. I value education. I study both geography and history. History is my inspiration, as it should be for all of us. Not long ago, there was one united Bengal, one vast entity that stretched from Rangoon to Patna, with Cuttack and Guwahati and Agartala and Chittagong in between. Bengal was glorious! Bengal was mighty! Bengali rivers were brimful of fish! Now there is nothing left except memories.'

'Well, you can't spend your life in the past,' said Mr Chatterjee, unable to help himself. Most of the shit he dealt with on a daily basis was because of people who simply could not let go of the past. He was firmly of the view that nothing good could come from history. And here he was, visiting it. He really ought to have objected more.

The priest grabbed hold of his hands, eyes gleaming. A lot of people had been grabbing his hands lately, keen on converting him to their cause.

'Not the past. Live for the present! Today geography is very fluid, and various types of wrong and absurd countries are coming into existence. Borders have no meaning. Districts melt away. Maps are misleading. Landlords have no say. We have been victims of partiality, but we must not lose heart. This is a time of great opportunity. This is a time of challenge for the Bengali nation. We must remain united in the face of opposition from non-Bengalis. This is a time for all good Bengali gentlemen to support each other!'

Mr Chatterjee had never been to Cuttack, and Rangoon might as well have been on the moon. But he could feel his spirits lifting. He might not be massacred after all. He was receiving special treatment from the police. He had never received special treatment from the police before. It was a heady feeling.

The priest was whispering.

'Who's the target? Gandhiji? Good choice. I approve. Where was he when the killings happened in Calcutta? Did he raise a finger? Through inaction he supported it. He is an enemy of Bengal. By eliminating him, you can make a statement on behalf of Bengal. Show them we are afraid of no one.'

This seemed rather unfair, given that the people in Calcutta had done most of the actual killing, but Mr Chatterjee chose not to quibble.

'I have to get to Gandhi,' he said. It was true. He had to save him. Who else was going to cure people like this?

'I'll drive you down personally,' said the priest. 'As a senior police officer I can get you right inside.'

Mr Chatterjee held up the end of his rope.

'Rascals!' roared the priest, and three constables materialized instantly. It was just like Star Trek.

'Take off that rope, and get another cup of tea. Is this any way to treat a gentleman?'

74

'Chinese people demand million-to-one ratio, as defined by Professor Zhu of Chengdu University!'

The General was trying to figure out which problem to deal with first— the problem of vodka, or the problem of aircraft carriers. Both were critical. On the aircraft carrier front he had to decide whether it was really safe to send a hundred-year-old carrier into the Bay of Bengal, which would soon be infested with shiny new Chinese submarines. Or was it more advisable to send in his other carrier, a mere stripling of sixty? Whenever he posed this question to the Admiral, he would shake his head, purse his lips and look faintly seasick. About the only edge the Indian Navy had was the power of democracy. This meant that Indian sailors, inflated by their love for liberty, would swim slightly better when their ships were sunk. Assuming the Admiral had been able to afford swimming lessons.

The vodka situation was equally grave. He needed lots of it. The vast majority of his fighter planes, which were of Russian origin, suffered from a crucial defect. They couldn't fly. When they did, they usually crashed, thus saving the Chinese the effort of bringing them down. The Russians blamed it primarily on the pilots, while emphasizing the need for more comprehensive maintenance contracts. There was no time for training, with the Chinese already mobilizing, so, after agreeing to pay exorbitant supplementary fees, the General had managed to convince a group of senior Russian technicians to fly down. They were coming to his house for dinner for which he needed vodka, lots of it. If he served them Indian vodka, they would be mortally insulted, and having drunk it, they would leave. He needed the genuine article. He had asked his orderly to get in touch with Balaji the Fixer, who fixed everything, but he was too busy with some special project for the Bank of Bodies and had said he couldn't help. Perhaps he could ask the Nepali Naxalites, who ran casinos and had all kinds of liquor in stock. To the best of his knowledge, they had been anti-Chinese for the last few weeks, so he might get lucky.

All this focus on liquor was making him thirsty, so he took a discreet swig from a silver hip flask, a parting gift from a Pakistani general, who had subsequently been vaporized. A nice enough chap, much worried about mullahs. With good reason, as it turned out.

He raised a silent toast to his deceased rival, and was interrupted in mid-swig by Captain Navalkar, who was giggling. Navalkar was at his workstation, ostensibly digging up intelligence, although he was probably surfing for porn.

'We'll be at war with China by next week. Sooner, if they launch a strike. I'm glad you find the whole thing so funny.'

'It really is funny,' said Navalkar, unabashed. 'These guys are insane! Just hang on while I forward this to my buddies. They could do with a laugh.'

Navalkar was intelligent, naïve and relentlessly cheerful. He was the one indulgence the General permitted himself. He kept him around because he raised his spirits. Assuming he was still sane, it was largely thanks to him.

'Morale is no doubt important, Navalkar,' said the General, 'but the Indian army doesn't actually have a position for a comedy co-ordinator, which is why I asked you to do intelligence.'

'But this *is* intelligence,' protested Navalkar, 'I'm analysing Chinese public opinion. Their opinions are awesome. Listen to this one.'

He swiped his pad. A miniature Jackie Chan materialized in mid-air. His expression was uncharacteristically petulant. 'Anguish of mother of murdered Chinese sailor is unbearable to watch,' said Jackie. 'Multiply Indian anguish one million times! Chinese people demand million-to-one ratio, as defined by Professor Zhu of Chengdu University!' He leaped into the air and vanished.

A small, blue dragon appeared in his place. It, too, was angry. Wisps of blue smoke curled from its nostrils. 'Chinese invented gunpowder, printing press, compass and paper,' declared the dragon. 'Illiterate India animals can never challenge China!'

The dragon was replaced by a small Aishwarya Rai. She was gorgeous, but annoyed. 'See how the dirty black hand is once more playing tricks,' she said. 'Instead of slurping gold and sucking silver, O leaders, take action against the enemies of the motherland!'

Navalkar beamed proudly, like a magician who had just performed a particularly good conjuring trick.

'Who on earth are these people?' asked the General, aghast.

'Patriotic Chinese citizens,' said Navalkar, 'can't you tell?'

'Patriotic Chinese citizens want to be Aishwarya Rai?'

'Apparently, some of them do. Others are more historically inclined.'

Chairman Mao appeared, looking youthful and deadly. He adopted the statistical approach. 'In last Corruption Perception Index by Transparency International, China ranked No. 72,' he said. 'India ranked No. 85. So much for democracy! Ignorant and smelly savages of India must be taught a severe and final lesson for daring to attack sacred submarine of China!'

The General opened his mouth to speak, but Navalkar raised a finger.

'Just one more,' he pleaded, 'it's friendlier.'

It was bound to be. It was Confucius.

'If someone did wrong,' said Confucius, gently, 'someone should apologize, rectify and compensate. This is basic courtesy. Indian hoodlums have killed Chinese sailor. They should compensate by handing over remaining Indian navy to China. We should then forgive our little brother, who is also our neighbour. Remember what I once said. If your neighbour is a monkey, he is still your neighbour. You may take away his banana, but then you must forgive him, even if low-rank people have their way with his mother on a regular basis.'

'Who *are* these people?' repeated the General, dazed by all the invective. It reminded him of the Officer's Mess on the day the Eighth Pay Commission results had been announced.

'The Chinese man on the street,' said Navalkar, 'at least, that's what their government thinks.'

'I don't understand.'

'The Propaganda Department employs approximately half the people in China to monitor the other half on the internet. Nobody knows which half is doing what, except for a few people at the top. Many of them also express spontaneous outrage about specific events as per government guidelines. They in turn get monitored by others. So they spend most of their time checking their own press releases, while genuine members of the public spend most of theirs looking for boobies. It's all very confusing. Sometimes they arrest each other. It takes weeks to sort things out. Almost everyone has done at least a year's hard labour. This makes them irritable, as you can see from some of the messages. In this way, the Propaganda Department keeps its finger on the pulse of the nation.'

'You mean to tell me they use the internet to gauge public opinion? They listen to loonies?'

'Well, most people are on the net in China. It's true that the loonies spend more time on it than the others. But what else can the government do? There's no point asking people directly. Who's going to tell them? People might think that the Young Prince is promoting homosexuality by doing it too often with the Firm Young Marshal. But if they complain too much they get sent to the Harmony Doctors for psychiatric reconstruction and attitude adjustment. Popularly known as the Beijing Brainfuck. They're highly advanced, biologically.'

'So right now the government thinks the people are angry?'

'The government wants people to be angry about other countries. It leaves them with less free time to be angry about the government. The Chinese people rise up and try to overthrow the government about once every hundred years. The Taipings tried in the nineteenth century, and Mao did it in the twentieth. They're overdue in the twenty-first, and the party is nervous. Besides, there's nothing much for people to do. They can't do religion, because it's all government-sponsored, and that's like praying to your local MP. They can't watch sports, because it's too boring. China wins everything all the time. They can't criticize the government, or throw chappals at ministers, because then they get sent to the Harmony Doctors, who readjust their brains. There's never anything good on television. So there's nothing much else to do on a Saturday night except burn down the Japanese embassy, for which buses are provided. It keeps the public satisfied, and it gives the Japanese something to think about. You don't have to worry about the Indian embassy. That was burnt down years ago, when the Bengalis sold Darjeeling to China, and we refused to ratify the deal.'

'None of this is very encouraging,' said the General.

'It's actually kind of circular,' said Navalkar. 'The Party fills the internet with powerful messages like Fuck the Indians, and Fuck Vietnam, and Fart in the Face of the Xinjiang Splittists. People get angry, because they want China to be strong. So then the Party gets angry, because otherwise they look weak, and then people get angry at them. The Party makes angry demands. The people get angrier. So the Party gets angrier. And so on and so forth. It's tricky. It's like walking a tightrope with your feet on fire.'

'They have to attack us,' said the General. 'They have no choice.'

So this was it. The End. It had been a long innings. He had fought the good fight. Most of it had been against his own people, it was true, but the fight had been good.

'That's what it looks like,' said Navalkar, cheerfully, 'but don't worry, boss. There's life in the old dog yet. I have a few ideas I want to bounce off my buddies in Bangalore.'

75

'At the age of sixteen,
I had my first illegitimate child . . .'

The Russian report was full of good news. Hectic activity had been detected between the Chinese missile bases of Da Qaidan and Xiao Qaidan, with missiles being transported from one to the other. Several people had already been shot for not moving missiles fast enough. This was promising. Da Qaidan had been built for launches against India, although no one had realized it until the strikes in '24, and it meant the Chinese were serious. There was plenty of activity around Datong as well, where all leave had been cancelled in both the 10th Air Army and the 2nd Artillery Corps, according to the Russians. Fleets of nuclear-armed bombers now stood ready, all set to rain death on the Gangetic plain. The Russian Ambassador had dropped off his report to the CA in person, before returning to Russia for urgent consultations. He seemed to be in a hurry, and had left without finishing his vodka. The CA disapproved. Nothing good ever came from hurrying. Some sections of society were trying to rush India into the twentieth century, but personally, the CA was against this. As a pragmatist, he saw 1895 as a more feasible target. Premature use of modern technology or thought processes was never advisable in India, as he himself could testify. His latest smiley drone initiative had not been a success. In an unconscious echo of Mrs Verma's mother, the CA had given instructions for smiley drones to float into kitchens, and give housewives useful tips on healthy cooking, but housewives were smashing them with whatever they could find close at hand.

His last encounter with CBI Director Sinha had also left him mildly disturbed. The man continued to bombard him with status reports about the telepath case, despite the fact that he had so much else to do. The last one he had insisted on delivering in person. He had seemed very perturbed. He had mentioned Shanti Nagar several times, even after the CA had made him tweak his nipples, both clock-wise and anti-clock-wise. It had been hard to make out what he was saying, but 'subversive elements' and 'child' and 'lathis' had cropped up often. 'Sir, please change your transport arrangement, sir,' he had said, in a desperate burst of lucidity, while continuing to alternate rotatory cycles with commendable zeal. Here he was grappling with the might of China, and Sinha was gibbering about Shanti Nagar. Except towards the end, when he had cried a lot, exhausted, and apologized repeatedly, and promised not to do a proper investigation ever again, and sworn that next time he would report whatever the Competent Authority wanted him to report, God promise he would.

The Competent Authority smiled at the memory. He rearranged his buttocks thoughtfully and sighed a happy sigh. Matters were proceeding according to plan. That he was a driving force in the destiny of the human race was something he had always been keenly aware of, but he was awestruck nevertheless. Thanks to the wheels he had set in motion, there was now frantic activity in far-off China. Missiles the size of skyscrapers were being transported hither and thither. Officers were kissing their wives goodbye, and looking through well-thumbed Hindi phrasebooks. Scientists were feverishly re-checking calculations, knowing that failure could lead to an entry-level job in the footwear industry. Members of the Central Committee were surreptitiously shifting their families to their secret havens in Honolulu. Decrepit old generals were studying orders with watery eyes, and signing them with shaking hands, remembering a time when life had been so much simpler, and all you had to do was squish people with tanks. And all this was happening because he, the CA, had willed it so.

The tragedy was that no one knew this, except for his minions, and they scarcely counted. Their files were his, to dispose of as he wished. With a flick of a pen he could send them from Airport Duty to Sewage Inspection, or from Geneva to Jahangirpuri. Even their lives post-retirement were his to command. He could put them in charge of inquiries which never discovered anything, or appoint them to committees which never met, or send them on study tours to countries with beaches. The adulation of such creatures, lavish though it might be, gave him no real pleasure. After years of dedicated service, he deserved more. The more he thought about it, the more deserving he felt.

Instead of getting Salman to novelize him, as he had originally thought, perhaps he should get a pet biographer, someone who would study his every move, and record his every word. But no mere scribe would be able to capture his greatness, or understand the masterful way in which he guided the fortunes of the nation. An autobiography was the only answer. It had worked for Gandhi. It had worked for Nehru. It had worked for A.R. Rahman. It would work for him. The moment he figured out how to type properly on his computer, rather than using two fingers, he would get started. He owed it to posterity. But why should he wait? He had minions. He yelled for Mehta.

Mehta appeared with his tablet at the ready.

'From 10:30 a.m. to 11:00 a.m. every day,' said the CA, 'I will be dictating my autobiography. Starting today. Let us begin. We will skip my childhood.'

Mehta began typing on his tablet.

'At the age of sixteen,' said the Competent Authority, 'I had my first illegitimate child . . .'

76

'Do you have any defects? Don't be shy, just name a price.'

'Shanti-bai, Shanti-bai, a big lady in diamonds is trying to buy people in front of Satyam Talkies!'

Little Sonu had burst into the room. He was extremely agitated.

Shanti-bai groaned. She was lying on her cot, about to receive a foot rub from Ranjeeta.

'Can't you manage without me for even five minutes?' she asked crossly. 'The moment I lie down, you start selling each other?'

'I didn't do anything,' said Sonu, hitching up his ragged pants. 'It was the fat lady. Tarun-da was saying she has a nose like Indira Gandhi!'

'There's a name I was hoping not to hear again in this lifetime,' muttered Shanti-bai. 'Hand me my umbrella,' she told Ranjeeta, standing up creakily. 'It's best to carry a weapon. No point in taking chances.'

Once she had her umbrella, she poked Sonu with it. 'Don't stand there like a statue, you useless child. Take me to Satyam Talkies.'

❏

It was all action in front of Satyam Talkies. Crowds were milling about, animatedly discussing prices. Shopkeepers in the nearby shops were following the action keenly, trying to understand the market sentiment.

Given that the ride to Shanti Nagar had been harrowing and fraught with peril, Mrs Verma felt she owed herself a small shopping spree. Hoskins had driven down the dirt track that led to Shanti Nagar like Michael Schumacher with a rocket up his bum, deaf to all entreaties, while conceding that the road was 'orrible. 'It'll get over faster this way, mum,' he had assured her, while driving the armoured Rolls Royce directly into a pothole. Once they reached Shanti Nagar, two of her guards had puked on her shoes. Most of them were still groggy. A few had tottered out, blinking in the sunlight, gripping their laser rifles with shaking hands. As an assault force, they lacked credibility.

Meanwhile, Hoskins had gone off to find beer, suffused with the warm glow of satisfaction that came from striking a blow against the enemies of the working class. It didn't matter what the colour of their skin was. He knew them when he saw them.

However, as she looked at the milling crowds all around her, Mrs Verma began to recover swiftly. The people here were so healthy! Prices were bound to be lower than Slaves R Us, because of lower overheads. There was the usual smattering of mutants and damaged people, but even they seemed reasonably well cared for. Shanti Nagar was unusually peaceful. She had already been here for fifteen minutes, and she was yet to see anyone being shot in the streets, and no one was molesting the women, not even the pretty ones. No wonder they were all so healthy. It was true she had come here to rid Pappu of his terrible curse, but she also remembered Sanjeev's pressing need for slaves.

'What's your price?' she asked a young vegetable seller. She liked the look of his forearms.

'I only sell cauliflowers, Auntie,' said the young man nervously, 'Try some. They're very good.'

Pappu ran up, breathless.

'Mummy, can I have some money for candy floss? They're still using coins here!'

Mrs Verma gave him some coins. Pappu ran off.

'Make sure the machine is imported!' she called after him.

'Don't worry!' he cried back. 'My hand feels right at home here.'

Her euphoria diminished. Would other parts of him also begin to develop minds of their own? She had to finish buying people and get back to her primary mission. Speed was of the essence. She turned back to the young vegetable seller.

'Do you have any defects?' she asked, urgently. 'Don't be shy, just name a price.'

The merchant standing next to him made an attempt to divert her attention. The sole item he had on display was a large, greasy drum. It appeared to contain some form of liquid. The stench was terrifying.

'Genuine cooking oil recovered from motor vehicles, Auntie!' he said. 'Try some, I'll give you a very good price. Your food will have a totally different flavour!'

'Really?' said Mrs Verma. 'Is it safe?'

She asked this more for form's sake than anything else. She shopped regularly for bargains at the Dead Circle.

'Auntie, for you, just five thousand rupees per litre. We only use motor oil from BMWs.'

The BMW was to Delhi what the camel was to the desert, realized Mrs Verma. It provided for them in many different ways.

'What about him?' she asked, pointing at his assistant, a large young man who was trying to hide behind the oil drum. She was not a woman whose attention was easily diverted. The oil merchant swallowed nervously, and looked around furtively. A large crowd was watching him with interest.

'Owneress, I could hire him out to you, although I would request that you keep him in Shanti Nagar, otherwise his mother will get very annoyed. He will keep most of the money. I will get a small commission. But I cannot do outright sale. Shanti-bai would cut off my balls if she found out.'

'Someone get me a knife,' said Shanti-bai. 'Make sure it's a sharp one.'

The crowd parted for Shanti-bai, and she strode through them to where Mrs Verma was carefully examining the large young man, trying to gauge his stamina. Size could sometimes be deceptive, she had discovered. Plus there was the matter of food to be considered. The large ones ate more.

Shanti-bai took a moment to size up Mrs Verma. The nose was genuinely disturbing, but the rest of her was familiar. Shanti-bai knew the type. In the days when she had been a councillor, many of them had voted for her, out of a sense of secret sisterhood, much to the dismay of the patriarchy. They were large and greedy, with a marked weakness for ghee and diamonds, but they were not completely immune to common sense. She knew how to handle women like this.

'Listen, why are you coming here and doing all this shouting? And what's the need for all these guns-shuns? Are you shooting some picture or what?'

'Please don't let her take me away, Shanti-bai!' begged the vegetable seller. 'I don't want to leave Shanti Nagar!'

'Where are you taking all these people, baba?' asked Shanti-bai. 'And are you just here for shopping or do you have some other purpose also?'

'I'm looking for a boy named Pintoo,' said Mrs Verma.

'Achcha,' said Shanti-bai. She adjusted her sari thoughtfully. A hush fell over the crowd, punctuated by uneasy muttering. 'Tell me your requirement. Perhaps I can help you.'

'My son Pappu is unwell. Despite owning our own doctor, we are unable to find a cure for him. I heard that this Pintoo has a knack for such things. I was told this by my iPod valet. Her cousin lives in Shanti Nagar.'

This was not true, although she liked the bit about the iPod valet. It added that whiff of authenticity. She obviously couldn't tell Shanti-bai that her psychiatrist had told her that Pappu was demonstrating classic symptoms of Alien Organ Syndrome, along with the early stages of Involuntary Psychic Confluence and that he could be cured by either reversing the procedure or destroying the source. Mrs Verma was very clear which one she preferred. But she would have to be careful.

'If you help me to find him, I can make a donation,' she said to Shanti-bai, who was obviously some sort of social worker. No doubt she was running an NGO. She knew all about NGOs. Donations were their main source of funds.

Mrs Verma was very close to being thrashed with an umbrella at this point. When Shanti-bai responded to her offer, she was brisk and cheerful, and very affectionate. The crowd dispersed rapidly. Whenever Shanti-bai spoke sweetly, it was time to get as far away as possible. Others had been fooled, and they had lived to regret it.

'It's very sweet of you to offer,' said Shanti-bai, pinching her cheek. 'Some might think you're trying to be naughty, but I know you mean well. You are making a mistake, however. The same mistake as my neighbour, Professor Gulati. He is a very educated person. He lives in the shack behind mine.'

'What did Professor Gulati do?'

'He tried to do two important things at the same time. His brain was very large, so he thought he could manage. He mixed up the issues of child nutrition, and his wife's complexion. At my request, he was trying to find a way to improve child nutrition in Shanti Nagar. He felt that if through genetic engineering he could manufacture a buffalo with extra chuchis, the milk output of the animal would improve. Biologically he was very strong. Mathematically, he was weak. I tried to explain this to him, but being a man, he was adamant. He spent many months on this project, while at the same time working on a fairness cream for his wife. She wanted to look radiant for an upcoming family marriage. As a result, his buffalos are now unnaturally pale, while his wife never comes out in public. This is what happens when you try to do two very important things at the same time. Now you tell me, what is the application of this story to your current position?'

'I should do the shopping later?' said Mrs Verma.

'I think so,' said Shanti-bai. 'Instead, you come with me. I'll take you to Pintoo. Then we'll see what's what.'

Mrs Verma felt a shaky tap on her shoulder. It was the surgeon. He was dressed for duty. He was wearing his medical backpack and his red-and-white combat helmet.

'It's time, isn't it?' he said, sadly.

'Yes,' said Mrs Verma. 'This granny is going to guide us. She knows where the patient lives.'

Pappu rejoined them, right on cue. His face was a mass of sticky pink, with bits of little boy peeping through. Mrs Verma could only recognize him from his clothes, which he was still wearing, thankfully. She grabbed hold of a sticky hand, taking care to ensure that it was the real one.

'Come, Pappu,' she said. 'It's time to take care of this hand nonsense, once and for all!'

Shanti-bai led the way, brandishing her umbrella. Two of the Self-Defence Force guards had just arrived and were standing at the edge of the crowd, trying to look inconspicuous, never an easy thing to do while carrying a semi-automatic weapon. They were keeping a low profile. As she walked past them, Shanti-bai leaned over and whispered.

'Stop playing kabaddi with your dicks and follow me.'

She had a feeling she was going to need them.

77

*'We must, however, insist on shedding of
blood as minimum qualification.'*

The Defence Minister was well known for his ruthless streak. As he droned on and on, some of the more intrepid members of the audience were checking out escape routes and considering daring bids for freedom, despite the jeopardy to their careers, using hard-won skills honed by years of fighting insurgencies. Others sank deeper and deeper into apathy and hopelessness. He showed them no mercy.

He was speaking in chaste and grammatically exact Hindi, which meant that at least half the assembled officers had no clue what he was talking about. But the minister was a stern advocate of the national language, and proud of his own proficiency. His children had gone to La Martiniere and UCLA, but that was only because their mother had insisted. Besides, someone had to learn the language of imperialism, in order to communicate on behalf of the nation with foreigners. His children would have the good fortune of playing this role. He turned a page and cleared his throat, taking a moment to peer at the audience through his spectacles.

The General groaned softly and tugged at his moustache. Sitting next to him, the PM stopped whispering into her phone and gave him a smile of encouragement.

'I have to go through things like this three times a day,' she said. 'Do you ever hear me moaning about it? Don't be such a baby.'

'You were probably listening to speeches like this *when* you were a baby,' said the General, 'in your mother's womb. The rest of us haven't had so much practice.'

They were at the investiture ceremony for the military bravery awards, the General because he had to be, the PM because a public place like this was ideal for making secret phone calls from her special phone donated by the Japanese ambassador.

'Government of India would like to issue a clarification,' said the minister, who spoke only in government third person plural. He should have been responding to the China crisis, but the investiture had already been scheduled. 'There are rumours that Government of India only gives awards to dead people. This is very wrong. Death is not compulsory for getting a medal. Even living people are eligible, although undoubtedly Government of India will give greater consideration to those who have made the supreme sacrifice. Those with black tongues allege that many of the winners have died by chance, and are not actual heroes. This is an insult to the martyrs of the nation. If there are any genuine questions, they can be posed in the appropriate forum. Meanwhile, if you demonstrate bravery, and you are still alive subsequently, Government of India will not hold this against you. So long as you have shed blood, chances of winning are always there. We must, however, insist on the shedding of blood as a minimum qualification. In this, we are inspired by the words of the immortal Netaji, whose pertinent speech we will now recite for you in toto and verbatim. As we face new challenges from China, it assumes added relevance. "Give me your blood," the immortal Netaji had said, "and . . . "'

The General pushed his fingers under his cap and massaged his aching temples. A missile strike at this point would be a blessed release.

'Hullo, Lee,' whispered the PM, 'is that you?'

She gave the General a discreet thumbs-up and grinned.

'Things are heating up, aren't they? You know this is your big chance.'

The Defence Minister paused briefly and took a sip of water, surveying the massed ranks of bureaucrats and officers before him. He gave a signal to his PA, and the cameramen lined up obediently. It was time for his big announcement. Years of effort would today come to fruition. His fights with the Finance Ministry had been epic, but eventually the Competent Authority had come down on his side. This was a big step forward. There was no way they were going to switch him to the Ministry of Rural Development after this.

'Government of India recognizes that true heroes deserve just rewards. It has been brought to the attention of Government of India that the pension for medal recipients has not been revised in the last forty years. Cognizant of this truly lamentable situation, Government of India has taken steps to rectify it. From this day onwards, all those honoured with bravery awards will receive an extra five hundred rupees every month as pension, subject to proper submission of all relevant documents to all relevant authorities, past, present and future. In order to differentiate between death and non-death cases, in the case of death cases, the widow will also be eligible for this pension, even if the original recipient is unable to collect in person, provided she does not remarry.'

Five hundred rupees was what the Defence Minister spent on cigarettes every day, but martyrs had different living standards. The assembled bureaucrats burst into wild applause. The paperwork for this pension increase had been rushed through in just eleven years. Inflation had caused some erosion in value, but it was nevertheless a tremendous gesture of support for the armed forces. The General smiled and shook his head.

The PM raised her voice to make herself heard over the din, taking full advantage of the fact that no one was paying her the slightest attention.

'Lee, this is your best chance in a hundred years,' she said urgently, 'they're distracted. Do what you have to do.'

She chewed the tip of her thumb as she listened.

'I'm not dragging you into anything,' she said. 'Just promise me you'll think about it.'

The Defence Minister smiled for the cameras, holding up a giant five-hundred-rupee note specially printed for the occasion. The widow of a martyr stood ready to receive it, petrified. There was a stampede as a posse of portly officials tried to fit into the frame. The army officers, who knew all about strategic exits, slipped out quietly, and vanished into the night.

The PM slipped her phone into her purse. She looked triumphant. 'I think he's going to do it!' she said. Her eyes shone and her smile was dazzling. The General stood up and held out his hand, which she gratefully took to pull herself up.

Her stamina wasn't what it used to be.

One thing still puzzled him. 'Where did you get the phone from?' he asked, as he followed her out of the hall.

'At a Japanese restaurant,' said the PM. 'It came free with the meal.'

❑

As the CA loosened his trousers and prepared for his siesta, leaning back in his big leather chair, he spotted a memo marked 'Urgent' on his table. It was the second time in two days that Mehta had used the word 'urgent' on a document meant for his perusal. He shook his head at this lamentable state of affairs.

He read the memo, frowning. Taiwan had declared independence. In a strongly worded statement, Prime Minister Lee had said that, in deference to the wishes of the local population, he was abandoning the fiction that Taiwan would ever rejoin the motherland. 'From today,' he had declared at a press conference, 'Taiwan takes its place in the community of nations, proud, brave, and free.'

They were certainly proud, thought the CA sourly. They might even be brave. But it was unlikely that they would be free for very long. The whole thing was laughable, like a mosquito goosing an elephant. It might cause the Chinese some very brief inconvenience. However, the inevitable forces of history, guided by his expert hand, were now in motion. Things were moving inexorably towards their logical conclusion.

❏

All evening and long into the night, the whispers spread through the streets of Calcutta. He is coming, they whispered, he is coming. The air was thick with the smell of blood. Weapons were unwrapped. Quotas were fixed. Revenge was sworn for offences yet to be committed. Trucks were loaded. Flags were unpacked. Neighbours eyed neighbours, and thought new thoughts. Passers-by estimated the value of goods in shops. Leaders pored over maps and deployed their forces. The British slept, exhausted, and dreamt of fish and chips, and fields of green, and revenge on Winston Churchill. Yet through it all, the whispers spread, and not everyone relinquished hope.

He is coming, they whispered. He is coming.

78

'I like Shakespeare, too, although I think your work has more impact.'

'You are a handbag!' said Natasamrat Ghanashyam Das, poking his young colleague in the chest for emphasis.

Mrinal gulped nervously, and his unnaturally large Adam's apple bobbed up and down. He was a tall, weedy young man with jug ears, buckteeth and slightly protruding eyes. He usually played the pitiful character in their productions, mainly because he was. Ghanashyam Das was unwilling to accept this situation. Ghanashyam Das believed that in order to be worthy of sharing the stage with him, each and every performer in his company had to achieve a minimum standard of histrionic excellence. Ghanashyam Das had sworn a mighty oath that he would turn Mrinal into a proper actor.

'Why are you trembling?' demanded Ghanashyam Das, poking him in the chest again and sending him stumbling back. 'Does a handbag tremble?'

Mrinal stopped trembling.

Ghanashyam Das pulled his hand back and slapped him hard.

'Ouch,' said Mrinal.

'Ouch?' said Ghanashyam Das. 'Did you say "ouch"? Have you ever heard a handbag say "ouch"?'

He pounced on one of the actresses who was sitting on the ground with the rest of the cast, clutching her handbag to her chest. The moment she had heard Ghanashyam Das utter the word 'handbag', she had feared the worst. The thespian snatched the handbag from her quivering hands, held it up and slapped it repeatedly.

'Is it saying "ouch"?' he demanded, as he assaulted the bag in a frenzy. 'Do you hear it saying "ouch"?'

He flung the bag to the ground and jumped up and down on it with both feet. The sound of an assortment of things breaking filled the air, but otherwise the bag was silent.

'How about now?' demanded Ghanashyam Das, even as he continued to jump up and down on the remains of the handbag. 'Do you hear it saying "ouch" now?'

He stepped off what was left of the handbag and brought his face very close to Mrinal's.

'Is this why I made you memorize Stanislavski?' he asked, enunciating clearly, his voice loud enough to bounce off the back walls. 'You must become whatever I ask you to become, both inside and out. Just because you are the son of a truck driver, you think you cannot be an actor? I am Natasamrat Ghanashyam Das, winner of thirty-four gold medals, felicitated on three separate occasions by the Theosophical Society. *Ananda Bazar Patrika* regularly refers to my performances as "unforgettable". The Maharaja of Burdwan wept when I played Karl Marx, and tore off his ruby necklace and threw it at my feet. The

Governor-General was overcome when he saw me play Alexander, and could not speak for days. The Chief Justice of the Calcutta High Court once disposed of three whole cases in one afternoon, without taking a single nap, just so he could reach the theatre on time. No theatrical achievement is beyond my capabilities. I can turn anyone into an actor. I swear I will make an actor out of you, even if it is the last thing that I do. Now go and stand in the corner facing the wall, and don't come back to me until you have become a handbag.'

Ali had seen Ghanashyam Das perform, so the Stanislavski reference puzzled him. His acting style had seemed more manic than method, particularly the parts where he beat his chest or laughed on demand. Ghanashyam Das had asked him to wait until he had finished conducting his workshop, and Ali had been watching with keen interest, having once nurtured ambitions of acting himself. He also had a plan—one that did not involve hideous acts of terror, like putting on a suicide belt and blowing up Suhrawardy.

Ghanashyam Das turned to Ali, wiping the froth from his false beard with a large, red handkerchief. The make-up man scurried across to him and deftly removed it, leaving his face free of vegetation.

'I was rehearsing for our next production,' explained Ghanashyam Das, 'Life of Ramakrishna. I have done Life of Hitler—foreign military leader, then Life of Netaji—Indian military leader. Now I am doing Life of Ramakrishna—Indian religious leader. Subsequently I will be starring in and as Life of Joan of Arc—foreign religious leader. In this way I will vividly demonstrate the brotherhood of man, including women. I see the question mark on your face. You are perplexed, is it not? How can the same actor play both a German man and a French girl, you wonder? Will the audience digest it? Let me tell you, I have devotees across the length and breadth of Bengal, even in Chittagong, where they cannot speak proper Bengali, and do terrible things to fish. My devotees can digest anything.'

'Gurudeb, you will receive marriage proposals from Paris afterwards,' said one of his cast members, 'it's inevitable.' He was a portly, sinister individual with a French-cut beard, who served as an understudy to the Great Man and nursed a secret ambition to play Caligula. He had already translated the script, written by Camus, yet another French person, and often left it lying around artfully where Ghanashyam Das

Shovon Chowdhury

might see it. He lived in the hope that Ghanashyam Das would eventually get over his heroic phase and see the virtues of a script full of orgies, gluttony, and plenty of declining and falling. In this he was mistaken. Ghanashyam Das was far from done with history—Napoleon, the Buddha and Jesus loomed large in his future.

Ghanashyam Das sat down on the edge of the stage, and one of his followers began fanning him with a peacock feather, left over from the Life of Shah Jahan.

'I really like the theatre, and I thought you were spectacular,' said Ali. Good reviews were the key to this man's heart.

'That is very obvious,' said Ghanashyam Das, 'since you are wearing a picture of Othello on your chest. I have often considered doing him. Such determination! Such character! Such pride! I myself prefer the biographical approach, but so far as fictional characters go, he is quite impressive.'

'I like Shakespeare, too,' said Ali, 'although I think your work has more impact.'

Ghanashyam Das acknowledged his praise with a gracious nod of his head, momentarily distracted by the sight of the make-up man combing the Ramakrishna beard. With minor alterations, it could be made to look just like the beard of Abraham Lincoln . . .

Ali cleared his throat.

'So, which of my performances is your favourite?' asked the thespian amiably.

'Netaji, of course,' said Ali quite truthfully, since this was the only performance he had seen.

Ghanashyam Das nodded happily. 'One of my greatest triumphs,' he said, 'over three hundred shows and still going strong. I was once held prisoner in Kankurgachhi, where the audience demanded that I perform the entire play all over again. They paid double, not counting the coins they threw on stage.'

'Sir, I have a proposition for you,' said Ali. 'I'm afraid there's no money in it, but you'll change the course of history. No one will ever forget your name.'

Ghanashyam Das was intrigued. Recreating history was one thing. Actually participating in it was a different sort of challenge altogether.

'Go on,' he said. His cast members huddled closer. They could sense drama in the air.

Ali told them his plan. He knew parts of it would tax their imagination, but these were people who could imagine Ghanashyam Das as Joan of Arc. They could handle it. There was silence for a while after he finished.

'It's as if I was born to provide this service to the nation,' said Ghanashyam Das, overwhelmed by what Ali expected of him.

'If tomorrow is to be the day that I die, I will die happy, knowing that I have reached the pinnacle of my career.'

The cast burst into an excited hubbub, debating the finer points of what needed to be done. They would need costumes, and make-up, and weapons, and a tea boy. Luckily no sets would have to be constructed, but the property requirements would be considerable.

'Hey, Mrinal!' shouted one of them. 'Go get your dad. We're going to need his truck.'

Mrinal was still in a corner, pretending to be a handbag. Much enthused by his new mission, he rushed off to find his father.

'Do you guys do pre-publicity?' asked Ali. 'We need to build some buzz.'

'Leave that to me,' said one of the young men, veteran of many a campaign from Jamshedpur to Jalpaiguri. His megaphone voice was unavoidable. 'By the time I'm finished, the whole of Calcutta will be buzzing!'

'Get the costume back from the dhobi,' commanded Ghanashyam Das, and retired to the green room to do vocal exercises. He had to prepare for the greatest performance of his life.

It was a long shot, Ali knew. He was running out of time. Direct Action Day was less than twenty-four hours away.

79

'That's where the Pope and David Beckham come in.'

The General was wondering whether he could give his guards the slip and creep out for a round of golf, but it seemed unlikely. They were an extremely able bunch of young men, completely unsympathetic to his need for fresh air. Besides, they were some of the few elite commandos actually performing military duties. They knew that even a minor slip-up would end up with them carrying shopping bags for a minister's girlfriend. They had no intention of messing up.

The General was in his Command Bunker, and he was feeling mildly claustrophobic. He had no choice. In the old days, the Indian army used to be of the view that fallout shelters were symbols of cowardice, fit only for wimps and sissies. As a result, during the last war, all the top brass had been wiped out in the first three minutes, which had hampered the war effort considerably. Since then, it had become mandatory for the commander-in-chief to skulk when war was imminent, so here he was, skulking. To an Indian army officer brought up in the finest traditions of leading from the front, it went against the grain. His father had charged up a hill at Kargil and here he was leading his troops from a rat-hole under Rajpath. It rankled deeply, but orders were orders.

The bunker had been built by the Bureau of Reconstruction, so it came with inherent handicaps. All the toilets were Indian style, because the CA took great pleasure in making his officers squat during times of crisis. Water supply was intermittent, and the General usually got his orderly to buy bottles of water from a nearby store, which was above ground, and would cease to exist in the event of a nuclear strike. There was a large supply of canned food, but most of the cans were at least a decade past their expiry date. If the Chinese nuked them again, the inmates of the bunker would die of either thirst or botulism. If the Chinese don't get us, the General thought gloomily, procurement will.

His gloom had no effect on Navalkar, who was whistling happily at his desk. He loved the shelter. All he really wanted from life was a sexy computer, a smooth connection and solid air-conditioning.

'All right!' said Navalkar, throwing up his hands, and knocking over his lucky teddy bear. The teddy bear eyed him from the floor reproachfully. It was wearing a T-shirt that said *I love Pune*.

'Beaten your own high score, have you?' inquired the General politely. Navalkar looked hurt.

'I'm working,' he said, 'in fact, I'm making major contributions to the war effort.'

'We haven't actually declared war yet,' said the General, 'you might want to wait till I give you the signal.'

'Oh, this is a pre-emptive strike,' said Navalkar, 'it's a Pearl Harbor sort of thing.'

He waited expectantly.

The General sighed. 'Fair enough, tell me all about it.'

'Listen to this,' said Navalkar. He tapped finger and thumb. A small, pink unicorn appeared on his desk, its expression stern. 'This declaration of independence is a slap in the face of the Motherland!' said the unicorn. 'The words of the filthy Taiwan splittist Lee are like the explosive diarrhoea of a rogue elephant'

'I had no idea you had such strong feelings about Taiwan,' said the General mildly.

'That's not me,' said Navalkar, 'that's someone on Renren. Here's another one. It's brief and to the point.'

It was David Beckham.

'Taiwan will be ours, or Taiwan will be dust,' said Beckham. His lips twisted scornfully. 'All those who think otherwise should wear green hats and join their mothers in a brothel.'

'Kashmir. Same thing,' said the General, 'except for the green hats. Didn't end well.'

Spider-Man swung in. His expression was malevolent. He leaped off the desk and clung to a wall, shimmering. 'Why are our leaders hiding like cowardly monkeys in the Forbidden Palace?' he demanded. 'Have they no shame? Have they no patriotic feeling for China? Chinese people will watch, Chinese people will wait, then Chinese people will remove the thing under the crotch and feed it to them, piece by piece, after thoroughly roasting over slow fire.'

'I like this one too,' said Navalkar, 'it's concise and anatomical.'

A small Pope appeared. His demeanour was ungodly. His invective was flecked with super-realistic spittle.

'Premier Wen is a cowardly dog,' spat His Holiness, 'may his grandchildren be born with unperforated anuses.'

'I think I get the idea,' said the General, 'the Chinese public is clearly very worked up over Taiwan.'

'Well, not yet,' said Navalkar, 'but they soon will be.'

The General eyed Navalkar thoughtfully. He knew Navalkar had been up to something. He had been uncharacteristically active recently, making mysterious phone calls and spending long hours hunched at his desk. From time to time, he'd been leaning back in his chair, looking up at the ceiling and giggling to himself like a virgin groom just before an arranged marriage.

'What exactly do you mean?' asked the General.

'Well, a few of us got together and decided there's no point hanging around waiting for the Chinese to drop the bomb. We need to take swift, decisive action, like Julius Caesar.'

'And here I was thinking that declaring war was the prerogative of the Prime Minister,' said the General.

Navalkar smiled bashfully.

'What exactly have you done?'

'Well, you just heard from all these angry Chinese people, right? All steamed up about Taiwan?'

'They seemed quite upset.'

'The thing is, they're not angry Chinese people. They're people in Bangalore, pretending to be angry Chinese people.'

The General was genuinely impressed. During the last war, they had suffered mightily at the hands of communist cyber ninjas, who had given a whole new meaning to the phrase party hack. His understanding was limited, but it seemed like his boys had done something clever.

'What difference will a few fake messages make?' he asked.

'It's not a few fake messages. We have 200,000 call centre people on the job, posing as virtual angry Chinese youth. Each one is posting ten messages every hour. Thousands more are coming online every minute.'

One of the few big cities left intact after the war, Bangalore remained full to the brim with hard-working vegetarians, and was blessed with a moral climate wherein they were undistracted by short skirts and other Western abominations. This made them phenomenally productive and helped the IT industry maintain its competitive edge, although margins were under pressure due to unexpected competition from Inner Mongolia. It was also the capital of the liquor industry, so dispositions were generally cheerful. Apparently every Bangalorean in the IT and BPO sectors was in the army now, fighting from the basement, just like him. I ought to give them a name, thought the General, like the 7th Bangalore Rifles, or the Auxiliary Mouse Corps.

'What will all this achieve?' he asked.

'Critical mass,' said Navalkar. 'A lot of people in China keep close tabs on the angry youth, so they know what to be angry about. They read the messages, get angry, and post messages of their own. This makes others angry, leading to more angry messages. The growth in angry messages should be massive and exponential. Some of the net police will have nervous breakdowns. Others will join the angry youth, adding to the confusion, and leading once more to the arrest of undercover officers by other undercover officers. The government will be unable to process all the information fast enough, which will delay their reactions, making people even angrier, leading to more angry messages, generating more information that needs to be checked, putting further pressure on the net police, who are by this time thinking of volunteering for Siberia. We could keep them confused for weeks.'

'Well done!' said the General, slapping Navalkar on the back. 'We should share this news with the PM,'

'I already did,' said Navalkar, 'I'm helping with her master plan.'

'Would you like to fill me in?' asked the General, with great restraint.

'The plan works at two levels,' said Navalkar. 'There's an angry youth level, which I have already shared with you. That's where the Pope and David Beckham come in. But there's also a Small Leading Group angle.'

'What's a Small Leading Group?' asked the General, imagining determined hobbits.

'The Young Prince is just like the PM. He doesn't really run anything, but the mandarins let him think so. They keep him well supplied with chicks and chocolates, and a private Disneyland with special rides that only he can enjoy. The people who really matter are the two hundred members of the Central Committee, who take time off from their businesses to meet once in a while. Most of them are related by marriage. Whenever they discover that someone is dead, they replace him with his nearest blood relative. They vote for each other once every two years. They run everything. They have to. They own everything.'

'It must be hard to keep track,' said the General.

'It is,' said Navalkar, 'sometimes they have to call up *The Economist*. The whole thing is too complex for one man to manage. There's a school of thought in China which believes that Chairman Mao was not just 60 per cent right and 40 per cent wrong, he was nutty as a fruit cake. They believe it was the pressure that did him in. To avoid a repeat, two hundred men in dark suits now do the same job. They form Small Leading Groups of three or four each. Each SLG takes all the decisions on a particular subject. There's a Small Leading Group for Taiwan, which is currently paralyzed with fear because Taiwan has declared independence, and everyone thinks it's their fault. Things are worse than they think. One of the members of this particular SLG is an enemy spy. He's a Taiwanese mole who was planted long ago as part of a deep-rooted conspiracy. Taiwanese spies are notoriously hard to detect.'

The General was impressed. They had a mole on the Central Committee. 'What is the spy doing for them?'

'More like what is he not doing for them. He's urging masterly inactivity. His colleagues are too terrified to think straight. One wrong step on this one, and they'll be exhibits at the Gulag Memorial in Siberia, now managed by the PLA. As a result, the government is doing nothing. This is making people even angrier. Our artificial angry youths in Bangalore help feed that anger.'

'Why don't I just hand over everything to you and go home?' asked the General.

Navalkar smiled modestly and looked down at his shoes. The General slapped him on the back again.

'Keep up the good work! Buck up the Bangalore boys, and don't let them take too many pee breaks. Give the enemy no relief. Keep messing with their minds. It's what we do best.'

'Don't you worry, sir,' said Navalkar. 'We'll fuck their ancestors to the eighteenth generation.'

He was getting quite good at Chinese curses.

80

'He kept saying "Hema Malini is coming! Hema Malini is coming!"'

Ram Manohar Pande spent the last day of his life doing what he did best. It was late in the evening, and he was making his preparations, chivvying along his juvenile task force with the choicest of abuses, and occasional pokes in the bum with his lathi. The rest of the villagers were making preparations of their own. While any actual acts of preparation were yet to take place, a lively exchange of ideas was in progress. As always, the village square was full of opinions.

'The most important thing is to protect the cows and the goats,' said Jit Ram, an elderly patriarch with a long white beard, 'they will suffer the most.'

'This is true,' said Mangat Ram, his contemporary and rival, a constant source of astonishment to everyone because he was the only fat person in the village. 'During the last bomb blast, over two hundred of my goats fell sick, and their milk became sour. Malti and Chhavi developed sores on their udders and died.'

The crowd made sympathetic noises, and wiped away furtive tears. They all remembered Malti and Chhavi, two of the finest cows the village had ever seen.

'Maybe we should propitiate the Big Cow,' suggested the village priest.

'Which Big Cow?' asked a callow youth, who had rotted his brain by watching too much television, as many in the village had predicted he would. The elders shook their heads dolefully. What was the village coming to, when its youth didn't even know about the Big Cow? The problem was there were too many young people, and not enough time to teach all of them properly.

'The world rests on the horn of the Big Cow,' explained the village priest patiently, 'she holds the world steady, otherwise we would all fall off, as any scientist could tell you. Sometimes, the Big Cow gets tired and then she shifts the world from one horn to the other. At times like this, the earth shakes, and the situation generally becomes difficult. That is what happened twenty-five years ago. I think she is tired once more, which is only natural. The world is very heavy. Plus population has increased, which is why sarkar is regularly doing campaigns like small family, happy family.'

'Where can we find this Big Cow?' asked the callow youth, who was actually quite a practical fellow, and would go on to run a successful roadside dhaba by installing a television in it, and charging a little bit extra whenever there was a cricket match on.

'Arrey, son of a donkey,' said the priest, 'the Big Cow is too big for you or me to see. If you did see her, you would go blind.'

'So what can we do then?' persisted the callow youth. 'What is the sense of telling us this if there is nothing we can do?'

'We can pray to her,' said the priest, sensing a once-in-a-lifetime opportunity. 'If all of you contribute ten rupees each, I will buy lots of good food, and perform a great puja. Once she receives our offerings, she will recover her strength, and then perhaps she will not need to shift the world to her other horn.' He added hastily, 'Although I cannot guarantee it.'

There was an uncomfortable silence. The villagers hid their annoyance as best they could. Thanks to births, marriages, deaths and innumerable auspicious days, enumerated by the holy calendar with suspicious frequency, the priest was already getting a lifetime's supply of ghee, bananas and dhotis, all of which he consumed on behalf of the Gods. They were not particularly inclined to add to his stash. In addition, most of them were pretty sure the upcoming convulsion had more to do with the army than the Big Cow. But it seemed rude to point this out, in broad daylight, in the village square. One had to respect one's traditions. Otherwise one would be rootless and confused.

The priest bustled off busily, thinking up new rituals as he went. He looked back over his shoulder as he left.

'There is no pressure on any of you. I'll start making arrangements. Those of you who wish to contribute, just come to my house.'

He smiled to himself as he walked off. The Big Cow was ready for milking.

Pande watched him go with a pang of regret. He was a Brahmin himself, and might well have stayed back in his village and spent his life doing what this man did. It was pretty easy money at the end of the day. But on the whole, he was more of a city person, temperamentally unsuited to rustic idylls. In addition, as a policeman, he was in a higher income bracket, with the added perk of being able to tread at will on the downtrodden.

Reminded thus of his role in society, he expertly planted his boot on the backside of the carpenter, who was squatting near his feet, fiddling desultorily with miscellaneous pieces of wood.

'Hurry up, motherfucker,' he snarled, 'I could give birth to two-three children in the time you're taking.'

'I'm doing the best I can, your worship,' said the carpenter plaintively, 'but my throat is very dry. If you gave me a little advance money, I'd wet my throat a little bit, then you watch how I work.'

'Shut your mouth and move your hands, chutiya,' said Pande.

Again with the money! What was wrong with these people? Wherever he went, people in Rajasthan were asking him for money. He blamed the local police. They were a disgrace to their uniforms. At least the little boys had made no financial demands. They were busy messing around with paintbrushes and a bucket of paint, practising on a large piece of paper while the carpenter did his job.

The discussion had shifted from the spiritual to the temporal.

'What do we do about compenshun?' asked Jit Ram.

Many of the villagers nudged each other, mystified. A few of them snorted. Who did Jit Ram think he was, pretending he knew English?

'That's a good question you've raised, Brother Jit Ram,' said Mangat Ram, 'we need to talk to gorment.'

'You will get nothing from gorment!' quavered another old man, bursting on to the scene with no advance warning whatsoever. He was even more ancient than the two village elders. His voice was hauntingly familiar.

Pande stared at him, astonished. It was the semi-comatose hookah-suckler whom he had met twice before near the entrance to the village. The villagers, who considered him to be more mineral than human, were equally nonplussed. A hushed silence fell over the congregation. The old man took up position in the middle of the village square.

'What compenshun are you talking about?' he raved. 'Last time, they took half my land to do their bomb blast. How much do you think they paid me? Four rupees per bigha! Can you believe it? Four rupees! I asked for eighteen, but they said, no, four rupees is enough compenshun for you. That too I had to give three rupees to the clerk, else I would have got nothing. We went to Delhi to meet Indira Gandhi and she promised to give more, but that rascal clerk stole everything! We will go back to Indira Gandhi, we said, you will get into trouble for this, and he laughed at us saying, go, go, nothing will happen, she may be ruling in Delhi, but I am ruling here. So don't talk about compenshun! Gorment will give you nothing! That Jagjivan, my neighbour, after the blast he went mad, he took off all his clothes and ran through the village naked with his noonoo flapping in the wind for all to see. Did gorment give him any compenshun? Nothing, nothing. We gave him buttermilk, but it did not help. He kept saying, "Hema Malini is coming, Hema Malini is coming!" After that, he had to be kept tied to his bed, and he would only stop shouting if we showed him a picture of Hema Malini. His wife used to say, see, now he has taken a second wife, that too South Indian, and beat him up regularly with a rolling pin. So much he suffered! What compenshun did gorment give him? Nothing!'

He brandished his hookah threateningly, enraged by the iniquities of the government, shouting hideous curses until two of his great grandchildren pushed their way through the crowd and dragged him off, still cursing.

No one said anything. The villagers were shocked into silence by this overdose of sex, violence and nudity.

'Perhaps we should go and meet Hema Malini,' said someone eventually.

'Don't be silly,' said someone else, 'we should all go and meet Indira Gandhi. Maybe if we all go together . . .'

'Indira Gandhi cannot be alive anymore,' said Mangat Ram, the voice of reason, 'unless she is some sort of djinn or spirit, as is rumoured by some. All this happened twenty-five years ago.'

'Someone else is the ruler now,' ventured a voice from the crowd, 'I think he is from the Bharatiya Janata Party.'

'Yes, yes,' said someone else excitedly, 'I think I saw a picture of him once. His face is like a jackfruit.'

'I know of this man,' said Jit Ram, solemnly, 'there are rumours that he drinks.'

'Then it is hopeless,' said Mangat Ram gloomily, 'even if he promises anything, he will forget about it later. My brother-in-law drinks, and he never remembers anything.'

'There is no point in worrying about compensation,' said Irfan, who had so far remained silent out of deference to his elders. 'This village always votes Congress, and the government now is BJP. We will get nothing from them. We should move with all our goats and cows to some neighbouring village. Then we should all pray to Allah, or Vishnu, as the case may be, and hope for the best.'

There were general murmurs of agreement. Irfan usually knew best, being a reading-writing type of person with the right attitude towards his elders. Besides, he treated his animals very well, exactly as their guruji would have wanted him to. Five hundred years ago, their guruji had seen the devastation caused by a drought, and understood the reason for their misery. Because they had abused nature, nature was punishing them. Accordingly, he had laid down twenty-nine rules, binding their lives to all things living, which was why they were known as the Bishnoi, or the Twenty-nine. Protect the trees, he had said, and do not slay animals, because otherwise, on your deathbed, you will hear the cries of all the creatures that you slew.

'What about the dogs?' demanded one of the little boys. 'We'll be taking the dogs too, right?'

'Yes, of course we will,' said Irfan, smiling at him.

The villagers dispersed, and hurried off to round up their livestock. The air was soon filled with dust, and the sound of braying.

❑

'Sarkar, I've finished,' said the thirsty carpenter, holding up a large signboard. It was slightly crooked, but it would do. 'Will you give me some money, now? There's a man I have to see,' he added, craftily.

'First you put up the sign and then we'll see,' said Pande, 'bring it with you to the site. Hey, you cut-pieces, you also come.'

Pande strode off towards the outskirts of the village, followed by the little boys, the thirsty carpenter, Irfan, and the small dog which had, suicidally, taken a liking to him.

The strange procession climbed up the hillock, and soon enough, they were looking down at the sand dunes that were the scene of frenetic military activity just a few hours earlier. A solitary guard stood on duty. There was nothing much to guard, except goats, and a large contingent of troops in the middle of the desert would have given the game away.

'Put the sign down,' said Pande to the carpenter, who did so, rubbing his throat piteously but wisely keeping his peace.

'Now you boys paint what I told you to paint.'

The boys went at their job with gusto, with much giggling and pushing and shoving. They got as much paint on themselves as they did on the board, but in the end Pande was satisfied with the result.

'Did you boys bring the football like I told you?' demanded Pande. The ball was produced, and one of them started dribbling.

'Stop that, sisterfucker!' barked Pande.

Irfan eyed him darkly, but said nothing.

'Two of you, go down there with the ball towards that army-wallah, like I told you. The rest of you follow me.'

Two of the boys ran down the hillock dribbling the ball, directly towards the sentry, yelling and whooping with delight. Once they were close, they veered away from him.

Shovon Chowdhury

'Hoy!' said the soldier, horrified. 'Hoy!'

If his hawaldar-major spotted this, he could face imprisonment up to three months, or a fine up to five hundred rupees, or both. He hitched his rifle on his shoulder and set off in pursuit of the miscreants, who were dribbling towards a goalpost somewhere in the distance.

Pande, the other boys and the carpenter quickly scrambled down the hillock and hid behind a sand dune, flat on their bellies, out of the soldier's line of sight.

'Put up the sign,' ordered Pande.

In truth, the carpenter was too weak and dehydrated to work any more, but he had developed a healthy respect for Pande. In a matter of minutes, the sign was up. Job done, they crawled back up the hillock on their hands and knees, the boys miraculously silent. What an excellent adventure they were having! Except that next time they would remember to wear pants while crawling through sand.

For a while, Pande stood on top of the hillock, his hands on his hips, filled with the satisfaction of a job well done. This was not an opportunity that he often enjoyed. The board was perfect. The writing was legible, the angle just right. He took a step back to admire his handiwork. He stepped back, onto the tail of the cheerful little dog as it were, who had been nestling fondly behind his feet. Unused to mistreatment by humans, the dog leaped up and bit him in the leg.

Pande drew his revolver. He was completely fed up with the way dogs had infested his investigation, right from the beginning—from dogs appearing miraculously in that rich man's house to that Bengali bitch and the trick she'd played on him with her neighbour's dog; pretending she wanted it dead while actually they were best friends. Enough was enough. He took careful aim.

The last three things that he ever remembered were the sound of a young boy screaming with rage, the sensation of juvenile teeth sinking into the fleshy part of his unwounded buttock, and the sight of Irfan's heavy, metal-tipped lathi, descending towards his head.

This case had begun with dogs, thought Pande, a split second before he died. It was only natural that it would end with one too.

'Hey, Hank, check this out.'

Hank came over to the monitor, which showed the barren sands of Pokhran, live via satellite. Embedded in a dune was a crudely painted

sign which said 'HELLO AMERICANS! NUKULAR BOM WILL
EXPLOD HERE!'

They had a good laugh about it.

'Like we're going to fall for that one . . .'

Hank went home and told his wife. She thought it was funny too.

Three days later, the Buddha smiled.

81

'That Pande was always going to die at the hands of a villager.'

Kader Khan, sixteen, proprietor of KK Mobile Shoppee, was watching
cartoon porn. He was developing a taste for it. It appealed to both the
adult and the child in him. His boys were working all around him,
hunched over their mobiles. One or two were playing games, but Kader
Khan didn't mind. So long as they repaired their twenty phones a day
and never asked for a holiday he was fine.

'Pintoo, check this out, man,' he shouted, 'once you see this, you'll
also want to be a rabbit!'

Pintoo was halfway across the room when he froze, and dropped to his
knees. 'Oh, my God,' he said, clutching his head. 'No!'

'What's up?' said Kader Khan, on his feet, instantly. 'Brothers, lend a
hand.'

The boys got Pintoo back on his feet. His face was ashen.

'What's wrong, Pintoo?' asked Kader Khan.

'I think I just killed someone,' said Pintoo.

'No, you didn't,' said Kader Khan, 'you're not capable of it. I've
known you since you were a kid. I don't know what all you've been
doing, and there's no need for me to know. There's no give and take for
me in that. But you should go home and rest. The others will make up
your quota, won't you boys?'

The boys raised a limited cheer.

He pressed a mobile into his hand. 'Keep this,' he said, 'I should have
given you one long ago.'

Pintoo tried to protest.

'Don't worry,' said Kader Khan, 'I'm deducting two rupees from your salary every month. That means you'll be working for me for the rest of your life, and at least one of your children is mine.'

'I killed someone,' said Pintoo.

'No, you didn't,' said Kader Khan. 'Go home and rest, brother.'

'Good thing you've come, Pintoo,' said Banani, 'we have to meet the babaji in half an hour, followed by this Competent Authority.'

She was sitting on the porch behind Tarun-da's house. The Ancient Headmaster and Tarun-da were with her. The view was terrible, with the nala in the foreground and the blasted ruins of the Red Fort in the distance, but it was quiet.

'That oily creep from the body bank sent us a message. Can you send different parts of a person to different places, Pintoo? If that guy gets any fresher, I swear I'm going to do something nasty.'

Pintoo sat down next to her. His legs were a little steadier now.

'Pande's dead,' said Pintoo. He put his hand on her arm. 'Don't worry, Uncle's okay. He's on his way to meet Gandhiji. But Pande's dead. He almost made it. I think he was a good choice. But he attacked a dog, and then a villager killed him.'

'Samrat almost got him, too,' said Banani. 'He was a good dog. I hope he's okay.'

'That Pande was always going to die at the hands of a villager,' said Tarun-da, from under a tree.

'Or a dog,' added Banani.

It was as much of an epitaph as Pande would get. He would have expected no different.

'It looks like your plan might not work, Pintoo,' sighed Banani.

'It was never going to be easy,' said Pintoo, 'but that's no excuse for not trying. Uncle is just about to meet Gandhiji. Gandhiji was super intelligent. He could think of something. And would you not trust Ali bhaiyya?'

Never having met Ali, Banani was not encouraged by this.

'Shanti-bai said we have to look at today, not yesterday. That's where we live. We know who's in charge today. The oily boy from the Bank of Bodies told us. We're going to meet this person for their business deal. It might be the only time. I don't think we should waste it.'

'I'm not going to kill anyone,' said Pintoo.

Banani put her arm around him. 'No one's asking you to, sweetie,' she said, 'but we may get only one chance.'

'I know,' said Pintoo, 'that's why I've been practising with Ranvir bhaiyya. I have a plan. I think I've learnt a new thing.'

'One Competent Authority will go,' said Tarun-da, 'another will follow. What will we achieve by this?'

'It's like cockroaches,' said Banani, 'cockroaches are tough. They can survive anything. They're the only creatures whose population has increased since the war. Cockroaches breed best in the dark. This Competent Authority and his friends, they're exactly the same.'

'In that case, what are we achieving?' asked Tarun-da.

'Once one of them is out in the light,' said Banani, 'the others will know we can see them.'

82

'Who dares call me a Hindu?'

At 7:30 a.m. on 16 August 1946, the Muslims attacked the Hindu barricades at Tala and Belgachhia bridges, erected to prevent them from attending the great rally called by Suhrawardy at the Ochterlony Monument.

At 9 a.m., the police told Brigadier Mackinlay not to worry. There would be incidents, they said, but not much violence. The troops could stay in their barracks.

At 10 a.m., the shops started burning in the north and the east. Smoke rose above the city, and mingled with the monsoon clouds. It was a typical Calcutta monsoon day, hot and sticky.

At 11 a.m., Hindus started attacking Muslim processions as they marched to their meeting at the monument. No one died, but many were wounded.

At 11:30 a.m., Gopal Patha gathered the men who had survived the fight with the Muslim League thugs at the Sangu Valley Restaurant. 'Two milkmen have been killed in Beliaghata,' he said. 'Their throats were slit in front of their children. This is a critical time for the country. If you hear of one murder, you must kill ten more. A ratio of ten-to-one—that is what I expect.'

At noon, the inspector general, the deputy commissioner and the additional secretary met, and wondered whether they might need the army after all. The police were confident, however, and declared that they would deal with it.

By 2 p.m., an immense crowd had gathered at the Ochterlony Monument, a teeming mass of humanity that covered the maidan and spilled over on to the streets. It was a holiday, and the atmosphere was festive. Many had brought their children along to see the fun. A few had brought tiffin, to eat after the show.

At 4 p.m., Husain Shaheed Suhrawardy stood up to speak. He drew his strength from crowds, and this was the biggest crowd he had ever seen. All of them had come to hear him speak! No one will forget this day, he thought. My name will live forever. In this, he was not mistaken. One of his aides, standing on the dais behind him, could see the smoke rising from College Street, just a few miles away, where the shops were already ablaze. He was perplexed. Did no one else see it? But if his leaders found it normal, who was he to interfere? He bit his lip and kept his peace.

Ali stood at the back of the crowd, near Chowringhee. He eyed the street anxiously. The truck was late. Timing was everything. It was a forlorn hope, but it was all that he had. What was keeping them?

'Is it time yet?' hissed a man just next to him.

'Not yet,' said another, 'Brother Suhrawardy will give the signal. Be patient.'

Ali looked around. The crowd was full of goondas, mingling comfortably with the happy families. Some of them held their weapons aloft, while the more discreet kept them hidden in the folds of their dhotis.

Suhrawardy stood up. The crowd fell silent. Somewhere, a child cried, his voice echoing eerily across the maidan.

'First of all,' said Suhrawardy, 'I want to thank all of you for your good work for Pakistan.'

A great roar went up from the crowd.

Suhrawardy raised his hand.

'This cabinet meeting in Delhi is all bluff. Nothing will come of it. As long as I am here, let me see how the British give Bengal to Mr Nehru!'

Another roar went up, although not quite so loud this time. Not all of them hated Nehru quite as much as Suhrawardy would have wished, but he was here and Nehru was not. It was a question of etiquette.

Ali took another look at the street. It was full of people. Calcutta Tramways had declared a holiday, because they wanted their employees to join the fun, so walking was the only mode of conveyance today. The streets were mysteriously free of rickshaws, and as he watched, Ali understood why. Scarcely a hundred yards away, three men separated a solitary rickshaw puller from his rickshaw, and hacked him down where he stood. One of them cut the little bell off the handlebar as he lay there dying, and they walked off, victorious, brandishing it aloft like a trophy. The little bell tinkled merrily. A few yards away stood a group of policemen, watching them, beaming with pride. They were direct ancestors of Ram Manohar Pande. It had taken generations of careful breeding to create him.

Meanwhile, Suhrawardy was getting into his stride.

'Direct Action Day is just the first step in the Muslim struggle for emancipation,' he said, 'we are all together in this. We will never be ruled by the Hindu bania, whose servant is Mahatma Gandhi. We do not believe in foolish tenets like non-violence, but I know you are all good people, and generally, Muslims have behaved well. If we are oppressed, then naturally we will retaliate, but otherwise, I urge you to keep the peace.'

A sigh passed through the crowd. People heard what they wanted to hear, and for those who were not sure, there were others to explain the message. Ali looked back down the street anxiously. Where the hell was that truck? He missed his mobile.

Suhrawardy was winding up. His job was done, and he knew it. By now many in the crowd could see the smoke rising from College Street, and they began to wonder. As they wondered, people across the city died silently. Some were not so silent, but they were too far away to be heard.

'Please,' said Suhrawardy, 'return to your homes now and continue to think of Pakistan. No one will molest you in any way, the police and the army have been given orders by me not to interfere. I have taken care of everything.'

That was the signal. The goondas melted away in twos and threes, drawing out their weapons, their footsteps quickening as they neared the edge of the crowd, eager to join the fray. As they emerged from the crowd they started grouping together and moving faster, first trotting, and then running, all their weapons out in the open, the choppers and

Shovon Chowdhury

the sharpened rods, the revolvers and the rusty knives. The police stepped aside. One or two of them cheered them on. They ran and they roared, like demons from the pits of hell. Cries of 'Allah hu Akbar' filled the air.

A trumpet blared, salvaged from the production of Life of Shah Jahan. The crowd on the main street parted, and through them marched the massed ranks of the New Bengal Theatre Society, dressed as soldiers of the INA. Babloo, who had misunderstood his instructions, had come dressed as one of the Greek soldiers from Life of Alexander, so they had kept him in the middle of the ranks, where he marched on proudly, his skirt swirling, his sword clanking by his side. As they marched, they sang the battle hymn of the INA. They did not sing it well, but they sang it from the heart, and their voices soared across the open field.

Behind them, slowly, majestically, came one of the largest trucks Ali had ever seen. On the back of the truck, on a raised platform, towering above the crowds stood Natasamrat Ghanashyam Das dressed as Netaji Subhash Chandra Bose, a steely gleam in his eye, a megaphone in his hand. This was the greatest day of his life, the apogee of his theatrical career. Like Suhrawardy, he had never had an audience this large. He intended to make the most of it.

An awestruck silence fell over the crowd. Even the goondas halted in their tracks, and nudged each other, pointing. Suhrawardy stood transfixed on the dais, as if seeing a ghost.

Netaji flung out an imperial arm, and the crowd waited with bated breath.

'Brothers and sisters of Calcutta,' he said, 'I come here today to tell you one simple thing. Give me your hearts' blood, and I will give you freedom!'

Ali groaned and clutched his head. He ought to have gone over the script once. The last thing Calcutta needed right now was more blood and thunder. Besides, which leader in his right mind repeated his speeches? It was like Abraham Lincoln touring America, re-reading the Gettysburg address, and maybe collecting coins in his hat afterwards. Nevertheless, the crowd went wild.

Netaji repeated his imperial salute. He grinned a heavenly grin. His jackboots gleamed in the pale monsoon light. The crowd fell silent.

'This city is in the grip of madness,' he said, softly, and then he raised his voice, switching emotional gears with a smooth facility that had gained him countless admirers from Darjeeling to Dhakuria. 'Look at you. I am ashamed of all of you! How dare you behave this way? Did you learn nothing from me, in all the years I spent amongst you? Have Bengalis become sheep, that anyone with a loud voice and a big stick can lead you wherever they want?'

Many in the crowd shuffled awkwardly. Netaji was angry with them.

'When we marched to save the country, we did not march as Hindus or Muslims or Sikhs. We marched as Indians. We marched shoulder to shoulder. We fought together as brothers. We died together as brothers. I left Islam Khan in the soil of Kohima. And Ratan Pal. And Jaspreet Singh. What would they say if they saw you now?'

A nearby goonda dropped his chopper, and looked at it, lying near his feet. Ali watched him closely. Was he crying?

'They followed me for thousands of miles,' said Netaji, 'they followed me without question. They followed me despite the fact that I had nothing to give them but the promise of freedom. Do you think any of them ever asked, "Is Netaji a Hindu, or a Muslim, or a Christian, or a Sikh?" Who here has the courage to speak this way? Who will stand up here and say, "You, Netaji, you are a Hindu, I will not follow you." Who dares call me a Hindu?'

He held out his arms and waited.

A shot rang out. Netaji fell, clutching his chest, a bloodstain swelling across his khakis. A moan went up from the crowd. They surged towards the truck. The truck was to soon vanish in the melee. Eyewitnesses would later claim they had seen Netaji alive, which led to reports that he was languishing in jail, where Nehru kept him locked up, or meditating on Mount Kailash, or hiding in Pondicherry.

Meanwhile, all hell broke loose.

The crowd surged in all directions, breaking free of the maidan and rampaging through the streets, blinded by tears, berserk with fury. People hacked at each other with scant regard for race or religion, wanting only to make someone pay. The police assaulted everyone in sight—indiscriminately, without fear or favour, their minds clear of confusion. Today there were no innocents, today everyone in Calcutta was guilty, and no judge or jury was required. The word spread like wildfire across the city, where arson and butchery were already in progress, and neighbour turned on neighbour with renewed fury, knowing it was all his fault, and his, and hers, and yes, even her children's too.

Thousands surged through Park Street, and Ali was carried along with them, helplessly afloat in a sea of enraged humanity. The street was strewn with debris, broken furniture and empty boxes, bedding and shoes and pots and pans, shattered glass and bloodstained weapons. Every shop on the street was burning. A young man poured kerosene on a sack, set it alight, and flung it through a window. Another man lay tied to a lamp-post, blood and brains oozing through a hole in his forehead. In front of a burning shop, a man squatted on the pavement quietly, an island of calm in a sea of madness, gripping a broken piece of glass with bloody hands, tying it to a stick to create a makeshift axe, intent on his task, oblivious to the chaos. The smell of blood mingled with the smell of smoke, a smell that no one left alive in Calcutta would ever forget. All along the street the cars were ablaze, some with their owners still inside.

The mob rampaged through Park Street. Ali managed to extricate himself as they dispersed down the by-lanes, his mind completely and utterly blank, his vision blurred by the smoke. As he stood there in the middle of the broad street, his vision began to clear, and he saw a khaki-clad figure lying just a few feet away, small and frail and hardly recognizable as human. Did it just move a little bit? Was it someone he could save? Ali forced himself to walk over. He bent down to take a closer look.

It was Afzal, the old INA soldier whom he had last seen standing on the corner of a narrow Bhawanipur lane, shaking his fist in defiance at the local toughs and crying 'Jai Hind!'

His throat was slit from ear to ear, and his dead hand lay over his breast pocket, protecting something. Ali gently lifted his hand, and reached into the pocket to remove what he knew lay over his heart. It was a tiny, tattered picture of Netaji.

'If I ever get back, I'll make sure they remember him better,' he said softly.

He raised his face to the sky in prayer, his cheeks wet with his tears.

The Great Calcutta Killings had begun.

83

'Even the mutants look clean.
Someone has been washing them.'

They walked past the Transit House, and the Temporary Shelter, and the Radiation Relief Camp, and the Foundation Stone Dhaba—constructed entirely out of foundation stones laid by various politicians over the years. They went through the Sixty Foot Road, and Netaji Nagar, and Naya Basti, and Goldie Nagar, and Shefali Nagar—named by the local boys for an actress they missed.

Soon they were all standing together in front of Tarun-da's little shack. In the past, fear of revolutionary speeches and the stench from the nearby nala had caused people to shun his residence, but now that Pintoo was in situ, it had become like the Ramlila Maidan. People were coming and going in extremely large numbers. No hawkers had set up outside so far, but it was only a matter of time. Inside, Mrs Verma, Pappu, her guards, Shanti-bai, and the two Self-Defence Force boys jostled for space.

Mrs Verma's guards were still groggy from their mistreatment at the hands of Hoskins the limo driver, but the charge-lights on their rifles were blinking, and the Self-Defence Force boys were raring to go. Shanti-bai sighed and sat down on the bed, so that she could hit the ground faster in the event of crossfire. She would have to be careful. One false word could lead to wholesale carnage.

'Oy Tarun!' she said. 'Bring the child and come here.'

Tarun-da emerged from the back with Pintoo. He blinked nervously at his guests. He was unused to so much military might in his living room. He preferred his violence to be rhetorical. The lady in the silk sari bore an uncanny resemblance to an aunt back in Barrackpore, famous for her volcanic temperament. And then there was Shanti-bai. He was second to none in his regard for her, but he preferred to worship from afar. Things got busy when she was around, and resistance was usually futile. But none of this was what made him nervous. What made him nervous was that Pintoo was vibrating like a tuning fork. He could hear his teeth chattering. So was the other little boy. He was shaking from head to foot. As he shook, his hand reached out towards Pintoo, dragging him forward like an eager retriever.

'Whee!' said Pappu.

'Go fetch the exorcist,' muttered Shanti-bai. Ranjeeta hitched up her pretty blue sari and ran off to fetch him. Mrs Verma pulled Pappu to her ample bosom, and staggered back. The boys stopped vibrating. Whatever force had possessed them, it was no match for motherhood. A hush fell over the room. Everyone could see the matching pairs of hands, attached to different boys.

'Body thieves,' hissed Shanti-bai. Her expression was ugly.

'Sisterfucker! It's them!' roared one of the SDF guards, and jabbed Pappu in the chest with his rifle. He drove them back till both mother and son were pinned to the wall. His body was frail, but his rage was great.

'I knew it was you!' said the guard. He was crying now. 'All of them died. All of them. My wife, my children, my little sister. All of them died in your mines. We wanted to live, but you showed us no mercy. My youngest son was such a happy little boy. He was born in your mine. All he ever knew was the hole, and the dust, and the rice husks for dinner. I was the only one who survived. I managed to escape during a Maoist attack, where they blew most of us up in an attempt to free us. I found my way to Shanti Nagar. It's the only place I know where poor people are welcome. But to see you here, now, in front of me, like this? I recognized you from the holo on Verma-sahab's table, which I saw once when I was serving tea. It was just a few days after my wife died.'

He jabbed Pappu in the chest, and the tears rolled down his cheeks. His finger trembled on the button.

'Why should I let you live? I have no family. Why should he? He killed mine to make money.'

Mrs Verma tried to speak, but there was something stuck in her throat. She never thought much beyond profit and loss, but right now, the profit was here, standing in front of her, crying. Shanti-bai got up from the bed, slowly, cursing her knees. She put a hand gently on the shoulder of the SDF guard.

'I've understood your case,' she said, 'now let it be. It's for me to determine what has to be done.'

'Let me finish them, Shanti-bai!' pleaded the guard. 'Let me finish them or they will eat Pintoo also. See, they brought a doctor!'

The doctor raised his martini glass in salute, but his heart wasn't in it. Even he was horrified by the young man's story.

Mrs Verma found her voice.

'I didn't come to take anything,' she said. 'I came to give it back. That's why I brought the doctor.'

This was true. Ever since she had rescued Ramu from the Bank of Bodies, Mrs Verma remained capable of doing many things, but killing little boys was not one of them.

'I can confirm that,' said the doctor. 'This is a totally new approach, but I'm willing to go along with it. You ought to make up your mind, though. All this detachment and attachment is very bad for the patient.'

'Why did you bring the army, then?' asked Shanti-bai suspiciously.

'I've heard many stories about Shanti Nagar,' said Mrs Verma, 'people say you conduct unspeakable rituals, and feed on human flesh, but everyone looks quite normal to me. Even the mutants look clean. Someone has been washing them.'

'I don't want it,' said Pintoo. A hush fell over the room.

'You can take it if you want,' said Pappu in a very small voice. 'It's been looking for you.'

'I don't want it,' repeated Pintoo, firmly. 'Here's the new rule. Whatever's attached to anyone, it stays attached to them.'

The guard lowered his rifle and stepped back, and was promptly disarmed by his colleague. 'I'll talk to you later,' said Shanti-bai. She pulled Pappu away and made him sit on the bed. 'Let's get you some biscuits,' she said.

Ranjeeta came in, panting slightly. 'Shanti-bai, the exorcist is here! He wanted to sleep with me but I told him later. Also Banani-didi wants Pintoo to join her outside. Some meeting-sheeting is happening. There's a big car waiting at the main gate, with some fancy people inside,'

'Go get us some tea and biscuits,' said Shanti-bai, 'get rid of the exorcist. Give him some money. And keep your panties on.'

She turned to Mrs Verma.

'Would you like half a cup?' she asked.

Shovon Chowdhury

84

'I think it is time for me to go.'

It was past four o'clock on the thirtieth of January when Mr Chatterjee reached Birla House. He leapt out of his tonga and flung the money at the tonga-wallah. His namesake, the priestly policeman, had made all the arrangements to get him to where Gandhi was, but had drawn the line at dropping him off in his jeep. 'It looks bad,' he had said. He had promised that no one would interfere with him inside.

He was late. Gandhi addressed the public at five sharp, every day. He rushed through the small gate. The policemen on duty hardly gave him a glance. They were supposed to be looking for a Maharashtrian murderer, but their scope for success was slim. They were all from villages in north India, and it had been quite a while since the Marathas had come riding through. The crowd was bigger than last time, simple people mostly, here to see the man they loved. Except one of them.

Mr Chatterjee scanned the faces anxiously, seeking signs of malice, wishing he could remember what Nathuram Godse looked like. There were quite a few foreigners, he noticed. Not in uniform. Journalists, probably. If Godse succeeded, the news would be around the world in a flash. Where was he? Which one was him? Was it that man? He was dark, and grim. He looked like he was hiding secrets. The man reached down and lifted his little boy onto his shoulders, helping him get a better view. The little boy whispered something in his ear, and his face broke into a smile.

It was hopeless. He wouldn't save Gandhi this way. He would only know when the assassin drew his gun, and how could he catch a flying bullet? He was no Rajnikanth. There was only one way to do it. He had to keep Gandhi safe in his room. Gandhi was a devotee of the truth. Only the truth could save him now.

❏

A few minutes later he was inside, and appalled at how easy it had been. The place was devoid of policemen, because their uniforms clashed with the drapes. The house was undoubtedly the house of a rich man, with marble floors, high ceilings, crystal chandeliers, and a faintly Grecian air. He stood there on the sprawling verandah, wondering which way to go.

A liveried footman walked past him with tea on a silver salver, not the least bit surprised to see him. He was well dressed and therefore above suspicion.

'Which room is Gandhiji in?' asked Mr Chatterjee. 'There's something I have to give him.'

It was the lamest possible excuse, but his brain wasn't working too well.

'See that door over there?' said the footman. 'Bapu's in there.'

He hurried off with the tea. He took pride in serving it hot.

Why did Godse bother with all the plotting? Why did he even need a revolver? All he had to do was walk in, take directions, find Gandhi in his room, and strangle him. Bare hands and a little enterprise, that was all he needed.

The door was open. Mr Chatterjee walked in.

The room was very spare, with plain, whitewashed walls, a simple cot and a small stool. On the stool were a spectacle case, and a copy of the *Gita*. A walking stick stood propped against it.

Mahatma Gandhi was sitting on the cot, bare-bodied, in his loincloth, a light shawl over his shoulders to protect him from the winter chill. He sat silently, hunched over, tiny, looking at his feet. He was the saddest man Mr Chatterjee had ever seen.

He stood looking at him, not knowing what to say.

Eventually, tentatively, hating himself for disturbing his silence, he cleared his throat.

Gandhi looked up at him, his expression dull, but as he looked more closely, a glimmer of interest showed in his eyes.

'There's something different about you,' he said.

Mr Chatterjee said nothing.

'Come closer,' whispered Gandhi.

Mr Chatterjee stepped forward. Gandhi reached up and felt the fabric of his shirt with expert fingers, mumbling silently to himself. He peered closely at the buttons. To Mr Chatterjee's embarrassment, he lifted his shirt, and examined his belt buckle. A fleeting expression of wonder crossed his face.

'You have come from very far away,' he said, 'your journey must have been a strange one.'

'It was,' said Mr Chatterjee.

Gandhi sighed, no longer interested. Once more his face clouded, and his chin sank down on his chest.

'How are you feeling?' asked Mr Chatterjee.

'How am I feeling?' asked Gandhi slowly. 'It's a long time since anybody asked me that question.'

He took Mr Chatterjee by the hand and made him sit next to him.

'Sometimes I feel it would have been better if Shukla had never taken me to Champaran. He was very persistent, that boy. He kept following me around for days. He kept talking of Champaran, a place I had never heard of, and of indigo, a plant I had never seen. I was just back from South Africa. All I wanted to do was run my ashram, do some good, breathe the air of my native place. He followed me everywhere. Lucknow, Kanpur, Sabarmati. Wherever I went, he was there. I could hardly understand his strange Bihari dialect. Prasad used to translate. He kept saying Bapu, you must listen to this boy, what he is saying is important, what is happening there is wrong. You must go to Champaran. He was not my follower then, this Prasad, but he was interested in me. Occasionally he would spend time with me. The funny thing is, the first time I went to Prasad's house, they did not let me use the bathroom, because they could not make out my caste.

'Before I knew it, there I was, in Champaran, thanks to that boy who would not take no for an answer. In my first few days in that alien place, Shukla would run errands for me, and try to make me comfortable. Slowly others like Prasad joined, but in the beginning, that young man, whose thick Bihari dialect I could barely understand—he was my sole supporter. Where would I be today, but for him, I wonder? Did he do the right thing, by pursuing me as he did?'

'How can you even say that?' protested Mr Chatterjee. 'We're all free because of you.'

'What kind of freedom do you call this?' asked Gandhi.

Mr Chatterjee had no answer to that one.

They sat together for a while in companionable silence, shoulder to shoulder, as the shadows lengthened across the room.

'Sometimes I think that everything I did was wrong,' said Gandhi, some time later. 'People support me for a while, but in time they find me tiresome, perhaps even evil. Bhimrao was always blaming me, saying

Bapu, you talk about Harijans, but it's all talk, you do nothing for them in reality. So I told Kasturba that she must adopt an untouchable girl, so that people could see that Gandhi's wife has become the mother of an untouchable. She did, and her name was Lakshmi. I thought it was a good thing. But see what happened. All the textile merchants of Ahmedabad used to support my ashram through their donations. After Lakshmi came to our house, the donations dried up. Now they spit at the mention of my name. I am a Gujarati, and now even Gujaratis curse me. Maybe everything I did was wrong.'

'That's not true,' said Mr Chatterjee, 'they remember you very fondly, where I come from. Many regret not listening to you more.'

'Is that really true?' demanded Gandhi, searching his eyes, gripping his wrist with his bony fingers.

Fixed by his piercing gaze, Mr Chatterjee was unable to lie.

'Not really,' he admitted, 'but your picture is everywhere. All the kids who go to school can recognize you.'

'An idol,' said Gandhiji, exasperated, 'you turned me into an idol.'

He felt something under his grasp, and lifted up Mr Chatterjee's wrist. It was his wristwatch.

'Remove that watch,' said Gandhiji sternly, 'you must give up all foreign items. That, at least, I must still insist on. You cannot sit with me and pretend to respect me, and wear such a thing.'

'It's Indian,' said Mr Chatterjee.

'They make such things in your India?' asked Gandhiji, wonderingly. He grinned his gap-toothed grin. It made him look like a happy child. The moment was fleeting. His expression soon darkened again.

'And I wonder what price you paid to produce it,' he said sadly.

He sat there morosely for a while, his mouth moving silently.

'Sir, please, don't go,' begged Mr Chatterjee, desperate, 'I have come here from the future, as I think you have understood, although how you can believe it I do not know. There's a man outside waiting to kill you. If you go outside he will shoot you in the chest. You will bless him, and then you will die. You must not die. There is still a lot you can do, and things don't really work out so well for us, up ahead in the future. We need you.'

Gandhiji shook his head stubbornly. He looked at his own watch.

'It is past five o'clock. I am late. I am never late. Punctuality is very important.'

He rose briskly from his cot, leaning on his stick. He was sad, but spry. Mr Chatterjee never called anyone father, but he did now.

'Bapu . . .' he said.

Gandhiji smiled at him sadly. It was a smile of ineffable sweetness, a smile that Mr Chatterjee would carry in his heart till the end of his days. He could see that he had believed every word.

'I think it is time for me to go,' said Gandhiji gently.

85

'Give me marching Chinese soldiers.
Give me tanks.'

The Chinese troops moved back from the border. Chinese missiles sank back into their silos. Chinese tanks rolled back to the inner provinces.

Even as these developments were taking place, ordinary citizens were rising up all over China. Hundreds of local officials had been dragged out of their mansions and their limousines, and people were taking turns kicking them. Geriatric leaders gazed nervously at their guards and fiddled tremulously with their false teeth. Concubines packed up their jewellery and mumbled into their cell phones, telling their mothers they would be coming home soon, with presents for everyone. Villagers boarded trains for cities, and no one asked them for permits. Executioners crept away quietly, leaving their tools behind. Petitioners burnt their petitions, because the time for petitions was over. Judges sat alone in their chambers, and reflected on the true nature of justice. Jailers fingered their keys, wondering, while prisoners rattled their bars. Mothers spoke softly to their children, asking them to watch, and remember. Freedom, they whispered. Remember the word, remember the sound of it, never let it leave your hearts. Freedom.

❑

The Angry Old Man was holding out his mike to the farmer, trying to stand as far away as possible without actually stepping out of the frame, as his aroma was richly rural. He was talking to a common person, so he was being sternly sympathetic.

'Is there a nearby fallout shelter you can go to?' he asked, sympathetically. For once, he was glad to be out in the field, even though it was smelly. Just a few hours ago he'd been in a studio, sitting round an imposing mahogany table with six celebrated journalists, who were all either completely out of touch with reality or, in the case of two of them, senile beyond redemption. While hobnobbing with them had helped confirm him, in front of the nation, once more, as a leader of his profession, the drivelling had been very hard to bear.

The villager looked at him silently, eager to please, but puzzled.

His Hindi was a little rusty, but he translated the phrase 'fallout shelter' as best he could.

'Ah,' said the farmer, 'shelter.'

He thought about this a bit. Perhaps this TV channel was running some kind of promotion, where shelter was being offered to lucky winners? He watched TV all the time, and he knew all about consumer promotions, although he had never actually qualified for one, not being in a position to buy refrigerators, or motorcycles, or even five bottles of Pepsi in five days. But he understood the basic principle well enough.

'Well, shelter is certainly a problem,' he said, hopefully, 'my roof has many holes in it, and everything gets wet in the rainy season. So in case your channel is offering free asbestos sheets, sponsored by Everest or Charminar . . .'

'But what would you do in case of radiation?' asked the Angry Old Man, sticking to his angle with single-minded dedication. He never let facts interfere with angles.

'We don't get any of that here,' said the farmer, correctly interpreting this to be a medical term, 'for that, you would have to go to the Health Centre at Chhabua, which is eighty kilometres away. I had taken my sister-in-law there once to deliver her baby, but there were no doctors, so we came back again. The child was born in a taxi, which is what everyone in the village calls him.'

The Angry Old Man missed this opportunity to focus on the heartwarming reality of village life, as a kind of poignant coda or sidebar, because a stream of information was coming in on his earpiece. He swung around to face the camera, somewhat creakily.

'More after the commercial break,' he said, 'when we share with you some dramatic new developments, which could transform the destiny of India. Stay tuned!'

436   Shovon Chowdhury

'Quick,' he said to the crew, 'put up a blue screen behind me. Cut out the location and put on a graphic. We've got some breaking news.'

'What kind of graphic do you want?' asked the graphics person, live via satellite from New New Delhi. 'Should I do you a mushroom cloud?'

He'd been working on mushroom clouds for the last twenty hours straight, studying footage from the last war, and had developed some really nice ones.

'No, you fool!' said the Angry Old Man. 'Give me marching Chinese soldiers. Give me tanks. Give me Chinese fists waving in the air.'

The graphics person was crushed, but he was a trouper. He gave him some tanks. They were actually Pakistani, but he was hoping no one would notice, what with a legendary personality giving scoops in the foreground and everything.

The Angry Old Man turned back to the camera. 'Ladies and Gentlemen, there have been dramatic developments across the border,' he said sombrely. 'Even as we discuss the possible consequences of war here in the heart of rural India, China has exploded. Enraged by government inaction in the face of the challenge from Taiwan, the Chinese people are protesting violently against their government. The government has arranged for official buses, so that angry citizens can spontaneously congregate in designated areas and abuse Taiwan, using phrases from the *Little Book of Protest*, but analysts are saying it's a case of too little too late, and the public is in no mood to listen. In related news, internationally famous godman Dharti Pakar has urged the followers of Falun Gong in China to rise up. Here's what he had to say . . .'

Dharti Pakar appeared on the screen, smiling serenely from his floating lotus.

'We at the ART OF BREATHING™ believe in attaining peace and harmony through breathing,' he said, 'so do my brothers and sisters of the Falun Gong. Let us rise up against our oppressors, wherever they may be, and breathe together. To understand my technique fully, please log on to www.artofbreathing.com. We accept all major credit cards.'

The Angry Old Man came back on. 'Let's get a quick reaction to this truly stunning development from one of India's leading editors.'

They switched to one of India's leading editors, who was fast asleep, his mouth slightly open, his chin resting against his chest. The secret to his appalling longevity had always lain in taking naps whenever and wherever he could.

'Mr Mehrotra,' said the Angry Old Man, 'MR MEHROTRA!'

The leading editor woke up and automatically delivered a sound bite.

'As usual, the Hindu fundamentalists are fishing in troubled waters,' he said, firmly. 'It's quite typical, really. All part of the Parivar's agenda.'

'Thank you, Mr Mehrotra,' said the Angry Old Man, putting a finger to his earpiece. 'There's more coming in here. A truly powerful statement, from the online version of the *Beijing Youth Daily*, which has demanded, "the strongest protest, the loudest voice, the angriest action, the darkest midnight, the most barbarous outrage, the deepest pain, and the strongest support."'

He paused for a moment, to let it all sink in.

'We are not sure exactly what that means,' he admitted, 'but the significance is inescapable. Our expert analyst Subramaniam, just back from Geneva, will be analysing it for us shortly.'

He paused for a moment, listening.

'Ladies and gentlemen, the news just keeps pouring in. Even as we speak, in an unprecedented move, the Supreme Leader of China is making a self-criticism in front of the Central Committee, many of whom are awake. This is completely unheard of. Could this be the end of Chinese civilization as we know it? In yet another disturbing development, Little Kim, the Sexy Leader of the autonomous region of Koguryo, formerly known as North Korea, has demanded the immediate conquest of Japan so that, and I quote, "the glorious nation of China can finally gain control of Tokyo Disneyland".'

He fixed the camera with his piercing gaze. It was time to mould public opinion.

'The question today, ladies and gentlemen, is one of the utmost importance. Does this mean we can breathe easy, and pull back from the brink of oblivion? Or is this our golden opportunity to finish off our ancient enemy once and for all? Join me, at 9 p.m., right after this commercial break for the panel discussion with six eminent journalists, "The Nation Ponders."'

❑

Navalkar, the General, and the PM weren't pondering. They knew.

'I think we should frame this,' said the General, holding up the single sheet of paper reverentially, 'we may never see anything like it again.'

Shovon Chowdhury

'What is it?' asked Navalkar.

'It's an official letter of apology from the Government of China, regretting any recent misunderstandings we may have had. They sent it to the CA's office, but they sent copies to both the PM and me as well. They know how things work here.'

The PM gulped down her champagne, not the safest thing to do at her age, but when would she ever see a day like this again?

'We're out of it,' she said, 'thank God. I think I'm going to retire now.'

'Do you really think their government is going to fall?' asked Navalkar, still unable to believe how things had worked out.

'I have no doubt,' said the PM, 'once the senior citizens are out on the street, there's no going back.'

This was true. The inmates of a retired persons' home near Beijing had ventured out, and in an unprecedented public display of outrage and incontinence, had assaulted a nearby police picket with their walking sticks. The police had offered no resistance.

'So we really did win the war,' said Navalkar, in wonder, 'who would have thought it?'

'We didn't actually fight a war,' said the General, soberly, 'which is just as well because we would have lost it. Not just because the Chinese army is stronger, but because the Chinese nation is stronger. Stronger, healthier, richer, smarter, more advanced in every way. All their children eat three square meals a day and go to school. They just happen to be a better country than we are.'

The PM looked up at him, feeling both hurt and, in some odd way, responsible. But she said nothing.

'Well, all right, sir,' said Navalkar, who had always known all this and had never let it bother him, 'let's not get depressed at a time like this. We've pulled it back from the brink. And after all, didn't someone once say that the best way to win a battle is to avoid fighting one?'

'Someone did,' said the General. 'His name was Sun Tzu. He was Chinese.'

❑

The CA had been monitoring the rapidly unfolding developments with disbelief. When the official apology from China arrived he yelled for Mehta, before he realized he was still at home.

He didn't know who had sabotaged all his carefully laid plans, but he would find out, and they would pay. Meanwhile, what was required was quick decisive action. He would reveal himself immediately. He would address the nation across all national channels. He would permanently reset the anti-surf mechanisms on all TV sets, so that no one could miss his speech. The anti-surf mechanism had been made compulsory for all TV manufacturers in India by a special ordinance he had passed a few years back, in response to requests from numerous advertisers. It ensured that anyone who tried to switch channels more than once in five minutes received a mild electric shock through their remote control. The shocks increased with the frequency of surfing.

Just to be sure, he would cancel all other news coverage so that his face was all people saw, which was only as it should be. His greatness would have a calming effect. He would explain the need for a forward policy with regard to China. Not that he needed to explain, but when the bombs started dropping, he wanted people to know why, and take solace in the fact that it was all part of a master plan, guided by his masterly hands. He would then go down to the bunker, where he would override all the command protocols, arm the missiles, and ask Mehta to fetch the black bag with the nuclear button. The disinfection would begin.

It was time for him to come out of the shadows, where he had never really belonged. It was time to tear off his mask and leap out at the public, who would soon come to adore him. He was the Competent Authority, after all. He had the competence. He had the authority. He had the chair. He had climbed up the hard way, step by bloody step, smiling at idiots and bowing to fools, clutching his madness close to his chest until he had reached this position of power. By now he was more heaven-born than those dolts from the foreign service. It was his God-given right to decide what to do, and nothing and no one would get in his way.

86

'There are some poor people in the reception!'

'There are some poor people in the reception!' whispered the yummy receptionist, in hushed tones of shock and horror.

Guru Dharti Pakar pushed the supermodel off his lap and stared up at the intercom, unable to believe his ears. He had often feared this day would come.

'Are you sure?' he asked. Perhaps they were holograms. It might be a Halloween prank by American devotees.

'I'm sure,' said the Guardian of the Gates of Heaven™ tremulously. She tried to get up, but she had lost all sensation in her legs.

Ranvir was standing in the fountain. It seemed like a waste of perfectly good water, so he had decided to take a much-needed bath. She watched, paralyzed, as he raised his dhoti and sat down. He emitted a happy sigh as the water cooled his fevered loins. Pintoo was running his hands over the glowing, life-size cutout of Guru Dharti Pakar, trying to figure out where the power supply was. His fingers left grubby streaks all over its pristine, white surface. The ancient headmaster, who had insisted on accompanying them, was supine on one of the snow-white sofas, fast asleep. A thin line of dribble trickled down his chin, forming a slowly expanding damp spot on the fluffy white cushion. Banani, who was wearing a crumpled cotton sari and absolutely no diamonds, had picked up one of the glossy ART OF BREATHING™ brochures and was leafing through it. Her expression was disrespectful.

Completely paralyzed by the shenanigans in the holy sanctum, the yummy receptionist had failed to notice the distinguished gentleman with the excellent hair who was standing right in front of her. The distinguished gentleman rapped his knuckles on the desk peremptorily.

'I'm so sorry,' said the yummy receptionist, flustered, 'I have no idea how these people got in. I'll call security and have them removed immediately.'

'Please don't be concerned,' said No. 2, oozing charm from every orifice, 'they're my companions. I'm from the Bank of Bodies, with subordinates from our Shanti Nagar office, here to meet His Holiness.'

A bleating gargle echoed through her headphones. It was Guru Dharti Pakar clearing his throat.

'Were they real?' he inquired hoarsely.

'It's all right, boss,' she said, trying to ignore the fact that Ranvir had taken off his dhoti and was now washing it in the fountain.

'They're with the Bank of Bodies,' she informed her boss, 'an officer is here to see you, and he brought the poor people with him.'

That was when he remembered. How could he have forgotten? Today was the day they were meeting the Competent Authority, with the little miracle worker. This was an even more golden opportunity. Guru Dharti Pakar had many fat cats under his thumb, but no one was fatter than the Competent Authority. Once within range, he was confident of mesmerizing him.

'Send them up quickly,' he ordered his comely devotee.

She turned to No. 2.

'Please, follow me. Guruji awaits you eagerly. He has interrupted his afternoon meditation just so that he can meet you.'

No. 2 smiled invitingly at Banani, who showed him the finger and gathered her unruly flock. She let the ancient headmaster be. It was a long time since he had slept in such comfort.

'So now we're meeting God?' asked Pintoo.

'Just a silly old man,' said Banani, 'don't let him get too close, and if he offers you anything, don't take it.'

No. 2 smiled to himself. Pintoo's powers were unnerving, and the woman's attitude was shockingly anti-business. But viewed collectively, they were nothing more than a bunch of simple-minded peasants. Quite similar to his board of directors. Fooling them would be child's play. His plan was simple. Once the child had been displayed to the CA and the meeting was over, he would engage them in charming banter. While they were distracted, one of his men would creep up behind the child and hit him on the head, rendering him unconscious. He would wake up to find himself alone in a padded cell, and they would only give him food if he did what they asked.

They emerged into a great hall at the end of which sat Guru Dharti Pakar in the lotus position, his eyes closed, an expression of supreme bliss on his face, ensconced on a slowly revolving marble lotus, floating a few feet above the floor. He used it as an alternative to his levitating throne, to impress special guests. As they approached, he pressed a button with his toe, and the lotus gently descended to earth. In his right hand he held a long-stemmed orchid, imported at great expense from the Amazon rainforest, and lovingly spray-painted silver. He had spent many years in Delhi, and he knew the score. People here liked things shiny.

He raised his right hand in benediction. 'Greetings, my children,' he said, 'I thank you for sharing your auras.'

'Is that beard real?' asked Pintoo, pointing.

'It is entirely real, my child,' replied the holy man, 'I keep it glossy though the regular use of ART OF BREATHING™ organic shampoo, which you can purchase from the gift shop downstairs. Alternatively, you can order through our website. We deliver within fourteen days, and accept all major credit cards.'

Banani eyed his beard thoughtfully. It was genuinely lustrous. Her own hair had been thinning out lately, and she was constantly on the lookout for a good shampoo.

No. 2 decided to get down to business.

'Your Holiness, please see a quick demonstration from the child, and then let us move,' he said.

Guru Dharti Pakar raised a perfectly manicured hand, which he, doubtless, kept soft and glowing with the help of ART OF BREATHING™ Hand Lotion.

'My dear son,' he said, in a tone of mild reproof, 'the time for business will come. First let us breathe.'

He closed his eyes.

'I'm already breathing,' whispered Pintoo to Banani.

'Hush,' said Banani, 'just do what he says. It'll make him happy.'

'Empty your mind of all thought,' trilled Dharti Pakar, 'become one with the universe. Breathe with me.'

It was actually quite relaxing. They breathed. Harmony prevailed.

Dharti Pakar opened his eyes. He smiled at Pintoo.

'I have heard much about you, child,' he said. 'Please accept this small gift with my blessings.'

He held out the gilded flower.

Banani had told him not to accept anything from the man, so Pintoo pushed. The flower vanished.

'Don't worry, old man, it'll come back soon,' he said, grinning, 'it's in the same place, just earlier. Would you like a ride?'

Dharti Pakar looked at No. 2, and swallowed.

'You spoke the truth,' he said. 'He can perform wonders.'

'Your Holiness, you wanted to see proof. You have seen it. May we please go now?'

'How did you get him to join you?'

'We have an understanding. We suspend operations in Shanti Nagar, they help us promote Religious Joy.'

And how long will it be before you double-cross them, wondered Dharti Pakar. The game was complex. The stakes were high. He would need to keep his wits about him.

'What about the government?' he asked. 'Has the Bureau of Reconstruction cleared the files? Is this why you want me to meet the Competent Authority?'

'Yes, Your Holiness,' said No. 2, 'there have been a few misunderstandings with the Competent Authority. Your Holiness is highly regarded in government circles. I propose that we go together. A small demonstration from Pintoo, combined with your presence, should be sufficient to win him over. Once we have his signature, nothing will stand in our way.'

Dharti Pakar rubbed his hands together. His eyes gleamed as he contemplated the possibilities.

'Why are all of you so excited about meeting this CA guy?' asked Pintoo suddenly. 'Does he have an extra head growing out of his shoulder or what?'

Dharti Pakar closed his eyes and assumed an expression of deep devotion. 'Compared to the CA,' he said, 'all of us are nothing. The CA has the power to demolish houses and convert them into latrines. The CA knows the number of everyone's Swiss bank account. The CA can eradicate illiteracy with the flick of a pen. The CA can collect in advance, and refund at leisure. The CA can bestow petrol-pump licences and cooking gas connections, and also he can take away. The CA commands the power of invisibility. He can build invisible hospitals, and fill them with invisible doctors. He can make vast quantities of minerals travel invisibly across the land. He can create miles and miles of irrigation that no one will ever see. The CA can redraw the borders of states, just because their shapes displease him. The CA can prevent dengue by declaring Section 144. The CA can command Air India to fly him wherever he wants. Nothing is beyond the scope, purview or grasp of the almighty, all-seeing, all-knowing CA.'

Banani and Pintoo exchanged quick glances.

Dharti Pakar raised a benedictory hand, encompassing all of them with a single fluid gesture, like a magician about to perform a particularly good conjuring trick.

'I, too, can control the flow of time,' he declared, 'thanks to the many years I have spent meditating in the Himalayas. I could transport all of us to the Competent Authority in the blink of an eye. But the effort depletes my aura, rendering me temporarily incapable of serving the needy. Therefore, although it is imperative that we bring matters to a speedy resolution, so that we can swiftly commence our endeavour to uplift the nation, I would rather not make haste through spiritual means. Let us use conventional methods instead, and proceed to the abode of our ruler without further delay.'

He turned to No. 2.

'Your limousine or mine?'

87

'I did teach you one thing, didn't I?'

As he neared his office, the Competent Authority saw that India Gate had collapsed again, burying the recently erected statue of the Dalai Lama. India Gate collapsed about once every eighteen months. It had been a mistake giving the contract to the Agriculture Minister's nephew, he realized. His only previous experience had been in Low Income Housing. But it had been the patriotic thing to do. The alternative was to accept French assistance. As creators of both the Statue of Liberty and the Eiffel Tower, the French had considered this project to be right up their boulevard, but they had expected it to be referred to as Le India Gate. The Agriculture Minister's nephew had been the only local candidate to match the tender specifications, mainly because he had written them.

There was still an excess of substandard people. That was the problem. Every walk of life was infested with them. That was why further cleansing was required. Further delay was unacceptable. This was not a time for television broadcasts, uplifting though it might be for his subjects. This was a time for action. He would reveal himself later, to the more compact population that remained.

The car drew up in front of the Bureau of Reconstruction building, which looked just like any other government building, except for the many smiley drones flying in and out. They chattered constantly. 'Flood relief will be reaching you shortly,' said one. 'In cases of non filing of FIR, please file an FIR,' said another.

The Competent Authority had called ahead to warn Mehta that he was coming. His bunker was now well stocked with imported chicken legs and fresh carrots. While he was a strong proponent of healthy eating, sometimes, when no one was watching, he surrendered to the dark side. His hammock would be waiting, with his well-thumbed copy of *Mein Kampf* in a smaller hammock right next to it. The ever-faithful Mehta would have readied the button, and the codes to launch the nuclear missiles. They would be lying on his table, along with a few last files he might need to sign. Mehta's face appeared in the car window again, shimmering slightly. The drones were interfering with the transmission.

'Sir, the Bank people are coming, sir,' said Mehta, 'accompanied by several poor people, sir. Should we confiscate their ID cards and book them for non-possession of ID cards, sir?'

'That is not good governance, Mehta,' said the Competent Authority, disapprovingly. 'Seat them in my room. I will give them five minutes.'

A representative sample of the population would be in his room when he pressed the button, including poor people, the first he had met in years. It seemed fitting. The Chinese would take a few minutes to respond, leaving him enough time to drive down to his VVVIP bunker. He could perhaps take a moment to explain to the poor people why he was doing this. They had a right to know. Who else was he doing all this for, if not them? The car stopped. The Competent Authority emerged. He bounded up the steps to the elevator. He was feeling unusually energetic. 'It is a pleasure to have you inside me, Mr Authority,' said the elevator, 'and may I add that you are looking particularly handsome today?'

The Competent Authority had a quick look at himself in the mirror. It was true.

'You have reached your floor in complete safety,' said the elevator, 'this journey was brought to you by Khemka Elevator Company.'

The Competent Authority stepped out of the lift, dreaming of fire and flexing his thumb.

❑

Guru Dharti Pakar's limousine was like a VVIP temple on wheels. It had a holo projector, a refrigerator and a bathroom from which Tarun-da had just been rescued. Each seat had a little silver dispenser filled with scented napkins. In the background, Shri Shri Yo Yo was softly singing a gentle ballad dedicated to his mother.

Banani was observing Dharti Pakar and No. 2, who were at the other end of the limousine. She was trying hard not to vomit. They sat close to each other, whispering warmly, like young lovers in the first flush of love. Talk about unholy unions, she thought, they'll be giving each other blowjobs next. Ranvir sat next to her, gripping his lathi, knees pressed together, teeth clenched. He was ready for battle, just like Pintoo had told him. Tarun-da sat quietly, clutching a rough jute bag with strings.

The limousine drew up in front of the BoR building. A few smiley drones floated above, observing them carefully. 'Citizens! If you can have children, avoid using condoms!' said one of them, but it kept its voice very low.

No. 2 emerged first from the car, and courteously held open the door for Banani. She ground his instep with her heel as she stepped out, smiling sweetly in his face.

Two guards with laser rifles were standing in front of the guardroom. It was a short distance from the main BoR building, so that the guards could confront outsiders without offending the masters with their presence. One of the guards was listening into his earpiece.

'They want us to take them to the boss,' he said.

'What, these people?' said the other guard. 'Is he going to cook them or what?'

'All that I don't know,' said his comrade, 'when we get there, you can ask.'

'Ranvir bhaiyya, you stay near the car,' said Pintoo. Ranvir hesitated. The guards here were professionals, ex-army, most likely. The thought of leaving Pintoo in their hands bothered him. Banani leaned forward and whispered in his ear. Ranvir's face lit up. He assumed position in front of the guardroom, gripping his lathi.

The others followed one of the guards inside to the elevator. The elevator welcomed them. It was reserved, but polite.

❑

Sensing a certain urgency in the air, Mehta bypassed the waiting room and led them directly to the CA's chambers. The unpacking of the nuclear launch button and codes had also instilled in him a strong desire to flee. As per Indian tradition, the CA had made no provisions for his servants. But flee where? Perhaps if he lay on the floor directly underneath the CA's hammock, he might be able to survive while New New Delhi was obliterated. He wondered what they would call it the next time. Newer Delhi? Newest Delhi? Extremely New Delhi? Or would they shed the last vestiges of colonialism, and call it Nayi Dilli instead, like most of the residents?

The Competent Authority was at his desk, gazing fondly at the nuclear button. It was big and red, with a thumb shaped indentation in the exact shape of the Competent Authority's thumb. This was more for reasons of comfort than security. There was nothing biometric about it. It was purely mechanical. The Competent Authority was above scanning in any form. He was the only person in the country without an Aadhar ID card. Someone had to be outside the system, in case it was compromised.

'Dear fellow citizens,' said the Competent Authority, 'you have come at a very momentous moment in the history of our nation. Our reconstruction efforts have been unacceptably slow. Third-class people have infiltrated every walk of life. It is no longer possible to distinguish third-class people from normal people. Therefore, in order to secure a better future for our descendants, a thorough cleansing is required. The last PM I served, the Man of Steel, also had a similar thought process. Perhaps that is why he instigated the first war, in his frustration, although due to lack of adequate precautions, he was destroyed. I am pleased that a mentor of the younger generation is here, in the form of this underprivileged youth I see in front of me. He can watch in awe, and perhaps later tell the story to his fellow descendants, as they gaze up at the stars together under a moonlit sky. This will be because their housing will most probably not have been constructed by then. But I promise you that this time, we will place much greater emphasis on the speedy construction of low-income housing. Fewer people will lead to greater efficiencies. See what happened in the case of Singapore. And now, by the power invested in me by this chair, I shall input the codes and press this button. If any of you have any last words, you may speak them now.'

Pintoo pushed. The chair vanished. The Competent Authority fell to the floor with a thud. 'Mehta,' he bleated weakly, 'Mehta.' He put his hands on the desk and tried to pull himself up. His face seemed a little less fleshy now. There were little beads of sweat on his forehead.

'You will be booked under Section 506 for criminal intimidation, as per the Indian Penal Code of 1861,' he said, hoarsely, 'as well as for Sedition, under Section 124. Your Income Tax files will be put under scrutiny. No roads will be built in your locality. No tubewells will ever be repaired. Your reimbursements will be unavoidably delayed. As and when you become eligible for government benefits, you will not receive said benefits.'

He dragged himself up to his knees, but he was visibly weaker, and deflating imperceptibly, like an elderly balloon. His voice was fading as he spoke. 'No coal mines will ever be gifted to you,' he gasped, 'no poor people will ever be uprooted for you. No banks will be forced to give loans to you. Quickly rectify your mistake, and we may give some consideration to your youth and inexperience.'

His eyes were open, but unseeing. He groped blindly for his chair. Pintoo had sent it to Shanti-bai's room, where she was settling down for a nap. She took one look at it and yelled for Ranjeeta.

'Bring me the kerosene!' she said, 'jaldi! And don't forget the matches!'

'This is what everyone was afraid of?' said Pintoo, looking down at the CA, sitting in a heap on the floor. 'He's just a fat little man! Can't you see that? He's like Vinod's uncle Babloo chacha, except Babloo chacha has more hair. And all of us were too scared to do anything about him? How many goondas could he hire? More than the whole population?'

He stepped forward and slapped the fat little man hard, once on the left cheek, once on the right.

'See?' he said. 'That didn't need special powers or anything!'

The fat little man burst into tears.

'How can you treat me this way?' he burbled. 'Don't you know I can declare curfew in your area? Tomorrow who will attest all your documents? How will you manage if there is no one to sort out all the jurisdictions? What about flood relief? Who will distribute flood relief?'

His weeping intensified. He held out his hand, limply, for a handkerchief, a pale, pudgy shadow of the man he used to be, forlorn and chair-less. Mehta handed him a handkerchief, also weeping, and left to do one last sweep of whatever money he could find. It had been a great game as long as it had lasted, but now his number had come up, as he had always assumed it would. Mehta had recognized this the moment he had started down this road. The inevitability had always lent him a certain recklessness, which had increased progressively over the years. He would have to be quick, but his fingers were nimble. Once he was done, he would hop into the friendly elevator, confiscate the CA's car, and make a swift dash to the Haryana border. In the ensuing chaos, he could well establish his own kingdom, although some of the privileges due to kings would be denied him, owing to the lack of available women.

Dharti Pakar and No. 2 were dumbstruck, and clutched each other in terror. No. 2 deeply regretted not getting the file signed earlier. Tarun-da stood poised behind them, a look of intense concentration on his face, bag in hand. The two of them could see vast quantities of rupees vanishing into thin air, which was never a good thing. Plus, they were surrounded by hostile poor people. The peril was palpable. Only their supreme intelligence could save them now. The wily guru was the first to recover.

'My child, you may have grievances against the government,' said Dharti Pakar, 'but a certain amount of adjustment is always required. Violence is never the solution. As young Jesus said, you should at least wait until the person turns the other cheek. Take deep breaths, and allow me to massage your aura.'

'You should have packed some winter clothing,' said Pintoo, and pushed. Dharti Pakar disappeared.

'Where did he go?' asked Banani, who was keeping a sharp eye on No. 2.

'He's a holy man,' said Pintoo, 'I sent him to the Himalayas. He can think about God in peace and quiet.'

'What about oily boy?' asked Banani. No. 2 gave her a look of reproach. When it came to women, he preferred naked hostility to sarcasm. Their relationship was still at a very early stage. A lot of work would be required.

'The child's life is obviously very valuable,' said No. 2, smoothly, 'we would be happy to provide him with Full Body Cover. He will be entitled to a Privilege Discount, and we'll waive the Return After Use clause.'

'Now, Tarun-da!' said Pintoo.

Tarun-da pounced on No. 2. He had been dreaming about pouncing on No. 2, that capitalist swine, from the moment he had met him.

'I can offer you significant stock options . . .' said No. 2, as Tarun-da jammed the jute bag over his head, pulling the strings tight and muffling the rest of his proposition. He tied his hands behind his back with the other end of the string.

'Mgmf,' said No. 2, from inside the bag. He was just like the Chairman, at last.

'Are you couriering him somewhere?' asked Banani, who was ready to believe anything by now.

'The Bank of Bodies is still running, Auntie,' said Pintoo, 'we're going to need a hostage.'

❏

Mehta was just getting into the CA's BMW when Ranvir descended on him like a hound from the depths of hell. 'Unbuckle your pants,' he hissed in his ear, as he grabbed him by the scruff of his neck.

He paused for a moment and turned to the guard.

'May I?' he asked.

As a fellow professional, he owed him courtesy.

'You are our guest,' said the guard, smiling, 'just don't do any breaking-shaking.' Ranvir dragged Mehta, kicking and screaming, into the guardroom, and shut the door behind him.

The guards outside grinned. One of them lit a bidi.

The silence was broken only by the blood-curdling cries of Mehta, growing progressively fainter, as Ranvir did to Mehta, relentlessly, what Mehta had done, for many, many years, to the nation.

❏

A few days later, in Shanti Nagar, Mr Chatterjee was saying goodbye to his wife. Tarun-da had gone back and brought him, weeping, from Gandhiji's funeral. Pintoo had sent him. While practicing with Ranvir, Pintoo had discovered that he could send and bring back people he knew, and along with them, others, because he could feel them, and touch them. Tarun-da had helped with Mr Chatterjee. Of Ali, Pintoo could find no sign, although during his trip, Tarun-da had heard rumours of a man who was searching for Netaji and noticed that throughout Calcutta, in tea shops and colleges, and mansions, the songs of Bob Marley were spreading.

'Are you sure you can do this?' asked Mr Chatterjee.

Banani gave him a quick peck on the cheek.

'Don't worry,' she said, 'I've been practicing with Pintoo, too.'

'Does it have to be you?'

'This was my idea, Hemu,' said Banani, 'we've left generations of kids in the dark, because we never had enough teachers. We need more teachers. We need teachers who can teach them to be teachers. Each one will create more, and in just a few years, Hemu, things could be so different! Why should we be a country full of children with no future? If we do this, we could change that. Don't you see?'

'I do,' said Mr Chatterjee, 'but won't these teachers have families? Why will they come with you?'

'I have all of time to choose from,' said Banani, 'and we have fewer children to teach now. I just need a few of the great ones. I have hundreds in my notebook. It's what my grandmother would have expected me to do. I'm sure some of the teachers will come. Some will have no families. Some will do it for the country. Some will come for the adventure. Don't you think I can convince some of them?'

Her eyes were shining. Personally, Mr Chatterjee couldn't have refused her anything. He hugged her tight.

'Come back safe,' he said, 'I did.'

Mr Chatterjee stepped back. Banani turned to Pintoo, who was standing nearby, smiling.

'Send me off, then, Pintoo,' said Banani, 'send me off, and bring us both back. Then I'll get the next one.'

'OK,' said Pintoo. He waited. He knew Banani had something more to say.

'I may not be as good a teacher as some of these people,' she said, tapping the notebook, 'but I did teach you one thing, didn't I?'

'You did,' said Pintoo.

'And what was that?'

'You can't change the past,' said Pintoo, 'but you can change the future.'

'Good boy!' said Banani, ruffling his hair. 'What are we waiting for? Let's get started!'

Banani smiled.

Pintoo pushed.

ACKNOWLEDGEMENTS

More than anyone else, I have to thank Nilanjana Roy, for sticking with me through thick and thin, despite all the cats that were crying for her attention. If any one person has to be blamed for all this, it would have to be her.

Chiki Sarkar was an early victim of this book. Her advice and encouragement were very helpful, at a time when I was hanging around in Jaipur trying to feel literary.

I don't know much about editors, but Dr Davidar is clearly a lion amongst them. Everyone should have their book done by him. I'm particularly grateful for the bunker, and his calm in the face of mounting hysteria.

Simar Puneet was ruthless in identifying the stinky bits, and relentless in the pursuit of absconding characters. She made me look much better than I deserve.

When Marysia Juszczakiewicz of the Peony Literary Agency decided to invade Delhi, she was lightning quick. Her enthusiasm was infectious, and her efforts on behalf of this dubious enterprise have been awe-inspiring.

Thanks are due also to Aienla and the Alephs. This has been a lonely process, but in the end it felt like bringing it home. I hope they liked the coconuts.

Most of this story has been ripped out, naked and quivering, from the headlines of the past decade. It's been a depressing decade. Luckily for me, whenever I felt my faith in human nature ebbing, I just had to look across the room, or pop my head around the corner. Ruma, Pia and Shyon are not just people I love, they are lovely people. Coco, of course, is better than any person, and she knows it. Together, they were my fortress.

Till the next time.